JASMINE J

C000102644

Bestselling Author of:
MR SOON COME
&
THE DEVIL I KNOW

For Marcia
"Enjoy!.."
Love, Jasmine 20/11/06

XAYMACA BOOKS
(Going Where Others Fear To Tread)

♥

'Xaymaca Books supports the Sickle Cell cause'

Published & Distributed by
Xaymaca Books
PO Box 10886
Birmingham
B5 7YX
West Midlands
Great Britain
Tel/Fax 0121 440 2459
E-mail: xaymaca@book1.freeserve.co.uk

Copyright ©2006 Jasmine Johnson

The right of Jasmine Johnson to be identified as author of this work has been asserted in accordance with the Copyright, Design and Patents Act 1988.

This book is sold subject to the condition that it shall not, by way of trade or otherwise, be lent, resold, hired out or otherwise circulated without the publisher's prior consent, in any form of binding or cover, other than that in which it is published and without a similar condition, including this condition, being imposed on the subsequent purchaser.

No part of this publication may be reproduced or transmitted in any form or by any means, electronic or mechanical, including photocopying, recording or any information storage or retrieval system, without either the prior permission in writing from the publisher, or a license permitting restricted copying.

A CIP catalogue reference for this book is available from the British Library.

Printed and bound in Great Britain by Mackays of Chatham

ISBN 0-9544175-1-8

AUTHOR'S PROFILE

Mother of one, Jasmine Johnson hailed from Jamaica as a teenager. She now resides in Birmingham, West Midlands in Great Britain. She has gained a BA Honours Degree in Media & Communication Studies from the University of Wolverhampton.

Jasmine draws her inspiration from life. She specialises in the theme of *'relationships'* and readers everywhere have expressed their admiration for her *'tell-it-like-it-is'* style. She has the ability to create *'virtually tactile'* situations, commanding her readers to *'react'* to every emotional situation.

As well as writing racy novels, Jasmine also writes punchy short stories and tantalising poetry, which she performs with a unique style of her own. Her debut novel **Mr Soon Come,** (published by The X Press) won her **The New Nation's Writer of the Year Award, 2001.**

Her second novel **The Devil I Know** is self-published, and was pleasantly received by readers everywhere. It was chosen as **Book Of The Month, April, 2004** - Robert Beckford Show - BBC Radio West Midlands.

She also writes for children. Her children's play, **'Thank Heavens For My Senses'** was performed by children at Regents Park Primary School in Birmingham.

One Sweet, Sweet Moment In Time, (a short story) and *Doilies For Her Front Room* (a poem dedicated to her mother Ruby Lurlene Johnson) were published by Writers Without Border in two separate publications. *Red Shoes And Severed Trust (*another short stories) was published by Avocado Press.

Jasmine is also a past student of Birmingham Theatre School, where she has gained Certificates in Acting. She has also taken part in the **'In Celebration Of My Sisters'** show, presented by The Write Thing, London.

She also gives readings from her novels and performs her poetry all over the UK. She is currently working on developing element of her work into a stage play.

ACKNOWLEDGEMENTS

Auntie Daphne & Uncle Labon / Auntie Joyce & Uncle Prosper
Uncle Lenny / Uncle Arthur & Madge / Uncle Roy & Millie
Uncle Errol & Madge / Uncle Venris & Auntie Luna.
My nieces Shari and Khamilah / My nephews Jerome and Amari.
My cousins: The Kings, The Harrisons, The Roses, The Goldings, The
Tsegahs and The Whites

Ikenna Morgan

*** SPECIAL THANKS ***

My Mum & Dad Ruby & Luke Johnson
My Dear Auntie Dorcas & Uncle Sony
My brothers and sisters Errol, Neil, Kevin, Yvonne and Jacqui
My brother-in-law Barry Shorter & cousin-in-law Byron Morgan.

Extra Special Thanks to:

My sister Jacqui Shorter for her patience in proofreading this novel, and for
always being there.
To my brother-in-law Barry Shorter who saved the day with
his computer expertise.
A big thanks to my Cousin and Best Friend Janet Harrison...
'Little Lady, big heart'.
Thank you for being there, come rain come shine.
'You're never too tired to listen'.
To my Dear Friend Sue Brown & daughter Jenai & son Jediah.
'Thank you'... You know why
*

Paulette Haughton... *'Thank you'.*
Father Hovis & Countryman!
'Thank you guys! Nuff respect! *'Real soldiers'.*
Mann Matharu, a *'Bombastic'* Graphic Designer... *'Thank you!'*
To my neighbours: Tony, Tom & Marie, Pansy, Pat, Ann & Ashley,
Ruth & Eddie.
*

And among many, one of my most faithful readers, *'Sonia Brown'* who
eagerly awaited this book!... *'Hope you like!'*
***

But most of all!!... ***To my Dear and only son Andre***
'Creativity is a gift from God'... May yours be forever *blessed, son.* Whatever
else you may do in life, keep writing those lyrics and mixing those tracks...
May your troubles be *'small'* or *'none at all'*, and may your 'fortunes' be *ten
times ten.*
And remember, son, it was *'you'* who told me, 'Mum...
'Pride And Persistence Pay Off'...
Let no one take you dreams away, son... *Love you*, Mum.

A special message to All My Loyal And Faithful Readers...
'Thank You!'...

First and foremost, for your patience. And secondly, for giving me the encouragement to keep on writing...

For your numerous acclaim-filled letters, phone calls and emails relating to my first two novels, **Mr Soon Come** and **The Devil I Know...**

For being liberal and opening your minds to reality and giving me the freedom to express myself; safe in the knowledge that there are people who *'appreciate'* life on pages...

For letting me be the writer I have always wanted to be: being able to express myself liberally, and expressing my Jamaican *'patois'* through my characters with pride, without having to strip my work of its *substance*, and my characters of their *essence*...

Thanks to all my Non-West Indian readers who have allowed themselves to relax and to discover that after all, *'patois'* is *'not'* double-dutch, but simply English words uttered and spelt with a difference...

Thank you for bombarding and pestering Waterstones, Borders, Harriet Tubman and all other good bookshops with your constant quest for **'The Day Hell Broke Loose'**... For giving me the drive and desire to bring you more *'unputdownable'* novels...

But most of all, Thank you for being the *'you'* I love: 'true to yourselves, honest, appreciative, encouraging, and recognising that whether we like it or not, *'passion'* is what drives us all'...

PS... Only about 20% of the words and phrases in this novel are written in Jamaican patois, but should you require a list of their meanings, please email: **xaymaca @book1.freeserve.co.uk.**

'Yours Creatively,

Jasmine,

'For I have only just begun.'

THE
DAY
HELL
BROKE
LOOSE

This novel is the sequel to Jasmine's first two novels, *Mr Soon Come* and *The Devil I Know*, (although you do *not* have to have read the first two to follow it). It is so cleverly written, it is also a 'stand-alone'.

However, should you wish to obtain copies of Mr Soon Come, send your requests to The X Press publishers at
vibes@xpress.co.uk
They will advise you accordingly.

And for copies of The Devil I Know, contact
xaymaca@book1.freeserve.co.uk
Depending on the volume of requests, a *'Print According To Demand'* service can be operated.

It was the popularity of both novels; the fact that they were both set in Birmingham, West Midlands, and with the overwhelming curiosity from her readers as to *'what had become of all those exciting characters'*, that gave Jasmine the urge to take up the unique challenge of the *'bringing together'* of the two completely different novels. The challenge was much too tempting for her to resist.

It had been a long time coming, but Jasmine is a lady who loves a challenge. Tell her she *'can't'* and she most certainly *'will'*. The journey was a mighty long and winding one, but every curve provided a significant *'lesson'*. And through it all, with every line infused with passion enough to move the hardest heart, it is safe to say, *'The Day Hell Broke Loose'* was well worth the wait!' She sincerely hope you enjoy reading it as much as she enjoyed writing it. ***So... here it is... from the depth of her 'creative soul'...   Enjoy!...***

CHARACTER RECAP: FIRST NOVEL - *MR SOON COME*

CONTEH - THE MAIN CHRACTER

A perpetual womaniser. He was married to the beautiful Simone, who decided to leave him after he pushed the boundary of infidelity a little too far. He contracted the HIV virus from Simone's best mate, Pam. Luckily, Simone was clever, and when Conteh thought he was making babies, she was wearing femidoms!

NICO (*featured in first two novels*).

Best mate of Conteh, Nico also contracted the HIV virus from Pam. However, the bitter and ruthless Jamaican Indian set himself on a vengeful mission: armed with the lethal weapon of HIV, he waves his evil wand of *'infection'* at every female who is willing to take a sip from his devil's cup.

LAWRENCE

Simone's new husband. The type of man every mother would like her daughter to bring home. He is so *'fine'*, every woman wants him.

SHEREE

(wasn't actually named in Mr Soon Come – just mentioned as Lawrence's ex-lover).

Lawrence's ex-lover, well before he met and married the beautiful Simone. But just when he thought the ashes in that fire had well and truly died, an ill wind blew, exposing the red, raw, obsessive smouldering that had lain dormant inside Sheree's calm head.

EVADNEY

The sista that was in love with a dread for the longest time. But when **GARNET** found *blonde-heaven*, he rejected her for **TRACEY.** Evadney was left feeling deflated and needed a shoulder to cry on, so she took a quick lick from Conteh (Simone's husband at the time). Evadney was their next-door-neighbour. Garnet's rejection however, caused Evadney to wonder if brothers had definitely discovered fountains of honey that flowed uncontrollably from the meeting of every white woman's thigh. Nonetheless, after Tracey left Garnet for a bigger, blacker Bongo Dee, Evadney promised him she would forgive, forget and marry him. *Will his soul be gently rocked in the bosom of Evadney's love?*

GONGO PEAS
Garnet's friend and best-man.

YVONNE
Evadney's friend and bridesmaid who had seen the thick and thin she had been through when Garnet rejected her for Tracey. Her advice to Evadney were well-meaning, but given or not, Evadney would have done what she felt she had to do anyway.

CARMEN, COLLETTE and JOYA
Three of Conteh's baby mothers who realised that they couldn't rest until heartbreaking Conteh *begged*. But what if the fumes from the *bad* they wish for him lurk somewhere in there not-too-distant future, waiting to devour their very souls?

JACQUELINE
An old ex of Conteh who wished she had never met him at all. She couldn't turn the clock back, and when the one secret she kept in the dark came unexpectedly out into the light, her *made-in-heaven* marriage swayed on the rocks. Keeping the truth of Cerise's father (Conteh) from everyone including Cerise herself, resulted in Cerise making a devastating mistake: she slept with her own father! The effect of that cause?… *the production of an incestuous child: her son was her brother. Conteh's son was also his grandson*

HENLEY
Jacqueline's Bajan husband, who felt betrayed after discovering that Jacqueline had lied to him for all those years about *who* Cerise's real father was: he wasn't some *run-away American* after all, but the one *Conteh Egyptian*. Henley contemplated returning to sunny Barbados. What will Jacqueline do?

CERISE
Daughter of Jacqueline and Conteh who gave birth to her own brother. Her father's son. Lucky for her, or an inexplicable fluke you might say, following her tenth check-up, neither her nor her child is infected with the HIV virus. But Cerise is bitter. In her silence, like the belly of a threatening volcano, she is bubbling inside.

MARCIA

The once *outwardly confident*, yet *inwardly weak* sista that tasted Conteh's juices and stayed hooked. A slave to his touch, she was driven by a spate of fatal attraction. After torching his gleaming BM, attacking his wife Simone in her own home and venting the residue of her anger on her red silk sheets, (*Conteh's fetish*), Marcia thought that was the end. But now, struggling with an undiagnosed mental illness, memories of the love rat are pushed once again to the forefront of her mind. *Now, it has only just begun.*

BEVERLEY

The happy-go-lucky lady that lost a red earring behind Conteh's loo seat after he dared to take her back to his house for a quick fix one night. While his wife Simone worked her ass in high *altitude*, he worked his off in a nasty *attitude*, for his own lecherous *gratitude*. Now, cursed with his legacy of HIV, Beverly is now *waiting to die.*

SHARON and MELISSA

Two close friends who were not partial to *orgy*etrical romps. A blonde and a brunette who had once *tasted black* and *couldn't turn back*. Still, black, white, yellow or pink, the fury of hell is no match against a woman scorned. Watching Conteh squirm may have been good, but when all anger is vented, and all that is left is the blatant reality of AIDS, which way out will the two ladies choose?

SANDRA

Conteh's straight-talking, *no-beating-around-the-bush* sister. She sees it and says it. And though her verbal deliverance might at times seem uncaring, tactless and cold, they often prove to be right.

JANET

Conteh's sister also. Caring, subtle and well-meaning, Janet is always there for Conteh, especially after him loosing Simone, his stretch in prison and the death of their dear mother, Gladys. Apart from himself, Janet understands Conteh the most.

BONGO DEE (*featured in first two novels*).

A bigger, blacker brother with more clout behind his slam than most black men in Birmingham. He is mean too, but white women love his wicked slam. *Lucy* was tasting this big, black berry. So was *Heidi*.

And so was *Tracey*. Three *living-blonde-proofs* that *'the blacker the berry, the sweeter the juice.'* Chat bout. But as the pot melted, they had no clue to the fact that more than a small sprinkling of a sinister *'someone else'* bubbled *potently* in the mix.

MENNA

The leader of the pack! *The Don't F**k With Me* chick.
The lady with a few fish to fry. Everyone knew that *Vengeance was hers*, but even Menna herself thought it was all over. Little did she know that the raging fire in her belly had not yet blazed to its fullest. From Birmingham, to Jamaica, to Canada, back to Jamaica, then back again to Sunny Birmingham, where will this determined *Queen of Justice* finally lay her blazing tiara? And before she decides to, how far will she go before deciding that the raging furnace has *definitely* burnt its last flickering spark?

CYNTHIA

Menna's sister. Strong, bubbly and fun-loving, she still yearns for a nice guy. But only a fairytale happening or an inevitable twist of fate will cook up a scrumptious man for Cynthia. With the strong sisterly love her and Menna share, will the winding path she treads with her sister lead her down the road to heaven?

ANGIE

Menna's close friend; a white woman who has and still is travelling the path of *black love*.   Recently parted from her 2Pac look-alike boyfriend, Angie is on the lookout again. Birmingham is pretty damn small. So… which coffee will be mixing with her cream next?

BLANCHE

Simone's mother: the mother-in-law every man would love to have. Blanche loved Lawrence to a fault. They played, at times, like two children.

SIMONE

The Delectable one…

Through it all, she remains as beautiful, sweet, without-malice, light-hearted and forgiving. But heartache is not just for the ugly, the bitter, malice-keeping, heavy-hearted and the unforgiving, so let's hope there are no surprises awaiting this sweet, undeserving angel. Let's hope her tears won't have to fall anymore. And let's hope we can all truly believe that *'unconditional'* love can be love that sacrifices *physical* love-making to its fullest, even when we're young enough to see it as impossible. Can we believe that the long and inexplicable journey in our search for love can sometimes take us back to where we had never dreamed we'd end up?

Question: *'How deserving are our individual fates?'*

* * *

CHARACTER RECAP: SECOND NOVEL - THE DEVIL I KNOW

LIJAH

The fallen brother who had come to realise that he was not worthy of the *Majestic* title *'RASTA'*. Caught with his pants down as he filled the need in Faithlyn, a sassy baby-sitter from Jamaica, his awakening was not just rude, but he had come to realise that there were still room in his life for another dollop of pain. After wild wranglings with Juicy Lucy (*whom* he shared with Baby Face Glen, *with whom* he shared his queen Gloria), and after tangling with vengeful Bernadette, plus coping with the death of his son Kunta, Lijah found a *'second-chance'* place to dwell: the arms of his queen Gloria. Lijah would like to think he is home and dry… a sleeping dog… but will restless Bernadette get a life and let him rest?

GLORIA

Lijah's woman. She left Lijah and fled to pastures new in Jamaica, but the greener grass that tempted her was nothing but a deceptive mirage. Now, back in Birmingham with Lijah in *The Devil She Knows,* the question still lingers… *'how much does Gloria really know him?'* Will they continue to help each other make it through countless nights?

FESTUS

Lijah's best friend. For years Festus carried the burden of the big lie he had chosen to live. Happenings from his childhood resulted in him physically violating his woman, Kizzy. And to add to it all, he took the wrong path and ended up in jail. Now, he's out and swears by Jah Cure's pledge: *to be a better man.*

KIZZY

Festus' ex and Gloria's best friend. Like Gloria, Kizzy jumped from a hot frying pan into a raging furnace when she left Festus. Her new man Baby Face Glen is no Angel. In fact he's the same devil Gloria had to seek refuge from! But Kizzy knew nothing of this. Now, she wants rid of him but chance would be a fine thing: *over his dead body*

FIONA

Fiona is Kizzy's adopted sister. She is bisexual. Mama Maya adopted them years ago when they were both babies. Just after shacking up with her girlfriend, Grace, (an ex-model) Fiona had a letter from Aunt Patricia in Jamaica, telling her that she was her blood-mother. Fiona was furious, especially when she read that her blood-father was Pastor Fontaine, whom, surprisingly, was also Grace's father! Hence, Fiona and Grace's relationship was suddenly incestuous! Fiona stayed away from everyone. She was bitter and had pledged not to forgive Aunt Patricia.

FARI

Kizzy's son. Eleven years old and the son Festus had always believed was his. But nothing could be further from the truth: a truth Kizzy could never tell him even if she wanted to.

ROY

Lijah's older brother. A policeman with an eye for the ladies, he has his fair share of troubles. Moving back to Birmingham from London, he is pleased that the family has patched up a few of their differences. He wants to cool it with Mitzi, and likewise, steer clear from Bernadette. But how narrow will his escapes be from the perilous paths both ladies had tread? For both of them, the *rose man* only knocked once, but once was all it took for *'game over'*.

FAYE

Lijah and Roy's sister. After fleeing England for France in an attempt to leave her family troubles behind, she is now back in Birmingham. Bernadette was her best friend, but after Faye took Pierre, Bernadette's French husband away from her. *How will it all end?*

LUCY

Lucy is full white and the half-sister of Kizzy who is mixed-raced. She is the daughter of Beatrice, a well-to-do white woman (now deceased) who had dabbled with Lothan, (Lijah's dad) when he was a young man and gardener to her husband. Lucy blamed Lothan for her mother running away and leaving her and her brother Conrad, after finding out that she was pregnant with a black child (*a taboo in those days*).

Armed with a slight touch of madness spurned from resentment, Lucy decided that since she couldn't get to Lothan, Lijah should pay for the *sins of his father*.

CONRAD

Lucy's blue-eyed blonde-haired brother. His mother leaving them as a child has affected Conrad in a serious way. He lives a life of crime from a very young age. Prison is his second home, and the act of *sodomy* towards his fellow cellmates has become a kind of addiction. *Will Conrad ever be stopped in his sodomizing tracks*?

BERNADETTE

Roy's ex, with whom his brother Lijah had dabbled. A sista who seriously needs to *get a life*. Her blackmail tactics are wearing thin, and seemingly, her brain cells too, but not as thin as Lijah's patience. Roy, however, had managed to keep her at bay. And like stale blood, her bitterness is curdling. *How short is her rope when measured against time?*

MITZI

The most recent of Roy's exes. She was a top model, earning more money than she could ever spend. But with youth only a passing attribute, money falling carelessly through her fingers like grains of sand, and Roy giving her the brush-off, Mitzi took a reality check: *'perhaps it's time I tell my daughter Shari who her father is'*. But before that, *the rose man must knock once*.

BABY FACE GLEN

A brother from yard who is dead set on digging up enough gold to see him ok. First it was *Lucy*. Then it was *Gloria*. Then *Kizzy*. After his deportation from England back to Jamaica, Glen is about to make another stop on England's shore. *But whose purse string will he be holding on to this time?* The plot thickens.

FAITHLYN

The young but feisty baby-sitter from yard, with whom Lijah got busy on his settee when Gloria was on a night out: she came back early and caught them at it: slap bang in the middle of the mix. Now back in Jamaica, with poverty a heavy chain around her neck, Faithlyn jumped at the chance when Baby Face Glen offered her the chance to make some dough from trafficking a few bundle of cocaine in her gut. *But how far will Faithlyn reach?*

LOTHAN

Lijah, Roy and Faye's dad, now living in Jamaica.

DORA

Lothan's wife and Festus' mother.

MAMA MAYA

Lothan's first sweetheart when she was a slip of a girl back in Jamaica in the fifties. Also Kizzy and Fiona's adopted mother. Mama Maya is now living in Jamaica.

AUNT PATRICIA

Mama Maya's best friend. Now living in Jamaica.

MONTIE

Festus' father, the Handsworth tramp. Dora's first husband.

HEIDI

A conniving Irish girl who tricked her way under Festus' roof by leading him to believe that she was pregnant with his child, when her and Bongo Dee knew different. *What will the outcome be?*

REDS

Lijah's friend. A Bob Marley look-alike. He finds comfort, as always, lying across his bed with his thoughts, mainly of Kunta and Papa Dread. He was always a peaceful dread, but life can find a way of driving drive the most peaceful of man to drastic irrational measures. Taking Rock out might have felt like justice at the time, but he was never gonna be able to put the trauma of taking a life into words. So when Mitzi contacted him to say she wanted to talk, he could never imagine that she had another shocking revelation for him.

SHARI

Mitzi's daughter. Too young to have lost two boyfriends (Damian and Kunta) to drugs and guns, and to be a mother of two, but that's the way it is. She had no choice but to grow up fast, and joining Ikesha and Andre (aka STAL – *STreet Anthem Lyricist*) in trying to make a positive blot on Birmingham's landscape, via a *D*on't *B*e *I*nfluenced campaign, she found the strength all black women must possess. But when her mother Mitzi said she wanted to reveal something to her, she wondered how sturdy her newfound strength would be.

IKESHA
Making a change in memory of Kunta...
Gloria and Lijah's daughter. She has emerged from darkness into light. She never believed she could ever emerge from under the dark blanket of rape, or even stop crying over the untimely death of her brother Kunta, let alone be strong enough to organise a campaign aimed towards uplifting young black youths and adults alike. *Will she, Shari and positive rapper Andre be able to make the message stick? ... THEY LIVE IN HOPE.*

****

NEW CHARACTERS JOINING THE PREVIOUSLY MENTIONED ONES, FINALISING THE LIST FOR *THE DAY HELL BROKE LOOSE*.

AMARI
Simone and Lawrence's son. He's five years old.

LANCE
A black Airline captain and husband of **MORAG**, a kept blonde. But that wasn't always the case. Morag is an ex-stewardess who was always touched with that good old *ants-in-your-pants* syndrome. One man could never satisfy her, so Lance had acquired her second-hand, from *one-careless-owner*: her first husband, dashing, debonair and white, Captain Frank Philips. So, although Morag was financially *kept*, sexually she wasn't *satisfied*. And with Lance's attention waning from her and more towards what everyone of us wants: *Money*, Nico decided to lay more than a little loving on her. Morag felt sweet. But Lance, the dashing black captain is somewhat of a spoilt child who wants everything. And along with his obsession for money, there was one more deep desire that was too hard to hold down. *Whatever may that be?*

CLIVE
The new First Officer in town, and the third black crewmember to take up the aviation banner of flying-high. He loves himself, money, fast expensive cars and his plush bachelor pad. Women are way down his list of priorities, but a mysterious fetish tickles his fancy. *What might that be?*

PETER

A *get-rich-quick-seeking* white guy from Menna's business past who would do almost anything to make a million. Whilst cooling out in Jamaica, he had a plan and wanted Menna in on it. With an eye for black women and an even wider one for Menna, he lived in hope. *But will Peter really retire in style as he planned to?*

GLENDA

The blonde who chased a more tempting bit of cheese, only to loose all she previously had, gaining nothing but an appetite for the *'fire-water'*. It helps her to forget, though only for short whiles.

CLAYTON

A Canadian born brother of Jamaican parentage, living in Toronto, Canada. A brother who had convinced himself that he had found his soul mate in Menna. He wanted her like breath, and after bearing his soul to this strong, fiery and mysterious lady, *can this son-of-a-preacher-man really hold her?* He's certainly willing to try.

VINCENT

A stranger that Menna and Angie met in an Italian patisserie at Heathrow Airport. Will Menna see Vincent again?

MARIO

A sexy Italian guy Menna and Angie met at Heathrow Airport the same day they met Vincent. But little did Menna know that Mario would play one of the biggest parts in her life yet!

ANDRE (aka STAL)
The rapper with a 'different' song to sing…

A quietly-confident rapper whose lyrics have no room for negativity, and one who looks forward to Peace, Love, Happiness and Prosperity. His motto is *'Pride and Persistence pay off'*. Joining Ikesha and Shari in delivering the *D*on't *B*e *I*nfluenced message might have pulled Andre away from his studio for while, but he couldn't be more pleased, since it also pulled hundreds of young minds towards *'fixing-up'*…*HOPEFULLY FOR A LIFETIME.*

Author's Note

This novel is purely a work of fiction. All characters, events and situations are solely the product of the author's imagination and bear no relation to any real persons, places or actual happenings. Any resemblances to true characters, living or dead, or actual places and situations are purely coincidental.

♥

Dedicated to all sistas who are keeping it real: *strong* in *spirit, positive* in *mind* and *rich* in the perception of *'self'*. And to all brothers who know what it is to *'keep it real'*… *'Respect'*.

'Vengeance may be sweet, but be careful in your quest to make it yours. For in your tasting, the *'lick'* may become a *'sting'* upon your tongue, and the bitter nectar of its twist may linger in your mouth...
forever.'
Jasmine Johnson, 2006

PROLOGUE

*S*imone woke again to a beautiful day. She opened her blinds and let the natural light shine in. The sound of her son's voice added the backdrop she needed. He was waking. Minutes later, he trundled into her room, his gentle feet gripping the soft carpet. He rubbed his eyes and said "Mummy," and it sounded as if it was his first word. Simone picked the big boy up as if he was a newborn baby. He felt her love as he clung to her neck, then he said, "Where's Daddy?"

"He's sitting in a big bird in the sky. Taking lots and lots of holiday-makers to some place in the sun."

"Is he gonna take us soon?"

"Yes. Of course he is."

And Amari smiled and said, "Good. Can I have my breakfast please, Mummy?"

"Yes, of course you can, son," Simone said, smiling back and marvelling at how much he looked like his father. A fine figure of a man: Captain Lawrence Hendricks. The man she loved unconditionally: as far as her idea of *unconditional* was. The man who had saved her from a life of misery from one Conteh. Conteh Gonzales. *Egyptian*. Once King-inna-di-ring.

La Desiderata. Second to Maya Angelou's *'Phenomenal Woman'*, it was her favourite poem. It means *'Things to be desired.'* She couldn't be sure of its real source, since the mystery which surrounds it isn't as inspirational as the poem itself. Some say it was found in a Baltimore church in 1692 and of unknown origin. Some say it was in fact written around 1920, whilst some say it was in fact 1906. Some say it is linked to The Old St Paul's Church, Baltimore, AD 1692. But apart from applauding the writer (apparently Max Ehrmann) Simone didn't give a damn. To her, it was simply *inspirational*, offering a simple positive credo for life. Each verse helped her through several past situations.

When she was with Conteh, a notorious soundman: the metaphoric *cow* that didn't know the use of his tail until it was chopped clean off, *La Desiderata* gave her strength whenever she was down. Hardly these days though. Being *down* that is. As far as she could see and feel, happiness lived *permanently* within the walls of the luxury home she now shared with her new husband, Lawrence, and adorable five-year-old, Amari.

1

Like a prayer, the framed words from the poem adorned a small space on her bedroom wall. And like a dose of vitamin, she would read a bit each day. And today, as she held Amari's hand, and just before she headed downstairs, she read...

> *Go placidly amid the noise and the haste,*
> *and remember what peace there may be in silence.*
> *As far as possible, without surrender,*
> *be on good terms with all persons.*
> *Speak your truth quietly and clearly;*
> *and listen to others,*
> *even to the dull and the ignorant;*
> *they too have their story...*

'Not all men are the same', she recalled her mother Blanche's words in her upper-class Jamaican accent, when she had told her she was going to marry Lawrence, this gorgeous Antiguan. And she seriously believed that. She needed to. For God knows, the sista couldn't stand another broken heart. The one she had was mended. Fixed. Healed. And now, it was signed, sealed and delivered to *Lawrence*.

And it was her mother too who had told her, when Conteh had ripped her heart to bits: *'You will overcome. You will overcome.'*

And after the wedding, she had said of Lawrence, *'Love him, but keep a little back for surprises. Your father has never failed to surprise me. I guess I surprised him at times too. No one is perfect. And no two days are the same. Today you can have sunshine, tomorrow a ruthless hurricane. The relics of some storms can be salvaged, while some, you'll just have start right over again.'*

"And what do my big boy want for breakfast today, then?" Simone asked Amari, giving him another hug.

"Weetabix of course, Mummy."

"Ok."

"After I've brushed my teeth, of course, Mummy."

"Oh... right... ok... I almost forgot," she said smiling. "I stand corrected."

And with a twinkle in his little eyes, Amari rushed enthusiastically to the bathroom.

Chapter 1

ℑt was 4am when Evadney hit the pillow. Her night at Banana Baits followed by a private party did it for her. With Father Jarvis and Country Bwoy doing their things as guest DJs, it was hard to pull herself away any earlier.

Evadney lay in the back room of her parent's house thanking heavens she had had her fix from Conteh well before the rumours that he was dosed with the deadly AIDS virus. She could have been one of his victims. Luckily, she escaped, though through shear luck, as opposed to being sensible.

In a few months time she would be moving out again, into a brand new two-bedroom house in Handsworth Wood. Along with her day job, she had worked the midnight shift at a reputable Supermarket in Small Heath. For a good while she wore the haggard facial look, with bags beneath her eyes big enough to hold her weekly shopping. Strong black coffee helped her through umpteen mad office hours. The sista had to do what the sista had to do, knowing full well that others took much easier ways out. Pole dancing clubs, for instance, are crying out for bodies like hers. But there are *types* and there are *types*.

Well, at least to her, (since some would dispute it) *giving some* to your next-door-neighbour's husband cannot be compared to having hundreds of creepy men leering over you as you slide up and down slippery poles in seedy joints. *Feh real.*

* * *

The decision to have Garnet back had deemed Evadney *'foolish'* by her friends and a few family members. They couldn't understand it. More so because she had lately appeared stronger and more assertive than she had ever been. Had it been when she seemed to have no words herself: when she was simply a ventriloquist's dummy, with Garnet's hand up her back operating her every move, it would have been more understandable.

Seemingly, Garnet had persuaded her to tell her friends to *'leave people's business and mind their own'*. And Evadney, *seemingly*, had sent out a non-verbal message to everyone. A message that read, *'I have forgiven Garnet for leaving her for a blonde'*. It was the *in-thing*.

3

It was all around her: one of the 21st century's cries for numerous sistas of late. One that Evadney herself had said is *'taking over like wild fire'*. She had once told Yvonne, 'Whilst every other nation's men took multi-culturalism to mean different races living together in harmony, our black men took it to the extreme. They took it to mean: *'I-must-leave-my-black-sistas-and-find-me-a-blonde'*. And whilst every race disappear behind closed doors to discuss the blatant migration, and whilst black women (for the fear of being labelled racists) stifle their feelings about being pushed aside like relics in a reject shop, black men continue to give out the message loud and clear. The message is... *'We prefer blondes. They are the new designer must-haves. And what the fuck are you gonna do about it!'*

* * *

Garnet's *second chance* came, however, not long after Tracey the *blue-eyed-blonde-haired* chick had dumped him for a bigger, blacker brother: *Bongo Dee*. Oh yes. Women *craved it* Bongo *gave it:* Rough love. There must be a name for a desire like that, and to add to it all, this *once-taste-black-can't-turn-back* blonde had told a friend of hers, *'The blacker the berry, the sweeter the juice'*. No messing.

Evadney's friends were convinced that she had become one of life's statistics: *a sista who will probably choose a BTN relationship, rather than stare miserably, night after night at a television screen. Better Than Nothing relationships* for the over forties, are by far, outweighing the *QFMR: 'Quest For Mr Right'*. And somewhere between these two equations lies a group of *HACSS: Hard, Ambitious, Career-Seeking Sistas*, who will *not* allow any man to fuck with their minds, let alone their hearts. *Period.* So, marrying careers that allow them to become *Ms Independents* is just what the doctor ordered. *Chat 'bout.*

However, looking at it from a different perspective, Yvonne, one of Evadney's closest friends *(one who had a narrow escape from a phoney English-American love rat called Marlon)* had surmised that after all, Garnet was *The Devil* Evadney *Knew*. She herself had no chance of knowing *Marlon* who was practically Dr Jekell and Mr Hyde. He had tricked her into a relationship just so he could get into her house. And when he had stolen himself away like a thief in the night, he took with him her passport and a gold pendant he had bought her in his staged affection. Later on she gathered that her passport was needed for some serious stripping-down. A British passport is of great value. Marlon had his plans. And the gold pendant had to go. His

American wife was coming to the UK. It belonged to her. So when he whipped it off Yvonne's dressing table, conscience had nothing to do with it. So yes, Yvonne had seen it all and whatever Evadney chose *to do* or *not to do* would be entirely up to her.

So, there was a whole lot of surmising going on, since, at the best of times, Evadney didn't discuss too much about her private life with her friends. Instead, she just kept right on living it, leaving the world and his wife to surmise. Rather than lying, or saying too much, Evadney said *jack*. And she had always known that she would say it best, if she said nothing at all.

* * *

Evadney emerged from the peaceful surroundings of the dim room. The light of the Sombre Sunday afternoon was winning. She drew the thick heavy curtains in the room she was temporarily occupying, letting in the natural daylight. At the same time she flashed her mind to Jamaica where her parents were at that present moment. With the hurricane season hitting tropical coasts everywhere, she hoped they would have a trouble-free time. She pulled her dressing gown around her and walked to the bathroom with her thoughts. She brushed her teeth, staring at her reflection in the mirror. But her mind wasn't there at all. Not on her reflection. In fact it wasn't even on the rendezvous that was about to take place in her parents' house just a few hours from then. It was on something she had been driven to do ever since Garnet left her feeling like shit. Something she wasn't sure she would be given the chance to do. Something that would give her sweet satisfaction. Something that stayed dormant under her hat like a centipede under an undisturbed stone.

* * *

Now, Evadney set the shower and stripped ready for a fresh. '*Sting FM*', she thought, '*must tune in*'. It was almost like a fix. 1:30pm and it was Country Bwoy's voice that glided on the airwaves when she turned the stereo on. His selection of music: mostly ones that suggested affairs, sneaky moves, hush-hush rendezvous and stealing love on the side entertained her, although in reality, she knew how it felt. She had experienced both sides: the giving and the receiving.

She climbed under the shower to '*Stealing Love On The Side*' and remembered what she did to Simone, a sweet, undeserving sista she once lived next-door to. It was that sordid event that forced her to sell up and move away. *Lust*. Such a dangerous urge for self-satisfaction. And she had always wondered what she would say to Simone should she bump into her again. Perhaps nothing. Perhaps the humiliation she felt would surface again, pushing words out of it.

But Country Bwoy didn't pull her guilt string for long, for it wasn't long before the noise of the cascading torrents would drown out *'Me And Mrs Jones'*.

* * *

2pm. Fresh and ready, Evadney stumbled down the stairs to meet what was left of the day. With ease, and almost as if the shower had washed away her previous thoughts, (or could it be the fact that that her favourite DJ was on the air?) she skanked across her mother's kitchen to Bob Marley's *Easy Skanking:* Whatever else it was, this theme song did it for her every time. Without knowing it, Birmingham's number 1 DJ had managed to place an extra spring in Evadney's step on umpteen Sunday afternoons. *Father Jarvis*. Larger than life… *No messing*.

Evadney opened the fridge, peered in and saw nothing she fancied to break her Sunday morning fast, so she reached for the box of crunchy nut cornflakes and filled a medium-sized bowl. As she showered the small, bronze, honey-coated flakes with ice-cold milk, she was oblivious to her own smile. A tinge of *deviousness*, mixed in with the contagiousness of Father Jarvis, you might say.

'Woah nah nah nah nah!' As usual, Father Jarvis was on form and he made Evadney glad to be alive. 'Good Aftanoon Birmingham and all surrounding counties! Good Aftanoon! Good Aftanoon! Yours truly di Grand-faada welcomes you to di most *talked about*, di most *chat 'bout* show dis side of the West Midlands! Just getting my fingers warm, people, before I open di phone lines! Yes… Yes'… *'We're takin' it easy'* he sang now, trying to match the voice of the legendary Bob Marley,

> *'Woah nah nah nah nah'*…
> *Excuse me while I light my spliff*
> *Oh God I gotta take a lift*
> *From reality I just can't drift*
> *That's why I am staying with this riff*
> *Take it easy, easy skanking*
> *Take it easy, easy skanking*
> *Got to take it easy, easy skanking*

> *You see we're taking it easy*
> *We're taking it slow, taking it easy*
> *Got to take it slow, so take it easy*
> *Easy skanking, easy skanking*
> *Oh take it easy, easy skanking...*

'Yeees, we're gonna take it *real* easy dis aftanoon, people. Nice an' easy. I'm still getting my fingers warm, just bear with... Laad! Laad! Dem start a'ready! People di phone lines nuh open yet! Gimme a chance! Gimme me a chance! Shantamatilda! Wha's di matta wid you? A'right! A'right! Laad mi seh dem killin' mi in 'ere a'ready!"

Evadney emitted a laughed – an extension to the smile that invaded her face the moment Father Jarvis hit the air. She was lifted. She had always wondered if this DJ ever had a problem or two of his own. So cheerful in his delivery of sweet reggae music, he was almost definitely infectious.

She ate her cornflakes then did a quick straighten-up of the house. It didn't need it, she had already done it last night, but it was force of habit. Her mother's feet had hardly touched the first flight of steps on the Air Jamaica jet when she took to de-cluttering her house. Years of *keep-for-no-reason* relics had held their grounds in cupboards, cove holes and tops and bottoms of wardrobes in her mother's house: her mother had called them *keep-sakes*, only the only *sakes* they served were the sakes of stealing space, making the massive house a claustrophobic nest. And later, of course, therapy for Evadney, since de-cluttering seemed to relax her.

* * *

2:10pm. This Sunday afternoon had come with a difference. It was wet. Dark skies loomed over the city almost with a vengeance, but it didn't matter to Evadney: Father Jarvis' voice had chased away the gloomy effect that grey skies usually had on her, making it feel warm. Cosy. In fact, as she watched the rain falling from the sky and on to the window, she felt glad she was indoors.

* * *

3pm. Time had flown. Standing at the front window, Evadney wondered if she should have invited *Sanchez* to her parents' house. Unlike Garnet, this guy looked tasty enough to eat. After saying no to

7

him for one too many times, she fell pray to his charm one afternoon when she bumped into him, as she strolled, alone, along a romantic walk in the Lickey Hills.

Pretty boys were never her things. Superficial paper-people she called them. Well, basing her conclusion on the few she had given brief chances since the split with Garnet, she concluded: they have no soul and nothing to prove. Nothing to prove since they lived on their looks alone. *'Good to look at'*. So up until now, she had left them well alone.

As it went, this time she was charmed. Perhaps it was the ambience of the picturesque Lickey Hills… the carpet of golden leaves beneath her feet… the hints of sunlight that peeps playfully like hide-'n-seek, or strips of magic in the rays of sunlight, maybe, that shone through golden branches. Perhaps it was the freedom of the hills, or perhaps it was the *jeans-wrapped-tight-come-and-get-me* ass (an asset of *Sanchez*, if ever there was one) that he consciously hoped she would take a good look at.

Something about this hunk sent her mind on a mission, charming a natural wetness from her previously *wash-and-put-away-like-a-best-dress* vagina. Whatever it was, right then, as she stood staring at the dark skies, this *sex-on-legs* was on his way to her parents' house. *Coffee and chat* was what he called it. Whatever happened, they would both, for a while at least, take in Father Jarvis, Revive Champion and connoisseurs of all connoisseurs. *Chat 'bout.*

'If Garnet could see me now. Shit. He would surely wish he had stayed put. Shopped in his own damn back yard… so to speak.'

* * *

Although she anticipated it, the doorbell startled her a little. After taking a deep breath and walking the short distance to the front door, Evadney opened it with a newly found confidence.

"Hey, girl, how yuh doin?" the hunk said.

"I'm fine, Sanchez… come in."

Before he accepted her invitation to step inside, the gorgeous-looking guy glanced quickly out onto and across the open road as if he expected a private detective on his tail.

"For you", he handed her a bottle of wine and kissed her left cheek.

"Thank you", she said receiving both the bottle and the kiss, "come in."

"And this," he swung his right arm from behind his back and handed her a slim, golden box.

"Oh… Thank you." She kept her eyes on the box, the curiosity lines on her forehead almost forming a question mark.

The box housed a single red rose.

"I know what you're thinking," he told her assertively.

"You do?"

"Yeap… *'It isn't real',* you're thinking." He stood, almost still in the passageway.

"Well… I must admit, I have never been given…"

"Well, to me, unlike the song, paper roses are the best."

"… Er… Go on into the living-room," she closed the front door, "straight ahead."

"No, you first. I'll follow you."

She smiled, tutted and proceeded to the living-room, knowing full well he wanted to look at her ass.

"You look *good,* girl."

"Thank you," she gestured to the big leather settee, "you're not looking too bad yuhself. And thanks for the wine… and the rose."

"Oh, it's nothing." He took her right hand and entwined her fingers into his and said, "May I?" but before she could answer, he planted a warm kiss on her lips.

It felt good. And he was certainly different.

"I hope it's to you're liking," he said as he pulled away. "The wine, I mean," he added when he saw the slightly puzzled look on her face.

"Oh, right, I'm sure it will be."

"You look like a woman of class… and a classy lady must have the best."

Evadney wasn't such a connoisseur of wines, but the bottle had a class about it, and since he mentioned the word *class,* she took his word for it.

"Sit down," she invited again, as she walked to the kitchen to chill the bottled offering.

"Nice place yuh parents got here," he called out to her as he relaxed on the settee.

"Thanks," she called back, "nothing like your own, though… can't wait. Not long now." She was back in the living-room now with her boxed rose. "I'll just let the wine chill a little," she added, walking over to the fireplace where she stood the box upright for show.

"You like it?"

"What?"

"The rose."

"It's a rose."

"Yes, but not a *real* rose."

"No, but you are the donor. You said it's special. I accept it whole-heartedly…"

"*Whole-heartedly?*… are you sure?" he tested her sincerity.

"I suppose it isn't the *gift*, but the heartfelt meaning from the *giver*."

"Yeah… Yeah… So… don't you wanna know *why* it's special?"

"Er… yeah. Yeah, I suppose I do… *why?"*

He smiled, almost cynically, but didn't reply.

"Well?" she asked, placing her ass in the single-seater.

"Hey… I don't bite, you know… come and sit over here."

"You're a fast mover, I can tell…"

At that moment the phone in the hallway rang and Evadney rose to answer it, "Excuse me a sec'," she said to him.

It was her mum, and as she chatted away, *Sanchez* spared some time to look around the older-generation-style living-room. It spelt care. Care for retirement. Stability. Nest egg. *'Lucky if you can live that long',* he thought, then looked around in time to catch Evadney walking back into the room. "C'mon. Sit here," he said, patting the settee and reaching for her arm at the same time.

Though a little apprehensive, Evadney did as he asked, smiling at him, though with scolding eyes, She reached for the remote for something to do.

Father Jarvis' voice sparked in the background, quietly but clearly, almost on a simmer.

"So, what d'you do for entertainment?" he asked her, "I never see you out in clubs. I see you out, but never clubs. Don't tell me you just keep this *coca-cola-bokkle* body hidden away behind four walls." As he spoke he moulded her left shoulder and played with the fingers of her right hand.

"Well, I had a great night last night. Banana Baits then a private party. Apart from the odd party or two, I haven't been out much over the past year or so. Work, work, work, I'm afraid. Houses aren't cheap… well… not the one I was buying anyway."

"I hear yuh. Still, life's too short. Too much work and no play will make you a dull girl."

Evadney chuckled. "No, I've reached my goal on the house front now. Party-wise, life has just begun for me. I'm ready to have fun. So where do *you* go then?"

"Everywhere. Everywhere there's life. Can't get enough of it. You can call me *Dracula*," he said cynically, then nibbled playfully at her neck. I used to go to the Scratchers Yard... Fern Gully... places like that. Gave them a rest now though. Lots of new places to go now."

Now Evadney's mobile cut in interrupting the flow. She could here it but she couldn't see it. It was in the room anyhow. She freed herself from Mr Handsome, discarded the remote and felt down the side of the settee into which she previously sat. There it was flashing at her... *'Garnet calling'*.

"Garnet, Hi... Yes... Ok... They're fine, Mum just rang... No, not now, I'm a bit busy right now... I'll call you... I'm not sure, sometime later... I will... Ok, bye... bye... bye... No, Garnet, not now, I'm busy... I can't... later."

Evadney clicked off, but like a child, she played with the phone as she could feel *Sanchez's* gaze eating into the side of her face.

"Him still luv yuh... dat's a fact... but you done know dat."

"Who?"

"Yuh man. Dat was him, I know. Di one yuh was deciding whether to give a chance or not."

"How do you know?"

"I've lived, girl." He reaches for her hand.

"De t'ing is... Do *you* still love him?"

"I'm not answering that," she said, almost as if he was treading where he had no place treading.

"Well, you don't need to answer. Women flex a little way different from men. If they love one man, it is very rare that they allow another man onto his patch. A man now... he can love his girl bad, but he'll still tek a lick if it's going."

"You should write the book of life. You seem to know it all."

"Not *all*. But I know one thing... *I'm* here... he's there... *I'm* touching you... he's not..."

"So?"

"So, *nothing*. I'm just trying to show you that life is one big game. Everybody plays the fool sometime. Not just men... women too."

"Listen, you don't know the half, so don't judge me."

"I don't know the half, but I know he hurt you. Real bad. And as for judging? *That* I don't do. All I know is, I'm feeling you right now.

11

Feeling you big time. Whatever game you're playing with your man, that's for you two to sort out. I'm not gonna lie, I wanna taste you, girl."

She was still standing, her fingers in his hand. She looked at him wide-eyed. She wasn't expecting his spiel to end like that.

"Call it what you want," he continued. "Lust… whatever. We can play. No promises, just good old-fashion fun. Ah nuh not'n. I know yuh neva invite mi 'ere todeh fi nuh coffee."

"Mmmm… I d'know…" Still she played with her phone, and he, with her fingers.

"What don't you know?… you *know* you didn't really ask me here today for coffee and chat."

Now, Evadney sat again on the settee, only this time, at the far end, causing their hands to stretch as he held her fingers.

He sensed something. Apprehension? Second thoughts? Whatever it was, he would soon coax it away.

"Listen… you're not sure what you want. When a woman is sure what she wants, she doesn't play. If you were satisfy with your decision to have him back, I wouldn't be here… either that or you're trying to give him a taste of his own medicine… like I said, I've lived. I know how some women's minds work…"

She looked at him with depth now.

"But remember," he told her, "things have a way of back-firing."

"What d'you mean?" she quizzed.

"Well… sometime we set traps for others and we trip an' fall right innah it, to raas… excuse di language."'

Evadney couldn't help herself. An attack of giggle*itis* caught her. She threw her head back and laughed so loud, the contagiousness of it caught *Sanchez*. Now, they both fell about laughing so much, it was as if they were old friends. She was much more relaxed than she had ever been the whole time he had been there.

"No… seriously though," Evadney said, wiping her eyes and settling into a kind of sombre, "I'm…"

"Listen," he said, moving closer to her, gently prizing the phone from her hand and placing it on the edge of the settee, "when was the last time you made love?"

"What?" She looked quickly at him, a little surprised at his extended forwardness. And the quickness of it too.

"… 'Cause I know seh him not getting' not'n… not yet anyway."

"How do you know that?... You seem to know everything, don't you?... If you know so much, you should be able to tell me *when* I last..."

"...Had a good seeing to?" He finished her sentence presumptuously.

If looks could kill, he'd be dead, "*Seeing* to?"

"No, seriously..." He drew even closer now and assumed a Barry White tone, "when was the last time you had the moist tongue of a man gripping your nipples?"

Evadney grew warm as she experienced his suggestion. Almost literally. It felt like making up with an old boyfriend. Father Jarvis played Gladys knight... '*Love is a dangerous game, Winners and losers, Pleasures and pain...*"

"I can tell," he relented, "you haven't been touched for a very long time."

"How can you tell that," her voice trembled as his lips brushed her soft neck... her left earlobe... her sensitive shoulder-blades.

Her resistance was slowly dying.

"When was the last time you had a man's fingers manipulating your tender nipples... moulding your firm, sensitive breasts." His whispers killed her softly. He had surely done this before. Several times before.

"Oh, Christ... what's with the questions?... Don't tell me you need answers," she hummed.

Now, he slid onto his knees, her slender legs enfolded his torso. *Fast mover*.

As she melted, he caressed her breasts, checking, but for a second, for the slightest sign of resistance. There was none.

"When was the last time..." he whispered, Father Jarvis helping his moves of passion with his fine selection of lovers rock, "...you had the firm hands of a man gripping the cheeks of your ass?" and now, he did just that: gripped her firm ass and would have loved to have shared the sensation it gave her.

"Mmmm," she hummed quietly, her wanting becoming unbearable.

"When was the last time warm tongue slid slowly down the crease of your back, teasing your sensitive sine. Sweet kisses showered your face... warm lips caressed yours?"

'*This is torture*', she thought, but it echoed only in spates of hums.

"When was the last time you had someone ventured through to find the path to your pleasure.... A man... slide... with expertise... his hard moist manhood inside you, reaching your g-spot… bringing you to a climax enough to have you floating?" Now he pushed her sarong-styled skirt away, revealing perfect legs. He kissed them, sweeping his warm moist tongue from her right knee all the way up to her inner thighs. There, he rested a while and lay his head upon the spot where her legs had met a perfect V. And now, for the first time, she reaches out to him. Caressed his head, holding it still against her stomach. Telepathically, they spoke.

Now, he resumed, kissing the base of the V, his strong tongue knocking firmly at heaven's door, asking to be let in, though the tightness of her thighs turned him on. He moved his head, but his nose, lip and the warmth of his breath maintained tactility with her inner thighs. He gnawed at them simultaneously, teasing the soft sensitive tissues.

She wanted him.

His bulge grew.

Their minds locked.

He pulled away again, now letting his tongue walk the length from her thighs to her navel, sinking it into its depth. Slowly, he opened her blouse. Reaching for the tiny clasp at the front of her sexy, laced bra, he unleashed the firmest breasts he had seen in a long while. 'Ohhhhh… what beauties', he marvelled inwardly. He coupled them. Kissed them. Moulded her nipples with eager yet tender fingertips.

She closed her eyes and sank into the taking. Now, her whole body shook when she felt his tongue wrapping itself around her left nipple, then the right…. left… right. 'Uh! Uh! Uh!' *Orgasm number 1.*

Then down, he went… down… down… down… and now, her hungry clitoris danced as it invited his eager, strong, busy tongue. 'Ahhh!… Ahhhh!… Ahhhhh!…' *Orgasm number 2.*

"Yuh like dat?" he whispered.

Her eyes remained closed. "Shhhhh," she replied, knowing that action would speak louder than words.

Now the sweep of pleasure, from the base of her woman, coming to rest in the fold of her clitoris, pulling sweetly at her ultimate pleasure zone, *almost* bringing her third and most almighty glory down. "Ahhh!… Ahhhh!… Ahhhhh!…"

Then, Suddenly, he stopped.

Just like that.

Stopped.

Up from his knees and straightened himself, leaving her to twitch.

She looked questioningly at him and was assured that just on the verge of an almighty orgasm, the man was *done*.

Leaving.

Ready to go.

She looked questioningly at him. *'What the fuck is that all about?'* she wondered.

"Are you ok?" he patronised.

"Yes… yes… fine," she lied.

"Did you come?"

"What d'you think?"

"I can never tell. You women make so much noise, I never know if it's the real thing or just the build-up. I know you sometimes fake it too." That was his idea of a joke.

She looked away and focused on the soundless TV. Father Jarvis' voice jabbed, his music positively torturing.

"Hey… come here," he reached for her and pulled her up towards him. "I know it seems as if I've just touched you up and is leaving, but I have to meet a bredrin at t'ree o'clock."

"You're… *leaving*?… *Now?"*

"Yeah, but we'll do dis again sometime… And if you'll let me, we could even go all di way… that is if your man doesn't put too tight a grip on you."

'If I'll let you? You didn't fucking try', she thought. She couldn't understand it. After all the hype, he didn't go for the kill, and now she's burning with desire. *Frustrated.* Being brought to the brink then left high and dry was no fun.

"Too tight a grip on me? No… no one puts a grip on me."

"Ok, I hear you. So I take it I'll see you again then?"

What she *really* wanted to say was, *'Aren't you gonna finish what you started?'* but she must try to play the lady, if it wasn't already too late.

"Ok," she said, as he led her towards the front door.

"I'll call you," then he reaches for her lips again. But this time, it was all too much for Evadney. It's been a mighty long time since Garnet left. And although she had a few dates, she hadn't had a bit since the time Conteh lit a fire in her. She gripped him, her tongue descending down his throat faster than he could think. Hastily, she unbuttoned his shirt, pulling it away from his body as if it was on fire.

"Whoa," he responded, pretending he was surprised.

Like lightening she loosened his jeans and groped his firm, sexy ass.

"I think you're hungry," he told her, knowing full well he held the handle. He had the power all right.

Kissing his nipples, his belly button, his thighs, she made him grow again from his shrunken position. And then, there and then, she gave in to her desires.... down.... down... down.... "Ahhh... Ahhh..." he hissed, leaning against the wall with a kind of mastery, his right palm upon her head, as if to bless what he was about to receive.

"Oh, girl... you are... ahhh!... you are... ahhh!... ohhhh! You are something."

"Here," she whispered, squeezing a condom into his right hand.

'Where the hell did that come from?' he wondered.

"Just like that, huh? You *are* hungry... here" he pulled away, "you put it on."

Evadney took the rubber sheath from him then stood up, still moulding his dick as if her life depended on it staying rigid. Within a few seconds, she carefully slid it over his hardness.

It didn't seem to kill his passion. He stayed ready.

It was upstairs that she wanted him, but halfway-up-the-stairs was where she had him. Sitting there on heat, looking down at the top of his head, her thighs around his head, she appreciated his tongue once again on her clitoris. And now, as she gripped the banisters she appreciated his hardness, *jabbing-teasing-jabbing-teasing* her pleasure-filled clitoris, before making its slow, firm entry inside her. And when the whole length of him was inside her, she stretched both her legs down, gripping him. Then... up again, allowing him to move his speedy ass to the rhythm of the moment, ignoring the invading discomfort of the stairs against her spine.

And then, when their passion ran over... showers.

Torrents of passion juice.

Inside her. Yes, inside her.

Deep, deep inside her.

You see, condoms have a way of *bursting. Only this time, this one was helped. Deliberately pierced by the tip of a devious finger.*

The world isn't perfect. Far from it. *Trust no one but yourself. No one.*

And now, when the moment had lulled into a nothingness, leaving only the trickling of clammy sperm, the waft of his aftershave and the sound of Sting FM, Evadney looked up. Her eyes met with those of her father's: his giant portrait looming over her, sending out his robust image. His eyes scolded her. And she could almost here him saying, *'Yuh dyam fool!'*

But it was later, as she sat in the bath, bubbles up to her neck, that Evadney meditated on this man's *out-of-context* words, as he pumped his juice into her, he had chanted: *'Paper roses… they are special…uh!… special… uh!… special because they never, uh! never, uh! never die… they live forever'… uh! uh!*

'So what was all that about?' Evadney had promised herself she would ask him when next she saw him.

Chapter 2

Conteh paced from room to room in his mother's house. He didn't know why, he just felt compelled to do so. It had been… years since his mother (dear old Gladys Gonzalez) passed away, leaving the house to him and his two sisters, Janet and Sandra. Conteh knew how much Gladys loved him, but he could almost hear her saying, *'I told you so'*. He could hear her saying too, *'Dat girl is going to leave yuh'*… and he remembered her dream, too… *The dream of the caged bird*… the dream that sadly came true.

Nothing had changed much since the last time Conteh visited his mum, in fact, the memories, coupled with the familiar kind odour of the house was so palpable, Conteh knew he could not live there for good. He felt he had let Gladys down.

Both Janet and Sandra had places of their own, and had no intention of living there either, but the selling of the legacied shelter was postponed until Conteh's return from jail - an event the girls were almost certain wouldn't be too long. Now, they would wait until he got settled, sorted himself out and was really ready to make some use of what was left of the rest of his life.

With Conteh's portion of the proceeds of the sale of the house, added to his bank balance (the proceeds of the sale the house he and Simone shared), he would have no problem buying himself a nice little roof.

But all he could think of as he paced from room to room was the day he was given the news that in the light of *fresh evidence*, his conviction was quashed. Only, the *evidence* wasn't really that *fresh* after all, since he had tried to tell them all along that a mysterious woman had walked into his shop with a bag that geld the gun and the merchandise stolen from the jewellers opposite. But when he had found out *who* the woman was, he had half told himself he deserved it, and so the *'name and blame'* was deemed a lame option. But when the reality of an horrific prison cell had kicked in, when his faith was weakened and he had cast the bible his dear mother Gladys had sent him aside, and when several cellmates had taken interest in his forbidden zone, the need for revenge on Menna became a must on his list of 'to dos'.

Taking revenge on the woman who had rendered him HIV positive, was never an issue. Pam loved life and would never have done it intentionally. And besides, AIDS had already taken her to the other side.

The house was quiet. Too quiet. In fact it bordered *'torturous loneliness'*. Even prison didn't feel that lonely, since there were always other suffering souls to share a cell with: even the ones who dared to try (but didn't succeed) that Sodomite thing.

Like food, Conteh needed music. *Nuff music*. It is his world. He recalled the first Saturday after his release: he had found himself in a cosy corner of the Million Dollar nightclub, taking in the '*History In The Making*' dance, when, among others, he had bumped into an old friend, Lijah Zephaniah Benjamin (another Birmingham brother who had tread the path of infidelity and had come awfully close to losing his queen and all he had worked for). Saxon Studio from London, V-Rocket from Nottingham and Kebra Negus from Wolverhampton were in the house... not forgetting Conteh's very own, (the Vibes Injection sound crew).

Ever since then, although he didn't know *why*, apart from paying a few visits to his sisters' abodes and visiting his idrin Nico, Conteh had remained a recluse, *almost*, popping out only at odd times to get food.

Today, he was alone with Jimmy Cliff, and although he wanted to, he didn't turn off his stereo. He had chosen to play CDs of sad song endlessly:

> *Many rivers to cross*
> *But I can't seem to find my way over*
> *Wandering I am lost as I travel along*
> *The white cliffs of Dover*
> *Many rivers to cross and it's only my will*

> *That keeps me alive*
> *I've been licked, washed up for years*
> *And I merely survive because of my pride.*

Today he wondered where Nico could be. It had been a while since he had seen him and he was a little worried. He had tried calling his mobile. Turning up on his doorstep. *Everything.* Conteh had even asked West Midlands police to check the whole thing out, but when they broke in, they found nothing but a well-kept flat and a bed that looked as if it hadn't been slept in for a very long time. Nico had suddenly become as illusive as The Scarlet Pimpernel.

> *And this loneliness won't leave me alone*
> *It's such a drag to be on your own*
> *My woman left and she didn't say why*
> *Well I guess I have to try.*
> *Many rivers to cross but just where to begin*
> *I'm playing for time*
> *There'll be times I find myself thinking*
> *Of committing some dreadful crime.*

Along with his sisters, each member of the sound crew tried to get Conteh out of himself, but it was almost as if a deep depression had gotten a hold of him. Each in turn would come to check their idrin to make sure he stayed on top: Federal G, Rin-Tin-Tin, Skankie, Polin Little, Little Tom, Racoon, Grinning Cat, Country Bwoy, Cyclone Quality, Cocoa and Knight. After a while when it seemed as if Conteh had won in his *'wanting to be alone'* stance, the guys had given in slowly.

However, it was on one of his visits to the shops that he bumped into Lijah, who was driving his Jeep in the opposite direction. He was a little shocked to see Lijah without his locks, but he soon got used to it. Lijah had invited him to a kind of get-together, or even a school reunion if you like, since most of the bredrin who was invited, attended the same school at one time or the other. *Handsworth Boys.* Gloria would be on some kind of *'bonding'* retreat with her company, (a trip she didn't really relish), since, as far as she was concerned, this *bonding* thing was a farce. This 'bond-with-me-today, chat-behind-my-back-as-soon-as-it's-turned was not her thing. And the fact that she didn't do the regular pub-glog she was already rendered the one that

'didn't fit in' anyway.   Khamilla and Shanique would be staying
with Shari in her new council flat, so Lijah decided to use the house as
the venue. Conteh had promised Lijah faithfully that he would come,
but Lijah had heard of his great withdrawal, and lived in hope.

The phone rang and made Conteh jump. Before he picked it up he
knew it was his sister Janet. Like their mother, Gladys, Janet was born
to care. Always trying hard to please everyone, with little time left for
herself. She is a born *'giver'* who is always reluctant when it is her
time to *'take'*.

"A'right, Sis'?… yeah, man, I'm a'right…. You're going over to
see Simone?… yeah, well, give her my love, yeah… I still love her,
yunnuh, Jan'. Still love her." But that was not new to Janet, who was
always reluctant to *'give her his love',* since, as far as she could see,
Simone already had love in abundance.

Although Conteh was kinda pleased that his sisters had stayed
friends with Simone, he replaced the receiver, wishing Janet had not
mentioned her tonight: *the woman who had taken more that a little bit
of his heart.* He had spent too many nights in prison wishing he had
never hurt her, giving her the chance to find the arms of an over-
charming, high-flying Antiguan captain, but he had long gone accepted
that *wishing* would never get her back. But the most hurtful things of
all were that this guy's ring had replaced his, and that she had given
him a son (the son he had always wanted with her)… that he had given
her a luxurious house… Car… *Everything.* That with this guy, she had
found true happiness and there would be no room in her head for him.
Ever. But most of all, with all said and done, Conteh was HIV positive.
And although he was a non-progressor (meaning his chances of
developing AIDS were low), he knew she would *never* want him back.

For a short while it was almost as if a presence had comforted
Conteh. He could detect a familiar odour. Some would call it *spooky.
Haunting.* Some would rather not experience it at all, but to him, it was
comforting. Familiar. An odour that only he could explain. The one he
had smelt when the prison gates had opened on his way back from his
mother's funeral. The one that would generate from her bosom, when
as a child, he would lay his little head there. A grown man, but if he
could just find his worry-blanket just then, he would be happy.

*I've got many rivers to cross
But I can't seem to find my way over
Wandering I am lost as I travel along
The white cliffs of Dover*

> *Many rivers to cross and it's only my will*
> *That keeps me alive*
> *I've been licked, washed up for years and,*
> *I merely survive because of my pride.*

* * *

Simone cut her conversation to address her son. "Five more minutes, Amari, then toys away, Darling," she said gently, looking over at him.

"Do I have to go to bed, Mum?" the sweet, five-year-old asked from his comfortable position in the corner of the huge lounge.

"Yes, Darling, as soon as you kiss Janet and Sandra goodnight."

"And Daddy," he corrected.

"Yes, and Daddy."

"Is Daddy going on a flight tonight?"

"Yes, Darling, he is."

"When am I gonna go with Daddy in his aeroplane, Mum?"

"Soon, Sweetheart, soon."

Janet and Sandra sat in the big leather settee, smiling as they listened to the conversation between mother and son. Less than ten minutes ago Sandra had listened, though subconsciously, to the sound above her head: the sound of the cascading torrents as Lawrence took his shower. He was humming a tune and she was sure it was Luther Vandross' *So Amazing…* it was a song she was familiar with. *Deep meaning.*

"I love my daddy," Amari said, still paying attention to his toys.

"Janet's heart melted. She looked at Sandra who was melting too. None of them had children of their own. Their brother Conteh, it seemed, had had their share.

"I hope so, Darling," Simone said, smiling, "I hope you love your daddy."

"Do *you* love my daddy, Mum?" the little boy asked innocently.

Simone, along with Janet and Sandra giggled, "Yes, Darling. I *do* love your daddy."

"A lot a lot a lot?"

"Yes… a lot a lot a lot."

Love has truly been good to me…

Sandra wondered if it was just her that heard the deep, round vocals that descended the stairs.

21

Not even one sad day...

'*Love lives here,*' Sandra thought, '*or does it?... Is this real? Does such perfect love really exist?*'

Or minute have I had since you've come my way...

She didn't mean to be sceptical. She was just being real. She had seen one too many betrayal. One too many couple '*living a lie*'. The hypocrisy of life had clouded her judgement, making it hard to believe true sincerity when it stares her in the face.

I hope you know I'd gladly go... Anywhere you'd take me...

As for her, (and she wasn't bitter) she had given up hoping that her prince would come.

It's so amazing to be loved,
I'd follow you to the moon in the sky above...

At the same time, the only thing Janet could think of was the fact that Conteh had allowed himself to loose this beautiful woman. And what Sandra didn't realise was that Janet had long gone picked up on, and believed in the harmony and love that she felt lived in the house in which they were sitting. She told herself that if anyone deserved a life like that, it was Simone. She couldn't wish better for her. She had had her fair share of tears. Janet was grateful that Simone was the person she was, for she had forgiven her after she had lied to her about the earring she had found behind her loo seat. She was simply trying to help her brother out of a sticky situation, but it had backfired. Simone understood.

No one would ever know how precious the gift of Simone's friendship was to her, but she would be lying if she said she hadn't imagined that the voice that hummed its way down the stairs and into the warm lounge, was that of their brother. And that she had wished him a cured and changed man who could be given one more chance with Simone.

"Hey, ladies!" Lawrence entered the lounge. Clad from head to toe in his pilot's uniform, he placed his flight bag on the floor. "Sorry I

can't stay and chat, but you know what it's like when duty calls."
Perfect white teeth sealed his words.

"Oh, we understand," Janet said, smiling back.

"Where are you off to, tonight?" Sandra asked.

"Just a short-haul. Malaga." He picked his big five-year-old up.
Amari had long gone dropped his toys and dashed towards him.

"Well, think of us here in boring Birmingham, won't you?"

"Well, I won't be seeing much of it, I'm afraid. Quick turn-round.
This is a matter of dropping my passengers off and turning straight
back."

Janet couldn't help wondering how nice-natured this man was.
Some guys would have problems with harbouring the ex-sisters-in-law;
maybe because of their own insecurities. But not this one. Or perhaps it
was because Lawrence knew he needn't be insecure, since there was
no way Simone would contemplate going back to a *HIV positive ex*.

But while Janet could see a *near-perfect* black man, Sandra's mind
was conjuring up all sorts. Hotel rooms. Countless lovers. Hot air
hostesses on stopovers from long-haul flights clambering all over
him…She really couldn't help it. As far as she was concerned, a man
like this could never have eyes for *just one woman.*

Simone was now standing next to her husband, waiting to relieve
him of their sweet son, who was hugging his daddy so tight, love had
made a heart-shaped haze around them. "Daddy's got to go now,
Darling. His passengers are waiting for him to take them on their
holidays."

Amari loosened the grip on his daddy.

"I'll see you tomorrow, big boy." He kissed his son's forehead.

Amari leaned now into his mother's arm as if he was a small baby.
Lawrence put his arm around her and kissed her. "See you tomorrow,
Honey."

"Can't wait," was her reply, kissing him back.

"Can't wait," Amari imitated.

Everybody chuckled, and the sweet child clung tighter to his
mother's neck.

"You're getting too big to be lifted," Lawrence teased him, as he
straightened his jacket with his left hand, and picked up his flight bag
with his right. "Ok, ladies, see you again soon." Now, his left hand
grasped Simone's right.

"Bye, Lawrence," the sisters said in unison as they watched the
family walk to the front door. "Have a good flight," Janet added.

"I'll try," the gorgeous, handsome specimen replied.

At the door, Lawrence paused to shake his legs. Whatever the reason was, he had been suffering from mild cramps. He had promised to get it checked out.

"Bad circulation, Darling," Simone told him. "And being cooped up in the cockpit of an aircraft won't help either. Make sure you walk around as soon as your co-pilot takes over."

"Yes, Mrs Hendricks," he said playfully, "I will." He kissed his wife and son goodbye and headed for his car.

After waving her husband goodbye, Simone walked back into the lounge. "Sorry about this, girls, just gimme a few minutes. Let me put this young man to bed... C'mon, Amari, go kiss Janet and Sandra goodnight."

Seconds later, they watched mother and son climbing the stairs.

"Is he real?" Sandra asked Janet.

"Who?"

"Lawrence."

"Wha' d'you mean?"

"He just seems... *perfect. Too* perfect to be exact. Are there *really* men like that?"

"Of course there are, Sandra. Don't be so negative. Just because our brother and so many other man are love rats, it doesn't mean all..."

"No, but... "

"But what?" Janet perplexed. "How d'you expect the man to be?... You know, it's true what they say about not being able to please us women... if a man is a bastard, we moan, if he is good, we try to find reasons why he is."

"So you believe he's genuine then?"

"Yes, I do, Sandra. Everyone is innocent until proven guilty. Stop being such a doubting Thomas... What's with all the negativity anyway?"

"You're right," Sandra said. "I shouldn't be so doubtful, but life has just made me conclude that everything that glitters too much is far from golden..."

"He's fast asleep, would you believe it? He must have been very tired" Simone said, ascending the stairs, forcing their conversation to cease for a little while. But it wasn't long before the three of them settled down to that good old girl talk.

Sandra was never one for beating around the bush. In fact there were times when she had gone so straight to a point, people around her had crumbled under the strain of embarrassment. Simone was used to her outspokenness, but she had noticed that for a long time after her and Conteh had split, Sandra, for her own reasons, had held the twenty-question session back. So tonight when she asked, "Do you ever think about our brother?" Simone was a bit surprised.

"Oh, Sandra." Forever the protective mother-hen, Janet intervened. "Simone don't want to be talking about Conteh, she's…"

"No, I don't mind talking about Conteh at all. It's not as if it's painful or anything. I've gotten over that hurdle. It's just sad… the prison thing. And worst of all, the HIV, thing."

"I know," Janet dropped her voice.

"But, *yes,* Sandra, I *do* think about Conteh. He was my first husband, of course he's gonna cross my mind from time to time."

"But not in a *missing* sense?" Sandra quizzed deeper.

"Sandra!" Janet scolded, "I don't think so." She answered for Simone.

Simone chuckled. She was *definitely* used to her ex-sister-in-law's *no-beating-around-the-bush* attitude. She respected it. "As a matter-of-fact, there are things about Conteh that I miss. The only thing that tore us apart was his cheating. That was too painful to bear. If it wasn't for that, we would have been together now."

"He loved you, Simone. *Really* loved you," Sandra told her. "The other day he was…"

"Sandra," Janet interrupted, "Simone is married now, she don't want to hear…"

"And I loved him too, Sandra," Simone butted in. "*Really* loved him. But he hurt me real bad. He would have taken my life if I didn't wise-up." She remembered telling them the femidoms story.

"Does it suddenly stop?" Sandra relented.

"What?"

"*Loving* somebody?… Does that just *stop*?… you see, I wouldn't really know. I've never really loved anyone that deep. Does it just switch off like that?"

"No. Not just like that," Simone asserted.

"I know you love Lawrence, but is there just a little spec of *something* left for Conteh?" Sandra's probe was beginning to feel like an interview.

"Well… let's put it this way, Sandra, I don't *hate* him."

Sandra smiled, "But that didn't answer the question."

"Sandra, leave it now," Janet said.

25

"Ok, let's change the subject of *Conteh*," Sandra said, looking at Janet, then back at Simone, "Simone, d'you think Lawrence is faithful?"

"Sandra!" Janet splattered. "You're something else, you are."

"Do I think Lawrence is *faithful*?" Simone scrutinised the question.

"Yeah. Do you?" Sandra looked at Janet as she waited for her answer.

"Well, let's put it this way... It's all about that little word '*trust*', and the way you feel inside. I stopped trusting Conteh because I was given reasons upon reasons why I shouldn't trust him. And even when every corner of our house was filled with doubts, I lived in hope. I gave him chances after chances, hoping that love would change something, but it didn't. Conteh didn't stop until he ended up screwing my best friend."

Janet sipped her black grape. She didn't know why she was feeling so uncomfortable. In fact, she didn't know why her sister insisted on probing into Simone's business.

"So you *totally* trust Lawrence then?"

"Yes. It isn't to say I *know* he's not cheating on me, Sandra. No one can ever really *know*, unless of course you have a crystal ball and are willing to use it to track your partner's every move. But my intuitions are usually pretty good. And if he is cheating, he's pretty clever. And although I'm the ambassador of women who shouldn't trust *completely,* I will still say, don't hang your man before you know he has definitely committed a crime."

"It's good that after our brother, you can trust... I would be paranoid."

"Lawrence is good to me, Sandra. From the life I had with Conteh, this is heaven. Financially, we're ok, although I will be going back to work in a year. We have a beautiful house in an affluent part of the West Midlands. We have a wonderful son. And sex? She chuckled, "sex is great. It isn't everything, but it's great. I love him deeply. And if someone up there is fooling me, all I know is, right now, it feels good."

"I almost envy you, Simone," Sandra said, smiling.

"But how can you envy me when you're not even sure if Lawrence is real?"

"Yeah, but even a false sense of security for a little while, if it makes you happy, will do me."

"Sandra!" Janet scolded her again. "*False sense of security*? You do choose your words, don't you?"

"It's ok, Janet, I know what she means," Simone showed how understanding she could be.

"Mum!" Amari called from upstairs.

"Won't be a minute," Simone assured the sisters, as she headed upstairs. "I thought he was fast asleep."

"Sandra," Janet couldn't help but choose the opportunity to goad her sister, "why d'you have to be so insensitive sometimes?"

"Simone don't have a problems with my questions, it's just you. And anyway, I'm just asking what *you* are frightened to ask. You know you want to know."

"Sandra, I would never ask anyone if they think their husband is faithful. Only *you* would do that. Yuh too dyam nosey an' tactless."

"Hah! Hah! Hah!" Janet's little bouts of discipline always seem to fail to do their intended jobs. Sandra was jolted into fits of laugher, but when she caught the serious stare from her sister, she settled into a wide grin.

"But happiness comes with the demanding calls of a child from time to time," Simone said, entering the lounge again.

"Weren't Lawrence seeing another woman when you met, Simone?" Sandra was off again.

Janet put her eyes up to the ceiling in disbelief of her sister's persistence. '*Is this pure inquisition, or downright evilness?*' she wondered.

"Yes. They had a mutual agreement. They both had no delusions as to where things were at, so when he told her he met someone he was really serious about, apparently, she was very cool about it."

"*Apparently*?" Sandra found a flaw.

"Well, that is what Lawrence told me," Simone assured her. "I am a woman, and although I have never entered into a *just-sex* relationship with anyone, I think if I ever did, I would become a bit more attached than to be able to just step aside unscathed, should he decide to end it. But obviously we aren't all the same."

"Have you ever met her?"

"No. Hopefully she's found someone she can look to for more than just sex. After all, it's been nearly five years now."

Janet's mobile rang. It was Conteh. She had forgotten he wanted her to pass 'round. Minutes later, the evening came to a close, but that was just one of many more to come.

* * *

With their father not around to help her and with the constant *toing* and *froing* of her children, the *too-skinny* blonde battled it alone, getting by on the *now-and-then* intervention of a few neighbours who, when the *not-so-perfect* is in their faces, didn't take the Englishman's *stiff-upper-lip-turn-the-other-way-go-indoors-peep-out-and-gossip* attitude. Instead, they tried their best to help her.

'You're lying!' Thoughts lashed like angry waves against her mind. *'He couldn't possibly love you!'* the voice of the irate black woman echoed like a nasty rebuke in her liqueur-drenched head.

It's a cruel world.

Everybody must be prepared for their share of cruel chippings hitting them in their faces for time to time. Only, for Glenda, they were *stinging like hell.*

The *once-gorgeous* now *bedraggled-from-drink-and-too-much-fags* white woman defeated the laws of control by successfully driving her two mixed-raced children to school.

Some days would be worse than some.

Today was a mediocre day.

Glenda had found that she loved him even after she found he wasn't as flushed as she thought he would be.

She hung around...

Waited for the impossible to happen...

It wasn't coming...

You see, his hands were already full and he had not bargained on her hanging on.

He told her he loved her, but he lied. For to his idrin and the black sistas he checked, she was like a grating abomination: and so he had denied her like Judas did, Jesus.

"Run along now, kids," Glenda told her children at the school gates. "See you later."

* * *

Simone did not realise that the lady that pushed aggressively past her and mumbled the word *'bitch'*, was someone that felt she had a reason to. She herself had no reason to be aggressive. In fact it was questionable as to whether or not there was an aggressive bone in her body.

At first, she didn't recognise the bitter female, but looking closer, she realised it was one of Conteh's ex-girlfriends, who, even now Simone had found herself a new husband, still thought she owed her something. But that wasn't entirely it: if the bitter antagonist had checked herself, she would have found that she was suffering from more than the average dose of bitterness. *Jealousy. Resentment.* In every way, Simone was on top, and the troubled sista knew it too well.

Asking Joya what the problem was would have been justified, but instead, Simone just smiled to herself and carried on, a verse of her much loved poem springing to mind:

> *Avoid loud and aggressive persons;*
> *they are vexatious to the spirit.*
> *If you compare yourself with others,*
> *you may become vain or bitter,*
> *for always there will be greater and lesser persons than yourself.*

Chapter 3

𝔂t was an hour ago since Lawrence and his co-pilot, Lance alighted from yet another long-haul flight, this time from the States. They hoped the customs routine and the crew-room paperwork wouldn't be so time consuming, but it was part of the game.

"That wasn't such a bad flight, was it?" Lawrence asked Lance.

"Well, we've had worse," Lance said.

"How's Morag anyway?"

"She's ok, I think."

Lawrence looked at him, "You *think?*... is everything ok with you guys, Lance?"

"I'm not sure, man. There's something going on with Morag... I' d'know, man... I'm watching a few things."

Lawrence looked puzzled.

"You mean…"

"I think she's having an affair."

"Really? What made you think that?"

"Well, I've seen a few signs. Nothing concrete, but enough to uphold my doubt."

"How come you hadn't said anything before?"

"Well, like I said, nothing's concrete. I asked her about a few little uncertainties, but she denied them all. Told me I'm paranoid… I d'know. What with these long-haul flights taking us away for days on end…"

"What signs have you seen, Lance?"

"Well, for instance, there were a few suspicious text messages in her phone…"

"You checked her phone!"

"Had to. Only after I started becoming suspicious… you've never checked Simone's phone?"

"No… never felt the need to. I trust her, man. To the max."

"Well, I never trusted Morag, not really. Remember how we met? She was with her first husband at the time. Captain Frank Philips. I don't know what she saw in me. Financially, I couldn't compete with Frank… a yacht… multiple country houses… cars… his bank balance… I often wondered if it was down to that cliché."

"What cliché?"

"You know… the once taste black thing."

Lawrence Laughed. "Why didn't you ask her?"

"I did. Especially when I realised that Frank was serious about divorcing her. I must admit, at the time I felt a little inadequate. It was ok when we were just fooling around. But when I had her fully, I…"

"So why did you marry her if you had doubts?"

"She said that was what she wanted. Me? I wasn't really sure *what* I wanted. Right now I'm not even sure if…" Lance paused. As if he had started to communicate something he shouldn't.

"You're not sure if *what*?"

"Nothing…"

"Marriage is a big step, Lance. I don't think it's one anyone should take if there are doubts. I didn't realise you felt that way… and you really feel she's having an affair?"

"Yes, I do, but I suppose there's something in the saying, *'blondes just godda have fun'*.

Lawrence chuckled, "Not just blondes, mate. If a woman have it in her to cheat, she will, blonde or not."

"Has anyone ever cheated on you?" Lance asked.

"Uh huh… I didn't tell you this before, but the American woman I was married to ran off with a rich Nigerian. It happens. No one's invincible. It broke my heart. I didn't think I'd love again, but look at me now… *Simone*. She's a dream come true, Lance. We are great together. You know what they say, 'one man's meat is another man's poison'. My ex-wife saw pound signs, but Simone sees the person in me. To her, the rest is a bonus. It still puzzles me though how the man she was with didn't see that he had a real gem."

"So, have you seen or spoken to Sheree since you broke up with her?"

They were nearing the entrance to the crew-room now. Lawrence chuckled, "Not *seen*. But I had just one phone call from her just after I married Simone. That's it."

"Not as often as before, but she still keeps in touch with Morag," Lance announced. "Since you introduced them, they built a kinda friendship. They keep in touch. Not often, but they do the odd drinks… birthdays, etc. I also believe that Sheree knows that Morag kinda look up to Simone. And with Simone being her rival, well."

"Morag looks up to Simone?"

"I think so. Just from a few things she said. Said Simone has something special. Someone she felt she could talk to with her problems."

"Well, that's women for you," Lawrence said. "They all need agony aunts from time to time."

"But anyway, back to Sheree," Lance said, "I've always wondered about your parting, but now you've confirmed you only had one call from her…"

"What?"

"Well, women aren't usually like that, are they?"

"Like what?"

"You know… just accept a goodbye like that. They usually cling tight after one night of sex, never mind five fucking years, man. C'mon, Lawrence, you must have found it strange… if it was like you said. The way she just let go without a fuss or a twinge."

"Yes, well I'd be lying if I said I wasn't expecting a little more force behind her reaction, but I found love, man. I didn't have time to ask why."

"Unless she had somebody else and was glad to be released."

"No. I don't think so. Besides, the arrangement we had? If she found someone, she needn't wait to be released, she could have gone."

"Well, like you said, you found love. Me? I'm shattered. Let's go home."

"Changing the subject," Lawrence added, "What d'you think of the new First Officer?"

31

"Who, Clive Saunders?"

"Yeah."

"He seems promising. Ambitious. Money orientated, but I can't say much. I can't seem to get enough myself. He seems ok."

"Is he married?"

"No. He loves life too much. Loves his cars too. Always on the lookout for the latest. I suppose he can afford it."

"You seem to know a lot about him."

"We had a few drinks and a chat at the flying-club the other day."

The two dashing men had picked up their flight bags and were heading for the lift that would take them to ground level, where their cars awaited them.

Home, they say, is where the heart is, and *home* was where they were heading. But unlike Lance who was going home to a wife that no longer interested him, rushing home to see his wife and five-year-old son was a novelty for Lawrence: a novelty that had not shown any signs of wearing off.

"I'll talk to Simone if you want. We can arrange dinner for you and Morag one evening. It might be just a phase you guys are going through..."

"Somehow," Lance stated, "I don't think so. I think we're on a downward slope."

"That bad?"

"Maybe worse."

The lift door opened and Birmingham International Airport seemed somewhat different to Lawrence. The short walk to the car park was a little strange. He could feel that there were more to the unsalvageable marriage of Lance and Morag, but the problem was theirs. And apart from hoping they would work through it, there was nothing he could do.

* * *

Turning the key in the door of their luxury house, creeping up the stairs and into Amari's room just to kiss his little forehead, always invigorated Lawrence.

After taking a shower, he climbed into bed and wrapped his arms around his woman. That seemed always to give him new life.

Simone turned, mumbled a sexy, "Hi Baby... how was your flight?"

"It was good. But I missed you. Couldn't wait to get home."

"I missed you too, Babes."

"More so after Lance started to tell me he thinks Morag is having an affair."

"Really?" Simone didn't seem surprised.

"Yes, it made me realise what a gem I have." He kissed her lips.

"Oh, Baby, that's so nice. You're not so bad yourself."

"Mmmm," he cuddled up close to her, "do you think Lance's suspicions are valid?" He shook his left leg. Cramp bothering him again.

"D'know. What evidence has he got?"

"Some text message business. He looked in her phone."

"Oh dear. I didn't see Lance as a snoop." She chuckled.

"I suppose he had his reasons."

"Well, I'm not one to get into people's business, but years ago, when I was with Conteh, and Morag was with Captain Philips, we had a jewellery party at the house. It was then I noticed what a flirt Morag could be."

"Don't tell me she was flirting with Conteh."

"No. She was flirting with Nico. I'm not sure whether they had a thing, but… well, let's put it this way, with Nico being the way he is and Morag… well, I wouldn't be surprised if anything went down."

"But… isn't Nico the one who's got AIDS?"

"Well, HIV positive… That was the same night he took Pam home. She didn't know at the time she had AIDS."

"Jesus. And isn't Nico doing that evil thing of going around deliberately sleeping with every woman he can get his hands on?"

"So I heard, Babes, but like I said, I don't know if Morag and Nico got it together. If that happened, Morag never said. She was never as open as Pam. She flirted openly alright, but actually admitting that she did the deed, well…"

"Apparently, she looks up to you," Lawrence told Simone, "so I don't think she'd tell you that."

"Morag looks up to *me*?… who said that?"

"Lance."

"I don't know about that. What I know is, she has been telling me that she thinks Lance has gone off her. She thinks he's not turned on by her anymore."

"Really? I wouldn't be surprised. Lance was trying to say something to me back at the airport, but then he stopped. They definitely have some problems, but they need to sort it themselves."

"D'you think it's solvable?" Simone asked.

"I don't even wanna think about it, Babes. Besides, why are we in bed talking about other people's problem when I'm dying to make love to you?"

"You started it," she said playfully.

And there it began.

He lifted the sheets higher and eased himself onto her.

He found the palms of her hands and lay his masculine ones over them, entwining his fingers into hers.

He stretched her arms outward.

Kissed her tender neck.

Descended gently to her tender breasts.

He took them timely into his mouth. Suckled. Licked. Kissed.

The beautiful Simone tingled with delight. "Ahhhh…"

"Tell me how much you missed me," he commanded in a seductive whisper.

"A lot."

"That's not enough." He bit her gently.

"A thousand times more than you missed me."

"Still not enough." He moved his strong tongue down to the centre of her navel.

"Ahh…. A million times, then."

"Still not enough." He moved to her sensitive side and took a lump of her skin gently into his mouth and suckled, "Let me hear you."

"Ahhh!"

There was no forest to wade through.

She was clean-shaven, just the way he liked it.

"I wanna hear you, Babes," he whispered, as if he needed the reply before he could go there.

But soon, he needn't ask, for when he reached her heavens, he kissed the top of her waiting flower. Prizing it gently apart, he thrummed her pleasure as he played sweet music with his warm tongue.

"Ahhh… Baby… I missed you… Missed you… Ahhh!" Her seductive whisper turned him on.

Time had flown. They were having fun. Pleasure lived within the walls of their bedroom.

Time passed.

And now, he pulled himself up and kissed her lips, at the same time, he eased his stiff manhood into her.

"Ohhhhhhhh!"

* * *

But at that moment, in the bedroom of a quiet house, the mood was somewhat different.   Lance was convinced that the aroma of another man lingered in his house. In fact it oozed out of his walls. He lay his flight bag down on the lounge floor and just stood there. He had no proof, but still he *knew* it.

Something was strangling him. He wasn't quite sure what it was. Jealousy? Paranoia? Or just plain old *someone's-been-playing-with-my-discarded-toy*?   Yes. *Discarded*. For only Lance knew what he really wanted. But everybody knows that no matter how old, raggedy and unwanted an old toy becomes, watching someone else play with it ekes out feelings of *selfishness*.

A stiff whisky was just what that moment ordered.

As he poured, he raised his head upstairs where she lay sleeping.

She would be waiting for him, like she always did.

Now, his head told him she had always waited for him with *seconds*. Leftovers. Another mans *leftovers*. Like she did, her husband, when he himself was *the other man*. Did she use protection? Surely this man's sperm must have settled mockingly in her, laughing as it mingled with his?

Lance poured the half-filled glass down his neck then headed upstairs.

"Lance?" Morag's tired voice called out. "Hurry up. I miss you."

Paranoia fluttered in his head. *'How much? How much do you miss me?'*

He switched the bathroom light on and looked around. 'Surely *he* was here?' In my bathroom... this other man. He must have showered with her... *yes*... he did. Made love right here... Under the falling torrents while I transported a flight full of passengers to the States...' He looked for a strand of hair. But *what* hair? Was he *black*? *White*? *Asian*? What kind of man was fucking his wife? For something told him that this man definitely existed. Someone was definitely sharing his chow-chow.

"Hi," Morag had said when Lance finally crawled into bed, "you took so long." She held and started to kiss him.

He stiffened.

She paused. "What is it?"

He looked away.

35

"Lance, you haven't touched me for months… what is it?"

"I'm tired, Morag. I need to rest. It's been a long flight."

"You're still not convinced. You think I'm…"

"I've had a hard day, Morag," he stressed. "Let me rest."

She prized back the sheets and plunged herself out of the bed.

Through the dimness of the room he watched her as she angrily dragged on her silk dressing gown and left the room.

Now, he lay there in silence listening to the clinking sound of glass against bottle. *Firewater*. Like a rock, she had ran to its rescue.

His mind drifted to another place.

Somewhere he'd rather be.

A place he had battled with in the past.

Forbids.

Despises.

A place where he himself tried to tell himself he didn't belong.

* * *

A week and two days to be precise and Evadney hadn't heard a thing from **Sanchez**, the man that screwed her senseless halfway up her parent's sacred staircase. When she had got, *'The mobile you have called is switched off'* for the third time, she planned on putting it down to experience. The *burst condom* episode bothered her a bit, but when her period had arrived, it was as if it made everything well. She decided which piece of her mind she would give him if ever she bumped into him again. Then she moved on.

Besides, she wasn't that bothered. Sanchez wasn't the only cook-ups rustling on her burners. Oh no. Someone she had met before she built Garnet's hopes up was on her mind. He might be a plane ride away, but that was ok. Holiday romances were ok by her. Besides, it won't be long before she would take that well needed visit to Jamaica. Just a few weeks after her parents' return.

To add to it all, Garnet had never been so tentative. He was showing her more attention than he had ever shown in the whole of their previous time together. She was lapping it up. However hard he tried, nothing could make up for him pissing off with the blonde Tracey, leaving her rejected. The tears she cried were unthinkable. And she hit the bottle for a little while too. Now, Garnet was certainly on his toes and she took pleasure on keeping him dancing. He had even proposed. Asked for her hand in marriage. *Chat bout*. She told him, *'I'll think about it.'* But were Garnet's hopes built on solid ground? Or were they shacked up on a mound of sinking sand? Only Evadney knew that. She was playing all right. And it wouldn't be over until the once-ditched lady got the throne. *Life*. It's filled with pleasure and pain. Winners and losers. Ordinary and extraordinary people who *seriously* don't know which way to go. *Feh real*.

* * *

'*Speak of the devil, she's sure to appear,*' was Lawrence's thought when he picked up the first message from Sheree. Coincidentally, it came just a few days after he and Lance spoke about her and the fact that she had taken the ending of the relationship so well.

He was somewhat surprised to hear from her after so long, so he quickly returned her call, thinking something was seriously wrong. But he soon found out that her sole intention was to invite him over for what she called an innocent drink and a chat, *for old times sake.* In the nicest possible way, he declined, knowing what a simple drink could lead to if a woman has her clever head on.

But when four subsequent messages were left: each one sounding more irate and desperate owing to the fact that her previous ones weren't returned, Lawrence began to wonder what was going on.

But today, when he sat having dinner with his wife and son and his mobile vibrated on the coffee table, he regretted picking it up. The last thing he wanted to do was to lie to his dear wife, so he was pleased when Simone didn't ask who it was when he switched his phone off after deliberately losing the nuisance call.

* * *

Farewell, I'm leaving...
Farewell, I'm leaving...

Henley picked up the last of his bag from the hallway and turned to look one last time into his now ex-woman's eyes. *19 years down the drain*. He had already said goodbye to Cerise and her son. They were sitting upstairs in her bedroom. Cerise hated goodbyes. It was her Dad that was leaving them. Not her *blood-father*... her stepfather. But nonetheless, the best dad there ever could be.

Jacqueline should have known that it would come to this: the secret of Cerise's real father being the father of her baby wouldn't keep its lid on forever. *Whatever is done in the dark will surely come out in the light.* Although it wasn't intentional, that was sick enough, but it was the fact that the woman he loved so much made a calculated decision to keep it from him that made him decide to tear himself away from the family he had loved for years.

Jacqueline loved him.

They had been through thick and thin. Even after Henley's mother had expressed her preference for a Bajan wife. Although we all *hailed from* and were *hauled from* the same continent - Africa, subtly, the senseless *Battle of the Islands* still stupidly prevails. *Trust.* The black and white thing may be *something*, but the subtle *'Island'* thing is *something else.*

Cerise sat cuddling her son. He was five years old and a picture of Conteh. How could it not be? With the jeans so closely entangled, it was either going to be a carbon copy, or a gruesome distortion. But he was a perfect little soul.

It wasn't for the want of *trying*. On Henley's part, that is.

In fact the relationship lasted a long time after the gruesome revelation, but when it is confirmed that you have been living a lie for so many years, things could never be the same again. In his *trying*, Henley had had promised to *try* to forgive and forget, but one too many arguments overshadowed his *trying*. Arguments they never used to have. When there is a *root canal* that feeds the hurt: the source of an unbearable pain: a reason for thoughtful nights, then every molehill becomes a mountain. And soon a naked truth is revealed: *'when you peel back the skin, revealing the basic elements of 'unconditional love', you will find that it is not that easy to give.'*

'But why do you have to go to Barbados?' Jacqueline had asked months ago after Henley had told her he was definitely going. *'You've been here for so long.'*

'Barbados is nice,' he had said. *'Life can be good there. Fresh start. Besides, I've lost a big part of me here in England. Never once have I kept anything from you. I need to get as far away as possible. It hurts.'*

'Henley, everybody hurts sometime,' she had said with sad eyes.

'You're never gonna understand my hurt. It doesn't take a man to come home and find his wife in bed with another man for him to hurt deeply.'

'Can't we stay friends, Henley? It seems as if you hate me.'

'No, I don't hate you. But selfish though it may sound, Jacqueline, I love you too much to ever start being just a friend.' And tears had welled in his eyes.

38

'You love me too much and you're walking away?'

'You're never gonna understand, Jacqui... you're never gonna understand.'

And she had cried.

And he had cried some more.

But his mind was made up.

So today as the final closing of the *physical* door emphasised that of the *emotional* one, Jacqueline knew that *cheating* wasn't the only thing that could bring a good relationship to a point of no-return. *Secrets* can do that too. Some secrets, when revealed, can be just as deadly as lying.

* * *

Come dong w'en mi call you Inez, come dong...
Come dong w'en mi call you Inez, come dong...

Three days later...

Bridge Town, Barbados...

Henley strolled down the High Street.

He browsed the shops.

Felt the sun on his face.

Watched beautiful ladies go by.

Bought flying fish from a street vendor.

Watched tourists busying themselves, soaking up the glory of an Island he had taken so long, for granted.

Now, he came to rest where young-looking old ladies sat, their wares in front of them, touting for English and American pounds.

Like a tourist, he pointed his video camera at them, assuming they would all love the attention. But when *'Tek di cam'ra out mi face!'* was the response he got from the oldest and seemingly *most-unlikely-to-protest* lady, he knew different.

'Straight', he thought with a smile. 'Say what you feel... say what you feel.'

Henley walked on.

It would take time... Time to forget her.

And like a clown, more tears would fall when there was no one around. It's the natural process of grieving.

You see, he had left his heart way back in Birmingham, England.

Jacqueline was on his mind.

Yes... it would take time.

Chapter 4

Sheree sat again, staring out at the front door through the tinted window of her top-of the-range Jag. She was a woman that had everything, and at one time she was satisfied with that. With a lover no more than a phone call away, everything was just so.

But now, he was gone.

Said his *Au revoirs* and married one of the most beautiful women in Birmingham. *Simone. One woman's sadness is another's joy*. That's the way of the world.

Stalking the man that had been her lover for the longest time (more than anyone would care to imagine) had become part of her life: a notion she would have previously counted as ridiculous.

"*Sheree?*... Is everything ok?" Lawrence said after walking over to her ride. He was wondering why Sheree was parked outside his house.

"Fine. Everything's just fine."

"Are you here to see me?... how did you know where I lived?"

"Small world," she said, looking straight ahead.

He was worried now. "What is this?" Lawrence asked when he realised that something was amiss. The words *'Are you stalking me?'* lingered on the tip of his tongue, but he held them back. "What are you doing sat outside my house?" He knew that would be the last thing Simone wanted. After that episode she told him about with Marcia who attacked her in her own house after being hooked on Conteh, that would be the final straw.

"I d'know..." Sheree turned and looked him in the eyes now, "Just watching the movements of a *perfectly* happy family, I guess."

'*Oh no. Not that fatal attraction shit,*' he thought. A puzzle-line found its way across his forehead as he saw the blatant cynicism in Sheree's eyes.

"You never return my calls, Lawrence. *Why*?" She was abrupt. Perhaps she was related to Bernadette, although they didn't know each other.

"And why do I need to explain my actions to *you*?... I'm a grown man. What is this, Sheree?" He was getting annoyed though he kept it down.

"I thought you had more manners than that." She slowly gaped her legs making the V on her black leather seat wider. She was no teenager. She didn't wear short skirts, just sexy-but-classy ones. So she must have come prepared, for the ones she wore was already conveniently pulled up.

Lawrence pretended not to see her gorgeous, though devilishly tempting, black, silky legs. "Sheree, I'm married now. I told you, I don't want anything interfering with my life."

"And that is why you can't return my calls?"

"No. It's because your intentions are not innocent. I would hate to think that my wife is returning calls to her ex."

"Is her fucking pussy made of gold or something?" she said matter-of-factly.

Lawrence looked around, then at his house. He got a little nervous. Somewhat shocked at Sheree's expression. She had always been so lady-like. "This isn't like you... What's gotten into you?" He spoke low as if he was sure someone could hear, not realising that his low dulcet tone turned Sheree on.

"I asked you a question... is her pussy made of gold?... the way you left me?"

He looked around again, then back at her, puzzled. "We had an agreement, Sheree. You were ok with it."

"Fuck the agreement, Lawrence! I'm human!"

"Shhhh... Listen... this is ridiculous. It's been five years. If you had found someone you would have done the same. We've already been through all this on the phone."

Sheree turned the key in her ignition.

She kept her eyes on him.

He waited for her to say something, but she didn't.

Just eased off... gently... gently...

Her action was message-filled.

The last look she gave was loaded.

Too loaded.

And Lawrence knew... she had only just begun.

'Should I bother Simone with this?... Tell her and be out with it? What if she's in danger from Sheree's weird strategy?' As he walked up his drive, thoughts rolled around in his head.

"Hi, Babes," Simone said when he entered the house.

"Hi," he said, giving her a kiss. "How was your day?"

"Good. But better now you're here."

"Mmmm." He squeezed her. "Where's my son?"

"He's having a nap."

Lawrence hugged his wife again. *'Why can't life be straightforward?'* he thought. For he knew now that it wouldn't be the mountain that would wear him out, but the niggling grain of sand that would come to settle in his previously comfy shoe.

* * *

A quiet corner of The Belfry housed her… It wrapped its arms around her like cuddles, fitting her into its surroundings like hand and glove.

Sheree was the type of black woman who, was it not for her skin colour, could pass for an upper-class white woman. Golf-club-swinging white men who retreated at weekends to boat houses, sailed in yachts, escaped to villas in Spain, and drank expensive whisky poured from thick cut-glass decanters, lit her fire a treat.

Alternatively, the black man Sheree would allow into her bed would have to be gorgeously handsome, suave, sophisticated and reeked *STATUS*… Like the high-flying Captain Lawrence Hendricks. But that was a problem: Simone had won his heart. Sheree knew that. But something made her want him *more.*

Lawrence hadn't the slightest clue that Sheree hadn't moved on, until a week ago when he found her sitting in her car outside his house. It was then that he realised just how *deep* some women can be.

The Belfry was where they first met, and now, unbeknown to him, Sheree would escape to its comfort from time to time. Choosing her usual quiet corner, she would reminisce. Tonight she had come to think hard about their last encounter. She wanted him. And although he had made no bones about telling her how much he loved his wife, still, she would try. *Time is truly longer than rope.*

Tonight, the man that joined Sheree was *drop-dead gorgeous.* And Status? Later she would find out how much he had to offer. If the *'Lawrence lock'* was too hard to pick, he might do for a while. And, so willing he was to *give it to her*, she figured it would take her mind off Lawrence for a bit. *At least.*

"Hi," the *look-good-enough-to-eat* man had said, "are you alone?"

"Yes. Is that a problem?"

"No. I was just wondering if I could join you."

"Stop wondering and get me a drink."

"Whoa… You are one assertive woman."

"I ask for a drink not a diamond ring. That's assertive?"

"Well… it's not *what* you asked for, it's *how* you asked for it."

"And I suppose you're gonna tell me that black women don't do them things...save it." She gave him her right palm to talk to. 'Cause I can't deal with that right now..."

"Are you uptight?" he asked her.

"Get the fucking drink or stop crowding me with your shadow."

"Ok, ok... Jesus."

"D'you need His help?"

"Sorry?"

"Jesus... d'you need His help?"

"Oh..." he smiled.

"Well leave Him alone then. He's busy helping others. Get me a drink. Gimme some company. And if you think assertion means uptight, you need to get out more."

"And what are you drinking...?"

"Sheree... the name's Sheree. Whisky... no ice."

"Ok, *Sheree*. Whisky it shall be." He turned and made for the bar, smiling to himself.

"...And yours?"

"Sorry?" he turned back to face her.

"Your name."

"*Tom*... they call me *Tom*."

"Is that your name? Or is that what *they* call you?"

"Thomas in full, *Tom* for short."

"A typical white man's name. Perhaps the surgeon who delivered you was called Thomas."

He walked the few steps back towards her, "You're kinda cheeky, aren't you, Sheree. I can't remember when *Sheree* was a typical black woman's name. Was your midwife a white woman?"

"Tom, you're sharp. We're gonna have fun... as a matter of fact, my midwife *was* a white woman, but no, I wasn't named after her."

The handsome man smiled then attempted his way to the bar again.

Sheree picked up her mobile and noticed a missed call. It was from Morag. Years ago. Lawrence had introduced them. One evening as Sheree and Lawrence sat there having a drink, Lance walked in with Morag. Morag was introduced as a friend. Later the reason was revealed to Sheree: Morag was married to a Captain Frank Philips. Lance and Morag were lovers. Though the two ladies weren't bosom pals, they stayed in touch. And since Sheree knew that Morag and her rival Simone had known each other long before she came along, at the back of her mind she knew she would always be the outsider. And when Lawrence ended the relationship and married Simone, Sheree felt something different. Something she herself found it hard to explain.

Sheree glanced over at Tom at the bar, then dialled Lawrence's number. She was pissed off at the automated message. She wanted to talk to him. Especially after her surprised visit to his house a few days ago.

"Why didn't you come with a girlfriend?" *Tom* asked, returning with two glasses of spirits.

"Funnily enough, I was going to call an old friend, Morag, but I figured she might be tucked up with her husband."

"*Morag*?" *Tom* seemed interested. He reached for his drink, hoisted it to his lips and peered curiously at Sheree.

"Yes, Morag. What the hell does her name matter?"

"No. It's just the name. It's… unusual."

"It is."

"Is she foreign?"

"No. She's an English woman. Blonde. Married to a black airline pilot."

Tom gulped his drink as if something shocked him.

"Are you ok?" Sheree asked.

"Yes… fine… Is this your usual haunt, Sheree?" he changed the subject.

"Well, it's certainly not yours. First I've seen you here."

"No. It isn't my usual. I usually go to places like…"

"The Scratchers Yard… Fern Gully…"

"How d'you know that."

"You look the type."

"Is there a *type* that go to Scratchers Yard and Fern Gully?"

"If you don't think so, you're seriously naïve, *Tom*… *it don't suit you.*"

"What?"

"Your name… *Tom*… You are definitely *not* a *Tom*."

"What am I *definitely*, then?" He hid his eyes in his glass.

"Are you… kind of… mixed?" Sheree asked.

"No. I'm not mixed anything. I'm full whatever I am?"

"And what are you? You talk with a Jamaican accent, but there sure ain't no Negro roots spurting out of that head." She smiled at her own wise crack.

"I am a person. Never mind the texture of my roots."

44

"Listen," Sheree said, "I'm only teasing. If your mother wanted you to be a *Tom,* then *Tom* you must be."

"Ok, Sheree, credit goes to *your* mother too... so, why have you decided to come and sit here alone?"

"Sometimes it's good to just sit alone. Listen to the sound of your own thoughts."

"And do they sound good?... your thoughts."

"Not right now, but I'm working on it."

"Looks like you have a plan for happiness," *Tom* said.

"My mother once told me, if you want something, go out and get it."

"Didn't she add, *'within reason'*?"

"I suppose it depends on how limited one thinks *reason* is."

"Well, Sheree," he sipped his drink, "from where I'm sitting, *'reason'* looks good. I would like to taste some of this *'reason'*... He sipped again. "Tell me... how limited is this *'reason'*?"

She looked at him. Gorgeously handsome, suave and sophisticated he most certainly was, but how was his *STATUS?* "The limit of this *'reason',"* she replied, "depends on the status of *the person* who's asking... what do you do for a living?"

"Usually women ask, *'What car do you drive'*?"

"Don't put me in your basket of women... what do you do for a living?"

"I work in IT. *Consultancy.* That's where the money is these days."

She beamed. "You're right. You can't go wrong there."

"What's the name of the Comp...?"

Sheree's phone rang, "Excuse me," she whispered to *Tom.* "Hello," affection coated her tone. "How are you?... What d'you mean *what's the problem?* I need to talk to you, Lawrence... Yes... why are you treating me like this?...What d'you mean *stop calling your mobile...*?"

Tom watched as Sheree clicked her phone off. It was obvious that the person on the other end called the shots and ended the conversation.

"Lover's tiff? Is that what you're working on?"

"Never mind me. I was asking the name of your company," Sheree jabbed.

But at that moment *Tom* looked up and saw a familiar face at the bar. The lady looked tentatively in his direction with a puzzled expression on her face, then she started to walk towards him. "Excuse me, Sheree," *Tom* hastened, cowering as he got up, "just nipping to the gent's."

"Excuse me," Evadney asked when she neared Sheree, "sorry to trouble you…"

Sheree looked at her with sarcasm, widened eyes and raised eyebrows. Her non-verbal expression said, *'What?'*

"… That guy that just got up…"

"Yes?"

"…Is his name *Sanchez*?"

"No… No, his name's *Tom.*"

"Oh… sorry, it's just that he looks remarkably like someone I know."

"No problem," Sheree said, staring at Evadney as if she was beneath her.

Evadney was now walking away.

"Tell me," Sheree sounded out…

Evadney turned back towards her.

"Does this *Sanchez* make *love* as good as *Tom looks*?"

"Evadney chuckled, half blushed and walked away without answering.

"It wasn't him," she said when she reached her friend, Yvonne. "God, that was like his double, though… Come on, let's go." They left the building.

Tom, peeping from around the corner, watched her go. He mopped his brows, gave it a minute or two, gained his composure then walked back to join Sheree again.

"Apparently, you've got a double," Sheree told him.

"I *have*?" he asked, still watching the entrance as if he feared Evadney's return.

"Apparently. Some woman came over asking if your name was *Sanchez*."

"*Really*?… well they say we all have a double somewhere… another drink?"

"Same again, please."

"Are you driving, Sheree?"

"No. I took a taxi here. My intention was to take one back."

"I can give you a lift… if you want."

"I don't mind either way. As long as I can have a skinfull."

"Are you sorrow-drowning?"

"An impossible task... my sorrow can't be drowned. It's like a damn floater. Keeps popping back to the surface no matter how much I try to flush it away."

He ignored her spiel. "I'll take you home... unless of course, *Lawrence* won't be at home waiting and get the wrong end of the stick."

"You know about me and Lawrence?"

"No."

"Then how d'you..."

"You called his name earlier when you were on the telephone, remember? *'I need to talk to you, Lawrence'* you said."

"Oh, right... I forgot... No... Lawrence won't be at home waiting. That would be wishful thinking on my part."

"Separate places, hey?"

"Lawrence is somebody else's guy."

"Oh... I see. You were having an affair."

"That's wishful thinking too. I just can't wash him out of my hair... And he's one of them."

"One of them?"

"One of them rare ones. Faithful to the fucking core."

"Like that is it?"

Sheree looked as if a big dollop of the blues suddenly hit her slap bang in her face.

"I'll get your drink." He almost rushed to the bar. Perhaps he couldn't deal with emotional situations.

Sheree dialled again. She was met with, *'The mobile you have called is switched off. Please try later'*. "Fuck you!" she said as she clicked and threw her phone in her handbag. She gazed around the place for a few minutes until *Tom* was back.

"One whisky," *Tom* said, placing the glass of spirit in front of Sheree.

"I have to go," Sheree announced.

"Now? What about your drink?"

"What about it?" She picked up the glass, downed it in one, then rose to her feet. She stumbled slightly.

"Are you ok, Sheree? How many have you had so far?"

"Don't worry," she said, throwing her bag over her shoulder, "not that many, I can tuck myself up in bed," she slurred slightly.

"Where d'you live, Sheree?"

"Solihull."

47

"Let's go. You can direct me."

It was clear that Sheree had had one or even two, too many, but it wasn't long before *Tom* was standing with her on her doorstep, somewhere in Solihull. Although it was a gloomy night, it wasn't hard to see that the area was plush.

Sheree fumbled for her key while *Tom* glanced at the spanking new TT that sat next to the top of the range Jag on her drive.

"Nice rides."

"Thanks. Are you coming in for a night cap?" Her posh accent made *Tom* wonder if she was born white and more *upper* than the upper-class whites. 'And how many black women say *'night-cap?'* Well, he hadn't met one before this one. However, he hoped she would ask. *'If only I could hit this classy ass,'* he thought. *'Well, pussy is pussy. Upper, middle, lower... yes... That's it. As long as I can hit her lower-middle section with an upper ram-jam, it would do me fine.'*

Seconds later, he browsed around a living-room that was out of this world.

"What d'you want to drink?" Sheree asked.

"The truth is, Sheree, I wouldn't say no to a coffee."

"No problem. Sit down. I'll put the kettle on."

"Milk, two sugars," he assured her.

"Fine."

"Nice place you have here."

"Thank you," she answered from the kitchen.

He raised his voice to meet the distance of the kitchen, "Beautiful face, wicked figure, nice house, wicked rides... what else can a woman like you wish for?"

"So you think there's happiness in all that?"

"Maybe not, but some people would give their right arm for a fraction of all you have."

"And some people will give their right arm for the one they love to love them back." She walked into her living-room and unsteadily placed his coffee on the coffee table.

"Does this *Lawrence* know how much you love him?"

"Don't make the blindest bit of difference," she was now about a foot away from him, "I think he's found in *her* the ultimate... *thing*... whatever that is. I envy her."

"You love him bad, don't you?"

"You could say that, yes... what about you? Have you ever loved somebody so much it hurts to imagine them with another?"

"Yes… and I still love her."

"So where is she now?"

"The last I heard, she was in Jamaica, but…" he reached for Sheree's right arm and kissed the back of her hand, "That's life…. So when was the last time you made love to this *Lawrence*, Sheree?"

"Around five years ago." She sat down by him.

"What?! And you still…?"

"I know. I should get a life, shouldn't I?"

"And make the most of it when you do."

"Is that what you do? Make the most of…"

"You've heard of the May Fly, right?"

"The May *what*?"

"The May Fly. Has a life span of only a day. And I do believe this little thing makes the most of it. Tomorrow we die, Sheree."

"That's true. I just can't get this man out of my fucking head, I told you."

"And it took you five years to realise?"

"No. I was just trying to hold it down… it didn't work."

He paused. Looked at her. "So… really," he pulled her closer to and kissed the side of her face, "when was the last time you made love?"

"Same answer… five years ago. Of course I've had sex. But not made *love."*

He reached forward and kissed her passionately.

"Come." He took both her hands. "Stand up."

"Sheree stood up, still feeling the effect of the firewater she had earlier.

"Let's dance."

"Where's the music?" she asked.

"The best dances are the ones without music." He held her close and felt her breasts against his chest.

"There are times I wish we could do this… me and Lawrence."

"It's ok. I'll be your substitute. For tonight, at least," He turned her around and rested her ass on his rising bulge.

She felt his throbs of desire, yet her mind was on the other side of town. On Lawrence.

Soon his hands found their way under her thin blouse, "You have such smooth skin," he whispered.

She breathed ecstatic sighs as his fingers manipulated her sensitive nipples, and his warm tongue played with the back of her neck.

"Mmmm…"

Now, he lifted her blouse clean over her head, and before it reached the ground, he had turned her 'round and was sucking on her nipples, licking her navel.

"Ahhhh."

Now on his knees, he gently pulled her down towards the floor, where he slowly removed her skirt.

"Oh… *Lawrence*…"

"That's not my name, but I'll answer to anything if the caller is as sweet as you."

"Oh, sorry, Tom."

He removed her sexy knickers now, blowing on her hungry vagina as if it was hot food. "I just want to *taste* you," he whispered. And that he did. Tasted the sweet juices of her clitoris."

"Ahhhh…. Ahhh…" Sheree was lost to the after effect of drink and the present effect of a busy tongue on her clitoris.

Now, he moved up and found her nipples again. She was in heaven… and now, his fingers played a sensational song on her now throbbing woman.

"Ahhh… *Lawrence,"* she hummed.

"Like I said… I'll be your Lawrence tonight."

"Oh… sorry, Tom…. Lawrence is stuck to my brain cells."

"It's ok," he whispered, "and now… I'm stuck inside you."

She needed no telling. She felt it. Her upper-class turkey stuffed with a lower-class sausage. "Ahhh! Ahhh! Ahhh!… Lawrence!"

'Call me what you like,' he thought, *'I seek now sentimental trophies. Uh! I'm getting some. Uh! That's enough for me. Uh! A nuh not'n. Uh! Uh! Ohhhhhhhhh!!!!!!'*

Tom rocked her world. And when he had emptied his load inside her, and when she had reached the highest climax she had ever reached in a long time, they were both drained.

"Oh…. my head," Sheree said the next morning when she woke in an awkward position in her bed. She vaguely remembered last night. *Tom* had obviously picked her up, negotiated the stairs with her dead-weight body and placed her there. *Vaguely*. Yet the memory of him emptying his load into her stood out so vividly, it was uncanny.

Now, she looked to her left a saw a strange sight.

A *red rose*, packaged in a long, slender gold box. It lay by her head like a morbid calling card. A note stuck with strong intent from its corner.

"What?" she asked as she reached for the bit of paper. She read it silently... *'Just a little something to remember me by. Something that'll never die. 'Paper roses... they are special... they never die... they live forever.'*

"Strange," Sheree mumbled. Then the realisation hit her... she had no contact for him. No number, nothing. But it didn't matter anyhow, for as the sperm of a stranger lay thick within her vagina, it was Lawrence that lay heavy on her mind.

But even if Lawrence had known, it would have made no difference at all.

For at that moment, he held her tight. His darling wife, that is. *Simone*. Morning had broken once again on their sweet harmony... their dovetailed bodies forming a perfect *S,* beneath the warmth of their duvet.

A seemingly *unbreakable* chain.

* * *

It was the end of another long-haul flight and Lawrence couldn't help but noticing that Lance hadn't made much conversation compared to other times. "Is everything ok, man? You haven't been your talkative self at all," he said to him.

"Nothing a stiff drink can't sort."

"Wanna talk about it?"

"Same old thing, man. Same old thing."

"You still think Morag's playing you?"

"No *think* about it. She is. The thing is, the way I feel, I think I can handle it now if she told me the truth. Just as long as I don't turn up to find this guy in my house. I'd kill him. Otherwise, I could handle the truth."

"You think you could handle it? Man, unless you have something or someone else to cushion the blow, I don't know if it can be that easy to handle. Speculating is one thing, but getting the hard-hitting truth can't be easy. People sometimes think they are handling things, but when it comes down to it, they're just putting up a front... Talking about that, you know the other day you asked me about Sheree...?"

"Yeah?"

"Well, I think I spoke too soon."

"Why? What's been happening?"

"I must have had at least eight calls from her since then...."

"I told you, didn't I? I told you it was a bit strange her accepting the closure so calmly."

"But that's not all…"

"What's that?"

"The other evening she was only parked outside my house."

"What?!"

"Yeah… it freaked me out a bit."

"What did she want?"

"It was weird… asking me things like *why didn't I return her calls* and all that shit."

"Oh dear. That doesn't sound good."

"I found her whole attitude strange – the fact that she was there when she wasn't supposed to know where I live is one thing, then when I asked her why she was there, she said something about 'watching the movements of a *perfectly* happy family' or some shit like that."

"You better watch that, man. That definitely doesn't sound healthy."

"Oh, the worst of it all was when she made some sarcastic crack about Simone's vagina being made of gold!"

"What?!" It wasn't funny but Lance couldn't help laughing out loud. "The woman's stalking you, man. Weird. Have you told Simone?"

"No. No I didn't. Didn't want to scare her. She had some shit before with an ex of her ex-husband. Turned up at her house and attacked her."

"Really?"

"Yes, so I didn't wanna scare her."

"Yeah, but I don't see Sheree doing that. She's after you. I don't think she'd trouble Simone. She seems quite level-headed."

"Level-headed! How can you use those words after what I just told you? A level-headed person doesn't waste time sitting outside someone's house for something as unconstructive as that?"

"No. I mean towards Simone. I seriously don't think she'll mess with Simone."

"I hope so," Lawrence said, flicking through his flight paperwork. "She's either crazy, or she's been watching too much damn TV."

"And you know, I thought you'd marry her?"

"Who, Sheree…?" Lawrence looked at him, "… Nah. Sheree was ok. Good lover in a physical sense. In fact, because of that, and not finding anyone I could call a wife, I just kept the bed thing going. Not in a disrespectful way. That's where we were both at…. But there was something missing. Couldn't put my finger on it, but there was definitely a void. But when I met Simone, I knew. It felt wholesome."

Lance paused and thought about Lawrence's last comment. He knew there was nothing wholesome about him and Morag. Used to be, but doubts have clouded his mind and spread a thick shadow over everything. However, he still felt for her. Not love, but something. At times he had been somewhat confused, but he knew that Lawrence was right – thinking he could handle the truth was one thing: having it in your face was another. But still, in all his confusion, he felt sure about one thing. One thing he was not yet ready to reveal to anyone.

"I still can't understand why Sheree would be lingering outside your house after all these years though. A few months after, yes, but not so long after you've been married. The last thing you want is any problems."

"Tell me about it."

"Are you *sure* she was ok with the split, right?"

"Well, I thought she took it fine. And it's been too long now for her to decide to change her mind, so that's why it was a bit worrying: the phone call, then her sitting in her car outside my house." Lawrence stood up and shook his legs.

"Women," Lance rounded off, as he finalised his paperwork for flight expenses.

Lawrence smiled as he shook his legs. "They make our worlds go round, hey?"

"Believe me. It's no joke… You're not still having cramps?" Lance asked.

"Yeah. Hereditary, I think. My father used to suffer from it badly." He smiled. "I remember back in the Antigua, there was a story about a man who suffered from cramps. Apparently, he was having an affair with another man's wife. As it went, the man came home one day and caught them in bed…"

"*Coitus interuptus* with a difference, hey? Heh! Heh!" Lance was amused.

"Indeed. Anyway, unluckily for this man, he couldn't run…"

Lance couldn't stop himself laughing. He knew what was coming.

"… Severe cramp got him in both legs. I heard that when the woman realised her husband was coming, she was urging this man, 'Get up an' run, Busta! Run! Quick! Run!… Well, he couldn't, could he? He couldn't move a muscle." Lance's Antiguan accent accentuated even more whenever he would exert himself frivolously.

"I suppose you could really call that *coitus crampus*, right?" Lance's laughter bounced off the walls and threw itself into every crook and crevice of the crew room.

Lawrence had never heard Lance laugh so much, and considering his mood earlier, he was pleased he shared his little cramp-in-bed story with him. He needed to lighten up.

"Well you have no fear a dat, Lawrence. You will never find yuhself in that position. Being caught in bed wid anadda woman is practically impossible for you, you're Mr Faithful himself. So wid anadda man's wife would be totally outa di question." Lance was relaxing. It was only when he was totally relaxed that he spoke patois.

In the midst of the frivolity, the door of the crew room opened and First Officer Clive Saunders walked in. "I can hear you two from the airport lounge," he exaggerated. "Life must be extra sweet for you both."

"I don't know about *extra*," Lance said.

"I hear it's for *you* though, Clive," Lawrence told him. "Too sweet, in fact. I hear yuh getting a sweet motor."

"Yeah. What else is money for if not spending?" the dashing black hunk said assertively.

"All I know," Lance said, "You can never have too much. Lately I've been thinking, *'show me a way to make a quick million, and I'll show you how quick I can walk out this door'.*"

"Really?" Lawrence asked. "You would give up flying if you made a million?"

"Well... maybe a bit more... a million isn't much these days, but I'm not joking... if someone tells me, *'now, this is how you can make a million or two,'* as long as it's not risking mine or anyone else's life, I'll do it."

"C'mon. You don't mean that?" Lawrence asked. "Reason has a limit, man. You have to think within it."

"I suppose so, but I'm good at weighing things up."

"Wait a minute," Clive said, "how the hell did we move from talking about *laughter* to *making millions*?"

"I think you mentioned life being *sweet*," Lawrence said. "So what about *you*, Clive? Would *you* do almost anything to make a million?... Think about it now... considering a million is nothing like it used to be."

"Well, I never had it, therefore I don't know how it *used to be*," Clive mused, "so... within reasons, yes. As long as it doesn't entail *physically* taking someone's life."

"Sounds like you would take someone's life *emotionally* though. Leave them standing like a man who loses his entire family in a fire. Just as long as you make your million," Lawrence joked.

"What are emotions compared to a million?" Clive bantered, though he meant it.

"Well," Lawrence rounded off, "I hope you two make your millions. *Me*? I must get home to my priceless family." He picked up his flight case and made for the door.

"Take it easy, man," Lance told him. "Don't worry about Sheree."

"Well," Lawrence said, "I hope she's as *level-headed* as you trust. I just don't know why she was outside my house... but like they say, '*there's none so strange as folk*'." He mimicked an old English accent he heard from the TV.

"Like I said," Lance told him, '*women*'."

"*Some* women, you mean," Lawrence corrected. "See you guys." He pulled the door shut and couldn't help thinking how pleased he was that aviation is appealing to more blacks in Britain now, than ever before. Brothers were reaching for the stars in more ways than one. But, as he made his way out of the airport building, he couldn't help thinking that although he had heard Lance's high-pitched laughter, there was definitely something amiss. *What*, he didn't know, but something was definitely up. Something much more than marital problems. Like he had something up his sleeves. Something that borders on *scrupulous*. Slightly shifty. But he had put it down to nothing more than another plan to try to get what he wanted from the airline. Lawrence was simply guessing. And besides, as long as it hadn't got anything to do with him, that was cool. Everyone around Lance was big and bold enough to look after themselves, including the airline bosses.

Chapter 5

Ҭwo weeks before the Handsworth Carnival. It must have been the day for it: placing flowers at their loved ones' graves had become a ritual for the two men, but today was the first day they had actually met at Lodge Hill Cemetery. In the midst of life we're all in death, so in the midst of clubs and pubs and restaurants and playgrounds and plush living-rooms, there are graveyards: *the final resting place.*

"Whaap'n, Bredrin?" Conteh said when he realised that the guy who was placing flowers not far from him, was his long-time bredrin, Lijah.

"*Wyait*!" Lijah alarmed, "Is you dat, Egyptian?!"

"Yeah, man."

"Mi neva realise seh I's suh close our old ladies were?"

"Nuh suh meah seh. Bwoy… small world, man. Even in deat'."

"Yeah, man. Trus' mi," Lijah said. "Mi madda, Nettie, mi son, Kunta, mi uncle, Stan, Papa Dread an' his queen, Norma." Lijah pointed as he summed up the loss of lives that affected him so deeply.

"Bwoy, man sorry, Bredrin. Mi know sorry cyaan help, but…" Conteh averted his eyes now to his parents' tombstones. His father, Sony, it seemed, had gone on a long time before his dear mother, Gladys.

"And to think," Lijah added, "if Gloria's parents weren't buried in Jamaica, they would have been here too."

"Serious," Conteh replied, realising for the first time, that there was, and will always be someone worse off than himself. He was there to respect two of his loved ones; Lijah was there for five. Then looked further up and saw Pam's headstone. She was his ex-wife's best friend. She was beautiful. Full of life. And sure had lived it to the fullest, until her living was severed by the dreaded AIDS. A cold shiver ran down Conteh's spine when it was brought home to him again with brute force. He had copulated sweetly with Pam. *Once upon a time.* He dragged himself away from his thoughts and changed the subject totally. "Mi 'ear 'bout dem man deh, Bredrin…. Jaro… Sugar… Bunti… Nuff shoot up an' t'ing, *feh real.*"

"Bwoy, I man don't even waan talk 'bout dem man deh yunnuh, Bredrin," Lijah stressed. "Not when I man come fi lay flowers at mi loved ones' graves. Nasty pieces of works, Bredrin. Yuh don' talk 'bout dem people deh w'en yuh doin' not'n sacred, Bredrin."

Conteh understood. "I hear yuh, Bredrin. I hear yuh."

"All dem man deh is responsible fi mi young son lying in dis cemetery right now." He forced back his tears. Time had passed but still they came. His wounds were not yet healed.

"Easy, Bredrin." Conteh realised he had touched more than a nerve. Ah feel yuh pain still. Kunta fi one shouldn't be here. Too young."

"Anyway, yuh still coming up to deh house fi dis get togedda mi tell yuh 'bout?"

Conteh hesitated. "Yeah man. Mi wi' reach."

"Yeah, man. Pass 'roun'. Locking yuhself away won't help not'n."

"I hear yuh, still."

The two men found themselves walking to their cars together. Conversation flowed easily. There was an air of affiliation about them. Conteh felt he could open up to Lijah, and visa versa. They both did time... Lost loved ones to the dreaded grip of death... Hit hard emotional times with their women... Women messed with their minds in return for them messing with theirs... And they were both weak when it came to the carnal flesh.

"Bwoy, nuff t'ings went down ova a period a time, yunnuh," Lijah announced.

"Nuff t'ings, Bredrin," Conteh agreed, but lucky fi *you*, yuh still have yuh woman. I've lost mine. She's now married to some Antiguan captain, Bredrin. One a dem *Highflya* man deh." His voice trembled, knowing that that wasn't his only problem.

"I nearly lost Gloria too, Bredrin. To some shotta in Jamaica."

"Wha'?!"

"Long story, Bredrin... still..." There was a pause. Lijah wanted to bring up the HIV thing he had heard about, and Conteh wanted to hear about what really went down with the shooting thing: when Jaro, Bunti and Sugar was taken out by some guy called Rock. They were both the best source for both stories right now.

"Anyway, Bredrin, yuh goin to di carnival nex' week?" Lijah asked, changing the subject slightly.

"Bwoy, mi not sure yunnuh."

"I man aggo tek a walk. Mi an' mi Queen, yunnuh?"

They had reached the final few footsteps out of the cemetery when a red Mercedes slowed. "Whaap'n, Bredrin!" boomed a familiar voice.

"Whaap'n, Faada Jarvis?! *Bombo claat!* Man cool?" Lijah asked, stretching his right fist to Birmingham's number 1 DJ.

"Yeah, man, man cool.... Whaap'n, Egyptian?" the jolly DJ enquired of Conteh, knowing of his situation: where he'd been and where he was at with the recluse thing.

"Man cool yunnuh," Conteh said, though his voice said otherwise. They touched fists.

"Bwoy," Father Jarvis continued, "long time... Di las' time I saw you was a while back at a dance at di Million Dalla Nightclub. I hear seh yuh jus' *lock off*, Bredrin."

"Bwoy, I jus' need some time to think, yunnuh."

"Time to think? You should have enough a dat, Bredrin. Where else could a man think more, than in prison? Although I've never been, I would think dat is w'at anyone would do most in a place like dat."

"Yeah, man, I's true. True..." Conteh didn't have much to say. All he wanted to do was to get away. Find the comforts of his mother's house again.

"Listen, Bredrin, yuh need fi come outa di 'ouse... Mi plannin' a dance. A Red Affair t'ing down at Banana Baits..."

Lijah interrupted. He could see this was gonna take a while. Gloria was waiting and he had to go. "Listen, Blood," he said, stretching his left hand out to the two men as he walked to his car, "man affi mek a move, yeah?"

"More time, Lijah!" they both said.

"... Yeah... mi 'ear 'bout dah dance deh," Conteh replied in response to Father Jarvis' earlier announcement.

"Yeah, well, dis is a special one. If I cyan remember," he cleared his throat simultaneously as a bantering jive, "from some rumour," he did it again, chuckling simultaneously after every joke-filled clearing, "I hear yuh *love* red, so yuh should enjoy it... oh... sorry, Bredrin, mi nuh know... unless di woman dem rip up dem red silk sheets an' wear dem... mi nuh know." He laughed at his own joke.

Conteh summoned a smile, then managed a chuckle caught from Father Jarvis contagious ones. "Rumours... Bwoy, it look like no secret is safe, is it, Bredrin?"

"Safe? Wha's di matta wid *you*? No secret is safe unless i's jus' *you* know it, Bredrin..." He emitted that infamous chuckle again. "So yuh coming?"

Conteh paused.

"Bwoy, mi cyaan believe a notorious soun'man like you jus' lock-off so."

"Nah, man," Conteh defended, "ah nuh so."

"Ah so, man. Yuh know seh yuh jus' *lock-off* inna di 'ouse. Yuh need to come from behind dem four walls, man. And not only to go to the cemetery. It's good to visit di dead, but di living need to see yuh out, Bredrin."

Conteh ignored all Father Jarvis' ramblings and said, "Yeah, man. Mi coming."

"*Yes,* Bredrin. Is dat mi waan 'ear. Mi not competing with Vibes Injection. Mi know seh dem nah play dah night deh, so yuh cyan come."

Conteh found another chuckle inside him and let it out.

"I even saw your sister Janet the other day," Father Jarvis said in perfect English now. "She said she would be there." He started his engine. "More time, Egyptian."

The men touched fists again and Conteh walked slowly towards his ride, as if he had no particular place to go; considering that earlier he wanted to *fly* home.

"An' don't fi'get di carnival!" Father Jarvis shouted as he sped off.

Conteh looked back. He couldn't help wondering if Father Jarvis was showered by God with a heavy sprinkling of *happy dust*, with which he was commanded to sprinkle over anyone who dared to let sorrow bring them down. He had the ability to make everyone forget their troubles for a while: men, women and children alike.

* * *

Behind these prison walls
Doing my paces, doing my time
Spending my restless nights
Visioning faces, oh they are crying, crying
Prison a no bed a roses
The levity it makes mi bawl
I wish that Jah could come and take us back in time…

Jah Cure's words had helped Festus through many lonely hours. He needed the small CD player Lijah had sent him and the wardens had allowed him to have. He knew Jah was on his side and was relieved when a compassionate prison guard listened to his complaint and had Conrad removed to another cell. But he had prayed that strength would be an attribute of Conrad's new cellmate.

Most of the time, he thought about his son. Fari was only eight years old when Festus got sentenced. Now he was twelve years old. And if he played his cards right, the good behaviour thing might work for him. He could be out of the God-forsaken place in a couple of months. He hoped luck would be on his side, since everything runs on one too many red tapes.

Kizzy. He thought of her nearly always in the dead of nights. He had seriously had more than enough time to wonder. Reflect. Reflect on how badly he had treated her. He needn't wonder why. He knew that all right. He knew full well that if it were possible to take his mind from the place where it lived, washed the foul residue of his childhood from its crevices and replace it with fresh uplifting things, he would have been a better man. It might have been a little too late to convince Kizzy, but, *maybe,* given the chance, he could use his harsh prison lesson to turn his thinking around. He could, perhaps, become a father to his son. A father with some fine examples to set. But then again, the *maybe* was a very big one. Sodomy is one thing if you are that way inclined. If not, Festus had come close to realising that along with the lining of his ass, he could lose his very soul. And a man without a soul is no man at all.

He thought of Lijah. The falling out they had when he made that move on Ikesha.

And he thought of his mother Dora whom he had disowned. The blame he lay with her.

And what had become of him? *Montie.* His father. Has the streets of Handsworth and the effect of alcohol claimed him yet?

Reflection behind prison walls. How vivid it can be.

> *Behind these metal bars*
> *To Jah Jah I'm chanting*
> *I pray for love divine*
> *I'm oh so sorry a man*
> *Deeply I'm hurting*
> *The price ordained to be mine*
> *Impossible to see the changes that I have made in my life*
> *All they see is just the boy I left behind...*

There was no question about it. Festus knew it. Or willing to try, at least. He chanted along with Jah Cure, knowing full well that all he wanted was a chance...

> *Cause I swear that I can be a better man*
> *Yes I swear if only you could understand*
> *The faith in me shall set me free reflection*
> *The faith in me shall set me free reflection*

Dah da da da da dah die

And I swear that I can be a better man
Yes I swear if only you could understand
The faith in me shall set me free reflection
The faith in me shall set me free reflection...

* * *

An affluent part of London was where she hailed from. So staying at her daughter's flat could be classed as a *come down* for Mitzi.

Year had passed and Shari had melted a little. Opened up and let her mother in... though the feeling that resided wasn't 100% kosher. It was, however, her mother.

A mother though, who had rejected her because she had chosen the *love of Kunta* over *University*.

A mother who *still,* until that minute hadn't told her *who* her father was.

A mother who's luxury flat in Kensington, London was once too good for her and her two boys.

A mother who had wished that drink had not messed with her brain the night her defences came down, allowing the sperm of Reds (a sweet Rastaman) to mingle with her egg, bringing forth his child.

Roy, a *well-to-do* black policeman was more Mitzi's thing. Thought her fanny was made of gold-dust, until she realised that no dick is made of gold, for as Roy fucked her, so he did his blonde wife, topped with a sprinkling of Bernadette, a mad bitch who was hell-bent on fucking he and his brother, Lijah up. When it comes to pum-pum, dicks have no partiality. *No sir.*

Shari was in London spending some time with Ikesha. They had grown real close since the death of Kunta (her man and Ikesha's brother).

Mitzi loved her own company, and in a funny kinda way, she relished being alone. But why was she in Birmingham?

Roy. Huh-huh... *Roy.* That same hunk of a policeman. Like fly followed shit, she followed him. Roy had managed a transfer from the force in London and was placed in the West Midlands. He had made a few friends. Things had worked out OKish on the family front. Things were never gonna be 100%, but between him, Lijah and Faye, they managed to secure *'amicable'*.

Ever since Lijah had turned up at Mitzi's flat in London and revealed to her that he and his brother were fucking the same *devil woman*, Bernadette, Mitzi had given Roy hell. Roy tried to end it, but she was having none of it. Maybe some strange *Fairy-Bad-Mother* was flying about sprinkling some obsessive shit into the food or drink that some black women had been eating of late. *Shit.* Mitzi, Bernadette and Sheree had certainly tasted some. *Seriously.*

About a week ago, Roy had popped in to see Mitzi at Shari's flat. After giving her a taste of what she liked, he explained how busy he was, and that he wasn't sure when he would see her again. After all, they weren't together. They were free agents. She knew the score.

So earlier, as Mitzi waited in her daughter's flat for the door to knock, she hoped that Roy *wouldn't* suddenly find some time and simply decide to *'turn up'*. It was his choice to become quaintly casual. And besides, in Mitzi's eyes, this new guy had passed her *'class'* test. *'Class'* then, you could say, was in the eyes of the *beholderess*. For when her eyes had first beheld him, and when his acting had convinced her that he was worthy of her company, and when he had seduced her with his suave, debonairing sexiness, her classy fanny had twitched, rendering her now, not the *shit-don't-stink* lady she thought she was, but simply another *horny bitch* who needed her *'heat'* cooling by the *red-hot-passion* of a *hungry dog*. Chat bout.

It's nature.

It calls.

And when it calls it has no partiality. Bitches or Ladies, Dogs or Gentleman… anyone will do.

"So, you were born in Birmingham then?" *Gregory* the *hungry dog* asked as soon as he got settled into Shari's settee. If only she could see her mother entertaining a strange man in her flat!

"Yes. That was a long time ago, though."

"Can't be that long," he flattered, "you look quite young." The handsome man looked a little tired. Slightly ashy around the eyes. Perhaps it was the heavy night he had last night. The measures of firewater. The multiple women in that *orgyetrical* setting. The countless missions he had accomplished.

"Thank you, but I'm a grandmother." Oh my God, she'd finally owned the title she had previously despised! *Grandmother*. Wonders would never cease.

"Do you think you'll live to be a great-grandmother?"

She looked at him, "Hope so… that's a funny question to ask. Do I look ill or something?" she asked, smiling.

"No…. No, just silly chit-chat, don't mind me… So remind me, what brought you to Birmingham now?"

"Well, a little of everything really. A few loose ends to tie-up. Between my daughter, her father and my…"

"… Your man."

"Well… *sort of.*"

"*Sort of*? He either *is* or he *isn't*?… All you women with your issues. You are all like wounded dogs walking around with your heads down, whining."

"Excuse me! That's not a nice thing to say…"

"Well… it's true, isn't it? Like troubled souls. Jumping from frying pans into fires. All that shit."

"Jesus… Do I look wounded?"

"It's not what's in the face, sista, it's what's in the heart."

Mitzi didn't know what to say. "What are you talking about?"

"Nothing. Don't worry," he leaned towards her, "may I?"

She leaned towards him and reciprocated a kiss.

"Do you want a drink, Gregory?"

"I'm fine… thank you. I'd rather *you*… *You* are going to be more thirst-quenching than any beverage in a cup," he sang like a cunning fox to an unsuspecting bird. And the cheese she held in her beak was sure to fall his way.

"*Going to be?*" she asked.

"Well, what I mean to say is, you're kinda *sweet*."

"Oh… thank you," she blushed.

He swung his body round and attempt to stretch out on the settee. "Come," he patted his lap with more familiarity than a king in his own castle. "Sit here."

"*What?*"

"Sit here… we might as well make ourselves comfortable." *Mr Confident or what?!*

Mitzi glanced up at the paper rose he had given her earlier and smiled.

"Perhaps I would if you had brought me *real* flowers. One artificial rose isn't…"

"So you don't believe in my reasoning that real roses *die* and paper ones *live* forever?"

"Well, that's your philosophy. I just like real flowers."

"We'll all have them in abundance. On our graves. And *still* they'll die."

"Christ you are morbid, aren't you?"

"Come," he patted his lap again.

She adhered.

"That's better," he said, his left leg stretched down the length of the settee, his right resting on the warm carpet. His impatient crutch awaited the touch of her spine. Now, he cuddled her waist and told her how good she *looked... Smelt... Felt.*

She lapped it all up along with the sweet kisses he planted on her tender neck.

"So... when was the last time you made love, Mitzi?"

"What a question to ask."

"You don't have to answer."

"I won't.... when was the last time *you* made love?"

"A long time ago."

"I don't believe that. A handsome man like you?"

"You didn't ask me when was the last time I had sex. *Fucked."*

"Oh... right... who was *she* then?... the woman you made love to a long time ago?"

"*She*?... one cleva bitch."

"Oh... I see... like that is it?"

"Damn right."

"And where is this *clever bitch* now."

"Last time I heard... in Jamaica."

"D'you still love her?"

"Damn right. But that's neither here nor there. I don't think she ever loved me."

"I take it you're bitter."

"Bitter? Isn't that a term for vengeful woman?"

Mitzi laughed.

"No. Men get bitter too."

"I suppose you could say I'm bitter, but this woman isn't the root of my bitterness."

"Who... or *what* is the root of your bitterness, then?"

"Are we gonna spend all evening talking about bitterness, when there's *you*... the sweetest thing I've met in a *long* time resting on my groin?" He nibbled her ears... groped her breasts... stretched both arms down to her waist again, sinking them into its folds.

"Hey!" She pretended a protest, feeling the deep intensity of his touch.

"Stop pretending you're not feeling me, girl," he mumbled in her right ear, " 'Cos I'm feeling you, *big-time*." His hands roamed now to her breaking dawn, and as she felt the heat of her inner sun, she felt the rising of his moon as it nudged and pushed against her sensitive spine. *'Ahhh...'*

He reached *up* now, resting his palm on her breast. "*Sweet*," he hummed. "Are you a model?"

"As it goes, I am." She prised his hands away from her breast. She was crawling up the wall, but displaying a *too-easy* disposition just wouldn't do.

"What's the matter, Sweetness? Don't you want me to touch them?"

"Well, let's put it this way, if you touch my breasts, I'm gonna be in trouble."

"Feh real? *Why?*"

"Nothing."

"C'mon... *why?*" He teased her earlobes with his tongue.

"Next to my clitoris," she told him, "they are my weakest spots."

"Really?"

"I can have an orgasm just from my breasts being touched."

"*What*?! Whoa... I's weh yaah seh?"

"Yes, so don't." Mitzi got up. "Excuse me, I need a drink." She headed for the kitchen. "Sure you don't want one?"

"No... I'm cool," he said, gripping his hot ferocious dog as if to stop it jumping out.

But Mitzi was surprised when a few seconds later, *Gregory* came in search of her. There, he found her taking deep breaths. He had surely stirred something in her and she needed to cool down.

"Are you ok," he asked, knowing full well he had got her just where he wanted her... in more ways than one: *On heat* and *in the kitchen*.

"Yes, fine... drink... I wanted a drink." She fumbled with the fridge door.

"Come here," he took her hand and pulled her away from the fridge. "What is it?"

"Nothing."

"Have I upset you?"

"No."

He hugged her and started to kiss her neck.

"Hey… take it easy…"

He kissed and gnawed at her breasts through her thin blouse and just the thought of his lips on her nipples sent Mitzi wild.

"You didn't need a drink, did you?" he said in a lustful mumble, his hands all over her.

"Didn't I?" she said, her voice weakening.

Cleverly, as he attacked the buttons on her blouse, he kept up his chest-pecking.

She was up against the fridge now. And with her blouse opened, bra undone and her firm breasts at his mercy, his hands roamed faster than the speed of light.

"*Gregory*," she whispered.

Defences down…

Desires burning…

He had caught her. *Vulnerable*. And she had climaxed before he even touched her down below.

And now… his firm tongue… Moving around her nipples. Warm… moist. "*Mmmmm…*" She held his head firm against them as if to say, '*don't stop, Gregory… don't stop.*'

He glanced up as if to check his progress. He saw her eyes. They were begging… begging… begging for more.

And now… his speciality… having a woman's ass against his bulge turned him on. Gently, he edged her towards the worktop turning her to face the wall, as he placed his hungry dick against her firm sexy ass.

"*Gregory…*" she whispered, without protest.

His dick bulged against her ass and as his firm fingers manipulated her over-sensitive nipples, she was elevated to ecstasy.

Now, skirt up showing her a perfect model's ass, he rubbed his palms firmly over the pouting cheeks and listened to her moan with desperate wanting.

Spread-eagled, he wound his right arm around her right hip and plucked a feeble thong that barely covered her entry. It fell like a feather to her daughter's kitchen floor.

Now, his left hand kept her crying vagina sweet.

Fumbling.

Touching.

Manipulating.

Sinking.

And now, his right hand reached for his stiff, eager manhood. It could wait no more. Like a savage wolf to raw meat, he let it loose.

And there it was... back-shot. Oh!

"Ahhh!" Mitzi groaned her appreciation. "Ohhhh! Gregory! Ahhh!"

A bite to the sensitive curve of her neck...

"Ohhhh..."

Fast, firm, deep thrusts....

One! "Ah!"

Two! "Ah!"

Three! "Ah!"

Four! "Ah"

Five! "Oh, Gregory! Gregory!"...

"Yuh like dat?" he asked in a sexy whisper. "Mmm?.. Yuh like dat?... Tell mi!" he commanded now in spates of hums and whispers. "Tell mi!" *Uh! Uh! Uh!...*

"Yes! Yes! Yes!"

Eighteen! "Uh!"

Nineteen! "Uh!"

Twenty! "Baby..."

"Ohhhhhh!... Ohhhhhh!... O, Baby! Baby! Baby..."

Then came the showers...

Showers of acid rain...

Rain with no barrel to catch its corrosive torrents...

No sheathed covering to protect her landscape...

No mercy from *Mr Paper Rose*.

No guilt.

Just plain old self-gratifying pleasure.

Now, he turned her 'round and kissed her, looking at her breasts. Groping them some more as if he wanted to own them. *"Sweet,"* he whispered, *"sweet."*

Mitzi had nowhere to put her eyes, so she rested them on her brand new thong... now ripped and discarded. *Discarded*: like her once-sparkling modelling career. Or the relationship she once had with Roy. *Discarded.*

And now, as the triangular bit of scarlet lace lay shamelessly on her daughter's kitchen floor, alien sperm trickled from her still throbbing vagina...

And that was the way it was...

That was the way her cookie crumbled.

Glory, glory, halleluiah... and what a joyful moment that was....*'Paper roses'*, he had said, *'they are special... because they never die... they live forever'*...

Chapter 6

𝔉estus appreciated the fresh breeze against his cheeks. It wasn't like the breeze he felt on days when he would trot around the prison yard on exercise days. This was different. But although the difference was supposed to come with illation, something was amiss. The *will* to embrace the outside world wasn't there. Maybe it would come, but just then, it wasn't there. Perhaps all his *will* was left behind: *not yet risen* from beneath a pile of prison sheets in which he had felt for a long time, that his pride, dignity and manhood were lost. *Taken* by Conrad: a burley blonde whose dick had recently found a new place to dwell. Maybe the first *will* that would come would be the one that would come hand in hand with a *way*: a *way* to eradicate Conrad. For every time he would try to focus on the *'better-man-now'* pledge he hoped would stay in the forefront of his mind, he would see the image of the man that invaded his space, time... after time... after time... But also, for some reason, something told him that Conrad would get his comeuppance. When he least expect it. Maybe *one day*, he would *try* to mess with another one of Jah's children. And maybe that day would be his last... *One day*.

The fresh wind that blew against his cheeks as he walked towards the entrance of the prison gates confirmed to him that HM Prison had truly released its grip on him. And despite his lack of *will*, things were better than a while back when he wasn't half the man that went inside. Just a shadow of his old self. And there was a time too when he was so broken, he had given up all hopes of ever wanting to try again on the outside. And on umpteen occasions he had asked himself what he had to offer the outside world. A world that would surround him for the second time around. But with words of encouragement from Lijah and a few positive inmates, and with Jah Cure's music taking him through countless nights, Festus knew that if he really tried, he *could* be a better man.

Seeing Lijah's car outside the prison gates was another breath of fresh air. Everybody needs at least one good friend. One that you can trust. One that can understand that sometimes some things can be hard to convey.

Lijah stepped a few yards towards Festus and reached for his right arm. They wrapped palms and pulled each other close. Like a Jamaican farmer would tighten the last noose beneath the belly of a donkey (only without the agony of the poor beast), the two men tightened their friendship.

"Man cool?" Lijah asked, feeling more than pleased to see his idrin on the outside again.

"Bwoy… man deh pon street again, Bredrin."

"Jah know," Lijah endorsed, as he released his friend and walked round to the driver's seat.

Festus opened the backdoor and threw in a solitary bag, slammed it shut, then opened the passenger door and got in.

He was going home.

Home to Birmingham.

But he knew that by no means it would be *'journey's end'*. He had a much longer way to go. He knew too that the road would be hard, since *sorry* seemed to be the hardest word.

* * *

Some might see it as being downright rude. After all, he'd been away a mighty long time. And Heidi had seen it now as *her home*, although it was *his house*, but when Festus pushed his key through the door of the house he had left her in, he felt no way. And when he heard a familiar voice shouting, "Heidi?! Ah yuh dat?!" he wondered who the hell else the calling male had expected to be pushing key. And when he walked through to his living-room, the look on Bongo Dee's drowsy, sleepy face was an image worth capturing.

"Wait! Bredrin?! Festus?!… Jeeesas C'ris'… mi neva know seh you deh 'pon street again, blood?"

"Firstly, yuh wouldn't know. It wasn't headline news… an' secondly, mi is *not* yuh bredrin!"

Bongo felt as if he had lost a little power.

Festus looked around his living-room, ignoring the presence of the man that was twice his size. Not much difference except for a lick of new paint. Kizzy's touch had left long time ago. "Where is Heidi?"

"Bwoy," big, strong, confident Bongo definitely seemed much more than a little sheepish. "Ah t'ing shi gone shoppin' yunnuh." He consciously reminded himself not to say *'bredrin'*.

"I'll wait." He placed his bum on his very own single-seater. It felt weird.

Bongo got up. "Yuh want a drink?"

"Seem a likkle weird, don't yuh t'ink?... A man asking' mi if mi want a drink inna mi own house?"

"Well... let's not pretend," Bongo perked up, "you and I know exactly what's been going on, so..."

"An' yuh an' I know dyam well seh Heidi is livin' in dis house because her pickney was meant to be mine."

"Whateva Heidi tell yuh is not'ing to do wid mi yunnuh. Dat is between yuh an' Heidi. I neva tell Heidi w'at to tell yuh."

"But yuh neva tell ar w'at *not* to tell mi either..."

There was a pause.

"... "Dat's why I'm here," Festus added. "Nuh worry. Man cool... ah nuh not'n."

Bongo stepped from the living-room leaving Festus sitting staring at the TV screen. He opened the front door and as he walked down the drive, he dialled Heidi's mobile. '*The mobile you have called, is switched off. Please try later.*' Not good. The least he could try to do was to alert her that she had an unexpected visitor. He climbed into his ride and drove some distance in the direction he believed her and her son would be coming.

In the meantime, Festus took the opportunity to ascend his stairs... to walk into his bathroom... his spare room... Fari's room. His heart began to hurt. *Fari.* He stood there remembering. A tear fell from his eye. So... wouldn't he just die if he knew that Fari, the son he thought was *his,* was *not* his at all? That he was a result of a rape carried out by his so-called friend *Jaro*? Oh Lord. It's a cruel world... but it's the only one we've got.

And now, he walked into the bedroom. *Memories.* They don't leave like people do. They *always* stay with you. It was Heidi's space now, but the bed was in the same spot. And the memories that came back to him were not the nice ones.

Not the one when he had made sweet love to Kizzy.

Nor the time when he had entered dear, sweet Ikesha.

The memory was of that terrible, terrible day... the whole thing surfaced in his head as if it was yesterday. And in his mind, like self-torture, he watched it... piece, by piece... by piece:

'*Where were you tonight, K'?*'

'*I went to see a friend.*'

'I said... Where... the fuck... were you, Kizzy?!'

'I'm not listening to this.'

'Who is he, Kizzy?... Fed up wid me now, yuh gone fin' man? All yuh 'oman is di same, yunnuh!'

'Festus, let me go! You're hurting me!'

'You haven't answered my question, Kizzy!' Whap!

'Are you fucking around on me, K?' Whap!

'Festus, for God's sake!... Weh yuh get dat stupid idea from?!'

'Stupid idea?!' Thud!

'Stupid idea?!'

'Festus!'

'How could you, Kizzy?!... How could yuh mek anadda man touch yuh?! Yuh t'ink I don't notice di way yuh sneaking 'round fi weeks, now? Who di fuck is he?!' Slap!

'Festus... Please!'

'Who is he, Bitch?!' Whack!... Rip! ... Whack!

'Festus! Stop it! Stop it!'

'Yuh jus' like me fuckin' madda, Dora!... Dat is exactly what she used to do! She used to tek adda man! Dress up inna dat nurse's uniform every night, pretending she's some saint, w'en all di time she was fuckin' out on me ole man! Dat is w'at turned him into a fuckin' drunken tramp, walking di streets of Birmingham like a dog, to raas! Woman! Dem is di root of all fuckin' evil!'

Festus could almost feel it now.

The shameful intrusive entering.

The ruthless hammering. He remembered too that he had not seen Kizzy. Just a *'fallen'* woman. In his eyes, she was a whore. A slut. A prostitute. *Everything she wasn't*. His corrupted mind had already devalued her, and so... his body had to.

"De root of all fuckin' evil! No wonder he used to beat the hell out of her!"

"Now she is livin' in Jamaica wid a new man! Retiring in style! Soaking up di sun, while me ole man walk di streets of Handsworth, lifting di lids of every bin he can fin'!"

"Festus! Stop it! What yuh talking about!"

"Festus... I thought... your... parents... died in a car crash?!"

"I had to run away!... Leave Bristol to bombo claat! I was only a yout'. I couldn't take it any longer! The root of all evil! Woman! Ugh! Woman! Ugh! Woman! Ugh! Ugh! Ugh!"...

71

But what Festus couldn't relive was what he *didn't* see... Her 'broken' spirit... Her no-avail tears... The old memories that he had caused to surface in her mind... the memories of her first rape. Her pain.

But among others, he had learnt one thing: he had learnt, however late, that the power of a man is most definitely *not* in his might.

"Kizzy..." Festus cried, as if she was there with him. "I'm sorry... Eheheheh," He was broken again. "Eheheheh!" *Crying.* "Eheheheh" *Louder. Louder.* He fell now upon the bed and imagined her there. *Kizzy.*

Memories...

They don't leave like people do... They *always* stay with you.

"Fes... tus?" Heidi was home. In the room. Her Irish eyes looking at him crying all over her bed... his bed... whatever. The bed to which he had taken her a few times after Kizzy had left.

Festus looked up. That was not what he wanted. Not to be seen crying like a baby. He stood up.

"What is it?... Why are you... crying?... I didn't even know you were... out?"

Festus felt a right spectacle. The little boy that stared at him looked cute. *Very cute.* But no way was he his son. It was like looking at a tiny Bongo Dee. *Chat bout.*

"Heidi," He shaped up and looked at her. "I haven't lost my mind. And don't think for a blood claat second I'm crying over you..." *Straight to the point.*

Heidi felt cornered.

Still, the little boy stared at the tear-stained face of the strange man in his mother's bedroom. He was puzzled.

"... I just want you to look me in the eyes now, and tell me this child is mine..." He waited for her answer.

Heidi started to smile. Not a happy smile. *Nerves.* They make us do the funniest things.

"Don't show me yuh blood claat teet' dem, Heidi! Plastic smile cyaan work a bombo claat! The child is Bongo's! Did you think I was gonna be inside foreva?!"

Perhaps he shouldn't have shouted. Not in front of the little boy. He made him jump.

"Sorry to scare you, little one," Festus said to the little boy in a calm voice. He pulled himself together and walked past Heidi and out of the bedroom. "Fin' yuhself a place as soon as possible, Heidi. Jus' ease outa mi house, yuh 'ear?"

Heidi stood there speechless. Her little boy looked at her with questions in his little eyes, gripping tightly to her arm. She had reached the end of her rope: best if she tied a knot in it.

Now, Festus pulled the front door shut behind him.

She wondered where Bongo was.

Bongo Dee, sitting in his ride outside the house watched Festus' disappearing back.

The dawning of a new scenario had arrived. For from every action, comes a reaction. *Feh real.*

* * *

House-guests can be like dead fish: after three days, they stink.... But this wasn't, and would never be the case with Festus. Lijah and Gloria had both agreed for him to stay with them until the Council found Heidi a new place to go. She had tricked her stay in a nice place for long enough, and now the roof Festus had inherited from Kizzy must be reclaimed.

It was two whole weeks after his release before Festus really got talking to Lijah about his life: *what, if, when, where* and *how* its scattered fragments could be salvaged. It was as if he needed that time to have lapsed before he really opened up.

"It aggo hard, Bredrin," he said as they sat in the living-room talking.

"Yuh sort out di house wid Heidi yet?" Lijah asked, taking a lick of his spliff.

"Well, she's got six weeks. The Council found her a place. The child isn't mine. Spitting image of Bongo Dee."

"I didn't think he was anything like you," Lijah said. I saw her in town with him once, and I doubted it from then. And when I heard that Bongo was touching her, there was no doubt whose pickney it was. The only way you can be given a jacket an' hold it, is if di pickney look just like di madda. An' if dat happen, an' yuh still doubt it, dere's DNA test an' all dat, dese days."

"Fari looks like Kizzy," Festus added. "Di bwoy don't have a single feature of mine... but mi *know* seh is *my* pickney, Bredrin. Kizzy didn't fuck 'roun'," he asserted. And he was right. She didn't *'fuck'* around but she was *'fucked'* around by Jaro.

"Mi glad yuh sort dat, still," Lijah said.

"Yeah, man. Ah Bongo Dee pickney. Ah nuh not'n."

"Yuh lucky still," Lijah told him. "Mi an' Gloria love Shanique, but Faithlyn try fi gimme a jacket. We decided to bring her up, but Shanique is Rock's child."

Festus paused before responding, and when he did he was practically crying. "I just can't wait to see my son... *Fari*..." He was overwhelmed by sadness.

Lijah knew exactly where Festus' head was at. *He who feels it knows it*. And Lijah had felt it. When Gloria had taken Khamilla to Jamaica, it felt as if she had ripped a large piece of his flesh away from him. And when he had made it to Jamaica and found them sharing a roof with Baby Face Glen: a man they had no business sharing one with, it was as if he was watching that bit of flesh being squeezed through a mincer, him feeling the painful mutilation.

"Yuh t'ink she'll give me a second chance?" Festus asked.

"Who?"

"Kizzy."

"Bwoy..." Lijah contemplated, "Kizzy deh ah Jamaica long time now, Bredrin. Shi mus' have man."

"I'm gonna try."

"Why not?"

"Not'n try, not'n done, Bredrin," he said sincerely. "Now mi know w'at Jah Cure mean... *reflection*..."

Lijah looked at his friend and listened. He knew where he was going too.

"... I spent nuff time reflecting on the way I treated Kizzy. It wasn't good. I was mixed up, Lijah. I had problems going on inside my head, man. I used to jus' kiss mi teet' w'en Kizzy used to tell mi 'bout therapy. *Counselling*. I used to t'ink it was rubbish. But bwoy..."

"Step by step, Bredrin," Lijah advised. "One day at a time."

"I wanna talk to her."

"Kizzy will listen, man."

"I know she will... but I don't mean Kizzy... ah mean mi madda... *Dora*."

"Yeah?!" Lijah was shocked. Most of all to hear Festus refer to Dora as *'my mother.'* Before, when he had confronted him about *two* crucial *twos* coming together to make one crucial *four*: that the *Dora* that was married to his old man Lothan, was in fact Festus' mother: the mother he had told everyone had died in a car crash, and that Montie the Handsworth tramp was his old man, Festus had said he didn't want

74

to talk about it: that as far as he was concerned, Dora might as well be dead. And although Lijah had heard from Kizzy about the domestic happenings that resulted in Festus whole-heartedly chopping himself away from his roots, he had struggled to comprehend the steadfastness of his stance on staying away permanently, even after his secret was out.

"Yeah, man. I won't be able to turn back the years, but going inside has made me realise that my anger towards my mother caused my own downfall. Kizzy… I abused her. *Physically… Mentally…*" He filled up.

"Easy, Bredrin. Mi glad yuh realise, still. Dora will be pleased." Lijah felt light for Festus. "Her an' di ole man are getting' old now. I'm glad I made peace wid di ole man… I would hate for one of us to kick di bucket, leavin' di adda one feelin' guilty."

"I want to go to Jamaica, Lijah," Festus said. His mind was made up.

"Yeah?"

"Yeah… Soon… but I don't want Dora or Kizzy to know I'm coming."

"Bwoy, dat wi' gi' Dora heart attack, man. I's *long time* yuh nuh si or talk to ar yunnuh, Festus."

"Years, Bredrin… years."

"To jus' turn up like dat… bwoy…" Lijah wasn't sure.

"Years… years…" It was as if he didn't hear Lijah's last concern.

"… I was a yout'…"

"Mi know, Festus," Lijah said as he watched his friend holding his head. He knew he was distressed, but he couldn't read his mind.

"De old man is dead, Lijah. Died on the streets of Handsworth while I was inside. He had a pauper's funeral." There was a finality in Festus' voice now. He knew there was nothing he could do about the past. All he could do now was to try to move forward. *Try.*

"Cheer up, Bredrin. I's carnival tomorrow, man. One day of niceness at leas'. Wi aggo tek a walk down deh."

"Dat a'right, still."

Lijah was a little glad to hear the jingling of keys. Gloria, Khamilla and Shanique were home. Their home-coming had saved him from taking his grown friend in his arm and rocking him like a baby.

Festus shaped up.

Every new minute would be a new start towards the future.

* * *

Bernadette forced her way through the thick carnival crowd to reach Lijah. He was standing with Festus, waiting for Gloria and the children to come back.

Lijah only knew about the fact that he was being chased, when he felt his ass being groped: some foreplay, only the man was in no mood to play.

He turned quickly to behold her… *Bernadette*. The woman who had a nasty hold on him. It had been a whole month at least since he had actually set eyes on her, but her phone calls to his mobile were still coming. When Bernadette was at a loose end: when her other male attendants were off somewhere, and she needed her welding done: *welding in the carnal sense that is*, she would call him. The saying, *'Yuh want di propa t'ings, call mi'*, wouldn't go amiss. And the job of refusing had not been as easy as Lijah like it to be, since the grip of blackmail can be tight. He had managed to strike a deal: *that under no circumstance would he sleep with her without a condom*. He had to protect Gloria. He was already rocking the boat. Tipping it over again wouldn't be good. She would probably kill him this time. However, Bernadette was surprisingly fine with the condom thing.

There was a time though, when there was no contact. And Lijah had got a little comfy, thinking it was peace and safety, until, bingo! It was sudden destruction again.

Now, a flush of heat overcame him. Festus knew of Bernadette, but not of the Rock thing.

Lijah looked around like a thief would, when ensuring he wasn't being watched.

"Bernadette?… I's weh yaah deal wid?"

"Just saying hello, Lijah… how are you?"

"I'm fine. My woman is around. I don't think groping me in public is the way to say hello."

"Well, *excuse me for breathing*," she said sarcastically.

"Ok, Bernadette, you've said hello. I would rather Gloria didn't see you hanging around me."

"You cheeky fucka!" she said, as if he was the one taking liberties. "Look how long you haven't seen me and this is the reception I get."

"A month, Bernadette. A month. You can hardly class that as long."

Festus looked simultaneously at both of them. He was puzzled at her attitude.

"That still wasn't a nice reception, Lijah."

"Did you expect open arms?" Lijah asked, getting really annoyed now.

"Don't push your luck, Lijah, you're still on borrowed time, remember?"

"I still can't believe this blackmail shit really makes you happy."

"This... *blackmail*? Or this... *black-male*?" she joked, ignoring his seriousness.

"Don't get clever, Bernadette."

"*Get?* I thought I already *was* clever." She got closer to his ear. "How else would I be able to command your company in my bed from time to time?"

Lijah was getting uneasy. Gloria would be back any minute. "Have you not seen my brother lately? Why don't you link him, Bernadette? Give me a break."

"How d'you know I'm not eating from both porridge bowls?"

"You *bitch*."

"It takes all sorts to make the world... and by the way... You fuck the best."

Lijah went hot. Festus was a little further away now. He felt he had to move. Giving them privacy one would expect.

"What kind of a woman are you! I told you, my woman is around! Why don't you f..."

"I was almost forgetting... your brother is a cop. Perhaps he would like to know how *Rock* died."

"You *fucking* bitch," Lijah said in a low voice, his teeth clenched.

"It would be hard to find a bitch that isn't a *'fucking'* one... and I just love it when you're angry... just as much as I love it when you fuck me."

He kissed his teeth. He was flustered more than ever before now.

Bernadette changed her tone, "Don't you miss me, Lijah?"

He couldn't believe the balls of the woman. He looked around again. "Bernadette, ah weh di blood claat... yuh sick yunnuh... believe mi!" His voice was low, yet it summoned more anger than when he shouted. He was staring daggers at her.

Bernadette reached out and touched his face. "I said, *don't you miss me*?"

As he prized her hand away from his face, he looked and caught the question in Festus' eyes from a distance, then, looking back at Bernadette, he said with stern assertion, "Like a fucking hole in the head."

"How d'you know what a hole in the head feels like? Did Rock emerge from the dead and tell you?" She hissed like a snake.

Lijah got hotter; especially now he caught sight of his queen, Gloria and the children walking back towards him with cones of ice cream.

"Move from mi, Bernadette. Gloria is coming."

"That's no way to treat a lady, Lijah, you know better than to talk to me like that."

"Cho… ease outa mi life nuh, 'oman? Move!"

"Maybe I will ease out of your life, Lijah… and maybe I won't… but if I decide to, Lijah, it won't be until *after* I decide that I want to."

"What did I do to deserve dis?" Lijah asked her. "Your grief wasn't with me in the first place. It was with my sister. And that's old news now. How long are you gonna be a chain around my neck?"

"Like I said," she assured him… "Not until I'm ready." She turned to leave, but turned back and told him, "By the way, I have stocked up on another lot of lavender oil… See you soon." And as if the devil had really gotten hold of her, she blew him a kiss!

Gloria got there just in time to see the disappearing back of Bernadette. She didn't recognise her from behind, and thought it was just another sista that Lijah was chatting to. "A'right?" she asked her man.

"Yes, Empress… you?"

"Mmmhuh."

He looked at Khamilla and Shanique whose cares just then were nothing but the creamy dribbles of vanilla liquid they were eagerly licking from the crispy cones as they watched the merrymaking of the exciting carnival day.

Festus drew nearer now. Both he and Lijah spoke to each other with their eyes. It was a serious situation. But what was the man to do? He was being pushed over the edge. Will he decide just to continue giving Bernadette what she wanted in exchange for a peace of mind?… You see, it was no different from a game of Russian roulette. Condoms have a way of bursting. Neither he nor Bernadette knew about the waiting bullet of HIV. Nico had ploughed her field and scattered his bad seed upon her land. And the pending pollination? It was lurking. Waiting like a thief in the night.

With the children behind, Gloria licked her ice cream and strolled along, linking her man's arm. She hadn't the slightest clue of her pending fate. No sir. Not even … the slightest clue.

* * *

Sleepy-eyed, Simone trundled downstairs to put the kettle on. She listened to the sound of her husband's engine as he pulled away from the drive. The musky-sweet odour of his body still lingered on her body, and the taste of his tender kisses still lingered on her lips. As the kettle hummed, she turned...

And there it was...

On the table.

An oblong envelope with her name on.

She opened it, pulled the note out and read...

Have I told you lately how much I love you?
Have I showed you how much I care?
Do you see the adoration in my eyes every time I look at you?
And feel the love when I hold you near?

'Tell me when I see you next'
Your dear husband
x x x

Simone held the card close to her chest, smiled and said, "Heaven must have sent you from above."

Chapter 7

"*How* was your time in Jamaica, Empress?" Garnet asked as he cast his eyes over the two suitcases on Evadney's kitchen floor. Independently she had made her own way back from Heathrow airport by train, rather than take him up on his offer to pick her up. He had literally just turned up: a few minutes after her black cab pulled in.

"Good. It was good. How have *you* been?"

"A'right. Mi did miss yuh dough, 'Vadney... Maybe next time I'll come wid yuh."

"You couldn't have missed me that much, Garnet. You're used to being away from me."

" 'Vadney, mi tellin' yuh seh mi did miss yuh. Yuh doubtin' mi?"

"No, Garnet. If you say you missed me, you must have," she patronised.

"Didn't you miss me, 'Vadney?" His voice was more formal now. Perfect English overrode patois.

She reached for the kettle and swung it under the tap, downing her answer with the noisy torrents of water falling into it. "I'm tired, Garnet. Just gimme a few minute to chill, will you?"

"You're too tired to tell me whether you missed me or not, 'Vadney?"

"Yes, *I missed you*, do you want a cuppa tea?"

Garnet looked hurt. He wasn't sure she meant it. "Are you sure you haven't got a man out there?" *What the hell? No point beating around the bush. He wondered, so he asked.*

"Like you had that blonde, Tracey?" she snapped.

"What's this, 'Vadney? Have we moved on from all dat? Or are we still there?…"

"Do you want tea or not?"

"No t'ank yuh..."

She poured boiling water on a waiting teabag.

"Are you sure you want to go t'rough wid dis weddin' t'ing? Cos I man not too sure seh yuh forgive mi fully yunnuh."

"I've practically just got in, Garnet. I haven't even sat down. The last thing I need is this."

"I think the last thing you need is *me*. I wish you would come upfront an' seh w'at yuh really feelin'."

"When did *what I feel* matter to you, Garnet? Did you not think about what I felt when you fucked off with Tracey?"

Garnet paused… "Why did you agree for us to get back together if that wasn't what you wanted, 'Vadney? You've been so cold."

"However cold I might seem, it can never touch your coldness. The only person that mattered back then, Garnet, was Tracey, so don't gimme yuh emotional crap."

"*So cold,*" he repeated, as if he didn't hear her last comment. *What would he have done if he knew that the mysterious Sanchez had thawed her a little? And there were more. A fat lot more.* But as far as she was concerned, nothing would ever square up to what Garnet did to her.

She picked up her tea now and walked almost aggressively to her living-room.

Garnet followed.

"Somehow, I don't feel welcomed here." He was apprehensive about sitting down.

Evadney flicked the TV on. "Do you know how I *really* felt when you left me for Tracey, Garnet?" As she asked the question, it was almost as if that was the very moment Evadney had come to the full realisation of the *nothing* Garnet had made her feel she was. A *worthless nothing,* that *in his eyes*, only a white woman could replace.

"Oh no…" Garnet put his head in his hands and tried to sweep away the frustration.

"*Why?*" she asked desperately, looking at him as if it happened yesterday. "It couldn't be for *status*. She had *nothing*." She looked at him now as if she had to have the answer there and then. As if she wanted to open his brain: do her own psychological autopsy to find the answer. "Is it because I couldn't have children?… or is it because you think *pearls* are more precious than *onyx*?"

"No… no… no." He turned his head to the side wondering why Evadney had decided to walk in from a two-week trip to Jamaica and started to ride an old subject.

"*No?*… Then you just *saw* her… *fell* for her and decided to *leave* me and *move in* with her?… I even heard you were pushing shopping trolley in Tescos… something you've never done with me? How did she get you to do that, Garnet?"

Garnet swept his palm over his locks but said nothing. Dejavu was devouring him. He had been there so many times, and wondered if the end would come. "You haven't forgiven me in the slightest, have you, 'Vadney?"

"You and I went back to Federation days, Garnet. We…"

"Empress, I t'ought we been t'rough all dat? Tracey and I are history now."

"Of course you are. Only because she left you for Bongo Dee."

"Can we just leave it, Empress? *Please.*"

"Did you call Tracey, *Empress*, too?"

" 'Vadney, *please*…" He paused. His eyes beckoned her and his heart begged again for full forgiveness. If only he could turn the clock back. "I realised long time ago that I was foolish. I shouldn't have…" He wanted to hold her. Sing to her. The song he sang to her the day she said she'd given him a second chance…

Natural African black woman I adore you… Empress…

"Is dat why yuh don't want mi to move in wid yuh or mek love to yuh until afta di weddin' day?… or are you having second thoughts about di weddin'?"

"No… no, Garnet, I'm not having second thoughts at all… The wedding day is on, Garnet. The wedding day is on. Don't worry about that." She sipped her tea as she listened to his deep sigh of relief.

"Empress, I know I've done yuh wrong… Hurt yuh badly. But if yuh lef' mi, I'll be a wrecked man…"

"Like I was a wrecked woman when *you* left *me*?"

"… After all dat rigmarole wid Tracey, I realised seh we were meant to be."

She gave him a loaded look. A look filled with a whole load of *telling*. But all he could do was wish he could read her thoughts.

* * *

Tender fell the rain…

Marcia sat almost analysing each drop that took purchase against her windowpane. With depth, she watched the individual droplets as they would fall, then trickle down the clear glass as if driven by a mission, mingling and losing themselves in the one that had fallen previously. There was beauty in the simple process: a beauty that only Marcia would see. Around her shoulders she had wrapped an infamous red, yet *far-from-perfect* silk sheet. Far-from-perfect since it was the one she had mercilessly ripped as the untimely hurt Conteh had delivered years ago, ripped her heart. She had not discarded it like Menna did. And although it was tattered and torn, a strange compelling had commanded her to keep it.

She had had a few mild stresses in her life, but was firm in her belief that falling so deeply in love with Conteh, then bearing the full blunt of his heartless treatment sent her over the edge. Conteh had rejected her. Told her he would *never* leave his wife for her. And she had lost it. *Totally*. It resulted in her being whizzed off to a ward in a mental hospital. Ever since then, Marcia suffered a series of mental breakdowns.

Of course she knew that if Conteh wasn't the source of the initial trauma, it might have been someone else. But as it went, it was him, so she had laid the blame for her first breakdown *firmly* at his feet. And with still no firm diagnosis for the series of mental breakdown she had suffered since, Marcia was less than pleased about popping some Goddamn pills for the rest of her life.

'*Ain't life a bitch?*' she thought as she fluffed and puckered her pillow in readiness for her afternoon nap. Lately, she had been feeling extra tired. Slowed down.

She eased her right shoulder onto her pillow, picked her feet up off the floor and curled her body up in a cosy ball as she continued watching the raindrops. It wasn't long before the therapeutic sound of the afternoon rain against her window would snooze her away into dreamland.

Tender... tender... tender... fell the rain.

* * *

My Bonnie lies over the ocean,
My Bonnie lies over the sea
My Bonnie lies over the ocean,
Oh bring back my Bonnie to me...

Sista Viola Prince tipped more water into the mixture and put her back into it, but her mind couldn't be more further from the dough she kneaded. *Marcia,* her beautiful daughter. It didn't seem so long ago that she sang to her sweet, petty little girl to sleep. She had even gotten tired of the song, and she wished Marcia would ask for another one. It was the only song for her, so every night Viola would sing diligently to her, until she would sink into a deep slumber. Now, like any mother's instinctive urge to comfort, she would sing it whenever she felt her daughter was on the edge of another breakdown. The song had new meaning now... for she wished she could have her old daughter back: she lay over the turbulent ocean of an undiagnosed mental illness...

Bring back, bring back,
Oh bring back my Bonnie to me, to me.
Bring back, bring back,
Oh bring back my Bonnie to me...

The day she was first called to the mental hospital had never left Viola's mind. There, she had found her daughter. *Rocking. Rocking. Rocking.* And she had laid her daughter's head upon the bosom from whence she once suckled, and combed her hair.

Conteh. She wouldn't forget his name. *Conteh Gonzales*: the heartbreaker who had tipped Marcia's scales. And without constant medication, they would never be balanced again, for she had entered the twilight zone of strong medication, and the taboo and stigma that goes with mental illness. If the leg, the belly, the heart or lung is sick, to society's reckoning, it's ok, but when it is the brain, you're a freak.

SECTIONED. That was the word that attached itself steadfastly to Viola's brain from that very day. Her daughter, *SECTIONED* in a mental hospital. It broke her heart. .

Viola stopped what she was doing. She pushed the residue of the *not-yet-tight* mixture from her fingers, washed and dried her hands and walked to the telephone. The dialling and the answering took forever.

"Marcia... Yuh a'right?... yuh jus' wake up?... Why don't you come ova fi dinna? I'm cooking stew peas an' rice... Yes but yuh haven't come ova fi ages... Yes, but yuh *one* an' Jesus innah di big flat... A'right... Yuh tekkin' yuh tablets?... A'right, me comin' ova wid some stew peas fi yuh... A'right, see yuh lata."

Viola replaced the receiver, walked back to her kitchen and resumed her job of cooking. She was tired of asking Marcia to come to church, though every week she would ask the brethrens to pray a special prayer for her. If only Marcia would stick to taking her medication, rather than insisting that she would try to *beat it naturally*. She had watched her moods swinging like a pendulum. She would swing from mad shopping sprees, to feeling low, to being depressed. And then there would be the over-charming Marcia one minute, then the over-abusive the next. But most of all, the *acute paranoia*. She would be convinced she was being followed. Someone was after her. Coming to get her. *'Why us, Lord?'* she asked her God, *'why us?'*...

> *Rock of Ages, cleft for me,*
> *Let me hide myself in Thee;*
> *Let the water and the blood,*
> *From Thy wounded side which flowed,*
> *Be of sin the double cure;*
> *Save from wrath and make me pure.*

* * *

It was from a distance that they stared at her. *Simone*... It was Jacqueline that recognised her, since Cerise wouldn't.

"That was the woman that your father was married to," she told Cerise.

"Really?"

"Yeap."

"She's *beautiful*."

" 'Course she is. But that didn't stop him sleeping around, did it?"

"Cashier number twelve, please," the computer in the busy post called out, and Jacqueline, Cerise and her *spitting-image-of-Conteh* son walked towards the waiting cashier.

While Jacqueline acquired the items on her list, Cerise strained her head to find Simone again, but she wasn't in sight. But minutes later as they stood wrapping a parcel and engaging in a conversation that probably should have been left for behind closed doors, a voice asked, "This is Conteh's child?" And when they had looked, they found Simone standing there looking without malice at the cute little boy.

"Er… yeah… yeah… it is," Cerise replied nervously."

Jacqueline looked at Simone, wondering if she had heard the *whole* and not just *half* the story.

"I wasn't eavesdropping, but you weren't whispering. And I don't think there are that many soundmen called Conteh."

The silence could be cut with a knife now.

"Hello," Simone said, now bending down towards the little boy.

"Hello," he replied coyly.

"How old are you?"

"Six."

"Ok," she said, smiling. Simone had heard about this little boy, but now it was fully confirmed. She was a mature woman and had no qualms with Cerise. She didn't do childish confrontations, besides she had left Conteh's stable long ago. And the dark idea of a child being fathered by his own granddad was something she wouldn't let distress her. Life was too short. She was gentle with herself…

> *Take kindly the counsel of the years,*
> *gracefully surrendering the things of youth.*
> *Nurture strength of spirit to shield you in sudden misfortune.*
> *But do not distress yourself with dark imaginings.*
> *Many fears are born of fatigue and loneliness.*
> *Beyond a wholesome discipline,*
> *be gentle with yourself.*

"You're Simone, aren't you?"

"Yes. And you must be Jacqueline."

"Yes… I am."

"Small world, Jacqueline… small world."

"I see your tolerance ran out… you left him," Jacqueline told her.

"We've all got our limits."

"Have you forgiven him for all he'd done to you?"

"Yes," Simone said. "I have. But Conteh needs more than my forgiveness to make it all right."

"He's the pits," Jacqueline said bitterly.

"I wouldn't say that. There are worse people than Conteh out there, Jacqueline. *Believe me*."

Jacqueline didn't know where else to go with the conversation.

Although not knowingly, Conteh had gotten her daughter (his own daughter) pregnant: It was the cause that resulted in the devastating effect of her husband Henley leaving and returning to Barbados… She was picking up her whole life and moving to The States, and all this woman could say was, *'There are worse people than Conteh out there?'*…

"Well, if there are, I hope I never meet them," Jacqueline said.

"Me neither, Jacqueline. Me neither."

Simone bade them goodbye, but long after she had gone, the image of her beautiful face remained in Cerise's mind.

* * *

"I knew you'd come," was what Bernadette said as she opened her front door to Lijah.

Silently he walked in.

She felt the aura of anguish that oozed from his very existence and saw the quiet storm that brewed deep within his eyes, yet Bernadette seemed to thrive on this. Why couldn't she just leave him alone? Was there a name for her illness? For it had to be one. *A strange illness*. There was no way that was simply *'sex-on-order-with-the-help-of-blackmail'*.

Lijah puffed on a spliff as he walked silently to her living-room. Placed his ass in the far corner of her big settee, he fixed his eyes on the TV. He wasn't taking it in. just a place to focus.

"Chill, Lijah," Bernadette told him. She was half-dressed.

He said nothing.

"Drink?" she asked.

He shook her a *'no'* then watched her wheeled her poisoned ass to her kitchen.

He eased forward and asked in a monotone, "Got an ashtray?"

Within seconds she brought him one. Lijah took a long hard pull, then rested his spilff in one of its grooved edges. "I want outa dis, Bernadette." He exhaled a thick puff of smoke. "No messin' dis time."

"You make it sound as if you've initiated into some sort of gang and now want out," she said, sitting beside him.

"It's worse," he told her, now making eye contact.

"No it's not. Gang leaders kill. *We're* having fun."

"Fun?! Fun?! Bernadette my family is at risk again. I don't want to loose them again..." *Oh the weakness of men.* You see, he was now melting to the warmth of her tongue against his neck, and the firmness of her wandering palm against his balls.

"Jesus, Chr..." he whispered, but was stopped as she gobbled his lips. Sunk her tongue down his throat. Pushed him backwards on the settee. "Bernadette..."

"This will be the last time," she whispered. "I'll leave you alone after this."

"I don't believe you," he mumbled as she loosened his belt.

"Are you really seeing my brother?"

"Is it an issue?"

"Ahhh..."He was pleasantly surprised. She was quick. Her warm mouth had devoured his stiff manhood.

"Well? Is it an issue?" she paused to ask.

"Not really," he mumbled.

"Well, just lay back and enjoy.

"Ahhh... ahhh... oh... ohhh... shit..."

"Why were you so harsh at the carnival, Lijah?"

"Ahhh!" he jerked backwards. "Shit!... What was that for?!" she had bitten him. "That hurts!"... But seconds later he eased again into her warped tenderness.

"Why did you talk to me like that?"

"Bernadette, you're blackmailing me. My woman was near... And you were getting too close... I told you..." His eyes were closed. "Ahhh... ahhh..." *Oh the weakness of men.* Give them a bit and they're like putty in your hands... even when their worlds are about to cave in around their feet. Bless their little weak little hearts.

Bernadette eased off. "C'mon, Lijah," she said standing up and pulling his arms. "Clothes off. I want to rub you down with some lavender oil."

"Bernadette, I don't know if we have time for all that. Gloria is expecting me soon and that lavender odour lingers, you know that."

"Ok, we'll leave it until another time…"

"You see!" Lijah protested.

"What?"

"I knew you were lying… you just said, *'We'll leave it until another time'*… I thought you just told me this would be the last time?"

"It will. Slip a the tongue… don't take any notice of that last statement…"

He stared suspiciously at her.

"… Get your clothes off anyway," she commanded, "I hate fucking with clothes on. I'll get the condoms."

He adhered as she ascended the stairs.

Lijah was sat nude on Bernadette's red carpet when Bernadette re-entered the room, also nude. A sense of dejavu hit him. He had been there before. She had done this before. He rose to his knees now and would be a liar if he said he wasn't about to give thanks for what he was about to devour. Something gave him wings. Maybe it was the *'This will be the last time… I'll leave you alone after this,'* he had heard earlier from Bernadette. "Come here." He took the lead now. With his face to her groin, he gripped the firm cheeks of her ass. Legs asunder and hands on his head, she looked up to the heavens. Eyes closed. "Ahhh…" she hummed as Lijah's tongue played sweet music on her clitoris. "Ahhh… are you sure you want this to be the last time?" she asked him.

No answer. The man was eating. Some strong tongue movements going on.

"Ahhh… Lijah… oh… that… is… so… *gooood.*"

"Condom." He stopped for a second. "Where is it?"

Bernadette handed Lijah the rubber sheath, then slowly knelt down. Creeping 'round behind him, she cuddled his back as he eased his lifesaver on. She kissed his neck. His back. His sensitive sides.

Now, Lijah turned and took her in his arms. He kissed her passionately. *"The last time?"* he whispered, wondering how sweet the poison of deception could be.

"Last time," she whispered back. "If you want it to be…"

He laid her down… His manhood ready… He prised her apart as he licked her tender, aching breasts. *"Last time?"* he asked again as if it was a part of the foreplay.

"Just enter me, and cut the fucking chat," she spluttered like a hungry prisoner.

"... Ugh!!... Jesus, Lijah! You're like an animal today..."

He pushed both her legs towards her head and thrust his raging anger deep... deep... deep her.

"Aw! Lijah! Ugh! Ugh! You're hurting me!"

"Is this the last time!"

"Yes!"

"Say it again!"

"Yes! It's the last time!"

"*Bitch!"* Bang! Bitch! Bang! Bitch! Bang! Bang! Bang!"

"Stop it! Stop it! Lijah, stop it!"

"And he did. *Stopped it.* But not until after he had ejaculated.

He rolled over and placed his left palm over his forehead.

His energy *drained.*

Her inside *throbbed.*

His mind *wandered.*

Her ass *burned* from the carpet.

And the condom?... what condom? It had long gone *burst.* Oh yes... *burst.* Well and truly... *burst... Burst.* Oh Lord... Lord, Lord. Lord.... *Burst.*

And *too late... Too late... Too late... shall be his cry.*

* * *

It was inevitable... Later that night Lijah was arrested by guilt and a thought that wouldn't leave his head. He had already taken great care in ensuring that the tinge of Bernadette's perfume that had lingered on him was gone. A shower took care of that, and since he was now domesticated and took his turn in filling the washing-machine, when he had piled the forensic-filled clothing in with some of Gloria's and the children's, nothing was suspicious.

But guilt could not be washed away. *No sir.*

He forced himself to look naturally into his woman's eyes when she spoke to him, but it was all an act. *'Natural'* didn't come so easy when he could still *feel* Bernadette's juices all over his dick... *see* the look on her face as he lashed her with his *rod of retribution...* and *hear* her cries of agony... smell her potent perfume as it oozed with her body heat out of her pores... And as for the taste... well, he could still hear her hums as his tongue played sweet music on her clitoris...

And the burst condom episode wasn't helping much. Apart from his brother, Roy, he had no idea where Bernadette had been. But that wasn't all. The words Gloria had said years ago on the night they decided to get back together surfaced again. She had uttered them when he was just seconds away from reaching her hungry flesh. She had stopped him in his tracks and said, *'We've both taken different turns from each other, Lijah. Eaten from different plates. We both don't know where we've been. We're big people. We might have been stupid before, but let's be sensible now. We need to take that crucial step of getting AIDS tests.'* And like an intended bullet from an angry gun, the words had returned to shatter his brain.

* * *

It was a rainy day in Handsworth. Shari pulled her hood of her coat over her head and scurried from her car across Soho Road straight into the West Indian food shop. She didn't have Menilek and Kunta Junior with her. They were at home with her mother Mitzi, who, as far as Shari could see, had mysteriously developed a liking for Birmingham.

A frumpy older woman edged aside almost reluctantly, to make room for her in the narrow isle. Now, pulling the hood off, Shari recognised her. And when she moaned everlastingly at the shop assistant about the size of their bread, the texture of the gizzardas, and the softness of the dumplings, Shari knew that this woman was nothing but a walking bag of cantankerousness, since the food they were selling were nothing short of *'the best a West Indian could get'*. This woman was simply bitter and needed to de-clutter her mind.

"How much is yuh bun?" the woman asked in a less than courteous tone.

"T'ree poun," the assistant replied.

"T'ree poun?" she kissed her teeth, "an' mi cyan mek it cheapa at home?" She was downright rude.

"Den gaah yuh yaad go mek it den nuh!" the assistant quite rightly told her. Politeness would be wasted on this woman.

"Gi mi a bokkle ah yuh strawberry syrup," she grunted, as if she begrudged putting good food into her body.

The assistant obliged.

"How much?" *Mrs Grumpy* asked, digging into her purse as if it had no bottom.

"Wid di res' ah yuh stuff…" she paused to tally, "five poun'."

The rude woman emitted a sarcastic cackle and the assistant caught the questioning eyes of the other five waiting customers, including Shari's.

90

Now, stretching a ten-pound note towards the assistant, the woman took the opportunity to look now into Shari's face. *"Hello,"* she said, jolted *purely* by the sudden familiarity of her face.

"Hello," Shari replied.

Then, as she took her change, reality hit her.

She realised *who* Shari *really* was and came over a little unnecessary.

Dudley Road hospital. Her mind was transported.

Zelda the cantankerous nurse was obviously flustered. Shame, one would guess, when she remembered the way she treated the young, pain-stricken Shari as she gave birth to Menilek years ago… *'Yuh tek di pleasure, now tek di pain!'* she had told her.

Or perhaps it was the *to*ing and *fro*ing of words between her and Gloria…

'Don't I know you?' Gloria had challenged.

'Mi know nuff people,' Gestapo Lil had said. *'Who is yuh parents?'*…

'Who my parents are, is not relevant right now,' Gloria replied. *'Besides, I'm not a child.'*…

'What a facety 'oman,' the grumpy nurse had replied perturb.

But she was even more shocked when Gloria spieled, *'Who knows, you might not have been much older than Shari when you had your first child in Jamaica, so comfort the girl and don't distress her. It's your job. Most of you older people forget that you were young once. And that you did the same t'ing di kids are doin' now. The only difference is, it would probably have been undaneat' a sycamore or mango tree. Or in some coffee grove or somewhere like dat. And in dem days you were marched home to the boy's parents, and he would have to marry yuh! In your case though, any man who got you into trouble would have probably ran miles.'*

Zelda hung her head down and left the shop without saying goodbye to Shari.

"Can I have a duck bread, one of those buns and three lamb patties please?" Shari asked.

"A'right," the assistant said, and as she placed the items on the counter one by one, Shari glanced out and saw the youth she had been trying for the longest time to link. "Excuse me," she said to the assistant who was now doing a mental tally of her eats. She stepped quickly out of the shop. "Andre!" she shouted, dead set on not letting him disappear.

91

The young man slowed up, and when he had recognised her, he started to walk towards her, cowering from the drizzly rain.

After a short sweet greeting, Shari wasted no time in asking for Andre's input into a campaign geared towards positivity.

"Yeah. No problem," he said. I'm working on my second album at the moment, but I would love to do it."

"Your second album?!"

"Yeah."

"That is what I like about you, Andre. You are so persistent in whatever you do."

"*Persistence* is a key to success," Andre said. "So is *Pride* in yourself."

"I'm sure it'll pay off," Shari assured him.

"I hope so," he said. "As a matter of fact, the title of the album I'm working on is *'Persistence and Pride.'*

"Really?"

"Yeah. It features some strong lovers rock. Something for everyone. Young and old."

"You've always had an old head on your shoulders, Andre… always."

"It's about keeping it real," he said. "Here's my contact." He handed Shari his card. "We'll talk more about this campaign, yeah?"

"Yeah. I'll call you." Shari said, tucking the card safely into her handbag and away from the dampness of the day.

"Laters," Andre said, as he walked away smiling.

"Laters," Shari said, returning to the shop to get her freshly baked wares.

* * *

"**I**'ve stopped asking myself *'what will people say'* for a long time," Evadney said, relaxing as Yvonne manipulated her waistline, searching for that comfortable fit.

"Look… you're a grown woman," Yvonne told her, adjusting the tape measure around her friend's waist.

"Worse things have happened in the world," Evadney said.

Yvonne smiled. It was an *honour* for her to be asked to make that special dress for her friend's wedding day, though she wasn't sure if the *pleasure* was one hundred percent. However, wishing her friend well on her decision to walk down the isle was the best she could do. She had always been there for Evadney. From way before the day she had told her what she had done with Conteh after Garnet had left her for Tracey. For a while, Evadney seemed to have gone into herself, then she seemed to have snapped out of it, met a few guys and… well, whatever, Yvonne had always been there. "You marry who the hell you want to marry. It's nobody's business. It's your own bed you're spreading. Only *you* and whoever you marry will lie in it. *Nobody* else."

"When Garnet left me, people talked. I felt like nothing."

"And they'll talk now. People will always talk, girl," the tall, well built, bosom-blessed Yvonne said. "And while they're talking about you, they're leaving someone else alone."

"So what do you *really* think of what I'm doing?"

"I've told you already. *You've* decided. It's *your* life. Every individual has to live with his or her own actions."

"It had hurt though, Yv'… really hurt."

"Of course it would. When a black man leaves a black woman for another sista, it cuts like a knife. When he leaves her for a white woman?" she kissed her teeth and rolled her eyes, "it cuts like a thousand knives, with salt being poured into the wounds. Let's not pretend the hurt is the same. Even the white woman he left her for, if she was honest enough, will agree that the hurt must be different. It's nothing at all to do with racism, though many would define it so. It's the residue of our history. It cannot be helped. We were made to feel inferior then, and our men are irritating it now. And it would be *politically incorrect* if we should express the way we feel about our men doing the mass exodus, so the only thing we can do is put up and shut up."

Evadney sighed.

"So, are you looking forward to your day?" Yvonne asked.

"Yes… I am."

"Well, sound a bit more cheerful, will you?" Yvonne told her.

"You just get this dress right," Evadney joked now.

"This is going to be a *perfect* dress, for a *perfect* day. Don't you worry."

Chapter 8

𝔜t was a quiet Sunday afternoon… Reds, the *silent river* of a Dread lay across his bed, the thick strands of his locks spreading the whole breadth of the top of his bed. Lying loosely upon his flat stomach, his red-gold-and-green belt was released, as if to free him of his little niggles. Thoughts raced though his ital-filled head. He felt that Papa Dread's spirit was with him – he could feel it: *a calm, peaceful, pacifying presence.* He felt a strong sense of forgiveness too, forgiving him for pulling the trigger that wasted the notorious *Rock.*

As he lay there, Reds could almost hear his own thoughts echoing… *'Why does Mitzi want to see me… it's been so long since we copulated… she was under the influence of firewater… it probably wouldn't have happened if she was sober…what does she want with me now?'*

The phone by his bed rang. He turned onto his stomach and reached over to answer it. "Lijah?… Whaap'n, mi Lion?… is weh yaah seh? Bernadette still ah badda yuh?… Bwoy, it look like sop'n seriously wrong wid di woman dem nowadays, Rasta… Wha?!… Yuh mek sure dat's di las' time, Bredrin… Me?… Well, Mitzi seh shi waan talk to mi… yeah, *the* Mitzi… Couldn't tell yuh, Rasta. Mi jus waitin' fi ar yah now… Yeah, man… Check yuh inna di week still… Bless."

And no sooner than Reds replaced the receiver, his doorbell rang. Quickly, he fixed himself up, then descended his stairs. Mitzi was early.

"Garfield, Hi," Mitzi said in a posh accent, "hope you didn't mind."

"Reds couldn't help feeling a little strange at the sound of *'Garfield'*. In a very long time, it had been the first utterance of his *real name* from a black person. He had been assigned *'Reds'* from way back in the days. Though he was not immediately mixed-raced, his remarkable resemblance to Bob Marley and his high complexion had warranted him the title *'Reds'.* He had answered to it ever since. Mitzi, however, had hardly called his real name, let alone attempted to use his nickname.

"Come een, Mitzi… go through to the sittin' room." He gestured with his right hand as he closed the door behind her.

As she walked, arms folded, she cast her eyes *left-right-left-right* as if she was a surveyor sent to inspect his property. And when she got to the living-room she stood, arms still folded, waiting to be invited to sit.

Reds didn't know why he was feeling slightly nervous in his own house.

"Sit down," he said, pointing to his settee. "Yuh want a drink?"

"I'm... fine thank you." Her arms were still folded, and though the dread's flat was immaculately clean and fresh with the aroma from sticks of burning incense, Mitzi perched on the edge of his settee as if a pack of fleas lay at the back, waiting to ambush her *'shit-don't-stink'* ass.

Reds reached for a full packet of Rizzla and a square tin that were sitting on his coffee table. "So to what do I owe the *pain* of your company?" he asked as he sat down and got busy with his fingers.

"No need to be inhospitable, Garfield."

"Well, I don't for one minute believe its gonna be a *pleasure... is it?*"

"Where's your lady, Garfield?"

He looked at her. "My lady?... Why?..."

"I just wondered."

"I haven't got a lady... after Damian's mother... well..."

"You're still a nice looking guy..."

"Don't patronise me, Mitzi, why the visit?"

Well..."

"And you can relax. There's nothing in my yard dat bites," he said without looking up from his spliff-building.

Mitzi relaxed a little. Who the hell did she think she was anyway?

"You were saying?" Reds reinitiated.

"Garfield, I don't know where to start..."

"That's why you should relax. If you're not rushing, I have all day." His nerves had left. He felt in control now. He had detected a slight weakness in her ability to deliver her mission statement, so it gave him back his courage.

"Garfield..."

He looked up as he lit his spliff, its first puff licking out a cloud of ital smoke. *'Well?'* his squinting eyes asked.

"Years ago... when you and I... can you remember?"

He paused. Pulled in another lick. "How could I forget? You were tipsy. You regretted it.... what about it?"

"Well... I... got pregnant."

Reds fixed his eyes on her as he gently pushed out the residue of his last drag. "You.... got... *what?*"

"You heard."

"You got *pregnant?*"

"Yes."

He lay his spliff down like one would, burden.

"So now, after all these years you come to tell me you *aborted* my child?"

"No… no I didn't."

Reds paused. Stopped in his tracks. "So… whaap'n to di baby?"

The baby is Shari."

"Reds stood up quickly and retreated to a corner of the room. From there he stared out at Mitzi. *Weh yuh seh?*"

Mitzi didn't repeat herself. She knew he heard.

"Shari… Kunta's girlfriend, Shari?"

"Yes."

"Shari is mi pickney?"

No answer.

"Blood cl…"

"Listen, Garfield, I know it's gonna take some getting used to, but…"

He sat back down and reached for his spliff again. "*Shari is my child?*"

She nodded a 'yes'.

"Then… why *now*, Mitzi?"

"I don't know. I just felt I had to."

"Bombo cl…"

"You don't have to use foul language, Garfield."

"Does Shari know?"

"No… I thought I'd talk to you first."

"Mitzi… can you remember my son Damian?"

"Yeah. He got shot, didn't he?"

"He and Shari had a t'ing going."

"Yeah, but I didn't know that until lately."

"And what if you did? Would you have told Shari then?"

"I think I would have had to."

"Who knows, Mitzi?… Gloria?… Lijah?…"

"Nobody knows. Just me."

Reds reached for his lighter. Perhaps it was the coldness of Mitzi that caused his spliff to go out so quickly. "Mitzi… you have robbed me of all those years of seeing my daughter grow up?… Supporting her like a father should?…Why?"

No answer.

"I'll tell you why, Mitzi… because you felt you were betta dan I man." He took a lick of ital.

"Garfield, I didn't come here for a fight. I just wanted to tell you."

"And you're *not,* Mitzi… not in the least… you're *not* better dan I man."

"Garfield, I'm going now." She got up.

Reds' stare was piercing.

Mitzi's arms were still folded. "I'll see myself out."

"Like you *saw yourself* outa Birmingham twenty-two years ago with my child in your womb?"

She was walking away now.

Reds positioned himself where he could see her leave. He was still shocked. And only when the door slammed hard behind her that it really began to sink in.

Only then that he realised that the killing of Rock had more meaning than he had first thought.

Only then he realised that he was not just a father, but also a grandfather of two.

Reds took another lick of his spliff then dialled Lijah.

* * *

Beverley sat alone in a London flat; waiting it seemed, *to die.* The flat was not hers, but her *once-wanna-be, now-big-time* singer boyfriend's. Well, now, they're just friends. Couldn't be anything else, least of all, lovers. It would have been he who their friends would have expected to bring HIV home, but Beverley beat him to it, although they weren't together at the time she stepped through Simone's door and copulated with Conteh. And luckily for this guy, who had more raw talent than any X-Factor host could ever wish for, Beverley found out about her little mishap before she managed to climb back into his bed.

Now, she sat, almost lifeless, in the dim, lonely room, thoughts filling her head. She remembered Nico, and how he was consciously and heartlessly sharing his fate of disaster with every woman he could get his *hands on* and *dick into.* Nothing she could do about that: each man is responsible for his own actions. But most of all, she remembered how Conteh let rip at her for carelessly losing a solitaire red earring behind his loo seat, causing Simone to find. *Shit.* It was then that she realised how much he *really* loved his wife, but she couldn't help but asking herself that same old question, '*why fuck out on your woman if you love her so?*'

The book that rested on her lap told of how HIV and AIDS attack each person's body differently. Different symptoms, different times – and sometimes they don't strike at all. Conteh and Nico had long stretches of good luck: apparently, the luck of Magic Johnson: *non-progressors*. Beverley, however, didn't have long to go, now. She knew it. Dying alone must be the loneliest thing anyone could ever go through. And Beverley had lifted her eyes and heart onto Glory, and asked the Lord to have mercy on her soul.

* * *

Everybody, everywhere tries to do the best they can in the name of survival. In the pockets of their own little worlds, they shake around like lose change, each one having the ability to make as much noise as they can: it depends on how much they have been *used* and *abused:* wrongfully *spent* by people who knew not the value of *respect.*

But not all noises are *bad*, and sometimes *good* can emerge from the *bad* that had been done.

Ikesha emerged for the last time from the room where she had been attending therapy for several weeks. The treatment was surely working. Facing her problem head-on was what she needed. It had been a while, but until she could face up to the fact that dealing with rape *inwardly* was no good, then she couldn't decide to seek treatment.

She had come a long way from the morning she woke to find herself lying on her living-room floor, her absent rapist long gone - a fist full of GHB drug on his person.

"Hi," Shari said, lifting her head from Ava Ming's *Once Upon A Lie*. "Everything ok, girl?" She addressed Ikesha with excitement as if she already *knew* that everything was just fine.

"Everything's fine," Ikesha said, pulling the door closed on the therapist. "C'mon. Let's go find a place that do some decent food."

"Well, you know there's no *Gloria's* restaurant 'round here," Shari bantered with a smile, as she carefully placed Ava's novel into her handbag. "This is London. Your mum's kitchen is in Birmingham."

"Trust me," Ikesha said, taking the lead out of the building, "Have you managed to speak to Andre Johnson again about the *Don't Be Influenced* campaign?"

"Oh yes, I spoke to him a few days ago. He's working on his second album, but he's quite happy to join us in forming a team that campaigns for positive changes – not just for youths, but for adults too… in fact, his words were, *'There have been so many things going on lately, it looks as if we need emphasise the message and tell them to fix up'."*

"That's Andre for you. Quiet nature, yet his lyrics are so positively loud," Ikesha responded.

"Believe me," Shari enthused. "Oh... he also said he will be working on a special Don't Be Influenced track."

"Whoa!! That sounds great," Ikesha said. "We have to start planning soon. There are lots to do."

"D'you think we'll succeed in putting our messages across?"

"Why not? We may be young, but not too young to see what's happening around us. Papa Dread is gone. I see no other elders taking up where he left off. It looks as if they have neither the time, patience nor even the Charisma to talk to youngsters who are willing to listen. Everyone seems to be so wrapped up in his or her own self-gratification. There's always somebody trying to get his or her own back on somebody else. Women using extreme measures to seek revenge on their exes..."

"I think that must be one of the oldest tricks in the book, Ikesha. People always want to fight fire with fire."

"Yeah, but they don't seem to realise that if everybody sings the same tune of anger, there will be no harmony." As she spoke, Ikesha spotted a food shop that called her with its colourful pictures of Ackee 'n Salt fish, callaloo, fried plantains, fried dumplings and every appetising meal from the West Indies. She pointed and walked towards it as she continued talking, leading Shari in its direction. "We cannot try to walk in Papa Dread's footsteps. Far from it. But every step towards *Positivity* and the welfare of our *'selves'*, is one less *Negative* one towards many tears that need not fall."

For a young girl, Ikesha seemed to have the oldest head ever.

"True," Shari agreed. They were now standing in the West Indian Takeaway, which was equipped with adequate seating facility for anyone needing to eat in. "You have always been mature, Ikesha," she continued, but I think you have grown like a thousand times more after the Rock thing... and even more after your session of therapy."

"You have matured too, girl," Ikesha told her. "Don't underestimate yourself. You are a mother of two at such a young age. You've lost two boyfriends to drugs and guns... and don't forget that you have been through a *Rock* experience too. Many would have crumbled at just the thought."

"I didn't crumble, Ikesha, because I had your mother. She was my rock. She was better to me than my own mother, but then everybody knew that."

"Well," Ikesha told her as they stood waiting to order, "Let's not dwell on the past. We have a future to at least *try* to prepare."

"Can I help you, ladies?" a fair-skinned brother with his hat placed backwards on his head asked.

"I'd like a fritter, a dumpling and a portion of ackee, please," Ikesha told him.

"Anything else?"

"Yeah, can I have a mango and pineapple drink?... Oh and one slice of hard-dough please."

He looked at Shari now.

"Just make that twice," she told him.

"Ok, that'll be ten pounds all together, please."

Ikesha handed the man a ten-pound note. "How long?"

"Ten minutes."

"Ok, we'll be over there."

A Jamaican woman with a fresh yard accent took the order from the man and walk real slow to the back, as if she was still walking in the Jamaican sunshine. *Real laid back.*

* * *

Lucy closed the door on her most recent fix and watched him drive away from her country house. She returned to her bedroom and lay upon her bed, still warm from his body, and toxic with his putrid perspiration worked up from an hammering session of *'no mess'* fucking.

She picked up the slim, oblong box and admired it's content.

Then, she placed it carefully upon her pillow.

He had enjoyed her kinky bondage.

And *she,* his expert love-making.

She had not known of the road he had chosen to travel.

Nor of the long, long way he wished he could go.

But she remembered his words as he made love to her:

'Paper roses,' he had whispered, *'they are special...uh!... special... uh!... special because they never, uh! Never, uh! Never die... they live forever'... uh! Uh!'*

Neville, he had said his name was. *Neville.*

And as she stroked her paper rose, Lucy dialled Bongo Dee.

The rose man was her evening meal... Bongo Dee would be her supper... tonight. *Lord, Lord. Lord.*

Lucky for Lijah. For while Bongo Dee was sampling her chow-chow, she was leaving him alone. In fact, she had not bothered Lijah at all since their last encounter. Strange, but it was so.

* * *

Marcia pulled the comb through her hair and worried not like she used to, about the volume of knotted breakage that came without effort into its teeth.

For so long, her once-beautiful hair had been left to grow wild and un-groomed beneath a hat that had become a permanent fixture to her head.

Nerves danced like crashing waves against the walls of her stomach, threatening to up-heave the mutton soup Viola had cooked for her.

Now, she scraped the cluster of natural dead hair from the comb and used it as a stress ball.

Her phone rang, but she ignored it, feeling pretty sure it was her mother – ready again with a whole heap of concern. When the ring tones had bounced for the last time off her wall of tolerance, she rose from the spot where she had been sitting for the past hour and walked over to her dressing-table. She picked up the bottle of Jean-Paul Gaultier and douched herself in its fragrance. It was Conteh's. He knew nothing of it though. She had bought it for him long after they had parted. She loved the smell and closed her eyes to savour it.

Once upon a time she had fallen in love.

Now she was simply falling apart.

The dream she once clung to was gone.

Now, she walked over to her bed and pulled out the drawer at its side. She ran her fingers over the long metal rifle with revolving cartridges. She loved that too.

LoveHateLoveHate. The line was thinner than she thought. *Much thinner.*

* * *

Carmen had heard about it and had come to see for herself. She parked outside the school gate and awaited her arrival.

The tired blonde swigged the last drop of whisky from a bottle she had not bothered to hide from her children.

'*Where's my daddy?*' the little girl had asked the day before, forcing Glenda to recall how he used to pop round occasionally to check on her. One of his idrins who knew of her had driven behind her on his way to the same school a few mornings when she was worse for wear had tipped him off. And he had seen for himself more than a few times. Seen her when drink had taken her beyond caring. And he would ready his children for school, and in a nervous disposition he would pull up at the school gate, glancing around to see who would or could see him, (especially anyone who knew he was married), or anyone who knew any of the other women he was seeing. He would cautiously open the back door of his car and urged his secret offsprings to *'run along'*. The teachers knew of their mother's plight and had accepted that he was *'just a friend'*.

And now, as Carmen watched, Glenda pulled away from the school gate. She followed, feeling like a stalker, but she just felt the urge to see it all for herself. But when Glenda pulled up in front of an off-licence, it wasn't worth thinking about. She stopped for a while in the middle of the quiet street and watched the way she hurried into the shop. Carmen shook head and drove on.

Chapter 9

*S*hari poured water on the waiting tea-bag and wondered what the hell her mother had to tell her. All she knew was that she was sitting in her living-room on tender-hooks, playing nervously with her *posh* nails. And to top it all, it looked to Shari as if something was definitely *sweeting* her in Birmingham. She didn't seem to want to return to London. And as for that *red paper rose* she had leant against the side of her bed, she wondered who would have had such a cold imagination. *Real* ones are more to Shari's liking.

"So what is it, Mum?" Shari asked when she sat now with her mother and two boys in her too-small living-room, nursing the cup of hot, freshly-made beverage.

Mitzi crossed her *posh* legs and folded her *posh* arms across her *slim* waist.

Shari took a sip of her tea and waited.

Mitzi uncrossed her legs and rubbed her *posh* knees and looked at her *posh* toes and…

"What is it?" Shari asked firmly.

Mitzi could detect an added strength to the maturity that Shari had developed over the past few years, and more so over the past few weeks since her, Ikesha and Andre had been gearing up for the *Do*n't *B*e *I*nfluenced campaign.

"Well... Shari... this isn't easy for me..."

"C'mon, Mum, it can't be that bad."

"Well it depends on what you class as bad."

"What is it?"

"... You know you kept on asking about your father?"

Shari's eyes widened. She placed her tea down on the coffee table. "*Yeah*?"

"Yeah, well... I... I think it's about time I told you."

"*About time? About time?...*"

Mitzi wished she hadn't started.

"I happen to be twenty-two... a mother-of-two... and you *only just* feel it's time to tell me who my father is?"

"Shari, let's not spoil our relationship. It's got much better than it had been in years..."

"Who is it?!"

Kunta Junior and Menilek looked round suddenly.

"C'mon, Shari," Mitzi said. "Let's go into the kitchen."

"What is it, Mum?" Menilek asked as his mum and grandma got up to leave the room.

"Nothing, son... just play with your brother, we'll be back in a minute."

"Well?... who is it?" Shari continued. "Do I know him?"

"Yes... You do."

"What?! I *know* him?... Who is he?"

"Who d'you know that looks like Bob Marley?"

"Shari stared at the floor as if the answer lay there... "Who do I know that looks like?... " She stopped. Looked at Mitzi.

"Lijah's friend," Mitzi threw in another clue.

"Lijah's fr... no... no... not Reds."

"Yes, Reds."

"Oh my God." She covered her mouth. "Look how long I've known the man... Reds is a nice man... Damian... Damian... he's Damian's dad... I went out with Damian... Damian was Reds' son... He was my brother... I slept!..." Shari was a gibbering wreck. It was as if the poor girl's brain was shaken inside its skull.

"Shari. Calm down. The kids."

"Calm down?... calm down?!... Calm down, you bitch!!!" She lounged at her mother and grabbed her by her *posh* hair.

"Shari! Stop it!"

"Mum?!" one of the boys called out.

Shari let go.

Stepped back.

"Mum?" Menilek stared at them both.

Stared at her mother as if she was an alien that had just landed. 'How *could* you?' she wondered.

Shari took stock of the situation.

In a few weeks time she hoped to stand in front of a crowd to talk about peace, love, happiness and prosperity among black people. About not allowing yourself to be influenced by anything negative, and yet, there she was about to crucify her own mother.

"Mum?" Menilek asked, "Why did you pull grandma's hair?"

Shari cuddled her son, but still she stared at her mother. "Why now?" she asked her.

"I don't know." Mitzi's eyes were averted.

Shari took her son's hand and returned to the living-room.

Menilek looked behind for his grandma. He was puzzled.

Kunta Junior sat, still playing with his toys.

Shari released Menilek's arm, reach for her cup and sat down.

Mitzi entered the room and sat in silence.

"Does Reds know?" Shari asked without looking at her mother.

"Yes… I only just told him the other day."

"So I'm the last to know who I am, hey?" she turned now to look at her. A lump buckled in her throat. She could kill her mother. Slap her face like she did way back when, in London. But something calmed her into thinking: *'I must be the change I wish to see in the world.'*

"Shari, you had to know sometime. It's either now or when I'm old…"

"What about all the times I've asked? When I desperately wanted to know?"

"Like I said, I don't know. It just feels right now."

"Did something happen in your childhood to make you like this, Mum?"

"Like what?"

"You're not real… you're… you're like that rose by the side of your bed."

Mitzi looked at Shari.

"Who gave that to you anyway? Roy? Is he the real reason you're hanging around down here?"

Silence.

"Well, Mum?"

"Don't you want me around?" Mitzi asked.

"I never said that, but I'm not sure you've suddenly developed a love for me, Birmingham and your grandkids."

"I'll be gone soon, Shari."

"I'm not pushing you out, Mum. I just need time to take all this in."

"I'm sorry." Mitzi's voice dropped.

"So what am I supposed to do now? Suddenly learn how to be a daughter to Reds?... What did Reds say?... Does he want a daughter?... What?..." The poor girl was confused.

"Shari, what will be, will be... Don't start stressing," Mitzi said matter-of-factly.

Shari got up to leave the room. She couldn't believe it. "Whether you stay or whether you go, Mum, you need to come to our meeting. You might learn a thing or two. It won't be just about young people being influenced. It will be about positive parenting. You might learn a thing or two."

Menilek was taking in the words from his mother's mouth, but they may as well be double-dutch, for he simply couldn't make sense of any of it.

Shari looked down at her perplexed son.

And there it was...

For the first time...

She saw the likeness...

He had his granddad's eyes.

And if Reds had told him, what had Lijah said after learning that he and his long-time idrin shared the same grandchildren? It would be quite a shock.

The world is as *strange* as it is *small... very.*

* * *

It was in the dead of the night when the call came, and although Lijah was woken from a deep sleep, he had no trouble recognising the voice. It was Dora... *Lothan had passed away.*

* * *

"Sorry about yuh ole man, Bredrin," Festus said to Lijah. He was sitting in his reclaimed house to where Lijah had brought him the news in person.

"In di midst of life an' t'ing," Lijah surmised. "He's had a good innings still."

"True. An' di good t'ing is, you can lay him to rest… my old man…"

"A'right, Bredrin," Lijah hastened, nobadda start dat now."

"Mi know," Festus agreed.

"So, yuh sure yuh want to come to di funeral?" Lijah asked Festus.

"Yeah, man," Festus assured him, "Life too short, Bredrin. Mi know seh mi cyaan mek up fi all di years, but mi need fi go. Mi need fi sit down an' face mi madda. Look her in di eye an' tell her sorry… Shame I cyaan exchange words wid yuh ole man, but ah so life go."

"Mi glad, Bredrin," Lijah told him. "When mi did mek peace wid mi ole man, it did feel good. Real good."

"When I was in prison, I wanted a madda. Badly. I don't know why…"

Lijah couldn't handle another dose of Festus' grief, so he changed the subject. "Yuh passport ready?"

"Yah, man… passport ready."

* * *

Taking a break from sunny Jamaica was on the cards for Menna, but no one could have told her that her next stop wouldn't be Birmingham, England.

Toronto, Canada was in her readings, but she would not have thought it.

Clayton hugged her shoulder with one arm and steered with the other. "I might not be able to give you a tour of communities in Birmingham, but I'll take you on a deeper tour of communities trying to mimic Kingston, Jamaica," he told her as he cruised around one of the large Jamaican-populated neighbourhoods in Toronto. "*Connection*, *Village* and *Jungle* are where you'll find all the Jamaicans you can ever wish for in Canada."

"Who told you I'm wishing for any Jamaicans? All I want is to see this place for myself. See if it's all its cracked up to be. What all the hype is about and all that," she joked. "Maybe, if ever I need a place to retire, Canada might do."

"Really?" the tall, sturdy, yet gentle brother asked.

"Why not? Somewhere I can chill. Away from the bad memories of Birmingham… Somewhere to enjoy the rest of my life in peace."

"You sound like an old woman who's got nothing but a few years to live, Menna. Chill out."

She smiled a deep smile, not forgetting that Clayton could read her expressions.

"*Bad* memories?" Clayton perplexed.

"Yes. Memories are like old wood. They must be cut away before one can move on."

"And do you have a lot of this *old wood* that need cutting away?"

"Enough. I think we all have them, Clayton. Some of us have more than some."

He looked at her, meaning to ask more, but he didn't. Instead he averted his attention to his duty of Tour Guide. "Down here is Village," he told her. "The area around St. Clair Avenue and Bathurst Street." He spoke as if she knew this *St. Clair Avenue and Bathurst Street*.

Menna could almost feel Jamaica. And if Clayton hadn't sped up a little faster than normal, she could have sworn that a guy in a bright yellow suit was a guy from West Kingston, Jamaica, who was apparently known for conjuring up and churning out fake passports like photocopying machine issues copies. Menna had heard of Franklyn's dealings from her brother, Errol. In fact it was the joke that Errol told along with the story that made her laugh. Franklyn had apparently fallen asleep around a domino table once. Rumour had it that he spoke in his sleep, repeating, almost song-like: *'A fee! A fee! Passport for a fee!'*

"Round here they call Jungle. More West Kingston. Lawrence and Bathurst area. They also call it Lawrence Heights."

Menna wondered how interested Clayton thought she *really* was in neighbourhoods trying to emulate communities in Jamaica.

"Ben Johnson lived in this community after he left Jamaica." Clayton looked and found a sign of disinterest in Menna's eyes. "Are you ok, Menna?"

"Yes. Fine. Are you?"

"I'm fine. You seem a little distant. Are you sure you want me to go on showing you around?"

"Yes. Of course."

"Cos I would hate to bore you to tears."

"A few things have brought me to tears before, Clayton. Boredom wasn't one of them."

But it was her sister, Cynthia that filled her head now. She was missing her more than she ever did since she did the dirty on Conteh and took that flight out to JA. They talked a lot, though. Cynthia was living at her flat while her own house was being rented. She knew everything was cool, but just then, that sisterly hug wouldn't go amiss. Besides, she wished she could snap her fingers and find her a nice man. Not *Mr Perfect*, since there isn't such a man. Just a nice guy who would see and appreciate the *'woman'* in her. Match her sense of humour and not change her. Make her happy. Cynthia was a good woman who graves a good guy. She won't just settle for *anyone*. So, instead, like a host of similar *good black women*, Cynthia waits on an empty stage for *'fate'* to turn a light on. And when a few weeks ago (though in a jovial banter) she had told Menna that she had given up hope on finding someone special, Menna seriously wished she could help.

Now, Menna followed her eyes to hip-hop fashion-filled stores.

Grocery stores filled with Jamaican delights invited all shoppers that needed them.

Posters promoting Jamaican plays and reggae artists who were scheduled to grace Toronto with their presence proudly plastered any available space they could find.

"Tell me when you are ready to go home, Babes. I'm not sure you're really enjoying this tour. You don't have to be polite, if you're bored, you're bored."

"Where would you say the best place is in Canada? To live, I mean."

Clayton slowed. His house is situated in the middle of Ward 1: Etobicoke North. This is where the largest population of Jamaicans could be found. "You don't *really* like the areas I've shown you do you?"

Reggae music blared out of a record shop on the left and made her want to get out and dance, but instead she rocked appreciatively in her seat.

"I do like the areas. But because you like somewhere, doesn't mean you can't ask about somewhere *nicer... better*."

Clayton parked up outside the record shop as if he needed the heavy baseline for a backdrop to his 'city-survey' chat. Or maybe he wanted to see Menna rock-away some more. "Well, according to some Economist Survey, Vancouver is the world's best place to live."

"Really? I heard about Vancouver. And how far is it from Toronto?"

"Not sure, but not a lifetime's journey..."

Menna listened tentatively.

"...Some intellectual took the time to rank a whole load a cities in terms of personal risk, infrastructure and the availability of goods and services..."

Menna stared at Clayton as he readily dished out the information she needed. He oozed intellect, but it was as if he didn't know how much. And from what she had tasted, he wasn't too bad in the bedroom department either: despite of what his past conquests had said.

"... And came up with their answer. They reckon Canadian cities are safe heavens. Not seen as targets for terror attacks."

"That's pleasing to here." She wanted to make love to him. There and then. Something was happening to her. But whatever it was, she knew it wasn't the *'falling-in-love'* shit. *Lust*, one might say.

"True. That is one of the reasons I am pleased that this is where I'm at right now. This rising terrorist threat in the USA, England..."

Menna gazed at Clayton, smiling.

He detected her penetrating gaze. It threw him slightly.

"... So the main uncertainties for people living in Canada are climate-related."

"I could cope with that," Menna said. "That is *if* ever I decided to live here."

"So? Do you think you would?... live here in Canada? Vancouver, maybe?"

"D'know. Haven't seen Vancouver yet. Is there a lot of black people there?"

"Not as much as Toronto, but you can't have it all."

"True."

He leaned towards her. "But there's one good thing..."

"What?"

"Wherever in Canada you decide to live..."

"*If*, Clayton, *if*."

"... I'll make up for all that." He kissed her passionately. She reciprocated *three-quarterly*.

"See that guy?" Clayton said when their lips had parted and he had glanced to his right.

"What guy?"

109

"The one in the yellow suit."

"Oh *him*. He looks familiar."

"He's from Jamaica. "*Mr Fix It*, they call him. I hear he can fix a fake passport for the most notorious deportee. I hear he's got his game down to a fine art. How he's gotten away with it for so long, God knows."

"I *thought* it was him. My brother told me about him. So what's he doing here in Canada?"

"He's got a nine bedroom mansion here. He flits backward and forward like you and I change our underwear. In fact there is a joke…"

"You mean, '*A fee! A fee! Passport for a fee'!*" Menna blurted.

"Yeah! You heard about that?"

"Yes. My brother told me… life's one big hustle, Clayton. *Mr Yellow Suit* has his game, we have ours."

"Only, there are some hustling that are just not worth the game. In the end, Mr Yellow Suit might have to let go of all that illegitimate loot. Lose all his gains."

"True. He's living for today. Tomorrow we all die."

"You sound as if you are empathising with him."

"I wouldn't say I am. Just stating a fact."

"Fact is, tomorrow he dies without respect or dignity." Clayton started the engine. "Are you hungry?"

"A little."

"Let's go find some real Jamaican food. I know a good food shop not far from here."

"So, Clayton, tell me," Menna pulled the arms of the handsome man tighter around her, then the sheets between which they lay, tighter around them both. It had been just over an hour since they got home from their tour of a small area of Toronto. "Do you like living here, *really*?"

"Where? In my house, or in Canada?"

"Both."

"Yes to both… Well, let's put it this way, Menna, like I said, Canada is where I was born. And although I might appear more Jamaican than Canadian, I will have to say yes, Canada is a good place to live. And if you're after that side of things, the nightlife in Toronto isn't that bad either.

"Who would have thought it, Clayton…?"

"Who would have thought *what*?"

"That I would find myself between the sheets, in some Canadian Ward, with…"

"…With the son of a preacher man?"

Menna laughed. Though in jest, it was exactly what she was about to say. Clayton, it seemed, had tuned into her telepathy. This was her second day with him in the Jamaican populated part of Toronto, and although she would admit she wasn't *in love* with him, she would say, (however corny it may sound) in a long time, *'he was the only man that could ever reach her spiritually, intellectually and something else she couldn't quite put her fingers on.'*

"I didn't think you'd accept my invitation to spend two weeks in Canada with me."

"Why didn't you?"

"I don't know… I just had a feeling I was nowhere near your type."

"Really? And what do you suspect my *type* to be, Clayton?"

"Even though you're intellectual, I see your intellect more of a rugged sort, if you see what I mean…"

"Er… vaguely."

"… I see you going for the more rugged type. What d'you ladies call it?… *Rough Diamond*."

"Really? You think I'm a *Rough Diamond* type?"

"Yeap. I think so."

"What made you think that?"

"Well, I am always drawn to women like you, and if at all I manage to pull any, in the end I always lose them to *Mr Rough Diamond*."

"Really?" She smiled.

"Yes, *really*. But I never learn. Women crave my brain. My intellect. But sooner or later they trade it in for what they call… well, in the words of the last lady I entangled with, *hot passion*."

"Is *that* so?"

"Damn right."

"And she *told* you that?"

"Yes. I asked her why and she told me. In no uncertain terms, she told me I wasn't passionate enough."

"Straight-talking lady, huh?"

"I guess she was. The guy she ended up with had all the passion she wanted all right. Plus enough for the whole female population of Canada. She ended up with a broken heart, but I don't suppose that will stop her going for the same type over and over again."

"Were you hurt?"

"Yes. But I suppose I'm no different from her. I have my type too. Human nature. We know what we want, whether it's good for us or not."

"Oh dear…"

"Well?" Clayton asked.

"Well what?"

"What do *you* think, Menna?"

"Are you asking if I think you are passionate?"

"Yes."

"Well, if you ask me, that is exactly the kind of question that can reverse the effect of something good. Especially *after* the moment. To me, it's like fishing for a compliment. Besides, I think a man ought to *know* when he's done some damage in the bedroom. But I suppose if the history of your past women is exactly like you said, I can see why your *'Halo Of Confidence'* has slipped."

"Ok… let's drop the subject," Clayton hastened. "Tell me one thing…"

"Ask away."

"Why did you *really* decide to come to Canada and spend two weeks with me?"

"You mean seen as I hardly know you, right?"

"Well, that's a part of it. And seeing as you haven't fallen *head-over-heels* in love with me or anything like that."

"Well, Clayton, falling *head-over-heels* in love…"

"…That would have been a bonus, Menna, I know. I wasn't expecting that."

She chuckled. "I decided to come because I like you… we got on great in Jamaica. Conversation-wise anyway, (and I know this is going to sound corny) but you are the only man that reached me in a long time."

"My name is *Clayton,* Menna, not *Billy Ray.*" A cynical smile covered his face.

"What?"

Clayton eased his lips closer to her right ear and sang…

> *Billy Ray was a preacher's son*
> *And when his daddy would visit he'd come along*
> *When they gathered around and started talkin'*…

Menna chuckled. She got the joke. And to add to it all, Clayton could sing!

> *That's when Billy would take me walkin'*
> *Out through the back yard we'd go walkin'*
> *Then he'd look into my eyes*
> *Lord knows, to my surprise…*

"How could I expect less? You were brought up in the church, your daddy a preacher man and all. Singing was a part of your sleeping and your waking, right?"

He ignored Menna's statement and question, though hypothetical, and carried on the playful singing…

> *The only one who could ever reach me*
> *Was the son of a preacher man*
> *The only boy who could ever teach me*
> *Was the son of a preacher man*
> *Yes he was, he was, ooh, yes he was*

"Ok, *Billy Ray*, point taken… as I was saying, conversation-wise, you have it."

"Uh huh?" Clayton readied himself to listen.

"You seemed a little different from the guys I usually go for."

"You mean a little different from the *Rough Diamond* type?" he joked.

"Well, if you say so… Secondly, I would be lying if I said it wasn't because I really wanted to experience Canada. I had heard so much about the place over the years, I knew that I had to see it someday, so when you invited me, I thought, 'why not'?"

"So I was right. It wasn't that you had fallen head-over-heels in love with me?" he had thrown that one in before, but he thought he'd try it from a different angle. If only just to establish how she *really* felt.

Menna laughed out loud as if the question was new and out of the blue. "I don't fall *in* love so easily, Clayton, let alone *head-over-heels*."

"Especially not with…"

"… The son of a *preacher man*?" She assumed his presumption.

"You tell me, Menna."

"No, seriously… the last time I fell in love…"

"It was with a *soundman*… *Conteh. Conteh Egyptian*…. A member of the Vibes Injection Crew from Birmingham, England."

Menna sat up and twisted round to face Clayton. "How the *hell* d'you know all that?"

"Birmingham, England holds a lot of clues to the person you are… or *have become*, that's for sure."

"Do I get an answer, Clayton, or are you just gonna ignore me and analyse me? How d'you know all…?"

"You've been talking in your sleep."

"Like *hell,* I was… Clayton, who do you know that I know?"

Clayton held Menna's gaze. "You *really* were that much out of it, huh?"

"What are you talking about, Clayton? Enough of the parables, man?"

"Menna, on our second date in Montego Bay…"

"Yeah?"

"You must have had one too many… you talked a lot…"

"What exactly did I say?" There was a desperate urgency in her eyes. "Tell me…"

"You seem worried, Menna. What are you mostly afraid you might have said?"

Menna cringed at the thought. There are things she would rather not reveal to Clayton. Or anyone for that matter. Who knew, *knew*. Who think they know, *think they know*. That was just it. Like some people in Birmingham who spend their lives wondering, *'Did Menna do a t'ing with Conteh?'* "Well," she said, "That would be telling. If I hadn't yet told you, that is… *shit*… that's why I don't…"

"Don't worry. You said nothing incriminating… at least I don't think so."

"What d'you mean you don't *think* so...? What else did I say?"

Clayton drew nearer and rested his forehead against Menna's. "Menna, all you kept saying, was, 'Conteh… Conteh Egyptian… the bastard! All he lived for was his sound, Vibes Injection… and hurting women, black and white…' And of course, I gathered he must be from Birmingham, England."

"Are you sure that was *all* I said?"

"Yes. A few other niggles, but like I said, nothing incriminating. Drink can be hypnotic. Most of the time, being under its influence can bring out the true feelings in people. So I gathered you either *were,* or *still is*, in love with this… *Conteh, Egyptian."*

"Still is, my ass! Fuck that!"

"Whoa! So it's turned to hate, then? Either that or you are in denial."

"That night?" Menna asked, ignoring Clayton's last statement, "did anything else... *happen*? I don't usually get like that?"

"Like *that?*"

"You know... out of control... to a point where I can't even remember what I said."

"Well," he cleared his throat as if readying himself for a speech, "I took you to your hotel room and made love to you."

"What?!" Her eyes widened.

"You were good."

Her brows knitted into a question mark.

"Oh, yes," he relented, "it was *soooo* good, I had a permanent hard-on for days after, just thinking about it."

"You love to take the piss, don't you, Clayton?"

"I still can't believe how much of a devil you were."

"Cut the crap, Clayton! I knew I woke up in my hotel bed, but I must admit, I couldn't recall how I got there, but don't take the piss. That is just *not* my style."

Clayton paused and stared half-seriously into Menna's eyes. "Do I *really* look like a guy that would do such a thing?"

Menna looked away. She was partly ashamed for seeming to have lost control.

"You know your brother, Errol was there. He made sure you were ok. Did he not tell you? Moreover, did you not ask him?"

"Ok, Clayton, don't get clever. I *did* ask Errol, as I couldn't remember much about the latter part of the night. He told me he made sure I was ok... but when you joked..."

"When I joked, you wondered if it might be true? You wondered if your brother would lie to you in league with some strange guy?"

"Let's change the subject, hey?" she commanded.

"You hate not being in control, don't you, Menna?"

"Damn right. Ever since I was a little girl. I can't help it. And if ever anything got the better of me, I don't let it rest. My mother always used to tell me, *'Be still chile. Calm down.'* But it's not that easy. Especially if I'm wronged."

"I can tell. Turning the other cheek won't ever be your thing. There's a fire still raging in your belly, too..."

Menna looked at him questioningly.

"I can feel it," Clayton assured her. "I can almost see the flames licking out of your eyes, yet a sexy sassiness still manages to remain."

She smiled.

"You have unfinished business, Menna. And you won't rest until you sort it. But if you ask me, it isn't true that revenge is good for the soul… It's not."

"Are you preaching to me, Clayton?"

"No. Just trying to tell you that I'm deeply in love with you. That I know this is just a fling for you. Even if you had to come all the way to Canada to do it. And I know too, that you'd never marry me…"

"What?!" She stared at him as if he had blasphemed.

"I must admit, it's a question I've been dying to ask for a long time."

"Clayton, *slow down*. Are you crazy? You don't even know me."

"My mother doesn't know my father. Even after forty years of marriage, she still doesn't know him. But still they're making life."

"Hey?"

"My father has affairs, Menna. Enough to make Casanova look tame. But as far as he's concerned, he loves her. And I suppose she has her own reasons for staying. Old habit, maybe, I d'know."

"Are you *serious?* Your father has affairs?… But he's a man of God?"

Clayton chuckled. "Well, he climbs a pulpit and preach hell-fire and damnation from his pew every Sunday, alright… but who says that makes anyone a *man of God?* You are a woman of the world, Menna. You've seen and heard enough to make you know that what the *eyes see* aren't always what the *head knows*. Just the other day a Deacon in my father's church was jailed for paedophilic behaviour."

"What?!"

"Why are you so surprised? The world is gone crazy. As we speak, something crazy is taking place. Something dark. Sinister. And things we didn't used to hear black people doing, they're doing them. Or rather, we're hearing of them."

"No… wait a minute… this Deacon was *in the church*… and *molesting children*?"

"You might heave at this, but not just children. He did it to his *own* children and *grandchildren*."

"Oh shit…" Menna dropped her voice and turned away, almost willing Clayton to stop. It was almost as if her skin was crawling away from her flesh. "Oh Christ…"

"And this was a Deacon the people respected. The whole church had him high on a pedestal."

"Ah... well," Menna surmised, "I guess no one person ever *really* know another fully... was he married... this Deacon?"

"Yes. Forty years."

"And did his wife not suspect *anything*?"

"I suppose she knew, but refused to accept it. I suppose she was wishing it were a bad dream and that it would eventually go away. But it didn't. Anything would have been better than knowing that her children and grandchildren would carry the scars of that atrocity for life, but I guess she couldn't see that at the time... I suppose, in the end, she must have wished that so-called man-of-God she lay next to night after night, was a womaniser instead.

"Like your father?"

"I guess so. He had his fair share of womanising, my father. But still, although he wasn't the perfect man-of-God, I would rather know he womanised rather than engaged in paedophiliac behaviour... Anyway, let's change the subject... *so?"*

"So... what?"

"Would you consider marrying me?"

"Clayton, seriously now, how long have you known me?"

"Just over six months."

"And you don't think that *marriage* is a bit too strong a concept for you to be tossing around so soon?"

"You mean considering that apart from fucking me, you don't feel any emotions, right?"

"Well, I wouldn't put it so strongly, but shouldn't emotions form a part of this *marriage* thing?... And of all the nice ladies in Canada..."

"Don't patronise me, Menna. I hear you... the answer is *no*. I'm a grown man. And I might not be *Mr Vibes Injection,* but I think I'm man enough to take *no* for an answer. You being patronising is not what I need right now. If I had found a suitable *Canadian woman*, I wouldn't be here mentioning marriage to you."

"Are you getting upset, Clayton?"

"No."

"I think you are."

He smiled.

"Clayton, I don't think I want to marry *anyone*, really. Or at least I don't feel like I do right now anyway."

"Point taken. I understand. Let's not sweat the small stuff, hey?"

"It's *small*? You think marriage is *small*? Some view marriage as quite big. Important."

"But there are bigger and more important things in life. I could name a few, but I'd only bore you some more." He chuckled.

"Listen, Clayton. Some years ago, I boarded a flight from Birmingham, England to cool out in Jamaica. Within that time, I tried to find out *who* I really am…"

"And have you?"

"No. But I suppose my journey has not yet ended. I need to revisit Birmingham. Tie up a few loose ends, then maybe start searching again."

"Why don't you just give it up? *Live*. Try to be happy. Who said it's ever a good thing discovering *who* we really are?"

"It depends on how the individual feels. Everyone's different."

"I think what you really mean, is that you need to kick up some *storm* before you seek some *calm*?"

"Sounds like you're preaching again."

"No. Just talking … listen… I can't explain the way I feel about you, but all I know is, in a long time, you are the only woman I feel I could love *unconditionally*. Of course I could be wrong. I just feel that way. Strongly too. We are, none of us perfect, but it's almost as if, if you should say, *'Clayton, I've killed a man'*, after hearing your reason for doing it, I'd still be willing to attempt a lifetime journey with you."

"Christ, Clayton, you are *deep*… Shit."

"It's *you*, Menna. You bring out the depth in me. At least once in everyone's lifetime, someone special comes along and stirs something in he or she. I suppose for you, it was *Mr Vibes Injection*. For me, it's *you*. And I know that it'll be a long time (if ever) before I meet someone I feel the same way about."

"*Unconditionally*, Clayton? Doesn't that mean…?"

"Yes. I know what it means. But it's the way I feel. I'm no Saint, but lying isn't one of my hobbies."

"Clayton, I… I can't marry you... you deserve a woman like yourself."

"And what might a *'woman like myself'* be like?"

"Sweet… Open. Honest. Undeserving of ones with chequered pasts."

"And I suppose you're trying to tell me that you are not sweet… not open… dishonest… and you only deserve to be with someone with a chequered past?"

Menna smiled.

And so did Clayton. He smiled and kissed her forehead. "It's ok, Menna. I appreciate you letting me down gently. I won't ask again, I might not be your type, but I have my pride to think about..."

She coupled his face between her palms and kissed him.

A silence followed...

"... But if ever you come to your senses," he added, "I'll be right here waiting for you. You said you like what you see of Canada. This is just the tip of Toronto, there are much more to see. Soon, you'll be on a flight back to Jamaica. Then at some point, I expect, you'll travel back to Birmingham, England. After that, I don't know, but I hope you find yourself. If you do, and you find that this *son-of-a-preacher-man* can possibly be a part of the *'you'* you find, then I'll be right here waiting for you."

"Christ, you sound almost poetic... Listen, Clayton," Menna said in a serious tone, "I've decided... from the minute I board that flight back to JA, I want you to start living your life. I'm flattered, but I want you to forget about me. I like what I see of Canada, and I'm glad you invited me, but even if I ever decide to come back, it wouldn't be fair. I don't..."

"... *Love me?*... you don't *love me*. Rub it in some more, why don't you?"

"Why do I feel we're repeating ourselves?" Menna asked. "We're beginning to sound like a couple of scratched records."

"You're right. I suppose, whatever I say, what I would really like to hear is that you'll come back and stay, but affection isn't something to be forced. It should come naturally."

Menna sighed and rolled over into a more relaxed position. She stared at the ceiling in the large room in which she had not long had sex with Clayton. "That's just it, Clayton. I can't pretend. Love isn't something one pretends or even plays at. And *marriage*? Well..."

"But love is something that grows, right? Because you don't love someone at first sight, it doesn't mean you won't love he or she at all. "

"You're right. I can't dispute that."

"And I'm a true believer in becoming friends with someone before that head-over-heels thing kick in. Passion is good, but it wears off... sometimes to find two people asking, *'what have we really got in common'*?"

"Yeah, but we've already messed that up. We've just had sex."

119

"And before that, *I* saw a true friend in you. And more. A strong woman who wants to be loved. I think you have so much love to give, but is probably looking beyond the realms of reality for a receiver."

"I'd like to know how you come to have so much faith in me," Menna told him. "I wish I had an ounce of that faith in myself."

"You have. Much more than an ounce. You ooze confidence, Menna. You know what you want, and you're gonna get it... In the end."

"Really, *Billy Ray,*" she teased playfully, "you don't say."

"Yes, really."

"And do *you* know what I want?"

"I don't *know.* I just *think* I know."

She fixed him an attentive gaze now. "What do you *think*, you know?"

"I think deep down, like most women, you want to find love. Unconditional love. You want to be able to trust... you've had your trust abused in the past. And like I said, I *think* you have some serious unfinished business to fix. Some you don't even know of yet. And maybe one day you'll confide in me."

"You sound as if you already *know,* never mind *think*. You talk like a prophet, Clayton. Like you can foretell the future, or even tell one's past. Is that a legacy of your daddy the preacher man?" she joked.

"No. There's nothing prophetic about me, Menna. Just a guy who has learnt to read people's eyes. Most of all, I can detect pain at a glance. And when it is disguised by the smiles of a clown...?"

Menna turned away. She had not realised she was giving off such strong vibes.

"You know they are the windows to one's soul, don't you?"

She looked a question into his eyes.

"The eyes."

"I know what you mean, Clayton. I just don't know if I like being read so deeply."

"Listen, Menna," he wrapped his left arm round her waist and gently kissed the side of her face...

She turned to face him again.

"... I'm a good listener," he continued. "You can trust me too. Like I said, we are, none of us perfect. And for the want of not becoming a scratched record, I'll be right here waiting for you." He kissed her lips again.

She didn't know why, but this time, she felt something deep within her. Not love. She knew that… but *something*.

Now, he nibbled gently at her tender neck.

"You are too sweet, Clayton," she whispered. "Like I said, undeserving of ones with chequered pasts."

"When you are ready to let me be the judge of *who* I deserve or *who* is undeserving of me, then we can proceed with this conversation."

She was now thinking how much she was beginning to like the mastery in him. Even if just to know that it was there. She couldn't stand a total pushover. Then she thought, *'what does it matter anyway? I'm leaving soon. And I'm not coming back.'*

He nibbled now at her tender breasts. "Until then, maybe the lady will allow me to make sweet love to her again." He was now descending towards her navel, and when his warm tongue pushed deep into its sensitive depth, Menna trembled, waiting for the ultimate pleasure. Having sex… making love… there's a difference. She knew what she was doing, but she also knew that Clayton was making *lurve*.

"When was the last time you were this intimate with a woman, Clayton?" she hummed in a low quivering voice.

"*This*… intimate?" he grasped her hips firmly with both hands as his strong tongue danced towards her clitoris.

And now, Menna cared not for the answer, for this sweet, sensitive *son-of-a-preacher* man had found her throbbing pleasure. His warm tongue *walked the walk*. *Talked the talk*. And now, he was *singing the song* of passion… a song Menna could never tire of hearing. She had already made sure he had saddled up. Though something told her he could never tame her.

"Come live with me, Menna," he whispered as he took her to a limitless height.

As she trembled against his lips, humming songs of ecstasy, he said it again. "Come and live with me. I can make you happy." He kissed her between every sentence. "This house is damn lonely and I don't want to settle for just anyone." Now, he pulled gently away, hoisting himself up towards her firm, protruding nipples.

She appreciated his lips against them, one after the other as his firm hands moulded them into edible mounds.

"You couldn't handle me," she whispered back.

"Try me." Now… firm yet gently, he eased his manhood into her waiting wetness.

"Ahhhh!" it felt like the first time.

"I've fallen for you, woman," he whispered as he squeezed her tight. He was loosing himself. His whole body was devoured by her touch as he slowly slipped... slid... slipped... slip... in... out... in... out of her warm moist tightness."

"Keep your feelings for another, Clayton. I'm no good for you," she murmured.

"Let me be the judge of that... *mmmm*."

"Shhhh," she commanded.

Clayton wanted to consume her. She felt and tasted too good... "Can I feel you, Menna?"

"What?"

"I need to taste you.... Feel you... Skin-to-skin."

"No. I don't do that. I don't know your history, Clayton. Besides, if you can say this to me, you must have said it to other women."

"No... never."

"So how can you tell that I'm safe? How d'you know I haven't got HIV or AIDS?"

"Instinct," he whispered, trying almost to emerge with her. Become one. "*Please*. Let me feel the warm juices of your vagina against my dick."

"You know Clayton, for the son-of-a-preacher man, you talk damn right dirty in bed," she told him, moving to the rhythm of his sweet strokes.

"And when will you realise that it's *you*." He thrust amorously into her, almost as if to emphasise the '*you*'. Her sigh of surprise aroused him more. "You do something for me, Menna... something magical..." Gently, he moved now, convincing himself that he needed this woman more than anything else in the world. Not just for a moment. Not just for two weeks. But for a lifetime. "Can I?"

"*No, Clayton*," she said in a pleasure-filled agony. "*No*."

"Just for a few seconds... I promise I won't ejaculate inside you."

"*No...*"

"Just imagine it... My warm, hard dick throbbing inside you," he whispered.

"No..."

"Our juices mingling..."

"No..."

He pulled out now as if to torture her into surrender.

She ached for him.

He descended *down... Down... Down...* until his lips met again with her throbbing clitoris.

"Ahhhh! Clayton..."

"How much do you want me?" he whispered.

She didn't reply. He already knew how much.

He eased off.

She throbbed. To a point of begging. But she didn't.

Then up he came. Towards her over-aching breasts. *Nibble. Lick. Nibble. Lick.*

"Ahhhh..."

And before she knew it, he filled her again... Down below. His warm throbbing manhood thrusting sweetly into her flooding depth.

"Ahhh! Ahhh! Ahhhhhh!"

He devoured her mouth. Merged with her. Became one.

Oh, that sweet river of joy that floweth like warm rain... Sweet... Sweet... Sweet river of joy...

And soon, she came to realise that his warm thick juices mingled deep inside her... *Without permission...* A discarded condom floating at the bottom of his king-sized bed.

Mercy please.

Mercy...

Mercy...

Please.

* * *

C'mon baby, let the good times roll...
C'mon baby let me thrill you soul...
C'mon baby, let the good times roll...
Roll along...

There was a wailing coming from her soul, yet tears failed to flood her eyes... The hardening in her throat pushed its thrusting force against her now bulging neck, and the urge to punch the walls disintegrated into the simultaneous clenching of her fists, her nails sinking mercilessly into her palms.

My mama may have...
And my papa may have...
But God bless the child...
Who's got his own...

Marcia tried to sing it away… the blues that is. Sing… sing… sing.
But not for long.
The force was stronger than she could ever be.

> *My… mama… may… have*
> *And… my… papa…*

Beauty forced its way back, making way for a fierce ugliness.

> *But… God… bless… the… child…*

Her eyes bulged with the telling of a gruesome tale.

> *That's got… his…*

Demons danced on the pile of carpet into which she stared.
She cuddled her knees and rocked into the corner of the room that
held her like the rock of ages. In her eyes, it cleft for her, hiding her…
She had long gone discarded the gun that the voice in her head had
told her to reach for, yet, she saw it still… at the end of her fingers. An
imaginary figment that wouldn't go away.
The banging of the front door took her to another place.
Her mind conjured up dogs.
Chasing hounds.
They chased, howled, snapped at her ankles.
Her chained ankles.
Now, she sprung from her safe corner and barred the door. Piled
pillows, chairs, anything behind it.
"You won't get me! No! No! You won't get me!"
She paused at the calling of her name from outside her bedroom
door. The voice was familiar, but in her head, it came in hostility. To
her, it came in the name of *'search and destroy'*.
"You're out to get me! I know! I know! But you won't! No! No!"
Now, the knife in her hand sparkled as a thin ray of light hit its
gleaming blade."
The sound of her name again. "Marcia?!"
Then the knock on her door.
Too close for comfort.

'*Protect yourself!*' the voice in her head urged, '*They're coming to get you!*'

She pushed the barricades from behind the door.

Her hand that held the knife found strength *ten-fold.*

She found strength ten-fold.

She swung the door open and stared viciously into the eyes of the woman that stood there, but she didn't see the concern in them.

"Marcia? Lord, help me, Marcia?!" the woman shouted, *tears* now pushing *concern* away.

'Protect yourself!' urged the voice in Marcia's head again.

And back went the knifed hand.

Then forward with a brute force, plunging itself deep into the womb from whence she came.

"Marcia?!" the voice of Sista Viola Prince could be heard over the hills of Birmingham and down below.

"Oh Lord!"

Marcia stared at the screaming woman.

Her eyes were piercing.

Bulging.

The veins in her neck and face protruded as if under protest.

She stared at the helpless woman at her feet.

'*What is that thing?*' she asked inwardly. '*That red liquid that is flowing... flowing... covering the silvery shine of the knife?*' Innocently, she held the guilty weapon.

"Marcia?" Viola whispered now.

"Mrs Prince?!" A policeman dived in.

"Top a the stairs, Gov'! Get an ambulance! Mrs Prince has been stabbed!"

"Marcia," Viola was still whispering.

Now, Marcia, in the belief that she had wings, headed for the bedroom window.

With bruises on her fingers, bruises on her toes, she shall hear her mother's whisper wherever she goes...

My bunny lies over... the ocean... my... bunny... lies over... the sea...

Viola drifted on the strings of an angel's harp.

Was that it for hr her?

Is that how she was meant to go?... Taken by the hands of her own daughter?

If it was… then if the life she lived was as pure on the inside as it was on the outside, Viola needn't knock on heaven's door. No. It would be opened diligently unto her by her Saviour's own hand. And then when she sits to lay her burdens down, He would explain to her, the real meaning of life.

But as the life seep away from her previously strong God-serving body, Viola worried only for her daughter…

> Rock of Ages…cleft… for… me…
> Let… me… hide… myself… in… Thee…
> While… I… draw… this… fleeting… breath…
> When… mine… eyes… shall… close… in… death…
> When… I… soar… to… worlds… unknown…
> See… Thee… on Thy… judgment throne…
> Rock of Ages… cleft for…me…
> Let… me hide…myself …. In….Thee…

'*What will become of her*', was the words that travelled on her feeble breath, as the ambulance men hoisted her, gently but urgently onto the patient's trolley.

Viola's will to hold on was strong, but so was the plunge of the knife that ruptured her inner organs. *Touch and go. Slim chance.* But she had faith. She hoped it would pull her through.

"Hold on, Mrs Prince," the friendly voice of an ambulance woman coaxed.

Viola heard but she couldn't respond. '*Marcia*,' she thought, '*My dear, dear Marcia.*'

A great big pot of red peas soup stood undisturbed on her hob.

* * *

This was her third breakdown and by far the worst… How will she survive this?

They told her she had plunged a knife into the womb of her dear mother.

And the flashbacks…

Oh, the flashbacks… *Horrific.* They confirmed it must have been true.

She saw it… *The red flowing liquid that covered the shining blade.*

She heard it… *The sound of her name from her mother's whispering breath.*

"No! No! Noooo!" oh, the agony of anguish… despair…

She had nearly committed a crime of *matricide*. And what would she have done?

Another dose of sedative awaited the beautiful lady.

'*Conteh*', she thought. *'Why is he still lurking in my head? Did I love him that much that his memories refused to leave? This love? Why must it be so cruel at times? Why don't it just leave when people do? Why must it remain to achingly mock the heart?'*

"Mum! Where are you?!" It felt as if the whole of her insides were aborting away from her… Plummeting… Plunging to the floor of the mental hospital.

"Your mum is in the hospital, Marcia," a ginger-haired nurse assured her. "She's in good hands. She'll be fine. Don't worry."

"Mum!… Come and show them that they're lying, pleeease…" she sobbed. "Come and show them I didn't hurt you!" She was in serious pain. *Physically* and *mentally*.

Whatever?… whatever?… whatever will the poor girl do?

Marcia was confused, but straight-minded enough now to realise that she couldn't stand what awaited her. *People*. What would they say?

She couldn't bear their contempt.

Their pitying eyes.

Their *not-knowing-what-to-say* glances.

The ones that would bubble and squeak behind their shielding palms.

And worst of all, she couldn't stand the pretentious bunch that would try their best to look at her with *normal* eyes.

Or the ones that would try not to look at all.

The fake empathy. *Nothing*.

The *'there-there'* sympathy.

So all and all, she couldn't stand anyone who *knew*.

And now that she couldn't tell *who* had seen her in action, now, in her semi-normal state, she could only see everyone around her as *'the jury'*… *'the unfriendly*… Not *for*, but *against* her. Judges and juries who had long gone convicted her of the crime of being a victim of mental illness.

She had stabbed her dear mother.

Nearly severed the hands that fed her.

And God… will He forgive her?

Marcia nursed a throbbing toe, a dislocated knee and four broken fingers. All of which were results of her *'I believe I can fly'* fantasy from the height of her bedroom window to the hard ground.

* * *

When Simone opened her front door to an unexpected knock, she wasn't surprised to see the most beautiful bouquet of flowers in front of her eyes.

"Somebody loves you," the deliveryman said.

"So I see," Simone replied.

And later when she read the accompanying card, it brought tears to her eyes. It read:

> *How sweet it is to be loved by you…*
> *Can't wait to see you and my son again.*
> *PS. His surprise is in his toy box.*
> *Your loving husband*
> *x x x*

Lawrence was on a long-haul flight to the USA. His mission to make sure his family never feel neglected was being maintained. *Highly.*

Chapter 10

𝔐enna stood amidst a loyal mob of sound-following gals and boys, taking in the *'Murder Before Disrespect'* sound clash in Mobay, Jamaica. She felt a strange sense of *belonging*. Memories of Conteh swam around her head like sharks that hovered for their next meal. It was him that wetted her appetite for these sound clashes. They had never been her scenes before she had met him. In fact, she would not have called it her scene now, but like drugs, something in the whole performance was slowly pulling her in: perhaps like a perverted voyeur would watch a situation in which he or she would not see themselves partaking. Reggae music was in her bones all right. But give her a good Lovers Rock dance any day.

Her stay in Jamaica had been one with a difference. One of mixed feelings.

Sad, since she had seen the burial of her dear grandmother.

Happy, since she had completed her novel, *Don't F**k With Me*: a task she had set herself to complete. And it was then, in a cosy little room in her grandmother's house, that she realised she loved him, *still*. But she had not forgotten that the line between love and hate is a considerably thin one. Feh real. And every time she crossed that line, she knew she had unfinished business to do.

But now, as she stood there beside her brother, him wondering why she was so fascinated with the battle of the sounds, a slight apprehension: she must now *return to Birmingham, England. She must face whatever music there was to be faced.* Or what music must be faced. Right then, the music she faced now was intensely physical, rather than mental: five world cup winners had taken to a stage to battle out a heat of dub plates, for yet another gleaming cup.

6am.

Morning crept in gently, spreading its light over the tired, yet loyal, tenacious crowd and Menna marvelled at how steadfast supporters and onlookers were. It was as if some of them had not moved from the very spot they stood from the moment they entered the arena some twelve hours ago.

"Yuh sure yuh enjoy it, Sis'?" Errol her brother asked.

"In a strange kina way, I did. I must admit it's a little different from the few I went to with Conteh. This is more… *raw,* I should say. Maybe its because Jamaica is where sound clashes were born."

"Ah true. Trus' mi. Soun' clash inna Jamaica beats all soun' clashes," Errol was proud to say.

"I don't doubt that, Bro'. But my feet are killing me." She looked at the sea of people who were now looking up at the stage as if God stood there. They must have the strongest feet ever, for they didn't seem to be showing the least sign of discomfort, or even the need to rest them.

World cup promoters, Scottish and Chung had long gone counted their chickens, which would surely hatch *nuff*. No one was allowed a freebie on the security-tight entrance: not even Eradication and his entourage, and the young Canadian made no bones about expressing his disapproval as soon as he had his chance to take his stand. He had come to attempt the *'upholding of his victory'* in the New York's sound clash, last year.

Pier One was almost heaving under the strain of jumping sound followers, as they showed their appreciation, flashing their sweat-filled rags in the air like a sea of whirlpools. They flicked countless lighters, blow-torches and even mobile phones into the air, and blowing horns of differing sizes seemed a crucial 'must'. The monumental event, also known as *'Jamaica's World Clash'*, honouring the success of reggae music has never failed to pull the heaviest crowds – not just from Jamaica, but from all over the world. This line-up featured five World Champions:

Powerful Coronet, World Cup winner, 1999.

Everest, World Cup winner, 2000.

Black Sea, World Cup winner, 2001

Eradication, World Cup winner, 2002

Alpine Peak, World Cup winner, Jamaica, 2002 and UK Cup winner, 2003.

Crazy Crew was the promising newcomer. *Very promising.* Besides, all the other sounds had to start somewhere before they got to where they were in the present competition.

"Crazy Crew didn't do too bad for a New Comer. Watch this space, dat soun' is goin' to cause some damage in years to come," Errol said.

"And what about Everest?" Menna asked.

"Everes'? Everes' nice, man. Everes' inna di business long time still. Stand a good chance. Win di firs' elimination round. T'ings look good fi Everes'." Errol was commentating so well on the whole thing, Menna needn't ask how much he loved sound clashes.

Time flew by.

Alpine Peak, the 2002 World Cup winner took the next three rounds by storm, chatting down his opponents with no mercy whatsoever, his energetic passion shining through his youthful looks, sending out a message to all who didn't know, that he must have been in dancehalls since his eyes were at his knees. *Chat bout.*

"Mi like Alpine Peak. Real Veteran still," Errol proclaimed.

"And what are his chances?" Menna asked.

"Bwoy… anyt'ing cyan gwaan yunnuh. It's *who* di people dem shout fah di mos'."

Though Menna wasn't such an expert on how the sounds were judged, she had come to rate Black Sea, the 2001 World Cup winner, and was surprised to see them eliminated first. Crazy Crew followed, then Eradication, who was the most pressured, as they had to live up to their surprise victory in New York the previous year.

"I quite liked Black Sea. They were good," Menna said, "shame they couldn't stay in."

"Yeah, but a nuh suh it go. It's di people's choice," Errol told her again.

The heat was a fierce one, and one by one competing sounds bit the dust of defeat, now leaving the battle between Powerful Coronet, Alpine Peak and Everest.

"So, of these three, who do you think will win?" Menna shouted now over the loud music.

"Well, again, anyt'ing cyan happen. Di Japanese bwoy dem good. So is Alpine, an' so is Everes'. Di t'ree ah dem good. So anyt'ing cyan happen."

"I hope they're all good losers. There's only one cup," Menna said, looking up at the drama-packed stage. She was fascinated at the hardcore way in which things were done in JA: *No messing. Raw and ready.* She could see how important it was for sound clash competitors to have broad shoulders and strong mental endurance for nuff hardcore *'cussing'.* There couldn't be any cry-babies in arenas like these. Being verbally insulted with *all-in-the-game* taunts, like being accused of fucking goats, cows, batty and sucking pussies needed nuff mental strength. Men have been known to kill for less, so these guys proved to be real mental toughies. When Menna first heard the insult, *'Suck unnuh Mumma!'* in a sound clash years ago back in England, her toes had curled, but she had soon come to realise that that was all in the name of the sound clash game.

"Yuh know, Sis'…"

"What?"

"Yuh don' seem di type to fall in love wid a soun' man."

"Where did that come from? I thought you were concentrating on the clash, not thinking about *who* I fell in love with."

"Well… mi was jus' t'inkin' bout yuh an'… w'at's 'is name?…Conteh."

"Why d'you say I don't seem the type?"

"Mi nuh know… yuh jus' seem…"

"I fell in love with a Jeweller, Bro'. Whatever else he was came after. And anyway, what's wrong with soundmen? They're pioneers in their own right aren't they?"

"Of course. But mi mean, yuh don' seem like a dancehall kina girl."

"Am I not standing here in one of the biggest clashes in the world, Bro?"

"Yes, but... I t'ink yuh jus' observing. Studying. Maybe yuh researching fi yuh book or sop'n."

"And I think you're observing me, Errol."

Errol laughed. "Or this might be a way of getting closer to him. Yuh neva know."

She gave him a look. "And anyway, not all soundmen's wives or girlfriends love dancehalls. Some soundmen don't even like their women going to dancehalls and clashes. Not as frequently as dancehall girls anyway."

"Was dat di case wid yuh an' Conteh?"

Menna ignored her brother. He didn't even know half the story, just bits he gathered from time to time.

She averted her eyes to the people again. She couldn't help it. She had always been a keen people-watcher who had a *more-than-average* eye for detail. She cast her eyes all around her, taking in faces, reactions, body-languages: things she couldn't take in so well a few hours ago when it was much darker. A handful of white Jamaicans, Chinese and Indians sprinkled themselves amidst descendants of original Africans. One of the Jamaican-Indians looked remarkably like Nico, but it wasn't him. She had long gone double-checked that. They say we all have a double somewhere and this guy was most certainly Nico's double.

Now, she clocked a familiarly looking woman as she moved across the crowd towards her. The petite mixed-raced woman followed a brother through the thick crowd. He had a cute face, yet his eyes were mischief-filled: at least Menna could detect it – even from that distance. She could have sworn this sista was a face from Birmingham, only it couldn't be, since the sista she had in mind wore dreadlocks. Of course it couldn't be her. Besides, she had a long-time man, and as far as she could surmise, they were inseparable. The thought of this sista being in Jamaica, away from her long-time and with another brother, was unimaginable.

"Yuh a'right, Sis'?' Errol asked when he noticed Menna's stretched neck and the intense question in her eyes as she watched the approaching woman.

"Yes... I'm fine. I thought I saw someone I know from Birmingham, that's all," she replied as the sista changed direction and disappeared, "but it can't be."

"It could be. People from all ova di worl' is 'ere fi dis soun clash yunnuh."

"You're right. But I still doubt it was her... So how is the clash looking to you, Bro'? You must have a favourite by now. Powerful Coronet? Alpine Peak? Everest?"

"Bwoy, Alpine is looking like a dead cert now yunnuh."

"Really?"

"Yeah man. 'im inna di lead up till now. Dere won't be any need fi a dub-fi-dub competition. Alpine aggo win, man. Mi feel so. No problem."

In a way, Menna wanted Powerful Coronet to win, but although they performed well, they had not won any round. In a funny kinda way, it was their mastery of the Jamaican patois that captivated her. She recalled hearing that from a very young age, the brothers, Johnny T and Peter (later to team up with Ganja Man, a Jamaican selector) threw themselves whole-heartedly into reggae music, when most people would never have imagined reggae to have touched Japanese soil. She recalled hearing too, that, in 2002, the 'Far East Rulers', first arrived in England for the UK Cup Clash and defeated several prominent sound systems at The Marcus Garvey Centre in Nottingham. Since then, Powerful Coronet has become a household name on the UK sound-clash circuit, and a favourite with fans worldwide. She loved their spirit, but unfortunately, that wasn't enough to pave the way in the clash.

"They master the Jamaican language real good, don't they?... Powerful Coronet," Menna said.

"Oh yeah. Dem good. Mi love dat. But dat is reggae music, Sis'. It breaks down all barriers."

"That's true."

"Dem come all di way from Yokohama, Japan yunnuh."

"So I heard."

"An' dem firs' win di Worl' Clash in America in 1999... people say it was luck, but dem soon prove dem wrong. It wasn't luck at all. Di Japanese bwoy dem know dem music, man. Powerful Coronet is a powaful force to be reckon wid, man. Trus' mi."

"They seem it."

It wasn't long before Alpine Peak was declared the winner, and Menna, her brother and the crowd alike were not surprised. The crowd cheered. Horns, whistles and pleasure-filled chanting filled the air. And it was then that Menna saw her again. *Kizzy.*

"It *is* someone from Birmingham, Errol. It's Kizzy. I know her. But she's cut her locks. Jesus. I didn't ever think she'd do that."

"Go talk to ar den nuh."

"She's too far," Menna said as she waved, trying to get Kizzy's attention.

Kizzy was looking her way, but she wasn't waving back. She obviously didn't recognise her and thought she must have been waving at someone else.

"Are you waving to the girl in di red dress," Errol asked.

"Yes."

"I know di guy who shi deh wid yunnuh."

"Do you?"

"Yeah, man. But yuh frien' mus be tough fi deal wid 'im"

"She's more of an acquaintance than a friend, but why must she be tough to deal with him?"

"Well…"

Before Errol could finish, someone tapped him on his shoulder. He looked round. "Whaap'n Fait'lyn?"

A young woman was standing there. "Yuh si Glen?" she asked in the broadest Jamaican accent.

"Glen?… no… no…," Errol told her.

"S'maddy tell mi seh Glen down 'ere. Mi frien' drop mi down 'ere. Mi waan some money fi buy food fi mi pickney dem. If yuh see'm tell 'im seh mi ah look fi 'im, y'ear?"

"Aright," Errol said.

Faithlyn walked off with her friend.

"Who's Glen, her baby-father?"

"Glen is the guy standing over dere wid yuh acquaintance."

"Oh. I see," Menna said, looking over at Kizzy, who, unless she actually fought the crowd and went over to her, was never gonna recognise her. "So why did you tell her you hadn't seen Glen?"

"Fait'lyn was neva his serious girl. He just had a baby wid ar. That must be his new girl. 'im used to have a girl name Gloria from Englan' before dis one."

"How come you know so much, Bro'?"

"People chatty-chatty yunnuh. If fresh news outa street mi nuh mus' 'ere? Dis mus' be di girl wid money. Dat's why Fait'lyn lookin' fi 'im. I's dat girl's money min'in' Fait'lyn pickney dem."

"Are you sure you're not the chatty-chatty one, Bro'?"

"No. I's people tell mi."

Suddenly, the crowd surged forward causing a sudden unrest. Menna freaked. Tripped on a rush of adrenalin. She hoped there wouldn't be a rata-tat-tat or a bang or anything. But as it went, it was nothing more than the occurrence of a common cry: two guys were fighting over a *batty-barely-covered* gyal. When will they ever learn? As well as entertaining music, pum-pum had always talked. *Loud.* And when pum-pum talks, men listen to the point of *manic.*

Pum-pum shook the tree of an infamous USA president.

It rattled the caged of a famous football manager.

And for one famous footballer, pum-pum bent his mind like he bent his spins.

Good old pum-pum. It rules, ok?

It has teeth too:

First it smites like a playful kitten.

Then it sinks its teeth in… and bites! And who gave it to women? The Almighty.

Only, he had not meant for it to be the *organ of glut.*

But from the beginning of time, men had glutted after pum-pum. And when you look at most of their down-falls, (bless their weak little minds) money and pum-pum are key players. *Feh real.*

Pum-pum…

Vagina…

Fanny…

Punani…

Who needs a goddamn monologue to name one organ? Call it what you may, it will always and forever be the organ that will drive men crazy? Wasn't it a Jamaican who had once said, *'Punani too sweet, it too sweet, it too sweet, Punani too sweet mi affi dilute it?'*

* * *

Menna had thought long and hard about what Clayton had said… *'Why don't you just give it up? Live. Try to be happy. Who said it's ever a good thing discovering who we really are?'*… *'I think you have some serious unfinished business to fix. Some you don't even know of yet…'* She didn't need Clayton to tell her about her unfinished business, she knew all along. But it was a few days after the sound clash in Mobay that she really got thinking. She decided to let go of the past. Cut away some of that *'old wood'*, so to speak, and move on. If the past was willing to let her be, then sure enough she was willing to let it be. After all, it had been a *mighty long time.*

It was on the bottom step of her deceased grandmother's house that she sat thinking - playing with a few ideas for the future. Ten minutes ago she had placed Ava Ming's *Once Upon A Lie* to her left, placed a cushion against her back and lounged backwards, taking in the now-bearable heat of the evening sun.

Only last night she ran a few ideas past her brother. Working part time for the Jamaican Tourist Board was fine, but the urge to return to Birmingham was quite strong. The urge to do it for herself again was calling, and among others, a publishing company for black books was one idea that came high on her list.

Mainstream publishers are doing their thing, and with most of them, black writers have to sell their souls, strip the essence from their work: become more *'mainstream'* so to speak, before they will even attempt to give them a chance. Menna had also decided that she neither had the time nor the patience to send her manuscript to a whole load of *'your-novel-doesn't-fit-our-criteria'* critics who probably hadn't even got past the first page in the first place anyway. She would try one: *Hot Cover Publishing*. And if they weren't interested, she would self-publish. What the hell? She was a risk-taker anyway. Whether she had something to loose or not. That was Menna: *the woman with fire in her belly.*

"So, what will it be then, Sis'?" Errol asked from the front seat of his Lexus. "A black publisha? Back to di nine-to-five? Perhaps yuh cyan start up where you left off inna Inglan' wid Black Star... An' den again, yuh novel might mek yuh a few millions." His engine was running as hot as the date that awaited him.

"Yeah, right. Fat chance, Bro'. I really don't think so."

"Yuh don' seem to have much fait' in yuhself."

"Oh, I have a lot of faith in myself. I just I doubt it will make me millions."

"Well yuh betta t'ink fas'. You'll be in Inglan soon."

Menna paused. An idea came to him. "What I need is a business partner. Maybe one that failed before and would like to start again. We could both look at publication in a big way."

"Well, Sis', mi cyaan help yuh wid dat at all." He revved his engine.

"I know you can't help me. I want a legitimate partner," she joked.

Errol laughed. "Si yuh lata."

"I thought you'd be taking the Jeep to impress your date!" she shouted as Errol pulled off.

"No. Yuh cyan use di Jeep todeh. If yuh stop t'inkin' long enough."

"I will... take the Jeep, that is. I doubt if I'll stop thinking."

"A'right! Lata!" Errol shouted again.

"Ok, Bro', see you later!" Menna shouted back as her brother finally sped away. And just a few seconds later he came into her mind... *Peter... Peter Walker.*

In the realms of a working partnership, Peter and Menna went way back, before she even new Conteh Gonzales lived and breathed.

Peter, a tall, handsome but gangly looking white guy was one of those white guys who tanned at the *thought* of the sun. Menna had accompanied him on one of his many visits to Jamaica. They were searching for Caribbean men for a bonanza issue of Men's Bodies Magazine. It was only a few days before the trip that Peter was placing bets with Menna on *who* would end up the blackest! And since Menna didn't sit out in the midday sun like sun-grabbing tourists did, Peter thought that his heavy bronze complexion was a fair match to her natural God-given one. It was an ongoing joke between them, one that past a few minutes away.

Before Men's Bodies, from 1985 to 1990, Menna and Peter rubbed shoulders at Key Chip, a fast thriving computer company that was pulling in more business than the MD could ever keep up with. Menna was the Accounts Manager and Peter was the Chief Accountant. Peter was left to oversee all financial matters: the MD trusted him to the max.

However, things came to a nasty head some time in 1990, when some bandulu dealings were uncovered at the heart of Key Chip's financial matters: several fictitious accounts were set up on Key Chip's Purchase Ledger. Every month for five years, cheques were made out to these accounts. And when, by sheer chance, the MD happen to ask to take a closer look at a few of his so-called suppliers, he was more than a little shocked to find that his company was paying out large sums of money to illegitimate companies!

Menna suspected everyone.

Everyone, including the tea girl.

Including too, a strange Italian man that popped into the office one day to have a meeting with Peter. Menna didn't know why, but she felt this guy was dodgy. Handsome and harmless to look at, but owing to the circumstances at the time, *dodgy*. Because of all that was going on, Menna couldn't help tarring him with the same suspicious brush she had tarred everyone else with. She had only seen this Italian guy once, but for sure, if she saw him aging, she would recognise him.

Before the MD could get to the bottom of it all, the fictitious companies were closed and all money taken, making it hard to trace the fraudster.

Everyone at Key Chip covered their asses real good, leaving all fingers pointing at Menna. For one, she was the one responsible for opening all new accounts. Secondly, they were all done using her password. The battle to clear her name was *hot*, but the victory was *sweet* when computer records proved that all those accounts were opened at times when she was away on holiday or out of the office. Someone took the opportunity to obtain and abuse her password. *Not good*. But someone should have told them they were fucking with the wrong bitch. Her time was longer than any fucking rope you could find. And as for biding her time, she was like a sitting duck.

Sharon, a blonde with whom Menna (unknowingly at the time) shared an infamous dick, was the Purchase Ledger Clerk at the time. Sharon took it real bad. She empathised with Menna to a level she was most certainly not expecting. Well before Menna decided to leave Key Chip, (she was suspended, since Key Chip needed proof before they could actually fire her) Sharon left. Apparently, this was in protest against the way Menna was being treated. Menna appreciated Sharon's loyalty, but felt a little bad that she should give up an ok job in the name of *'loyalty to a black woman'*.

When Menna had cleared her name, she took the company to tribunal and won a surprisingly huge sum. Let's say, it filled a few gaping holes. However, Menna couldn't help but think that someone was either out to get her, or simply to get rich at her expense. Whoever he, she or they were, they were willing to watch her fall. And she had pledged that if she ever found out who the fraudster was, she would deal with *him, her* or even *them* in a serious way. Feh real. She didn't know why, but something told her that one day... one fine day... she would find out... for she was lucky like that. Someone's guts were destined to become garters.

A while after that, Key Chip went bust. It was a shock to most people, since one minute the figures looked great, and the next it was rather unhealthy. It was then that Peter Walker launched Men's Bodies Magazine and deployed the creative services of Menna. With her tidy nest egg from the payoff she had from Key Chip, and the money Peter offered, things looked good, so she didn't decline.

For a while, Men's Bodies showed real potential, but in the game of business, sometimes when the road gets rocky, it gets rocky. Sadly, in 1992 it fell apart. Six months later, Peter hit the bottle, and Menna who was now the owner of Black Star Magazine was a little worried about him: more so when she heard that Glenda, his wife of ten years had checked out. Glenda figured that Men's Bodies was the first success of all Peter's *bright ideas* of working for himself, so she was not about to sit around for the next ten years waiting for the *'chance-sparking'* of another.

Glenda had good looks. Weekly manicures, pedicures, health farms and all that needed to be kept up. As such, she had no profession, so when the hands that steered the *'comfy ship'* in which she sailed for years showed signs of getting severed, the only thing this glamorous lady could think of was, *'jump ship'*. She then searched for any man that showed sign of having a few shillings to rub together.

For but a short while, the tables turned: Peter found himself on the payroll of Black Star Magazine. With the Experience from his own magazine, he had a lot to offer, but it soon became apparent that Peter's hunger for big money was beyond what Black Star was ever gonna be able to fulfil. She was sad to see him go, but Peter was a survivor and if he could stay away from the bottle and focus on his surreal need to make it rich, he would survive. So Menna wished him well with some avant-garde idea he was working on.

Not long after Peter parted company with Menna, Sharon became desperate for work and Menna could not decline her a job. After all not so far back she had given hers up to show loyalty to Menna.

And it was later that Menna would find out that way before she met Conteh, Sharon had had her heart broken by him. This led to Menna masterminding the greatest sting of them all: she had sent Sharon and her friend Melissa to act out an orgy with Conteh and Nico, with Garnet snapping away happily at the hot, steamy moment. The love rats were caught, hook, line and sinker, with Menna only too happy to send the hot snaps to Conteh's wife, Simone.

'*Peter... I wonder what he's doing now?*' Menna wondered. '*Perhaps he made his million and his wife Glenda came begging for him to have her back. It would be good to work with him again.*' Business-wise, Peter definitely had something, and Menna was a glutton for a good business head.

* * *

Pavaty! Pavaty! Dis yah one yah name pavaty!
Pavaty! Pavaty! Dis yah one yah name pavaty!

Faithlyn sat in a tenement yard in Trench town. A suckling baby at her breast, it really was a wonder how she managed to feed the rest. Well, she hardly *managed* at all. Things were hard. *Desperate.* Her two sons (by two different fathers – none of whom she ever saw) were born to her at just 15-years-old: the second being conceived only two months after the first one was born. When she was sixteen, she met Rock, a third baby-father and none-the-less, a notorious *bag-of-trouble*. She fell pregnant with his child.

Rock promised her a big life: one that he would buy from shady dealings. After Faithlyn's third child, she managed to get a family relative to sponsor her on a short stay in Birmingham, England. Rock was there and she wanted to be with him. So it was just after her seventeenth birthday that Faithlyn landed in Birmingham. She left her three young children with her aged mother, who could do with care herself.

With things not yet running for Rock in Birmingham, Faithlyn made do with small jobs, like the baby-sitting one she had landed with Lijah and Gloria, but she had soon lost that when Gloria caught Lijah with his pants down, giving her what she wanted… on her settee in her living-room! Oh yes, Lijah had tuned Faithlyn's piano all right.

Faithlyn fell pregnant again for Rock in England, only, she decided that Lijah would wear the jacket. So on that infamous evening when she dumped baby Shanique onto Lijah, she humped a suitcase filled with cash from his wardrobe: one she had trouble explaining to customs officers at Heathrow Airport as she tried to pass the tight cash-filled case through custom. So neither her nor Lijah benefited from a penny, since it was now the property of the police.

Faithlyn needn't worry about Shanique, the child she left in England. Gloria and Lijah were rendering special care to her. But now, beneath the shade of mango tree, a fifth child hung from her breast. A dear, sweet child that had no say in the choosing of its parents. A child who would not have chosen a father with the character of another infamous character… *Baby Face Glen*. A character Kizzy was wrapped up with. One she had not yet discovered to be much more ruthless than a sweet-talking taxi-driver. And from whom, previously, Gloria had escaped after finding out that Lijah, her old grass was ten times greener after all. *Chat bout.*

Only a few nights ago Faithlyn took a trip down to Mobay to find Glen. She was unsuccessful. He was with Kizzy. Glen had spotted her before she spotted him. And since ducking and diving was his speciality, she had no chance.

* * *

When Menna had first received the email from Peter Walker, she was somewhat surprised. It was only a few days ago that he had sprung to mind, and she had joked that Peter must have picked up on her telepathy.

She was surprised to get the email, however, she was not in the least surprised to hear that he was soaking up the sun, right there in Jamaica.

Of course there must be umpteen others, but Peter was the only white man Menna knew who visited Jamaica more often than a Brummie would visit the Bull Ring Shopping Centre. The unwavering entrepreneur must have tried almost every *get-rich-quick* trick in the book so far, in his attempt to make a million. He had sat with her on many occasions, discussing some of the most farfetched ideas she had ever heard of: all of which Peter had tried, tested, but sadly, failed miserably.

But Menna had never forgotten Peter's words when they parted last: 'I *will* make a financial killing, Menna… by *hook* or by *crook*'.

And Menna had smiled and said, 'Peter, hope it's by hook and *not* crook'.

And that was it. Menna had not seen or heard from Peter until this *out-of-the-blue* email.

'*Hi Menna*', the email had said. '*A little bird told me you are here in Jamaica writing that novel you had always wanted to write. Well, guess what? I too, am here in Jamaica. Not writing a book, however, just soaking up the sun at a most glorious resort. Maybe (if breaking from that computer screen won't stop your flow. And if you don't mind sitting with a failed white man on the balcony of his hotel apartment), you can come over for a chat and a glass of something. Catch up on old times back in 'not-so-sunny' Birmingham. Failing that, maybe I can come up, down or even over to see you, wherever you are. Menna, Jamaica is such a beautiful country. That saying is really true: 'nature had surely kissed the earth and called it Jamaica'. If you are here, please do not ignore this email. Would love to hear from, but most of all, to see that beautiful face of a loyal old friend'.*

Menna had smiled, finding Peter's reference to her as *'beautiful'* a little strange. Never in all the years she had worked for him, had he even made out that he had noticed her physical beauty. The only thing Peter appraised with passion, was her work: her tenacity, accuracy, ability to handle herself both in an accounts and a creative field: to handle an accounts department, and also to get a good story – her pride in her work.

'Perhaps', she had figured, 'the isolated distance of the electronics airwaves, and the non-existence of Glenda gave him confidence to tell me I'm 'beautiful'.

'Peter, Hi', Menna had written in return. 'Good to hear from you. In JA again, hey? Peter, I don't know why you don't just buy the island!' she joked. 'I can see you retiring here. Where are you staying? Of course I'd love to see you and catch up on old times. It's been a long time since Black Star, and an even longer time since Men's Bodies. And on the subject of 'men's bodies', have you put any weight on?'

But it was days later before Menna received a reply from Peter. 'Glad you agreed to come and see me, Menna. I am staying at El Greco Resort in Montego Bay. Its one of the new ones. If you haven't been, it's ideal for families, business travellers and pleasure seekers alike. It is only 5 minutes from the airport and is sitting breathtakingly on a high mountain plateau. The resort is surrounded by lush, tropical beauty with a spectacular panoramic vista of mountains rising from the aqua-blue waters of Montego Bay. It is a quiet retreat, Menna, yet only an elevator ride from the hustle and bustle of Montego Bay's popular 'Hip Strip.' The infamous Doctor's Cave beach, water sports, shopping, entertainment, casino gambling, restaurants and theme park are within walking range. So... am I relaxing? You needn't ask? Can't wait to see you.'

Peter had always had a creative way of describing anything. Back in Birmingham, he would describe something so vividly over the telephone, when you eventually get to see it, you knew his eyes were working like the lenses of a camera. He had a way of describing things with enough passion to make you wanna go, *uuuuuhhh*. There she was, in her own country, and it took a white man to emphasise a small section of its beauty so well, it made her realise how much her and a lot of other Jamaicans had taken it for granted!

'Peter,' she typed back, 'if El Greco sounds so breathtakingly wonderful, then try and stop me from coming over. I will talk to Errol. We'll plan a day when I'm not part-timing. He has the wheels. I'll persuade him to take the trip'.

"Yuh goin' ova to Montego Bay to si a w'ite man?" Errol had said with a cynical smile when Menna had asked him to take her. "So wha'?… yuh switchin'? Black men hurt yuh so much, yuh switchin' to w'ite men?" he joked.

"Listen, Bro' are you taking me or not?"

"Why not? A nuh not'n. Mi might even fin' a English girl dong deh."

"Peter is my ex-boss. He's always here in Jamaica. He wants to have a chat. I haven't seen him in ages. And anyway, why is it that when a man and a woman meet, it has to be sexual?"

"Cho, man," Errol said, "yuh know seh is joke mi mekin'… anyway, w'en you an' dis ex-boss is havin' unnuh likkle chat, what will I be doin'?"

"Errol, we won't be talking about anything we don't want you to here. He's my ex-boss, not my ex-lover. You can sit with us and have a drink, or you can take in the beautiful scenery of the El Greco resort… chirps a tourist or two… yuh just said yuhself, you might find an English girl."

"El Greco?" Errol made no comment to Menna's long speech, "Wha'? Is desso 'im deh?"

"Why? You know it?"

"Yeah, man. I met an English girl dere some years ago. Seh she was gonna sen' fi mi. Seh shi wanted mi to come uppa foreign. But from shi reach back, shi neva call mi. I reckon shi had a man. I reckon shi jus wanted to fulfil a fantasy. Taste a Blackman, yunnuh?"

"An she couldn't taste a black man in England, Errol?"

"Errol laughed. "Maybe that would be risking it. Shi was a bit stush. Toffee-nosed, yunnuh? Not di type yuh would expect to mek a black man fu…. touch ar. An' anyway, di black man dem inna Inglan' nuh have nuh substance. Dem weak. Nyam tomuch bake bean an' t'ing. Maybe shi wanted di real t'ing, yunnuh? Undiluted, yunnuh?"

Menna laughed and shook her head at her brother's raw, barefaced bragging. "Bro' you'll never change. Never."

"Errol laughed and said, "So w'en yuh want to go an' si dis w'ite man?"

"When are you free, Bro'?"

"Thursday is a good day. Si if dat good fi 'im."

* * *

Thursday seemed to have come in the blink of an eye and as Menna sat dosing in her brother's Jeep as they travelled from Kingston to Montego Bay, sleep took her into the land of dreams. She saw herself in a mansion somewhere in Birmingham, only it wasn't *exactly* Birmingham. This mansion comprised of ten bedrooms, all with its own en-suite, two bathrooms, a gorgeous kitchen, utility room and a veranda that overlooked the sea. And it was the calm waves and the vastness of the ocean sitting magnificently against the horizon of the perfect pure blue skies that she saw him. *Conteh.* Pops up everywhere, that man. There he was walking on the water towards her. *'Whaap'n Babes?'* she heard him say. *'Yuh a'right?'* He smiled, showing a perfect set of white teeth and cute dimples, and when he smiled the lines around his eyes made them laugh. And gleam. And call her again to the magic of their hypnotic gaze. Nico was behind him. He is lurking. Waiting to pounce. She felt it was a trick. She stepped back and seemed to have lost their images. Another step found her falling. Falling into an everlasting darkness. She couldn't stop. There was no bottom to this pit. Then the sound of sirens. And seconds later, she found herself inside a room in this mansion. But she was trapped. As if someone had locked her in. And though they weren't, her hands felt tied. She tried to open the door. *No chance.* She walked over to the big window and looked down. It was swarming with police cars, but the windows of the cars were blacked out. No movements. They were just sat there. Waiting for her. And although she could not see the men that sat in these cars, she knew that like eagles, *their eyes watched her.*

But suddenly, back to reality. The Jeep hit a bump and Menna was jolted back to reality. "Oh shit," she hissed.

"I's Wha' wrong wid yuh?" Errol asked, taking his eyes off the road for a second.

"Weird dream," she said, wondering what its significance could be. Now she was taking it literally. The only dealing she could possibly have with the English police is if they eventually found out that she was the bitch behind the All That Glitter robbery. The bitter woman who took revenge on a cheating, two-timing rat, by pulling off a robbery and framing the bastard. *'Fucka,'* she thought, and it was then that she realised that despite her pledge to *'let go'*, and despite her recent realisation that she *'loved him still'*, her anger had not yet subsided, but was still there, bubbling like a vengeful volcano. Perhaps it was the dream. Perhaps her anger would always be teased by his image. *Weird.* Sometimes she loved him. Then she hated him. But one thing she knew, when the hate hits, it was always stronger than the love. To a point of *'peril'*. Time didn't really heal. *No sir.* It didn't. *How long must this pendulum reaction continue?*

"How can you fall asleep and dream in the middle of such a beautiful day?"

"Oh, so dreaming is for dark, horrible nights are they?… although this one should have been." she added.

"Wha'?" Errol perplexed.

"Never mind, Bro'. How long now?"

"Not long." He looked at his sister, smiled and shook his head. He had never been able to understand her.

"Little weedy Peter. He was a good boss," Menna said out of the blue.

"You were dreamin' 'bout Peeta?" Errol asked curiously.

"No I wasn't."

"Yuh sure? Min' yunnuh… Min' yuh not secretly fallin' in love wid dis Peeta guy."

Menna smiled at her brother's self-amusement. "Shame Men's Bodies magazine folded," she continued. "But I suppose from every action comes a reaction, and if it didn't, Peter wouldn't be doing whatever he's doing now. And I wouldn't consider Black Star, and so my road wouldn't turn this way."

"And is it a good turn, Sis'?"

"Can't tell yet, Bro'', I'm still travelling. Only when I reach back in Birmingham that I'll be able to tell. Time."

"Anyway, changing the subject slightly… what about Clayton, the Canadian?"

"What about him?"

"Well, you dated him a few times in JA… Spent two weeks in Canada with him…"

"…And now you expect to hear wedding bells, right, Bro'?"

"No… But sooner or lata yuh wi' have to fin' yuhself a man, Sis'."

Menna laughed, "Like you've found yourself *a* woman? I know you have *several*, Bro', but not *a* woman."

"Very funny."

"No. Clayton is a sweet guy… Oh! By the way… talking of *sweet,* that night in Montego Bay… recap."

"When I had to mek sure seh mi likkle sis' got to bed ok?"

"Yes… were you there when I was babbling on about Conteh?"

"I caught some of it, yes. You have some serious hang-ups about that guy. He really broke your heart, didn't he, Sis'?"

"Did I say anything really…?"

"No, Sis'. I came along at the end when you were repeating some stuff about 'Conteh… Conteh Egyptian… the bastard! Living only for his sound, Vibes Injection… and hurting women, black and white… something like that. I just hung around to make sure you got to your bed safe. Not that I didn't trust Clayton, but after all, you are my little sis'."

"Less of the *little*, Bro'." Menna smiled. She had forgotten to ask her brother before now, and not that she doubted Clayton, but she was pleased her brother confirmed she didn't expose herself too much.

Soon the jeep was pulling into the resort. An arched bamboo entrance guided them towards the hotel's reception. As Errol eased into a parking spot, Menna looked up at the balcony of several one and two bedroom apartments, wondering which one housed the notorious Peter Walker.

"Menna?! Hi!" a familiar voice called out just as Menna was shutting the door to her side of the Jeep. She looked upwards to see a tall, bronze white man. *'Who is he?'* she thought, since she was sure it wasn't Peter. This guy that stared down and was waving frantically at her was stout. Muscular.

"I'll come down!" the man shouted, and it was then that his voice revealed that it *was* Peter.

"He must have been on some serious work-out shit," Menna said to Errol as they walked towards the hotel's reception.

"What?" Errol was half listening. His attention was attracted by an English rose who was more deep-blushed than bronze. She was collecting her keys from reception.

"Oh… never mind," Menna said, putting her hand up jokingly. "I can see you're otherwise engaged."

Seconds later they were within hugging distance of Peter. "Menna," he initiated a hug, "you look great."

"Then what about *you,* Peter? Great isn't the word. This is a new you. What's all this?" She punched his taut triceps playfully.

"Yes… nothing some wholesome hours in the gym couldn't solve."

"No… seriously… you look good, Peter. God I didn't think you craved muscles."

"Well, you don't have to call me *God*... and *no*, not *crave*, just *had to*," he looked at Errol in anticipation, showing an anxiety to be introduced.

"*Had to?*" Menna asked, ignoring his blatant quest to be familiarised.

"Yes... my Jamaican girlfriend wanted something to hold onto. Told me I was too *maaga*." He attempted patois.

Menna and Errol smiled.

"Your... *Jamaica*... *girlfriend*?" Menna perplexed.

"Yes... Charmaine. She was beautiful. Sweet. She had jet-black skin, and the most gorgeous figure you could ever imagine. Lovely square shoulders, a slender neck, thin waistline, pouty ass..." The man was almost aroused. "...Well... let's just say Charmaine was *Perfect*."

Menna looked at her brother amused and the look on Errol's face said, *'I wish I had a woman like that'*.

"So... what happened with you and Charmaine?" Menna had to know.

"I took her to England but she left me after a while. Found herself a richer white guy."

"Oh... so *not* so perfect, then?" Menna couldn't resist.

"Well... you could say that, yes... Aren't you gonna introduce me...?" He looked from her to Errol.

"Oh, sorry, how rude of me... but I couldn't get a word in anyway, Peter, you haven't stopped talking, but that's you, you haven't changed," she joked. "Peter this is Errol, Errol this is Peter."

"Errol, Hi," he reached for Errol's right hand and looked searchingly at Menna.

"Errol's my *brother*," she told him when she realised what he was searching for.

"Your *brother*? Oh... I see," he shook harder now and his eyes glinted. Menna saw them and quickly dismissed the thought of what she *assumed* Peter was happy about. *'No. This is Peter, my ex-boss... and besides, I'm into Black men in a big way. I just need to get one bastard out of my psyche.'*

"I thought..." Peter continued.

Menna helped him, "... You thought Errol was my *man*?"

"Yes," Peter chuckled, "I did. Come up to my apartment," he said, right arm outstretched into the direction of his apartment, his left around Menna's shoulder. As Peter looked in the direction of his right arm, Menna peered at his left that was sitting comfortably around her shoulder, and then at her brother - she was sure to catch the expected mischief in eyes.

Admittedly, Peter was a little forward. Back in England he had never been so tactile.

"Ex-boss, hey?" Errol mouthed. Menna read his lips perfectly and it was a job trying to keep a straight face.

As they attempted the stairs, the English rose Errol had seen earlier descended them. This time, their eyes locked, and if looks could *eat*, he would be her afternoon delight. *Seriously*. Her eyes said *'you can stick your black pudding into my pork pie any day.'*

"A'right, Sweetness?" Errol chirped.

She smiled, sending her deep-blush into a deeper shade of pink.

"Where's your boyfrien'?" he asked, wasting no time.

She slowed up. "What boyfriend?"

"A'right... dat soun' good. Mi comin' to check yuh lata, yuh 'ear?"

"Pardon?"

"Later... I'll see you later." He spoke perfect English for her ears. "Make sure you don't hide."

She smiled widely.

Now he watched her walk away, knowing it wouldn't be for long. He felt a rush of heat when she wiggled it much more than a little bit.

"Come on," Peter urged from a few steps up. "Let's find this apartment of mine."

Peter led them to a room that was the epitome of casual elegance blended with comfort and convenience. The apartment was amply air-conditioned and comprised of a gorgeous bedroom suite, which included a large bath and an ample closet. A casually elegant living area boasted a delightful tropical island décor, from the fully equipped kitchen to the comfortable, spacious great room. A crisp white French door and window was opened, letting in a fresh Caribbean breeze, and a cosy private balcony gave Peter the chance to enjoy leisurely breakfasts or romantic sunsets. Menna's creative mind grasped it in seconds, but she couldn't help thinking how complete it would be with a female company. But that was Peter's problem and she scolded herself for even thinking about that side of his life. Now she turned her mind to thinking of the beauty of Jamaica. "Peter, this is absolutely lovely," she told him.

"Let's sit on the balcony," Peter urged. "Would you guys like a drink?"

"I'm fine at the moment, thank you," Menna said.

"W'at yuh have, Peeta?" Errol asked in an undiluted tone.

"Peter chuckled. "I so love the Jamaican accent. You know, Menna, I marvelled at something…"

"What, Peter?"

"I marvelled at how, when a white guy shows interest in a black woman, and when they end up together, the black woman ends up trying to become more aristocratic in her speaking than the Queen herself. It amazes me how they miss the point. Apart from the exotic beauty of black women, white men also like their culture: otherwise, why not stay with a white girl? I want so much to learn the language. Black writers for instance… how many black writers are really true to themselves? How many of them write from their hearts? You know? How it's really coming out? Or do they spend so much time trying to please the non-black audience that the real essence of what they are trying to say gets lost?"

"That I couldn't tell you, Peter."

"And don't they think that white readers are inquisitive and want to learn?"

"But isn't it a catch 22 situation? If they write patois, the mainstream publishers won't touch them, so the only way they are going to be able to reach white readers is to hope for more black publishers, or do it themselves. So maybe they don't know what to do."

"True," Peter said. "What about you, Menna? Is your writing stripped of his essence?"

"Hell, no. Most of my characters have strong West Indian backgrounds, even if they're English-born. So when they're engaged in dialogue, I'm not going to have them giving it the *ok-yaw* and all that *la-di-dah* stuff. The black guys I feature are most certainly not the *Derrick from Big Brother* type. And that is not to say it's a bad thing to be *la-di-dah,* but that is just not where my essence lies.

"And anyway, white readers are under-estimated. Jamaican patois is not at all hard to understand, and the longer West Indian writers hide under the umbrella of the Queen's English, then the longer white English readers will take to learn."

"But Peeta," Errol said, "You're assuming dat all black writers know patois. Black and patois don't always come as a package yunnuh. Not all English-born West Indians cyan write patois, an' a writer have to feel comfortable wid what he or she is writing, and a lot a dem feel that it is a *come-down* to write patois anyway."

Menna looked surprisingly at her brother.

"I suppose it depends how the individual view the term *'come-down'*, Peter said. "If they see the new language of the people who were *'taken-down'* from Africa against their will as a *'come-down'*, then the *'come-down'* should be seen as a reminder to us all. It's a mind thing. If they see patois as negative, then maybe they should realise this... the slave-masters thought their languages were *rich*. The Africans thought theirs were *rich* too. So what should be said about two *rich* languages combined?"

Now Menna looked at Peter with a difference. She had never viewed it from that angle before.

"Patois is rich, man," Peter sounded like a Jamaican for a second.

"Yeah, man," Errol endorsed.

Peter rambled on and Menna listened with intent. She hadn't the slightest idea that his interest laid so deep.

"You want to learn patois, Peter?" Menna quizzed.

"Why not. Why does English have to rule?"

Errol laughed out loud as he tried to understand Peter's hunger for patois, when so many English blacks, and even the ones who were born in Jamaica tried so hard to shun it.

"Oh! Errol, sorry... you wanted to know what I've got to drink. Go look in my fridge." He pointed and Errol followed his finger to the kitchen, which housed a miniature fridge. "Help yuhself, man."

Errol opened the miniature fridge and pondered, conversing with his taste buds.

"Is that why you come to Jamaica every year, Peter?" Menna asked. She was now alone with him for but a short moment, "to learn patois?"

"No. Jamaica's got me spellbound. I love it. Love the food, the people, the Caribbean air, the mountainous views... well, I could go on."

"Not forgetting di girls, man." Errol came in on the end of the conversation.

"Oh... how could I forget," Peter delighted.

Errol placed his ass in the vacant chair. He arched his back, elbows on his knees, arms outstretched with his chilled Supamalt in his right grip. Expectantly, his eyes wandered as he looked down at the eager sun-worshipers that lined the edge of the swimming pool, and then he saw her again. The English rose he so desired. A Jackie Collins novel lay across her stomach. She pretended to sleep, but she watched him through dark lenses, imagining his dark chocolate stick stirring and causing her vanilla ice cream to melt.

But an hour passed and Errol had not moved, although Menna thought he would have long gone moved towards the eager, now lobster-red woman. But Errol was relaxed into the chair.

The conversation was good. It was holding him. But how it swung towards this topic was a mystery to both Errol and Menna alike. "And another thing, Peter added, as if he was simply talking about adding a spoonful of sugar to his tea, "There is something I would like to penetrate… Menna, this might come as a shock to you, but please don't judge me."

Menna looked at Peter, then at Errol, then back at Peter again. "What?"

"Have you two ever wondered about the drug trafficking business from Jamaica to England and America?"

There was a noticeable pause.

"From time to time, yeah," Menna told him, "*why*?"

Errol raised an eyebrow, shuffled his feet and his back found its arched position again.

"Have you ever heard of a white business man travelling on a British Airways flight being hassled or harassed by customs under the suspicion of carrying drugs?"

"No…." Menna perplexed, well, not on the news anyway, but I suppose there must be a few. And I don't think anyone - black, white or yellow can get away with that so easily these days, anyway. There are sniffer dogs everywhere, new strategy put into place, tighter controls. No matter if you're black, white, pink with spots on, the dogs will sniff out any drugs."

Errol said nothing. He just stared at Peter.

"Well, put it this way, Menna. I've lost track of how many years I've travelled to and from JA, and not once have I ever been stopped."

"Yeah, but have you ever carried anything?"

"No."

"Well then. Maybe that's it. If you did, you would probably be acting nervous. Jumpy. Then they'd have a reason to stop you."

"True. And if I carried anything in my suitcase, yes the dogs would have sniffed me out."

"Ok, Peter, I give in. What are you saying?"

"I am an ordinary-looking white man who travels often to and from Jamaica. Sometimes it's business, sometimes it's pleasure and sometimes both. And like I said, not once have I ever been stopped?"

"Yeah? Get to the point," Menna urged.

"Just imagine that being either of you guys travelling Air Jamaica?"

Menna and Errol exchanged glances.

"Can't you see what I'm getting at?"

"Kind of," she said.

"If I climb onto a BA Jet, sip G 'n T in first class compartment, climb off and strut through customs, what do you think the chances are of me leaving that airport with a gut full of cocaine stuffed in a load of condoms or some material like that?"

"Oh, Peter, that's absurd!" Menna alarmed. "Not that old trick? In fact, it's not even a trick anymore. How could you even think of that?"

Menna looked at her brother for support, but saw only an approving glint in his eyes. The two men had connected. Picked up on each other's telepathy. Errol was a baggage handler at Kingston International Airport, but the most he got to travelling these days, was the *'thought'*. A few acres of land he had recently sold allowed him the luxury of a Jeep. The Lexus was on its way out. He was managing ok, but it seems to take the utmost integrity and uprightness these days to refuse the chance of making nuff illegitimate dallaz.

"You see," Peter continued, "while they are so busy looking at Air Jamaica's passengers, and assuming that they are all desperate one-parent-families trying to make a quick buck from muling, the BA jet would have off-loaded an innocent-looking white man with cocaine of limitless street value.

Errol's eyes lit up even more. He was ready. And of course he knew that Peter wouldn't be telling him this if there weren't anything in it for him. "Are you planning on doing that?" He spoke perfect English as if there was a must.

"Would if I could. Worth the try. The only problem is, I would need to get connected. If this shit works, I wouldn't have to work again."

"Oh, Peter, what about the consequences. What if a condom or two burst in your stomach? You'll die. Would that be worth it?"

"I wouldn't be able to tell. I'd be dead." He smiled smugly.

"Christ, that's sick." Menna turned her head away.

"What if.... What if... what if," Peter was being cynical. "Menna, you have always been so damn over-cautious. What if a gunman attacks this hotel right now and blows all our brains out? What if the plane I'm travelling on in a week's time crashes? *What if?... What if?..."*

"So you would *really* be willing to take that risk, Peter?"

"Menna, life's *all* about risks…"

That was one thing Peter didn't need to tell her.

"Not only that," Menna added, "that shit might be mixed with all sorts before it filters down to the hands of innocent kids?" She recalled hearing of Kunta, the young son of Lijah and Gloria - old friends of hers: a promising young lad from Birmingham, who fell victim to the devil's food.

"And it might *not*. Menna, you worry too much. Do you really think that novel of yours is going to make you a million?"

"Don't you dare be cynical about my novel, Peter. It *might* make a million, and it *might not*. Just like a sachet of cocaine *might* or *might not* burst in your gut and your greedy ass."

Errol looked at Menna. He remembered the conversation they had a few days ago about her book, and how she expressed her doubt about it making a million. *He,* however, was the one who suggested that it *'might'*. It was Menna's prerogative to be modest.

Peter sucked nicotine from the stub of a cigarette. He had felt the lash of her tail, and it took him back to the stink she kicked up a Key Chip when she was suspected of fraud.

"Who the fuck wants to be a millionaire, anyway? Money like that only brings misery."

"Bwoy…" Errol spoke, "I wi' tek a likkle misery if I can hol' a million, yunnuh. Mi nah tell yuh nuh lie…. *Trus' mi*."

She cut her eyes at her brother and kissed her teeth.

"Think about it, Menna," the adamant Peter said, "I've trusted you with my thoughts. You can either be a part of it and become rich, or be out and hope your book becomes the best of the bestsellers."

Menna's eyes widened at the thought that Peter would even *think* of asking her to come in on such an idea, let alone expect her to say yes!

Errol slipped back into silent mode. Peter already knew he would be game.

Menna cast her eyes simultaneously to and from the contrasting pair: a black man and a white man: two completely different backgrounds. Now, *money* gave them an affiliating trinity: a date with the devil, one treacherous aim, and one destiny that diced with death.

"Listen," Errol said, rising from his chair, "I'm going downstairs. I'll leave you two to talk." He shook Peter's hand as if they had already made a deal.

"And if this woman promises you a ticket to England, Errol," Peter said, "don't believe it. They do it all the time. Women are full of tricks."

Errol glanced at the sunbathing English woman he was about to try and conquer.

"Nah, man. I don't fall fi tricks like dat anymore," he said, heading downstairs.

"Women are full of tricks, hey?" Menna asked Peter when Errol was clean out of sight.

"You should know that, Menna, surely. You take the biscuit for that one."

"What d'you mean?" she knitted her brows. *'What does Peter know? Does he know what I did to Conteh?'* she wondered.

"Nothing... nothing."

"So... what do I *take the biscuit* for, Peter?"

"Hey... Let's talk about good things. Like getting rich," Peter squeezed her knee. Kept his hand there for a good few seconds.

'What?' Menna thought, resting her eyes on Peter's eager knuckles, *'Yuh flying pass yuh dyam nest, bwoy?'*

He noticed her disapproval and took his hand away.

"This Jamaican sun has made you real forward, Peter... *presumptuous, man.*"

"Sorry... didn't mean to offend you. Being away from the stiff office environment... and you know what the sun's like. Push us guys' testosterone levels up sky high..."

"... And made you feel you can touch me seductively?"

"Menna, I touched your knee, I didn't..."

"Still presumptuous," she jabbed.

"Sorry... I was forgetting... my name isn't *Conteh Gonzales. Egyptian...*"

She looked at him with widened eyes.

"...The only man who could make you change from an angel into a monster." He lit a new cigarette.

"What the fuck... Peter, what d'you know about me? Have you been...?"

"...*Researching*?... like I said, Menna, let's talk *money*. "

Menna's head boiled but she tried to play it cool. Peter may have felt he had the handle, but she wasn't one for holding any blade for long.

"Listen, Peter, when I had your email and agreed to meet you, I didn't expect this... I thought of running an idea by you, but..."

"... You mean a publishing idea?... something like that?"

"Yes, sort of... how did you know?"

"Menna, that is old ropes. We've both been there. The T-Shirt is worn. We're getting old..."

"Speak for yourself, I feel twenty-five."

"Ok, good for you, I'm forty-two. My *white* wife has left me for a *black* man she *thought* had money... my *black* girlfriend left me for a *white* man she *knew* had money... so I'm about to get me some scandalous cash. I'm not about to piss around again in no fool's game anymore."

"*Fool's* game? Is earning an honest living a fool's game, Peter? So what d'you call drug trafficking, a wise man's game?"

"Like I said..."

She interrupted, almost as if it had just hit her, "Glenda left you for a Black man?"

"Yeap."

"I had no idea."

"She wasn't with him for long though," Peter hastened. "She soon regretted it. He gave her a couple of babies, stuck her in a corner somewhere away from his black circles. Now, from what I heard, she dances daily in showers of tears and the contents of a whisky bottle."

Menna was speechless. The image of Glenda was vivid against the walls of her mind. It didn't ring true.

"You look shocked, Menna,"

"Shocked isn't the word. Is she still living in Birmingham?"

"Yeap... apparently this guy thought she had money... well, you know how Glenda always look good, and of course she still had the expensive clothes, shoes etc., that I bought her..."

"So..." Menna perplexed, "*she* thought this guy had money, and cast her net... *he* thought *she* had money and cast his'..."

"You got it... The thing is, this guy was married and had several other women around Birmingham, black and white. He lied to her. She fell pregnant and the rest is history."

"So, how come you and Glenda didn't have kids?"

"Glenda always said she wasn't ready. I wouldn't force her... but anyway," he perked up, like I said, let's talk money."

"... Mmmm... well... nothing surprises me these days," Menna said, still on the subject of Glenda, " so... how d'you see me in all this, Peter?"

He looked at her curiously. "Are you considering?"

"I never said that. I asked, *'how d'you see me in all this?'* What would be my role? I most certainly wouldn't be swallowing any damn cocaine, that's for sure..."

"... Aren't you thirsty?" He got up, " Let me get you a Supamalt or something."

"Supamalt will be fine, thanks." She crossed her leg as if in readiness for business, and as Peter swung to the kitchen, she swung her eyes in the direction of her brother, who looked home and dry. He had most certainly *pulled.*

"Menna," Peter returned with a nice chilled Supamalt and his hot passion for talking business, "research is my thing. I've been doing my research on the Birmingham scene for a very long time."

"Big Brother, hey?" She was still curious to know why he thought she took the biscuit on *women being full of tricks.*

"Call it what you like. You know two guys who can take a *small amount* off my hands for a substantial fraction of the street value..."

"*I,* know two guys? I don't know any such people who deal in them things, Peter. Where did you get that information from?"

"Well, let's put it this way, Menna," he pulled on his cigarette, "*you* don't know that these guys deal in these things. Well, one of them will come as a surprise to you."

She looked at him and chuckled nervously, "Now you're scaring me."

"Who's Garnet, Menna?"

"*Garnet... Garnet... Garnet...* the only *Garnet* I know is just a photographer guy who used to snoop around taking incriminating photos for anyone willing to pay."

"*Was,* Menna, *was.* Since then, Garnet has linked with a guy called Bongo Dee... know him?" He paused and pulled in a long lick of nicotine as if to charge his batteries.

"No. I don't *know* him. Heard of him, though. Heard he used to be minder for an ex-lover of mine. Heard he's one of the guys who have taken over from Jaro, Bunti and Sugar, who were supposedly

Birmingham's biggest dealers. They were killed, I heard, in some shoot up a while back, by some guy named Rock."

"It must be the writer in you. You retain information like the memory of a damn computer," Peter said. "You even remember names. You must have a good source."

"My sister Cynthia. She keeps me informed on what goes down in Birmingham."

"Well, at least you know something. You know a lot, in fact."

"Yeah, well bad news travel fast…"

"But," Peter added, "some of that is old news now. Bongo isn't so big any more. The top dog that supplied him was penetrated by the pigs. They pulled the rug from under his feet. So there's no one to feed Bongo anything. And that makes Garnet even smaller. In fact the guys fell out over some woman."

"How the hell d'you know so much, Peter?"

"Well, all that's not relevant. I've been making enquiries. From what I heard, they might be interested individually. Nothing much is going on for them. They've both tasted that kind of life… but nothing's certain on that front as yet."

'*Garnet?* When I met him he was with some blonde called Tracey who snatched him from his long-term queen Evadney."

"No one can be snatched, Menna. The man must have wanted to go. His own free will, remember?"

"I guess."

"But I think it's the same woman. She left Garnet for Bongo and they fell out."

"So how did Garnet get wrapped up in the drug scene?"

"Quick and easy money, Menna… but notice I said a *small amount.* These guys will only be able to handle a tiny portion of what I intend to transit. I have bigger fish in England. Briefcase brigades. Just waiting to gobble up what I intend to traffic. I'm talking guys with the readies. No credit. Straight up. Money for merchandise. A lot of cash. No joke. Nice neat drop."

"What?! You must have a big gut. How much are you planning on swallowing…?"

Peter chuckled, "Menna, you worry too much. The real plan is somewhat more sophisticated than what I revealed to you and Errol."

"You mean you're not going to swallow sachets of cocaine?"

"No."

"So why all that spiel about swallowing and shit?"

"For one, it tested your shock level. Secondly, to prove that the chances of me getting through customs like I said, is pretty high. And three, to see your reaction to my proposal on that level."

"I want *you* to be the brains in this… well, I want you to talk to the guys."

"Me?!"

"Bring them in slowly. Let them know that it'll be worth it. I'm a white guy. They won't trust me if I approach them. They'll think I'm with the pigs."

"Peter you are crazy. Who d'you think I am? Some ex-inmate from Bad Girls, Prisoner Cell Block H… Within These Walls or something?"

"Much more sophisticated than anyone from those clans." He looked deep into her soul as if he knew something.

"Besides, I wouldn't have thought these guys would need persuading… And why would they listen to me anyway?… a woman?"

"You're not *just* a woman. You've got balls. And I think there's more chance of these guys listening to a sexy, beautiful black woman, *with balls*, than a strange white man who they'll view as the enemy trying to sting them."

"So… tell me… if you are planning on trafficking so much cocaine… you have these briefcase brigades waiting to snatch top portions off your hands… why the little guys in Birmingham?"

"These big fish are in it for a one lick. I would like to build a little family, so to speak. To keep me going. Something I can control without getting directly involved with these guys."

"But I thought you just wanted to make one big lick and that would set you up for life?"

"I might well just do that. If I can't get the guys in Birmingham on board, and if the first drop with the big fish goes sweet, then I might just settle. These guys might not agree. You might not want to be in on it. So that part might not materialise."

"I don't know, Peter. This is *way* out of my dept…. I didn't realise you were planning on me getting directly involved. I haven't been back to Birmingham for years. I can't just turn up and start trying to recruit suppliers"

"Trust me. It'll work."

"That's just it. I can't trust you because you don't know if it will work. And even if you did… Bongo?… Garnet?… Me approaching them with… nah. That's not me."

"Think about it, Menna. If you want in, I'll explain more."

Menna emitted a cynical snigger. "Peter, I admire your bravery, but I cannot agree to join you on this… Christ, I'm a writer. I can't get involved in drug-trafficking."

"But you rob jewellery shops?"

Menna choked on a mouthful of Supamalt, spraying Peter face with brown liquid. She looked around to make sure her brother was right there at the poolside with his newfound chick. Not even *he* knew of the trick she played on Conteh back in Birmingham. "What?!" she whispered sternly, "Shit, Peter, who told…?"

"Like I said, you've got balls. Why else would I ask you to be in on this?"

"Peter," she whispered again.

"Why are you whispering?" he asked cynically, smiling at her vulnerability. And almost as if he had triumphed, he reached for a tissue and attempted to wipe away the brown liquid that was now trickling into the corner of the small slit he had for a mouth.

"Sorry I splattered you," Menna apologised, "You took me by surprise."

"I'd love to."

"What?"

"Take you by surprise."

She paused. "What the fuck are you talking about, Peter."

"Chill, Menna… No worries about splattering me. I should lick my lips, really," he amused. "I suppose that's the only way I'm likely to taste your saliva. You never know how much I've fancied you, Menna."

She gave him one of her looks. "Peter… are you coming on to me?" She wasn't sure what to address first: Peter's *'but you rob jewellery shops'* comment, or his blatant *attempt to hit on her.*

He smiled and ignored her question. "… And by the way," he said, "your secret's safe with me. You've kept this one real tight. I must say I admire your bravery…"

She sighed and tried to take her mind away from Peter's little flirtatious moments. There was a bigger matter at hand.

"… I called you here, Menna, because we've worked as business partners before… Men's Bodies Magazine… Black Star… But that was then. This is now. I know the way you think… well, maybe not trafficking, but there is a fire in your belly. You are strong. I thought you'd…"

She glared at him.

"...Well, never mind, just think about joining me on this. It'll be a good lick. Just think, you'll be rich forever."

"Is this blackmail, Peter?"

"No, just giving you a chance to be financially free."

"And if I tell you once more that I definitely don't want to take you up on your offer?"

"Then, no problem. I will just have to trust that my secret is safe with you, as yours is with me."

"Peter, I did what I did back in Birmingham because I was hurt. This bastard tried to take me for a ride. I took revenge by doing a robbery and planting incriminating evidence in his shop. They say revenge is sweet and I guess I wanted to taste it. And further more, if I didn't protect myself, the guy would have given me HIV anyway."

"He had HIV?" he seemed interested.

"Yeap. And for all who want to know, I don't think it's over yet."

Peter was still thinking...

"You bear a mean grudge, Menna," He snapped out of it. "You're not one to be crossed. Don't you think he's suffered enough? Let it go."

"No. Not until I see him suffer with my own eyes. *See* him cry. *Hear* him beg. *Smell* the fresh sweat from his frightened brows. He will be *touched* but cannot touch. And he'll *taste* me... one last time. *Taste* me. I'll have the bastard wishing he were lucky... *Fucka.*"

Her anger turned him on. Made his dick jump. But a drag on his nicotine stick was all the soothing he was gonna get.

"What's all that about? I thought he was in jail anyway?"

"Not anymore. They've released him. New evidence."

"So... how are you planning on..."2

"Never mind... you were saying?"

"D'know, Menna. Like Errol Dunkley said, *'every man do his thing a little way different.'* That was what you choose to do to satisfy yourself, and from the look of things, you're still not satisfied... I just want you to respect what *I* intend to do to give myself freedom from the rat-race."

"Not *respect,* Peter. I can't give you *respect.* There are innocent kids on the streets of England who will fall victim from the source of your preconceived idea to become rich."

"So... I take it you're definitely not in then?"

"No."

160

"Ok."

"And how can you find satisfaction in putting people's lives at risk?"

"Menna, I can find satisfaction easily in counting my millions. Didn't you expect to find satisfaction by knowing that Conteh was sitting in jail for a crime he didn't commit?... I told you before, Menna, I *will* make a financial killing... by *hook* or by *crook*."

"Ok, Peter, we've been there before with the Conteh shit, I ain't going there again, but I think you'll be hit with more than a pang of guilt with this one. And you better be careful about the *'killing'* you intend to make. Things have ways of turning sometimes when you least expect it. Your little plan might turn and you might end up in jail or something worse."

"*Maybe*. Just *maybe*. I'll cross that bridge *if* I ever come to it."

"One more thing, Peter?"

"Yes?"

"When did you become so..."

"Streetwise?"

"Yes... and callous with it too."

"The day the phrase *'money talks'* was a confirmed reality. The day my wife and girlfriend left me for men they thought had more money than I had."

"More *hard-earned* money. Glenda and Charmaine left you for guys who they *thought* had *hard-earned* cash."

Peter sniggered, and in his sniggering was a message.

Menna didn't ask. She was all talked out.

"... You mean as hard-earned like the cash that will be earned from this cocaine traffic?... Listen, Menna, Charmaine left me for a big, fat white guy who was at the receiving end of a cocaine run. How fucking *hard-earned* was that?... dirty money, clean money... it's still fucking money to me."

"You really believe that?" she asked him seriously. "You don't think that dirty money have no prosperity, whilst hard-earned cash will prosper?"

"Ok... tell me this, Menna... If you stumble upon a million pounds in the street..."

"Yes?"

"It isn't yours, you just found it in the streets, but you know that it is money from drugs, whatever..."

"Yes..."

"No one is around… you had no part in the *coming about* of this… dirty money, as you'd call it…"

"Uh huh?"

"You could walk away with this money with no hint of a trace…" he looked directly into her eyes, " would you *keep the money*, or would you take it to the police simply because you think it was *dirty?"*

"Well, that's different."

"How? The money is *dirty*. Full stop."

"Well, I suppose if I didn't rob anyone…"

"Tread carefully now. Remember you robbed a jewellery shop so you're not all that righteous."

"Yes, but it wasn't for my *gain* though, Peter. I didn't keep the jewellery."

"You *gained* satisfaction from Conteh's incarceration…. go on."

"What the fuck is this?" She could box him.

"Well?… would you take the money?"

"Yes. I'd take it… I'd take the money. Why not? I didn't rob it. I didn't do any cocaine run. I didn't kill anyone. It was just there. The police would only claim it after a while anyway, so why not?"

"So your problem is not with the *'moral hygiene'* of the money, just as long as *you* are not involved in the process of its illegitimate earning?"

"I suppose so."

"Another question…"

"Yes," she said, now with attitude.

"Your man is a drug dealer…"

"Well, I can stop you there for a start, because unless he's doing that shit without my knowledge, he wouldn't be my man in the first place."

"Ok. Say he was. He had bought you lots of nice clothes. Jewellery. Everything. Then later you find out where the money came from… do you give the stuff back?"

"No. Because I didn't know in the first place. But I probably wouldn't take anymore."

"Ok… that's all."

"Are you testing me? What's that all about anyway? The chance of me stumbling across millions in the street is a million to one."

"I just thought you were so righteous, you'd say you'd take it to the police. You've always been so fucking righteous. Always was. I noticed that from Key Chip."

"Oh… yes…" Menna alerted, "Key Chip… Now you come to mention it, did you ever hear anything from that shit that went down? Who the fuck tried to make me out to be a fraudster?"

"I don't think it was *personal*, Menna. Whoever did that was trying a thing. However they made the buck, they'd just do it. Fuck the person who would take the wrap."

"And that's what make my blood boil, Peter. To think that I could have been finished there and then. My credibility taken. Gone. Just like that. I'd rather go to prison for the revenge thing I did on Conteh, than to be branded a thief." A fresh anger rose inside her.

"Calm down. That was ages ago. You've moved on. Key Chip paid you a tidy sum."

"You don't understand, Peter. If I had gotten hold of the person who nearly fucked me up then, I would have killed he or she. And if I ever get the chance I'll still kill them!"

Blood rushed to Peter's face. He didn't expect such fresh anger to surface after so many years. "D'you know I suspected, Sharon," he asked.

"Who?"

"Sharon."

"Sharon?!"

"Well, she always worked late at the office. Lots of opportunities there to open a few fictitious accounts. She was the Purchase Ledger Clerk, for God's sake."

"No… I don't think… Nah… Nah… she came to work for me at Black Star after you left."

"*Did she?*"

"Yes."

Peter looked surprised.

"She even helped me with a little personal score we both had to settle."

"And did you… *talk* much about Key Chip?"

"Not much. In fact, looking back, every time I mentioned it, Sharon seemed a little uncomfortable, so I took that as a sign to leave it alone."

"*You see. I told you.* I think Sharon knew much more than she tried to let on."

"But *why* would Sharon try to set me up?"

"I don't think she would have been trying to set you up. Like I said, it wouldn't have been personal. Just trying a thing. She was always hard-up, remember?"

"Peter, that don't make sense."

"Why not?"

"Large sums of money had been paid out to these fictitious companies for five years. If it was Sharon, why would she be always hard-up?"

"D'know. To take any suspicion away from the situation I guess… just in case the situation should come to light."

Menna started to think. She traced every step in her mind trying to revisit all Sharon's moves. Could it have been her? The last time she saw her was when she bade her goodbye and thanked her for pulling off that incriminating orgy with Nico and Conteh - with the help of her friend Melissa.

"Do you still keep in touch with Sharon, Menna?"

"No. We exchanged mobile numbers, but it's been a while. Besides, the last time I rang her, the number was dead."

"I doubt if you'll hear from her again. Perhaps for the best."

"The best! If it was Sharon, I'll wring her fucking neck! I told you, if I get hold of the person who nearly fucked me up, I'd kill them! Sharon or not!"

"Hey… Menna… Calm down… haven't you heard of that poem that says…"

"Poem?"

"Yes, it goes something like…

> '*Go placidly amid the noise and the haste,*
> *and remember what peace there may be in silence…*

Menna allowed her anger to subside a little. Listening to Peter quoting poetic lines had to be a first. It didn't suit him, but the words were heavy… *until she realised.* "Placid?! Me?! Fuck placidity…"

"And what about the *peace that may be in silence?*'

"Stop it, Peter. Yuk. It doesn't suit you, all this… quoting poetry shit."

"But something suits *you.*"

"What?"

"*Anger*… it makes you beautiful. Turns me on… kinda."

"Fuck off, Peter."

"It's true," he assured her.

"You're crazy."

"I know you don't check white guys. Most black women don't. Stuck in their roots. Unlike a lot of black guys all over, who see nothing but white women these days."

Menna lifted an eyebrow. "And why d'you suppose that is, Peter? Seen as you know so damn much."

"Why do I suppose *what*?" he asked with confidence. "That the majority of black women are stuck in their roots? Or why the black man/white woman craze is sweeping like wild fire?"

"Tell me all, Peter. You seem to be the professor on it all. And since you seem to be up on the psyche of men from the African Diaspora, shoot… I'm listening."

He smiled at her sarcasm. "Well, it could be psychological… the black man's quest for white women over their own black women, that is."

"*Psychological*?" Menna played dumb.

"Yes. Even though these black guys don't know it, and will give you all the excuses they can find; most of them blaming black women."

"C'mon, Peter, tell me more."

"Well…" Peter climbed a high horse, "Let's look back at the story of slavery… the white slave-master, when he wanted sex, he used to say, *'Get me a wench'*. And it would probably be a black man who had to go fetch this slave – one of his own women… Yet this black man would look up at the slave-master's wife, knowing that if he so much as brush a single hair on her head, he'd be either flogged silly, or even hung."

"Yes?"

"But that isn't to say that the white woman, sitting up their on her pedestal didn't crave the strong, sturdy body of a black slave. It was just that it was a definite no-no… wasn't allowed."

"Yes… go on."

"So, for both the white woman and the black man, it was the *great forbidden*. And you and I know that when you deprive someone of something, when they get the chance, they will take it in abundance."

"Ok…"

"Nowadays, white women are available to the black man, ten-to-the-dozen. Times have changed. She is no longer on her pedestal, so the black man is taking what he didn't dare touch."

"Uh huh."

"In the case of the black woman now, it is the flipside of the coin. The white man was always forced upon her. Against her will. So now they have their own free will, the majority are choosing *not* to indulge."

"Is that so?" Menna played dumb.

"So, whilst the majority of black women would spend their whole lives looking for that *perfect black man*, black men have no problem choosing a white woman over them. To them, it is gold dust. What they couldn't have is now liberally opened onto them. In a way, they see it as a kind of... *Status*."

"*Status*?"

"Come on, Menna, don't pretend. Blacks know it, whites know it... ok, name all the black celebrities on TV, then show me a good handful with black partners... well, the English ones, anyway. American celebrities seem to be a bit different, though not entirely."

Menna stared at Peter. She had never heard a white man speak so openly about the subject before. Usually they would shun the subject. Get a little jumpy. Liken it to *chips being on shoulders* and shit like that. "I didn't know you were that deep, Peter?"

"*Deep?* Because I said the things everyone else is thinking? Check out the Chinese and the Asians, for example. They didn't go through the slavery shit, yet they aren't so quick to shun their women in such abundance. Yet, the black man who spent his whole life crying, *slavery!* Is now spending the rest of it chasing the daughters of the slave-masters."

"Are you sure you're not a black man in the body of a white man, Peter? And isn't your message a little mixed? You love black women."

"Of course I do. But you're getting me wrong. I'm not saying its wrong, and I'm not saying it's right. You asked me a question and I'm explaining what I *think* the explanation is... My reasoning on an obvious *scale-tipping* scenario..."

"Perhaps the Black man is tired, Peter. Perhaps he's tired of the *struggle*. Tired of crying when no one's listening... Perhaps it's about time he lay his burdens down."

"Everyone's got his own different reason for everything, Menna. A little way different, like I said. So understand me then... I'm tired of the financial struggle. Perhaps it's about time I lay *my* financial burdens down."

"I still say there are other ways than drug trafficking..."

"I've given up trying to persuade you… but I will say… although I know it'll be a *no*, but I'd like to take you on a proper date."

Menna looked around as if she expected to see another Menna in the room. "You… would like to take *me*… on a date?"

"What's wrong with that?"

"Er… nothing, nothing."

"Y*es*, Menna, it is *something*. Tell me… Either you don't check white guys, or you don't check *drug-trafficking white guys*, or…"

"Whoa! Can I speak for myself?"

"Feel free to turn me down, why not?"

"Give me your card, Peter."

"That's a start," he fished for his wallet, "here… this is my luxury apartment in London. You can call me anytime. In fact, you can turn up anytime. If I'm at home, I'll welcome you. I'm going back to London in two weeks. Then I fly back to JA two weeks after to talk to a couple of guys will be key players. Without them, the big delivery wouldn't happen. If everything goes ok, I should be back in London mid September to deliver the merchandise and collect my loot. Can't be too exact with time though, but call me."

"You really mean business, don't you, Peter?"

"Every last word, Menna."

She kept her eyes on his card. "I may well turn up for this date."

"Peter looked through her. He remembered how hard it was to keep from hitting on her back in England. He knew she was one of those *pro-black* women. Not racist. Just *pro-black*. Ain't nothing wrong with that. But he had hopes. *High hopes.*

A knock on the door told them Errol was back.

"One second," Peter said, glad for the opportunity to walk away that second. You see, he was *rising*. After all, Menna was *one sexy black woman,* and the thought of her coming to see him at his luxury apartment in London sent his thoughts racing. Charmaine might have been hot, but the thought alone of being between the sheets with Menna, would have him coming in his right palm for weeks.

* * *

Meanwhile, back in Birmingham, it was Faye's time to meet '*Mr Paper Rose*'. Apart from the Sunday afternoon at Evadney, these days, like Dracula, he only seems to come out in the dark, and it was at a petrol station in Moseley that she saw him.

"Hello, Sweetness," he chirped.

167

"Hi," she snarled. She might have taken Pierre off Bernadette, but she hated creeps, drop-dead gorgeous or not.

"I haven't seen you around. Are you new in Birmingham?"

"No. I was born here."

"Wha'?... How come mi neva si yuh before?"

She glared at him.

"Married?"

"What's it to you?"

"Just making conversation."

"Try the weather, my marital status is not for discussing with strangers."

He beamed at her sarcasm. "So a date is out of the question then?"

"Damn right," Faye said, wheeling her ass out of the petrol station shop.

The rose man felt a little put out. He wasn't used to rejections. In fact he didn't get many. He had the face to launch *'the opening'* of a thousand fannies, so I guess you could say, *'better luck next time, Mister.'* And that he could count on. *Most definitely.*

Chapter 11

"What time's your take-off?" Peter asked Lance as they sat sipping soft beverages in a secluded corner of the lounge in Kingston International.

"A good few hours yet. We have plenty of time to talk," Lance assured him.

"Heathrow landing?"

"Yeap."

"You could do this with your eyes closed soon," Peter said.

"I do now."

"A far cry from Handsworth Boys hey, Lance?"

"You bet. Those were the days."

"And you were gonna be a footballer. You were the best all-rounder in our year."

"You were gonna be a lawyer, Peter. So what happened?"

"Things don't always turn out the way we want them to. *You* were adamant you were gonna make a million by the time you were thirty. That didn't work out did it?"

"I suppose I would if I had made it as a Premier footballer," Lance said with a chuckle.

"I thought flying planes paid as much."

"It's ok, but not *that* ok."

"Still. There's hope yet," Peter said.

"Ok. Tell me more about this *hope*. What progress have you made on this operation? Two weeks is just around the corner."

"First things first, Lance… What about your fellow crew members? Have you spoken to them yet?"

"Not yet."

"Not yet!"

"Peter, this isn't like asking the guys if the want to pop out for a pint."

"Lance, you said yourself two weeks is just around the corner. You're either gonna try to bring them in on this, do it without their knowledge, or don't do it at all. The choice is yours."

"I don't know, Peter. If I decide to go with either of the first two options, I need some more reassurance that this thing is as safe as houses."

"Houses aren't as safe as they used to be anymore, Lance, so I can assure you, that is *not* the assurance you want. But I can assure you this operation is full-proof."

"Really? Even with Airport security being much tighter than it had ever been over previous years?"

"Lance, trust me on this. I've spent a long time perfecting this."

"So… you're telling me you have *perfected* the art of *the perfect crime*?"

"Near enough."

"Have you got the whole police and security forces here in Jamaica and in England on your payroll or something?"

"Not the whole. Just *some*."

"What?"

"Couldn't do it without, Lance. Everything will be tip-top. From the docking of the Columbian ship here in Jamaica, to the off-load of the merchandise in Britain."

"So why is it that with all your reassurances, I still feel that something's amiss?"

"I can't answer that. I can only assure you that everything will be fine."

"I still think there are too many cooks, Peter. How much can you trust that Errol guy? And that Baby Face Glen? How much have you checked them out?"

"Let's put it this way, these guys are small-timers. The money they'll be making just to move stuff from the ship to the lock-up in Kingston is more than they've ever made or will make for a very long time."

"Yes but what if things go wrong? How can you be sure than one of these players between here and England won't shop you? And how can you be sure any of these bent cops are in it to sting your ass?"

"Gut feelings, Lance. We all need to rely on a little *gut* from time to time."

Lance paused. "Two million is a lot to pass up. But this is risking my career. If things don't run smooth we're all fucked for life."

"Even if things go wrong, nothing will fall on your doorstep."

"Yeah? Assure me on this one."

"Just play the innocent. You know *nothing* about 200kilos of class A drugs worth £20 million being hidden in the roof lining of your 676's baggage container."

"As easy as that, hey?"

"As easy as that."

"And what about the speculation? The media and the people who won't believe me and my crew?"

"So you're going to tell them then?… your crew."

"Don't know yet. Lawrence is a straight kinda guy. Plays by the rules. Shit, this man won't even have a fucking one-night-stand even if there is no way his wife would find out, he's hardly gonna agree to be a player in a cocaine run. No way can I see him going for this."

"The thing is, can you see him passing up two million? That's the thing."

"This is Lawrence, Peter. Perfection walking. I'll have to think hard on this."

"What about the other guy? Clive?"

"Possibility. Tricky though. You can't really say until you put the situation to the individual. Talking about the subject lightly might be a way of testing the waters. We've had conversations like this before. Just in a bantering kinda way. And I pretty much know that Lawrence is set. Like I said, Clive is a possible. But the last thing I want is to suggest it, they don't approve and pull the fucking plug on things before it happens."

"Well, think carefully. Sleep on this. If you don't want to go through with it either with the guys or just yourself, let me know. There's another strategy, although this one is more solid. But you need to let me know pretty sharpish."

"So... tell me, Peter... how did you manage to persuade the authorities to get involved?"

"You mean, how did I *persuade a few bent people in authority* to get involved?"

"Yeah."

"Money talks, Lance. And when someone is already bent, he or she don't take much persuading anyway."

"Yeah, but how did you know how to make contact? How did you know who these guys were, etc?"

"Research. Over a year of research. Caution. Attention to details. Before you know it, you have a ready network. Like I said, money talks."

"Corruption at all levels, hey?"

"Lance, if you can show me a team of men in high places without a few bad apples, then I'll show you a man that's an island. There are bad apples in every high place you can think of. Corruption is everywhere. Even in politics. Of course these bad apples don't always spoil the whole bunch, but nonetheless, they're there."

Lance thought for a few seconds. "So... from the Columbian ship, to the lock-up, to the Aircraft, to its off load at Heathrow, to its despatch to its final destination...?"

"Yeap... What about it?"

"You see no mess-ups?"

"I see no mess-ups."

"And if it all goes ok, how can all us soldiers be sure that you won't run off with our cuts?"

"So now you're questioning my honour?"

"Put yourself in my shoes, Peter. I could hardly go running to the police to lodge a complaint."

Peter laughed. "There are people waiting to take it off my hands. No dribbles. Big swoop. The merchandise will be stored in a warehouse in London. Friend a mine. As soon as I get my money, the code will be sent to my look out at the warehouse. The merchandise will then be fork-lifted onto a waiting company truck."

"You'd get your money before they inspect their merchandise. I thought that would have to be a synchronised deal. How do they know they can trust you?"

"They do. *They know* that *I know* that they are *not* to be messed with. I'd have to leave the country."

"And then?"

"And then arrangements will be made for the payroll. Most of these are bent cops and security staff. Can you see me running off with *their* dough?"

"Sounds good."

"But if you do go through with it, Lance, have you decided how you're going to get this cash tucked away? I'm sure you know that with all this money laundering tightness, it won't be easy; you can't just walk up to the local branch of you bank and say *'can I put this in, please?'* Banks and trading companies are obliged to inform the authorities if they're approached with suspicious sums of raw cash. You can't even buy a motor with a whole load a cash anymore."

"So, what about you? How will you do it?"

"Now that's something else I'm trying to perfect. I have a friend. He's the business. Used him before for smaller things. I heard he's stepped his game up to beat the fraud-busters. I'll be putting him to the test again."

"Sounds like a 007 guy."

"There will always be people constantly trying to beat any new system the law might try to put into place. It's like a game of chess. Everyone tries to make a cleverer move. As soon as they find a way 'round the last loophole, financial gangsters find another one. Money makes the world go round. A sophisticated game of cops and robbers I'm afraid."

"Don't the thought of prison frighten you, Peter?"

"Yes. But so does flying. I still take the chance."

"Tell me, Peter," Lance looked him straight in the eyes now, "how the hell do a white guy from England manage to command such operation in the heart of Jamaica?"

"White guy, black guy, yellow… green…" he leant forward as if to drum home a point. "*What's the colour of money*, Lance?"

"I hear you… I hear you…" His thoughts pulled him away for a few seconds… 'Money… it talks… No doubt about that'…

Dirty cash. He wanted it.

* * *

'You fucking bastard!' She slurred, spittle flying all over the settee. *'You fucking piece a shit',* she spoke into the bottle as if her antagonist was swimming in the lethal liquid. *'I loved you, in the end, you bastard!... but you were ashamed of me... It was as if I didn't exist... You kept me in the corner... I must have been an embarrassment to you and your world... You fucking... fucking... fucking...'*

Glenda?!... Oh my God, Glenda?!" The faithful neighbour rushed in again. Why are you doing this to yourself?"

'I hate him... He never took me to any of his black functions.' She took a swig from the bottle. *'Yes, he could come to my functions... On my territory... I wasn't ashamed of him... But never once...'* She swigged again. *'Why d'you suppose that is?'* She looked for the answer in her neighbour's eyes, although she had convinced herself she already knew. *'My kids have black sisters and brothers... I doubt if they'll ever know them.'*

"Glenda," the neighbour pleaded, "Not in front of the children. They shouldn't be seeing you like this. And you can't keep on driving when you're like this. You'll kill yourself. Cause an accident. And the children... They're not safe... It's a wonder you haven't been stopped already."

'The bastard!' Glenda shouted, her children staring at her unbelievable sight.

* * *

When the Air Jamaica jet touched down at Kingston International, Lijah and Gloria experienced an inevitable dejavu. And though the door had not yet opened to let them out, a familiar heat surrounded and welcomed them.

"Are we in Jamaica now?" three-year-old Shanique asked.

"Yes," Khamilla, the assertive eight-year-old told her.

Only Festus knew the volume of nerves that danced within his belly. English-born, yet the *Jamaicanness* he had assumed for years would now be given a reality check.

This was the second time in years that Faye and Roy would touch the soil, smell the air or even feel the barmy breezes of the island of their parents' birth upon their faces. Faye, for one, would not fail to see Jamaica for what it was, *originally*: the island to which her forefathers were taken: off-loaded by a bunch of people-thieves who once went to Africa in search of wealth. Wealth that did not belong to them. And in their searching, they saw. And through brutal force, shackles and chains, they *conquered*. And in their greedy quest to own the world, they stripped these people of their African names, giving them their own. And still, in modern days of judicial rights, it is said that an apology is *not* warranted, since back then, slavery was *not* illegal. And Faye had long gone asked herself, *'how could the brutal dragging-away of a people from their own land, packing them like cargo into inhumane spaces with not even room to breathe, let alone sing the Lord's song be 'legal' in the first place?'*

Faye peered with her thoughts through the window of the aircraft as she watched dwarf-like men rallying around, ensuring the safe delivery of the set of aircraft steps. She wondered how many of them *knew* how they came to be on this now tourist-craved island. How many of them *realised* that their surnames bore no significance at all to the roots of their African ancestors, but to a bunch of slave-traders who mistook the *'colour of their skins'* for *'power beyond all powers?'*

Roy sat reading a paper to the very last. You would have thought he had another two hours flight ahead of him. He showed no urgency. And neither did the sign of the least anxiety spawn from his *'too-cool'* being. Perhaps it was his Air Force training. Or even that of the police force. *Keep a cool head even when the world about you is panicking.* Whatever it was, as far back as anyone could remember, Roy kept a cool head.

He kept a cool head when his mother Nettie argued non-stop with his father Lothan about his mysterious affair.

He kept a cool head all through his Air Force career.

When his blonde wife found out about Bernadette, filed for divorce, and rang him dry.

When he had come to realise that for a while his dick was delving into the same black-hole as his brother Lijah's. *Bernadette.*

And when his new woman Mitzi had discovered the existence of Bernadette, lashed out hysterically, slapping him about the face, she had not ruffled a single feather of his. Roy had simply restrained her and said, in a calm voice, *'I have no time for this, Mitzi. I'm gonna take a shower. I have to go to work. The streets of London are heaving with criminals. Not so long ago, there was another shooting.'* And then he kissed her as if nothing had happened.

"Home sweet home," Lijah said, even though he himself was a born-bred Brummie. But *home*, they say, is where the heart is. Lijah didn't know why, but his heart was always in JA.

Gloria smiled. Only herself and Khamilla could truly relate to the Island with the most familiarity: they had recently lived there for a good while. *'Baby Face Glen,'* she thought. And if she never set eyes on this dude again, it would be too soon. But *Kizzy and Fari?*... she couldn't wait to see them. Only it would have been good if she knew the trouble Kizzy was having with her man. And even better still, if she knew *who* this man was. *Lord have mercy.* Whatever happened to good old communication between friends?

Getting from the airport tarmac, through to luggage checks, then finally to the point where they could actually see their van, took the usual laid-back Jamaican time - *Totally tropical pace'.* Lijah reached out and touched fists with Renta, the chatty taxi-driver who took him all the way from town to country in his taxi on his prior visit to Jamaica. Luckily, he managed to link him again. Renta was a reasonable man, and Lijah trusted him to charge a reasonable rate, with no invisible extras added on – like a tyre bursting on his way to pick them up. Or a blown exhaust. Or anything that would make a few extra English pounds.

"Blessed," Renta said, addressing everyone. "Sorry yuh affi come to funeral, but ah so life go yunnuh."

"Yeah, yeah," Lijah agreed, while Gloria smiled, getting acclimatised again to the heat that was now thawing her winter-weathered bones.

Faye's reflection was somewhat lighter now. From thoughts of the descendants of a stolen people, her mind rested now on her first visit to Jamaica as a little girl: the pretty, unblemished feet she brought there were returned blemished. Mosquito-eaten. The bussing, blood-sucking insects knew fresh blood when they smelt, it and sucked mercilessly like a swarm of miniature Draculas. This time she came equipped with all sorts of lotions and potions.

But Festus was the quietest of them all. Had this been some time before his incarceration, he would have displayed a happy-go-lucky style. Now, he just nodded. And in his silence, like a reader would conjure up images of scenes in a book, so he conjured up an imaginary place where his mum Dora would be sitting at that very moment.

A most beautiful Jamaican girl around seven years old smiled at Khamilla and Shanique. Long artistically sectioned strands of her hair, caught by numerous rainbow coloured bubbles hung beautifully from her head and sat gracefully around her shoulders. "Hello," Khamilla said, but the sweet child withdrew playfully behind her mother's skirt.

Roy simply smiled a businesslike *'load-us-up-and-let's-go'* smile.

* * *

An hour and a half later, the van was negotiating the steep and rocky road towards Lothan and Dora's house.

Everyone but Festus was fast asleep.

The sound of the engine aroused a maaga dog that had lain dozing under a guava bush at the edge of his yard. The perturbed beast ran towards the van, barking fiercely and gnashing at it as if it knew no danger. At one time Festus was sure it was caught under the wheels of the moving vehicle, since after a thud, its tone changed from a masterful *I'm-defending-my-territory 'Wrah! Wrah! Wrah!'* To a *cowardly-panicky 'Harrr! Harrr! Harrr!'* Renta showed no desire to stop, and when, in his silence, Festus looked back in the direction of the disappearing *harrrings,* the skinny beast was scurrying away at the speed of lightening, glancing behind as if to make sure the offending vehicle wasn't following. Or as if it was saying, *'Bastard!'*

Now the racket seemed to have brought the van's other jetlagged passengers to life. Simultaneously, they lifted their sleepy heads and eyes to see pleasant old ladies with tartan head-ties standing with hands behind their backs, staring indiscreetly at the van-load of foreigners. They need no telling *why* they came. The whole village was part of the *death-celebrating life-mourning* event summoned by Lothan's passing. "A'right?!" some shouted as they waved.

They all waved back.

Festus in particular waved with meaning. He felt a strange *belonging*. Only he couldn't understand: England was his place of birth, yet it took a scattered bunch of laid-back waving villagers to make him feel that he was *home*.

Reflection.

Further up the road, a brood of clucking hens that had sensed the danger of an approaching mongoose made their way from the heart of a coffee grove to the safety of their yard. The *puck-puck-paaak!!!* from the frightened feathered friends seeped through Festus' silence.

Reflection.

Vultures circled the noonday sky making it known that they knew that some carcass lay dead somewhere. Festus watched their circling as they readied themselves to swoop down anytime soon.

Reflection.

A donkey was braying in a not-too-far distance. The van drew closer and Festus saw the grey, overworked animal. It had stretched the whole distance of the rope that hugged its neck at one end, and a coconut tree, the other. Festus watched it's wide teeth as it brayed, and wondered if it was a grin of protestation, or an expression of incarceration.

Reflection.

A cow mooed.

Goats bleated, echoing trembling bahs! around the mountainside.

Birds stole sweet nectars from ripened mangoes before they would fall to the ground to waiting children.

Camouflaging lizards gripped dry-grey tree trunks as if to show it *belonged* to them. Green ones perched threateningly, fore-legs hoisted, waiting it seemed to jump.

The odd pig or two grunted, wondering, one would expect, *when* their day of slaughter would come.

Reflection.

Festus had seen and heard it and assumed it all, but nothing could have prepared him for the strangest sight of all: *the sight of his mother, Dora.*

A mother he had not seen since he was just eighteen years old.

When he had left Bristol for the big city of Birmingham, with nothing but a *'grip'.*

When he had ran away from the sight of one too many beatings - his mother the recipient.

The sound of one too many denials, outweighed by showers of accusations: his father Montie spitting out one two many, *'Women cannot be trusted!... 'Pretty woman nuh good!... 'Woman is di root of all evil!* For that she was... Dora: *a pretty woman.* But Monte's condemnation had clouded Festus' eyes. To him, she was *ugly*, he beauty devoured by images of infidelity. *Ugly* since it was her betrayal that drove his beloved father to drink. And later, to assume the undignified post of *The Handsworth Tramp.*

Back in England, Dora had no chance.

The van pulled into a clearing adjacent house.

The morbidity they all expected was non-existent.

There was no weeping.

No wailing.

No gnashing of teeth.

Instead, a group of men sat around a table banging out dominoes, talking loud and drinking white rum.

Women busied themselves over bubbling pots, and if you weren't careful you'd be seasoned. Curried. Jerked. Whatever.

For now, Lothan's death was *celebrated.*

Later, maybe, it might be *mourned.*

Celebrate the dead and *mourn* the living was where it was at just then.

And now, Lijah saw them…

Four beauties and old friends of his: Judd, Dorr, Dawn and Paula. The last time he had seen them was the last time he had made the *kill-two-birds-with-one-stone* journey to JA in 2003. He wanted to sort a few things out with his old man in Point Hill, and to see his queen, Gloria and his daughter Khamilla in Kingston.

Now, the ladies clocked him and drew enthusiastically closer to the van, remembering that last time he had come *without* a girl. But now it was different. Gloria was larger than life.

"Whaap'n Lijah!" Judd asked confidently, as if no one else was around.

Gloria looked at the *woman of substance* that spoke to her man with more familiarity than *just good friends.*

"Tell me nuh?" Lijah reciprocated her question with a question. It was like dejavu.

"Is weh yaah seh?" Judd beamed a sunshine smile.

"Who's that?" Gloria asked through her teeth and in a low voice.

"A friend," Lijah assured her.

Now, all Renta's passengers were outside the van. Roy wiped perspiration from his brows and glanced discretely at Paula, who could give Bernadette and Mitzi long runs for their beauty. Dawn herself had not noticed Roy's desiring glances, but Dorr clocked him.

Now, Faye looked at a tall, slim man whose strong white teeth she had seen well before she saw his face. *'Smiler'*, she thought. But she looked away again when the woman by his side gave her a *'tek-yuh-yeye-affa-mi-man'* look.

Smiler was Leon: Judd, Dorr, Dawn and Paula's older brother. Back in the days, this guy could charm the hind legs off a stubborn mule. And with the dashing look to go with it, there were always rival worries! *Chat bout.* Leon was standing with his back flat against the wall of the temporary tent, built especially for the nine-nights' singing, drinking and celebrating. His left leg was firm to the ground and the sole of his right foot pressed firmly against the wall of the tent. The can of beer he held in his right hand added a kind of *cool* kick.

James, Leon's younger brother and another *fine specimen* of a man sat to his left.

Renta stretched and walked over to a nearby bush. He looked left-right-left right, undid his zipper and rolled out his dick as if it was a *too-heavy* weight of meat. Now, as if to mark a separate territory, he pissed a long, pressured piss that could have put the falls of Niagara to shame, sending a cluster of shama-macca bush into shame. The sound of the splattering showers against the innocent bush teased Festus' bladder.

He was looking at a woman that was looking curiously at him.

Minutes later, Dawn was looking at Festus' back, as he shook residual piss from his dick, protruded his ass, pushed it back into his y-fronts, zipped up and turned 'round to face the music, *in more ways than one.*

Festus knew it had to be her. *Dora.*

It was the eyes.

The same eyes he had always seen looking back at him each time he would look into a mirror: for whilst he had taken his susceptible nature and the ability to be tripped up by life's downfalls from his father, Montie, he had taken Dora's *eyes.*

But earlier, seconds before he had turned to the call of nature, Festus had put up that good old *front* as he turned a body glazed with a coat of *confidence* to the edge of the bush that Renta had previously christened with potent piss. And as he stared into the cluster of shama-macca bush, he wondered why they looked so sad. Pissing in a corner of an English street had never felt so *ok.* But, 'w*hen in Rome'*, he had thought… *'when in Rome'.*

Reflection.

* * *

A certain degree of anxiety was to be expected, but not even Festus expected this, so when the group of women left their pots unattended to hurry, scurry and fan Dora back to life, they all stood aside and waited for them to *make it ok.* Poor Dora's heart couldn't take the surprise, so her legs buckled beneath her.

Blood drained rapidly from her head.

For years Festus had told people she was dead, whilst she was live and kicking. And now, in a matter of seconds, he could have literally killed her with his *shock appearance*. That would have been the last thing anyone would have wanted. *Two deaths in one family... at the same time.*

When Dora was fully revived, accepted that her prodigal son had *come home* at a strange but *way-over-due* suppertime, they were left alone in the peaceful confines of a back room to talk.

Valuable years were lost.

No chance of them being found.

But it was a start.

The first day to the rest of their lives.

And a darn good start too.

Life is short.

Shorter then we all think.

And making peace with our loved ones is all too often taken for granted.

For Festus and Dora, the rest would be *history*.

History-In-A-Peaceful-Making.

Chapter 12

"Who the fuck is Faithlyn?!" Kizzy screamed at the top of her voice. "And how the fuck did she get my mobile number?!"

"Hol' yuh mout'!" Baby Face Glen retaliated, clenching the edges of his mouth to stop himself hitting her. "Is who di fuck yuh t'ink yuh shouting at?!"

"Listen! Is you mek yuh matey calling mi number yunnuh, Glen! Telling mi she's got you child! I don't need to be fighting over no man! So just go to her and all the others! I don't need this! Just fuck off!"

He glanced around. No woman had ever dared to talk to him like that. "Is weh yuh seh?" his eyes narrowed.

"You heard! Fuck off!" She turned her back on him.

Life, it seemed, had turned Kizzy into a warrior. Venomous words have now formed an intricate part of her vocabulary.

"Blow!" In a matter of seconds, Baby Face had swung her 'round and planted a thunderous box across her left cheek. Kizzy felt the immediate raising of her skin as the five fingers and palm of his heavy right hand wailed her tender skin. She held her jaw and looked curiously at him opened-mouthed and wide-eyed.

She was lucky. This was the first time he had shown her his true colours, but she had noticed his anger growing from strength to strength as soon as she started to tighten her purse string. Baby Face was kept sweet for a long time with the money from her bloodmother's Will.

"What the fuck yuh doing?" Kizzy had *seriously* acquired a new vocabulary. Wearing out the *F* word was not a habit she had intended to form. When she was a robe-wearing, head-wrapped queen, it was almost sacrilege.

Baby Face had turned his back now, feeling no way about laying another on her if she pushed her luck.

Kizzy's mind was catapulted to the last beating she got in England, some years ago from Festus. *"What did you just do?"*

Mi don' waan lick yuh again yunnuh, Kizzy. Jus' hol' yuh blood claat mout'!"

"Yeah?!... She walked towards him. "Yeah?!... You gonna *make me*?!"

He turned to face her. "Yuh deaf?!"

"Bastard!" Still she held her face.

"Blow!" The dainty lady lost her balance, stumbled and fell against the worktop in Mama Maya's kitchen. She was only cooling out there for the day. Her own house not so far away was spared the wrath of the violence. Mama Maya had gone shopping with Fari and Aunt Patricia.

Now, looking up at her man from her stepmother's kitchen floor, she felt belittled as he looked down at her as if she was a piece of shit. "Get out," she said as if her voice had lost its life.

"So wha'? Yuh gwine mek mi?"

"Get out..."

"Mek mi nuh!"

"Get out, Glen! Get out! Get out! Get oooout!!!"

Her screams rattled his already quivering cage.

Now, he curled the corner of his lips angrily, eased his right foot back, and was about to bring it forward with a bitch kick, when... "Not in my house! No! Not in my house!"

Oh yes... Mama Maya was back. Back to save the day. "Kick her an' yuh have to kick mi as well!" She placed her shopping bag on the kitchen floor and rushed towards her adopted daughter, pushing the evil antagonist out the way in her passing. Apart from her stinging face and her feelings, Kizzy was not that hurt, but still, she lay there on the floor. "Yuh a'right, Kizzy?"

181

"Yes… Yes, Mum. I'm all right.

But by the time Aunt Patricia trundled in with the rest of the shopping, the sound of Baby Face's engine was disappearing down the road.

"I warned you about Dat Bwoy dyam hurry-come-up bwoy, Kizzy! … I knew he was trouble! …He was only afta yuh money! What if I didn't come?!… He would have killed you!… Come… Get up…" she calmed. "Don't let Fari si yuh like dis."

But only Kizzy knew how much she *wouldn't* want her son to see her *down* again. She recalled that nasty day, back in England, when Festus had lost it. Her son's voice echoed in her head now… *'Mummy! What's wrong with your face?! Has Daddy been hitting you again?!'*… *'Don't worry, Fari,'* she had said. *'Mum is gonna be fine.'*… *'You wait 'till a get my gun! I'm gonna shoot Daddy! Shoot him! Shoot him! Shoot him!'*… *'Fari! Don't ever talk about shooting anyone! D'you hear me?! Ever!'*

"Mum!" Fari came running in, all excited. He had stopped down the drive to talk to his friend. "Mama Maya bought me a new Bob Marley T-shirt!" At ten years old, unlike most ten-year-olds in Jamaica, Fari was still a child.

"Good. You can wear it to country tomorrow. Uncle Lijah, Aunty Gloria, Khamilla and baby Shanique will be there." She kept the red-wailed side of her face away from him.

The two older ladies looked at each other and spoke through their silence.

"I know. I can't wait to see them… Didn't Auntie Ikesha come to her granddad's funeral?"

"No."

"Why?"

"I don't know, son. There could be lots of reasons. We'll ask Auntie Gloria tomorrow."

"It's gonna be a long way to country, man."

Kizzy smiled, though she had worries on her mind.

* * *

Lothan's burial service took place on the Saturday: three days after the posse from England had landed.

Chosen once again for his verbal mastery and his dry sense of humour, Venris White was ready to deliver yet another strong eulogy. As he stood there in his smart suit looking *out at*, *into* and *around* the crowd, he needn't ask how popular Lothan really was, but only *some* of the history of his life was of relevance to Venris: from Jamaica as a young man, through to more mature years in England, and then his returning to Jamaica to finish his days.

Speaking ill of the dead was not in the game of eulogies. Besides, if infidelity were all his sins, *he was a Saint*: if leaving his sweetheart in Jamaica and marrying another in England, even when the *other* was his brother's sweetheart, and also the best friend of his own sweetheart left in Jamaica, *he was a Saint.*

And if making love to a white woman, bringing forth a child (Kizzy) of whom his wife knew nothing about was another of his sins, *he was a Saint.*

And, if later, making love to his invalid wife's *new* best friend (Dora) as she lay in an invalid bed in the room above his head, her hearing the pleasure-filled sounds of his lovemaking was the other of his sins, *he was a Saint.*

And if Lothan were a *Saint*, there would be no ill to be spoken. God rest his soul, for he is just a man.

And even if he weren't a *Saint,* Venris would still eulogise him as being *'good'*. And the pastor would proclaim his as *'going to heaven'*.

Secrets. They are little packets of *hush-hush*, designed to be kept undisclosed either forever, or for a set period of time. But the tasks of keeping the *forever* ones are arduous. For it is a fact that *'if it happens in the dark, chances are, it is likely to come out in the light.'*

So... asked to realise, analyse and then criticise, what could a proverbial *'fly on the wall'* have told of the secret lives of everyone within? All these *'relatives from England'* that had come to pay their *'respects'* under the roof of this Jamaican church? ...

Take Gloria for instance: Back in England, in reaction to Lijah's infidelity (with a blonde Lucy, Faithlyn a seventeen-year-old babysitter from Jamaica and then his brother's ex-girlfriend, Bernadette), picked up with one Baby Face Glen, a notorious *gold-digging-woman-beating-get-rich-quick-seeking* dude from Jamaica. But Gloria did not reveal her secret rendezvous with Baby Face to her best friend, Kizzy, not even after she was living with him in Jamaica!

Then there was Kizzy, best friend of Gloria's: Whilst Gloria lived in Jamaica in the house she inherited from her mother Hortence Fontaine, back in Birmingham, Kizzy had ran to Lijah for a shoulder to cry on, and a listening ear, after her long-term man Festus (who needed serious therapy) had beaten her silly. Inevitably, Kizzy and Lijah, both lonely and hurting, fell into a moment of passion. *Gloria knew nothing of it.*

And too, whilst Gloria was in Jamaica, a notorious character called Rock, who could have passed for a relative of Baby Face Glen's, and who had already killed her son, Kunta, raped her daughter Ikesha with the help of the rape drug GHB. *Gloria knew nothing of this.*

And after Gloria had suffered from the brutal hands of Baby Face Glen in Jamaica, she fled with her daughter Khamilla back to England, only to find that Lijah was left with a *jacket that didn't fit*: Faithlyn, the obliging baby-sitter (who was the pivotal reason for their break up) had fitted him up with Rock's baby, Shanique. In their getting-back-together, Lijah and Gloria decided to keep the child. Lijah was, and still is, living under the spell of Bernadette's blackmail. *But Gloria knew nothing of this.*

And it was well before all that, that mixed raced Kizzy had found her blood-mother, Beatrice: a wealthy white woman whom, in her attempt to avoid shame, disgrace and condemnation, discarded poor Kizzy in a children's home, where Mama Maya who had an abundance of love to give, found her. And it was from Beatrice, that Kizzy found out *who* her real father was. *Lothan.* Lijah's father. Lothan had played away from home, yielding to the temptation of Beatrice, whose curiosity to taste a black man's dick was too overwhelming to control. But for Kizzy, it was too late. Her and her half brother, Lijah had already had sex. *Lord have mercy. Lijah still, even now, had no idea that Kizzy was his half sister.*

And Faye: Lived a good part of her life thinking she was Lothan's daughter, when in fact she was Lothan's brother's daughter. The man she had called Uncle Stan. For way back when, in Jamaica, her mother, Nettie was Stan's girl, but when she came to England, loneliness drove her to betray Stan with Lothan. In the meantime, Lothan had left his own girl in Jamaica. Mama Maya. *Sweetie:* who was Nettie's best friend! *Whole heap a passa-passa.*

So, as it went, Faye tried to run away from herself. She left for France, where life took an unexpected road: she found herself with her friend Bernadette's man, Pierre, a gorgeous Frenchman, who, as it went, turned out to be bisexual! *Oh Lord.*

And Roy: He too had his fair share of ups and downs.

Married a blonde.

Fucked about with his ex-girlfriend, Bernadette, who was fresh back from France with the weirdest mission to accomplish.

Roy's wife caught him, filed for divorce and rang him dry.

But all through this, Roy had Mitzi, a toffee-nosed bitch whose career meant more to her than her daughter, Shari, kept it going on.

And to add to it all, Roy later made a strange discovery: as he two-timed Mitzi with Bernadette, Bernadette two-timed him with his own brother, Lijah! *Heaven help them all.*

And Festus: *Poor old mixed-up Festus*: with whom Ikesha, after her terrible rape, had the strangest encounter. She had gone to her Godmother, Kizzy for a listening ear, not knowing Kizzy had left Festus. And Festus, at a low ebb, needing love and affection, had taken advantage of Ikesha's vulnerability. And in the heat of their passion, Lijah had rumbled them. Busted Festus' ass. *But Gloria knew nothing of all that either.*

And later, Festus took the right road to hell, only to realise that doing the night-shift in a *tyre-making, spirit-breaking, blood-sucking* company was a million time better than just one night in a prison cell with a *back-breaking, ass-piercing, spirit-stealing* sodomite called Conrad. What Festus needed was *help. Therapy.* Not added extras to his problem like the act of sodomy... Conrad. *Say no more.* But Festus knew, also, that justice comes in the most unexpected ways... If it *'goes around',* chances are, it is sure to *'come around'.* Sooner or later, Conrad's comeuppance will come.

And Mama Maya: *Poor Mama Maya.* Whose heart Lothan had broken, not realising that it would have affected her *forever.*

Mama Maya had never loved another man again... *ever.* No sir.

And Aunt Patricia: Made love to a pastor way back when, in England, resulting in the production. *Fiona, a bisexual female.*

Aunt Patricia, like Beatrice, gave her daughter up for adoption, and when the uncanny turn of fate manifested in her close friend Mama Maya adopting both Kizzy and Fiona at the same time, they both swore it was for a reason. A pre-written fate, you might say.

And Fiona's father?... *Pastor Fontaine* – Gloria's dad. *God rest his soul.* Father too of Grace, the beautiful ex-model Fiona had fallen in love with, only to later realise that it was *her very own sister. Lord, Lord, Lord.*

So Gloria had several sisters: Fiona and Grace were just two in a wide ocean of (as Pastor Fontaine must have viewed) *'insignificant others'.* But she knew nothing of it. Just of passing rumours. Worst of all, Fiona was Gloria's sister. Gloria was Kizzy's best friend, yet none of them knew *who, what, when, where* and *why.* The whole thing is as complicated as pieces of a jigsaw puzzle that had been mistakenly placed in the wrong box! And if you allow yourself to think too hard about it all, chances are, your brain might explode.

And then there was *Dora*:

The opportunist nurse with a sexual thirst. Well… she's human.

Dora was Nettie's friend, but Nettie had no sexual use for her husband Lothan, *then* a strong, virile, fine figure of a man. So, in the midst of Dora's sedative-assisted care for her leg-less friend, Nettie, she cared for Lothan by rendering that well-needed 'sexual healing'.

But when you add it all up and compare the reckoning to other happenings around the world, they weren't such big deals after all. For whether we want to believe it or not…. *'All our houses are made of glass.'* Chat bout.

So there it was. A church filled with ordinary people.

People who had chosen ways *they thought* were the best ways out of their own individual situations.

People.

Imperfect people.

That's all we are.

After all… Show me a family or an individual that is perfect, and I'll show you an Eskimo that goes shopping for ice.

Lisa and Camile King, two adorable sisters, blessed with voices of angels rendered songs to thrill all souls.

Only God, the dead and DJs can unite the living with such abundance.

Not that the latter could *ever* be compared to the Almighty.

There were no seats left in the church, and even standing rooms were seriously vied for.

Dora sat in the front row. Veiled in black, she mourned her husband, yet at the same time she experienced the strange feeling towards a son she had pushed from her womb one cold day in a hospital in Bristol, England.

Faye, Roy and Lijah were experiencing different levels of emotions, having attended their uncle Stan's (Faye's father's) funeral back in England a few years back.

Khamilla sat quiet, not liking the fact that her granddad lay speechless in a funny shaped box called a coffin, whilst Shanique, not blood-related, but still too young to know that, or what the whole service was really about, looked on.

Judd, Dorr, Dawn, Paula, Leon and James came with their respects and paid them with true reverence.

Aunt Patricia wiped a tear from her eye.

Mama Maya wiped a lot. After all, she was Lothan's original sweetheart. *Sweetie*. She had often wondered how life would have turned out if she had got to England before her friend Nettie. If only her father had sorted out her passage to England much sooner. But each time, the answer *'what is meant to be, shall be'*, came back.

Kizzy held her hand, knowing what she was feeling, although she still could not comprehend a love like that. Mama Maya must be one in a handful of women who had loved once, lost, and never tried again.

Lijah looked across the crowded church and saw Mama Maya's tears.

He reflected now on the conversation he had with his father a few years back. And it was only after putting a few things together, he had come to realise that *Sweetie* was *Maya*.

Lijah went there again in his mind:

'Dad... who is Sweetie?... Along with everything, I should have asked you long ago. Mum cried. Said she was being punished. Shouldn't have done it to Sweetie. What did she...'

'She told you about Sweetie?'...

'No, Dad. Not in details. She didn't tell me who Sweetie was.'...

'Sweetie was the girl I was supposed to marry, Lijah. She was my sweetheart. She was Nettie's bes' frien'. I came to Englan' wid di intention to send fi Sweetie. Nettie's faada sent for her before I could send for Sweetie. Nettie's faada died in a terrible accident at a foundry he was working. Nettie shared the same rented house with me and a few others. In those days, we who came, were all lonely, Lijah. All lonely. I was lonely an' Nettie was lonely. Plus, she was grievin' ova di deat' of ar faada. Well... all an' all... one t'ing led to di adda. We couldn't stop ourselves. We fell in love. She fell pregnant with Roy in 1957. I decided to do di right t'ing. Marry her.'...

'What?!... So what about Sweetie?'...

'I couldn't even tell her myself. Not even in a letter. I had to let her hear it through di grapevine.'...

'Isn't that a bit low, Dad?'...

'All of us do low t'ings in our lives, Son. Is your life perfec'?... Son, when yuh live inna glass-house, yuh should neva t'row stones'...

'Sweetie lived in Birmingham?'...

'Yes, Son. Sweetie is closer dan yuh t'ink.'...

'Wha' d'you mean, closer than I think? Do I know her?'...

'Son. I've suffered enough. I'm old now. None of us are perfect. Let me just have me last days in peace. Don't ask me any more questions. I hope God has forgiven me, Nettie, Dora... everybody. Di Bible seh He is a merciful God...'

So Lijah had known that this was the lady Lothan told him about: the lady that never marry. And there he was. Her first and only love. Lying motionless in a morbid coffin.

Kizzy was now looking Lijah's way.

The remembrance of their passionate encounter was so vivid it unnerved her.

She wanted to *wish* and *will* it away.

But most of all, she wanted to change the fact that Lothan is as much her father, as he was, Lijah's. For although unknowingly, they had incestuously copulated.

Festus was sat in the row behind Lijah and his family. He had crossed the *Dora* bridge, but the *Kizzy/Fari* one was still to come.

But as he sat there watching his mother, he remembered his father, Montie again... *'Died on the streets of Handsworth. Buried in a pauper's grave. Does Dora know?'* he asked himself as he watched her falling tears and the dignitary proceedings of *'the respected dead'*.

* * *

It didn't seem long before the sun sunk low, then eventually disappeared beneath the horizontal mark of the tranquil Jamaican sky. The evening brought a welcomed chill: just enough to cool the excruciating heat that had prevailed all day. Currents tripped in and artificial lights took precedence over the natural daylight.

Owing to the vibrancy of the merry-making, it was hard to tell that someone had just been buried.

The temporary make-do tent was now heaving with people.

The veranda was packed with no place left to sit, stand or even promenade with ease.

The large stretch of concrete yard was heaving with people who had earlier filled their bellies with *curry this, curry that, jerk this, jerk that...* everything that you could think of that was worth cooking to nice-up the celebration.

The sound-system in the far corner boomed, helping to turn the sad occasion into a party.

Judd, Dorr, Dawn, Paula, Leon and James, the authentic residences of JA, along with a few others who had simply *'stopped by'*, sat around the edge of the concrete square yard having a conversation with Roy, Lijah, Faye and Gloria.

Festus, however, ceased the moment with Kizzy. For the longest time, they sat in an almost private corner, talking. Earlier, he couldn't tell her how sorry he was for treating her the way he did back in Birmingham.

"I know you might think this is prison-talk stretched out, Kizzy, but I'm a better man now. I did my time. All I'm asking is for a chance. Everybody needs a second chance from time to time."

"Festus, we've been apart for a long time now. Lots have happened in-between."

"Yuh have a man?" he asked, seriously wanting the answer to be *'no'*.

Kizzy paused, her mind moving to her face that bore the mark of Baby Face fingerprints not so long ago. "No, I don't. But he don't think so."

"*He,* don't think so?"

"We're finished. Well... I finished with him yesterday. But I know it's not the end of it. He's not gonna take it that easy."

"Didn't he treat you good?"

"No. He had women, Festus. One of them called me the other day. Told me she had his child... when I confronted him, he slapped me across my face..."

Festus looked away. He was the original *'pot'*. How the hell could he call Baby Face *'black'*?

"... And if Mama Maya didn't come," Kizzy continued, "he was about to kick me." Kizzy struggled to stop herself from crying.

"Kizzy... sorry 'bout dat." He wanted to hold her.

"Why are you sorry? You didn't make it happen... Mama Maya didn't like him anyway. You know how she can sense things."

"Like she sensed me?"

Kizzy said nothing.

"I wonder if she would ever trust that I can be a better man?" Festus asked desperately.

But Kizzy didn't answer that. Instead, she said, "I wonder why I have to attract the same type of men... you did that to me. Slapped me down... then put the boot in." Her voice trembled. "And I loved you so much."

Festus felt something warm around his heart. He knew she meant it. She had loved him deeply, but he wished she could have said *'love'* in its present tense, as opposed to *'loved'* in its past. He looked around. No one was looking their way. Everyone was occupied with his or her own little moment.

"Kizzy," I'm going to get therapy. I *know* I can be a better man. *Seriously.* I want you back. *My son... Fari.* I want to have him 'roun' me again, Kizzy."

Kizzy looked away. Fari isn't Festus' son, but what you don't know, won't hurt you. He loved him. "Festus... what happened? That robbery? Why?" She had always wanted to know.

"Kiz', I know I was over forty, but I was just a boy... believe me. I'm grown up now. I had a lot of time to reflect on things. I need that chance, Kiz'... *please.*"

Kizzy saw Fari walking towards them. Earlier, he was playing with a group of children by the clearing adjacent the house. As he approached, the DJ played Jah Cure's *Reflection*, and Kizzy wondered if Festus had requested it at that crucial moment...

> *Dah da da da dah die*
> *Dah da da da dah die*

This song took mi t'rough nuff crazy nights, in prison, Kiz'. *Nuff,*" he told her.

> *Behind these prison walls*
> *doing my paces, doing my time*

Kizzy hugged her son.

Fari looked at Festus. He was two years older than the last time they saw each other back in England.

> *Spending my restless nights*
> *Visioning faces, oh they are crying, crying*

Festus' eyes were almost filling up.

> *Prison a no bed a roses*
> *The levity it makes mi bawl*
> *I wish that Jah could come and take us back in time*

"Are *you two* gonna get back?" the handsome young boy with adorable locks asked his parents.

They both looked at each other.

"You've been talking a *long* time," he said, smiling.

Festus felt a twinge of hope. He didn't know what to say. There was a pause.

> *Cause I swear that I can be a better man*
> *Yes I swear if only you could understand*

"I hope so, son," Festus said, his eyes on Kizzy, searching, one would expect, for reassurance.

"What did you want, son?" Kizzy asked, not answering her son's question or acknowledging Festus quest.

"Nothing. Just come to make sure you're ok."

> *The faith in me shall set me free reflection*
> *The faith in me shall set me free reflection*

"Ok. Well I'm fine, thank you."

"Good," Fari said. "Are you ok, Dad?"

"Yes, son… yes… I'm ok." Festus wanted to treasure the feeling. It was an inexplicable one.

"Good," Fari said, turning now and running back towards the children.

> *Dah da da da da dah die*

"He looks after you, don't he?" Festus said.

"Yes. He does."

"So what d'you say, Kizzy?… To us." His eyes pleaded.

"Festus, we'll talk about this another time. It's not as easy as that."

He sighed. Relaxed. What else could he do?

And for a while, they sat in silence, Jah Cure still *telling*. Stroking his pain and killing her… softly…

> *Behind these metal bars*
> *To Jah Jah I'm chanting*
> *I pray for love divine*

I'm oh so sorry a man
Deeply I'm hurting...

Festus reached for her hand, and caught only her little finger.

The price ordained to be mine

Kizzy stiffened slightly.

Impossible to see the changes that I have made in my life
All they see is just the boy I left behind

Reluctantly, he pulled back.

And I swear that I can be a better man
Yes I swear if only you could understand
The faith in me shall set me free reflection
The faith in me shall set me free reflection

Dah da da da da dah die

Silently, they sat, talking only with their minds.

Don't judge me wrong
Cause now I'm stronger than I was before
I was young and unwise
Didn't you hear my cry
Impossible to see the changes that I made in my life...

It was ok.
For a while, at least...
But suddenly, it fell upon them all.
A blanket of unexpected darkness that is.

All... they... see... is... just... the... boy...

The sound system died.
"What's that?" Kizzy asked.
"Power-cut, I think," Festus said, not being able to see Kizzy, but for her shiny earring.

192

"Oh Lord. I don't like it," she said in a low panicky tone.

There was no moon, and the stars above were few, so there was pitch blackness for miles.

People panicked. Not that they weren't used to darkness, but it was just how long before light would return.

"I's a'right, everybody!" the DJ shouted, mainly for the benefit of the *dark-frightened* English visitors. "Nuh worry! Wi soon get powa again!"

People remained in their clans, talking, laughing and waiting for the moment of light again.

In the distance, Kizzy could see a glaring pair of eyes. "What's that?" she asked as it drew nearer. She was dead scared.

"It's a dog, Kiz'. It's ok."

"Nuh worry, Inglan' girl," a Jamaican man said, "I's only a daag!"

But seconds later, in the distance, the headlights of a vehicle of some sort could be seen and its labouring sound heard as it struggled up the hill towards the house. That was a bit of a relief for everyone. *Light.*

But not for long.

About thirty yards from the house, it stopped.

The lights went off.

It's engine shut off.

"Heye, sah!" the DJ shouted in jest, "come closa nuh! Whoeva yuh is!… Wi need some light up yasso!"

But nothing.

On the other side of the yard, Gloria was panicking. She didn't like it. Neither did Faye, Khamilla nor Shanique.

The men acted like soldiers, camouflaging their fears with laughter and chit-chat.

And then… something sinister.

A figure lurked suspiciously in the dark.

Why didn't he or she speak?

A cool breeze ruffled the leaves of a nearby tree.

Dogs barked as if to warn of the approaching menace.

"Oi!" Another man near the sound box shouted. "Is who yuh?!"

Nothing.

"It mus' be a duppy or a gunman!" someone joked, but it really wasn't funny.

Then, someone produced a flashlight and turned it towards the spot where the vehicle had pulled up.

Kizzy thought she saw someone hiding behind the big mango tree, but she couldn't be sure. This was country in Jamaica. Pitch-black darkness meant just that. *Pitch black darkness*. And with stories of duppies and shit like that... well."

"I'm gonna try and find my way to the house, Festus. I don't like this," Kizzy said.

"It's just as dark as outside, if not worse," Festus told her.

"Yeah, but it's inside. I'll feel safer there... Fari?!"

"Yes, Mum?!"

"Are you ok?!"

"Yes. I'm just sitting here waiting for the light to come back on!"

"Gloria?!"

"Yes, Kizzy! We're all fine."

A burst of laughter spread over the place. "Unnuh English people 'fraid a dark eeh?" someone joked.

But no sooner had his flippancy thinned out into the air, there was light.

"Yeah, man!" the DJ shouted, whilst everyone else emitted their own elation.

Jah Cure was back in form as the speaker box pumped.

But... that wasn't the end of the drama, for when Kizzy looked around, a new figure had appeared beside her. *Baby Face Glen*.

The world is a small place, and Jamaica even smaller.

Finding her was no problem.

He had heard she was at a funeral in Point hill, St. Catherine, and had driven all the way to see what she was up to.

"Glen?" Kizzy perplexed, her heart beating. "What are you doing here?"

Glen looked at Festus and wondered why the two of them were sitting alone, and not in a bunch like everybody else.

"Why? Mi not welcome 'ere?"

"How did you know I was here?"

"Nuh worry 'bout dat." He pulled on his spliff and glanced at Festus with squinted eyes.

"Mum! Are you glad the light's back now?" Fari came running back. "Hello, Glen," he said when he realised it was him.

"A'right big man?"

"Was that you in that car?"

Glen didn't answer. All he wanted was to talk to Kizzy. Alone.

Festus felt the vibe. He got up. "I'll leave you two alone," he said, walking towards Lijah and the others.

"Whaap'n, Festus?" Lijah asked when he got there. "Sort out?"

"Well, look like ar bwoyfrien' come, Bredrin. Di lurka in di dark."

A sense of curiosity got Gloria. She hoped Kizzy would bring him over soon. They all looked in the direction of Kizzy and the mysterious *boyfriend*. And too, they all detected that all wasn't well. Kizzy's defensive body language and the way she was talking didn't seem like someone that was *pleased to see her man*.

Lijah looked closer. *'No... it couldn't be... no... not Baby Face'*, he thought. "G?" he alerted Gloria.

"Yeah?... what is it?"

"Is that *who* I think it is?"

"Who?" She couldn't see properly.

"Look good, G. look good," Lijah urged," wanting company in his uncomfortable discovery.

Gloria looked. "Oh my God!..."

"I's wha'?" Festus asked curiously. "Who is he?"

"No!..." Gloria said, covering her mouth. "Don't tell me..."

Festus looked at Lijah for an answer.

Lijah didn't know where to start.

Everyone else sat staring curiously from Kizzy and Baby Face to Lijah, Gloria and Festus.

"I's who dah bwoy deh?" Judd asked, knowing that the anxiety was spurned by his presence.

"Long story," Lijah replied.

"I's who, Bredrin? Yuh know him?" Festus demanded.

"We both do," Gloria said.

"Yeah?... How?"

But the bangarang between Kizzy and Glen was now getting to a stage where help was needed.

"Only a blood claat disrespectful person would find his ass to a burial-yard to harass and manhandle a woman," Lijah hissed.

"Get off me, Glen!" Kizzy shouted, trying to wrench her arm out of Glen's grip.

Festus was the first to move towards the scene. He saw red. And this *'red'* almost felt as if he was the only one entitled to abuse her.

Lijah followed.

Then Roy.

"Yuh nah leave mi a bombo claat!" Glen raved.

"Leave her alone?" Roy said, although he was a good few steps behind Festus and Lijah. His police instinct kicked in, but this was Jamaica. Not Britain. Baby Face was a bad bwoy and wouldn't have given the slightest of a damn.

"So wha'!" Glen let go of Kizzy and muscled up to Roy who was now in front of him. "Yuh gwine mek mi, *Missa Englishman*?"

"If I must?" Roy told him in that cool but firm voice.

"Come den nuh! Come, yuh likkle blood claat!" He was up in his face now with a vengeance.

"Kizzy?!" Mama Maya came running from the house. "Lord have mercy!"

"I don't want no trouble," Roy told Glen, still calmly. "Just don't manhandle the lady. It's my father's funeral. We don't need any trouble."

And only then, as Glen glanced around at the others, that he saw and recognised the familiar faces... Lijah... Then Gloria... Then Khamilla.

He spun now like a gig.

The wind went from his sail. Just a little.

A few other Jamaicans had gathered around.

They all looked at him. Stared him out.

He stepped back without saying a word. Back... back... back... then he turned to Kizzy and shouted, "Yuh t'ink mi done wid yuh yet?" he kissed his teeth. "Mi nuh done ah bombo claat!" He made his way back towards his car.

The crowd that had gathered round the scene was now dispersing.

Minutes later the crowd settled again into the event of sending off Lothan in *peace*.

But *peace* wasn't the word, for when the *rata-tat-tat* of a lethal weapon chilled the air, panicking screams could be heard for miles.

"Faada, help us!" Dora pleaded.

"Heavens above!" Mama Maya shouted.

"Blessed Jesas!" Aunt Patricia joined in.

Then, the starting of an engine followed.

Then the moving away of the lurking vehicle.

Fari gripped his mother's hand tight.

Festus didn't know when he had done it, but he found himself holding Kizzy. *Tight*.

No one was hurt. Lucky for them, the bullets were fired into the air.

And when Gloria had caught her breath, she looked at her friend. Her eyes said, *'We need to talk.'*

She knew, but Kizzy didn't.

Share and share alike, so the saying goes. But this sharing ran deeper... Same dicks, different tricks... *Lijah*... *Baby Face Glen*. As it went, they had both been eating from two familiar bowls.

So all in all, this was no simple passa-passa.

Passa-passa times ten was more like it.

* * *

Menna stretched, wiped the sleep from her eyes and yawned - almost like a lioness...   She had England on her mind.

She fumbled through her closet, clawing at a mound of classy garments, which should not have been mounded at all, but hung in an organised sequence the way they always used to be.

Like the song, she found her *cleanest-dirty* shirt, though not *'dirty'* in the sense of the word. It was worn once, but Menna wasn't in the habit of wearing her garments more than once before the next laundry. However, Kelly-Ann her helper had been ill. Tomorrow she planned to *do-it-herself*.

She showered, spruced, then stumbled out to meet the day.

After filling her glass with cool coconut juice, walking to the veranda and placing her ass on the wicker chair, she sighed, cast her eyes over bordering Lignum Vitae. Now, she fixed them on the blue skies.

Like her thoughts, the sun was rising.

And there it was again...

Like a mocking song...

In the distance somewhere, she could have sworn she could hear him calling...

Conteh. His voice echoed through her head like a *fresh* and *happening* nightmare.

Blame. It had long gone found a place in her head to dwell.

Asses. There were a few to be kicked. *Still.*

Funny... she was missing *something*...

Suddenly she felt the void... those good old revive dances Father Jarvis used to put on.

Her feelings were mixed now.

'Hello, Birmingham,' she thought... *'How are you?'*

197

* * *

Baby Face Glen jabbed the air with bony, evil, women-beating, trigger-pulling fingers. The big metal bird that took his girl, Kizzy and her son, Fari away, seemed to laugh mockingly at him through teeth of steam as it took to the open skies.

Glen had floored his gas pedal to catch her after hearing of her plan to visit England, but he was minutes late. As far as he was concerned, Kizzy was planning to leave his silly ass for good: then, the purse string would be well and truly cut.

"Yuh wait till ah ketch yuh bombo claat!" he lifted his head and spoke to the sky, as he watched the aeroplane becoming smaller and smaller. Aboard was the whole England posse. Kizzy had planned to take the journey back with them a few days after the funeral. The talk she had with Gloria helped her to make that crucial decision. Selling her house in Jamaica and moving back to Birmingham might just be what she would do, for it was obvious that Jamaica was never gonna be big enough for her and Baby Face Glen. It was a thought.

She loved it in Jamaica, but the only way she would be able to live there in peace now, is if Baby Face left the island. But she knew he had no plans to leave. He was already deported from Britain a while back, so that wasn't going to happen. Besides, he didn't seem to have two pennies to rub together. The taxi service that he ran went under after he was caught in some drugs thing or the other. Whatever other pending scheme he had bubbling was of no interest to Kizzy.

It was past time she shaped it.

Chapter 13

Innovatively it sat on a delicate glass shelf in their elegant bathroom… Beautifully gift-wrapped, she knew her husband was being a *sweetie* again…

A Diamond necklace fit for a princess.

"Where have you been all my life?" Simone whispered to herself as she admired the expensive piece of jewellery.

"Mum, look what Daddy left me!" Amari shouted. He had woken and had come to find her. "An aeroplane."

"That is so sweet," Simone said, averting her eyes from her own precious gift and admiring the miniature model of a 767 jet.

"What's that?" Amari asked, looking at the piece of jewellery his mother held in her hand.

"A Diamond necklace, son. Daddy left it for me."

"Ahhh… you can wear that to a ball."

"I know… I can."

* * *

"**H**appy?" Evadney asked Garnet as they sat over plates of ackee-an'-salt-fish garnished, with steamed callaloo, accompanied by slices of hard-dough bread, fried dumplings and salt-fish fritters. *Auntie Carry's* kitchen had nothing on this.

"Yeah, man," Garnet replied, easing a portion of delicious ackee onto the corner of his bread. He took a bite. "Happy isn't the word, Empress," he chomped happily.

"Evadney looked closely at him. "Yuh love yuh Jamaican food, don't yuh?"

"Wha'?" he said reassuringly. "Den nuh mus'. It's di best."

She was still looking at him. A question swirled in her head, but she wouldn't ask it the way it wanted to come out. Instead, she rephrased it… "When was the last time someone cooked you food like this?"

"Mmmm…" He tried to remember. "Yuh was di las' one to cook mi food like dis, Empress."

"So long ago?"

"Yes." He chomped on a fried dumpling now.

Still, she looked at him.

He noticed her intense stare, paused and said, "Wha'?"

"Nothing… did you have a good sleep last night?"

"Lovely, 'Vadney…" he took a sip of *'real'* hot-chocolate, *Jamaican style*. "Lovely. Your bed is so comfortable. Whe' yuh seh it was? *Aatapeedic*?"

She nodded. "Orthopaedic, yes."

I've been missing out…" he bit into a fritter and wondered what had *really* gotten into his head when he left her… Then he remembered… Tracey had put her mouth where Evadney's had dared to tread. *Heh-heye!* Oh the calling desires of the carnal flesh.

For the first time since Evadney had told him she was taking him back, Garnet had stayed the night with her. *No sex*. Said she was holding out until the wedding night. Garnet was just getting used, one would suppose, to what would be his *permanent* new dwellings after the wedding day.

Or perhaps she wanted to show him how *luxurious* it could be in her solely-acquired house…

The warmth of her bed…

The bounce of her stair-carpet after he had walked nude from her shower…

The touch of her soft, cared-for hands, nimble fingers tipped with modern, well-manicured nails…

The newly acquired fragrance she had smoothed over her toned body…

The way she moved in bed: *New. Innovative. Sensual*…

Maybe it was to give him a taste of the *'new woman'* she had become…

Or maybe she wanted him to taste the joy…

The joy…

The joy…

The joy of having her back

"Pleased with your suit?" she asked now.

There wasn't much left on his plate. Two mouthfuls if he was lucky. "Yeah man, Empress. Pleased wid mi suit. But even more pleased wid mi new *bride-to-be.*" He squeezed her right knee.

"And I hope *I'll* be pleased with *my* new husband," she said with a look of *'hope'* in her eyes.

"You'll see, Empress… you'll see." The last mouthful off ackee greeted his taste buds. "Bwoy, 'Vadney," he shook his head and chewed happily, showing his appreciation to the end for her West Indian culinary expertise, "Dis is one a di t'ings mi did miss 'bout yuh. Yuh cook *sweet*." The man was in heaven and a satisfying belch wasn't far off. *Belly full*. And if he a fowl, he would be wiping his beak on the ground.

"I can't believe Tracey didn't cook you breakfasts like this *every* Sunday morning?"

"Well…" he leaned his head coyly. He was searched for an answer.

"Just make sure Gongo take care of that ring." She cut him off as if she already knew the words he was struggling to find. "It isn't cheap. I know that cut *deep* into your savings." She smiled.

"Nothing's too expensive for my Empress." He pushed a truly empty plate aside.

She stared at the empty plate and wished the saying, *'the way to a black man's heart is through his belly'* was completely true. Maybe it *used to be*. But nowadays, everyone knows that that shit is as worn as an overstretched elastic band. Good food plays a big part all right. But there is something else in the mix. A crucial ingredient. White women know it. Black men know it too, but they're not telling the black women what it is. Could it be that its no use telling her since she don't have it anyway? The mystery of it all will stay as hidden as the Kernel's recipe.

Now, Garnet stared at her, feeling pleased that she had finally warmed towards him. He was becoming relaxed.

Although he didn't get not'n, last night was good.

Real good. Just cuddling her was heaven.

He had tasted 'the other' grass, but one thing he knew for sure, he had no desire to go no place else again. No sir. This time he pledged to keep his ass quiet. Stay put.

Yeah man, Garnet was home-to-roost.

Comfy.

He was almost '*born-again*'.

In fact, the dread was *glowing*. His flowing locks were swinging with a difference now. And if you listened carefully you could almost hear the sound of the swaying strands: they hummed like the branches of a willow tree... er... or could it be that they were *weeping*? You see, willows weep. Oh yes... *they weep.*

* * *

It seemed like forever since Angie sat patiently waiting for her friend Menna to emerge from gate number 11. Previously she had watched flights taking off and landing.

Butterflies fluttered in her belly.

She had not realised how much the anticipation would get to her.

It had been a while since that infamous ritual *'burning'* in her back garden. That infamous day when Menna had attempted to *'leave all memories of Conteh'* in a pile of ash. The *red silk sheets* he had introduced to her bed were gathered in a *less-than-adorable* pile, along with desperate, irate, nasty, *cussing* notes from Conteh and Nico: Notes expressing their anger at being given a taste of their own medicines. Even now, Angie would smirk every time she remembers the shrewdness and balls of her friend. Being two people at once in order to get the better of two guys took some balls, and Menna had it. *Real*

201

balls. Angie herself was not at all adventurous like that, but just being around Menna, or any *woman of substance* for that matter, would excite her. Menna had a definite *'Don't fuck with me'* style. One that must have been lying dormant for a while, and Conteh seemed to be the final *'tipping of her scales'*. The last straw. Like she had said to Angie at the time, *'The bastard has just pressed the wrong fucking button.'*

So, *'the burning of her sheets'*. Menna had told her it was a *'transition from the past'* so to speak, and Angie had agreed for her to do it in her garden. But when Menna laid a single red rose upon the pile of silk, poured the paraffin over it and set it alight, admittedly, at *that* moment, Angie wondered if her friend had lost it. Especially when she took the trouble to analyse the way the flames had changed the once-beautiful silk into a dark, useless pile of *nothing*.

Angie got up and started to pace up and down the waiting area of the airport lounge, but it wasn't too long before her wait would end. She looked towards the entrance to gate number 11. Droves of black people trundled through:

Some looked like real fresher Jamaicans.

Some looked like American blacks who had wandered onto the wrong flight.

A few older black couples pushed high trolleys that looked as if their contents were too heavy for their wheels to withstand. It seemed they had brought the whole of Jamaica back.

"Hey!" A lady with a chic pair of sunglasses over her forehead shouted. She looked like Whitney Houston *when Whitney Houston looked like herself*. She was waving frantically in Angie's direction. Angie turned and looked behind her to see who this woman who had just stepped out of vogue magazine was waving at.

"Ang'!"

Angie looked back towards the woman, still unsure. Christ it had been five years. *Shit*. It *was* Menna. Jamaica had done her real fine. She had topped up her God-given tan and sported a fine hue. She wore a thin, black, sleeveless dress that hugged her body like it had no intention of letting her go. And where did she get that chic hair-do? *Damn*.

As Menna came closer, Angie rushed towards her. She would hate to make a fool of herself by rushing to hug a stranger.

"Menna?!" She hugged her. "Girl yuh look good. No wonder yuh didn't wanna come back." Angie sounded blacker by the day.

"Angie," Menna pulled away to look at her friend. She held her at shoulder's length and looked her up and down. "What you done to your hair?"

Angie's hair was kind of... *burgundy*.

"I dyed it, silly, what d'you think I did with it?"

"It's great. But girl you know black men prefer blondes."

"I see you haven't lost your sense of humour, Menna."

"No... Whatever else I've lost, I need a little bit a that to keep me sane."

"Shall we get a coffee?" Angie asked, anxious to do the *sit-chat-catch-up* thing.

"Why not?" Menna agreed. "Let's find a patisserie, there are enough of them around here."

Like ebony and ivory, the *rootsy* chick and the *English rose* trundled off to find cups of warm wet beverages.

"Is that all the luggage you brought?" Angie asked on their travels to find coffee.

"You know me, girl. If it's not needed, don't take it. If I could have thrown my passport in my handbag and head for the airport, I would."

"You would?"

"Yes. But you know... us ladies need clean nickers. *Daily*." She laughed out loud.

Angie laughed with her. They were just outside the entrance of a fine looking patisserie. "You haven't changed, girl," she told Menna... "C'mon. This one will do."

* * *

"So tell me, Ang'," Menna said after they had ordered coffee and some damn expensive cakes that looked as if they could be blown away like farts in a wind. "What have *really* been going down in Birmingham since I left? I've heard a few little bits from my sister Cynthia. She has been trying to keep me up. You know her. Don't miss a trick. But lately I've been missing out on the real deal.

"And you think *I* know the *real* deal?"

"For all you know, Ang', you might know the most important thing, but don't even know that it *is* the key to all."

"Yeah, right... I'm that same reserved white girl you left back in Birmingham, Menna. I'm not an expert on what goes on in the black community. Especially now since Roy and I are finished. I don't really go to any reggae dances anymore. I went once with a black girl from work, and the looks I got from a few women… well, it was as if I was there to take their black men away."

"Your coffee and cakes, Madams." A fine figure of an Italian waiter placed their coffee and cakes on the table. *"Enjoy,"* he said, almost as if to *garnish* his service.

Menna paused and looked intensely at the handsome man, who couldn't help but return her mysterious stare. In fact, she made him nervous.

"… Not as much as my friend would like to enjoy *you*," Menna cooed, something cynical going on in her eyes.

"Menna?!" Angie blushed and so did the waiter.

"Nice aftershave by the way," Menna said assertively now, "what is it?"

"Jean-Paul Gaultier," the handsome man said, still blushing.

"Mmmm," she replied, looking into his eyes and stirring her coffee, her right leg draped over her left, managing to exude a sexy-classy look. "I bet he's not as sexy as you."

"Pardon me?"

"*Jean-Paul Gaultier…*" She lowered her head, sipped her coffee, but kept her eyes raised, maintaining a now hypnotising eye contact with him… "I bet he's not as sexy as you."

"Menna?" Angie said under her breath, leaning slightly towards her. "What have you been eating in Jamaica, girl?"

"What's your name then, handsome?" Menna relented.

"Mario." He chuckled.

"Nice name, *Mario*." She bit into her croissant. "And what do *Mario* do for a living?"

"M*e*?" He looked perplexed. "I'm a waiter. Can't you see?"

"No… I mean for a *real* living."

Mario smiled nervously and in his urgency to leave, he turned away from her.

"Mario?"

"Yes?" He turned back.

"Have you ever been to Birmingham?"

"Birmingham?… No… no I don't think so."

"Oh… Ok, you just look a little familiar."

"Sorry, I have to go. I have other tables to serve."

"Sorry, Mario, I didn't mean to take up so much of your time. Thank you for the service."

"No problem."

Menna watched Mario and detected the curiosity lines that furrowed across his forehead.

"Menna, what was all that about? *'Have you ever been to Birmingham,'* Angie mimicked. *'You just look familiar'*... my ass. What chat-up lines?"

Menna smiled almost mischievously.

"I can't believe you, Menna. Poor Mario."

"And *what* may I ask can you see *poor* about Mario, Angie?"

"Well, I don't mean *poverty* poor, I mean…"

"You mean *woman-takes-the-upper-hand-and-chats-man-up* kinda poor?"

"Menna, I haven't seen you for five years, you call and say pick me up from the airport, I pick you up, you spent the last ten minutes chatting up an Italian waiter and…"

"…And *you* need to lighten up." Menna sipped the last of her coffee. "I have strong instincts, Angie. Trust me. I was a journalist remember."

"Meaning?"

"D'you want another coffee? Or should we just hit the road to sunny Brum?"

"I suppose we'd better hit the road, traffic and all that. And you'd better put this coat on. This isn't Jamaica you know. This is England. Those designer sunglasses won't be summoning any heat waves. Trust me."

"Damn right," Menna said, taking the Cashmere coat from Angie and standing up to get into it. "Back in a bit," she said, stretching her left arm through a sleeve.

"Where you going?" Angie perplexed.

"To see Mario. It would be rude not to tip him."

"You've definitely eaten something in Jamaica. You have always had fire, but you have never chased men like that."

Angie smiled now as she watched Menna flirting again with Mario.

"Knows what she wants," a handsome hunk of a black man said to Angie. He had been sat watching Menna's play and wishing *he* were Mario.

"Sorry?"

"Your friend. A real go-getter. Know what she wants. Not many black women are like that. Not English black women anyway. That's why they often view white women as easy. White women see what they want and go get it. A black woman now, she sees what she wants, plays so damn hard-to-get, the go-getting white women whips what she had wanted from under her nose." Mr Observer ended his statement with a high-pitched laugh, the end of which Menna came back to catch.

"And what about you?" Angie asked him, "Do you like the go-getting type?"

Menna was now listening tentatively.

"I must admit," the hunk replied, "I'm a bit old-fashioned... I do like old-fashioned girls. I believe if a woman chases *one* man, she'll chase *as many* as she can. And the one-night stand thing? As long as I'm single, I'll take it, yes. I'm a man. But I would *never* dream of marrying a woman that let me have it on the first night... 21st century or not." He released his Sunday Times to answer his mobile.

"I see you've pulled, Angie," Menna took the chance to joke.

"Actually, no. He was talking about *you*."

"*Me*?"

"Yes. He was watching you flirting with Mario. Said you're a real go-getter."

"*Really*?" She turned now to the brother who had now finished his call. "Perceptions can sometimes be deceiving, you know. I was never good at getting what I want on the men front. Especially when it came to commitment. The ones I met had always had other commitments. Like *marriage*."

He chuckled. "That's the cry everywhere, Sis'. I must admit, men are weak. But then again, perhaps God shouldn't have made women so appetising I suppose." He chuckled again.

"What about you? Are you married?" Menna asked.

"Was. We got divorced. And before you cast judgement, Sis', no, it wasn't my fault. I came home and found her in up against the work-top in my kitchen with my brother."

"Oh dear... so sistas are getting down with the hot stuff, hey?"

"She wasn't a sista. She was a brunette. I know black women only call other black women sista. But before that, that same brother's wife, (*a sista* by the way), booked a dirty weekend away with her white boss whose wife would have sworn blind her husband had never, or had no wish to taste the exotic fruit. So you see, everyone's at it."

"Ouch," Menna said, flicking her fingers flippantly. "Messy." She picked up her bag. "I hope I don't bump into your brother now. I would have known his life's story." She smiled.

"I doubt if you will. He doesn't live in England."

"Good to know. I would hate to see your brother blushing."

"He's not the blushing type."

"Have you and your brother made peace then?"

"No. We haven't spoken since then."

"Shame to lose your brother over a quick romp up against a work-top in your kitchen. You cannot replace a blood-brother, but women are ten-to-the-dozen."

"Women may be ten-to-the-dozen, but not *'good'* women. If that was the case I'd be settled long ago."

"I guess there's sense in that," Menna said, "but you will agree that losing a brother over a woman can never be worth it."

"There's sense in that too… Maybe one day I'll find it in me to forgive him. It's been a while, but I haven't found that forgiveness yet."

"It doesn't come easy, does it?… *Forgiveness*. Especially when you've been hurt to the core."

"You've got it. I suppose my brother had a touch of my father's weakness back then, when it came to women. My wife seduced him and he didn't have the willpower to say no.

"Sounds like someone I know. His father womanised and so he seemed to follow the same intense path." *Conteh* filled her head.

"But from what I heard," he continued, "my brother is a changed man. I hear he's very choosy with his women. Waiting for *Ms Right*, I expect."

"And he might find her. Where there's life, there's hope… I hope you find your *Ms Right* also."

"I doubt that, but if I don't, I guess I'll have to settle for *Ms Part-Right*." He beamed.

"Menna laughed. "You're funny. Anyway, nice meeting you…"

"…Vincent," he assured her.

"And don't worry, Vincent, I don't go around chatting up strange men *without a cause*."

"No doubt. We all have our needs. How better a *cause* can you get?" Vincent said with easy flippancy and Menna giggled at his quick-wittedness.

"C'mon, Menna," Angie urged, "let's go. Sorry, Vincent, don't mean to be rude but we have to travel to Birmingham."

"Birmingham? Wha'?… Been on the news a bit lately hasn't it. Like the Wild West I see. Nuff gun man an' t'ing… pure shottas dong deh."

"I shouldn't underestimate the gun *women*, Vincent," Menna said. "They exist you know. Believe me."

"Really? In Birmingham?"

"Not just in Birmingham, everywhere."

Vincent emitted a kinda pooh-pooh chuckle. "Gun women in Birmingham?" he patronised. "What a somet'ing?" he bantered like an old Jamaican man, though he couldn't be more than thirty-eight years old.

Menna liked that. "You have a wicked sense of humour, Vincent," she told him.

"Makes the world go 'round," he said with a smile.

"I used to have a *very big* one," Menna told him.

"And you don't have one now?"

"Oh yes, I still have one. But it's not as big as it used to be. We should never let our sense of humours go completely... but my big one went to sleep a while back, and I guess when it woke up it lost some weight... Long story. Maybe it'll surface to its fullness again sometime."

"Sooner rather than later, Sis'."

"Yeah. Maybe as soon as you find forgiveness for your brother," she joked.

"Maybe." He smiled.

"Take care then, Vincent. Might bump into you again some day. It's a damn small world."

"Well, you never know. The last time I passed through Birmingham was a few years ago when. Vibes Injection was having a clash with David Rodigan and this other sound... *erm*... can't remember."

"Really?"

"Yeah. I didn't stay the whole night though. I was with a girl I met a few days before. I was staying at hers. She was ready to go so I had to leave."

"But I bet you didn't complain though. Had your oats early."

"Menna?!" Angie scolded.

"No," Vincent said with conviction. "Not that one. That girl was propa, man. I never conquered. Fiery though. I remember that. She was fiery, but had nuff morals. Said she would neva do a quick t'ing wid any man."

"What happened to her?"

"We just lost contact. Shame, cos I really liked her. Given time, she would have been the first woman I would have proposed to. It just felt right."

"So how the hell did you manage to lose contact with this *Miss Propa*?"

"I think she changed her number on me. And I'm not one of these guys to just turn up on a woman's doorstep unexpectedly. Besides, she had my number. If she wanted to, she could have called."

"Shame," Menna said. "Looks like your *chance of a lifetime* is gone with the Birmingham wind."

"Damn right... Funny though. A friend and I went to a clairvoyant once... just for fun. This woman spooked me out. I swear, she told me all about this woman. Told me that she was my soul mate. And that our paths are gonna cross again. And that it was going to be a second chance. Said I should take that chance when it comes and accept it for what it is: the chance of a lifetime."

"You don't really believe in all that paranormal stuff, do you?" Menna asked.

"Nah. As I said, me and my mate just went for fun. Spooky though. She told me about this woman as if she had sent someone to spy on us prior."

"Spooky," Menna said.

"Anyway, about a month after Birmingham, I left England... Got married."

"To the brunette you found in bed with your brother?"

"Yeah. And the rest is history... as they say."

"Gee. That's some story, and although I'd love to hear the rest, for the third time, Vincent, we must go. Besides, you could talk for England!" Menna bantered.

"So I've been told. But only when I feel comfortable with the people I'm talking to."

"My sister would love you. Or maybe not. You two would be competing with each other for the *talk-for-England* trophy."

"Is she married?... your sister?"

"No. She had never even come close either. Don't even know if she wants to. Good men are hard to find."

"You ladies always say that, but half the time you are looking in all the wrong places, accepting advances from the wrong guys and starting on the wrong footing, then months later you start shouting, 'Dog! Dog!'"

Menna laughed out loud. "You should be on the stage, Vincent. *Seriously*. But on that note, we *must* hit the road."

"To the *Wild West Midlands*, hey?"

"If you want to put it like that, yes."

"A'right, Sis', take care. Mek sure you drive carefully, yeah?"

"She will," Menna said, smiling in Angie's direction as they walked now towards the exit.

Vincent kept his eyes on them and couldn't help thinking how much of a good company they were.

Now, they were just a few steps outside the door when Angie asked, "So, do you have a date with *Mario* then? I saw you flirting even more when you went up to *tip* him, if that's what you call it."

Menna stopped to secure her handbag. "Angie, do you really think I've become such a big flirt?" she glanced back and found Mario looking out at her.

"Well…" Angie surmised, "you could have. They say time can change people."

"I'm still an old-fashioned girl on that front. Twenty first century or not, I still like being chased."

"So Vincent was right about you then?"

"What?"

"Nothing."

"Angie, I've seen Mario before."

"Have you?"

"Yeap… and he's no damn waiter."

"*Isn't* he?"

"No. I reckon Mario owns that joint and a load others."

"What makes you think that?"

"No man with such a gorgeous *everything* spends his days serving coffee to hungry passengers. It's a fucking front."

"Really?" Angie sparked, looking back in Mario's direction.

"Hey!" Menna scolded. "Where's your tact? Left with Roy I expect… C'mon, let's get to this car of yours."

"Oh, sorry," she toddled off when Menna tugged at her right elbow. "He didn't see me looking… so… what is his *behind-the-scene* job then? *Gigolo*?"

Menna laughed. "Between you and Vincent, you've had me laughing more in the past hour than I've done for five fucking years."

"So… *Mario*… who is he?"

"The Italian Gigolo," how about that?"

"Sounds great for a novel… oh, by the way, that novel, did you ever finish it? You could have written five in all that time you've been away."

"Damn right I have. But I don't know if any publishing house will be brave enough to put it out."

"Why?"

"Well, firstly, it's brimming with attitude… I go where other writes fear to tread. I say what people think and wait for others to say for them. It's too hot to handle, Ang'. I think I might have to publish it myself."

"Oh no… I'm having goose pimples already. I hope you're gonna let me proofread it."

"If you want to. But don't blame me for you wearing out too many vibrators. It is also brimming with hot steamy sex scenes. You'll be quivering at every page. Mary Whitehouse would have a nervous breakdown."

"Maybe I won't need vibrators. Not if my new date proves to be ok."

"Oh. New date, hey?"

"Yes. He's taking me out tonight, so we better get a move on."

"Well, I hope there won't be heavy traffic. I would hate your date to be messed up."

They reached the car now and Menna hoisted her *not too heavy* case into the back of the Estate vehicle. "If I fall asleep on the way, you won't mind will you?"

"No. You must be jetlagged. I'll just talk to myself," Angie bantered. "I'll keep asking myself who *Mario* is. And maybe if I ask long enough, I'll give myself an answer."

"Yes. And the answer will be, *'Italian Gigolo'.*"

"In your own time, Ms Jarrett. I know how full of mystery you can be… talking of mystery, I didn't get a chance to meet that Nico you were seeing."

"You didn't, did you?"

"No I didn't. One minute you were seeing him, the next he was…"

"You haven't missed much. Apart from him being a good looker and a knock-out between the sheets, that's about it."

"He really fell for you didn't he?"

"So I believe."

"Both he and Conteh."

"Both he and Conteh..." Menna paused for a bit. Almost like a frozen computer screen.

"Are you ok?" Angie asked.

"Yeah... fine." She finally pulled her seatbelt across her chest and fastened it. "Let's leave those two alone. Tell me about your new date."

"Who Ricardo?"

"I don't know? You're supposed to be telling me."

"Well, let's say, I'll tell you about him after our first date."

"Go girl," Menna said, reclining her seat in readiness to relax. "Anyway, like I said, I hope you don't mind if I have a snooze."

"Anyway," Angie said, "if you fall asleep, how are you gonna get the low-down on Birmingham? You talked so long to Mario and Vincent back there, it was as if I didn't exist."

"Oh sorry. *Mario* was a *must*, and *Vincent*? Well he was just a loveable parrot. Laad di man cyan chat." The broadest patois took over. "But don't worry, we'll catch up. Besides, I don't want to go straight to my flat. We'll go to yours. Need to see if that burnt patch is still there littered with the ashes of red silk sheets."

"Your mad girl," Angie told her.

"Mad is good, sometimes," Menna said. "What time is your date anyway?"

"He's picking me up at eight."

"Oh, we'll have plenty of time. Don't want to get in your way of turning into Cinderella... If that's possible."

"You cheeky thing, you." Angie put her foot down.

* * *

They had both lost track of time, and before they knew it, it had flown by. However, Menna managed to leave Angie enough time to get ready for her date with *Ricardo*.

As she emerged from the taxi, she paused to take a good look at her old surroundings. It felt a little strange. Weird even. Perhaps she shouldn't have come alone. Not for the first time anyway. Good if her sister Cynthia was around but it wasn't to be.

As the taxi pulled away, she shrugged off the heavy rush of nerves that bubbled in her belly. It was inevitable. And again, for about the hundredth time, she reminded herself that pulling off a robbery, planting the evidence: gun and all on your antagonist, boarding a flight to Jamaica to watch the waves while your antagonist stew in jail, didn't happen every day. She was a good black woman whose scales had been drastically tipped by the wrath that love can sometimes bring.

She looked around her.

Lots had changed since she left.

Five years is a mighty long time. Untold things had happened in one, let alone the five long ones she had spent away from her flat. Her sister Cynthia had promised her she would look after it until she decided to return, but when six months turned into a year, a year into two, and when Menna decided to get Cynthia to sell her Mercedes sports and had the money wired down to her in Jamaica, Cynthia decided that her sister didn't intend to return anytime soon. And since she was spending more time in the luxury flat than she was at her own house, and since Menna was paying mortgage for a place she wasn't co-habiting, she decided she may as well live there. Menna wouldn't entertain strangers living in her place, so Cynthia rented her own place out.

For some time though, luxurious as it might have been, Menna's flat didn't come with the added luxury of *peace*. For a whole six months after Menna had left, Cynthia had to put up with nuisance visits from Nico. His best friend Conteh was doing time for a crime Menna had planned, committed and fitted him up with. Menna had peppered both their sorry asses with a clever trick. Nico wasn't going to give up so easily, so the bitter Jamaican Indian had become the soul member of a *search and destroy* crew. Chat bout.

It took a long time to persuade him that Menna had left the country. The visits ended eventually, but not without the help of West Midlands Police. Harassment is a crime. *Period*. And besides, Cynthia had decided to *keep* her sister's flat, but she was most certainly *not* her sister's *keeper*.

Now, Menna entered her flat.

She paused in its entrance.

Before she attempted her living-room, she was pulled to her bedroom. She stood gazing at its plushness that Conteh had loved so much. Cynthia had decorated, but she had not diverted much from Menna's taste.

And now... *Dejavu*. Menna remembered how she had pulled, in anger, the red silk sheets from her bed. The red silk sheets that Conteh had loved so much. The ones that wrapped so nicely around both their bodies.

She didn't realise that the memory would surface with such strength.

The memory of his touch, that is.

His *sweet* kisses that had at one stage become *bitter.*

She thought the feelings would be a nothingness. But she was wrong. So terribly wrong. There they were... the memories... in her face... in her space. Pulling at her mind like magnet would, steel.

She hated him now.

Hated him for making her a slave to his memory.

She walked to the living-room casting her fingers against the walls of the corridor as if to tell them she was here. A vase filled with beautiful flowers stood like a peacock on her coffee table. She smiled and warmth filled her belly. A note leant purposefully up against it: *'Hi, Sis',' it read. 'Welcome home. It must be strange, but take your time. There is rice-an-peas and chicken in the fridge. I only cooked it yesterday. The chicken is yummy, even if I say so myself. Should be even nicer now it's a day old with all the seasoning soaked in. (Smiley face). I would have liked to have been there for your arrival, but you had to go and change your date. As I said, I had already planned to visit Tricia, an old school friend in North Carolina. I hardly told anyone you were coming back, so you should have some peace. Time to settle in. PS. Thought the flowers would be welcoming, seeing as I'm not there! Luv. Sis'. Cynthia.'*

Menna couldn't help thinking how thoughtful her sister was. She hadn't changed. Always had her best interest at heart. Good old *'Mother Hen'* Cynthia... in the nicest possible way.

Menna left the TV alone.

The silence was great just then.

She placed her ass on the new settee. Cynthia had mentioned in an email that she was going to get one.

From her sitting position, she looked around her living-room.

Calm.

Peaceful.

The aura of the room was soothing...

But not for long. For as she leant back to relax and get used to the fact that she was really home, the telephone rang. It startled her. It was either Cynthia calling from North Carolina, or someone calling for Cynthia.

She eased forward and picked it up. "Hello?"

"Hello," the male voice at the end said.

"Hello?" Menna said again with apprehension.

"Hello."

"Who is it? Are you after Cynthia?"

"No… I'm after *you*, bitch!"

"Who *is* this?!"

"Yuh lef' yuh memory inna Jamaica?" the attitude-laced voice said.

"Nico?" She stood up.

"Yes, yuh bitch yuh!… Welcome home, baby…. welcome home… time longa dan rope…"

"How did you know I was back?"

"Neva min'… long run, short ketch." His voice was tinged with a whole lot a vengeance now. Five years didn't seem to have changed anything.

"Haven't you got a life, Nico?"

"As it is, not really. Borrowed time… but not life as I used to know it."

"And what's that got to do with me?"

"Not a lot. But we have a score to settle, you and I."

"I don't think so."

"You *know* so, Bitch!!!"

Menna dropped the phone. *Literally*. It hit the wooden floor with a force that brought home all her fears.

The realisation had truly come.

She must face the music. After all, it was already in her face.

Face it like the woman she had become.

"Oh shit", she whispered as her ass hit the settee again. *'Nico'*, she thought, *'Nico… one of the flies I had flicked mercilessly from my soup. How the fuck did he know I was back?'*

After the blood had left her head, she breathed deeply, as if to fill her body with *'hear I come'* juice… magic, whatever.

She stood up, stretched, almost like Tarzan would beat his chest. She looked into her full-length mirror that adorned her living-room wall and beheld herself: *sex on legs*. And then, something filled her in abundance: a strong shower of strength. "Here I come, you bastards," she spoke into the mirror. "Here I come… I'm ready for you. May the better fucka win."

* * *

Angie woke to the morning melodies of singing birds… Something was in the air… *Love*, she had called it, and as far as she could see, and as deep as she could feel, Roy her ex could eat his heart out. *Ricardo* had laid it on her *real good.*

Getting up to have a shower last night after the steamy little romp was the last thing on her mind. You see, showering meant washing the memory of this *'pretty bwoy'* away.

But shower or not, there was no chance of his memory disappearing anyway, since it lingered there still…

Not just in the aroma of his aftershave…

Not the shedded strands of his hair that lay like a signed testimony on her pillow…

Not the memory of his warm tongue swirling around her nipples… her navel… her clitoris…

Nor the odour of stale sperm after the mishap of a burst condom…

No… Ricardo's memory was also in the sight of a slim, golden box… in which lay a beautiful red paper rose.

'Menna,' Angie thought as she gazed at the *scarlet token* through sleepy eyes. *'I must ring Menna. Now I can tell her all about my date.'* She rolled over and hugged her pillow tight…

'Paper rose,' she recalled his chants as he convulsed under the influence of a mighty climax, *'they are special…Oh!!… They never die… Oh!! They live forever… Ohhhhhh!!!!!…'*

Chapter 14

"*Hi*," said one attractive lady to another… Rackhams were where they were both at.

"Hi," Simone looked puzzled.

"I recognised you from way over there."

"Are you… *Marcia*?" Simone asked. She looked a little nervous.

"Marcia?" the attractive lady quizzed.

"Oh… just one of Conteh's…"

"Oh, *Marcia*. The lady that has escaped from the mental home? I *look* like her?"

"Just a little. Around the eyes."

"Then I guess there was something about the *look around our eyes* that drew him."

"You are...?" Simone was curious.

"Did she not come to your home one time?" She ignored Simone's question. "Marcia… Did she not attack you?"

216

"You heard that?... Who...?"

"Yes, I heard. But not from Conteh. Bad news travels fast, you know that."

"Yes... she did attack me. That was pretty scary." Simone still awaited enlightenment as to *who the hell* this woman was.

"No doubt... No. I'm not Marcia... I'm Menna..."

Simone stared intensely at Menna now. "You sent the video and the pictures?"

"Yes... but I'm not crazy. Not like..."

'*A face to the voice*,' Simone thought. "... Menna, Marcia isn't crazy. She's ill."

"Oh, Simone. Dear old Simone. You are so sweet."

"I might be sweet, but I don't like being patronised, thank you."

"No, I mean it. I didn't mean to sound patronising. *Nice* is good, Simone. But it doesn't suit us all. I tried *nice* once. Didn't work for me. But I can see it's working for you, so go girl."

"Well, I can't spend my life being bitter. Besides I've found happiness."

"So I heard. Men like that are rare, Simone. Hold onto him. Tight. Cherish him."

"I've never looked a gift horse in the mouth, Menna. As far as I can see, I have a precious man. I will cherish him until the day he gives me cause not to."

"You loved him didn't you?"

"*Loved* him?"

"Conteh."

"Of course I did... He was my husband."

"And now?"

"Why all the questions, Menna?"

"Sorry. How could I ask you that?"

"I don't hate him," Simone said with conviction. "We all have lessons to learn in life. I guess Conteh was one of mine."

"Damn right. And that makes for all of us."

"Conteh loved me too, Menna. He just couldn't say no..."

"...To fresh pussies?"

Simone laughed. For the first time in the conversation she felt relaxed.

"Babes, I'm just over here!" Both ladies looked towards the voice.

"Ok, Babes!" Simone replied.

"Your husband, right?"

"Yes," Simone chuckled. "Who else is gonna call me *Babes*?"

"From *bad* came *good*, hey?" Marvelling at how absolutely gorgeous he was, Menna kept her eyes on Lawrence.

"You could put it that way, yes."

She turned back to Simone. "But I suppose when you got that video and pictures of that infamous orgy of Conteh through your door, you thought, *'Bitch. Whoever sent this is trying to wreck my marriage'*."

"No. It hurt me deeply, but if I had heard about it and asked Conteh, he would have denied it, so I suppose it was a blessing in disguise that you sent it."

"My intention was not to be nasty, but I heard you were a nice lady. You didn't deserve to be strung along like that. Besides, look what happened. The AIDS thing."

"Yes. I wasn't all together stupid though. I protected myself. Took control in the bedroom. Conteh loved it, but I was just making sure he didn't come to realise I was using femidoms."

"You took control, used femidoms and he didn't catch on?"

"No… not once. I maintained control in the bedroom. He liked that, so it worked."

"Clever."

Simone paused. "Is this real?"

"What?"

"The ex-wife in conversation with an ex-lover."

"Yes," Menna said. "I suppose it's the *ex* that made the difference. If you were still together and in denial, this conversation wouldn't be happening."

"True." Simone could almost touch the overwhelming strength of Menna's personality.

"But your husband…" Menna said, looking 'round again at the hunk. "He's *drop-dead* gorgeous. Keep your eyes open. The world is filled with female vultures. Ravenous and ready to swoop down on men like that… married or not. Women with good men have to fight to keep them away from snatchers."

"I don't intend to fight," Simone said, half smiling.

"You don't?"

"No. If I have to fight to keep a man, it means he didn't want to be kept in the first place. As far as I can, I try to know him. Keep my eyes open, yes. Temptations will always come. It is up to the individual to resist it."

"Damn. You're one astute lady. You were too damn clever for Mr Vibes Injection, that's for sure."

Simone ignored the comment. "If Lawrence loves me, and wants to be with me, he'll resist all temptation."

"Hi." Lawrence was standing next to them now; his tall, virile figure covering them like a protective shadow.

"Hi," Menna said, wondering if God could make her one just like him. *Ouch*. She could almost feel him. Couldn't help imagining. *Mmmm*. What the hell? No harm in imagining. We all do it. And besides, any woman who couldn't *'feel'* this fine specimen would most certainly be lacking something. He oozed sex appeal.

"Darling, this is Menna."

"*Menna*?" he said, reaching for her hand and looking questioningly at them both for assurance.

"Yes," Menna said. "Just a shadow from your dear wife's past."

He chuckled. "Oh… I see…" There was a strong recollection in his eyes.

"Anyway, Simone, must dash. Nice meeting you…" Menna said.

"You too, Menna," the beautiful Simone said.

"Lawrence," Menna turned to him with intent. "Your wife is a gem. *Know it*… but I'm sure you do."

"Sure I do," he told her.

"Anyway, I must dash." Menna said walking off and flittering her fingers to both of them.

"Is that really *the* Menna?" Lawrence asked as she walked away. "She sounds like a lady with a mission it seems."

"Yes… *the* Menna. And I suppose she could be on another mission. Who knows?"

"Babes, you never cease to surprise me."

"*Me*?… Why?"

"Just the way you two stood there chatting to her like old friends."

"Babes, you know me. Grudges and bad memories are like old wood. In order to move on, you have to cut them away."

"Whoa!"

"Besides…" she added…

"Uh huh?"

"If I was still carrying the memory of a bitter past, how could I put everything into loving you and our son?"

He paused as if the idea of her *loving him* was fresh news. He placed his bag of goodies in the middle of the store and kissed her.

"That looks so good," a voice said.

"Menna," Simone turned and smiled, "I thought you were gone."

"Very rarely seen," Menna commented.

Simone and Lawrence chuckled as they watched the attitude-filled lady leave for the second time.

* * *

"**We**'ll talk about North Carolina in a bit," Cynthia said as the kettle in Menna's kitchen boiled. "What have you been up to for the past two weeks?"

It had been only ten minutes after her arrival. Rather than going to her own house, she decided stop at Menna's. Earlier, the hugs and kisses were abundantly plenty as the excitement of seeing each other after so long could not be contained. It was so real, it was almost tearful.

"Nothing much... I visited Angie a few times... did some shopping... oh, guess who I bumped into?"

"Who?"

"Simone... Conteh's ex-wife."

"Really?"

"Yes. We talked."

"Did you?!"

"Yes... She's ok. Nice husband."

"So I heard. I heard he's nice looking."

"That's an understatement, Sis'. The man is *edible...fucking scrumptious."*

"Down, girl," Cynthia joked."

"No, he's solid. Looks like he knows where his bread's buttered too. He's a loyal man. I can tell."

"We all need one of them," Cynthia said. "Tea?"

"No. Yuh love too much tea. I'm gonna have a Baileys."

"And you love too much firewater."

"Oh..." Menna said reaching for her bottle of Baileys and ignoring Cynthia's comment. "you'd never guess who rang."

"Who?"

"You haven't guessed yet."

Conteh?"

"Nope."

"Who then?"

"Jamaican Indian."

"Nico?!"

"Yeap… Nico."

"What?! How did he know you were back?"

"Beats me."

"So what did he have to say for himself?"

"Some shit. In fact, I thought he'd turn up on my doorstep by now."

"Menna, be careful."

"I think you should be telling Nico that, Sis'. He doesn't scare me one bit. If he wants trouble he's come to the right place. I'm ready for the bastard. I have a plan and I'm gonna execute it… trus' mi."

"A plan?"

"Yes. I'll tell you in a couple a weeks."

"Charming. Keep me in suspense why don't you?"

"So how was North Carolina?" Menna asked.

"It was good. I'm planning another visit."

"When?"

"Not sure. I'll tell you as soon as I am. C'mon," she said, walking to the living-room. "I wanna hear all about Jamaica, your trip to Canada, Clayton… every dyam t'ing."

"In what order," Menna joked.

"It's up to you."

"Ok. There are some things I wanna ask you also."

"What things?"

"Remember Kizzy? The mixed-raced dread?… Festus' woman...?"

"Yeah…?"

"I saw her in Jamaica."

"Yes. She lives there now."

"So I realised… How come she left Festus?"

"Long story. Lots about Gloria and Lijah too. I know I told you a bit, but there are lots more… God, I sound like a right gossip don't I?"

"No you don't. Things happen. People will talk."

"True… Now c'mon… Clayton. Start with Clayton. Is it serious?" Menna sipped her Baileys.

"Serious?… D'know… I'm not sure…"

* * *

Sheree had lost the bounce in her steps for a while… Lawrence was simply not giving in to her *begging*.

221

She was obsessed with him and if only she could recognise it as a form of illness, she could seek help. Instead, she acted as if she had no life, spending most of her days spinning from hours of pining, to hours of erratic thoughts.

And it is a mystery why people who are hurting leaned foolishly into sad, heart-wrenching songs. Today, she lay across her settee with a G&T in one hand, *Tom's* paper rose in the other, and Lawrence on her mind:

> '*Don't leave me this way*
> *I can't survive*
> *I can't stay alive*
> *Don't leave me this way...*

* * *

The returning of her body to Jamaica was the least of the formalities… She knew the risk, yet she took it.

First she was petrified, the knowledge of the harsh penalties swimming around in her head… but she tried it: the *bravery* thing.

She felt the fear, but did it anyway.

A desperate measure that promise hope. But the only chance she had was a *hope-in-hell's* one, for the toll of a diverted and troubled flight had got her well before the sniffer-dogs at Heathrow Airport ever did. '*Keep your head up*', Baby Face Glen had told her. '*Look confident. Nuh badda gwaan jumpy-jumpy an' fool-fool. If yuh get t'rough, all yuh problems will be ova*'.

But now, a grandmother with hope-filled eyes waited in a tenement yard in Trench Town. A young baby torn away from the breast of her mother lay nuzzling at her breast. *Searching.* Searching for the familiar smell of his mother.

The other three boys kicked rock stones to pass the time. "Wi aggo rich, y'ear," the older boy told his little brother. "Wi aggo rich. Mamma aggo bring back nuff money from Inglan'. Shi gaan work fi wi." He backed off his mango-stained shirt and twirled it around.

"A lie yaah tell," the younger boy replied, "Jackfruit seh mama gaan ah Inglan wid *nuff* dope inna ar belly."

"Jackfruit?" he kissed his teeth. "Weh Jackfruit know? Yuh wait 'till mi ketch 'im. A gwine bus' 'im 'ead."

It was just one of the 60 small packages of cocaine that burst, covering the lining of Faithlyn's gut like snow falling for the first time

222

on tropical land. The other 50 packets lay there like the autopsy findings of her last meal.

650 grams of cocaine.

650grams of false hope lying in Faithlyn's stomach.

And now, the cry from her mother and children back in Jamaica would echo even louder:

> *Pavaty! Pavaty! Dis yah one yah name pavaty!*
> *Pavaty! Pavaty! Dis yah one yah name pavaty!*

May the Lord have mercy on her soul.

* * *

Not many people liked him… Even his mama had lost the will to care.

And there he was…

Heathrow Airport…

He had arrived.

Desperation was his driving force.

Desperation is a force that can drive a man to the gates of hell. And if he was already halfway there, it would not *drive*, but simply *nudge*.

He looked now, not *frantically* around him, but *nonchalantly* ahead.

Several aims.

Several journeys' ends.

Several fish to fry.

One destiny.

They asked him no questions… he told them no lies.

And so, like a mustard seed would pass through the eye of a storm, he breezed through HM Customs… *easy*… And like a triumphant magician, he mocked them. *'Fool-fool security'*, he had said as he grinned, strolling towards the exit of the busy airport, his thoughts… *'A fee! A fee! Passport for a fee!'*

Baby Face Glen. Who else? Yes, he had arrived.

Once again his feet had touched the *King's High Way. English* soil. His previous deportation? That was history… And on that *less-than-fine* day, a chill wind blew across the City of London… across England's plains… For from beneath the tropical skies of Jamaica, to that of suburban Britain, *he came*… But it was urban Birmingham that would feel his presence most. Oh yes. And if some only knew of his *'second coming'* they would shiver vigorously in their urban boots.

They would be very afraid... Lijah... Gloria... Kizzy... And *Lucy*. Yes... Dear old *Lucy*.

No, there weren't much loving waiting in the heart of Birmingham City for Baby Face Glen. But then the feeling was mutual. He too had brought none.

No... no love awaited him at all. Oh... sorry, except of course, *'the love of one lady'*: one calculating lady. So calculating that she had misread a *gruesome minus* for a *promising* plus. Yes. This lady waited unsuspectingly for Glen's sorry ass... the hope of *greener grass*. And that wasn't all: she waited too for his deadly hand... *in marriage. Holy matri-'Money'*... Lord have mercy.

But before Baby Face did anything, he needed to make a stop. His drug mule didn't make it and he needed an advance before the big deal that was pending with Peter Walker materialised. His intention was never to return to Jamaica. No sir. *Over his dead body*. So marrying a woman with English citizenship would seal his plans.

* * *

"Oh, Darling," Simone exclaimed to herself when she opened her wardrobe and found the most beautiful evening dress you ever did see. She gasped and could hardly get her breath.

They had seen it together in an exquisite boutique.

She had expressed her admiration for it.

And now, he had bought it.

Was she dreaming?

She held it up against her perfect figure before putting it on.

It was most definitely made for her.

Chapter 15

*S*ophisticated cocaine-detecting equipments were put in place... Tight anti-drug-smuggling measures vigilantly taken.

So how the hell did an unthinkable amount of Class A drugs pass undetected under the noses of Customs Officers at Heathrow Airport?

The answer? It's blowing mockingly in the winds of corruption.

While authorities waited for gang fights over the spoils of the proliferation of past hauls in the inner cities, 100kilos of class A drug, the street value of £10million had found its way to the safe heaven of Peter Walker's luxury flat in London. The harm and misery it would bring to umpteen people was not Peter's concern. All that concerned him was the fat proceeds that would line his pocket. And even after he paid his ferrymen, there would be enough for him to retire. An old money laundering friend would help him see to that.

Earlier, two Captains and a First Officer stretched their legs as they emerged from the confined cockpit space of a 767 aircraft. *One* of the Captains and the First Officer knew of the cargo they carried. The other, unsuspecting and innocent, had ridden unawares, on the waves of a wrecked career if the cargo was picked up by Customs Officers. The publicity would soar through the roof of the world's media. And what would his wife think? This captain knew nothing of it, so, innocently he cruised the M1 motorway with guys he thought he knew. Which one of these captains were in for a shock? Only time would tell.

Things aren't always what they seem.

> *Man to man is so unjust, children*
> *You don't know who to trust*
> *Your worst enemy could be your best friend*
> *And your best friend your worst enemy...*

* * *

"**D**rinks at mine when we get to Birmingham, guys?" Lance asked as his Land Rover Discovery cruised the M1.

"I'll see how I feel when I get to Birmingham," Lawrence replied. "I haven't seen my wife for days. All I want to do right now is to fall into bed next to her. You should do the same, Lance."

Lance shuddered at the thought. Lawrence didn't realise how much he had gone off Morag. *Literally*. He was sure she was having an affair, but proving it was another thing.

"She might not even be home when I get there, Lawrence. Our flight wasn't due back until tomorrow, remember? She wouldn't be wasting precious time at home. She'll be out... having fun. It's her birthday tomorrow. She usually start celebrating days in advance."

Clive said nothing. Instead he kept his eyes out the window as if the streets of London interested him. In fact his mind was on the unbelievable sum he was promised. *Just over a million.* A tidy sum. To him it was a dream.

"You and Morag need fix up," Lawrence voiced his reason. " Sort your marriage out."

Lance emitted a cynical, sharp spate of breath through his nose for a laugh. "It's you and Simone that put the *P* and the *M* in *Perfect Marriage,*" he stated. "Some of us have just given up."

Lawrence smiled and dismissed Lance last statement. "Wake me up when we get to Birmingham, will you? I'll tell you then if I'm coming to yours for a drink."

"You have to anyway," Lance told him. "You left your car on my drive, remember? And you too, Clive. You'll both be there anyway. You can't just shoot off like that, you might as well come in."

"I'm not sure about coming in," Clive replied. "I'll let you know when I get there. I have no wife to go home to, but I know I'll just be fit for my pit after this journey. Wake me up when you get there too."

"Are you two sure you're not brothers? Apart from the fact that you look so fucking alike, you are developing the same *'cat-on-a-mat'* ways."

"We can't be brothers," Lawrence joked, "Not unless Clive's mother visited Antigua in the past and copulated with the late Mr Hendricks. And I'm fine with my *cat-on-a-mat* ways, thank you. You see, there is a beautiful tabby cat waiting for me. Her name is Simone. Her furs are black, fluffy and shiny, and when she purrs against me…"

"Shut the fuck up!" Lanced said playfully.

"Well… I couldn't expect better." A pleasing chuckle followed Lawrence declaration for his wife, who at that moment slept like a baby in their marital bed.

Clive chuckled with him. "What was that idiot's name…? The one she was married to before?"

"Do I care what his name is?" Lawrence asked in a tired voice. "The man is an asshole, that's all I know."

"Ohhhh! *Bitchy*, hey?" Lance emitted.

"No, Lance. I don't bitch. I just state facts."

"Anyway, less of this," Lance said. "How come I drew the short straw to do all the driving then?"

"You're the most alert," Lawrence told him."

"That's true. I can't deny that. You two are becoming old men. Sorry I've got no fluffy slippers in the back there."

"Very funny," Lawrence said.

"No comment," Clive mumbled.

"And don't you be getting no cramps round there, Lawrence."

"I think I've had my fair share of cramps in the airport in Jamaica."

"Good. I can't be doing with lifting you out the car."

Lawrence ignored him. "So, no one waiting at home for you, hey, Clive?"

"No, mate."

"You may not have a wife, but surely you have a lady friend to drop in on? She can give your tired ass some TLC."

"Either that or tired me out some more," he said, almost in protestation.

"Nothing wrong with that. Your next flight isn't for a week… you have got a girl haven't you?"

"Women can be demanding to your bank balance and draining on your brain at times. Both financially and mentally depleting is no good."

"Financially?! Come off it, Clive, you're rolling."

"Yeah, right."

"You're single. Everyone knows that a flying profession pays well. It's just a pity more of us blacks don't take it up."

"Perhaps most brothers are frightened of flying," Clive said. "Well, as often as we do anyway." He laughed. "Anyway that's the least of it. Life's not all about spending money on women."

"I can't believe you've just bought a brand new Mercedes SLR and you're talking about spending a few pounds on a woman."

"A few pounds? I can assure you they cost more than that mate. A bloody bind too."

"If you have a woman that's worth it, it won't be a bind. I spend untold amount on Simone."

"Good for you. If she gives you satisfaction, why not? As for me, my car gives me more satisfaction than a woman."

"What?!" Lawrence laughed. "Are you serious?"

"Damn right."

"Tell me more about this car that is more satisfying than a woman then. Does it make love to you or you to it?"

Clive chuckled. "Well, you could say that… Apart from its cascading brushed aluminium exterior and sleek interior?" he rattled on, "And apart from the fact that it's automatic, has a 5.4 engine, 8 cylinders, 636 horse break power… maximum speed 334 and accelerates at 0 – 100 in 3.8seconds…? It's a dream. What woman is more exciting than that?"

"Yes, but can this *dream* car give you a good healthy orgasm?" Lawrence asked cynically.

"Oh, I get my healthy orgasms all right."

"*Palm*ela, hey? You don't wanna be using your palms too much you know."

"This conversation is getting out of hand," Lance joined in. "I thought you two wanted to sleep."

"Whatever you say, Lawrence," Clive said adamantly, "I still love my car."

"Your car sounds exciting," Lawrence added. "Though I think every heterosexual male needs a woman, even if it's just for sex. I will never compare a car to a woman. *However,* I would like to test-drive this car of yours... see if it's all it's cracked up to be."

"Any time, mate. Anytime."

"Wouldn't want one though," Lawrence hastened. "I'm not single anymore. Can't see Simone, my son and myself fitting in it. And anyway, I still think if the right woman comes your way, your car will take second place."

"Big *if* though."

"What d'you reckon, Lance?" Lawrence asked.

"Leave me out of this one, mate."

"Anyway, you've been quiet," Lawrence challenged. "You've only put two sentences into this car/woman debate."

"I've been concentrating mate," Lance said. "We have a good few miles to go yet."

* * *

In any given hour, in any one day, millions and millions of things happen in juxtaposition. Births, deaths, marriages, break-ups, lovemaking, head-kicking... you name it. But how likely is it that two deserving double-dealing love-rats would meet *'rather-be-dead'* fates at the same time? *More likely than you think.* Perhaps they were more than best mates. Perhaps they were more like identical twins. Some say one experiences pain when the other is. Pleasure too. Who knows?

For Conteh, this was a definite case of *'Bad Wednesday'*.

There was nothing left of the man to take, but still, like bounty hunters chasing a reward, they wouldn't leave him be.

He was HIV positive.

He had lost his mother.

Lost his wife.

Lost his dignity.

He did time in a hell-hole.

Fathered a child by his own daughter.

He was no longer King-inna-de-ring… but still they hunted him down like hounds to the call of a bugled horn.

Like vultures to dead meat they circled above his head, swooping down on him at every given chance, trying their hardest to pluck every last ounce of flesh from his already naked bones. *Women scorned.* Never underestimate them.

To start with, the quiet Wednesday afternoon quickly turned into a *not-so-quiet* night for Conteh. The neighbours to his left decided to have the biggest Barney of all, and he was convinced they would eventually come through the wall and into his living-room. Thank God Gladys didn't have to go through this. She had passed before the fiery couple moved in.

It was the same old story. Someone had been cheating. It always ends in tears. Break-ups. Loss of trust. It's true: *cheating is a thing that's sure to bring two unhappy people to a point of no return.*

His sister Janet had invited him to a dinner-party at her house. When he declined for choice of his own company, she had told him that she *might* pass 'round with some dinner. It was a strong *might* since the *will* was a bit difficult: leaving her visitors would be tricky, so Conteh wouldn't be surprised if she didn't show.

'*I can't see you going to Father Jarvis' Red Affair, yunnuh, Bro',* Janet had said, '*if you can't even come to my house because there's a little gathering, how yuh gonna go to a big event like that?'*

'Nah, man. I'm definitely going to that."

"Why? Because it's a *RED* affair?' she had joked.

And Conteh had smiled and kissed his teeth.

* * *

It was 7am. The morning came with a cold crisp opening. Evadney felt it and thanked heavens it was Saturday. She pulled her duvet tighter around her neck and pulled her knees up towards her elbows, rendering her body *foetus-like*. She felt cosy with her thoughts: one of them? *How far she had come.*

Now, she marvelled at how vivid thoughts and imaginations could be just at that moment: the moment halfway between sleeping and waking. Or when she had woken, realised it was a *stay-in-bed* morning and was slowly sinking back into a sweet sleep. Well, it was one of those moments. The image of her special day ran vividly through her semiconscious mind like a joyous premonition.

She saw her guests, each and every one of them, their extra-special outfits threatening to outshine hers.

The chic hair-dos that black women seem to have an edge on obtaining.

Sophisticated hats on the heads of those who would choose to wear them: mostly church people.

Boutique shoes to die for.

That's black people for you. Weddings, Christenings and funerals bring out the best in their *cut-above-the-rest* dressage. Like ten Sunday mornings all in one, you could say.

Relatives she had not seen in years would be there, but the only *nearby* relative of Garnet that was sent an invitation was an old aunt that lived in West Bromwich. Evadney already knew *she couldn't make it*. She suffered from chronic arthritis and had already returned her declination along with a well-wish.

The rest of Garnet's relatives were *not so nearby*. Garnet's elder brother was in The States. High up in the Military. *He couldn't make it.*

His sister who was just a year younger than him was in Jamaica. Neither she nor Garnet could afford the air-fair, so… *she too couldn't make it.* And only Evadney knew why she was more than pleased with all the *'couldn't-make-its'* from Garnet's side of the family. It was *her* wedding day, hence, *her* prerogative to be pleased at whatever she wanted to be pleased with.

Garnet's parents – God rest their souls, had passed over to the other side and would no doubt have been disgusted with the way he treated Evadney. *Still.*

So, as it went, all the rest were most of Evadney's family, and a host of people from her parents' church, (although the wedding would not take place there – a decision that had caused umpteen church sisters to sussu-sussu). Also, a host of fair-weather friends of both her and Garnet's. Fair-weather friends whom had heard of the devastating day when she was *dumped*, but left her to swim to shore in her own sea of tears… *alone.* And all of whom thought she was mad for having him back, but accepted the invitation to their wedding anyway…

People love drama.

Flaws.

Imperfections.

Things to sussu-sussu about.

The negativities of life conjure up juicy exciting topics of conversation. People's disasters are some people's joy. And Evadney had known that some would come to the wedding just for the *experience*. Just to voyeur perversely at two people using a whole heap of vows to patch up something that was previously brutally severed. It would be worth the watching.

But she thought of the handful of *genuine* people too: the ones that seriously helped her through her tearful times. She thought of people whom she *had invited*, and ones she *would have loved to invite*: Gloria and Lijah, who she heard developed big problems of their own. Ikesha, Kunta (God rest his soul), Kizzy and Festus, Fiona, Reds, Papa Dread (God rest his soul), Mama Maya. She knew them all. But of all those people, only Gloria, Lijah, Ikesha, Shari and Reds would be there.

So yes, of all the others that made up the 150, it could be easily said that they were no more than fair-weather friends, together with the huge congregation from her parents' church.

And not forgetting of course, her *loyal all-weather friend*, Yvonne.

She sunk again into a sweet sleep, but an hour later, she woke to the ringing of her landline telephone.

She opened her eyes and glanced at the clock that was aligned with them. 11am, yet it seemed like it was only just a few minutes ago that she was thinking about her wedding day. She listened to Garnet's voice filling her voice box. At that present moment he was having a great Stag-week in Spain with Gongo Peas and two other friends, courtesy of Evadney.

" 'Vadney?… are you there? Pick up if yuh diddeh… A'right, jus' to seh wi 'avin' a good time. Good Stag-week present. T'ank yuh, Empress. Mi cyaan wait 'til Sat'deh, Empress. Officially you'll be my bride!"

Evadney smiled, stretched and twisted her ankles in a circular motion as she contemplated rising to meet her day. She imagined Garnet and his mates in the sun. They were due back in England with no time to waste: the coming Friday night – the night before the wedding, to be precise. Garnet had made sure that every single thing was *ready, set* and perfectly *good-to-go*. He had known that he wouldn't be seeing Evadney on the night before the wedding anyway, so he was satisfied with reaching his flat, climbing into a hot bath, and psyching himself up for his special day.

The church ceremony was scheduled for 11am, so he had plenty of time for a lie-in.

But his outfit wasn't all Garnet that had made sure was *ready, set* and perfectly *good-to-go*. For months since Evadney had given him a *yes* to her hand in marriage, he had been boiling up some serious *lead-in-mi-pencil* brew: *strong-back, chainy-root, iris-moss*... well, let's put it this way, it had been a while since Garnet touched his Empress, *'Vadney*. And although he hadn't told anyone, he had developed a serious complex when Tracey left him for Bongo Dee. Garnet had put it down to Bongo Dee's higher degree of *sexual potency*. But now he had his queen back, he had to impress. The wedding bed must be greeted with an oiled spine. *Chat bout.*

Evadney climbed out of bed and reached for her stereo. Sting FM sent sweet reggae music into her head.

Shower.

Dress.

Breakfast and a short helping of Saturday morning TV.

Now, she cleared the top of her huge Italian table and laid a pile of *'amendment-to-the-reception-venue'* leaflets, a pile of envelopes, eight sheets of printed addresses and two pens upon it. She sat down and started what she had known would be no less than an arduous task. And when at 12noon she heard the doorbell rang, she knew it was her friend Yvonne.

"You know that sending out over 150 *'amendments-to-the-reception-venue'* leaflets will take ages, don't you?" Yvonne asked as she waded her no-mess womanly ass through the door.

"I know," Evadney replied, "that's why you're here to help me, girl. You're not moaning are you?"

"Jus' put di kettle on."

"Yuh neva drink tea ah yuh yaad?" Evadney joked.

Yvonne swung her a playful cut-yeye.

"The kettle *is* on."

"Trust your computer to crash at dis crucial time, man. Writing out all those addresses. *Oh Lord.*"

"Don't worry, your fingers will get nuff exercise."

Yvonne opened the tea container and her eyes wandered for a cup. "Are you gonna give the people an explanation as to why you're changing the reception venue?"

"No. What should they care? The new venue is much nicer. They'll understand."

"Oh dear," Yvonne said.

"What?"

"Heh! Heh! Heh! Heeeeye!!!" Yvonne emitted a deep belly laugh that showed the size of her diaphragm.

"What yuh laughing at?... I suppose that's just how people laughed when they received my wedding invitation, hey?"

"Yuh have any biscuit?" Yvonne ignored her friend's question.

"In the tin above yuh head. Yuh jus' min' yuh cyaan fit inna di bridesmaid dress on the day."

Yvonne kissed her teeth.

"It won't be too much inconvenience for the people anyway. Instead of driving to A, they'll just be driving to B. I'm not asking them to change their outfits... you are supporting me all the way aren't you Yv'?"

"Of course I am. Don't be silly. I'll be there for you all the way. Even when my reasoning doesn't get through to you."

"I heard what you said about this wedding. It's my own bed I'm spreading..."

Yvonne sat down at the table with her tea and a mound of biscuits she had no business eating. Well, not after moaning that she needed to lose weight, and certainly not after having a dress to fit into pretty soon.

"You better exercise after that," Evadney joked as she stared at the pile of biscuits.

"And you better clean out dem ears of yours good on Saturday."

"Why?"

"To hear the whispering comments of all your guests."

"Am I bothered?" Evadney said, mimicking the tone of some comedian woman she heard on TV.

"You're not, are you?" Yvonne paused to look at her friend now. "You know, Evadney... there was a time when you couldn't even mash ants. Now there seem to be a fire in you. A *don't-give-a-damn* fire."

"I know. It's that fire that all women have in them. The one that lay dormant until a man comes along and pour fuel on it. All women have it, believe me."

"Well, on Saturday you'll be a married woman. That day will be something. It'll be an historical day for you, your husband and all your guests."

"C'mon, let's get these envelopes backed and stamped."

"Laad mi sorry fi dat pos'man. Him gwine develop a hernia from your post alone."

"Yuh funny," Yvonne said, writing the first address on the back of a freshly sealed envelope.

"How are they doing in Spain anyway? Heard from Garnet?"

"Yes. Left a message this morning. They're having a great Stag-week."

"Eh eh," Yvonne said cynically.

But as Yvonne took the last sip of her tea and grabbed a nearby pen, Evadney couldn't help recalling when she had presented Garnet with the Stag-week tickets. *'Trying to get rid of me?'* he had joked. *'No, not really,'* she had said, *'you go get some sun in them bones. Revitalise. You're gonna need the energy on your special day....* *'Really?'* he had asked. *'Let's put it this way,'* she had said, *'I'm gonna make sure it's the most unforgettable day of your life.'* And when she kissed him, Garnet's eyes filled up. *'Why are you crying?'* she asked him. *'Because mi wish mi madda was here to witness dis. Mi weddin' day.'* And he had held her close and wished he could push time forward to the time when he could make love to her. Especially now she was looking the best she had ever been since the day he had caught sight of her as she wiggled her innocent ass past him to find a seat at a Federation meeting in Handsworth way back when. *Sweet.*

"Centennial Centre, look out!" Yvonne joked, breaking the silence.

* * *

For Nico, however, it was a definite case of *the net closing in*, and Wednesday night was as good as any.

Morag kicked off her shoes and showed pretty toes.

She stepped fairy-like across her huge lounge.

She poured herself a Cognac and took a sip.

Now, she filled the second glass just the way he liked it, but as she sat now, listening to the noise of the shower, and as she waited for the moment that he would descend the stairs, she couldn't help wondering how unwell he had been looking lately. Unlike the way he looked when they first met at Simone and Conteh's jewellery party years back.

"Are you gonna want some food?!" she shouted upstairs. "We can get Chinese in if you want!"

"No... I'm fine..."

Morag was a little startled as the voice came from right behind her. She didn't hear his footsteps ascending the stairs, but as she turned towards him, she could tell that there was only one thing he was hungry for. "Nico, Darling... I didn't hear you coming."

"Don't worry, you'll *feel* me *coming* later," he told her, running his fingers through her blonde hair.

"Very funny. How come you're not hungry?"

"My appetite for food left ages ago," Nico told her, now reaching for his glass of Cognac.

"That can't be good. Loss of appetite is never good."

"So they say," Nico replied uncaringly, sitting beside her now.

"I can't wait," Morag said.

"What for?"

"To *feel* you *coming*."

He chuckled.

"It suits you," she said out of the blue.

"What?"

"My husband's dressing gown. You bring out the life in it."

"So does your husband's pussy," he groped her knickerless fanny and kissed her, "it brings out the life in my dog."

"You dirty *so-and-so*," she whispered in his ear.

"Are you sure he won't be home anytime soon?" Nico enquired.

"Sure. Right now he is probably lounging in a hotel room in Jamaica. He'll be back late tomorrow. Bringing back a 767 from Jamaica"

"*High-flyer*, hey?… still, even the *highest of flyers* can be brought down by pum-pum."

Morag laughed. *Vagina* was more her term for the tempting bit of flesh that lay between her thighs, but since she had started dealing with Nico the raw Jamaican term, *pum-pum* had become one of several on her newly acquired list of Jamaican words, though whenever she would utter it, it never rings with true authenticity.

"Why don't I feel the need to say, *'lucky him?'*… your husband?" Nico asked.

"D'know… *why*?"

"Well… *I'm* here with you…" he groped her firm breasts. "… And *he's* not. The other reason I'll keep to myself."

"What other reason, Babes?"

He didn't reply.

"Are you ok, Nico?"

"Why?… wha' yuh mean, am I ok?"

"I just think you're looking a bit… ill. That could be the reason why you've lost your appetite. I think you should have a check-up at the doctors."

"When I loose my appetite for this," he groped her again, "then you can start worrying." Her reached for his glass and took another sip of

Cognac. Then, placing his glass on the sideboard behind him, he stood up and pushed her gently down onto the settee, rendering her in a lying position. "When was the last time I told you how beautiful you were?"

"Yesterday," she whispered, appreciating his sweet, manipulative touches.

"Do you love me?" he asked in a whisper.

"You know that," she whispered back, melting under his influence as she felt his warm Cognac'd tongue on her clitoris. Hoisting her right foot curiously towards his groin, she let her toes do the walking. Finding his bulge as hard as rock, she knew she would enjoy her birthday gift.

"C'mon," he said rising gently to his feet. "Let's go upstairs… soil the sheets once more before your husband gets back tomorrow. You can get him fresh ones." He picked her up like a baby and headed for Lance's bedroom. *Disgraceful.*

* * *

In the meantime, on the other side of town, Conteh couldn't be too careful.

It was dark.

Rain poured down in abundance and he hoped the showers would be a blessing like his mother had always said whenever it would pour.

"Oh, there she is," Conteh said, rising to his feet when his doorbell went, "good old Janet." His belly hung out for rice-an'-peas. Although it wasn't Sunday, that was what Janet told him she was cooking. He could almost smell the aroma already.

The shadow on his doorstep crouched under a large umbrella as the rain pelted down from the heavens. He smiled, knowing how much Janet hated the rain.

He opened quickly, "Come in, Sis'! Come in! What a rain?"

The lady did.

Stepped right into the dark porch, a hood covering her head and most of her face, the only thing in her hand was a big umbrella.

"Weh di dinna deh, Sis'?" he's a little puzzled now.

The lady turned her face outside. She held her gloves between her teeth as she shook the rain from her umbrella.

"Are you alone, Conteh?" a glove muffled voice asked.

"Yeah, man… yuh have a cold, Jan'? Yuh voice soun'…"

Her back was towards him as she leant the canvassed shelter up against the wall. Now, she turned to face him… "How do I sound?" the

236

lady asked in a sarcasm-laced tone. "Like an old flame, I hope?… And… *dinna*? What *dinna*? Who's bringing you *dinna*? Can't you cook for yourself?"

And it was then reality hit him, as he stood with the intruder in the dark porch. She was the same height and build as Janet, but it *wasn't* Janet at all… No sir.

"Don't you have a light in your porch?"

"Menna?! Fuck!"

"Language, Conteh," she scolded sarcastically, as he rushed towards the switch for the passage light.

"Menna?!" he alarmed as he walked back to the porch. "Bombo cl… What yuh…?!"

Dear old *Menna… Lord, Lord, Lord.*

"… What am I doing here? Wait… In a short while, you'll see. All will be revealed."

Conteh needed to pinch himself. It was happening all too quickly for him.

* * *

It had been literally six minutes since Nico lifted Morag from the settee and transported her to her bedroom.

Six minutes is a mighty long time.

She had moaned.

Groaned.

Sighed.

And died the *little death.*

Nico was laying it on. *Thick.*

And whilst he stole *love on the side,* his idrin was about to be *taken for a ride.*

But how rocky would it be for Conteh?

* * *

"That's not a very nice welcome," Menna had said after Conteh's surprised reaction. "I asked, *'who's bringing you dinner'*?" Menna insisted.

Conteh was speechless now.

"It's ok, I'm not a ghost," Menna assured him. "It's really me. And this time I'm not here to buy a ring… by the way, you smell *lovely.* Just had a fresh, did you. I see you still haven't lost that hygiene thing. You always had that edible freshness about you?"

237

He sweated, and though he tried to disguise it, his bottom lip quivered.

"Surely you didn't expect *never* to see me again, *Lover Boy*? Well, that might have been the case, but I needed to talk to you before AIDS kicks in and takes all the glory."

Still, they stood in the porch. Cat did a runner with Conteh's tongue.

"How is *it* these days?" God knows where she got the nerves from, but she reached out and groped his balls as if to assure him of what she meant by *it*.

"What the f…" he eased back and pushed her hand away.

"Stop pretending you don't like it," she mocked.

"Listen," Conteh said, "let me close the door, it's cold. You're obviously here for a reason. Let's at least keep the heat in, since I'm sure your ` visit is a *cold* one."

"No… leave it!" she ordered, "there are others. Aren't you the lucky one? The *unforgettable* one."

"*Others*?" He looked out into the darkness. "Wha' yuh mean, *others*?"

"*Patience,* Conteh, *Patience.* Didn't your mother tell you it's a *virtue*?"

* * *

"**O**h, Nico… Darling… Ahhhh! Ahhhh!" Morag exclaimed from her face-down position in her marital bed.

"Oh, Morag," he whispered back, covering the whole of her back with his eager, sex-greed body. "Uh! Uh! Uh!"

"I'll get a divorce… *Ahhh*! We can be together… *Mmm*… for good…"

"I can't do the commitment thing, Morag. Uh! I like it like this. Besides I can't maintain you like your husband can."

"It's not just about that," she despaired. "I love you…" She thought she was in heaven but she was falling further into hell. And there were only two choices for her landing: *a rock* and *a hard place*. "… You do love me don't you, Nico?"

No reply… just lecherous noises.

"Nico…?" Morag searched again for an answer, but when Nico caressed the right side of her neck with his tongue, then sucked mercilessly into its sensitive nape, the need for a reply wasn't so great. "Oh, Baby," she hummed.

And when he hoisted himself up by both arms and plunged a doggy-deep back-shot into her, summoning an orgasmic tremor, she had soon forgotten about *commitment*.

Oh, the pleasure... the pleasures... the pleasures of the carnal flesh.

* * *

Menna's phone rang before she could answer Conteh's *'Wha' yuh mean, others?'* question. "Hi," she said assertively. "Yes. Come. The coast is clear. *Mista Lova-Lova* is *all* alone. Until, of course the caring *dinner-lady* shows."

"Who yuh talking to?" Conteh perplexed, "who yuh tellin' to come, Menna?"

"Who are *they*, more like. Don't worry. I wouldn't bring *strangers* to your house? *They* are all old paths where *this dick*," she grabbed his crutch again, "once tread."

Though he was angry, he was rising. Having his dick groped by a sexy lady was sure to have that effect.

"Menna… is weh yaah deal wid? What's goin' on? You can't jus' come…"

"… But I *can*… and I *have* come to yuh yaad."

"This is trespassing."

"I might be trespassing, *but only for a little while*, but *you*? You have taken lives, just because you hated wearing a condom… Just because you are sex crazy. Just because you couldn't stay faithful to your beautiful wife, Simone." Menna's warm kissable breath was on his face, but all Conteh could do was to keep his eyes on the slightly ajar door, where the mysterious *'others'* lurked.

"*Who* is bringing you dinner? You never answered."

"My sister… Janet."

"Means nothing to me. I never did meet any of your family, remember? Not your mum, *God rest her soul*, I heard she passed away?"

Conteh couldn't understand it. It had been so long. What was Menna doing? He was still looking through the crease of his front door. "Who have you invited to my…?"

But there they were.

Larger than life.

He needed no verbal answer.

They piled in now, making it look like a rehearsed piece.

"Fuck!" He covered his face and peeped through the creases of his fingers, "Fuck! Fuck! Fuck!"

Carmen, Colette and *Joya*, three of his baby mothers walked in. None of them greeted him. Instead, they cut him with their eyes from brick-set faces, and with the vengeance of simmering volcanoes, they breathed hot breaths all over his pitiful face. And as if bad cases of rigor mortis were permanently set in, their arms were folded argumentatively across their chests.

"Shit," Conteh hissed, moving back to make room in his own porch, as if he had to.

The porch was getting crowded now.

Following them were another two women he had least expected to see with this bunch. Five outstretched fingers spread across a pale forehead, pushing back a mop of blonde hair. This lady could be called *'the blonde with attitude'*, for today, she had a lot more than way back when Conteh had fucked with her heart.

Behind her, swinging her head to the left, the second lady flicked sloping strands of brunette hair from an even paler forehead. She smiled, only this smile was most certainly *not* a playful one. It was like a poisonous kiss…

Sharon and Melissa. Who else?

A blonde and a brunette who had once had Conteh and Nico in no less than the cleverest *STING* of all. by Menna's order, they had staged an orgy. Garnet the snoop had clicked happily away, enabling a host of hot, steamy snaps to be brought right home to Menna, who in turn forwarded them to dear Simone.

Melissa closed the door behind her indicating that that was the lot.

Conteh felt cornered now.

Nowhere to run.

Nowhere to hide.

"Fuck… A weh di raas…" he whispered.

"Shall I lead the way into your living-room?" Menna asserted, "or shall we follow you, *Mr Heart Breaker*?"

"Yuh is one facety raas yunnuh, Menna."

"Ok," she stepped forward, " I'll lead. Where is it?"

"Yuh lucky seh mi is not a violent man."

"Not *physically* anyway," Menna said. "But *emotionally* your one of the most violent bastards out. So don't think that because you didn't physically hit us, you didn't violently hurt us. That's a fucking false sense of security… where's the fucking living-room?"

"It's straight ahead," Conteh tried to assert an upper edge. "Yuh facety blood claat… You have ten minutes. You can all have your say, then go?"

Menna laughed. "Listen *Bwoy*… I's not *you* runnin' dis show, so shut di fuck up!"

"Wait! Yuh cyaan come inna people house an' talk to dem like dat?"

"*Can… just have*. And what the fuck are you gonna do about it?"

"Unnuh sick! Dat's unnuh problem? You're all fucking crazy!"

"You heard Seal," Menna jabbed, '*we're never gonna survive unless we get a little crazy*."

Conteh stood now in the doorway of the living-room looking over the heads of all his ex-conquests. Eye contact was almost impossible now the light was much brighter. He was shaking.

"Sit down," Menna told him.

"It's ok, I'll stand this one out if you don't mind."

"I said, "I's *we* a run t'ings, not *you*! Sit di fuck down! In the middle of the floor, to be precise!"

"Wha'?!"

"Sit down in the middle of the floor… yuh deaf?"

"Fuck off! Get the fuck outa mi house!"

Menna kissed her teeth, "Make him," she gestured to the gang."

The five women pounced on Conteh and brought him to his knees. In the process, he fell a little too hard and jarred the base of his spine.

"Strip him."

"What?" Conteh alarmed. "Unnuh really gone mad?! Not ova mi dead body to raas!"

"No," Carmen opinionated, "Let him do it himself."

"Good idea," Menna agreed.

'*Didn't I dream this shit a while back?*' Conteh thought.

"Geddem off, *Lova Bwoy*," Sharon exercised her patois.

He gave her a daggered stare.

"Now!" Menna urged. But it was the gun against his chest that convinced him.

"Weh yuh get dat t'ing?"

"What does it matter? Strip!"

Conteh started to strip. "Yuh not gonna get weh wid dis a raas."

"Why aren't we gonna get away with this, Conteh?" Carmen asked. "Who yuh gonna tell?… the police?"

They all laughed.

241

'Is he *really* HIV positive?' Melissa wondered. He still looks *damn* good.

"Faster!" Menna urged.

He kissed his teeth.

A loosened belt.

Loosened buttons.

Zipper down.

"Stand up!" Menna shouted.

He looked at her questioningly. "I thought you wanted me to…"

"Stand up! Yuh chat too much! Did you eat chicken batty or sop'n?"

He did. Stood up, that is.

"Geddem down."

And so he did, showing a fat bulge of *meat-and-two-veg* through a pair of Calvin Klein's.

"Aren't you meant to be dying? Should you look so fucking good?" Melissa still needed to know. It was like a compulsion. It was almost like double-checking the *'use-by'* date on the packaging of delicious food she would hate to throw away.

"Now what?" Conteh said, looking just at Menna as if she was the only one in the room.

"Loose the CKs. We all wanna look once more at the perpetrating weapon.

"Is this your idea of a joke, Menna? Only from where I'm standing it's more like fucking perversion."

"Lay down," Menna said calmly now, ignoring his surmising.

He did… laid his body down like a lamb to the slaughter. And without protestation too.

"Help him, Melissa," Menna ordered.

The brunette heeded Menna's order and rid Conteh of his last piece of garment.

Now, he lay there looking a little pathetic, with a *'now what'* look on his face. Surely he had had a dream like this, but this was *reality*. Surely they weren't here to *cut his dick off* like in his dream? Perhaps, like in that terrifying dream, Simone would walk in a minute with a knife in her hand to give the *'do it!'* order.

The doorbell rang. *'Janet'*, he thought. He looked at Menna.

"Leave it," she said sternly.

"Conteh! It's me! Janet! I've got yuh dinna!" Janet shouted through the letterbox. She knew how deep her brother could sleep of late.

Before his incarceration and when he would find himself in numerous beds as his dear wife worked, he had mastered the knack of not falling into coma-like sleep, after he had given it to any given one of his lovers. But these days, *Deep Sleep* was his holiday home.

Conteh wanted to shout back, but the gun Menna held in her right hand spoke to him.

"Conteh?!" Janet tried the set of keys she had always had when their mother was alive. "Conteh?!… are you sleeping?!" Janet was now convinced Conteh was there as his keys were on the inside of the door, preventing hers to work. She dialled the house phone on her mobile: that might wake him up.

All five women looked at the ringing phone on a small table by Conteh's head.

Now, Janet tried his mobile, which, although she didn't know it, vibrated on the fireplace, with six women staring at it. She went to his voice mail.

Now, the avenging six listened to the shuffling sound of a plastic bag, the clinking sound of Pyrex dishes, followed by the pulling of the key from the lock. It told them all that Janet had given up and was leaving. They all knew too, that his dinner was left. Janet had carefully tied it around the handle of the door like her mother would. Bless his little cotton socks.

* * *

In another man's bed… With another man's wife… Drained from his almighty orgasm, Nico slept like a baby.

He and Morag were wrapped around each other.

Morag was in a deep sleep too.

Earlier, she recalled their *'mid-sex'* conversation and a little dejavu had surfaced.

The conversation was similar to the one she had years ago with Lance, as he screwed her senseless whilst her husband Captain Frank Philips was away on a long-haul flight…

Only, Lance wanted to marry her. *Commitment* people call it.

Nico didn't. *Commitment* was the farthest from his mind.

Whatever else she must live with, Morag must live with that too.

In harmony, they snored. His right leg was laid across her bum as she lay on her belly.

Emotionally, he was cold.

Callous.

243

Selfish.

Almost paralleling with *evil*.

But in a funny kind of way, so was she. Did she give a damn about Lance's feelings? *No.*

Tomorrow would be a new day.

New sheets were already prepared for the changing of the bed.

Tomorrow was when she expected Lance home.

Tomorrow… Tomorrow… only a day away…

* * *

"**Ok**," Menna resumed, "your *'sista of mercy'* is gone. Back to business."

"Well?" he perplexed.

"Firstly, what have you got to say to all these women? You've given them the HIV virus… Not me. As you know, I always take control over my own body. *No glove, no shove."* That's me.

From his *grounded* position Conteh looked at each one of the other five women consecutively. He didn't just hate being naked in such a situation, but he felt that his soul was naked. Naked in the presence of an *unforgiving* jury.

"It wasn't deliberate. I'm sorry. I was given it by someone, you know that."

"By someone you fucked behind your wives back? Wasn't it *Pam?* Your wife's best friend, I heard. I heard she's now dead."

Conteh felt a rush of heat and mopped his brow.

"Bad news travels fast. Good ones are always the slowest, but I also heard that your dear wife was clever. She used *femidoms*. Hah! Hah! Hah! Haaaahhh! Protected herself. So when you thought you were getting the *real thing*… Hah! Hah! Haaahhh!…"

Menna's laugh was infectious and it had the other five in a frenzy, each decibel of mockery drowning Conteh's very soul.

"… I had always wanted to meet her in person," Menna continued. "And I did. The other day, like I told you. She's *truly* beautiful. What were you thinking of when you fucked around on her."

Conteh's heart pained at the unbearable reminder. *Simone. Oh, he loved her so*. "Ok… Do what you will to me. Torture me, whatever. Even with the heating, it's cold in here. Get it over with."

"Have you forgotten?" Menna moved close to him and whispered into his ears, "I's *we* runnin' t'ings." He smelt her perfume and remembered it was the one she wore when they played on her living-room carpet the night of their first date. The night she had took him to the penultimate limit, then told him, *'I never fuck on the first night.'*

"Ok, *Sharon*… do your thing," Menna said, as she moved back to her perch. "And listen," she addressed Conteh now, "if you so much as try to touch any of these women, you're fucking dead."

"How yuh doing, *Heartbreaker?"* Sharon asked mockingly as she tied the blind-fold around his eyes. She was about to start the administering of some torturing moves. "It's been a mighty long time… wouldn't you say?" Now, slowly, she traced her fingertips around the outline of his pouting lips. She kissed the sensitive points at the corners of his mouth.

Conteh leaned his head. This *receiving-but-not-responding* thing was gonna be tough. There was a method in the bitches' madness, but he wasn't about to find out too quick.

She remembered the time when she was *under it*. Now, Sharon took his left *thumb* into her mouth, her lips, teeth and tongue administering a mini blow-job. In turn, she slowly gave the same treatment to all ten fingers. Luckily, like Menna said, Conteh had just had a fresh. It helped.

"Ok, Sharon, that's enough." Menna commanded, *"Melissa*… do your stuff."

Conteh smiled.

"And you can wipe that fucking smile off yuh face, yuh fucka!" Menna told him.

He did. In a spilt second.

Melissa continued the lip treatment. Using the tips of both forefingers, she applied gentle pressure along the length of his top lip and then along the bottom.

Conteh quivered. Tempted to touch, but the gun *dared* him to.

His neck, ears and toes felt Melissa's sensual touches now. She sucked, nuzzled and nibbled his neck sending him on a fast-track to arousal.

They watched him rise.

A whole lot of hard-on and nowhere to plunge it.

He reached out to touch her.

"Don't touch her!" Menna commanded.

He dropped his hands to his side.

Melissa relented, whispering words like, *'wet', 'hard', 'tongue'.*

He rose higher. *Hard as Rock.*

"Ok, Melissa, that's it… *Colette*? Do your stuff."

'How did this thing happen to be?' Conteh wondered. *'How did they all manage to get into this together? It is obvious* **who** *the ringleader is...* **Menna**. *She has more balls than a bull. But how did she manage to rope them all in. These women have minds of their own. Orgy-type rendezvous were never their thing... well, not so much Sharon and Melissa, this would be their thing, but Carmen, Colette and Joya? No... It didn't make sense. Menna must have used this 'Group Dynamic' thing on them real good... and if they hated me that much, how come all this tactility?'* ...

Colette's touch pulled him from his thoughts.

She started by licking his nipples. Then, it became firm sucking.

He gasped. He needed to touch. It was all too much.

She moved her tongue swiftly and teasingly around each nipple in turn. She traced the line from his chest to his belly button where she sunk it into the fold of his navel and licked. One of his weak spots. *Ohhhh.*

"No..." he agonised. "You can't do this. It's torture."

"Shut the fuck up!" Menna commanded.

Colette relented. She kissed the whole circumference of his belly.

Down...

Down...

Down...

And there she was... on the brink. Conteh anticipated the ultimate pleasure and sighed at the thought at what he thought he was about to receive. But his thinking was nothing more than *'wishful'*. Colette wasn't that daft.

"Ok, Colette, that's it."

But Colette disobeyed. She held his rigid dick in the palm of her hands, twisted and yanked! *Ouch!*

"Ahhh!" Conteh railed up. "Shit!"

"Lay the fuck back down!" Menna jabbed him with the powered pistol.

"This is fuckries!" He held his dick. "Jesus..."

"You know you're enjoying it," Menna whispered in his ears. "*Joya...* your turn."

Joya came equipped. Feather in hand. And what she did with her feather, her lips and fingers were enough to send Conteh over the erotic edge. He was driven crazy.

"Joya, that's it... *Carmen*... your turn." She looked at Carmen who was sat in deep silence all through this.

Of the three baby-mothers, Carmen was the strongest natured.

"Take'em off, Conteh," Carmen commanded.

"What?"

"The blindfold. Take'em off."

Menna looked at her. She was the leader of the pack, how *dare* Carmen try to take control? "They stay on, Carmen," she intervened.

"No. I want them off. As well as feeling but not touching, I want him to *look* but don't touch."

"No. They stay on," Menna asserted.

Carmen gave Menna a *look*, then preceded. She pounced on him giving a repeat of the previous four ladies' performances.

How could Conteh be expected not to touch?

"Hands off, Conteh. No touching!" Menna asserted again as he tried it.

"What do you six women want? My soul?"

"Shut up! You don't have a soul, yuh fucka!"

"Ok... whateva yuh seh," he reached for his own dick. He needed to be relieved.

"Leave it! Yuh wanka!"

"What?! It's my body."

"Ok, ladies, leave us now. Go into the kitchen or somewhere. I need to talk to him."

Carmen looked at her.

"*Alone*," Menna told her.

And like faithful little soldieresses, they filed out of the living-room and into the kitchen.

"You've all got your pieces," Menna told the girls, "he might try a t'ing. If you hear me shout, rush in and blow his fucking brains out." She pulled the living-room door to, enclosing her and her naked subject.

* * *

Morag lay there unable to move, seeking solace between the warm, yet *cold* sheet of her marital bed.

It would have been good if she had heard the footsteps of her approaching husband, but the effect of after-sex relaxation had taken her to an almost unreachable depth.

"Who the fuck are you?!" Lance's voice pounded into her brain as he shouted at Nico, who was snoring deeply, seconds before the angry question reached his head. "What the fuck are you doing in my bed?!"

'Fucking yuh wife,' seemed the most appropriate answer, though by no means the wisest.

Nico sat up and wiped his brow. Still half asleep on Lance's side of the bed, he was cornered and didn't know what the hell to do. One thing for sure, he knew he needed firstly to gather himself. Collect his thoughts. Waking up fully would help.

Morag was still clinging to the sheets, trembling… trembling… The whole situation had rendered her mentally and physically paralysed. She couldn't move. Just trembled.

"Is this what you've been doing all along, Morag?! And yet you denied having an affair?!"

She was definitely in a state of shock.

Whilst the questions were now moving in Morag's direction, Nico stole the moment to *'slide'* snake-like out of Lance's bed, but his movement re-attracted Lance's attention away from Morag. Nico held onto his balls and walked sideways like a crab, in an attempt to retrieve his clothes: he had left them there in the corner of room.

Lance couldn't believe what was happening.

His eyes caught Nico's bare ass, and for a few seconds, *he kept them there.*

He looked again at his wife, feeling more humiliation than jealousy.

Nico couldn't find his clothes but he had no voice to ask Morag where the hell they were.

Lance's heart began to pound.

He wanted to hit out.

Unleash his anger…

In the meantime Nico panicked.

"Bastard!" Lance lounged at Nico who was now wishing Morag wasn't such a tidy freak and had put his clothes somewhere.

"Easy, Bredrin!" Nico put his hand over his head and cowered, leaving his dangly bits on show. Lance was about to kill him. *Literally.*

"Lance?!" A voice called from downstairs.

Morag wanted to, but couldn't make the voice out. Both their cars were left on the drive when they left for their last flight, but *who* was shouting? Was it *Clive* or was it *Lawrence*? Whoever it was, he would see her for who she was. *A scarlet woman.*

The voice from downstairs gave her strength to move her ass. She climbed out of the bed and felt the heavy burden of shame upon her back. Pulling her dressing-gown on, she tried to stop Lance from killing Nico.

Nico was on the floor now.

His face was battered, yet Lance was showing no signs of letting-up.

Showers of kicks greeted his groin.

His left side was repeatedly kicked as he lay doubled-up on the floor.

Now, like a raging maniac, Lance was stepping in his head.

"Lance! Stop it now!" Morag shouted.

"Lance?! What's going on, man?" The voice was still calling from downstairs. The person had decided it was best not to go up.

Morag closed the bedroom door as if to shut the mystery caller out. She still wasn't sure, but decided that it sounded like Lawrence.

Lance dragged Nico to his feet and pressed his naked, battered body face-up against the wall, twisted his right arm behind his back and stretched his left high up against the wall.

"Haaaah! Easy nuh, Bredrin! *Please!*" Nico begged.

Now, Lance pressed his whole body up against Nico's and breathed his hot, angry breath on the back of his neck and down his spine.

Nico felt a little weird, especially as Lance's hard dick was a little too close for comfort to his naked ass. "Get the fuck away from me!" Nico protested, feeling that all wasn't well with the tactile encounter. Something told him that Lance wanted to *be* that close and he shuddered at the thought.

"Lance?!" Morag said, "Let him go now!"

"As if he was suddenly released from hypnosis, Lance released him, and like a freed rat, Nico hit the stairs. *Nude*. At the bottom he saw the image of a man standing in the dim kitchen. Nico had no time to investigate. He was out of there. *Freaked.*

"Sit the fuck down, Morag!" Lance said after, slapping her face with brute force.

"Bastard!" she protested.

"Don't move!" With purpose, he left the room and descended the stairs.

"Listen," his uniformed guest said, "I'd better go. You have some shit to deal with."

"No," Lance coaxed. "Stay. Pour yourself a drink."

"What?! At a time like this?"

"Yes. Stay. I'll be down in a bit," Lance's voice was calm. Too calm. In fact it bordered on the brewing of a devastating storm. *The calm before it, that is.*

"Who was that guy?" his guest asked. "He left in the nude."

"D'know. Obviously her lover… Pour a drink. I just need to sort the bitch out." Lance ascended the stairs again.

And when he got there, he found Morag praying… *Hard.*

* * *

Conteh was really wishing he could die. Now he knew that if a piece of meat had feelings, that was probably what it would feel like.

"Take'em off," Menna ordered now she was alone with Conteh.

"What?"

"The blindfold… Take'em off."

He did. "You have always held the handle, haven't you, Menna… while everyone else held the blade."

"Yes… and didn't you just fuck with the *wrong* woman, hey?"

"Can I get dressed now?"

"No."

"Why didn't you take part in this… *sexual torture?* And what is it all about, anyway?"

"Don't worry, I don't showcase to no one but myself." She took her top off, exposing firm, pouting breasts. Conteh sighed. The memories of bygone days came rushing back.

"Menna… explain all this to me… I don't understand…"

"Listen," She sat by him on the floor, "I was just playing hard in front of the others. *Touch me.*" She led his right palm to her left breast. *Firm.*

Conteh looked questioningly at her. *'What was she up to?'* he wondered, but still, he couldn't help but grope them. Well, wasn't he madly in love with this woman? Was she not the best thing after Simone? *Shit.*

"Did you miss me, Conteh?" she tantalised.

"Y… Yes… I did. I hated you at one point for setting me up, but I missed you."

"Well… I know I could never walk in Simone's shoes. None of your *'bits on the side'* could. She's clearly special. And I know that if you could have her back, that would be cream in you coffee, right?"

"True. But that will never happen," he said.

"Damn right… And that's the trouble with most of you fuckers… don't know how to make your women at home your starters, main course and dessert until she check clean out of your lives…"

He was staring at her breasts. Amazed at how firm they had remained, even though she was way past the age of a teenager. Perhaps it was the fact that she didn't have children.

"… You don't know how to spice up what you already have," she relented. "See the beauty in all her ways. Instead, you go around telling other women they don't exist. That you live alone. With your parents. You have no landline telephones. Crap like that. You even deny your own children to get some pussy."

"Ok, Menna. I get the point. *Please.*"

"But you and I?" Menna said softly, "we had something, wouldn't you say?"

"We both know that, Menna. But this torture thing…"

"Remember *this*?" Out of nowhere, she pulled a slit of cloth she had cut away before the ritual burning in Angie's garden. "Your favourite… *red silk*… remember? It was you who introduced it to my bed."

"Menna…?"

"Where did it come from? This fetish for red silk?"

He connected with her eyes.

"*Maggi*, wasn't it?… your love doctress? when you were a mere inexperience wham-banner…"

He was shocked. How could she have known?

"Maggie, who taught you how to love… Maggie, who taught you that a woman is like a rose, and should be handled like one…" Constantly, she eased the slit of silk over every part of his body. "… That she must be nurtured with passion before she could be expected to bloom…"

"Menna, how did you…"

"… "That she must be tended with care too."

Her tactility was driving him wild, but her constant reminder of how he was supposed to treat a woman wouldn't be missed. He could do without it.

"… And didn't Maggie tell you too, Conteh, that if a woman is not treated right, she could turn into a *prickly thorn*."

He averted his eyes from the slit of silk and focused again on her firm, black breasts.

"Kiss them," she told him, easing the miniature slit of silk over his face.

He looked at her, *puzzled*.

"Like you used to… *Remember*?"

"OK, Menna… what's the catch? You came here with my exes, tortured me sexually… I was forbidden to touch any of them… you held a gun to my head… these five ladies are in my kitchen and now you are trying to convince me you *yield* my touch?"

"I said, *kiss them.*"

He did. *Ohhhhh.* Catch or not, how could he resist? The memories. He trembled under the force, the taste of her nipples as they mingled with the warm juices of his tongue.

"That feels good, Conteh," she whispered, easing herself off the floor and up onto the edge of the settee. Her groin, now level with his head, she lifted her skirt up.

Conteh looked at her, his eyes asking *'why?'*

"C'mon… you know you want to," she told him.

He admired her long, silky, sexy legs, rubbing his hands all over them. *Ohhhhh.* It had been a mighty long time. Easing back the gusset of her laced knickers, he *tasted* her. Resting his tongue first at the top of her clitoris, he began with a gentle tease… And when it was impossible for him to control his desires, he dined with the ravenous hunger of a beast. *Ohhhh… Ohhhh… Ohhhh…*

They both knew that HIV could not be contracted through saliva.

It was hard for Menna to control herself, and minutes later, Niagara Falls had nothing on the almighty orgasm that followed. *Ohhhhh.*

"Don't you want to *enter* me, Conteh?" she whispered. "Imagine it… *deep inside me… Hard… Wet… Throbbing.*"

"No, Menna, no more torture, please. It isn't fair."

She ignored him. "Close your eyes, Conteh… just for a few seconds…"

He did.

"Image it… Imagine you inside me… for old time sake…"

"No… no… no…" Conteh whispered, sinking his head into Menna's lap to muffle the sound as he cried now like a baby. He was hungry. There was a feast, yet he couldn't devour, and he knew that Menna's wish was to take him to the brink of desire.

"Did you imagine it?" she whispered.

Sob, sob, sob.

"Now…" she whispered sternly, "you remember the night you left me high and dry in my flat?" She massaged his head. "You didn't want to make love because I insisted you wore a condom… remember?"

He remembered all right. He sobbed, wetting her thighs.

"You left me gagging… You climbed into your car drove away… went… remember?"

"Ok… I've been through the mill and back, Menna. I'm all beaten up. I'm lonely. My wife… she's… she's…"

"Left you?… Gone?… We all know that."

Sob.

"Yes, you bastard… the wife you told me you didn't have. You *lied* to me. Even when I asked you outright. Said you lived with your mum and four sisters… remember?" She held his head between her two hands and tilted his face towards hers, "*Why?*"

She watched him cry.

Watched his tears flow down his pitiful face.

'Will these tears ever be enough to match the floods his women cried?' she asked herself. *'So many hearts you broke.'*

"Ok… I deserve all I got… I…"

A shuffle in the passage alerted them, "Menna!" Carmen called, "What's taking so long?"

"Gimme another five minutes," Menna assured her, "Just talk amongst yourselves. I'll be there in five."

Conteh caught his breath.

"Menna," he looked purposefully into her eyes, "the robbery… *why*? Why so harsh. Prison was hell. Did I hurt you that bad? I didn't deserve that."

"*Conteh… Oh Conteh…*" She shook her head. "*Conteh, Conteh, Conteh…* you have no idea, have you? Not a clue. Conteh, women have *killed* for less what you put me through…"

"Yes, but you were already playing me at my own game. You were fucking my bredrin, Nico. My best mate… So *why*…? You went to the extreme."

"Yes… Nico… that reminds me. That *bastard*. I heard he's going around dosing every woman he can with the HIV virus."

"Menna, Nico is a big man. I don't answer for him. He must know what he's doing."

"Yes… *he* knows what he's doing, but innocent women *don't*." Menna spoke as if Conteh was the perpetrating serial infector. "He should be made to walk around with a permanent warning on his back, saying, *'I AM HIV POSITIVE'*. And if I had anything to do with it, he would. Nico needs to be exposed… seriously."

"Like I said, Menna, not my business."

"And you can tell him from me, Conteh, not to call my number again. How the hell he knew I was back, God knows, but he's been calling and leaving shitty messages on my answer phone. This isn't the Menna that boarded a flight to JA not so long ago. I know he's dying, but I'll finish the fucker off quicker than he expects. Let's see how brave he'll be when I bump into him."

"Menna, I'm not Nico's keeper. In fact I don't know where he is. He's not been at his flat. The police even went 'round. I asked them to. It's strange, he don't call me anymore…"

"Well, unfortunately, he hasn't crawled under a stone and died. He's been calling me."

"Menna… when did you become…?"

"Such a hard bitch?"

"Well… yes."

"The day I was fucked about once too often… Don't worry. I know how to deal with Nico. And it's most certainly not taking a sharp blade to his fucking dick. That would be too damn easy."

"Bwoy, Menna, yuh heartless."

"And you'll find that behind every heartless woman was once a bastard man."

Conteh sighed.

"And anyway, when did you start being *heartful*, Conteh?"

"Is it *me* that made you so heartless, Menna. Did I *really* hurt you that much?"

"Not just *me,* Conteh. There are five women lurking in your kitchen that would rather see you *die* right now. Lucky for you, I used this strategy. Nothing like wanting, or being teased with something you can't have. For me, dying is an easy way out. Or… perhaps you'd rather…"

"No. I wouldn't rather be dead. Life's precious. There are treatments on the market now to control HIV. I've changed, Menna. Too late, but I've changed. I might even go back to church."

"So you waited until all your chips are down before you take a chance on God?" Menna sniggered. "Get off me." She pushed him away like a leper, kissed her teeth and stood up. She shaped up, buttoned her blouse. "Stand up."

He looked up at her.

"I said, stand up."

He did. He soon realise that having a taste of her clitoris, and giving her an orgasm didn't make things ok, or even mellow her slightly. But he wondered how anyone could use *passion's heat* to be so *cold*. Easy. It is man's greatest desire, and don't women know it. So how better to tease, torture and tantalise?

"Put your hands behind your back."

"Menna, I's wha' dis now?"

"Hands behind your back!"

"Have some mercy on me nuh, Menna?"

The five girls came rushing in at the sound of Menna's raised voice.

"It's ok, girls," Menna assured them, as she placed Conteh's wrists in a pair of handcuffs. "Up against the patio door."

"Menna... Jesus."

She fastened the handcuffs to the handle of the patio door. "I'll leave the keys. In three days time I will text your sister from *your* phone, telling her to come and release you."

"From *my* phone?"

"Yes. I'm taking it. That was her that called you last, her number will show."

"Menna don't take my phone, *please.*"

"One good thing, Nico might call leaving you a message telling you where he's hiding."

"Wait a minute... Did you say *three* days?"

"Yes," Carmen answered for Menna. Now it is *us* that will be keeping you waiting, you bastard! A flipside to the coin, hey?!"

"No... you can't do this... I might need the toilet... Food... how am I gonna survive?"

"You will," Menna moved closer and whispered in his ears, *"we did."*

"Yes, but *did you,* though? *Did you* survive? Is this survival? You've turned into mad bitches..."

Menna moved in with raised brows and widened eyes as if for the kill.

"... You've stooped to my level," he started so he finished.

"Blow!!!" Menna planted the first blow to his left cheek, "Cut the cheek, yuh fucka!"

"Blow!!!" and another one from Joya.

Then Colette.

Then Melissa followed by Sharon.

Conteh's face swung *right-left-right-left-right*.

* * *

When Morag escaped from Lance's grip and hit the stairs like Nico had earlier, she couldn't get out and into her car fast enough.

But it was only when she got outside that she could confirm who was really in her house.

Lawrence.

It was his car that was sitting purposefully on her drive.

And why did he decide not to intervene?

Why was he just standing there in the living-room like a *see-no-evil-hear-no-evil* monkey?

* * *

Carmen was the last of the ladies to land Conteh a vicious blow.

The harshest saved till last.

She pulled back and winded him with none other than a sharp right hook. Straight to his gut. "Goodbye, Conteh. See you in hell."

"Not if I see you first," he screeched.

Now, he watched the ladies filing, one after the other out of his living-room. Menna hung in the doorway while the others walked towards the front door that led to the communal car. But it obviously wasn't over for Carmen as yet. She breezed back past Menna and headed again for the human target. "Oh... I just remembered," she said sarcastically, rolling her sleeves up and reaching inside her for strength. She pulled back again and landed him one right in his *two-meat-an'-veg*, "this is for *Glenda,*" she continued, "remember her?... one of the white women who is a mother of *some* of your children?" She was in his face now...

Conteh's eyes widened for two reasons: *agony* and *surprise*: the punch to his dick, and the '*How did you know about Glenda?*' question.

"There's *more?*" Menna asked, staring at Conteh with a puzzled look and shaking her head.

"... *One of* the women," Carmen continued, "you kept in the background for years. *One of* the women you denied... You drove her to fucking drink."

If looks could kill, Carmen would be dead, and if he could release himself, he'd personally kill her.

"I remember once… years ago, *you bastard,*" Carmen continued. "I called you on your mobile… there was a baby crying in the background… *remember?* I asked you whose baby that was… *'I'm babysitting for a friend'*, you said… it was later I come to realise the baby was *yours*. You even denied your own children. Looking back, you must have seen the word *'stupid'* written on all of our faces. I'm so glad Simone left you. She deserves better that a little piece a shit like *you,* yuh fucka!" She turned and left the room.

Conteh kept his head down. He had no answer for himself. The once over-confident, perpetual liar and serial cheat who spun women more yarns than he would ever care to remember, was lost for words. At that moment, he recalled how many black women he told, *'I don't check white women'. Why?* God knows. But now, as he stood there, pitifully attached to the patio door, there were about three teenaged, and about seven younger ones, all mixed-raced, scattered around Birmingham. Children his ex-wife didn't know existed. Children who would most certainly develop deep complexes at the thought of being *denied.* Not good. *No sir.*

"There, there, there, my little poochie-woochie," Menna mocked in a patronising baby-talk voice, as she pinched his left cheek, *hard,* "what's the matter?… baby being cornered by his past?… what a shame. Never mind." She took a deep breath, then added in a more serious tone, "We could have been good together, you and I… but so could you and your wife. Who's sorry now?" Now she too turned and left the room, flicking the light off and leaving him in pitch darkness, but not before picking up her umbrella. "I'll lock the door and push the key back through the letterbox!" she shouted. "At least your sister's key will work when she comes to rescue you!"

"Menna!" he despaired, "don't leave me like dis, *please!*… Menna?!… Menna?!"

But the only reply he had, was the clinking of a Pyrex dish against the inside of the porch, followed by the anger-filled slamming of the front door.

He had spread his bed with enough lying, cheating and dishonesty, and now, he was lying on its troubled, uncomfortable springs. *Feh real.*

His heart sunk.

His spirit died. What was left of it, that is.

Back in the days he had it all…

All the spirit in the world…

In abundance… *Spirit-a-di-pum-pum*… Feh real.

* * *

Fairweather friends: Morag and Sheree… They both suited each other. Which was why it was a bit of a shock as to why Sheree decided to take a thirty minutes car journey to personally post Morag's birthday card and vouchers from Rackhams through her door. Last year, although she posted it on time, it arrived three days late. Sheree wasn't that bothered when it got there, but when Morag gave her a big piece of her mind she decided to force the effort this year. The card and vouchers were bought in advance, written up and placed in a drawer. But it was an hour ago as she hunted for an item of underwear, that she found it. Morag's birthday was the following morning: hence the *spur-of-the-moment* decision to take the thirty-minute journey to her house.

'*Yeah,*' Sheree spoke to herself when the *bat-out-of hell* driver in the silver Mercedes flew past her around five minutes from Morag and Lance's house. "*So you've got a fucking Mercedes SLR, but you don't have to drive so fast. It's not a fucking motorway,*'

Her mobile rang but she left it to go to voice mail. In less than ten minutes she would be free to return the call to whoever wanted her. It was just after midnight. She didn't expect any life at Morag's. She would drop the card without making a sound, then leave.

But things don't always go to plan.

Sheree slowed up when she recognised Lawrence's car behind Lance's Land Rover Discovery. Morag's car was missing.

'*Shit,*' she thought, '*Lance and his friend Lawrence are obviously having a boys night in. Love to see you, Lawrence. If I had known you were here, I would have spruced up a bit.*'

She reversed a few yards from the house, got out and walked careful up the drive with Morag's card in her hand. Gently, she lifted the letter hatch and eased the card through, trying not to make too much of a rattle, when sounds from the inside met her ears:

She heard voices.

Men's voices. Inexplicable tones.

Groans.

Sexual groans.

The expression of *pleasure.* Or *pain,* even.

The giving and the taking.

Adverse love-making, some would say.

Diverse, others would say.

258

Sheree paused. She let the flap down gently so it held the card firm in the mouth of the letter box, lest its falling would disturb a flow.

What was she hearing? Could it be the TV? Her curiosity became hungry, but how could she satisfy it?

Nosey, she might be called, but that was the least of her worries. She tiptoed round to the side of the house, where, lucky for her, there were no probe lighting. And *bingo*. Just what she had hoped for: the small gate was carelessly left unlocked, and as she carefully lifted the latch and proceeded down the path that led to their backyard, Sheree felt like a criminal. She was familiar with the entrance, as she had used it with Morag once before when she had locked herself out and was trying different measures to get in.

Sheree's heart pumped as she followed her nose down, round and into the backyard. Luckily, the darkness wasn't a pitch-black one – it was light enough for her to see where her feet were going.

Reaching an appropriate spot in Lance's back yard, she stood there...

Staring...

Staring...

Staring in on a sight she had not expected to see. No... not in a million years:

Two sturdy, bare-assed males.

She could hear her own heart beating now.

One spread-eagled and facing the wall.

She covered her mouth as if to stop herself emitting her thoughts.

The other behind.

Her mind swung to bygone years...

Searching...

Searching...

Searching for telltale clues of Lawrence's bisexuality. For actions of non-interest in her. But no... there were none. So how come?... did he just suddenly *discover*?...

Moving...

'Oh, Lawrence... no... no... no', she thought.

Grooving... enjoying.

Was this the lounge in her friend's house? No. Couldn't be. More like a corner down in Sodom and Gomorrah?

Sheree's heart palpitated more and more. She wanted to scream. She kept her mouth covered to stop herself, then fumbled her way back up the side entrance and to her car. She couldn't remember how she got in, but she had sat there for a few seconds before the thought came to her. Acting on it would be risky, but she felt she had to. For selfish or unselfish purposes – whatever. She opened the boot of her car and retrieved the in-built-flash-censored camera that still held a half-used film. *'I need this evidence'*, she told herself. Luckily for her, her expert developer friend could help. Leaving photos like that with the average film-developer on the High Street would more than likely attract police presence.

But it was when she sat in her car again that she finally spoke to herself in depth: *'Lawrence and Lance. Lovers. Their marriages are farces. Now I know why you found it so easy to refuse another bit, Mr Hendricks. Why mess with another women, when the one you have is just for show? But why get married? It's the 21st century. Or did you think Simone could straighten you?'*

Sheree pulled away from the area. Slow… slow… She felt she knew the score: Lawrence and Lance were most certainly *not* alone. Bisexuality was not partial to creed, colour or race. Many men have done what's pleasing in the eyes of society. But without a doubt, when the sun sets, and the world about them sleep, they *seek*, *find* and *taste* the controversial nectar of a *society-condemned* fruit.

* * *

Simone was jolted from a sweet dream by the frantic banging on her front door… It frightened her. First she thought of the police and worried for the safety of her husband, then she thought, *'No. The police wouldn't knock so frantically.'*

She got out of bed, pulled on her dressing-gown and headed downstairs.

"Who is it?" she asked anxiously.

"It's me. Morag."

"Morag?!" Simone opened the door now to find Morag standing there with a face like a dropped pumpkin.

"Morag?" what happened to…?"

Morag stepped in. "I'm in real trouble, Simone."

"What trouble? What is it? Have you been attacked?"

"Yes, but it's my fault."

"Who did this to you?"

"Lance."

"Lance?!"

"Simone, I had some one at the house. We were actually…"

"What d'you mean you had someone at the house... not another man?"

"Yes. Lance wasn't due back until tomorrow. He just turned up."

"Lance is back? Then so should Lawrence be... He's probably on his way home then."

"Simone, I left your husband at my house. He was there. All the time Lance was laying into me."

"And what did Lawrence do?"

"Nothing. He just stayed downstairs."

"Lawrence? No... I can't believe that, Morag, I really can't believe that. I don't think he would just stand there and allow a man to beat a woman..."

"Well, he was in the living-room. Lance beat my lover up. Threw him out. Then he started on me. At first I wasn't sure who it was downstairs. It was only when I ran out the front door to my car that I realised. Lawrence's car was on the drive."

Simone paused. "Sit down, Morag. Let me get you a drink." She searched for explanation. *'Why would Lawrence allow this to happen without intervening?'*

The bronzed blonde lady sat on the edge of the settee. She was cold. The only thing that protected her was her dressing gown, which was more than could be said for Nico. Only God knew where he had got to, and *how*, since he was clad in nothing but his birthday suit.

Minutes later, Simone entered the room with *the Englishman's answer to everything*: a cup of tea. "Just a second, Morag, I'll get you some proper clothes", she said handing the distressed lady the cup. But no sooner than she attempted to go upstairs, the sound of rattling keys.

"Darling?" she said curiously as her husband walked in. There were questions in her eyes. "Hi."

"Hi," Lawrence said, "how come you're up?" But Lawrence's question was answered when he looked past his wife and saw Morag sitting in his living-room clutching a cup as if for dear life. As he got closer, he saw her battered face. "Morag?... are you ok?"

"Why didn't you stop him?" she asked Lawrence with hateful eyes.

"Sorry?... Stop *who*?"... Lawrence stared even more at Morag's face.

"Don't play the innocent, Lawrence... why didn't you stop him?"

He walked slowly towards her. "Stop *who* Morag?" The question of *'What happened to your face?'* was lingering on his tongue, but the fact that Morag thought he should have stopped *someone* doing *something* made him *reprioritise*.

"*Lance!*... Why didn't you stop Lance when he was trying to kill me?!"

A puzzled look engulfed Lawrence's face. "*What*?... Lance did this to you?"

"Why are you pretending? I know I was wrong, Lawrence, but he could have killed me!"

"Morag... whoa...whoa... slow down... what are you talking about? You think I'm pretending?" His tall figure stood over her now. Arms folded and like a fly on the wall, Simone hovered near, waiting to hear her husband's explanation.

"You just stood there in the living-room as if you wanted it to happen!"

"Morag...slow down..." He looked at his wife as if for help, then back at Morag. "You've lost me... totally. Morag... *please*... what gave you the idea that I was in your living-room when...?"

But just then, the anger seemed to have left Morag's voice. It was as if she was doing a rethink. "Was it not *you* that was standing in the living-room earlier when Lance and I were having a fight?"

Lawrence smiled now, but not amusingly – more like *with relief*. "Morag, if you saw someone looking like me standing in your living-room earlier, it must have been Clive."

"Clive? But it was *your* car on the drive..."

"Yes. Of course it was my car on the drive. That's because I left it for Clive. It was his idea. I took him up on the offer of taking his Mercedes SLR for a spin. I only intended to have a quick spin there and then, but he insisted that I took it home and have a proper spin tomorrow. I didn't even come into your house. See for yourself, Lance's car is outside on my drive."

Simone breathed a sigh of relief then headed upstairs to get Morag some proper clothes. She had heard her husband's explanation and it satisfied her mind. She knew there had to be a feasible one. Lawrence wasn't the violent type, and standing by while a man lay into a woman wouldn't be his style. But she couldn't help wondering now, *why* Clive didn't try to stop it, regardless of *who* was right or wrong.

"Sorry, Lawrence," Morag apologised, "I thought..."

"It's ok, Morag," he emitted a cynical chuckle. "Perhaps it's not such a good thing that me and Clive look alike after all... So... what happened?" he asked, going back to the situation at hand, why did Lance *do* this to you?... Your face is a mess."

Morag hesitated. Dropped her voice. Averted her eyes. "It was my fault. I... I had someone there."

"What d'you mean, Morag?"

"I didn't expect Lance back. He said the flight was scheduled to be back tomorrow."

"You mean Lance caught you with another man in his house?"

"More than that, Lawrence. We were in bed."

"What?! You had another man in your husband's bed?!... No... no... I don' wanna hear that," he lay a bunch of car keys on the fireplace. "This can't be true." He looked at Simone who had just walked back in the room with a pair of jeans and a jumper for Morag. Simone shrugged her shoulders helplessly.

Morag kept her eyes on her feet.

Lawrence told himself that Lance's tales about Morag's suspected affairs were right.

"Lance hasn't touched me for months, Lawrence... what difference does it make? It's as if he went off me."

"Listen, Morag, I don't need to get into your business. Your personal life is your personal life - that is something you two need to sort out... and I'm not saying I condone affairs, but I suppose if you felt you needed to, you could go some place else... a hotel room... to the guy's place... whatever... but that's Lance's house... his bed... Jesus."

"I don't even know where he is," Morag said, crying.

"Is he not at home?"

"No. I don't mean *Lance*... Nico."

"Nico?" Simone piped up.

"Yes, you know Nico?" Morag assured her.

"Not... *the* Nico."

Morag said nothing.

Lawrence looked shocked. "You don't mean that *Nico* guy who's got..."

Simone stopped him with a look. "Darling, I think I heard Amari calling, could you just..."

Lawrence took the hint and left the room. "Jesus," he said under his breath.

"Here," Simone said, handing Morag the change of clothes. "Put these on. They'll fit. I'll go get you another cup of tea."

The tea-making and the clothes-changing didn't take long, and soon the ladies were sat together like a counsellor and her client.

"Morag," Simone was sat on the settee opposite. "Have you been sleeping with *Nico*?… Conteh's friend, *Nico*?"

"Like I said, what difference does it make? I don't seem to interest Lance anymore. If it wasn't Nico, it would have been someone else."

"Yeah… but that's just it. It would have been better if it *was* someone else…" Simone got up, walked over and sat close to Morag. "Morag… have you been using protection?" She felt a slight touch of dejavu. It didn't seem so long ago that she had a similar conversation with her late friend Pam, for whom she had cried endlessly since AIDS claimed her life.

"Why?"

"*Wh*y?… you're having an affair, and is asking *why* you should use protection?… Don't the possible effects of unprotected sex worry you?… what if you… pick something up?"

Morag looked at Simone as if she could detect something more than a mere little lecture in her voice. Her eyes asked, *'What is it?'*

"Morag… you can remember Pam, right?"

" 'Course I can. How could anyone forget Pam? She died of AIDS."

"And you can remember the jewellery party at my house."

"Yeah… That's where I first met Nico."

"Well, you can't have forgotten that Nico left with Pam."

"I know. But he just gave her a lift. He said nothing happened. He didn't sleep with her."

"Oh…" Simone rolled her eyes in disbelief. "And you believed him right?"

"Morag said nothing. Supposedly she had come to *realise.*

"Morag, if there was one thing Pam didn't make any bones about, it was telling me *when* she slept with someone, *how*, and most certainly *who*. And believe me, Nico was definitely one of them."

Morag's face was a shadow of death and fear walked through the valley of her eyes. "Please tell me you're joking, Simone."

"I wish it was a joke, Morag, but Pam wouldn't tell a lie. With Pam, what you saw was what you got."

"But, that was a long time ago…"

"Look, Morag, we're all educated enough now about HIV and AIDS. An HIV carrier could look more healthy than you and I. That's what makes it so dangerous."

"Oh my God," Morag whispered in total despair.

"How long have Lance stopped showing interest in you? Have you slept with him since you started sleeping with Nico?"

"No... I haven't... I haven't been sleeping with Lance for ages. And I haven't been sleeping with Nico all that long either... about six months. In fact he hadn't called for a long while after the jewellery party. I didn't think he would. When he called, he had to remind me who he was. As I said, Lance wasn't showing much interest in me, so I decided to meet up with Nico for a coffee... the rest is history."

"So Lance isn't in danger then?" Lawrence asked. He stood now at the door of the living-room. He wasn't eavesdropping, but he couldn't help hearing it all.

"No... Lance isn't in danger. I definitely haven't slept with him after Nico."

"Jesus," Lawrence said, both in relief and disbelief.

Morag felt *judged*. She rose quickly from her seat and the urgency to leave took precedence over everything else. "I have to go. Thank you for listening."

"Why don't you let Lawrence drive you home, Morag? Or stay until the morning. You are totally stressed."

"No... no... I need to go."

"Are you going home? Are you sure Lance has calmed down?"

"I'm going home... yes... I don't know if he's calmed down... She turned and looked at the couple she had envied ever since they got together. And although she had spent more sociable hours with Sheree, Morag knew that Simone had a heart of gold. She knew this couple were meant to be. "It's my birthday tomorrow," she said almost out of context. "What a shitty fucking birthday present."

Simone hugged her. What else could she do?

"See you guys," Morag said, fighting back another fits of tears.

Simone and Lawrence held each other as they both listened to the disappearing sound of Morag's engine.

"What a mess," Simone said.

"Mess isn't the word." Lawrence looked deep into his wife's eyes.

"*What?*" Simone asked, seeing the depth of his stare.

"Nothing. Just appreciating my blessing."

He smiled.

"Why can't people be straight with each other?" he asked hypothetically.

"D'know... I guess that's human beings for you."

"Poor Lance. That must have been pretty shitty. Walking in to find another man in your bed with your wife… *Jesus."*

"You like Lance, don't you?"

"I can't say I've been given any reason not to like him. He's an all right kinda guy. I think he's planning something at work. Maybe to do with pay, I don't know. I could feel it. But he's human like the rest of us – *not perfect*, but overall, he's ok."

"C'mon," Simone said, taking his hand. "Let's go to bed."

Chapter 16

"*No*," Simone said with pleasure. "Don't tell me… not those shoes?!" She had seen them in a boutique.

He wasn't even with her.

One thing for sure, he knew her taste.

She gasped as she admired the most beautiful piece of footwear that sat in the middle of her living-room.

A man with sensitivity. Lawrence. Really… what a man?

* * *

"Yuh sure yuh don't want to go to the Red Affair dance tomorrow, Empress?" Lijah asked Gloria, as she fluffed her cushions for what must have been the tenth time. Her Hoover was appreciating a rest. Her Obsessive Compulsive Disorder for cleaning wasn't yet diagnosed, but surely it was there. She knew it too, but it wasn't taking over her life, so it was nothing to worry about.

"No, Lijah, you know we don't have no babysitter. If Shari was here we could have left Khamilla and Shanique with her. But she is still in London with Ikesha."

The word *'babysitter'* will always be a phobic word to Lijah. After all, who could forget Faithlyn? "They are spending a lot of time together, aren't they?"

"Yes," Gloria said. "Good. From what they've been telling me, it's all positive."

"What? Yuh mean that *Don't Be Influenced* thing they're doing?"

"Yes. Looks like we're gonna have two people in our family to be extremely proud of, Lijah. The idea and how they're gonna run it, sounds wicked. They seem to have it all planned. They've got funding and everything."

"They're working with that young DJ aren't they…?"

"Yes," Gloria assured him. "Andre Johnson… STAL, his street name is. I hear he's brilliant. Write some serious lyrics. Positive messages in all his tracks an' dat."

"We need more ah dat, Empress, trus' mi."

"I have always known that Ikesha would do something like that, but her brother Kunta getting caught up in drugs and dying only made her more determined. I'm so proud of her."

"I know, Empress."

"I'm so glad that I'm one of the mum's that know her daughter pretty well. Ikesha talks to me about everything."

Lijah swallowed hard. First it was the talk of a *babysitter* that got him. Now, it was the pang of guilt. He knew full well that Gloria didn't know Ikesha that well. She didn't tell her *everything*…

Rock…

The rape…

Ikesha had begged him not to tell her, and although he knew this was just to protect her mother's emotions, it didn't help the guilt he was feeling just then.

"Yeah… yeah… true," he said through clenched teeth.

"She said she wants to concentrate on talking to young people about being positive, self-value, drugs, guns, date rape… that GHB drug t'ing…"

Lijah looked at her… "Guns? She's gonna talk about guns? But what does she know about guns, G?"

"Well, it's like saying, *'what does she know about Date Rape?'* She don't know anything about it personally, but I suppose she just wants to be the ambassador for positive young people…"

Lijah felt even guiltier now. He felt as if once more he had betrayed Gloria. She was Ikesha's mother. Surely she should know that Ikesha was raped.

"… Getting young people to be more careful," she smiled, "Lijah don't you think our daughter was born with an old head?"

"Yes… yes…"

He wanted to tell her that their baby had been raped by Rock.

The same guy who shot their only son.

The same guy who had beaten Shari up.

He wanted to tell her too that he and Reds had taken care of him.

That he had made sure Rock could never touch his family again.

But would that make it ok?

"And what will Shari and Andre be doing?" Lijah asked, pulling himself away from his guilt.

"I think they are all there to push positivity from all angles, Lijah."

"But they have to come a different way yunnuh, Empress," he replied with conviction.

"I know, but Ikesha an' Shari think that with them being so young themselves, young people might listen. Different from adults talking down to them all the time."

"Bwoy, we can only wish them luck, Empress."

"Three positive young people, hey?" Gloria said. "Perhaps they can teach some of us adults a thing or two."

"Believe me," Lijah said.

"Why don't *you* go to the dance, Lijah?"

"Without you?… nah man."

"Why not? You can wear that nice red shirt you wore in Jamaica. That really suits you."

Lijah looked unsure…

"Go, Lijah. Get Festus to come out. I was speaking to Kizzy earlier. She said she wasn't going. I'm thinking of inviting her 'round. We haven't really spoken properly since we left Jamaica."

Kizzy… another pang of guilt for Lijah. Third time unlucky. He felt a thousand butterflies fluttering in his belly this time. Gloria's best friend. *He had fucked her*. And if only he knew she was his half-sister, he would die. "And you have lots to talk about haven't you?"

"You could say that."

"Good her and Festus are trying to work things out. That damn Baby Face Glen."

Gloria paused. "I still can't believe how small the world is."

"It's even smaller than we're thinking now, G."

"Gee wiz."

"Yuh t'ink Festus will be up to dis Red Affair t'ing?"

"Ring him, Lijah. Or go check him."

He looked at her, half sure about stepping out without her to an occasion that sounds so good. Farther Jarvis' dances are always swinging. "Are you sure you'll be ok?" Or maybe he was frightened Kizzy might come clean about their mad, passionate moment.

"Yes. I'll be fine. Kizzy will come 'round. Fari can sleep here. Like I said, we have nuff catching-up to do."

* * *

268

Janet had only asked her guests' excuse while she nipped out for a few minutes to bring her brother some dinner. But ever since she got back to the house, no conversation could take her mind off him. She was preoccupied with the notion that something was *seriously* wrong. Conteh was a deep sleeper, but with all that banging and shouting she did, surely he would have woken. She knew he hadn't gone out.

"We'll talk soon," Janet said to her last guest but one. "Thanks for coming, we have to do dis again."

"Sandra," she said now with intent as she hurried back to her lounge. Her sister was sitting there on the settee, her feet curled beneath her, as if she had no particular place to go anytime soon. "Come wid me," Janet stressed.

Sandra drained the last drip of wine from a bottle into her glass, staring at her sister.

"Where to?" she perplexed.

"To Conteh's"

"Why? What for? Didn't you just bring his dinner over?"

"I didn't want to say anything when the others were here, but when I went round earlier, his keys were in the door, so I *knew* he was there, but I rang, banged, shouted… *everything*… but nothing."

"Yeah, but you know he's a deep sleeper these days and…"

"Come on, Sis', I don't like it. Let's go 'round."

"Oh, Christ," she grinned cynically, "you're so dramatic. You're not expecting to find him hanging from the ceiling or something like that, are you?" Sandra downed the remainder of her wine in one gulp and replaced her glass.

"Oh, don't talk so morbid, Sand', it's not funny."

"You are seriously worried, aren't you, Jan'?"

"Yes," she jabbed, "jus' come."

Sandra considered herself *told*. She lifted her ass from her comfortable position and walked towards her jacket, "Come on then, *Mother*."

"Shut up," Janet retaliated playfully, though obviously still unsettled.

The sisters headed for the front door, leaving the after-dinner mess until later.

It wasn't long before they were on Conteh's doorstep. Janet rang the bell again, only this time she wondered *why the lights were off when it was previously on* and she had noticed too that *the dinner was gone from the door handle. 'Conteh must have taken it,* she thought, *'so why couldn't he just ring and say thanks?'*

"He must be gone to bed," Sandra said, "let's go."

"No. I'm going in." She fumbled in her bag. "Why would he just take the dinner, eat it, then climb into bed without ringing to say thank you? He's not that rude, Sand'."

Barely above his next-door neighbour's shouting, f'ing and blinding, Conteh could hear the chatter on his doorstep. If only he could get his sister's attention. "Jan'! Sandra! I'm in here!" *No use.* Drowned out or even mingled in with the sound from next door. He gave up trying.

"Jesus," Sandra said, listening to the fiery shouting, banging and screaming that were coming from the house next door, "I think they're about to kill each other, don't you?"

"They're always arguing. Conteh says they never stops," Janet told her.

"Anyway," Sandra said, "what if Conteh's got a woman in there?"

"Sandra, yuh sick? *Woman?* Our brother is HIV positive. *Woman?"*

"Oh, Sis', you're so naïve. It doesn't stop some people you know."

"Conteh isn't like that, Sandra. He might have been a love rat, but he won't knowingly put people's lives at risk. Not when he know he's HIV positive."

"He could use a condom. There are married couples where one is HIV positive you know. They just use tip-top protection."

"Listen, I don't want to discuss my brothers sex life, I just wanna find this goddamn spare key, I used it earlier, where the hell is it?" she said, still fumbling frantically into her handbag.

"Here's mine," Sandra handed her sister her key, squirming from the noise of next-door's feud, "But I don't know how you expect it to work now, it didn't earlier."

But a split second after Janet took the key, her mobile bleeped. Automatically she checked it. "It's from Conteh," she said. Now they both eased into the text. *'Hi, Sis' it's me. Sorry about earlier. I was upstairs… had company. Crucial moment. Couldn't come down. Still with her now. Don't worry. Condoms. Give me a couple of days, Sis'… it's been a long time… I'll call you… oh… thanks for the dinner.'*

"Oh, shit," Janet said.

"Told you," Sandra said, feeling she had won. "It doesn't stop people, Sis'. It's a good thing the text came before we pushed the key and went in... hah!"

"Shut up."

"Hah! Hah! Hah! That would have been embarrassing. We could have walked in on them."

"No we wouldn't. He's obviously in the bedroom with her. You can see the front of the house is in darkness. He would have heard us and shout, *'Don't enter the bedroom'*, or something," Janet said as she walked back down the drive. At the same time, she pressed the *send* button on her *'Ok, Bro'. I'll wait for your call'* message. She replaced her phone in her handbag and returned Sandra's key.

Sandra chuckled, "Our brother. HIV or not, he still wants his nookie. Hah! Hah! Hah!'

"Don't be disgusting, Sandra."

"Well, it's true... isn't that what his text said, Sis'? *Ah want mi some nookie tonight!* Sandra sang, *'Ah want mi some nookie tonight! Hah! Hah! Hah!'*

"Well, at least he's ok," Janet said, starting the engine and smiling at her sister's flippancy.

"Well," Sandra added, "I'll tell you one thing... if that condom burst, whoever she is, she won't be ok. Shi faat."

'Ok,' was the text that Menna returned. Being in control of Conteh's phone was proving ok already. If his sister was convinced that he was *getting some* with a condom, then that was ok for her. *Plan A* was well and truly taken care of.

* * *

Friday closed with a strange feel about it... 11:30pm... Menna sat, her eyes fixed on a woodlouse trundling across her laminated flooring. *'Little things'*, she thought, *'but don't underestimate them... they eat through wood. It's a part of their survival mechanism... Women.... they're often underestimated too, yet when pushed, they can be seriously deadly'*.

It was two whole days since the avenging six had left Conteh in bondage in his own house, and still no sign of a phone call from Nico coming through on his phone. Menna expected it. In her attempt to flush him out, she had sent a text to his mobile, pretending to be Conteh. She had waited... and waited... allowing all other calls that came through to go through to voicemail. She ignored the text messages: *after reading them of course,* but not one iota from the notorious Nico.

But it was as she sat pondering, that the idea came to her.

It was a long-shot, since Conteh had already told her that Nico was un-contactable. He had called her number the day she had landed and a few times since, trying to intimidate her, so now, she'll call his' in the name of *PEACE.*

It wasn't surprising. Nico's mobile was on voicemail.

He was a little laid-up.

Licking fresh wounds an' t'ing.

How was Menna to know that he was still aching from a gruesome ass-kicking from a black Airline pilot? Running nude into the bitter-cold night was the last thing he had expected, and stealing a semi-wet jeans and a make-do jumper from a nearby washing-line didn't stop him catching a nasty chill.

Menna got her sweetest voice out, and as soon the tone on Nico's voicemail kicked in, she started: '*Nico... Hi. It's me, Menna. Well, Jade to you. Whatever. I know you're pissed off with the way I played you and Conteh together, but I had my reasons. Anyway, it's time to put all this behind us now. I come in peace, Nico. Truce and all dat. I would like to meet you and Conteh for a mature chat. Tomorrow night would be nice. At my flat. 8pm sharp. Oh, by the way, Conteh has already agreed to come. He thinks it's a great idea. Making peace is the least I can do. You can call Conteh to confirm if you want. He told me he tried to call you but couldn't get you. I hope you will come, Nico. Menna.*'

Menna lived in *hope.* She hoped Nico would call, in which she would let him go to voice mail. But better still, she wished he would call Conteh's mobile...

A minute past midnight.

The *hope* game had played its course.

Conteh's phone lit up with '*Nico calling*'.

Menna let it ring out and into voicemail.

Seconds later when the message alert came, she listened with a cynical grin on her face, '*Yo! Bredrin! Bombo claat... What a turn up fi di books?... Menna waan talk to raas claat. Yeah, man. Dat good. Shi tell me seh yuh agree to meet. It feel a likkle strange, but dat good still. Next t'ing she'll be telling us she's going to church, Bredrin. Chuckle, chuckle. Call mi w'en yuh get dis message, addawise, I'll see you at her flat tomorrow. 8pm sharp shi seh. An' Bredrin... sorry mi neva call yuh or return yuh text an' t'ing, but I'll explain w'en mi si yuh. Right now mi mash up... Long story... A cat came home while I tried to play Super-Mouse to raas... Still... talk to yuh tomorrow.'*

Menna couldn't have wished for better. The worst that could have happened was for Nico to ring Conteh's home phone and talk to him direct. But since Conteh couldn't reach the phone from his captive spot, she needn't worry. Failing that, Nico could pass round and knock him up. Likewise, he couldn't get to the door either.

She took pleasure in texting back: *'Yes, Bredrin. Where have you been? Tried nuff time. No reply. Glad yuh a'right still. Yes, see you at Menna's flat tomorrow. 8pm. Sharp. Yes, it's a likkle strange but when I spoke to her, shi sounded genuine. Dah church t'ing deh possible still. Shi seem repentant an' t'ing. Good that shi wants to talk, man.'* She hit the send button.

Seconds later the phone rang. Whoops! *'Nico calling'*. He obviously wanted to talk. She left it be. It went to voicemail. *'No worries, Bredrin,'* the voicemail said. *'Just wanted to talk to you before tomorrow. No worries. See you at 8'.*

Menna didn't reply. She was convinced that Nico would show.

But for Menna, the next day came with a more acute strangeness than the one before.

It felt weird.

It could be likened to an artist anticipating a stage entry: rushes of adrenalin pinching her from time to time throughout the day. For whilst half the black population of Birmingham got ready to rave later at the fall of night, Menna prepared for a crucial *'shake down'*. Her helpers were waited in the wings of a beckoning phone call...

A phone call that would beckon them to come running.

An ass was getting to blasé for its underwear.

And that ass needed to be kicked. *Seriously.*

Time. It is surely longer than rope.

* * *

One is lonesome... Two is company... And three is a goddamn crowd. *So they say.*

7pm. Saturday. A cold November night.

A troublesome trio adorned in red from their heads to their toes, were sure to grace the entrance of the Banana Baits nightclub. Father

273

Jarvis had used his magnet charm channelled through his music to pull them, but before that, these sistas had a mission to accomplish.

There was a time when Birmingham wasn't big enough for the three of them:

They shared the same dick.

The dick of a notorious soundman… *Conteh Gonzales*. Chat 'bout.

For a while, they shared the same reason for screaming…

And now, that desperate need for screaming needed to be avenged.

One reason

One aim.

One gruesome destiny. Feh real.

But now, they shared the same mirror in Joya's flat.

A mirror into which they stared, catching a glimpse at their images, almost as if it was the last.

"Ready?" Carmen the leader of the pack (for now at least) asked.

"Damn right," Colette confirmed.

Joya nodded, "Uh huh." She pressed her scarlet lips together as if they were part of the plan.

"Then let's go," Carmen commanded.

Watching Conteh squirm on Wednesday night was just a portion of justice served. But what they were about to do before they make the big entrance into Banana Baits would simply be *another speckle of justice*.

Justice served up for umpteen *wronged* women all over Birmingham. Working under the spell of the subtle *Group Dynamic theory*, someone was about to be hung out… *to die.* Lord, Lord, Lord.

When the doorbell went, Menna was wondering who had turned up so early… 7:15 was not a scheduled time on her agenda, and she had stated to all, *'sharp'*.

"How do I look, Sis'?" Cynthia asked as she brushed past her sister in the doorway. She had stopped by simply to show off her slinky little red number and to try to persuade Menna come.

"You look good, Sis'," Menna said, looking down the corridor, "but then red always suited you… anyway, I didn't know you were coming 'round."

"So I have to announce my *'coming 'round'* now, do I?" Cynthia said with attitude. "It was ok for me to look after your yard while you swan around in JA, but…"

"You know I don't mean it like that, Sis'."

"Then what *do* you mean?" She hadn't taken her eyes out of Menna's full-length mirror since she walked in, "you've never said that to me before."

"Anyway, I *should* say it to you. What if I had a man here or something?"

"That's true… but I didn't think…" she looked questioningly at her sister.

"You never do. And anyway, you're going to this dance early aren't you? You know these dances don't start to hot-up until at least 10/11 O'clock."

"No I'm not going straight, I have to pick up a friend in West Brom. By the time I get there (considering she won't be ready) advise her on a thousand different outfits, blah, blah, blah, drive back to Birmingham, find parking…"

"OK, Sis', I hear yah." Menna was getting fidgety.

"So you're definitely not coming, Menz?"

"No, Sis'." Menna glanced at her watch. She was hovering, her body language shouting, *'C'mon, Sis', go!'* And in the nicest possible way, she wished she were gone, like *yesterday.*

Cynthia detected Menna's anxiety. "What's the matter? How yuh so jumpy? Yuh *are* expecting someone, aren't you? It look like yuh definitely waan mi out a di way." Her brows knitted into an acute state of curiosity.

Menna smiled and said, "No I'm not expecting anyone. Do I really seem jumpy?"

"Yes. That's probably why you're not coming. Yuh have man ah come. Yuh dark horse, yuh."

"No, Cynthia, I'm not coming because all that *red* will only remind me of that *red silk sheet shit* me and Conteh had going on. Besides, he'll probably be there, him and that damn fool, Nico… No, Sis'… I have better things to do."

"Well *excuse me*," Cynthia said sarcastically.

Menna knew all too well that the only dance Conteh would be doing is the *'I want to piss'* dance. And that was if he had not already done it on the floor!

"Mi gaan," Cynthia said as she headed for the door. "Well *I* haven't got anything betta than Father Jarvis keeping me dancing all night," she said sarcastically, wheeling her ass through the door.

"Enjoy yuhself, Sis'," Menna told her, glancing again at her watch.

7:30pm *'Shit. Cutting it fine'*, she thought, as she closed the door behind her jolly sister, hoping she wouldn't bump into anyone coming towards her flat.

* * *

It was inevitable that as the moment drew near, Nico would be apprehensive... He still *loved* her. Or at least, like a pendulum, his feelings had straddled across the thin line between love and hate.... Not so long ago he *hated* her and wanted revenge.

It had been five years, and there he was hoping his face wasn't so bruised.

HIV positive but still wanted to look his best for the first woman he had ever loved.

His flat was a mess.

His ribs hurt from the encounter with Morag's husband a few days ago.

And the chill he had caught was giving him a run for his callous deeds.

8pm sharp, Menna had said.

He splashed Jean-Paul Gaultier about his face...

Ran his fingers through his Coolie hair...

Took a deep breath and left his bachelor's pad.

* * *

The room wasn't big enough for both of them.

"C'mon, Janet, get out the mirror now, man, you look good," Sandra urged.

"Ok, ok... eager beaver, five minutes," Janet said.

"I'm really looking forward to this," Sandra said. "You know when Father Jarvis plays, no one can sit down. That's why we've got to get going. No good wasting half the night in here."

"Yeah, but don't you think 7:40 is a still much too early to leave out?"

"Maybe. But there's a nice lounge area. We can sit and have a few drinks before it starts buzzing."

"*You* can have a few. What will *I* be having, water? I'm driving."

"Don't be so extreme Jan'. There are other non-alcoholic drinks than water. And I hope you're not moaning... I drove last time, *remember*?"

"Mmmm..." Janet seemed a little distant.

276

"Isn't red a passionate colour?" Sandra said, admiring herself in the mirror her sister had just freed.

"Feh real. But to some, it spells danger… Conteh said he was definitely coming. I wonder if he still is?"

"It all depend on if he can let go of that woman. Hah! Hah! Hah!" Sandra laughed as if the idea was funnier than anything she had had to imagine in a long while.

"Yeah, right, like he'd still be holding her now," Janet nudged her sister out of the mirror, "yuh funny."

"Well… he text said '*Give me a couple of days,*' didn't it?"

"That's true, but that was *Wednesday*, Sis… Wednesday, Thursday, Friday and today Saturday? Nah, man. I thought he would have called by now. Still, I think he'll come. Perhaps he'll take her… then we'll see who this woman is."

"D'you think he'll wear red if he comes?" Sandra asked.

"No."

"He shouldn't have a problem. Remember that thing we heard… about his fetish with red silk?" Sandra smirked.

"Yes, but that was meant to be for his women's beds, Sandra, not *him* wearing it. I don't think a lot of men will… I can't see Conteh in a red shirt anyway."

"Can't you?"

"No I can't… I'm just wondering what he's doing that he had to hibernate for so long. He can't be… *doing it* all this time, he'll be drained."

"*Doing it?* Jan' *I* used to be the prudish one. Now listen to you? *Doing it*… don't you mean fucking?"

Janet gave her sister an *I-can't-believe-you* look and said, "You're something else. If Mum could ever hear you."

Sandra leaned her right leg in a suggestive pose, jerked her hips flirtatiously, and boomed, "I want mi some nookie tonight!"

Janet, almost falling for the wind-up, said, "Don't be so *disgusting*. C'mon. And no dirty dancing tonight, you're with me."

"I'll dance how the Goddamn hell I like. You know music is like an aphrodisiac to me."

"Don't I know it?… but you just behave… action speaks louder than words, and we're all judged by the way we act."

"Jan'…" Sandra said.

"What?"

"Cut the Vicar's wife crap. We're going to a dance, not to church." She took one last glance in a nearby mirror, pressed her scarlet lips together and fiddled with her hair.

Janet raised her eyebrows at her sister. And as they headed for the front door, it was hard for her to be totally convinced that all was well with Conteh. Something was niggling her, but mentioning it to Sandra was totally out of the question.

* * *

It was just past 7:45pm.

Nico didn't know why, but he felt a compelling urge to pass by his idrin's house before venturing to Menna's flat.

He had previously hid his sorry ass away from him, since Conteh's lectures on his callous and deliberate '*infecting*' stance were getting on his last nerve. But now that he needed his hand held, Nico felt no way about searching out his idrin.

Although he had received the text telling him that Conteh would be at Menna's tonight at 8pm sharp, he was still a little apprehensive now that the time for the crucial rendezvous was fast approaching.

'*Turning up together would take the edge off t'ings,*' he thought. '*After all, it's been a long time. One minute I was tasting her sweet flesh, (through sensitive condoms of course) the next, I was listening my best-mate freaking on the fact that the woman I was screwing in my home-movie, was not Jade, but Menna! We had both fallen hook, line and sinker with her. She had tricked the fuckin' pants off us to raas!*'

He hadn't gotten over it. *No way.*

But now she called a truce, he was game. Not'n nuh wrong.

Why he didn't ring before, was neither here nor there, but why he decided to get out of his car and knock, even though he could see that Conteh's house was in pitch darkness, was a mystery. Perhaps it was because he heard shouting, but if his detection were better, he would know it was Conteh's neighbours arguing. *Again.* But this time, loud music acted as a backdrop to the feuding drama. And like it did when Janet and Sandra came, Conteh's voice was lost in it all.

He knocked once, "Yo! Conteh! Yuh diddeh, Bredrin?!" he shouted through the letterbox once, but it would be his last. To his reckoning, Conteh was clearly not there and must have made an early start to Menna's.

"Oi! Nico! Bredrin! Is dat you?" Conteh despaired again. But he knew that it was yet another hopeless quest. And it was no good trying to alert the people next door. Not even in their quietest moment. This was definitely not something he'd want them to know.

Nico climbed into his car and checked his watch.

7:50. He was cutting it fine but traffic permitting, he would make it.

* * *

It was 8pm… It seemed ages since Cynthia had left Menna… Half an hour is a pretty long time.

Sadly, it takes only minutes for an earthquake, a tsunami or even a bomb to wipe out whole cities. So in thirty minutes, to Menna's surmising, a lot had happened.

She knew her relaxation technique ok.

Long, deep breaths took care of her nerves, so when she opened the door to a nervous, sheepish-looking Nico, she was pretty much *in-control*.

"Hi." She widened the door and stepped aside, "glad you could come, Nico."

He stepped in, looking around unsure. "Whaap'n?… where's Conteh?"

"He called," Menna said, leading the way into her living-room. "Said he's running a little late. Had to stop off somewhere before he comes. He'll be here, don't worry." She gestured now to the three-seater. "Sit down, Nico."

He did. Apprehensively. On the edge.

"Relax, Nico. It's me. Didn't we have good times together?"

"What shall I call you?… *Jade? Menna?*…Which one are you going by these days?"

"*Menna*. We've all worn that T-shirt, Nico."

He looked around as he eased slightly back into the settee. He needed a comfort zone, so he placed his right elbow on its edge, his left parallel to the top, then, as if it were a ritual, he joined the fingers of both hands forming a symmetry. Their tips met, forming a pyramid, its tip pointing unintentionally at Menna.

"Drink?" She walked over to her drinks globe.

"Er… no thanks… no, I'll wait until Conteh comes."

"Friends to the end, hey? Even to the end, you're doing things together."

"*To the end*?" He eased back to the edge of the settee again, losing his pyramid. "Soun' like yuh about to tek me life or sop'n." He chuckled.

'*Isn't it already taken?*' she mumbled.

"What?"

"Nothing."

Elbows on both knees, arms out-stretched and the fingers of both arms entwined, he looked around again as if he was sure someone would jump out on him.

"Are you always this jumpy, Nico?" She was good at reading body languages.

"Can I have that drink, please? Change mi min'."

"Good. Nothing like a *shot* of something to calm yuh nerves… What'll it be?"

"What yuh got?"

"Whisky, Brandy… wine, Supa-T…"

"Gimme a Brandy nuh? *Neat*."

"And there's also that new drink, if you wanna try it…"

"What new drink?"

"*Cure-Fi-Aids*? Have you tried it yet?"

Nico got up and kissed his teeth. "Yuh fuckin' wid mi head, Menna… I knew you were up to sop'n."

"It's a *joke*, Nico. You used to have a sense of humour. Chill."

He paused and checked her eyes.

In them he saw not tricks, but *luring* magic. He remembered how sweet she was between the sheets. *His dick jumped again.*

"Lighten up… c'mon…" she cooed.

He sat down again, only this time he wasn't as relaxed as he was before. He sat practically on the edge, eased both elbows onto both knees again, and clasped both hands into one fist, making a stand for his chin. "It's the first time I've been to your place, Menna. Before I had the chance, you took off to Jamaica… *How was* Jamaica anyway?"

She handed him his neat brandy. Their fingers touched. The last time they touched was on a cosy night, way back when. As she lay up in Nico's bed, a desperate Conteh stood on his doorstep, wondering why he couldn't come in.

The feeling moved Nico. She was the only woman that managed to capture his heart, and the only one sensible enough to insist he used a condom.

"What yuh done to yuh face?" she ignored his question on Jamaica.

"Got into a fight."

"Really…?"

"Yeah… over a stupid parking space."

"Oh dear."

"So… *how* was Jamaica?" he asked again, wishing not to dwell on Lance's ass-kicking.

"We'll talk about JA when Conteh gets here. Just relax, I'll be right back."

He watched Menna as she left the room. *'Mmmm… that ass,'* he lusted, grabbing his crutch as if to stop it jumping out and finding her *'sweet heaven'*. Now that he was alone, he relaxed a little more, taking a good look at the classy surroundings.

Bleep! Bleep! Hastily he retrieved his phone and opened the freshly-arrived text. *'Soon come Bredrin. Yuh reach yet?'*

Nico felt light. Learning that his friend was on his way made him happy. *'Yeah man. Mi deh yah. Hurry up. Feel a little strange,'* was his reply.

'Why?'

'Not sure. Jus strange. How long will you be?'

'Ten minutes. Had to make a little stop. In a bit.'

'Ok… bwoy, mi naah tell yuh no lie… I could fuck her. Shi nice!' was Nico's final text.

Menna covered her mouth to stop herself giggling too loud, and from her crouched position over the edge of her bed, she typed, *'Easy, Bredrin. She's out of bounds. No harm in dreaming though. Battery going. See you in a bit.'* She pressed *'send'*, waited a while, then placed Conteh's mobile under her pillow. "I won't be a minute, Nico!" she shouted to her waiting guest.

"No problem!" he shouted back after reading the last word of his text.

Then Menna reached for her own mobile and made a call. "Hi," she whispered low. "Where are you ladies?… ok… yes… he's here… yes… like a caged fucking bird…" she fight back the giggles. "See you in a bit… ok…" She clicked off… Took a deep breath.

"Your friend is running late," she said, walking assertively back into her living-room, where she found Nico much more relaxed than he was before.

"He'll be here in a bit. He just text me."

"Ok… I guess he's a little *tied up*, hey?" She knew her cynicism would go right over his head, but she said it anyway.

"*Was*, I think. He's on his way now though. No problem."

Menna sat opposite Nico now on the single-seater, looking confidently at him.

He wasn't so sure about this. Her stare was a little domineering. "*What*?" he asked, feeling more than vulnerable. She was penetrating his very soul.

"D'you have a spliff?" she asked in place of an answer to his question.

"Yeah." He fished a small neat plastic sachet from his breast pocket and shook it. "Good Sensi," he said.

"Nice," Menna said.

The doorbell went and a weight lifted from Nico's shoulders. As far as he was concerned, his bredrin had arrived.

"Buil' up, nuh?" Menna told him, handing him an ashtray, then walking to the door.

In the seconds that followed, Nico made himself more at home, and his palm ready to wrap his mate's. Knees apart, he crouched forward, the edge of the coffee table, sheets of Rizzla and a packet of Sensi taking a third of his focus. The other two-thirds antenna'd towards the mumblings that came from Menna's front door.

'*Shouldn't I be hearing Conteh's voice by now?*' he asked himself, head down as he sprinkled cigarette into the middle of the Rizzla.

"Nico... *Hi*."

Nico raised his head to a familiar voice... "*Joya*?... a'right?" He looked beyond her. "Yuh come wid Conteh?"

"Hello, *Nico,*" Colette said now, stepping in after her.

"... *A'right*?" Nico didn't know what to think. Still he looked beyond the threshold.

"How yuh doin', *Nico*?" Carmen entered like the final sealant.

Suddenly, Nico lost interest in the art of spilff-building. He knew all Conteh's baby mothers all right, but as for their connection with Menna, it was a mystery. "I didn't know you ladies were friends?" He looked at Menna now, trying to work out what the hell was going on. He checked his watch and realised that ten minutes went five minutes ago. '*Where's Conteh?*' he wondered. "Excuse me, ladies," he said, reaching for his phone. He dialled. It rang out... Under Menna's pillow to be exact.

"In competition with Magic Johnson, are we, *Nico*?" Carmen asked.

"Sorry?"

"You and Conteh. Got the secret to the AIDS thing, hey?"

"What yuh talking about, Carmen?"

"Well, apart from your bruised face, you look a bill of health…"

"So do you all. Bills of health… That's the thing with HIV… it has no prejudices. It hits the good, the bad, the ugly, the rich, the poor… and the beautiful," Nico said with conviction. "I was forgetting, apart from Menna, you're all infected, aren't you?"

"Yes," Carmen said, "Only some of us are men and women enough to hold our own shit… but the I guess the words, *'Taking it like a man'* are like swear words to you, Nico. That's why you're still charming your way into the beds of umpteen women, infecting them."

He shrugged his shoulders, but heaven knows he wanted a spliff like breath.

Like a rehearsed piece, they all took up seating positions near to him.

Feeling cornered, he asked, "What is this? Where's Conteh?"

"Tied up, I expect," Menna told him for the second time. "Facing a cold, naked truth."

"What?… What yuh talking 'bout?"

Nobody answered.

"Is this your idea of a fucking joke?" His eyes wandered simultaneously to and from each member of the bunch, as his heart pounded like a drum.

"*Joke*?" Menna asked. "Who's laughing?"

Nico kissed his teeth and placed his hand on his aching ribs.

"Your face, Nico," Menna asked. "This *parking space* you were fighting over?…What was her name?"

"What the fuck yuh talking about?"

"Didn't the *Cat* that own the *parking space* come home while you tried to play *Super-Mouse*?"

Nico got up. His brain was twisting in his head. Only then it all started to become clear… Conteh's phone… she must have it… *but how the hell?*… "Listen, I'm leaving," he said.

"Really?" Menna asked him "Who said?" She looked at her three helpers, "Did any of you guys said Nico could go?"

"No way"… "In his dreams"… "Let him try." Carmen, Colette and Joya voiced their feelings consecutively, drawing closer to Nico and penning him in. One by one, he made eye contact with them, and when he got to Carmen he said, "What have I done to these three? They're Conteh's women…"

"You hurt *one* sista, you hurt us *all*," Carmen told him. "And believe me, you've dished out an awful lot of death-kisses around Birmingham."

Nico needed no more explanation. Knowing she was the head of the game, he looked at Menna and said, "Nice one, *Menna... Jade...* whateva... *nice one.*"

"And even nicer still, Nico... Buff!!..."

An old hockey stick took his balance.

He held his head and looked simultaneously at them.

His knitted his brows. Questions filled his eyes.

"... I know your intention was not to *go down alone*, Nico," Menna said, "but *enough is enough*. You have infected enough women now. Stop it. Buff!!"

"Bitch!" he shouted as he stumbled back and fell ass-down into the settee, jarring his aching ribs.

"When will you stop, Nico?" Joya asked. "When will you stop fucking around with intent?... When the whole female population of Birmingham is infected?"

Like a dying man, Nico's whole body was convulsing.

"Is he dying?" Colette asked. "Shit, Menna, the idea wasn't to kill him, we're not murderers."

Suddenly, he stopped shaking and slumped into the settee.

"Shit!" Colette whispered.

She drew closer to him while the others looked at each other.

Colette felt for a pulse.

Shook him.

Placed her hand upon his chest to check for breathing, then... suddenly..."Bitch!"

Jesus. Nico grabbed her neck! She screamed.

"Fuck!" Menna shouted trying to get an angle to give him another bitch clout.

He was in a real frenzy. Squeezing Colette's neck! Hard!

"Help!" Colette screeched through half-blocked windpipes, and like a brood of panicking hens, the others jumped around.

Nico had no mercy...

"Help!" Colette squealed.

Lips pursed...

"Colette! Are you ok?!" Joya shouted.

"Hell, no!" She kicked. Scratched. Struggled.

Jaws clenched...

"Let her go, you bastard!" Carmen kicked his shin repeatedly.

Muscles protruded from his neck...

"Let her go!" Joya bit the top of his right arm. "Shit!" She remembered. Drawing his blood into her mouth wouldn't be good.

Eyes bulging... bulging... bulging... they threatened: 'I'll fucking kill her!'

"Lick him again, Menna! Lick him wid the hockey stick again!" Carmen shouted, "He's gonna kill her!"

But Menna had been trying all the time to get an angle on his head. She wanted to knock him out, but he had Colette too close to him.

Then... suddenly... Buff!!... Why didn't someone think of that before? The sole of Carmen's right foot met with balls, crunching the living daylights out of his *'wand of death'*.

"Ohhhh!" He let Colette go." Ohhhh!" He leant into the pain of the perpetrating organ. "   Ohhh!" The pain in his ribs was of little significance now. "Fuck!... Oh shit!... Shit!... Shit!..."

Joya hugged Colette's shoulders. "Are you ok?"

"Jesus," Colette said croakily. *Cough, cough, cough...* "I thought I was a gonna... Shit..."

Menna had no time for being noble. Buff!! Hitting him while he was down was just what the doctor ordered.

Nico found a little strength.

Just enough to glance up at the hockey stick.

Blurry-eyed, he stared at it as if it controlled itself. Metaphorically speaking, he didn't know what hit him. "*You... fuckin'   fuckin'... bitch...*" he protested, sounding like Don Corleone in his last days. Even at the edge of his life, Nico was unrepentant.

Buff!! The icing on the cake.

He was out... consciousness leaving him...

Fading voices fluttered around him as he slowly slipped away...

'*This won't be easy,*' he heard someone said.

'*I hope we can pull this off,*' said another.'

'*This is dead-weight, you know that don't you?*' another said.

'*Piece a cake,*' said the most assertive Menna. '*We haven't been eating yams, green bananas and cornmeal dumplings for nothing... unless of course, you guys have abandoned good old Jamaican food.*'

Nico heard the voices, but he couldn't respond.

He felt sure he was going to die.

Although he was brazen with his rude, threatening and intimidating phone calls, he had now convinced himself that the only thing that

stood between Menna and *'borderless revenge'* was Menna herself.
She was obviously the ringleader and there was no doubt that
something had driven her to *ruthlessness beyond comprehension*. But
then... who the hell was he to judge!

This was ordinary, mundane Birmingham, West Midlands.

These were four black women who at sometime or the other
marvelled at Friday nights on Broad Street: gasped at *drunken-
skirtless-don't-know-how-the-hell-I-got-home-last-night* white girls
who are forever unrepentant about drinking so much that the notion of
'enjoying myself' means nothing more than *'I-don't-know-what-the-
fuck-happened-last-night-but-I-loved-it-any-way.'*

These were ordinary black women whose *week-day-nights*
wouldn't see them dead in pubs or clubs. Yet, there they were taking
revenge to the extreme.

Question: *What is madness? Who is* and who *isn't?* And has it
somewhat outgrown its definition? *Possibly*. Or perhaps not. Perhaps
giving bastards like Nico their just deserves requires a little sprinkling
of *madness*.

Nico tried to summon up desperate last words, *but nothing*.

And now, like a silent witness, an un-built spliff lay open,
witnessing the beginning of a harrowing tale that was about to unfold.

Harrowing to some, *justice* to many...

Many women in particular who had taken passionate sips from
Nico's potent devil's cup.

Hours later, back at the Gonzales' house, midnight found Conteh in a
desperate state.

He needed the loo. *Badly*.

His bladder was full.

Droplets of piss dribbled from time to time down his sorrowful
pathetic legs, and there were no telling how long he could squeeze
back a pile of shit that sat at the rim of his ass, desperately ready to be
dumped. Doing it on the floor right where he stood was not entirely out
of the question, since what goes in must come out. He is human. And
when nature fights, it always wins. *Feh real*. If the boys from the Vibes
Injection crew could see him then. *Heh Heh! Heeeye!!!*

"Please, God, help me," he whined. "Help me... help me... help...
meeeee." But it wasn't too long before he fainted from sheer
exhaustion.

Crouched in the corner like a drunk, with wrists of a prisoner, slept the once-smooth operator, the familiar scent of his mother endeavouring to comforted him.

Poor, poor Conteh.

* * *

Father Jarvis pulled his red Mercs into a *lucky* spot... *Lucky,* since he was *lucky* to find one.

His Red Affair dance was already packed out.

Of all the other happenings around Birmingham that night, this one had obviously pulled the biggest crowd, without a doubt.

Country Bwoy had long gone followed his belly into the club and was entertaining the already large crowd of ravers.

"What di hell is dat," Father Jarvis asked DJ Clashington who was emerging from his ride at the same time. They both fixed their eyes on a blanket-covered *thing* that hung like a slaughtered pig from a nearby lamppost near to small car park in front of the club.

"Some Halloween t'ing," Scorcha the dancehall queen piped up from behind.

"*Halloween?*" Father Jarvis quizzed.

"Yeah. This girl told me." She slammed her car door shut. "They're gonna pull the sheet off at midnight I hear, and it's gonna light up... sop'n like dat."

"But is it Halloween season?" DJ Clashington asked.

"Well," Scorcha replied, "These people choose any time for anything."

"My Gaaaad, my Gaaaad," Father Jarvis exclaimed in that forever bantering tone, "dem betta mek sure seh dem don' bun down di place."

DJ Clashington laughed. "As long as it's a *TREAT* and not a *TRICK*, that's all dat matta."

They all laughed now.

"Faada Jarvis," Scorcha said, "Shouldn't you be in the dance already?"

"It still early, man. Early, early. Country Bwoy a do 'im t'ing, yunnuh?... Warming up."

"I can feel it's gonna be a good night," she said.

"Den nuh mus'?" he cleared his throat mischievously. "Bwoy, yuh outfit look ready, Scorcha. Red really suit yuh," he told her.

"Thanks. Suit mi temperament... *passionate*," she cooed.

"My Gaaaad, my Gaaaad," he joked, chuckling at her banter.

As they, all three, headed towards the entrance to Banana Baits, Father Jarvis holding a case filled with revives, Mr Chatbout, another one of Birmingham's finest DJs joined them. He was pressing his right palm against his right jaw.

"Whaap'n to you, Chatbout," Father Jarvis asked.

"Bwoy, teet'-ache ah kill mi, sah. But I couldn't miss dis Red Affair dance yah."

"Yuh nuh have *teet'-ache,"* Father Jarvis told him. "Dat mus' be a *pin-rake,* neva min' teet'-ache. If *real* teet'-ache did tek yuh, yuh couldn't move, let alone come to dance." He chuckled.

"Mr Chatbout laughed, knowing that at that moment, he was feeling nothing compared to what he felt earlier, but he was pleased to know that Monday morning however, the offending tooth would be history. "Is wha' dat t'ing deh hanging from di lamppost, Bredrin? He asked.

"Some Halloween t'ing, mi hear," Father Jarvis told him. Some midnight light-up business… me nuh know."

Mr Chatbout had second thoughts about kissing his teeth. Sucking air through the gap in his pained tooth would not help one bit. *Ouch.*

Country Bwoy's voice met them as they entered. Mr Chatbout, DJ Clashington and Scorcha stopped by the bar, whilst Father Jarvis continued on his way towards the stage, where a deck awaited him. It was a journey that would take him past the lounge. A sea of *red-adorned* females sat watching him, catching, nonetheless, some of the *happy dust* he seemed to sprinkle around (even via his radio waves) without knowing it.

"A'right Da'lin'?" He stopped and greeted an old acquaintance with a kiss on her cheek.

"Yuh look sharp as always, Father Jarvis," Janet told him.

"I don' know about dat," he said, receiving her compliment with pure modesty.

"Hi," Sandra said. She was standing there eagerly waiting to be introduced. Apart from hearing his voice booming out of Sting FM, and catching distance glimpses of him as he worked his musical shows at a few weddings, she had not met him *personally*.

"Oh, this is my sister, Sandra," Janet said to Father Jarvis, who was showing signs of *'wanting to hit his musical deck'*.

"Please to meet you, Sandra," he said politely, shaking her hand at the same time.

"Please to meet you too…"

"Nice… nice…"

"… Can I just say," Sandra added, "you are a *great* DJ."

"T'ank yuh, t'ank yuh. You are very kind," he said with modesty.

"No, it's the truth… you have real musical prowess."

Janet wanted her to shut up now. *'He's got the message, surely,'* she thought.

"My Gaaaad," Father Jarvis said, chuckling. "My Gaaaad." He blushed now in a way that would not be remotely identified as a *blushing*. "I hope you enjoy the night… anyway," he continued, looking now at Janet, a sudden spark of interest in his eyes, "Egyptian coming?"

"He said he was," Janet replied, "but I don't know," she smiled cynically, "I think Conteh is in love. Locked down with some woman."

"Wha'?" Father Jarvis asked, then he tried to take back the perplexity that went with the question. Well, the infamous rumour had spread. Nuff tongues had wagged. Bad news had travelled fast. So the *'locked down with some woman'* part seemed a bit *carelessly tossed* by Janet.

Sandra jabbed Janet discretely, an action that used to be the other-way-around. It was then that Janet realised that she shouldn't have made that banter. "No, I'm just joking. He should be here," she rounded off. *Phew.*

"Well, I hope so. Di man need to get out more, yunnuh?… yeees… yeees… Wha's di matta wid you?"

"True," Janet replied.

"Anyway, I must go an do my t'ing," Father Jarvis announced, "Enjoy unnuhself, a'right?" he told them, moving now with intent towards the stage.

"There is a DJ missing!" Country Bwoy bantered. "Faada Jarvis, weh yuh deh?!"

Father Jarvis smiled as he headed towards the short flight of stairs that led to the dance floor. As he moved across the dance floor and towards the spot where Country Bwoy stood, he glanced to his right and beheld a host of women dancing with their own images in the mirrored wall that gave the room a false sense of *'space'*. He couldn't help but smile to himself.

"Yuh reach?" Country Bwoy asked the obvious.

"No… mi nuh reach. I's mi shadow."

Little in size, big in presence. That's Father Jarvis. When he had entered the room it was almost as if a gaping hole was filled.

Some have it. Some don't. His musical prowess, coupled with his jolly, contagious energy was undeniable. *Simple.* And through no fault of his own, women gravitated to his aura like bees to honey. Chicken around corn. Steel to magnet. Or even bench to batty. Now, greedy begging eyes followed him, inquisitive minds searching for answers to his contagious existence. But like always, the *born-with-music-in-his-veins* DJ took no notice. No sir. The soul intention of this confident Sagittarian was to get his hands on his deck. The night promised to be a bombastic one.

You see... DJs came...

And DJs went...

But this Father Jarvis is a Boss Selecta. Here to stay. *Chat bout.*

"Mi t'ink it was *you* dem string up outside, Faada Jarvis," Country Bwoy bantered for the benefit of everyone's ears.

"What yuh talkin' 'bout?" he asked as the crowd laughed in reaction to Country Bwoy's statement.

The crowd knew not what he was on about, until he announced, "Listen! Everybady, listen! I don't know how true dis is, but mi jus' had a text within di las' few minutes"... Di text seh! Listen! Listen!... Di text seh... Dere is a man! Yes, tie up!... Outside!... Pon a lamppos'... Anybady waan go tek a look... unnuh run gallang! As fi me... I don' have *no* intention of looking at *no* nakid man!... So, ladies!... Genklemen!... Everybady!... If unnuh waan si some frozen balls!... Heh! Heh! Heyee!... Unnuh run go look!!... As long as unnuh come back inna di dance!"

Of course the place was in uproar. Only Countryman could deliver bad news with such dry banter. Laughter spread itself to and from the four corners of the room, mingling with the sweet reggae music.

"Country Bwoy!" Father Jarvis responded, "wha's di matta wid *you*? I's who sending you dem tex' deh! People! Dere is only one t'ing hanging from di lamppos' outside... it is some Halloween t'ing!... If dere is a nakid man hanging from a lamppos' outside right now, I believe his..." he cleared his throat to indicate an innuendo, '*you know what*' will be an icicle right now! Frozen balls, fi true!" he cleared his throat mischievously again. "Yeees!... Yeees!"

More laughter ripped through the room.

But of course, still, no one believed, until minutes later when legitimate sources confirmed it *was* true. The news moved now like wild fire through the dance and seconds later there was a mass exodus:

droves of perverted voyeurs were soon gathered outside to see the peculiar sight. And *peculiar* it sure was.

Roars of laughter filed the air. Sniggers, opened mouths, frozen expressions, everything went in that historical moment, for as sure as hell there he was... Unveiled since Father Jarvis and crew scrutinised the so-called 'Halloween' *TRICK*, a naked man hung helpless from the Birmingham City Council's lamppost. *Lord, Lord, Lord.* Above his head a well-prepared sign that wasn't there earlier, read:

> *'MY NAME IS (the name was smudged)*
> *I ALSO HAVE SEVERAL OTHER ALIASES.*
> *I AM A SERIAL KILLER.*
> *MY WEAPON IS MY DEADLY SPERM.*
> *FOR THE PAST FIVE YEARS I HAVE BEEN INFECTING*
> *COUNTLESS WOMEN WITH THE HIV VIRUS.*
> *NOW, MY TIME HAS RAN OUT...*
> *I AM CAUGHT... HUNG OUT TO DIE.'*

And from his dick, hung a card with yet another crucial message... It read:

> *'DANGER!!!*
> *CONTAMINATED MEAT!!"*

"Stand back please, everyone! Stand back!" A black policeman ordered, cutting through the curious crowd with a blanket in his hand. In the line of his duty, a straight face was required, but under the circumstances it was hard to keep one. So, with difficulty, he tried to squeeze back the hysterical laughter that threatened to break loose from his belly. *He is human after all.*

Another three officers followed.

"Is he dead," an onlooker asked.

"Looks like. He's lifeless anyway. It's freezing. Surely he'll catch pneumonia."

"How the hell did he get up there," Janet asked, getting a little closer.

"That's what I'd like to know," Sandra second. "Jesus."

"Oh my God!" Janet alarmed, though in a low voice.

"What, Janet?... What?" Sandra asked.

"It's *Nico*. Jesus, it's *Nico*."

"Which *Nico*?"

"*Nico*! Conteh's friend, silly. Jamaican Indian, Nico!"

"Oh shit," Sandra said. "So it is… I didn't recognise him with his clothes off… Hah! Hah! Hah!"

"Sandra, it's not funny." Janet covered her mouth and tried to be serious. Even though she had heard of Nico's AIDS-Spreading antics, she felt some compassion for him. *'Regardless,'* she thought, *'being strung up, nude, on a lamppost' in the freezing cold isn't funny.'*

Janet looked around her. Everyone had different expressions. At first, a considerable amount of females laughed uncontrollably. But suddenly, for some, the laughter had *stopped*. Jumped straight back down their throats. They had picked up on the blatant reality of *who* it really was. At a closer glance, the shell-shocked females had come to realise that the *'crucified'* man was no stranger after all. No sir. For they had mingled with him. Some still had paper roses above their beds. On their fireplaces on their walls. Dressing-tables. One in particular still had traces of his fluid deep inside her vagina. *Still… Ohhhh dear.*

You would have thought by now, that most would have heard about *'Nico, the deadly serial-sex-killer'*, but *no*. How could every single woman possibly know Nico to look at? How could they possibly suss, especially when he went by so many aliases? *Impossible.*

Cutting him down from the lamppost wasn't a task the policemen relished.

The blanket that covered him was no way adequate to shield him from the cold.

Nico wanted to wish the moment away.

Only minutes before, he had gained consciousness.

Shit. He could have died, but one thing for sure, he had no intentions of telling the police *who* had hung him out to *'die'*.

"Nico!" a man shouted from the spectating crowd. "Bombo claat! Yuh get ketch to raas! Heh! Heh! Heyeee!" It was Bongo Dee. But if he knew what Nico knew, he would shut is damn cake-hole. You see, it wouldn't be long before Bongo would discover that the *'cool breeze'* he was feeling at his tail was in fact *'fire'*.

Slowly, helped by the boys-in-blue and ambulance-men, Nico was guided towards the comfort of the waiting ambulance, hypothermia threatening to devour his ass. He shivered uncontrollably.

Frostbites had already started to eat away at his dick, and with the old wounds from Lance's pummelling, the stacks of comeuppances were seriously against him.

Now, safe within the ambulance and away from prying eyes, he cried like a baby.

* * *

Through it all, Menna had watched non-stop from her car. She was parked there for a good while. But only when the ambulance was clean out of sight that she started her engine and headed out. *Another mission accomplished.*

Carmen, Colette and Joya walked right back in and took their places on the dance floor, grinning like a bunch of Cheshire cats with tickling sticks up their asses.

"Heh! Heyee! What a somet'ing eeh sah?!" Country Bwoy echoed now. "Mi nuh know!... Nico?!... Pretty bwoy, Nico?!... Hanging nakid?! From a lamppos'?! *No... No...* Mi cyaan believe it!... Even dough mi si it wid mi own eyes, mi still cyaan believe it!... W'at I want to know is!... is *who* did tie 'im up deh?!... Heh! Heyee! Mi nuh know!... Mi nuh know!... Anyway, people! Nico is in good hands! Hospital food fi a few days an' he'll be as right as rain! Dat show is well wrapped up!... An' dis show mus' go aaaan!... Tek a listen!" He gave them a Beres track.

The room was still buzzing as ravers changed notes about the incident.

"What yuh drinking?" Carmen asked the other two avenging queens.

"Brandy," Joya said.

"Same again," Colette said.

"I *could* believe mi eyes!" Father Jarvis added his piece when he got the mike. "Dere was no doubt as to w'at I saw hanging from dat lamppos' outside... I know a nakid man w'en I si one! Well, after all, I am a man, so I should know w'at a nakid man look like! But I agree wid Country Bwoy! I would like to know is *who* tie 'im up deh!!... Heh! Heh! Heyee!... *Shantamatilda...*"

He kicked out Justin Hines *'Sinners, where you gonna run, where yuh gonna hide...'*

The crowd was ready for him.

They roared, so he pulled up and came again.

* * *

It was 1am... Menna sat outside Conteh's house like a triumphant stalker. She had long gone patted her own back for the earlier Nico incident.

She text Janet from his phone: *'Sis', wherever you are, I need you to come round the house. I'm in trouble. Mek sure seh yuh have yuh key, Sis'. Come as soon yuh can.'* She pressed the *send* button, then dropped Conteh's mobile back through his letterbox.

The sound startled Conteh. He thought someone was breaking in, and if that was the case, what the hell could he do? "Who's there?!" he shouted.

Menna walked back to her car that was parked under a big tree that had robbed it of most of the streetlight and that was good. She wanted to *see* without being *seen*.

She sat and waited.

Fifteen minutes later, she smiled to herself when Janet's car screeched to a halt outside Conteh's house. She watched the two sisters rushing frantically up the drive to his rescue. But it was only when she saw a light flicked on, that Menna drove away.

The girls were in. Her work was done.

* * *

Sandra was perturbed. *Pissed off* was more like it. The dance was kicking and she had to leave. Dragged out by her merciful sister to save her brother yet again. "I can't believe," she moaned. "The night was just ready, man. The music was just..."

"Shut up, Sandra!" Janet said. "Our brother is in trouble! You've moaned all the way! Yuh too fucking selfish an' insensitive!"

"Don't swear at me."

"Well shut di fuck up den."

"There you go again."

"You're moaning about music when our brother is in trouble..."

"Story of his life," Sandra mumbled.

"... Don't you care what might be the matter with him? You saw the text."

"His fingers must be ok... he text you."

Janet looked at her sister and gave up. They were in his house now. "I wish he would put a bulb in this porch," she moaned as she stepped into the dark porch, tripping over her own Pyrex dish, kicking Conteh's phone and stepping on some keys.

"Jan', is that you?!"

"Yes, Bro', it's me!"

"And me!" Sandra shouted.

"Are you alright? What trouble are you in? We were at the dance!… I tried to call you straight after the text, and no reply! Why couldn't you phone instead of texting? Conteh?!" Janet stumbled down the corridor and tried to find the light switch for the passage and landing. Bingo! *And then there was light.* "Why is that bag with the dinner sitting in the porch?… Conteh?!… You're scaring me now…"

"Sis'?!"

"Yes, Bro'?! What's wrong?… This is scary… Why was the house in darkness?!"

"Go upstairs and find a towel before you come in, will you?!" His voice boomed out of the darkness.

Janet felt even more scared. She looked at Sandra who looked how she felt.

"A *towel*?"

"Yes, just get one before any of you two come in here!"

"Ok!" Janet handed Sandra the bag of food and belted upstairs. *'Blood'* she thought, *'he must be covered in blood. Why else would he need a towel? He was attacked.'*

She grabbed the towel that was hanging in the bathroom and darted back downstairs, but in her haste and panic, she tripped, fell and skidded on her ass until she reached the bottom of the stairs. She hit it with a thud that jerked and jarred her back, sending a sharp, shooting pain up her spine.

"Are you ok?!" Sandra who was standing there asked. She didn't know where her concern should be now, on her sister's back (Janet held her back and her face wrinkled in pain) or her brother's mysterious plight.

"Yes, I'm fine," she jabbed, stretching the towel out, "take it to him."

"I'm scared. What's in there?… What…?" Her apprehension was acute.

"Go, Sandra! *Ouch!*"

"A'right! A'right! But is your back…?"

"Go!" Her back concerned her, but what with her brother? Why is he in the dark asking for a towel?

"Ok! Ok!" Sandra said, walking cautiously towards the living-room door. It brings back memory of when, as a child, her mother Gladys would send her for the belt for her own thrashing. How she used to walk slowly into the living-room where her mother stood waiting.

"Bro'?" Sandra called out.

"Come... But don't turn the light on yet!"

Sandra pushed the door. She could see her brother standing in the dimness of the room. He stood there like a slave, his pitiful figure silohetted against the patio window. *"What?... What happened*? Why are you standing there in... the... nude?"

"Just cover me with the towel, Sis', questions later."

"Ok... ok... I see." Sandra acted like she knew. *'Sex games, hey?'* she thought, looking away as she fastened the knot in the towel, *'no wonder you wanted to be left alone'*. "There," she said when she had finally secured the big bath towel around her brother's waist.

"Sand'? Is he ok?"

"I think so."

"You *think* so?" Janet held her back.

"Now turn the lights on and try to get these... *things* off my hands," Conteh urged.

"Things?" Sandra asked as she switched the light on, covering her mouth in the meantime to stop herself from laughing too much.

"It nuh funny, Sis'."

"No.... I guess not... It isn't. Finding my brother, *in the dark*, *in the nude*, *in handcuffs,* with no other players in sight... *no*... it isn't funny... not funny at all. Hah!"

"Sand'?!... Conteh?!..."

"Hah! Hah! Hah!" Sandra fell on the floor, holding her belly, her brother's weak and feeble state not yet registered, "Hee! Hee! Hee!"

"Sandra! What's funny? Conteh?... *Ouch!*"

It suddenly dawned on Conteh that his sister, Janet, the backbone of the family was talking to them from the bottom of the stairs.

"Sis'?!... Yuh a'right?!"

"No. I think I've broken my back!"

"What?" Laughter found its way back down Sandra's throat.

"The keys for these cuffs!" he urged Sandra. "There!" He pointed with his chin.

Sandra realised now, that despite her brother's high octave, he was in a pretty bad state. But still, she found the whole thing highly amusing and couldn't get shot of the laughter that flooded her belly. Worst when she found herself unlocking a pair of handcuffs!

Seconds later, Conteh rushed upstairs the quickest he could. He needed a shower and Jan needed care. They both did. Dudley Road Hospital, here they come.

Later, he would clean up the pile of excrement that nature wouldn't let him hold. He had managed to kick a cushion over it, though it didn't stop Sandra wondering what that *'smell'* was.

* * *

They were Diamonds... The most delicate pair you ever did see... They matched that elegant necklace she had found in the bathroom.

"What a man...? What a man...? What a *mighty good* man you are, my dear husband?" Simone asked hypothetically as she tried on the elegant pair of Diamond earrings. "What a mighty sweet man you are?"

Chapter 17

𝓜enna had tried desperately to get in touch with Sharon the brave blonde, but to no avail. She needed to talk to her in more details about a text she sent her.

The text led her way back to Key Chip, the computer firm where they both worked.

Menna's phone was playing up, so when she got to read the mystery-filled text, it was already weeks old. *'So that is why Sharon had been so helpful to me?'* Menna had thought after reading the text. *'She carried out the orgy.... Helped me out at Black Star... Helped me to kick Conteh's ass... and all that time... Why did she take so long to tell me about the Key Chip fraud? Considering that if I weren't out of the office on those occasions, I would have been seriously set up? Shit!'* But Menna was just speculating. Sharon's text said nothing of the sort. It simply stated that she wanted to *'Tell her about it'*.

Menna had been chilling after accomplishing her *'Pay-back'* mission. Her and her crew were brave, but she also knew that what goes around what goes around often comes around, and there were no telling how Nico and Conteh might react. She had been lying low, for a while, but by hook or by crook, she *had to* find Sharon.

All she had was her mobile number, and she wasn't answering that. The address she had for her was an old one. She had moved when Menna was in JA. Still, she had pledged not to stop until she found her.

It was early Saturday evening, two weeks to the day that Conteh was released from his bondage, and when Nico was hung out to die. Menna pulled into the block of flats and slowed up. What she was about to see was most unexpected?

"Stand back, please, stand back," the policeman urged the inquisitive mass that gathered like a bunch of perverted voyeurs, to stare at the two *body-bearing* trolleys.

Menna climbed out of her car and walked almost sided-by-side with an old but strong looking lady. They, both strangers, spoke at once, "What's happened here?"

"Oh dear," the old lady said, keeping her eyes on the *not-too-good* sight. "It doesn't look good."

Whatever had happened, Menna just hoped Sharon was home.

"What happened, Officer?" the wide-eyed old lady asked a nearby policeman. She was obviously coming from her shopping trip when, like Menna, she was confronted with flashing lights, busy police and ambulance men and the curious bunch of on-lookers, most of them from her block. Her already wrinkled forehead gained a few more lines when she beheld the two trolleys bearing sheet-covered bodies. The old lady tried to squeeze her way through, as if getting closer would allow ex-ray vision. Menna followed.

"Do you both live in this block, " the policeman asked.

"I don't, Officer. Just visiting," Menna said.

"I do," the old lady replied.

"What number?" he stressed, holding on to his radio as if his life depended on it.

"Number 12… what happened?"

"Were you acquainted with the people at number 13?"

Menna stumbled, slightly. Number 13 was the address she had written down. Surely it couldn't be Sharon?

"Yes…. Well, not *people*, just Sharon," the old lady replied. "Lovely blonde girl… what happened?" She looked again as the ambulance men pushed the second trolley into the back of the ambulance then closing the door.

Menna's chin dropped.

"We can't say for sure," the officer told the old lady, "but at the moment I don't think there's any foul play here."

"Pardon? That doesn't answer my question, young man. Is one of those bodies Sharon?" the old lady asked.

"I'm… afraid so, Love," he answered in a low voice.

"Jesus," Menna said in an almost whisper.

"What happened?" The old lady was beginning to sound like a scratched record. "She lived right opposite me. She used to get my shopping sometimes."

The policeman edged the old lady up the grass verge towards her flat. "If you must know, there was a suicide note."

"What?!" Menna whispered again. She had followed them although she weren't invited to.

"Really?" the old lady questioned. "*Suicide*?... *Sharon*?... but she had everything to live for..."

But Menna knew differently.

"Apparently not," the officer said.

"... So who's the other one?" the old lady quizzed.

"A friend, apparently. *Melissa.* The note said something about *bowing out gracefully* before AIDS made it impossible to do so."

"AIDS?.... AIDS? Oh dear... was the other lady a brunette, Officer?"

"Yes, she was, do you know her too?"

"Yes... yes... Pretty girl. Loved life too. They both did. Often reminded me of myself when I was their age. What a *terrible* thing. Oh dear...but *gracefully?* There's nothing *graceful* about *suicide*?"

The old lady's voice became more and more distant to Menna. You see, she had walked away. *Unconsciously.* Walked away from the scene. She had not realised how close she really had become to Sharon.

And there it was – a blonde and a brunette who had played a dangerous game of *kiss-and-tell.* A game Menna had sent them to play: with Garnet snapping away happily at their planned orgy: an orgy where the infamous Conteh and Nico were caught... *hook, line and sinker.*

But little did the obliging *sisters-of-mercies,* Sharon and Melissa know that one day, they would be *hoisted by their own petards.* They were best friends. The pact they made to OD on more than handfuls of pills was sealed when their last breaths were taken, not long, one after the other.

Another mournful day for two families, but still, the world keeps on turning.

Menna sat motionless in her car. Just then, time was of no essence.

She stared long and hard into space, the hustling and bustling of the morbid activity acting as a backdrop to her nightmare... '*Is the sun ever gonna shine anymore?*' she asked her inner self.

* * *

Simone was lying in her husband's arms. They were sat on the settee in their cosy living-room. Amari played happily with his model aeroplane.

"Why don't you call your mum later," Lawrence asked. "We haven't spoken to her for ages. I miss her bubbly voice."

"You just become a big kid every time you get talking to Mum, that's your trouble." She said playfully.

"That's no *trouble,"* he said. "I'm lucky to have a mother-in-law that I love so much. With all the mother-in-law jokes around, I should be grateful," he said, squeezing her tighter.

"I remember the time she came without you knowing. Great surprise that was. Your face. You were like a child."

Lawrence chuckled. "It's her personality. Blanche brings out the child in me."

"She loves you," Simone told him as if he didn't know.

"I should hope so," he said, kissing her.

"No," I mean like a son. You are special to her, Lawrence. I think if we ever break up, she would be more devastated than I'd be."

"Charming."

"No, I'm not saying I wouldn't be devastated. It's just the way my mother speaks about you. Your pedestal is so high... well, let's say you're her *brown-eyed* boy."

"Mmmm, that is so nice." He squeezed her again.

"I'll call her later... How's Lance ad Morag doing, anyway? Are they still talking divorce?"

"Definitely. He's not budging on that at all."

"Oh dear... Doesn't anything remain sacred anymore, Babes?"

"Human beings, Babes. It's the way of the world."

"Look, Daddy!" Amari came rushing over. He was filled with excitement. He had laid his aeroplane down and picked up a sheet of paper. "I forgot to show you this."

"What is it, son?"

"It's a picture of us... this is *you*... this is *me*... and this is *Mummy*."

"Did you draw this?" Lawrence asked.

"Yes, of course."

"Oh, this is brilliant, son."

Simone was smiling. She had already seen the picture. A typical child's drawing, only the five year old managed to draw a man hugging a woman. In between them is a little boy. He's looking up and smiling at his parents. They are both smiling down at him. It was a picture of true *happiness*.

"I'm going to put it in a frame, Daddy. And put it on my wall."

"Don't Mummy and I get one for our wall too?"

"Oh…" he was thinking. There's only one picture. "I will have to draw another one."

"But it won't be identical, will it?"

"Oh… that's true."

"I know," Lawrence said, "I'll take a photocopy."

Yes! Good! Like you did with the story I wrote at school."

"That's it, son… that's it."

* * *

Menna smiled cynically as she held a rare cigarette at the corner of her mouth. She read out loud the title of her new novel: *Don't F**k With Me'* … The novel that had seen many hot days in Jamaica. It was one of the reasons she had escaped to the Island in the first place. She smiled even wider as she remembered the phone call that came only the day before. *'Ms. Jarrett?'* the voice had said. *'That's me,'* she had answered apprehensively, thinking some *search-and-destroy* crew was on to her. God knows she had done some serious damage over the past few months. *'My name is Jane McConnell. I'm calling from Hot Covers Publishing… 'Yes?'* Menna perked. *'We're calling to say we're interested in your novel Don't Fuck With Me.'* *'You… are?'…* *'Yes. Can we arrange a meeting with you?'*

Menna could not remember the conversation that followed, but she could remember floating. Hot Covers Publishing had become one of the most prestigious publishing houses of recent times. For them to call her, was something. But Menna promised not to get too excited. Not just yet. She still had unfinished business that needed fixing. Her finger was already on the trigger, so to speak, and she was most certainly gonna *pull it*. *'Ruthless'* had become her middle-name. She had returned from Jamaica with a new lease of life…

Like Clayton said, there really *was* a fire still burning inside her. And of all the businesses that needed fixing, this one will be fixed with more vengeance than the rest.

Yuh t'ink shi did done?… No sah… Shi jus' ah come!

301

* * *

Menna didn't know why she came... Perhaps it was the hype... The hype that pulled any lover of reggae music like the tempting urge of hot sex. Or maybe it was that subconscious *thing*. That *thing* she had developed ever since she had met Conteh. That magnetic urge to be a keen voyeur of the exciting activities of sound-clashes.

Her seat in the arena was quiet. Almost *private*. Obscure to most, yet the stage view couldn't be clearer to her.

She felt relaxed. No aching feet. Unlike in the Murder Before Disrespect sound-clash in Jamaica a while back, when Pier One in Mobay told a story or two.

The Rubba-Dub Girls had managed to pull off the *'Inna Englan' Cup Clash, 2005'*.

Five sounds took to the stage to strut their stuff. Another musical battle had begun.

Ganja Man and Bobo Ranks compared with style. Ganja Man was adorned in an outfit so original, it gave off an *'I-believe-I-can-fly'* look. Looking like an overgrown eagle, he placed a permanent smile on Menna's face.

Bobo Ranks was his usual bubbly self.

The place buzzed with vibes. Earlier Menna had concentrated on the rainbowed mix that lined the back of the stage:

A white woman sat on a pedestal throwing a confident look out into the crowd.

An Italian with dread-locks long enough to make all Rastas sigh.

White men that could probably tell Jamaicans more about Jamaica than Jamaicans know themselves.

Fresh Jamaicans, straight from yard. Umpteen body languages mixed, entwined and melted their differences into each other, bubbling up a rhythmic pot that was licking out a message that said, *'reggae-music-have-no-colour'.*

The energy was seriously contagious.

Menna turned to her left and caught the eyes of Federal G, an old member of the Vibes Injection crew. The brother smiled a *knowing* smile at her. She nodded one back, hoping he wouldn't come over and chat the pants off her. She was simply *cooling out*.

And there he was... a breath of fresh air... Young Cyclone Quality: A young veteran if ever there was one. A young man (Menna had gathered) whose feet had touched Jamaican soil more times than most

Jamaican-born who had made their life in Britain. Apparently, the young DJ's quest for the best dub-plates was becoming unmatchable.

Cyclone Quality hit the stage with fresh energy: more *zing* than a freshly squeezed lemon. Like an unexpected whirlwind, he hoisted the crowd out of themselves. The other four members of his crew stood proud behind the deck. Straight out of Birmingham, there was no question as to whether these *young bucks* would be going places *inna di sound-clash t'ing*. Move over oldies… Not *out*… just *over*. Make room. These hopeful Young Bloods are here to stay. *Chat bout.*

"Hellooooo!!! … Yeeeess!" Cyclone Quality was in full swing. The crowd roared and you could tell *where* in the arena most of the Birmingham massives were. Cyclone loved it. "Dat's what I'm talkin' about!" he showed his approval of the crowd's response. "Nice!… 'ear weh meah seh?… Yuh si dem set ah yout' yah?" he asked hypothetically and the crowd roared. "Wi nuh normal!… Wi come straight from Birmingham, Handsworth!" The Midlanders were in the house all right. In full force. The whole of Handsworth by the sound of things. "Si weh meah seh?" Cyclone said, inlets of confidence lining the soles of his shoes. The crowd roared again. Uncontrollably this time. He tried to calm them, "Hol' aan!…" He put his right hand out to the crowd like Jesus would in the calming of the sea. "Dat ah di leas' of it!… Big up mi *bad man* frien' dem from Winson Green!… *Roar*. "Big up mi *bad man* frien dem from Aston!" *Roar*. "Mi *rude bwoy* frien' dem from New Town!" *Roar*. "Mi *bad man* frien' dem from Ladywood!" *Mighty Roar*. They were with him. All the way. Like loyal soldiers to their commanding General. The young man commanded roars that had the remaining sounds shaking in their musical boots. *Feh real.*

His energy was seriously contagious.

Menna had only averted her eyes from the energetic young man for a few seconds, when a woman with a *so-perfect-it-could-never-be-her-own* hair-do passed by in front of her, her uncovered *too-nuff* ass brushing the side of her face.

"Ca'lie?!" the woman called out in the freshest Jamaican accent. Her call was directed at a man that blinged like a Christmas tree - seemingly, her man. "Is weh di raas you did deh, las' night, Ca'lie?" She talked as she walked, unable to wait, it seemed, until she was next to him. "Yuh neva even tell mi seh yuh was comin' to di clash!… Yuh is a raas claat fucka yuh nuh, Ca'lie!"

The brother looked at her, wishing he had a spliff.

303

She reached him now. "Is weh yuh did deh las' night, Ca'lie?!" she repeated.

Carlie, the handsome, yet tough-faced man glanced at Menna. She didn't know why, since she couldn't help him.

"Yuh is fuckries yunnuh, Ca'lie" the angry woman relented. "Yuh si as soon as mi get my stay inna Englan'?" She kissed her teeth long and hard as if it was fuel for the rest of her statement. "As soon as mi get my stay inna Englan' ah gwine leave yuh raas. AIDS deh 'bout an' yuh jus' a fuck roun' fuck roun'… yuh gwaan…every rope have a en'!" She turned her back on him. Everyone looked at the pending feud, having just taking in the whole of their business.

Carlie pressed his teeth together, showing a forced-back anger. The muscles in his jaws moved, telling the height of his fury. He spoke now to her naked back, "Wha's di problem, Punty?"

She turned towards him now. "Ho' yuh mean w'at's di problem? Yuk t'ink mi nuh know seh yaah fuck Grace?"

Carlie walked off and Cyclone Quality took Menna's attention again. She had missed a bit, but now he shouted to his selecta, "Bugles! Play wi bad man tune nuh, man?!"

Bugles, a wicked selecta flicked on a track from Cobra. The crowd roared and the usual taunting began as Cyclone threw taunting words at the remaining sounds in the competition. Who couldn't take it shouldn't be in the game. "Mi gwine kick up unnuh bombo claat!" he told them. The crowd roared again. "Yeeeess!" he sounded like a Jamaican preacher. Now he jumped with frantic rhythms into the air, jabbing it with his fingers. He needed no gym, this guy. Heart pumping and sweat bursting, the crowd was putty in his hands. "Yeeeess! Dis roun' yah nice! Ah feel good yuh si!"

Menna's mobile buzzed in her pocket. She answered it. The call commanded her to leave her seat for a quieter place. "Hold on a minute," she told the caller. "I'll just find a place where I can hear myself speak." And it was at that place, about a hundred yards down towards the back of the arena she found him. *Conteh.* Standing there. Alone. With sad eyes. But then it could be because she knew he was: *sad,* that is.

They were both shocked to see each other. *He* shifted from one leg to the next as if he wanted to take a piss. Butterflies bubbled in *her* belly, their wings tickling its walls like torture, yet her face oozed *confidence* as she said, *'and-what-are-you-gonna-do-about-it?'*

She took her call. Stood right behind him to be precise, her voice pouring mercilessly into his ears. She watched him twitch. She knew he wanted to look back. Move, even. She loved it. Being in control had become a drug for Menna. An addiction. Perhaps it was an illness set on by one too many men trying to fuck with her head.

"And guess who is standing right in front of me?" Menna said down the phone to Cynthia. "Mista *Lova Lova*... Mista *'Dick-Couldn't-Keep-Still-Till-Him-Dip-It-Inna-Hot-Callaloo'*."

Conteh turned 'round and stared a *'why-can't-you-just-ease-off'* dagger into her eyes.

"Mr *'I'm not married'*, she continued. "Mr *'Nuff Baby mothers'*... Mr *'Wife-Lef'-Im-Raas'*."

Conteh was surprised at Menna's raw Jamaican tongue. Although she was born there, living in England from a teenager, she had lost it. But now, it seemed, she wasn't ramping. It was spending the recent years in Jamaica that gave her back that original *Jamaican-gyal* attitude. When she needed it, it worked for her. When she wanted to be *Miss Posh*, that worked for her too.

"Take care, Sis'. See you soon. Shame that stomach bug got you, you would have loved it," she said now in that posh English accent. "Oh, the clash is heavy. Impartial might even come back with the cup, who knows... Yes, there are a few nice-looking guys, but you can't go by look, Sis'. Look what happened with *Conteh, Egyptian*...." And when she was done, she flipped her phone shut and walked confidently back past Conteh. But not before the devil in her had its way: she grabbed the left cheek of Conteh's ass, filling her right palm and squeezed. *Hard*. The sudden, unexpected (and to his opinion) *dyam outa-aada action* made him jump. And his eyes widened as he watched her walked back from whence she came, as if nothing had happened.

A bredrin looked at Conteh and smiled a *big-up* smile. He thought Conteh had pulled. But he was wrong. *So very wrong*. In fact, if anyone, it was Menna that had pulled a *very long straw*.

For something to do, and to try to alley his nerves, Conteh folded his right arm across his waist, using it to grasp his left elbow. He ran his left palm over his face in disbelief, then left it covering his mouth. But there was nothing he could do about the hot flush of embarrassment that overcame him. It was so intense he thought that everyone could see his soul. In fact, he felt they knew the whole score. He felt that the recent torture back in Birmingham was etched upon his forehead. *Shit*.

When Menna reached her seat, Carlie, the protagonist was standing in his usual place. Punty, his antagonist was nowhere to be seen. She took a deep breath and praised her recent action.

"Were you in Jamaica at the Murder Before Disrespect clash?" Menna looked in the other direction to see who Carlie was talking to. No one was looking his way. She looked back to find him staring at her.

"I's *you* meah talk to, lady," he assured her.

"Me?" she pointed to her chest.

"Yes."

"Yes… yes, I was there… were *you*?"

"Of course I was dere. When I miss a soun' clash, I mus' be in my grave, to raas claat." It was obvious that the notion of swearing in front of a lady was a norm. *Built in.* A nuh not'n.

"Oh… right."

"Yuh love soun' clash?" he asked.

"I'm still deciding whether I can call it *love* or simply an *addiction*. Maybe there's a connection that draws me. Something from my past."

"Laad-a-Gad, yuh soun' intelligent, eeh? *Posh*. Yuh don' soun like a woman who would like soun' clash.

"*Really*? How should I sound? Like the woman who just told you, you *fucked* Grace?" Attitude laced her tone.

He chuckled. No. More of a *slack* cackle. "Yuh soun like a lovas rock kina girl."

"Right."

"Anyway, don' watch not'n," he said, trying to put a little cream on Punty's action. "Ah so some woman stay. Dem 'ear a likkle 'ear seh, an' dem tek it tu'n one bag a bombo claat stress." He kissed his teeth. "Anyway, mi did due fi lef' ar from time. Shi too dyam miserable. Every night mi come een shi jus nyngy-nyngy inna mi ears, to raas." He kissed his teeth again.

Menna took in his body language and saw that he needed a spliff for a prop. She smiled. *'You slag your woman off in front of a complete stranger that you are trying to chirps, and expect to succeed?'* she thought.

"Anyway," he relented, "I's a woman like *you* mi would like, yunnuh? Yuh look cool. Nice. Like yuh would jus' 'low a man wid 'im freedom... mi like dem kin'a woman deh, yunnuh? Mi cyaan tek di miserable one dem at aaaall."

"You mean you like the women you can walk over?…"

306

"No… a nuh so…. Easy nuh. Is wha' duh yuh?"

"… The women you can find at home *still* waiting after you've come home from screwing the whole world of women?"

"No… mi nuh mean dat? Mi jus' mean seh yuh look… andastandin'… yunnuh?"

"Oh," she emitted a cynical chuckle. "I am. *Understanding. Very.* You'd never know how much."

"Yeah, man," he grinned, stupid enough to think they had hit the same level of understanding. "Den mi nuh tell yuh?… cha." He leaned his head and looked at her: it was his idea of *sexy*.

The irate woman came back. Right in the middle of that *sexy* look. She gave Menna a dirty look. No. More of a *dutty-cut-yeye*. One that, if you let it, could make you feel as if someone had just walked over your grave. Or turn you into a pillar of salt, even. But Menna was neither dead yet, nor did she fancy walking for one moment in the shoes of Lot's wife. *Chat bout.* So she averted her eyes to the stage again. Besides, she had better (or *worst*, even) things on her mind. *Things to do. Places to go.* In three days time, for instance, she must make a trip down to London. *Oh yes.* She needed to see a white man about a score. An unsettled score…

Peter Walker… The man behind the Key Chip fraud… The man that very nearly wrecked her career. He had no conscience. None at all. But she was on his tail all right. This sista leaves no stone unturned.

* * *

'*What a difference a plane ride away from Birmingham, England made.*' Menna thought as she sat next to Clayton in his proud SUV. When she had rang to tell him she want the break, he wanted her there like *yesterday*.

Clayton was growing on her more than she had thought possible.

"Are you ok?" Clayton asked, taking her hand and gripping it tight.

"Damn right."

As Clayton manoeuvred the sturdy vehicle with mastery, she remembered when she had blown her fuse at him for daring to enter her bare-backed, after she had expressed her wish for him *not to*. Although it took a while for her to calm down, he had managed to allay her fears by producing a medical certificate, signed only the previous day, proving he was *not* HIV positive. Since he couldn't be sure the *she* wasn't, she still thought it was a bit reckless at the time.

"I'll say this again, Menna, if you ever decide that you want to come and live permanently in Canada, Menna, I promise I'll make you happy," he told her as he exit the Allen Expressway and headed west along Eglinton Avenue. "We didn't come this side when you were last here, did we?"

"I don't think so." For several blocks, Menna could see droves of Jamaican restaurants, bakeries, barbershops and hairdressers. Birmingham, England filled her head.

"The Jamaica Gleaner Company office is round here somewhere, I think," Clayton relented.

"Clayton, don't get your hopes up. I didn't take this journey to Canada to do a second recce or anything. I just needed a break. And anyway, I'm still contemplating where I want to spend the rest of my days."

"The *rest of your days*! Woman, you talk like an old lady who is about to snuff it."

"Menna smiled. "My sister has a friend in North Carolina, USA. She has given us an open invite, should we want to go there... see if we like it... Do the green card thing."

"The States... *mmm*." Clayton pondered.

"I didn't say it was a definite. It's an option."

"Have you not thought about the terrorist thing? I told you, Canada is one of the safest countries to be right now with terrorism on the up and up. This is a safe heaven, Menna. It isn't seen as targets for terror attacks."

"Are you sure that wasn't a sales pitch, Clayton? To get me to buy your idea on coming here to live with you?" she asked with a smile.

"Sales pitch, maybe, but however you look at it, it's true."

"I believe you. But like I said, moving countries is a big upheaval. It needs lots of thinking about."

"Yes, but you did it before. You went to live in Jamaica."

"I wouldn't call that such an upheaval. I was born there for a start. Secondly, when I went back the last time, it was on a whim. I didn't sell my flat and I left most of my belongings, so no, I didn't' *upheave* at all."

"So, why are you torturing me?"

She looked at him. "What d'you mean *torturing you*?"

"Each time you visit me, Menna, you give me hope. Whenever we make love, I feel I'm getting closer to you. Like I said, I feel you're the one, but I can't make it happen if you don't want it to…. It takes two of us."

* * *

Baby Face Glen wasn't the type to wait to be called when it came to cash that he was owed. Having Peter's address wasn't exactly a guarantee, but it was a form of security.

It was 9pm when he turned up at Peter's flat. Prior to his arrival, the security cameras were all out of order. Apart from human eyes, there were no captured evidences of prior visitors to the block. Just that of Baby Face Glen.

Glen looked around suspiciously before walking up to the intercom, but as it went, he pushed the main door before pressing the communication button. The door was open. Faulty, one would guess. So Glen simply walked through. Soon he would be on the doorstep of Peter's flat.

Would Peter be pleased to see him? Glen was angry. As promised, Peter had not called him the day before to sort out the meeting for today, so he came *unannounced.*

The big deal had not long gone down. As far as Glen was concerned, fresh cash was supposed to be lurking. Nuff of it. *An unthinkable amount.*

Though Peter's door was opened, Glen knocked… went in…

Minutes later, Glen emerged outside the building. He looked around suspiciously, then hurried away like a chased man. In his hurry, he bumped into a lady coming home with bags of shopping. She saw the terror in his eyes: eyes that looked like those of a fugitive. Even the newly fixed security camera saw it. The look in his eyes, that is.

* * *

It was the early evening News that drew Glenda to what was left of her senses. Drink had taken most of it, but the headline seemed to have knocked her sober. The black newsreader announced the shocking news almost as if she was talking solely to Glenda. *'Two men were found dead in a London flat early on this evening. They are thought to have died around 9pm last night. A man was caught on camera hurrying away from the apartment block. It has been revealed that one of the dead men, Peter John Walker, a forty-two year old and owner of the exquisite flat, was a known drug-trafficker, linked with cocaine trail from Jamaica to numerous destinations in Britain. The other man, Martin Backer is known as a small time crook.'*

Glenda stood up but fell right back down again. The full-on facial image of the man sprawled all over her TV screen was more than a shock. It had been a while since she had seen her ex-husband's face. Within that while, Peter Walker had seen the shores of the Jamaican coastline about as much time as Glenda had sunk bottles of whisky. When money flowed for Peter, Glenda stuck around, but when the chips went down she left him for a black guy who she figured had cash to spare. But she was wrong. This guy just didn't toss his cash around too lightly. In fact *he* thought *she* had cash in abundance. You see, Glenda always looked good. With her fine clothes, shoes, make-up and jewellery. And the pretty car Peter had bought her. The pretty car that soon lost its prettiness as soon as the service and upkeep couldn't be maintained. So, as her pretty car was *driven* away to a dealer, so Glenda was *driven* to drink. This guy had nothing to give her. Besides, he was married and had another umpteen *hangers-on* to attend to. Well, hanging to just his dick, to be precise.

"What is it, Mummy?" one of Glenda's *grown-up-fast* children had asked as Glenda stared wide-eyed at the TV screen.

"Nothing… Nothing, son… Nothing."

Chapter 18

*G*arnet woke to a beautiful morning… Spain was behind him now. For the first time in ages he heard the singing of birds. He wasn't sure if it was simply his imagination, but whatever it was, it was beautiful. *'Tweet-tweet-twiddle-de-tweet-tweet-twiddle...'* Nice.

He opened the bedroom window of his bachelor's pad and said, *"Give thanks."*

Late last night as he lay in his bath soaking away, one would suppose the *stress of bygone years*, he floated on air and thought he was dreaming. Then he realised it wasn't a dream at all, and told himself he was one of the luckiest men on earth. He told himself that the fact that Evadney had really given him a chance, and was ready to take him down the aisle of *matrimony* was a *wonderful stroke of luck*. Eh! Eh!… *Backside*. And if he had grinned any wider, the corner of his mouth would touch his ears. *Oh, happy days*.

Only a few days before he flew out to Spain, he spoke to an old idrin from back in the day when *Rasta* was *Rasta*. *Lijah Zephaniah Benjamin*. Lijah had empathised with him and told him to cherish this. Forgiveness like the ones they both had didn't come often. Lijah's story was somewhat similar.

Lijah and Gloria were invited to the wedding. That much Garnet knew. He didn't know much of *who else* were invited, since Evadney took care of everything... *bless her*. All he needed to do was to turn up at the church in his suit, with his best-man, Gongo Peas and a shiny *have-and-to-hold* ring.

Gongo Peas also told him how lucky he was. And today, when Garnet remembered how radiant Evadney had been looking these days, he said, *"Give thanks."* He had not tasted her flesh for the longest time. Like newly weds of days gone by, she said she would save it for the wedding night. *Ohhhh... Sweet anticipation*. He could almost feel the moment, and said, *"Give thanks."*

A sharp suit hung like a stag's antler from his wardrobe door.

His natty-dreads groomed to every last strand, even though the wedding was still hours away, and his *free-from-scissors* beard groomed to the tops. *Dapper dread!*

The gold crown he sported blinged even more that morning. Almost as if it could *feel*, and so radiated his *happiness*.

And today, for Garnet, *happiness* was a thing called *'matrimony'*.

And with nowhere to vent his happiness, he sang:

'Natural African black woman I adore you...Empress...

And as he floated from the bedroom to the bathroom, he could have sworn that in the distance he could hear Angel Gabriel singing the same song...

'Natural African black woman I adore you...Empress...

And as he splashed cold water on his face, he *knew* he was more than ready. Ready to make his solemnly-sworn *Have-And-To-Hold* pledge. *Chat bout.*

* * *

Garnet and Gongo Peas had travelled lightly... Gongo's BM was adequately gleaming - enough to meet the standard of any wedding limousine. *How yuh mean*? The brothers looked sharp in their *groom & best-man* suits an' t'ing. *Chat bout*. The church was an evenly proportion of black and white members. It was a little *out-in-the-sticks* and Garnet had wondered why Evadney didn't just use a Pentecostal church, or even a nearer one, and if the truth be told, he couldn't even remember her explanation as to *why* her parents' church wasn't good enough. All he wanted to know was that she was going to be his *bride*.

It didn't seem that long before Garnet found himself facing a Vicar in the big, intimidating stain-glassed church. It felt a little *cold* too, but then it could be down to his nerves. The congregation bellowed:

> *Come to a wedding,*
> *Come to a blessing,*
> *Come on a day when happiness sings!*
> *Come rain or sun,*
> *Come winter or summer,*
> *Celebrate love and all that it brings.*

Garnet felt a little lonely up there for a while as he waited patiently for his bride.

> *Thanks for the love,*
> *That holds us together,*
> *Parent and child, and lover and friend,*
> *Thanks to the God,*
> *Whose love is our centre,*
> *Source of compassion, knowing no end.*

Tick followed *tock* followed *tick* followed *tock*…

> *Love is the gift,*
> *And love is the giver,*
> *Love is the gold that*
> *Makes the day shine;*
> *Love forgets self to care for the other,*
> *Love changes life from water to wine.*

He waited…

> *Come to this wedding,*
> *Asking a blessing,*
> *For all the years that living will prove*
> *Health of the body,*

Health of the spirit,
Now to you both we offer our love.

… And waited…

He couldn't help thinking that the song was a little premature.

He mopped brow…

His silk collar began to choke him.

'Is this a dream? Where is she?' he asked himself… *'Come,*
'Vadney man… come…'

And *Tick* followed *tock* followed *tick* followed *tock*…

And then…

Oh my God… and then… *Oh Lord*… a woman who seemed as if
he had simply walked straight off the street and into the church with
one sole purpose, walked bravely up the long, lonely aisle. She handed
the Vicar a note then simply turned and walked back down the aisle
towards the exit again. *Just like that.* Just like a postman would walk
into a corner shop and hand the shopkeeper his post.

The congregation that had already sang one too many songs rang
out a unison murmur as if they *knew* what the note entailed.

The Vicar took the note, stared at it, then looked at the
disappearing back of the messenger.

Garnet looked anxiously at the Vicar. *'Surely not'*, he thought.
'Dear God, surely not.' He turned and looked at his idrin, Gongo Peas
who had leant forward, his elbows on his knees and his face in his
hands. He was peeping through his fingers as his heart pounded against
his chest.

There were no golden moments in that silence. *No sir.* It was
strangling.

As the congregation kept their eyes on the Vicar, he kept his on the
note - long after he had read it, that is. Then, he looked at Garnet with a
telling heap of sorrow in his eyes.

Garnet saw it. The sorrow in the Vicar's eyes, that is.

He needed no note.

No explanation.

Suddenly the jigsaw fitted too *perfectly cruel* for words. *Jesu*s. He
turned again and looked at Gongo, but what he really wanted to do was
to run…

Run!

Run!

313

Run like hell! Out of the church! Out of the gaze of prying eyes!…
run!… run!… run!…

"Garnet," the Vicar said after he had moved closer to Garnet's ear.
"We need to have a word in the vestry."

Garnet felt his knees going. He reached for his locks. *Anchor.* He
needed them. The long *once-roots-an-cultured* strands that had long
gone lost their *roots-an-culture.* "Wha'… wha'… what is it, Vicar?"
His voice was higher than he intended, and since the congregation was
now at a *pin-drop-silence* level, they had no trouble hearing.

"Ladies and gentlemen," the Vicar spoke diligently to his
congregation. "There is a slight technicality in today's ceremony. The
organist will play on. Please accompany him by singing hymn number
two, whilst the groom and I sort a few things out in the vestry."

Garnet turned and looked again at Gongo who was griping the ring
in his pocket now. Then he tried to see if he could see Evadney's
parents. Any of her family. Friends. But he couldn't see anyone. Just
strange faces. Old white men's faces pursed with pity. Old white
women's with that sorrow-filled smile. Old black men and women with
'we know' faces. They stretched towards him. Distorted. Harrowing.
Caving in on him like the walls of a consuming nightmare they spun
round and round making him dizzy.

The congregation stood to the beckoning of the Vicar, and as they
watched gowned man disappeared with Garnet towards the back, they
raised their *not-so-cheerful* voices into a song.

Gongo Peas got up and left the church, wandering out into the
churchyard for air. Something told him there would be trouble ahead.

No moonlight.

No laughter. No love.

No romance…

Just plain old *trouble* ahead. Bam-bam… Passa-passa… War inna
Babylon.

In the meantime, back in the vestry, Vicar John Cashmere tried to
find the best way to deliver the message to Garnet, who, already
knew… the best way to tell him that the message read: '*Dear Vicar,
this is a message for Garnet. Please tell him for me, Vicar, to keep
waiting. Please tell him that if he waits long enough, Tracey might
come. He had chosen her over me before. Left me when I needed him
most. And today, Vicar, I have chosen someone else over him, just
when he needs me most. And as you read this note, I will be marrying
that person. And Vicar, tell him that if he measures the hurt that he's*

feeling right now... the shame... the humiliation... the cut of rejection
that made him feel like nothing... tell him for me, Vicar, that my hurt
was ten times worse the day he left me for Tracey. Tell him for me,
Vicar, that the price he's paying now is a 'cut' price. You see, Vicar,
Garnet cut me. Sliced me up into a thousand pieces. And although I
patched myself up, the wounds will never heal. Today is his time to be
sliced up. 'None of my love'... Evadney.'

Evadney it seemed had lost her heart.

Can hurt really make a person that calculatingly bitter?

It was the dreadful bawling: the heart-wrenching gnashing of his
teeth that swept its way from the vestry, through the congregation and
out into the churchyard that dragged Gongo back in. As if he was the
only one in the whole building, he strode swiftly up the aisle, in front
of the congregation and across to the vestry, where he found his idrin
holding the killer-note in hand, squeezing it vengefully as he bawled,
tears, spittle and snort tainting his once-perfect suit. "Woooyee!
Woooyee! Jeeesas! Why 'Vadney duh mi dis, Gongo?!... Why?!"

Gongo took the piece of paper from his mate's hand. Tears had
fallen on the words, causing the ink to run. "Jeesas C'ris'," Gongo had
whispered when the gist of it hit him. "She had never really forgiven
you, Garnet. The planning of this whole day was a farce, man. She's a
fuckin' bitch!"

"Would you like a cup of tea, Garnet?" the Vicar was helpless and
Gongo's profanity made him a little uncomfortable. *Tea* was all he had.
He had given prayer a second thought since it would take a *miracle* to
reverse this.

"*Who* has she chosen over me, Gongo? Who?!!... Who is she
marrying?!!"

"Garnet," Gongo said sternly, "listen, Bredrin... Dis is terrible.
Really terrible, but 'ear dis, Bredrin... yuh have to pull yuhself
togedda!... Yaah 'ear mi?!"

"Gongo," Garnet said, lines of slime and bubbles of froth gathered
in his mouth like trimmings to the mockery. "Why shi neva jus' tell mi
no, Bredrin?"

"Dat would have been too easy, Bredrin. Her plan was to soak yuh
up. Dis is di worse kin'a fuck-up to raas claat."

"Woooyee! Laad! Laad! Laad! Woooyee!"

"Garnet! Bredrin! Easy, man, easy... Stop di bawlin', man..."

"Mammy! Mammy! Oiyeee! Cough! Cough! Choke! Choke!"...
He stopped. Suddenly. As if a realisation had just reached him....
"How mi gwine face all dem people out deh, Bredrin?"

"Easy, Bredrin," Gongo was as helpless now as the Vicar with his
cup of tea.

"A nuh not'n. Yuh don't even know dem people out deh. It's jus'
di normal congregation of dis church. Yuh lucky seh it wasn't a full
black church. Dis woulda been more shameful."

"Yuh don't t'ink shi is getting married in her parents' church, do
you?"

"Bwoy, your guess is as good as mine."

"Evadney *really* hate mi dat much, Gongo? Hate mi dat much dat
shi plan all dis?... sen' mi to Spain?..."

"Yeah, man. Shi sen' yuh to Spain to get yuh outa di way, so you
don't bump into anyone who would mention anyt'ing. *Woman*,
Bredrin, *woman.* Deadly! Dem can be fuckin' clever w'en dem want to
be... *Spain*," Gongo kissed his teeth. "More like *Costa Del Decoy* to
raas."

"I'm not going out dere, Bredrin. I'm not facing that crowd.
Strangers or not."

"Yuh don' have to face nobaddy. We'll jus' slip out di back. Di
Vicar will have to explain to dem."

"Yes. Yes," the Vicar assured Garnet. "I'll just say that due to a
little technicality, the wedding won't be taking place today."

Garnet wiped his face.

Blew his nose.

But he couldn't reach his heart. If he could, he would have taken it
out, washed it, and put it back in again. Wash away the pain. And
before that, he would have had to put it back together again. For it was
broken into a thousand pieces. And there were no telling if it could
ever be put back together again... *Humpty-Dumpty... eat your heart
out.*

As Garnet and Gongo slipped out the back of the church that
Evadney had no intention of getting married in, the despondent Vicar
delivered the *murmur-raising* news to his congregation, who had long
gone worked out the real meaning of *'a little technicality'.* To put it
bluntly? *Ditched.*

* * *

In the meantime, as Garnet bathed his pained heart, a quiet registry office on Broad Street saw the back of a brave *blushing* bride and her mysterious groom. Evadney and her new husband linked arms so tightly, the term *'till death us do part'* seemed as if it would live up to its true meaning.

Apprehension and doubt spread over the faces of the few that were chosen to witness the formal ceremony:

Pearl and Percy, *her parents*.

Yvonne, *her best friend*.

Two other old school friends, Joy and Rebecca.

No more, no less.

Later the small party would join an even bigger one at the Centennial Centre for food and beverages. And that would be all. No speeches. Speeches could stay. In fact, the only speech that was on the agenda was a *'tradition-breaking'* one from Evadney herself. Previously rehearsed, it would be *short*. Straight to the point. But *sweet* would be debatable.

"Just a few pictures at the Botanical Gardens, then we'll head down to the Centennial Centre," Evadney said to her parents and friends who were heading now towards two cars: Yvonne and Rebecca had travelled with Joy in her car. Evadney and her husband had travelled in Pearl and Percy's car. And all was well. *No need for limousine.*

"Percy," Evadney's mother, Pearl said to her husband as she crossed the road to the car. She looked back to see Evadney and her new husband still standing by the entrance of the registry office talking to a black woman who, seemingly, was with the next wedding party. "Mi don' feel good 'bout dis at all. A funny feelin' jus tek mi, Percy, tek mi. If mi nuh mine sharp, it wi' fly up inna mi head an kill mi."

"Pear, stop yuh foolishniss."

"No, Percy, ah true… a tormented feelin'." She sighed a desperate *'heye'*. "I hope Evadney know what shi doin', yunnuh." She looked back to see if her daughter had started to walk towards the car.

"Yuh have to leave dese young people to do as dem please, Pearl," Percy surmised. "Yuh cyaan tell dem how to run dem life."

"Dere is going to be 'ruption, Percy. 'ruption mi tellin' yuh… dis is no likkle somet'ing."

"Pearl, we are here because we are Evadney's parents. We have to leave her up to her own device. Ah fi dem problem. Mek dem sort it out."

317

"Percy, I know w'at yuh saying, but it won't be as easy as dat. Mi was *shock*, Percy, *shock* w'en Sista Vennah tell mi seh shi hear dat Evadney plan church wedding' jus' to have revenge on Garnet."

"So yuh mean seh Garnet really dress up an' gaan to a church?" Percy asked.

"Yes, Percy! Sometime yuh gwaan like yuh not 'earin' w'at mi sayin'!" She kissed her teeth and climbed into the car.

"Mi not 'earin' yuh, Pearl, because yuh not talkin' plain!"

"How yuh mean mi not talkin' plain, Percy? Yuh mus' dig out di wax outa yuh ea's dem!"

"Tell mi in English how it go, Pearl."

"How yuh mean *tell yuh in English*? Yuh nuh andastan' Jamaican?"

Percy laughed.

"Evadney neva forgave Garnet for leavin' her for dat w'ite girl."

"Well wi all know dat," Percy told her.

"As yuh know, only di few of us here was invited to di proper weddin'."

"Yes."

"Garnet an' him frien' Gongo was sent on a wild goose chase to some far church... Him also believe dat di reception would be at the firs' place dat was printed on the first invitation dem. Yuh rememba?"

"Eee heh? Ah weh yaah seh?"

"So w'en him lef' di church vex, he might go to dat place."

"Shit."

"Percy stop yuh swearin'!... So anyway, dat is why Evadney sen' out new leaflets las' week changin' di venue."

"So..." Percy asked, "di people at di reception?... dem expectin' Garnet to turn up?"

"Yes, Percy, dem expectin' to see Garnet."

"So... Evadney go t'rough all dat fi di sake a revenge?"

"Yes, Percy. Dat is what mi tryin' to tell yuh."

"Pearl, I t'ink Evadney playin' wid people's lives yunnuh."

"Dat is w'at a mean, Percy. I don' see Garnet tekkin' dis t'ing lightly. Dat is why mi tellin' yuh mi have a bad feelin' 'bout di whole t'ing..."

"But Pearl... what if you did dat to mi?"

"Percy why yuh have to tek bad somet'ing mek laugh all di while?" She kissed her teeth and pushed her bosom up.

318

Percy was well and truly *told,* and only the hint of a smile stayed on his face. But deep down, he himself was nervous about the whole thing.

* * *

Trust the Saturday traffic to bring Simone to a standstill just outside the registry office where Evadney stood with her new husband. "Oh," she said to Lawrence, "She's getting married."

"Who's getting married?"

"Evadney... My ex-next-door-neighbour... the one who..."

"Not the one Conteh..."

"Yes. That's her... good luck to her though. I wish her all the best."

"You know, Darling, sometimes I wonder if an angel had kissed you at birth."

"Why?" she asked, chuckling at what she thought was an OTT comment from her husband.

"I truly believe that if someone should kill you, and you should somehow come to life again, you'd forgive that person."

"Really?"

"The woman slept with your husband... well your *then* husband... and you wish her all the best."

"Well, what's wishing her bad things gonna do? You know that when people do selfish things, there's always a reason. Garnet treated her bad. I was angry at the time, but I guess she was lonely."

"And you see that as a good reason to mess with your man?... and for you to forgive her?"

"Well, no, but... I blame Conteh. Evadney had no loyalties to me. He should have resisted."

Lawrence smiled. "I knew you had a unique quality. That's one of the reasons I married you."

"Oh, I thought it was my cooking," she joked.

As the traffic eased, and before Simone attempted to pull away, she turned on impulse to find Evadney looking her way. There was no doubt that she had recognised her. Evadney didn't look away. She held the stare. But there were no animosity in her eyes. In fact, they said... *'Sorry'.*

Simone felt her lips spreading.

A smile appeared.

Evadney caught it and was grateful.

She followed the car with her eyes as it left that section of Broad Street.

Seconds later, she opened the back door of her father's car and climbed in. Her husband followed.

Percy and Pearl felt obliged to drop the conversation about the bombshell their daughter dropped on Garnet.

"Ok, Dad, let's go," Evadney chirped.

Joy started her engine and followed Percy.

* * *

There were no doubt that the organisers and catering staff had piled on a good spread for this wedding reception. The hall was decked and festooned with bows of the most beautiful flowers. A beautiful array of silk ribbons tasselled and draped around them. The most glorious displays of *'On Your Wedding Day'* helium balls one could ever wish for.

The tables were set for kings, queens, princes and princesses, so the rows of *Toms, Dicks, Harrys, Marys, Janes* and *Joe Bloggs* that occupied them felt like *royalties*.

Pearl and Percy sat more *nervously* than *proudly* at the top table.

Close friends of the family sat near, whilst mere acquaintances sat further.

The aroma from the curry, rice-an'-peas, chicken and whatever else there were, mingled with, and travelled up the noses of the *good, bad* and the *indifferent*.

Pastor Brown, the local pastor sat smiling as he always did, though the question of *'why didn't Evadney ask me to join her and her husband's hand in marriage?'* was still on his mind.

Everyone who knew *his* or *her* DJ will know that there are many *called* ones in Birmingham: all of them fit to feed the city with *sweet reggae music*.

They will know too, that there are a *chosen* few.

Simply put, *'Many are called, but few are chosen.'*

And they will know too, that although the deliverance of reggae music is neither a race nor a competition, for the people, there is *one winner... Yes sir.*

The people's choice...

The DJ who for years has lit up the lives of every listener that stayed faithful to STING FM, come rain, come shine.

And Evadney had always known that *no other DJ* would be *chosen* to grace her wedding day.

None other than the man himself… *Father Jarvis.* Yuh done know.

With over sixteen trophies to his belt, this maestro had not a goddamn thing to prove. He just goes on *doing his thing. Chat bout.* When he plays, he makes the people's hearts sing. A gift, one would guess, but he has it.

So there he was… on the wedding day… *doing his thing.*

The music he pumped out made everyone want to get up and move, never mind sitting there waiting to be fed, but that was just it, black people danced only when the time is *'appropriate'*, even if the music is tickling their asses with a vengeance.

Feet tapped frantically beneath dazzling-white tablecloths.

Heads nodded happily: even ones of church-goers.

But in the *feet-tapping-head-nodding* hour, tongues wagged too.

Tongues wagged uncontrollably about the *most wagable* subject at hand: *'the mysterious husband switch'.* Oh dear… *What a la-la?*

The Benjamin family had arrived a little late and their seating positions were a little too far from the itty-gritty of things. Gloria for one, would have liked to take a closer look at Garnet's rival. Herself, Lijah, Ikesha, Shari and Reds sat together in that order.

Reds was feeling overwhelmingly uneasy sitting next to his daughter, but not half as uneasy as Shari was feeling. Since Mitzi had enlighten them both on the *blood-ties* thing, none of them had taken that crucial step towards each other to familiarise themselves in a *kinship* way. Funny, but that was just the way it dropped. But that was another dilemma. The drama in this room was already too much. There would always be later.

"This is shocking, G'," Lijah said to Gloria. "This is a real twist. The invitation clearly said Evadney and Garnet. What's happening?"

"Everyone is as puzzled as us, Lijah," Gloria said in a low voice. I don't know what's happening. This is the strangest wedding reception I have ever been to."

"D'you think it was a misprint?" Ikesha asked.

"No, I don't think so. If it were a misprint, surely she would realise not long after, and then correct it? Even when she sent out the *'amendment-to-venue'* leaflets she would have mentioned the mistake."

Shari said nothing. Her mind was on her brother, Kunta. In fact, it was rarely off him at all.

Reds, who was a little too far to have heard what was already said, eased forward to catch Lijah's attention. "I t'ought Evadney was marrying Garnet, Bredrin."

"Nuh suh meah seh, Bredrin. Sop'n funny goin' aan, man. I was invited to Garnet's reception, not some strange man."

"Who is he anyway?" Reds asked.

"Bwoy, I don' know yunnuh. All he's doing is holding his head down."

"Maybe him hiding," Reds joked.

A group of men walked in and hovered for a while.

Looked around the room.

Took in what they supposedly wanted to…

Then one of them, looking over at Evadney and her husband shouted, "Dis is fuckries! Downright fuckries!" *That was it. They walked out again.*

Then… an excruciating *hush*… a thick blanket of *silence*. A silence that could drive hardened criminals out of their minds.

But Father Jarvis broke it and played on.

"Percy…" Pearl said, her voice shaking. "Mi tell yuh… mi tell yuh seh mi had a funny feelin' bout dis…"

Percy looked at Evadney. "Who are dose people, Evadney?"

"I don't know, Dad. Maybe some of Garnet's friends."

"Wi don' want no trouble yunnuh, Evadney." Pearl told her. "Dis is meant to be yuh weddin' day."

"Is it true dat yuh made a fool a Garnet, Evadney?" Percy asked, "fool him up an' sen' him to some church like yuh was gwine marry him?"

"Made a fool of him, like he did of me, you mean, Dad?… This is *my* day. Let's not spoil it." She motioned to Yvonne who seemed to have understood, because she got up, walked over to Father Jarvis, whispered in his ears, then walked back to her seat again.

Immediately, the music stopped. "People!" Father Jarvis shouted over the microphone. "I do believe we have a short speech from the *bride!* Heh! Heye!… Unusual, but we are livin' in di 21st century!" Father Jarvis knew part of the score. Not all, *just part*. And although he didn't agree with certain things, as far as he was concerned, it was nobody's business but the bride and groom's. His job was to *Entertain* with a capital *'E'. Chat bout.*

Father Jarvis knew about the *skin on the top of the porridge,* but what bubbled below would be as much news to the fun-loving DJ as it would be to everyone else. Had he known that earlier, poor *Billy-One-Mate* Garnet (his only mate then being Gongo Peas) was left waiting in vain for a bride that would never show, things might have been a little different. Two wrongs could never make a right. He knew Garnet. And later he would learn that whatever he had done to *receive* this treatment must have really cut Evadney to the core. But did he *deserve* it? Surely this was the lowest form of revenge?

Evadney stood up. *Sista Sledge-Hammer*.

Her husband squeezed her hand, still holding his head down as if there were people in the room he'd rather not make eye contact with.

He had a hard face. As if he'd seen life, and that the *life* he had seen wasn't good to him.

"Hello, everybody," Evadney commenced. "I know there are a lot of you sitting there with questions on tongues. One main question to be precise… and that question is, '*Why isn't it Garnet that is sitting here with me*?'

A rush of murmur filled the room as people anxiously awaited the reasoning from the horse's mouth, yet, not even a movie could deliver the amount of drama that was in store for them on this peculiar wedding day… in Birmingham. *No sir.*

"Well," she continued, "I suppose it's the flipside of the coin. A flipside to the question *I know* you all must have asked when you had the invitation to this reception. You must have all said, '*I though he rejected her for a blonde? How come she took him back?… How come she's marrying him?*"

Another spate of tuts, murmurs, eyebrow raising and even giggles followed.

"Well, I guess there are lots of flipsides happening today. I guess this will be the most peculiar wedding reception you have ever been to. So what? Adds a little drama to all our lives…"

The crowd laughed.

"… Garnet chose someone else over me back then… and now… *I've* chosen someone else over him." She rested her hand on her husband's shoulder. "I know this must be the most unusual reception you have ever been to, but I wanted it this way. I also want you all to be *happy* for me. I've come a long way. *Please*… pick up your glasses… even if it's just filled with water…"

The *clang-clash-shuffle-shuffle* happened almost in unison. Glasses were held in every able hand. Except a few people who decided to *sit on the fence*. Including Reds and Lijah of course. They obviously felt a sense of *loyalty* towards Garnet. Toasting to his rival's happiness just wouldn't do.

"I'm asking you," Evadney continued. "To toast to me and my new husband…"

But suddenly!… Before she could utter his name!…

Panic!

A visitor had arrived!

Glasses hit the tables again.

"Oh, Saviour help us!" was Sista Vennah's idea of discreet.

"Look who's here!" another church sister said in a high-pitched whisper.

Then… *hush*… *hush*…

All eyes were on *him*.

One man… One man and his anger… Garnet.

He needed no invitation. After all… was it not meant to be *his* wedding day?

He came like a lone ranger.

Was it to claim his bride? The life of her groom?… Or had he simply come to ruthlessly mow a meadow of hurt and shame, casting the debris of humiliation aside once and for all? *Jesus*…

Garnet's eyes found the perpetrating couple now, and like an eagle, he held them in his vision.

"Laad have mercy, Percy!" Pearl almost filled her tenna Lady, *bless her*.

"Faada, help us!" Percy exclaimed.

"Dere's not'ing I can do, sah!" Father Jarvis shouted.

"No, not *you*, Faada Jarvis! Mi mean Faada God!… Evadney! Look yah nong! Look weh yuh cause wid yuh dyam stupidity! Everyt'ing crash!"

" 'Ruption, Percy! 'ruption!" Pearl shouted. "Mi tell yuh! Why couldn't Evadney jus' marry di man widout trickin' Garnet?!… Laad have mercy!" She raised her hands to the heavens.

"Stop unnuh noise!!…" Oh dear… *the husband* spoke. "*Bombo claat!…*" He found his true *disrespectful* voice now. "*Stop unnuh blood claat noise!*" He stood up.

A woman screamed, obliterating the sea of panicking murmurs.

"*Shalamashalamashalama!*" Pastor Brown ketch di spirit as soon as reality ketch him.

Evadney looked at her husband. *Shocked.* Never mind the others, but he was addressing her parents. *Telling her parents to shut dem bombo claat?* No... it wasn't happening.

"Dis likkle *pussy bwoy* cyaan duh not'n a *blood claat*!!" Baby Face Glen proclaimed. Surely it had to get worse before it got better?... *Why was he reaching into his breast pocket?* ...

Father Jarvis eased away from his box.

A few big men edged around. Drew closer to the bubbling feud with all good intentions, but could they help?

Gloria looked at Lijah... Lijah looked at Gloria... the one common question in both their eyes... *'Why didn't we notice before?' Shit.*

There was something different about *him*, but it was most certainly *him*.

Gloria felt sick. She wanted to heave.

Goose pimples gathered at the back of Lijah's neck.

Then anger.

Real anger.

Surely he must leave his seat and help Garnet to kick this dude's ass? This was *his* territory now.

This man claimed his family in Jamaica.

Ill-treated Gloria.

Threatened his very existence. Had him shaking in his boots. Then he had the cheek to disrespect his father's funeral not so long back. The illuminating familiarity between he and Rock was uncanny. Although Rock was dead, they seemed to pop up in every corner of his life. But *Baby Face Glen?* ... it all started with Lucy.

Gloria turned away, the memory too much to bear.

"What is it, Mum?" Ikesha asked, clearly recognising her parents' recognition of *'Mr Husband Of The Year'*.

"Nothing... nothing."

"D'you *know* that man?"

But as Garnet got closer, the crowd panicked more, saving Gloria from giving an answer.

Something devastatingly sinister was about to go down.

A few people with young children had left their seats and were heading towards the entrance. Some were in search of a safer place within the building.

Garnet looked like a zombie. Still clad in his wedding suit an' t'ing, locks flowing *fine* down his back, tears still staining his wrecked, grief-stricken face, it was hard to tell that the brother had woken that morning with the *birds and hope*. Now, as far as he was concerned, humiliation had taken his pride and thrown it up against every pissed-up, profanely graffitied wall in Birmingham. The fact that he had done practically the same to Evadney some years ago, wasn't the issue. Right then, *he* was feeling it, and this much he knew: he knew that *it stung... Hurt... Pained... Jabbed.*

"Ease off, Pussy Bwoy!" Baby Face Glen shouted, his hand still resting on his inside breast pocket. "Whaap'n, yuh 'ave a problem?"

But Garnet took no notice. He just glided closer. Only *he* knew what filled his head - past conversations... Conversations that gave him hope. Security... *'Is that why you don't want me to move in with you or mek love to yuh until afta di weddin' day?... or are you having second thoughts about that?'...* *'No... no, Garnet, I'm not having second thoughts at all... The wedding day is on, Garnet. The wedding day is on. Don't worry about that.'...* And so it was. *On.* Only, the *wedding day* wasn't his. And he knew he would *never* trust again. Never.

The dirt he had *'sent round'* had now *'come around'*, flicking a pile of nasty gravel into his eyes. But right then, he didn't want to *'see'* no reasoning. All he wanted to do was to *'kill di fucka'*.

The crowd got more restless.

"Garnet?"... Pearl coaxed. "Fi a quiet life, Garnet, *please*... t'ink carefully now, Garnet... nuh fallah di devil..."

"Garnet?" Percy's false teeth clanged. "Listen to mi, Garnet..."

"Somebody stop them!!" a hysterical woman shouted. "Can't you see what's gonna happen?! Where are all the men in the place?! Has anyone called the police?!"

"So wha'? Is dead yuh waan dead, bwoy!" Baby Face Glen's anger turned his deep, dark skin *blue*.

A few more men drew nearer, wondering what they should do. It didn't take a fool to realise that this day could mark history in a big way. And if the truth be told, the men that gathered around were more frightened of meeting a bullet, than anything else. They felt pretty sure that Garnet had come just with fists of fury, but there was something in Baby Face Glen's eyes they couldn't trust. They were no heroes. And getting plugged for someone else's shit wasn't on their agendas.

"Mi nah tell yuh again yunnuh, Pussy Bwoy!" Baby Face warned. "Mi wi' pop a gun aanda yuh bombo claat!"

Lijah remembered. It was the very same words he had used to threaten him back in Jamaica.

But then... Sirens! Singing in the distance... *Draw mi nearer!
Draw mi nearer!*...

Loud sirens. Someone had obviously seen it fit to engage the *boys-in-blue* via a mobile phone.

Evadney whispered to Baby Face, whose eyes were wandering anxiously from *outside* to *in*. Sirens made him more uneasy than his love rival, Garnet...

Another deportation was on his cards...

Kizzy had left him...

Faithlyn came to a terrible end; his little scheme too hard to *swallow* by her desperate mother in Jamaica...

Peter Walker was dead and he had not collected his dues from the *big traffic*...

Evadney was his last hope...

The Jamaican police weren't his friends. And neither was Garnet. So wherever he looked, *the view was dim*.

Garnet got *nearer*... *nearer*... *nearer*.

Now, Baby Face Glen was right off-guard. The sirens had disorientated him.

"Easy, Garnet!" Father Jarvis voiced his reason. "It's not wort' it my frien'."

But Father Jarvis' voice was nothing but an echo in a dream.

Garnet moved closer. The voices of his *stolen* guests cradled him with discomfort.

A *too-loud* brook babbled and splashed in his head and serenaded him a *mocking* song. And still, past conversations with Evadney filled his mind, brimming its edges like the spoils of a broken damn... '*Empress, I know I've done you wrong. Hurt you badly. But if yuh lef' mi, I'll be a wrecked man. After all dat rigmarole wid Tracey, I realised seh we were meant to be'*...

The heavy rusted iron bar was cold and hard to the touch as it rested mercilessly against his back like a cruel pillow. And still, he remembered... '*Natural African black woman I adore you... Empress'*...'*Happy with your suit?'*... '*Yeah man, Empress. Pleased wid mi suit. But even more pleased with my new bride-to-be'*...

"I don' like dis at all at all at all," an older lady who sat cuddling her handbag and shaking her head from side to side said. "Why don't someone hold Garnet? Somebody gwine get kill!"

.... '*And I hope I'll be pleased my new husband'*... '*You'll see, Empress... you'll see'*. And only then, he realised how *mocked* he was.

Only then, he realised that the *husband* she hoped she would be *happy with* was not *him* at all. Too hard to swallow. *Was he laughing at him too?... this... new man? Was he?*

"Where are all the real men in this place?" a posh-talking woman with a frightened looking white man by her side shouted, "could someone try to stop this before someone gets hurt?!"

The most burley of all the men listened to her and started to walk towards Garnet, but when his mobile rang, something told the crowd he was glad to be called away from the dilemma at hand. He wanted to live.

.... *'Just make sure Gongo take care of that ring... It isn't cheap. I know that cut deep into your savings'... 'Nothing's too expensive for my Empress'...*

To everyone's surprise, Garnet stopped moving. *Suddenly.* He twisted his head like a robot, averted his eyes from Baby Face Glen and focused his stare at Evadney, almost as if he was looking for something in her eyes that would tell him it was *all a dream... 'Trying to get rid of me?' ... 'No, not really, you go get some sun in them bones. Revitalise. You're gonna need the energy on your special day'... 'Really?'... 'Let's put it this way, 'I'm gonna make sure it's the most unforgettable day of your life'... 'Why are you crying?'... 'Because mi wish mi madda was here to witness dis. Mi weddin' day'...*

Evadney got a little hot under her wedding dress. *'What was Garnet thinking?'* for she could *feel* his intense thoughts. That was not the way she planned it. Right about then, Garnet was supposed to have crawled under a stone and died from the effect of a broken heart. *But no.* There he was. Like Frankenstein.

And now, he looked back at Baby Face Glen. *'Were you laughing at me too?'* Garnet asked himself. *'Did you help her in this plan to make me a laughing stock?... A stooge?... Where were you when me and Evadney grew our first locks together? Where?! Where were you when we twisted and left... twisted and left... threw our combs away... where were you when I cried when she cut her locks... Where?!... Who di fuck are you anyway? Where did you come from?'* The urgency to wake the heavy rusted iron bar grew *stronger!... stronger!... stronger!...* So strong that it literally guided his right arm towards it. And as he reached under his jacket like a Samurai and pulled it out, more hysteria than ever flooded the room.

"Heeeelp!! Heeeelp!!" Evadney realised just how far she had pushed this man. *Revenge* was *revenge*, but this *ditching-at-the-altar* thing had taken the biscuit. Her screams dragged Baby Face back to the trouble at hand. "Is weh di blood claat yuh gwine duh wid dat t'ing, Pussy Bwoy?!"

Garnet lounged forward.

Power fell upon him.

And when he planted the heavy iron bar in Baby Face's head, the hounds of hell hounded in readiness for their supper.

"Garnet, noooo!!… Call an ambulance, somebody, pleeease!!!" Evadney had lost it. Brain scrambled.

Yvonne covered her mouth. What was she to do?

"Whoooo!! Whoooo!" Pearl had certainly flipped. "Percy! Whoooo! Laad, Percy!"

"Percy was standing. Hovering. He needed help. "Garnet?! Laad have mercy! Yuh waan to en' up inna prison?!" he shouted.

Screams…

Screams from everywhere…

But Garnet was not phased by the screaming. *No sir*. None of it. It was as if a sudden madness had taken hold of mind, telling him that nothing else mattered… *Nothing else.*

Now, he focused his attention again on Evadney.

"Yuh betta not lay a hand on mi daughta!" Percy asserted, standing in front of Evadney.

"Run, Evadney, run!" Pearl shouted.

A few men got closer for the protection of Evadney now, as it was a little doubtful how much Percy could do. The man they feared had a bullet was down.

From behind Percy's back, and trembling, Evadney kept her eyes on Garnet.

Their eyes locked now.

Fixed.

Stared.

A silent language.

In her shocked state, Evadney could feel ten thousand poisoned arrows aiming for her soul. She averted her eyes now and realised that a host of people had gathered around Baby Face Glen's twitching body. The force of the iron bar had claimed a grooved spot across his head.

Weary of Garnet, she refocused her eyes on him, only to find he had never taken his off her. The silence was deadly, proving that unuttered words can jab like the points of a thousand daggers.

"Garnet," Lijah coaxed, "put down di iron bar down now, Bredrin."

But all Garnet did was gibbered. The first sound he uttered since he entered the room. *Whispered. Gibbered. Jabbered. Whined* like a whimpering dog that had stepped on macca bush. He leaned his head from side to side like a simpleton. Where were they? *The words*. Or a word, even. Why didn't they come?

"Garnet?" Gongo Peas was there now. By his side.

But still, Garnet looked at Evadney.

And then... he found it. *The word*. One word... one three-syllabled word.

Found the word and a voice to propel it. A voice that was earlier all cried out.

First, it was an undetectable whisper. No one heard it. All they saw was just the meaningful moving of his trembling lips, his fingers still wrapped around his weapon... '*Delilah.... Delilah... Delilah...*' Until it came like a hurricane, pushing his larynx out the way... *Delilaaaaaaaahhh!!!!...Delilaaaaaaaahhh!!!! Delilaaaaaaaahhh!!!!*

Evadney shuddered. Jerked from her shocked state.

Before that, she hadn't even felt Yvonne's hands around her shoulders.

'*You marry who the hell you want to marry,*' Yvonne had said. '*It's nobody's business. It's your own bed you're spreading. Only you and whoever you marry will lie in it. Nobody else.*'

People covered their faces to hide the shock that had distorted them.

Garnet sunk to his knees. The iron bar fell from his grip, taking what it seemed, was left of his *being* with it. Fits of tears found his tear ducts once again, tracing the old tracks of the earlier shower. *When a man cries, he cries.*

And now, for the first time in his whole life, beastmen laid their hands upon Garnet's shoulders. And he didn't even see the crowd as they led him to their car.

Baby Face Glen twitched for the last time, the floor of the reception hall a temporary casket – his hand still resting on a shooter that lay dormant in his breast pocket... *A fee! A fee! Passport for a fee!*

The angels of hell opened its gates... *and welcomed him.*

... And there it was... the hole that Evadney had dug for Garnet in the name of *revenge,* had opened up even wider and took her in. She had fallen slap bang in the middle of it. *Hoisted*, even. *Hoisted* by her own petard.

Revenge may be sweet... but how nastily bitter it can be, when at times it backfires... Dig not a pit for another's downfall, lest ye fall first into it.

* * *

The Central News team wasted no time in telling of the *'rivalry wedding reception killing'. 'It is revealed that the killing of the groom at a wedding reception held at the Centennial Centre today, was a love-rivalry killing. The groom, a Jamaican and former deportee, who had re-entered the country on an illegal passport, was killed by a single blow to his head with an iron bar. It has also been revealed that he was the same man wanted in connection with the death of Peter Walker and Martin Backer, two men found dead in a London flat some weeks back. The groom's attacker is said to be the former boyfriend of the bride, who had waited earlier in another church for her, but she didn't turn up. As a form of revenge, she had sent him on a wild-goose chase. The plan was that genuine wedding between her and the now deceased man, would coincide with the trickery-church-wedding.'*

* * *

In the meantime, while the world around them turned *upside-down*, Lawrence and Simone lived in their own *downside-up* world. A world most would see as a *fairy-tale* world. *Perfect.*

Every thing was *just fine.* Mellow. Riding on the wings of doves.

A fine house, with a fine couple, with a fine son.

Love had not only lived, but seemingly, it was *born* in their house...

Bred in its walls.

Love was in their sleeping...

In their waking...

Love danced on their lips as they spoke...

Cushioned their steps as they walked....

Love... Precious *love.*

It was midnight. The Saturday night belonged to them... It wasn't unusual for them to do this... *dance... dance... dance* the night away in the cosy dimness of their living-room.

Amari was sleeping, and there were no doubt about how happy his dreams were.

The happy couple knew one thing: that they said it best, when they said nothing at all, so they did. *Said nothing*, that is. Just *danced*...

331

danced... danced.   And listened. Not just to the serenades of Luther Vandross, but to the beating of their own hearts. *It felt good.* So good. As *good* as *good* could ever be. They had found soul-mates in each other. *Companionship.*

From where they were standing, and by the way they both felt, surely that was *true love.* What could possibly upset such a happy home? *Nothing... nothing at all. Nothing...*

It was as if Luther Vandross was there in person...

> *Love has truly been good to me*
> *Not even one sad day*
> *Or minute have I had since you've come my way*
> *I hope you know I'd gladly go*
> *Anywhere you'd take me...*

"Are you happy?" Lawrence whispered.

"Yes. I am... are you?"

"Yes. Very happy."

> *It's so amazing to be loved*
> *I'd follow you to the moon in the sky above*
> *Ooh...ooh...ooh...ooh...ooh...ooh...ooh...ooh...I'd go...*

They danced... and danced... and danced.

> *Got to tell you how you thrill me*
> *I'm happy as I can be*
> *You have come and it's changed my whole world*
> *Bye-bye sadness, hello mellow*
> *What a wonderful day...*

He pulled her closer. Pressed his cheeks against hers. "Simone... I'm so glad I found you."

"Ditto. Too many men let pum-pum turn them fool." She was serious, yet the flippant way she expressed and sealed her statement made Lawrence laugh. And when his laughter had subsided, and the warmth of her body reminded him of how lucky he was, he helped Luther along, singing sweetly in her ear...

It's so amazing to be loved
I'd follow you to the moon in the sky above
Ooh...ooh...ooh...ooh...ooh...ooh...ooh...ooh...

"Ok, *Luther*," she whispered jokingly.

And it's so amazing, amazing
I could stay forever, forever
Here in love and no, leave you never
'Cause we've got amazing love...

"Damn right," she bantered.

Truly it's so amazing, amazing
Love brought us together, together
I will leave you never and never
I guess we've got amazing love...

"So..." He kissed her. "Mrs Hendricks..."

Ooh, so amazing and I've been wondering
For a love like you

"Yes, Mr Hendricks?"

"Could I please have the pleasure of your company in our marital bed?

"Er... let me see..." she bantered. "I do believe I can."

And now, like a feather, he lifted her. And kissed her. And as he ascended the stairs he thanked God for sending her to him. But not before he thanked Conteh. The goddamn greedy mouse that lost his mouthful of cheese, just for the sake of trying to taste one too many bit.

But most of all, he thanked God for sending him that *special woman.*

The only woman that he could love *above all others*...

The only woman who could keep him *away... away... away* from his hidden *'self'.*

Amari snored gently.

Lawrence laid his wife gently upon their marital bed.

Luther's voice followed them, sweeping his romantic voice into every kiss...

Every touch…
Every taste…
Every thrust…
GentleHardGentleHard….

I'd follow you to the moon in the sky above…

And as the rain pitter-pattered against their window, adding to the romantic backdrop of Luther's voice, perfection had found a brand new meaning…

I'd follow you to the moon in the sky above…

Chapter 19

"Glenda!' oh, Bejesus, Glenda!" The neighbour panicked and tried to pick the legless woman up off the floor. It was the desperate crying of the older child that alerted her. Once again, Glenda had tried to drink her troubles away. She had left Peter, but hearing of his death had brought out some sort of *hidden emotions*.

* * *

Now, a man that buys his woman sexy underwear is the man of every woman's dream… And when he buys the best? Well… judge for yourself.

Yes… Simone was convinced she *was* in heaven.

In the five years she'd been with Lawrence, his loving tender care was steady, but his generosity moved steadily up each gear, not *too-much-too-often*, lest it looses its real meaning. But just enough to keep her sweet.

Her appreciation for this unique man seemed unwaveringly strong.

For like she said, *'Heaven must have really sent him from above.'*

* * *

Earlier, Lawrence had kissed his wife and son at the door and watched them walk to the car. He was on one of his weekends off, and planned on doing some manly chores around the house.

"Don't spend too much," he had said to Simone jokingly.

"You know I will," she had said as she opened the back door for Amari.

"Bye, Daddy!" Amari had shouted as he climbed in.

"See you later, son!" he had shouted back. And when Simone had started the engine, she had turned and looked at him. They both returned blown kisses.

And it was not long after that, and for the first time since he went to jail for a crime he didn't commit, Simone was confronted with her ex-husband. It might be hard to believe, but their cars were positioned around the same vicinity of the spot in the NCP car park where Conteh had filled the need in her best friend, Pam. He knew it, but Simone didn't. All she knew, was the fact that he looked very uncomfortable. It was only when she had pulled into a vacant space next to him and looked to her left that she had seen him. Seconds later, he looked to his right and their eyes met, but Conteh looked away quickly. Shock maybe? Simone took it as a sign that he didn't want to talk to her. *Fair enough.*

Conteh didn't know what to do, though he felt it was rude to just pull out and drive away, so he hesitated in his car and hoped she would just get out, lock up and go. He was already a wrecked man. Menna and her gang had picked at what was left of his ass like vultures at dead carcass. He had tried his best at fixing himself up to meet Joe Public. Felt there were only so long his sister Janet could rally 'round him, doing all his shopping and that. He didn't look anywhere near his best, and from what he could see, Simone looked more *beautiful* than ever.

Simone climbed out of her car. She had nothing to be bashful about; her head could be held up high. After all, *he* was the perpetrator. She bent down, tapped on his window and waved.

Conteh waved back and felt obliged to leave the comforts of his car.

"Hi," Simone said, at the same time opening the back door of her car to let Amari out. "How *are* you, Conteh?"

"I'm ok... *you*?" He was shaking.

"I'm fine."

"I can see that." He found it hard to look into her eyes now they were standing so close. "How are you, Girl," he asked, doubling up on his concern. *Nerves.*

She smiled and said again, "Fine." She could detect his nervousness.

"Is this your son?" He was looking at Amari who was looking curiously back at him.

"Yes. Say hello, Amari."

"Hello."

"Hello, little man," Conteh, said, when in fact, what he wanted to say was '*You should have been my son... I had your mother first.*' But he knew that all the *horse-dead-an'-cow-fat* in the world was never gonna make it right. Like his mother Gladys used to say, '*Wha' gone bad a morning, cyaan come good a evening.*' No way.

He looked at Simone who knew what he was thinking. When they were together, he had desperately wanted them to have a love child. And when news of her pregnancy for Lawrence had reached him, he almost had a heart attack. "It's been a long time," he told her.

"Just a bit," she replied. "You look a little tired."

"I feel it," he replied. Telling her of his recent *tortured-then-tied-up-nude-for-three-days* ordeal wouldn't do.

I heard you are at your mum's house now."

"Yes. I suppose you hear a lot about me. Good to know you and my sisters stayed friends, still."

"Why shouldn't we? They did me no harm."

"True."

"I miss your Mum, Conteh. I loved her so much."

"She loved you too. Everybody knew that."

"But not even her love for me could have kept you from..."

"Ok." He stopped her. "*Please...* Let's just pass these few minutes amicably, yeah? Life's short... too short."

And there were more she could have asked him. Talked about. Queried. But she was bigger than that. New pages have been turned for a long time. And besides, she felt he paid his price. So rather than *ask*, she *told* him, though not in a vindictive way. Only because it popped into her head: "I saw a friend of yours the other day... Menna."

"Really? You... met *Menna*?"

"Yes."

He was shocked about that, but now, a new worry... 'when had Simone seen her?... *Before* or *after* she and her entourage had tortured him. And if it was *after*, did she tell Simone?' "You spoke?" he asked her.

"Yes... we spoke."

"I saw her too," he covered himself. *Just in case*. "And I wish I never set eyes on her again."

"Oh. Right. I see." Simone had no idea of Conteh's present worry. Knew nothing about his little encounter with the avenging queens.

"No more old stuff, Simone, please."

"It wasn't my intention to bring up old stuff... what made you think I was going to?"

"I know. I know you weren't... Simone, *I'm sorry*. I'm just tired. Mentally... Physically... Every which way."

She looked into his eyes and her look spoke volumes. "Look after yourself, Conteh... I mean that." She turned to leave him, not knowing how much he craved her tactility.

He wanted to hug her.

To be hugged by her.

To be comforted by her.

For her to tell him that she had forgiven him, although his sisters had already told him.

He wanted her to kiss away his pain.

Erase the tracks of his tears... for only Simone *could*. Only her.

He was just a man.

An ordinary man.

And back then, he was just a *boy in a man's body*. A boy who did not know which way to go.

"I'm trying," he said, engaging her attention again. "But I think right now, it will take greater powers than my own to make me right again."

She looked at him and *knew* he meant it.

He saw it. The question in her eyes.

"And yes, Simone... I know what you're thinking, but no symptoms as yet, *thank God.*"

"You know you don't have to develop AIDS, don't you?"

"I know. It's been a while, and nothing's happened. I just hope it stays that way. Apparently, I'm a non-progressor."

"A *what*?"

"Well, some people develop AIDS from HIV very quickly within the first five years. They are called progressors..."

"Right. I see."

"... Before I started to take the HIV drug that prolongs the symptoms, my virus load was undetectable anyway. There were no AIDS-related symptoms showing. My immune system is obviously keeping the virus under control. I can't complain."

Simone stared at Conteh. It was as if it was someone else that was standing there talking to her. "Conteh, you sound like a professional. You seem to be an expert on the subject of HIV and AIDS."

"I need to be. I'm just glad that with the help of a drug, my body is resisting the thing. Like I said, it's been a while, and no great crisis. I think it's God, Simone. I prayed a lot when I was inside. I think he has answered my prayers. All I can say is, I'm glad you protected yourself. You might be a progressor... and I couldn't live with myself if..."

"D'you still see Nico, Conteh?" She ignored his direct statement, but leaned into a sub one.

"No. But *Nico* is *Nico*."

"Is he *really* deliberately infecting women still?"

"So I heard. Fortunately for him, he is a non-progressor too. Which might be more than can be said for his victims. The women Nico is infecting might develop the damn thing and die, while Nico live forever."

"You know what I find amazing?" Simone asked.

"What?"

"If Nico was going around, secretly clubbing people over their heads and leaving them to die, he'd be reported by now. Yet a lot of people know that he's a serial HIV infector, yet he's left to roam free."

"Yes," Conteh said, but even if he's reported, you're gonna have to prove that he's actually slept with people... and only the people could prove that."

Simone thought about Morag, but felt no urge to tell Conteh of Nico's latest victim. Well, the latest *she* knew of. What difference would it make? "You had one weakness, Conteh. *Women*. You couldn't help it. Apart from that, you are quite considerate. Unfortunately, womanising is one of the things women loathe the most... including me."

"I'm a changed man now, Simone. Perhaps I needed to go through all I've been through before I could come to my senses. But it's too late. I've lost you... for good."

"I hear what you're saying, Conteh, but I still think that only God can change you. Too many times when we were married you told me you had changed... until you brought another woman through my door."

Conteh held his head down. He knew no words could even begin to compensate.

Amari tugged his mother's arm slightly. He was getting a little impatient.

"I'm coming, Darling," she assured him.

"I just wish…" Conteh attempted to express something.

"I have to go now, Conteh." She cut him off deliberately, knowing what was coming. "You take care now."

"And you, Babes."

She looked at him thinking *Babes* was a little too cosy.

"Until the day I die, you will always be my *Babes*," was his answer to her look.

"We are all entitled to our opinions, Conteh, but I doubt if my husband would agree with that."

"He's a lucky man, your husband."

"He knows… And I'm a lucky woman. We both know. We appreciate each other."

"Point taken." That cut him like a knife. "I'm pleased about one thing though…"

She looked questioningly at him.

"… I'm pleased I didn't shatter your trust in men completely."

"So am I."

"Is he as perfect as my sisters said he is?"

"No one's perfect, Conteh. But if I have to compare what you did to me in the past, to how Lawrence treats me now, it would probably look much nearer to *perfect* than you had ever been."

"So… he doesn't lust after other women?"

"Maybe he does. He's a man. But lusting after something, and going after it, are two different things, wouldn't you say?"

Silence.

"And if he ever lust after anyone, bring her back to my house, then I'd leave him just the same as I left you."

"I said I was sorry, Simone. *Really* sorry."

"I do believe you are sorry, Conteh. Only, *sorry* got here just a little too late, don't you think?"

He wanted so much to say the words to her, but there was another pair of ears, so he mimed, *'I still love you.'*

She read his lips perfectly, but when he asked, "What about you?" she said, "Take care, Conteh." She waved at him as she walked towards the lift that would take her and her son into the shopping centre.

"Take care, Simone," he said, climbing back into his car and feeling like the crater in his heart had just suddenly widened.

He watched her.

Watched as she disappeared.

Watched as if he was sure that was the last time he would see her. Watched as she walked away from the car park where he had sat for another ten minutes before he could turn the key in his ignition. Without knowing it, she had taken another bit of his heart. A Junior Delgado track came to him:

> *Don't break my heart*
> *Don't break my heart*
> *You really don't love me*
> *You really don't care for me*
> *You really don't love me*
> *You really don't care for me...*

An hour later back at his house, Conteh was experiencing heartache with a difference, and if Simone had seen him, she would have crumbled. The tears he cried would have torn at her heartstrings. Whoever said that time heals? He had always known that seeing her again would rip him, but he had underestimated *how much*. The face he had put on in front of her was brave. *Very brave.*

'*Dear God*,' he had said, '*I know you are a merciful God. Is it too much to ask? Will it ever be possible? Just to hold her once more... Please... I know I have done her wrong. And I know she has a new husband now. I would never try to break up her happy home. Besides, I am HIV positive, she would never want me again. But all I ask, Dear Lord, is for the chance to hold her... just once. I beseech Thee.*'

She was his first *real* love.

And she would be his last.

She was his present... his future... his past.

* * *

When his mobile rang, Lawrence assumed it was Simone. It was about two hours since she had been gone, and he assumed she was ringing to say she was on her way back. But when he checked, no number came up on his screen. "Hi," he said apprehensively.

"Hi… Don't hang up," the person had said. And when he had recognised the voice, it reinforced the notion that it would probably be a good idea for him to acquire a new number.

"Sheree, what is it this time?"

"I need to see you… It's urgent."

"C'mon, Sheree, we've been there before. This is harassment. It's got to stop. I told you I'm happily married."

"*Are you*?"

"What *is* this?"

"*Well*? Are you *happily* married?"

"Sheree, what's gotten into you?"

"Don't know. Just as long as it wasn't your *dick*. I *know* where it's been."

"*What*?"

"Does *she* know?"

"Does *who* know *what*?"

"Does your beautiful wife know that you're bisexual?"

"What?!" Lawrence was suddenly spun into a fit of uncontrollable laughter. "Well, I credit you for being the most persistent person of all times, Sheree, but this tactic stinks."

"Lawrence I *saw* you… you and Lance. I have the evidence to prove it."

Lawrence paused for thought. "*Evidence*?"

"A few days ago I came round to drop Morag's card…"

"Wait a minute… you say you have *evidence* to prove that I'm bisexual?… you saw me and Lance?…"

"Do I detect some kind of *interest*, Lawrence?"

"What evidence?"

"Pictures… pictures of you and Lance doing the *nasty*."

Lawrence paused again. A jigsaw puzzle was fitting. Maybe not nicely, but it was fitting nonetheless. "Where are you now, Sheree?"

"I'm at home."

"D'you live at the same place?"

"Yes. I'm still in the same house. Like *you* haven't left my head, I haven't left my house. Perhaps I should. Perhaps it would help. Get you out my fucking head."

"You know it's not ladylike to swear… Can I come over now?"

"D'you know how long I waited to hear you say those words? And look *when* you're saying them? Just when I happen to stumble upon your deepest, darkest secret."

"Sheree, I'll see you in a bit."

* * *

Lawrence knew why he had to battle the Saturday traffic to the other side of town to see Sheree, but although it was innocent, he couldn't help feeling that he was betraying his wife. Perhaps he should tell her. What if Sheree documented his visit somehow for her own use? Like she had with the so-called *evidence* she was about to show him? Simone was due home in about an hour and a half. He figured it was time enough to execute this task.

"Hi," Sheree said when she had opened the door to the man she had no way of getting her heart back from. "Come in."

To Lawrence, it felt like dejavu.

"Would you like a drink?"

"No thanks. I'm not stopping."

She smiled a cynical smile.

"Where are these… *pictures*?"

"And don't think I'm bothered about you taking them. I have the negatives."

Lawrence stood and spoke with his body. To Sheree, there were no bisexual traits blaring out at her, but she put it down to the fact that black men who found themselves in that position, are best at disguising what they *know* they would be most *persecuted* for. "The pictures please, Sheree?"

She walked over to a drawer in the kitchen and retrieved a small brown envelope. "Do you *love* Simone like you keep professing?" she asked as she smugly handed him the envelope. "To my heart and soul," he said with conviction, as he opened the envelope with urgency.

As he shuffled, looked, shuffled, looked, so Sheree shuffled the memories of their past relationship in her head as she looked at him, imagining all sorts.

Lawrence felt a little peculiar as he took in the images. "When did you say you took these?"

"Why d'you need to ask? D'you do this often… in the same position… in your flight uniform?"

He ignored her. "On the phone you said it was a few days ago when you went 'round to drop Morag's card… was it the night before Morag's birthday?"

"Yes. It was."

"It wasn't me that Lance was buggering that night."

"*That night*? Why? Did he do you *another* night?"

"Very funny… It wasn't me." He was still looking at the pictures.

"Yeah, right. *I saw your car,* Lawrence. Pull the other one." She leant against her worktop as if she had got the thrown.

"It *wasn't* me." He remembered the conversation with Morag in her distressed state when she thought it was he that was at the house that night.

"Don't take me for a fool, Lawrence. Even when you're holding the evidence in your hand, you're telling me it *wasn't* you."

"The picture isn't very good," Lawrence went on, "but if you had looked close enough at the shoulder of the recipient's jacket, you would have seen that the number of stripes made him a *First Officer*. I am a Captain. I have more stripes."

Sheree lifted a brow questioningly. That made sense. She drew closer now and looked at the pictures with more intrigue.

"When you told me you had pictures, I had to see. Of course I knew it *wasn't* me. *Couldn't* be. But I had to see the pictures myself. Just to see if Lance was *really* gay." He turns to leave.

She followed him. "So *who* is the other guy in the picture? He looks like you."

"Not my business to say."

"I'll ask Morag," Sheree said. "She must know which First Officer comes to her house."

"Have you said anything to Morag as yet?"

"No. But I will."

"Sheree, you're a grown woman. You do what you like. But think carefully."

"So *you* tell me who it is then."

"You already know that one of them is Lance. Ask Lance who the other guy is. He might tell you. I have to go. My wife and son are either home, or are on their way home."

Sheree saw Lawrence in a way she had never seen him before now. More intriguing. Noble too. *Noble* with a capital *N*. She wanted him more now. This guy was *rare*. Could even be *one-of-a-kind*, who knows. Every woman would love a man like that. "Lawrence?" she said in a low voice.

"Yes?" Holding onto the door handle, he turned to look at her.

"Can't we just be… *friends*?"

"Sheree, being *just friends* won't be enough for you. And if you're true to yourself, you'll know that it's not really what you want, and what you want I *can't* give."

"Why couldn't you love me the way you love *her*?... see in me what you saw in her?"

"Because I couldn't. I don't control that. And what I see in her just wasn't in you. They say beauty is in the eyes of the beholder, and I guess, not just the physical, everything about her is beautiful."

She felt a little hurt. The truth sometimes does that. She reached for his free hand and met with stiff fingers. Clutching at straws, she clasped her fingers in his and drew herself close to his back, feeling the warmth of his manly body, though, emotionally, she knew he was cold towards her. Not that he had forgotten where they'd been, but she had allowed him to become resentful of the way she tried to put a *spanner* in his *marriage works*.

"Sheree," he eased away firmly but gently, but still she pulled herself closer to him.

He turned round to face her fully, as if to give her a lecture, but she pulled up to him and rested her body close to his, pressing her groin against his, rubbing his ass and forcing a kiss. *She wanted him real bad.*

He turned away from her kiss and eased her body away from his, fixing her at arms length. "Sheree," I don't want to hurt your feelings, but I don't know how to get through to you... this *can't* happen."

She moved closer still and threw both arms around his neck. He felt her moist lips on his neck and it was then he knew that *firmer* actions had to be taken if he *really* wanted to stop Sheree from harassing him sexually.

"Sheree..." he said, prizing her off him with the intention to open the door and finally go, but Sheree closed her eyes and inhaled his warm, invisible, fresh, untainted breath. The musky manly scent that oozed from his body. She remembered his *good loving*.

Lawrence looked at her and realised that this woman had it *real bad.*

Would he give ar wha' shi want mek si gwaan? A firm hard seeing-to that would last?

"I know I have no chance of getting you back, Lawrence, but I just want to make love to you. *Just once*."

Suddenly, Lawrence dropped his keys right where he stood.

The pictures too.

344

He snatched Sheree up in his arms and walked sternly, but quietly up her stairs, the muscles in his strong, sexily-bowed calves protruding.

Sheree stared hopefully at him, her arms around his neck. She anticipated *heaven*. *'Oh, happy day'*, she thought, wondering what swayed him.

When he got to her bedroom, he laid her firmly on her bed. "Just once?" he asked her, as if to make sure she wouldn't harass him again.

"*Just once*," she whispered. "I *ache* for you, Lawrence. I'm trapped. Sometimes I wish I could be *her*. Just for a second."

As she spoke, Lawrence undressed her.

"Oh, Lawrence," she said as his firm hands pulled her skimpy underwear away from her. "You won't regret this... I promise. This will be our secret."

But Lawrence said nothing. And when he was done undressing her, he just stood there and stared at her as she stretched her hands towards him, inviting him to come. He saw not a nude, sexy woman, but someone *possessed*. Someone who was willing to use blackmail to get him into her bed. *Perhaps she knew Bernadette on the other side of town. A fly in Lijah's soup.* Or perhaps there are more women like that, than one could ever imagine.

"Lawrence?... What is it?... Why are you staring at me like that? Aren't you gonna get undressed?"

"Yes... I am... Just a minute, Sheree... I won't be a minute. I'm just popping to the bathroom," he told her.

"Hurry up, Babes. I can't wait. I'm burning up."

But it was the deadly silence and the length of time Lawrence seemed to be taking that made Sheree call out his name. "Lawrence?! Where are you?"

No answer.

"Lawrence?" She got up now to investigate. He wasn't in the bathroom. By now, Sheree had known deep down, but still she rushed downstairs and checked the kitchen...

The living-room...

The study...

Nope. Gone. The gorgeous man had left the building. *Period.*

Sheree rushed nude to her front window and stared out into the open road. There Lawrence's car was. He was simply sitting in it looking at her.

She grabbed her mobile and dialled his number.

He was expecting it. "Yes, Sheree."

"Why?!… Why, you bastard, why?!"

"Tell me, Sheree," Lawrence replied in a calm voice, "If the guy in these pictures was me, *what then*? Would you still want a bisexual guy?"

Silence.

"Well? Would you?"

Silence.

"You *would*, wouldn't you? You'd still want me. And so you'd use the pictures to blackmail me… that's it, right?"

"Lawrence, I *love* you."

"No, you're *mental*, that's what you are. What you felt for me has turned into something else. You need help. What you're doing is stalking me, and if it keeps up, I'll have to get the police involved."

"Why the humiliation? Why did you just?…"

"Because I *love* my wife… and if *telling* you isn't working, I thought *showing* you would. Not every man makes pussy turn him fool, Sheree. I will *never* betray her. *Never*. We had an understanding before I met Simone. We both agreed that when we found that special someone, we would call it a day. Move on, Sheree. *Get a life*. Get over me."

"You bastard!!!… Bastard!! Bastaaaaaaard!!!"…

Lawrence clicked off and hoped that would be the end of it. He drove home to Simone and his son.

An hour later, Sheree was still curled up in a ball on her bed: the very spot where Lawrence had left her waiting in vain. And as tears fell uncontrollably onto her pillow, the voice of Brandy seeped mercilessly into her head:

> *Have you ever loved somebody so much*
> *It makes you cry*
> *Have you ever needed something so bad*
> *You can't sleep at night*
> *Have you ever tried to find the words*
> *But they don't come out right*
> *Have you ever, have you ever…*

* * *

Simone prepared dinner and Lawrence hovered by her side. "Guess who I saw in town today?" she asked him.

"Who?"

"Conteh."

"Really?"

"First I've seen him since he went down."

"And what did he have to say for himself?"

"Daddy!" Amari came running in. "We saw a man in the Car Park today."

"Did you?"

"Yes. And he called mummy, *Babes*."

"*Really?*" Lawrence asked, looking at Simone playfully, but waiting for a reply from his son.

"Yes. He said until he dies, Mummy would *always* be his *babes*."

"*Really?*"

"Amari!" Simone scolded him playfully.

"And what did *Mummy* say?"

"She said, '*I don't think my husband would agree with that*'."

Simone smiled as she looked sideways at her son, not believing how much he had logged her conversation with Conteh.

"And what did the man say?"

"He said, '*He's a lucky man*'."

"And what did *Mummy* say?"

"She said, '*We're both lucky*'… and some other stuff… '*preciate*' or something."

"And what the man say?"

"He said goodbye. Then he sat in his car. And he was looking all sad."

"Was he now?"

"Yes… Can we play football, Dad?"

"We will tomorrow, son. Tomorrow."

"Ok."

Go watch TV. I'll be there in a bit."

"Ok."

Lawrence walked over and hugged his wife. You can always trust children to tell it like it is. No words were needed. Just a word-filled kiss.

* * *

"You seem a little quiet," Simone told Lawrence that same evening as they relaxed after dinner. "What's on your mind? Are you thinking about Morag and Lance's situation?"

347

"In more ways than one, Darling. I need to talk to Lance. I'm gonna take a trip over to his house." He glanced at his watch.

"You haven't spoken to him since, have you?"

"No. I thought he would have called. But we don't know if Morag told him she came here that night."

"True… Are you gonna ask him about what happened?"

"Well, it's really none of my business, but Morag *did* come over in a state, and I suppose, although he hasn't said anything, if he eventually found out that she came, he'll be wondering why I hadn't said anything… but there's something else." His mind rested on the pictures Sheree had given him earlier.

"Really?"

"Yes, but I'll tell you about it after I've spoken to Lance."

"Like that is it?"

"It's a little awkward. Need to get the facts. But trust me, after I've spoken to him, I'll tell you all about it. It's not something I want to discuss over the phone, so I definitely need to go over."

"Ok," Simone said. Her curiosity showed. "What time are you going?"

He got up. "I think I'll go now… I'll just give him a quick ring to let him know I'm passing by."

Seconds later, Simone sat listening to her husband's side of the conversation with Lance, which confirmed to her that Lance was ok with him passing by.

"How long will you be?" she asked when he clicked off.

"Not long." He pulled on his jacket. "I'll call you when I'm leaving."

"Ok," Simone said, putting her lips forward to receive his kiss.

"See you later, son," Lawrence said to Amari who was drawing in his picture book.

"See you later, Dad."

"Mummy?" Amari had said when he heard the door pulled shut.

"Yes, Darling."

"Do you like that man?" he said without looking up from his drawing.

"*What* man?"

"The man in the car park. The one that said… '*Until the day I die, you will always be my Babes*'."

Simone became curious. "*Why*, Darling? Why d'you want to know that?"

"Because I like him."

She looked closely at her son. "What d'you like about him?"

"I don't know. I just do."

"Oh… ok… I see."

"Do *you* like him, Mum?"

"Er… he's ok…" She was puzzled.

"Would you marry him if you didn't marry Daddy?"

Simone sometimes forgets how mature for his age Amari could be. "Why all these questions, Darling?"

"I don't know."

Simone sat forward on the settee. "Come over here Darling. Come and sit by me."

Amari lay his felt-tip down and walked anxiously over to his mum. He sat down and Simone cuddled him. "Son?"

"Yeah?"

"That man in the car park… *Conteh*. His name's Conteh."

"*Conteh*?"

"Yes. Mummy used to be married to him before she met Daddy."

"Did you?!"

"Yes. But sometimes things don't stay nice. Grownups sometimes mess things up. They make mistakes… some make little ones, and some make big ones. Then they have to go apart."

"Did Conteh make big mistakes?"

Simone smiled. "Bigish ones, yes."

"Oh… but Daddy don't make mistakes, does he? So you won't have to go apart."

"No, Daddy's not made any mistakes… well, not yet anyway."

"Is that why Conteh is sad? Because you go apart?"

"That might be a part of it, but I'm sure there are other things."

"I think that's *really* why he's sad. That's why he said, '*Until the day I die, you will always be my Babes*'."

"Do you now?"

"Yes. But you're Daddy's Darling, aren't you?"

"Yes. I am. And so are *you*." Simone smiled and hugged her son.

"So Conteh could have been my dad, then?" the forward five-year-old asked.

"Er, well, if he *was* your dad, *you* wouldn't be *you*?"

"*How* wouldn't I?"

"Er… I think we'll have to talk about that another day… ok'"

"Ok."

"Another ten minutes more drawing, then you'll have your bath, ok?"

"Ok." Amari trotted over to his drawing. "I'm going to make a nice picture for Grandma tomorrow, Mum."

"Great! She'll love that. Two more weeks an she'll be here."

"Is she gonna go back to Jamaica? Or is she gonna stay with us forever?"

"No, she can't stay forever, Darling. Grandma's got her own life in Jamaica. She'll be going back. But you will remember not to tell Daddy that she's coming, won't you?"

"I won't forget."

"You remember that it's a nice surprise for Daddy, and if you tell him, the surprise will be spoilt."

"I won't forget, Mum. I don't want to spoil Daddy's surprise."

"Good boy."

* * *

Simone didn't know where the time went, but time had certainly flown by. She woke from her nap an hour after she had tucked Amari up in bed, to find that Lawrence was not yet home. She lay there. *Still.* Recalling the questions from her little boy. *What was all that about?* And then the conversation she felt she wanted to have with him about Conteh. But that wasn't all: *Conteh* had filled the dream she had while she slept. But as she lay there, her mind cleared of everything else, she realised something, and wondered if that was being disloyal to her husband. Her *realisation* that is. Perhaps it was the fact that she had seen him physically for the first time in ages. Or perhaps that he had said words that her son had repeated. Or the fact that she knew he meant them. But whatever it was, the *realisation* was real… '*she loved him… still*'.

She turned, took a deep breath, squeezed her pillow tight beneath her head and relaxed as she recalled a conversation with his sister: *'And I loved him too, Sandra. Really loved him. But he hurt me real bad. He would have taken my life if I didn't wise-up.'*

She could hear her son's breathing. It relaxed her even more. She hadn't realised how tired she was. The shower she had should have woken her up, but it didn't. Lazily, her eyelids drooped again, and as sleep took her slowly, thoughts filled her subconscious… '*I'm pleased I didn't shatter your trust in men completely'*… '*So am I. Take care, Conteh.'*

* * *

When Lawrence got to Lance, he found him with a face like a wet weekend. Or more like a Bull Dog that had been slapped ten times across his face with a wet mackerel. But Lawrence knew it couldn't have been anything to do with what he had come to talk about.

"What's up? Someone died?" Lawrence asked when Lance opened the door.

"Might have been better if someone had."

"Like that is it?"

"Life sucks right now, I know that much."

"Is Morag's here?" he asked as soon as he reached the lounge.

"No. In London, somewhere. I don't give a shit."

"Point taken… How long is she gone for?"

"Until we've sorted this shit out," Lance said. He reduced the sound on some reality shit on the TV and discarded the remote as if it had done him some wrong. "Drink?"

"Just a coffee will do, I'm driving." Lawrence kept his eyes on him, the image from the pictures he brought frolicking strangely around his head.

"Gimme a minute," Lance said as he walked from the lounge to the kitchen, barely looking at Lawrence. "How did you find Clive's car the other night?"

"Life could have been better if someone *died* and you want my opinion on a *fast car*?"

"Well, I won't be talking about my problems just yet, so why not talk about a fast car? *And* whatever you've come to talk about, of course."

Lawrence responded to the question, knowing full well it was useless chit-chat just then. "The car's nice. It moves well."

"Excellent motor isn't it!" Lance shouted now, as the distance stretched between them. There was a lump in his throat.

"Well!" Lawrence shouted back, "*5.4 engine, 8 cylinders, 636 horse break power, 334 max speed and accelerates at 0–100 in 3.8seconds*?! What do you expect?!"

The clinking of cups filled the space of a response and Lawrence glanced at a medium-sized wedding photo of Lance and Morag. Of all that's been going on, he was surprised to see it so prominently *up*. But like everything else, it could have been an old habit. Like just another bit of ornament.

"*Well*?" Lance said expectantly. He was back in the room now, holding out a cup of coffee for Lawrence. "What's this little thing you wanna talk about?"

"Thank you," He took the cup. "*Little*? Did I say *little*?"

"Not directly. I'm just assuming."

"Well, it might be a little bigger than you've assumed, Lance." He wasted no time in handing Lance the snaps then stood up and placed his coffee on the coffee table. He then walked over to a far corner of the room, not feeling sure why he did. Then he watched as Lance flicked the photos over-under-over-under, real fast, raising his eyebrows at the same time.

Lance paused now and looked over at Lawrence, quickly emitting, "Who the fuck took these?"

"Who's the other guy in the photo?"

"I asked you *who* took these, man?"

"The person who took them thought the other guy was me. That's why I'm here. She took them to use against me."

"*She*?"

"Yes… Sheree. She took them on the same night you caught Morag with that guy."

"So you know about that too, huh?" He felt exposed.

"Bad news, Lance. It travels fast."

Lance dropped his shoulders and walked over to the settee. He sat down and placed the photos to his left. "Who told you?"

"I'm glad you recognised that beating up your wife is more important than *buggery-with-consent*."

"*Who* told you, Lawrence?"

"Look, it's none of my business. I only mentioned it because Morag was pretty distressed when she came over the same night."

"I wondered where she went, the Bitch! Did she tell you the guy was in my bed?"

"Yes. She did. And talking of bitches, you asked me how I found Clive's car… how did *you* find *Clive*?"

Lance stood up, stepped to his drinks globe and retrieved a bottle of whisky. "So that's why you've come? To play righteous? Scrutinise and judge me?" His back was up. His voice stern. He felt cornered.

"When have I ever tried to play righteous with you, Lance?" Lawrence's voice didn't lift an octave. He was calm.

"So you've come to give me the *why-didn't-you-tell-me-you-were-bisexual* shit, right?"

352

"No. I've come to let you know that Sheree's got the negatives. If you don't mind Morag knowing, fair enough. If you do, then it's a different matter. I can't see Morag holding that down if she gets hold of it. Not now you two are separating anyway."

"What the fuck was Sheree doing in my backyard anyway?! Fucking snooping?!"

"She came to drop Morag's birthday card off. She saw my car. Must have heard you two."

"She came with a fucking camera?!"

"So why didn't you tell anyone you were bisexual?"

"Anyone?! Tell anyone?!"

"Well, like your wife, for instance?"

"Fuck her! And fuck you, Lawrence! I don't need this."

"I know something bigger is bothering you. Yuh sure yuh don't wanna talk about it?" Lawrence offered.

"What are you now? My fucking counsellor?"

"Why are you attacking me, Lance? Am I the root of your problem?"

"Because I'm *fucking* sick of walking in your *fucking* shadow all the *fucking* time!"

"*What*?… What's that supposed to mean, Lance?"

"You know you're the airline's brown-eyed-boy."

"No. I don't know that. And if I *was*, shouldn't you be pleased that the company has a *brown-eyed-boy*, as opposed to the expected *blue-eyed-boy*?"

"Fuck you, Lawrence! Just leave, will you?!"

"Lance, what's the problem? Because you have one… A big one."

"Lawrence, I've asked you to leave."

"It isn't about my *brown eyes* at all, is it? You just hate anyone progressing a little further than you. Captain Frank Philips for example. It was jealousy wasn't it? That's why you started messing with Morag. Ok, you married her in the end, but I'm still not sure what you're all about."

"And what the fuck are *you* about, Mr *Fucking Perfect*?! What?! You and your perfect life! With yuh perfect wife! And yuh perfect…"

Lawrence folded one arm across his waist and pinched his chin with the other. His brow slightly knitted, he stared at Lance, but was seeing a stranger.

"… And yuh perfect *fucking* everything! No wonder we couldn't tell you about the fucking cocaine run!!!"

"*Excuse* me?… No wonder you couldn't tell me about the *what*?!"

Lance went silent. Like a tyre that had suddenly had a blowout at 90mph. Still… inside he smouldered.

"Did you say something about a *cocaine* run?"

"It was all in fucking vain anyway." He downed half a glass of whisky and was pouring another.

"You're talking in parables, Lance. C'mon. Educate me some more." Lawrence's curiosity heightened.

Lance poured another measure of whisky down his throat. "What the hell… the flight we took from Jamaica…"

"Yes? What about the flight we took from Jamaica?"

"It had around 100kilos of class A drugs, the street value of ten fucking million pounds hidden in the roof lining of the luggage container."

"*What*?! What the fuck are you telling me, Lance?! On the aircraft you, Clive and I took back from Jamaica?… it trafficked drugs?"

Lance nodded a yes. What else could he do? He had started so he had to finish.

Lawrence paused and traced the whole flight back in his mind, all the way to Heathrow Airport… So *how the hell* did this shit pass undetected under the noses of Customs Officers at Heathrow airport, with all the cocaine-detecting equipment and tight anti-drug-smuggling shit they are meant to have in place?" He asked in a stiff, stern whisper.

"Beats me. Peter should know."

"*Peter*?"

"The guy who headed the operation."

"So where's this *Peter* now."

"Dead. Headline news. Remember those two guys on the news the other day? The ones they found dead in a London flat? Peter John Walker, drug-trafficker, linked with cocaine trail from Jamaica…?"

Lawrence looked lost. Of course he had heard the news, but that wasn't his concern just then. "So how and where the hell did you meet this *Peter*? How the hell did you get pulled into something like this? Lance... are you *that* desperate to become rich overnight? Fuck, man, we're airline pilots not drug-traffickers!"

"Don't patronise me, Lawrence, I know what the fuck I am!"

"And you didn't patronise me when you put my career and reputation in danger?! I thought we were friends! I trusted you! If that shit had gone wrong, who would have believed I wasn't involved?!

Would you have told them?! You and Clive watched me take an aircraft from Jamaica to Heathrow, laced with 100kilos of cocaine, came home, fucked and hope all would be fucking well?!"

Lance said nothing. What could he say?

"Jesus Christ… And how d'you know it's the end of it because this Peter guy is dead, anyway? What if someone talks and the trail is traced?"

"How?"

"I don't know fucking *how*, Lance? I just know you nearly got my ass into some shit I knew fuck-all about! And the only way I'm hearing about it is because it simply slipped out because you're upset because you didn't get yuh fucking cut!… Jesus, Lance… What on earth were you thinking of?"

"I'm sorry, man."

"You're *sorry*?… You put my whole career in jeopardy and you are simply *sorry*?"

"There's nothing else I can say."

"Listen," Lawrence said, "I'm leaving. I have to think about this thing in more depth."

"The pictures," Lance said as Lawrence walked away.

"What about them?"

"Has Simone seen them?"

"No. But shouldn't you be more worried about *Morag* seeing them?"

"Fuck Morag… and what do *you* think of me now?"

"On what front? Drug-trafficking? Or your sexuality?"

"The latter."

"Well, let's put it this way: in years to come this is going to be so *in-your-face,* staying in the closet will be a thing of the past. MPs are coming out daily. TV dramas are nothing without it in their storylines. Soon, the only *lity* MPs will be judged by is the Qua*lity* of their Abi*lity* to lead their parties, and not by their Sexua*lity*."

"You and I know that the judging takes a different road when it comes to being black and gay or bisexual. Our people don't accept that kinda a thing so easily," Lance said.

"Our people were brought up on the scriptures, Lance. My mother used to quote them at the end of every sentence."

"I had no intention of being found out, Lawrence… If it wasn't for this…"

"Should a been more careful then."

He ignored Lawrence's last comment. "One of my uncles in Jamaica... back in the fifties... he was persecuted. Everywhere he went, people used to shout, Battyman! Battyman!... I watch people being persecuted now. So how could I ever come out?"

"We've all got our problems, Lance. This is yours. I can't help you. You'll have to deal with it. I just can't get over the cocaine thing."

"I didn't think you'd take the bisexual thing so lightly."

"It's your body. You do what you want. Just as long as you don't put anyone's life at risk... talking about that, as you were swinging it both ways, did you cover up with Morag when you..."

"No."

"And *Clive*?"

"Yes. Clive wouldn't have it any other way. He's very hot on protection."

"I can't believe I'm having this conversation," Lawrence said, making another step closer to the door.

"I thought you'd be more condemning," Lance told him, "never mind worrying about my safety... or is it Clive's and Morag's safety you're worried about?"

"Would condemning you stop you being *who* you are, Lance?"

"I suppose not."

"Well. There you are... Look, Lance, *you are* what *you are*. When I was a little boy back in Antigua, there was a man in his twenties. He was gay, and although he tried to hide it, it was known to a lot of people. My mother used to quote scriptures like: *'If a man lieth with mankind, as he lieth with a woman, both of them have committed an abomination'* and loads more of the *Sodom and Gomorrah* things. My mother lived by the bible."

"So your mother would see me as an abomination then?"

"She would, but she won't be *seeing* you, will she? So you won't affect her."

"I tried to keep it locked down..."

"You said."

"Be somebody else. Please society... All that."

"Lance, my father used to say, *'Try as he may, a man can never escape from himself.'* So I guess you were fighting a loosing battle." Lawrence looked at the wall as he spoke to Lance. For some reason, he found it hard to look into his eyes, and Lance was not sure whether he was hiding his *true* resentment of his sexuality, or if he just hated him for the cocaine run madness.

"What's with the eye aversion, man? I might not have been upfront and honest with you, but right now I need a friend."

Lawrence had no problems looking at him now. "*You* need a friend? Like I said, Lance, you're upset because you didn't get your payout. You didn't need a friend when you messed with my future, did you?"

Lance looked away.

"Listen," Lawrence told him again, "I'm going. My intention is never to fly with you again. I don't know how we're gonna get this over to the airline, but it's a must. I never want to be rostered with you again, Lance. If a white man had done this to me, I would have felt a little less betrayed. I guess money talks louder than anything else in the world."

Lance was a big man, so when Lawrence closed the door behind him, he looked pretty pathetic standing there like a scolded child.

* * *

Lance poured a drink when Lawrence left his house. He was in turmoil.

He couldn't help himself… well, perhaps he could if her tried, but trying was too distant a thought.

Cursed with more than his fair share of the seven deadly sins, he was on the brink of self-destruction… *Greed… Lust… Envy.*

He craved riches to a point of peril.

Lusted after the wives of they who have it, seeking to *take*…

Destroy… or even *own:* Not just *physical* riches, but the *spiritual.*

Lance had envied Lawrence's strength. His uprightness. His perfection.

He wanted to touch, feel, taste what he had… Simone. But he dared not try.

He *wanted to tread* the path his tread.

He *wanted to be* Lawrence.

He *wanted to touch* him.

He *wanted him… Wanted him… Wanted him.*

* * *

It wasn't the keys turning angrily in the lock that woke Simone from her second, but longer nap, but the clinking of the whisky bottle against the glass. Lawrence needed a stronger drink than the coffee he had at Lance's.

"Hi. You've been a while," Simone said as she descended the stairs.

"Yeah. I didn't expect to stay this long."

"You said you'd call when you were leaving Lance."

"Sorry, Darling, I forgot."

"Was Morag there?"

"No. In London or something."

"So what was it?"

Lawrence kept his head down as he stretched his free hand out to her. "Come," he whispered.

"*Darling*? What is it?"

He cuddled and kissed her, and with his arm around her, Lawrence walked despondently to the couch. He set his drink down, sat and pulled his wife down on his lap.

"C'mon. What is it? You're scaring me," Simone said.

"There are lots."

"*Lots*?"

"… The other night you asked me if I liked Lance…"

"*Yes*?"

"I told you I couldn't say I've been given any reason not to like him… that he was an all right kinda guy…"

Simone nodded periodically, waiting for the punch line.

"I told you he was human like the rest of us… *not perfect*, but overall, I thought he was ok…"

"*Yeah*?"

"Well, he's all that, except for the *ok* bit… he's not *ok* at all."

"Why? What's he done?"

"Simone…" he looked with purpose into his wife's eyes, "… the last flight we took back from Jamaica trafficked over 100kilos of cocaine."

Simone pulled back, swallowed hard and raised her brows.

"Yes," Lawrence answered her puzzled expression, "you heard me right."

"What?!!…"

"Lance, Clive and some white guy named Peter were behind it. I knew *nothing* about it… If that shit was uncovered, Simone, I would have been finished."

"Tell me you are joking."

"I wish I was… what was he thinking, Simone?"

"So... if it wasn't uncovered… you mean it got through Customs?!"

"Apparently. Remember the news a few days ago? Two guys found dead in a London flat? Peter Walker and some other guy?"

"Yes, I remember."

"Well, apparently, Peter Walker headed this thing from Jamaica. He managed to get Lance to agree. Lance knew I wouldn't agree, so obviously did it without me knowing."

"Oh my God! So... if it went ok, they would have taken the proceeds from the spoils..."

"... And I would have been none the wiser."

"Jesus." She held her forehead. "... Does Morag know?"

"Perhaps it's best if she don't. They're both bitter with each other. If she wants to ruin him, she would love to wave that bag a shit in front of the Customs' fan. Between them and the police, they would sure find a way to make that trail visible again, just to make examples of someone."

"I just can't believe Lance would do such a thing to you."

Lawrence reached for his drink.

"So you're sure that's the last of it?"

"Hopefully. I don't know if anyone else was involved. I just hope no one decides to turn this stone one day, just when we think it's all dead and buried."

"Jesus... *Lance*?... Is he that desperate for money?"

"Money talks, Darling. Many a souls are sold for cash. It's the root of all evil." Lawrence knocked back his drink.

Simone could feel that something else was up. "Anything else?"

"Er... no... nothing else..." He touched her face. "I take it my son's in dreamland?"

"Yeah... had a funny conversation with him after you left."

"Did you?"

"Yeah... he suddenly started to ask all these questions about Conteh."

"About *Conteh*?"

"Yeah. Wanted to know if *I* liked him, because *he* liked him... and would I marry him if I weren't married to you... and if I had married Conteh, would he be his dad... the honest truth is, Darling, I was shocked at his questions."

"He's no five-year-old, that one... what did you tell him?"

"Fact is, I sat him down and told him."

"You did?"

"Yeah. Well, he obviously couldn't understand how he wouldn't be *him* if Conteh were his father. I told him I'd explain another time. Oh…he was quite pleased that Daddy doesn't make mistakes, so we won't have to go apart."

Lawrence chuckled.

"He also assures me I'm your *Darling*."

Lawrence looked at his wife then cuddled her. "You are."

She hugged him back.

Lawrence looked into the distance of his mind.

"C'mon," Simone said, standing up and taking his hand. "Let's go to bed. We need to sleep on this *Lance*, thing."

"Ouch!" Lawrence winced. He was unable to move with the uncomfortable effect of yet another attack of severe cramps in both legs.

"Not cramps again? I swear it's getting worse, Darling. Either that or you're getting old," Simone joked.

"You're as old as you feel, Darling," he said, "and I feel like a very young man, thank you very much."

"And don't *you* feel like a young woman?" she joked.

Lawrence laughed as he shook and rub his leg to get his blood circulating again. "That's better," he said after the best part of five minutes.

And as they descended the stairs, Simone recalled a verse from her favourite poem:

> *Enjoy your achievements as well as your plans.*
> *Keep interested in your own career, however humble;*
> *it is a real possession in the changing fortunes of time.*
> *Exercise caution in your business affairs,*
> *for the world is full of trickery.*
> *But let this not blind you to what virtue there is…*

"I'll just go take a shower," Lawrence said. "I won't be long."

"I'll keep your side of the bed warm," she told him.

Chapter 20

℈t was late evening. Less than an hour ago, Lawrence had taken another flight from Jamaica and was pulling onto his drive when he spotted her vehicle...

Sheree.

What the hell was she doing parked a few yards down from his house again? This was the second time he had found her outside his house, and now it bothered him. How many other times had she been there? Was she watching his family while he wasn't around?

Lawrence parked up, got out of his car and walked towards the tinted-windowed ride.

Sheree spent no time in winding down her window. "Hi."

"What are you doing here?" Lawrence asked, perplexity shaping his brows.

"Isn't it a free country? Do I need permission to park on any street I like? I pay my road tax, you know?"

"No... you don't need permission to park, but I find it strange that this is the second time I've found you lurking around my door."

"Your *door*? I'm yards away from your *door*, Lawrence."

"Listen, Sheree, I don't know where your head is at right now, but I seriously think you're stalking me and my family. You've either been watching too much damn TV, or you're truly sick. Like I said, if it keeps up, I'll get the law involved." He walked away from her.

"And what will you tell them?! That your ex-woman is parked on a street for which she pays her road-tax?!"

Lawrence didn't respond. Instead he took his manly figure up his drive, pushed his key and entered his house where is wife and son awaited him.

"Hi, Daddy!" Amari shouted.

"How yuh doin', son?" Half his mind was absent. He had left it outside where Sheree lurked.

"Fine." He gave his daddy a hug.

"Good flight?" Simone asked, giving him a hug and a kiss.

"Yes. It was ok." he pulled the curtain slightly and peeped out.

"What is it?" Simone asked.

"Did Amari play out today?"

"Yes. Why?"

"Just wondered. It's such a cold day."

"Darling, he's got a coat. And you know I never let him go from my eyes view."

"I know."

"Why the over-protectiveness?"

"What are we having for dinner, Darling?" he asked.

"Lamb."

"Great. But I bet it won't be as nice as your mother's," he bantered.

"You cheeky devil."

Lawrence laughed. "Anyway, don't you think it's about time she visited?"

"Why?" She looked at him suspiciously, wondering if he had sussed her little surprise.

"Because I miss her. And to think I've flown to Jamaica so many times."

"Yes, but that's work. She understands… You really miss her, don't you?"

"You bet. She cheers me up."

"Charming. And I *don't*?" Simone joked.

"You know what I mean. And talking to her on the phone the other day made me miss her more." He made his way upstairs. Amari followed, remembering not to spill the beans about grandma Blanche's pending surprise visit.

"When will you be ready to eat?!" Simone shouted after him.

"In about half an hour!" he shouted back.

"Ok!"

No sooner had Lawrence got to their bedroom, he glanced through the blinds, only to see Sheree slowly driving off. He couldn't see her face through the tinted windows, but he *knew* her eyes were on his house.

"Daddy," Lawrence looked and saw his son behind him.

"Yes, son."

"A strange lady spoke to me today when I was playing out with my friend."

"Really?" Lawrence was anxious. "And where was this strange lady?"

"She was in her car outside the house… across the road… she said you were her friend."

Lawrence bent down towards his son. "Son, you know you're not to talk to strangers, don't you?"

"I didn't speak to her. *She* spoke to *me*."

"Then what did you do?"

"I came inside and told Mummy."

"What did Mummy say?"

"She told me to stay inside with her and watch TV with her."

"What's the panic?" Simone asked. She had heard the tail-end of the conversation.

"This… *strange lady*…"

"Yes, he told me. Said she was talking to him. Said she was your friend."

"And it didn't urge you to see *who* it was?"

"Darling, I'm hardly gonna come out my house, cross the road, just to see who someone who said they knew you was. Whoever she was, she must have friends or family 'round here. I've seen her vehicle there several times."

"Really?!"

"Darling? What's the panic?"

"Nothing… I just don't want my son talking to strangers."

"Ok. But I think she's harmless, though. She looked like a sensible black woman."

"I'll just have a shower, then we'll have dinner," he said. Clearly he was uneasy.

"Ok," Simone replied, looking puzzled at him.

* * *

It seemed a while since Lawrence had left Lance with that unsure feeling. He had betrayed him. Lawrence knew of his hidden sexuality, yet, although Lawrence seemed quite understanding, he still wasn't sure how he *really* felt.

Although his thoughts weren't, it had been a bright day, and the night hadn't turned out too bad either. It was one of those nights where, if you were lonely, you wouldn't say no to a bit of *passionate-filled* company.

Lance had wanted to do this for a very long time after Lawrence had showed him the pictures of his hot steamy session with Clive. He had also expected a call, or even a visit from Sheree, but it didn't happen, so tonight was the night.

A phone call before his sudden appearance would have been good, but Lance obviously didn't feel it was that important or even courteous.

"Lance, Hi," Sheree said, surprised to find him standing on her doorstep. It was only hours since her little confrontation with Lawrence outside his house, so she assumed it was him, come to give her a bigger piece of his mind than he already had. "Morag isn't here…"

"Can I come in?" Lance said, ignoring the statement about Morag.

"I thought you were Lawrence."

"Why? Are you expecting him?"

"No… no…"

"Well? Can I come in?"

"Er… yeah… yeah…" She widened the door and stepped back to let him in. Curiosity filled her eyes. "Everything ok, Lance?"

"Yeah… yeah," Lance said.

"Go through." She motioned to her lounge. "Drink?"

"No. I'm fine."

"Sit down," she told him.

"I'm not really stopping."

"Well, it must be important. You drove all this way for a few minutes?"

"You could say that, yes."

"Why didn't you call? I might not have been in."

"Sorry, I…"

"… No, it's ok. No need to be sorry. It's just that you could have had a wasted journey." Apart from wondering why he came, Sheree was looking deep into his soul. The image of his ruthless buggery had surfaced. She remembered his naked ass as he hammered Clive's, and now she told herself that must be the reason he came. Lawrence must have showed him the pictures and told him *who* the photographer was.

"This is nice," he said, glancing around her exquisite lounge. "You decorated since the last time Morag and I came."

"I should think so. That was a long time ago."

"True."

"… So what is it, Lance? To what do I owe the pleasure of your visit?"

"I think you know, Sheree."

"Ok, let me guess…"

"… Have you said anything to Morag?" He cut in.

"About what?"

"C'mon, Sheree. You know what I'm talking about."

"Oh… I see… the pictures."

"Yes… the pictures."

"No. I haven't told Morag. I only took them because I thought the other guy was Lawrence. His car was on your drive…"

"Sheree, I'm not a freak… I'm bisexual. I like men and women."

"Who said anything about you being a freak, Lance? Each to his own."

"Will you?"

"Will I *what*?"

"Tell Morag."

"No. That's your business."

"What would you have done if the other guy was Lawrence?"

"D'know."

"I had no idea you were so hung up him."

"So he told you, hey? Told you I've been *stalking* him. Is that the word he used? *Stalking*?"

"Well, is that what you've been doing?"

"How dare him discuss me…?"

"It's not like you think. He was a little concerned, that's all. Who wouldn't be? There's nothing wrong with you being crazy about him. He's a nice guy. But you'd be concerned too if you suddenly find your ex sitting outside your door."

"What d'you suppose she's got that I haven't?"

"Who, *Simone*?"

Sheree didn't reply.

"Didn't you ask him?"

"I know this might sound as I've lost every little bit of my self-esteem, respect, everything, but I would have seriously settled with being the other woman… but he rejected me."

"You know Lawrence. Loyal to the core."

"Loyal is not the word… Anyway, I thought you came to talk about the pictures. What have my hang-ups on Lawrence got to do with anything?"

"Nothing… Just making conversation."

There was a noticeable pause.

"I've been a fool, Lance," Sheree broke the silence.

"Why?"

"I got a little crazy. I was letting my feelings run away with me a bit too much."

"We all do crazy things from time to time, Sheree."

"I was outside Lawrence's house this evening as well. Just a few hours ago. That's why I thought it was him at the door."

"What were you trying to achieve by sitting there?"

"Like I said, I got a little crazy. The mystery of the mind, I guess… Sure you don't want that drink?" she offered again.

"Yeah, why not? Go on then… Got any Brandy?"

"Sure." She walked towards the kitchen.

"And Sheree," Lance said.

"Yes?"

"Thanks for not telling Morag. I know our marriage has ended, and I know she had her lover in our bed, but this…"

"No worries, Lance. You've got your troubles, I've got mine."

Seconds later, Sheree was back with two glasses of Brandy. "Should you? You're driving aren't you?" she asked him as she handed him his glass.

"One won't hurt."

"This is the second time you've been to my house, isn't it, Lance?" She placed her ass on her floor and her glass on the coffee table.

"I believe so, yes."

There was another pause…

"How does it feel?" she asked Lance.

"What?"

"You know… having feelings for both sex."

"I don't know how to describe it… I fancy men, and I fancy women… simple as that."

"Ok… so… is it 50/50?… I mean, do you fancy both sexes the same? Or do you fancy one more than the other?"

"It depends. A sexy woman can turn me on just as much as a sexy man and vice versa... Can you understand that?"

"No. I can't say I can. I've only ever fancied men."

"I didn't choose this situation, Sheree. It chose me. I didn't wake up one morning and decide I that want to fancy men and not *only* women, as the norm would have it. Who would want to choose a situation that they know they will always be persecuted for?"

"Right…"

"So if it's wrong," he continued, "then the blame must rest somewhere else within this universe. Not with me."

"Right." She wanted to ask more, but felt it would be a little intrusive, which was a little strange, considering she found her ass in his backyard with her camera.

"And if you'd like to know, I've always fancied *you*."

"What?!" She was a little surprised. "*Me*?!"

366

"Yes, Sheree, *you*. "It's true. But you were Lawrence's ex. I fancied Simone too, but…"

She looked at him. "You fancied your friend's wife?"

"Look, lots of men out there are fancying their mates wives. Fancying someone doesn't mean you have to act on it. We're human beings. Feelings are feelings."

"True. I suppose so."

"Anyway, you can talk, you fancy Lawrence."

"Simone isn't my friend. And anyway, he was my man for a very long time."

"Fair enough… So how come a beautiful woman like you don't have a man?"

"D'know. I suppose if he's out there, he'll come."

"And if he's not?"

"Then I guess he won't. What do I know? And anyway, I've decided, there isn't anything wrong with living without a man. Lots of women are opting for the single life. Less stress and all that. Get a little sex when you want it, then your bed is yours."

"True."

Another pause…

"Nice rose," Lance said, looking at the content of a gold box on her fireplace.

"It's not real… but it will live forever."

"What a concept? I've never looked at it like that before. Who's it from?"

"A friend when I was in need."

"Ok… Well, if his *deed* satisfied your *need*, what more could you wish for?" Lance said with flippancy.

Sheree reflected on him for a few seconds. *Tom.*

Another pause.

"You're beautiful," Lance swept an unexpected compliment. "You know that don't you?"

"*What*?"

"I said you're *beautiful*. Anyone told you that lately?"

She blushed. "No. But thanks. Pity your friend didn't see it."

"Sure he did." Lance gave her a deep look.

Sheree got a little uncomfortable. She didn't know where Lance was going with this, though, bisexual or not, she thought he was handsome too. "You're a handsome man too, Lance."

"That's debatable."

"You're also very modest."

"And you're also very sexy with it." He ignored her *'modesty'* compliment.

She blushed deeper. Sought refuge in her glass of Brandy.

He so her rush for cover. "… Sheree?…"

"Yes?…"

"Come here…"

"*What*?"

"Come here… *please*." He stretched a hand and reached for her.

"Lance, I'm…"

Slowly, he stood up. Taking both her arms, he pulled her from her sitting position, at the same time, checking for resistance.

"Lance?…." She was puzzled. It was all a bit quick. *She* was Morag's friend. *He* was Lawrence's friend. He was bisexual. "What's this?"

"Please don't resist me, Sheree… please," he said in a low, desperate voice, now pulling her close.

"I…" His lips were now on her ears… her neck… now, her lips…

Hiss kisses sweet…

As sweet as candy… ohhhh…

She couldn't… Wouldn't… and didn't resist."

"I want you, Sheree," he whispered. "Oh, God, I want you so much."

"Lance… I had no idea… Is this just lust?… What…?"

"*Shhhh*… whatever it is… I just want you…"

She was responding now… *wildly… passionately… eagerly…* ohhh!

"Can I?" he asked in an eager whisper, as if his life depended on it.

"What?" she whispered back.

"Can I fuck you?" Somehow, his crude, shameless whisper turned her on.

"Oh… Lance… I… Shouldn't you say *make love*?"

"Can I?… *Please*…" he ignored her query.

"What do you have with Clive anyway, Lance? I thought you were…"

Again he ignored her question and devoured her mouth hungrily.

"Lance…" It was all… all … all too quick.

He wasted no time. Now, he rid her of her blouse… Then her bra… Her right nipple was in his mouth… then her left… then her right… ohhh…

"Ohhh... Lance... Ohhh... Ahhh..."

Now, her lounge carpet received their hot bodies. No need for the bedroom. *No sir.*

Her skirt was gone with the wind...

Her black laced underwear, history...

Now, ravenously, he devoured her tongue, her neck... her breasts... ohhh!

"Lance... Jesus... Lance... Ohhh..." She hummed in ecstasy.

"Sheree... oh... Sheree... I've *got to* fuck you.... Need to... I have always wanted to..."

And now... the ultimate pleasure... His tongue on her quivering lower lips... *Ohhh!... Ohhh!... Ohhh!...*

She was in heaven...

Hot passion.... Hot, steamy passion... *Ohhh...*

Now, her heavens opened...

His hallelujah went in...

No condom...

In!... *Bare-backed...* In!... *Wet....* In!... *Juicy...* In!... *Hard...* In!...

"Oh, Lance!"...

In!...

"Oh, Lance!.. Lance!..."

In!...

"Oh! Ah! Ooh!"...

In!In!In!In!In!!!!!...

"Oh!... Oh, Lance!... Lance!... Oh!... Ahhh!... Ahhh!... *Lance... Lance... Lance... Ohhh... Ohhh... Oh my God... Lance..."*

* * *

It was the very next day after Lance visited Sheree, leaving her with a bellyful, that Lawrence decided to pay her a visit. She was expecting him sooner, so She was not at all surprised to see him on her doorstep. After the little confrontation outside his house the evening before, it was inevitable. Every time he tried to call her after what his son and Simone had said, she would cut his calls by clicking the off buttons on her mobile.

"Yes?" she asked sarcastically as she opened the door.

"Can I come in?"

"How can you be sure you'll be safe in my house?" she asked, widening the door to let him in before he could answer her question.

Silently, he walked through to her living-room with purpose, as the torment of her little idea of *stalking* was beginning to stink. "Ok, you *know* why I'm here," he told her.

"Do I?" she asked.

"Cut the fucking crap, Sheree! What the fuck d'you want?!"

She winced as Lawrence hardly ever used profane language. Not that she had heard anyway.

"You don't swear. What's this? A new you?"

"I don't swear to ladies, but I'm not so sure you *are* one... What were you *really* doing outside my house?"

"It's a free country, Lawrence," she told him. "I can park my car wherever the hell I like."

"I had no idea you had this in you... *really*," he told her.

"What? The ability to react to being rejected?"

"Play another tune, Sheree."

She gave him a cut-eye.

"Listen," he asserted, "I don't know what your game is, but just stay the hell away from my family."

"Or?"

He stared at her. "Are you *real*. That is some TV madness you're imitating. This is the real fucking world... what were you doing talking to my son about being my friend?"

"I just love it when you're angry," she said.

More and more Lawrence realised that madness is far *deeper* or more *shallow*, than he had ever imagined. "Listen..." he walked backwards slowly. "I'm going... I thought you were much more intelligent than that, Sheree... I really did."

"Don't worry," she said, "it's the last you'll see of me."

He didn't believe her, but he told himself that if he never saw her again, it would be his dream come true. If she could just disappear, he would be happy.

"Let yourself out," was all she said. Nothing else.

And so he did. Let himself out. Without the slightest clue that Lance had been there the day before, straddling his old path.

* * *

It was as she stood in the queue at Boots that Simone noticed that same distant look in her husband's eyes again. He was stood away from the queue holding Amari's hand. Ever since that trip over to see Lance that night, Lawrence constantly slipped into a world of his own, staring out into a distance, where seemingly something mind-consuming lived. She had asked him once or twice what the matter was, but he insisted that everything was ok. He had never been like that before, and she was convinced the drug-trafficking stunt Lance had pulled was laying more heavily on his mind that he had previously thought it would.

'Later I'll ask him again,' she thought. *'Perhaps this time he'll say.'*

* * *

Menna may have thought she had won the battle, but the war had not been won... *Not yet anyway*

It had only been two days since she actually got back from her well-spent trip in Canada. She hadn't even unpacked her suitcase. Neither had she had the chance to call her sister Cynthia, or her friend Angie to let them know she was home. And if she had time to sort out her faulty mobile, she would have realised that Cynthia and Angie had called to remind her that they would be flying out: Cynthia was off to North Carolina, whilst Angie was off to Spain. Through pure coincidence, (like both her mobile and home phones) they had chosen the same time to go away, but with Menna being so preoccupied with other extraordinary stuff: unlike the *run-of-the-mill-nine-to-five-go-home-cook-eat-watch-East-Enders-bath-sleeep-nine-to-five-again* black woman, she had clean forgotten. As for her home phone, that needed sorting since the night she threw it up against the wall after she picked up a call and found Nico on the other end. In and outgoing calls are fine, but retrieving her messages from her answerphone was a problem, since the red light no longer flashed at her, indicating she had any, and even when she checked, it gave her nothing. So, there too, lay un-retrieved messages from Cynthia, Angie and others.

"*Nico*... Hi... what...?" she said when she opened her front door to find him standing there. She was convinced it was going to be mother-hen Cynthia coming to find out why she hadn't called to say she was back.

"... What am I doing here?" Nico looked left then right. A kind of *coast-clearing* drill. Now, he held the gun so close to Menna's chest, she had no choice but to freeze. *Literally*. "Need you ask, Menna?" he continued, pushing her inside and closing the door behind him. "Thought you would have figured that one out for yourself, a cleva *bitch* like yuh, and all dat." He was confident.

371

"Where did you get that thing?" She stared at the deadly piece of weapon almost as if it was the first time she had seen one. Pointing one obviously carried a different rush to having one pointed at her. Now she knew how Conteh must have felt.

"Where did *you* get the one you used to pull off that jewellery shit... you know... the one you used to pull off that neat robbery just so you could set-up mi bredrin, Conteh?" Continuously, he budged her further towards her living-room.

But all she did was stare at the gun as Nico edged her towards her settee.

"Guns are the easiest shit to come by these days. You should know. Birmingham is getting more like the States. *Wild West Midlands they're calling it now.*" He pushed her now into a sitting position, and for the first time, the corner of her settee was of no comfort at all.

"Nico... put the gun down. We can talk."

"Talk? Really? Like we *talk*ed a few weeks ago when you and your fucking entourage of *She Devils* strung me up outside Banana Baits?" He chuckled with deep vengeance, then perched mockingly on the edge of her coffee table. "This feels good, Menna. *Real* good. Not like a few weeks ago when you bitches had me stuck between a rock and a hard place, *as they say.*"

Menna searched for a verbal escape.

"I didn't think I'd get another invite," Nico said, "so I invited myself. I came a few days ago too. Twice. You must have left the country." His sarcasm was spot-on.

"Nico, listen..." She would have clutched at any useless, puny straw now, in order to try to gain the slightest bit of control. "You and I... we..."

"Blow!" The back of his left hand connecting with her attractive face told her to cut the bullshit. He would have no mercy. "Don't try that coochie-coo shit with me, you bitch! HIV hasn't got my brain yet! In fact, as you can see, it hasn't got hold of my body too tight yet! I might be the walking fucking dead, but mi not lying down yet to raas!"

Menna stared at him. She had certainly become a hard bitch; though it would be true to say she wasn't yet ready to die. "So why the gun?... Are you gonna kill me?" she asked him in a mediocre voice, her left palm resting on her stinging cheek.

"Oh *yes*. Surely you didn't think I'd spare you? You're gonna *die*." He teased her sexy, supple lips now with the barrel of his small weapon, and at the same time, she saw the horror in his eyes.

He looked her up and down, his eyes saying, *'But not before I fuck you.'*

Menna tried to hide the terror in *her* eyes. Shaking in her boots didn't suit her image. She had taken on the image of *Sista-Hard-Stuff* and must not make her vulnerability show. *'There can be no courage unless you're scared'*, she thought.

"Humiliation," Nico continued. "I didn't realise how much it could cut. Shame. Disgrace. And it did, Menna. *Cut.* Hanging from that post, nude in the freezing cold was one thing…" Lines of perplexity gathered around his forehead. "…But having all those people staring at me… recognising me…"

"Nico, but you were going around infecting innocent women…"

"Are you God?!" he shouted so loud, she jumped. "Are you some sort of avenging queen or something?!" He was almost frothing at the mouth and the tone of his voice jolted her into a new realisation. A realisation that he was *really* angry. Livid. Desperate to get his own back. In fact, he wanted to get his own back well before the stringing up thing. She had simply poured fuel on an already raging fire.

"I *loved* you, Menna…" His voice dropped into a desperate, plea-like tone. "In fact, you were the *only* woman I ever loved. But you fucked me up. You played me and Conteh off like fools. You were clever though." He sniggered. "You made condoms your friends…"

Still she kept her eyes on the gun.

"… But not tonight… *Clever* won't have a chance to play… Condoms won't be your friends tonight… no way…"

She looked at him in shock. *Horror*. The obvious question filled her eyes. Did he mean what she was thinking? No… surely not.

"… Tonight I'm gonna *taste* you, Menna… *Jade* … You can be whoever you like tonight, I don't give a fuck… Skin-to-skin… I'm gonna *taste* you."

"Nico, no." She was calm. Trying to hold it down.

"What's the worry? You're gonna die anyway, so what's a little HIV between old lovers?" He touched her face.

"Really, Nico, let's talk about this."

"Ok…" He stood up. Grabbed his crutch and squeezed it as if his desires were burning. "We'll talk."

She searched for the catch in his eyes. "You want to *talk*?"

"Yes… *in bed*."

"What?"

"I said… we'll talk… in bed," he stressed sarcastically. "*Get up.* Lead me to the bedroom. You've seen mine, remember? But I've *never* seen yours… what was it you said when I asked you what was the mystery with keeping your address away from me?… oh yes, I remember… you said, *'There's no mystery at all, Nico. I'm just not ready yet. You're just not used to it. Don't tell me you haven't done the same to women in the past.'* He mimicked her voice with attitude.

Menna gave him ten out of ten for memory. That was exactly what she told him, and if her memory served her right, it was word for word. She recalled the night too. It was a funny night. Her and Nico were chilling at his place. A few minutes before her spiel about not being ready to take him to her place, Conteh was on the doorstep, with not even the slightest clue that the *Jade* that Nico had in his bed, was his very own *Menna*. It seemed a long time ago. Since then, she had seen Jamaica with a difference. Visited Canada, a place in which she hadn't yet ruled out retiring. *He* flashed through her mind. *Clayton*. If he could have seen her then. The only man who could ever reach her. After Conteh, that is. *Clayton*… the *fine* son of a preacher-man.

Nuff things had happened. Unexpected things from the past came to light.

She had *searched*…

Found…

Destroyed…

But now, as she walked with a false sure-footedness towards her own bedroom, a gun to her head, a new realisation hit her: she had come to realise that *she* was now the target of a *Search-And-Destroy* crew.

Bang! Bang! Bang! They were now inside the bedroom when the banging on the front door surprised them both.

Nico stopped and averted his attention towards it.

Menna hoped this person would be her saviour, but it would be a little difficult, since he or she would have to get in first.

Nico walked backwards to the bedroom door and pushed it to a *near-closed* position, leaving it slightly ajar so he could listen. Still, he pointed the gun at Menna, his eyes telling her to *shush*.

"Menna?! Are you there?" It's me, Cynthia!"

The tension inside the bedroom heightened.

Nico walked back briskly, the daring in his eyes rocketing tenfold.

Menna could do nothing but listen to her sister's voice.

Nico listened too.

" 'Xpect she's busy," a woman's voice said. She had only moved in a day after Simone returned from Jamaica.

"Meaning?" Cynthia asked.

"Your sister, isn't she?"

"Yes.

"She's got a visitor. I followed him up the stairs earlier."

"Really?"

"Yes, but he didn't notice me though."

Nico didn't like what he was hearing. He was clocked, so if he did anything foolish, there was a witness.

"Yes. Quite handsome too," the middle-aged white woman said. Menna recognised who she was from her voice at the outset. She knew how much her sister Cynthia loathed people who are quick and willing to tell other people's business, but she also knew that tonight, this gossip was kind of pleasing to her ears. Menna having some male company could do no harm. She hadn't yet told her how serious she was about Clayton.

"Oh yes," Cynthia bluffed. "Quite tall... dark..."

Menna knew her sister was bluffing. Digging for input.

Nico, however, just wished they would move away from the door. They were making him uneasy.

"Yes. Tall, dark and handsome."

"Lucky her... I'll come back another time then."

Nico was pleased as the voices trailed off. He had things to do.

Menna, however was not so pleased.

Nico looked over at the bed and gestured with his eyes.

* * *

In the meantime, Cynthia wished she had seen her sister before she took her flight. She was a little old-fashioned like that. As she reached for the handle of her car door, she wondered who this hunk was that her sister hadn't told her about. She climbed into her car and reached for her mobile. She dialled Menna's house phone. She didn't expect her to pick up, but when it clicked to her answerphone, she rattled, *"Hi, Sis'. I'm sure you know I came 'round a few minutes ago, but I know why you chose not to answer. I don't blame you. Have fun. And I don't need to tell you to be careful. You are the Queen of Sense! Listen; don't forget I'm flying to The States; in fact I'm on my way to the airport now. Have you been getting my messages? I don't know, Sis', I haven't heard from you and you've been back two days now.*

How was your time in Canada anyway? Try calling me if you get a chance – maybe after this hunk is gone. If not, we'll speak when I get back in a week, ok?"

But the only thing that Menna heard was when the phone rang. And later, if she came out alive, she still wouldn't get her message. The plan was to get both her phones sorted some time that week.

She lay there still. Nude. Shaking. She hoped Nico would not do it. He had dared to take his clothes off and lay beside her. She was cringing.

"You might be a bitch, but your are one beautiful woman." He moved his face close to her neck and breathed deeply. "You smell gorgeous too. You always did," he whispered, then he cuddled her. Ran his tongue down her right breast. Took her nipple into his mouth and sucked hard.

Menna closed her eyes and thought of a place far far away. Anywhere to take her mind away from the *there-and-then*.

The gun was still in Nico's right hand.

"We loved you… me and Conteh." Again he kissed her nipples. Kissed and licked the sensitive area beneath the pit of her arm. Running his right wrist over her body, from her knees up to her left breast, he breathed sighs of pleasure.

"Nico… the gun… careful… what if it goes off?"

"It will only go off when I'm ready, Menna… unless, of course, you disturb it."

She felt his manhood rising and throbbing against her outer thigh, its moist, clammy tip making her wonder if even *that* was safe. She cringed.

Now, he changed position. Stretching his right leg over her, he sat in a knee-crouching position, his dick standing like the Olympic torch over her V. The gun still in his hand.

She looked up at him in terror, thinking, *'Please… don't.'*

Ambidextrously, gun in his right hand, he moulded her breasts with his left. Touched her face. Swept it up and down her body.

Menna stiffened. She wanted to retaliate, but she had to think sensibly. "Nico, don't. *Please.*"

He ignored her. Looked her in the eyes as he moved his busy left hand now to inner thighs.

"No!"

"Shut the fuck up." He didn't shout. Just a calmly. As if to show he was enjoying his warp perversion.

376

His dick *boinged* to a stiffer attention.

With firm fingers, he manipulated her clitoris. "You used to like this... I remember," he whispered, closing his eyes.

"Please, Nico." Her mind wandered. Tried to find a way to defeat him.

He opened his eyes and lifted his gun-filled hand as a warning.

"Nico... *please*."

Now he parted her knees. Hoisted them up as far as they could go. *'Oh no,'* she thought. *'Oh please don't.'*

And now, he placed his knees between her outspread legs, then spread his body over her with one intention.

'There can be no courage unless you're scared'... *'There can be no...'* Whoosh! Courage overcame fright and Menna twisted with a sudden force, thrusting them both to her left, her on top of him: only they were that far over the edge of the bed, the force of the action landed him buff! On his back. She fell on top of his right wrist, causing a slight sprain.

She was no weakling, and he, no giant.

Nico's eyes widened with surprise, and when Menna seized the gun from his aching wrist he searched his mind for his next move. "What the fuck?!... Oh Jesus!" he shouted when she stood up quickly now, and planted the sole of her right foot in his groin, teaching the molesting organ a lesson.

Nico twisted to his left, doubled up in pain as he nursed his aching dick.

"Yuh fucka!" Menna protested, stepping over and away from him with purpose. But when Nico grabbed her left ankle with his left hand, she was most certainly caught unawares. "Let go, you bastard!" she shouted, pointing the gun at his head.

"Go ahead... shoot," he said with confidence. "Let's see how brave you are! Go on! Shoot!"

"Don't tempt me, Nico! I will! Let go of my foot, you shit-head!"

"I love it when you're angry," Nico said, dropping his voice. "Turns me on." The pain in his right wrist had subsided. It was now idle and the devil had found work for it. He reached now for her other ankle, rendering her awkwardly helpless. "Now what yuh gonna do, *Miss Cleva Bitch*! Yuh dead to bombo claat!"

"Nico! I'll shoot!"

"No you won't. All mouth and no fucking nickers, that's you."

377

Menna searched herself and wondered if she could *really* shoot anyone.

Nico yanked once on both her ankles, unsettling her balance.

"Nico! Noooo!"

But Nico didn't hear her plea. He rose briskly to his knees and yanked harder; causing Menna to topple over, face down on her bedroom floor, hitting her forehead against her mobile phone. She had left it there to charge earlier. And before she actually hit the floor, she had tried to grab the side of her square dressing table. She missed, and its protruding edge caught her wrist causing a nasty cut. Blood flowed from the fresh cut, but Menna had no time to take any notice, Nico had over powered her once more.

"Jesus, Nico! Are you crazy?!"

"Maybe I am. Maybe you and your crew were a little crazy a few weeks ago when you strung me up?"

Twisting her round to face him in the angriest mood she had ever seen, he slapped her hard across her face. She felt it. Then the force as he pushed both her knees up and back, nearly touching her shoulders. Anger must have made his manhood rise again. She thought she had crippled him for a while at least when she had planted her right foot on it, but the avenging snake seemed to have hissed its way back to life.

But the gun.

It was still in her hand.

How was he to know she couldn't really shoot anyone?

Wasn't he at all frightened she would pull it through desperation?

Apparently not, for as he looked deep into her eyes, she read his unspoken words.

His lips that were once quite tasty before she fled England, and before she discovered he was HIV positive, now tasted bitter. She flashed her head from side to side protesting against his venomous kiss.

And now…she felt it. Throbbing. Not *inside* her, but *against* her pubic. *'No, Dear God, No,'* she thought. "Nico… please don't… you're HIV positive. Please don't enter me."

"Like I said," he said in an evil whisper, "What's the worry? You're gonna die anyway, so what's a little HIV between old lovers?… And try that sudden shit again, and I'll kill you quicker than I intended to."

"Nico…"

He kissed her neck… Licked her breasts. "Noticed I 'low yuh wid di gun. I won't even restrain your wrists or anything."

"Why? Is it not loaded?"

"Find out for yourself. It's in your hand. Shoot me."

Menna was baffled.

Still, Nico pressed hard against her knees. She was fit but not that fit. "Nico, you're hurting me."

"Really? You hurt me not so long ago. Have you forgotten? I thought you were so tough, *nothing* could ever hurt you, Menna."

"My wrist… it's bleeding. I'm losing blood."

"You're not listening. I said you're gonna die. Loosing a little blood is the least of it."

Menna's mind raced. Looked like the end of the road for her. She had come to the end of her rope a while back: perhaps she really should have tied a knot.

"You've really fucked me up, Menna." he pushed hard against her bent-back knees.

"Aw!"

"I can never face the public again. Not after that stringing up thing. Country Bwoy laughed at me! Faada Jarvis! Missa Chat Bout! Levi Clashington! Lady Mutiny and Sandra Irie! Every raas claat body who knows me!" He was *A*ngry with a capital *A*. And maybe if he had stopped to check himself, he would have realised that *A*nger is one letter short of *D*anger. That letter is *D*. It represents a mound of negative nouns: *D*estruction… *D*evastation… *D*eath.

"Yes, Nico but you…"

"Blow!" he planted another box.

She held her cheek. "You get off on this shit don't you?" Blood from her wrist stained her face now.

"Maybe… I'm gonna make sure that no one find you when I'm done with you."

"What d'you mean?… Nico? What d'you…?" She panicked.

Now, he rested the shaft of his hard dick against the insides of her thighs and moved it up and down with frictional force.

Menna tensed and tried to find a way to make sure Nico's fluids didn't get anywhere near her vagina, and at the same time she wondered what he meant by his last statement. She asked again, "Nico… what d'you mean you're gonna make sure no one find you when you're done with me?"

He ignored her, but still he moved. *Up. Down. Up. Down.* He was enjoying it. She could tell. "What a way to go, Menna?" he said in his sick temperament, eyes closed. "What a way to go. This is fucking nice. Sweet. *Mmmm*... You are fucking sweet. *Mmmm... Mmmm... Mmmm*... Why do we have to die? *Ohhhh*..." His voice trembled. "... Whether you like it or not," he whispered, "I'm gonna enter you... *now*..." Slightly, he lifted his ass in readiness for his sick entry.

"Nico, no! If you do, I swear I'll shoot you!"

Nico paused and calmly said... "Like I said... go ahead. I'm not restraining you. But make sure when you pull that trigger, I'm well and truly dead... and let me tell you this... if you scream again... *I'll fucking kill you.*"

She wasn't sure about this. She didn't want to die. Not like that. Not there. Not then. Things to do. Places to go. People to see. Life to live... Clayton... Cynthia... And money to spend. Yes. *Nuff* money. *Unthinkable* money. Its source? A most surprising one.

And now, *it* touched her vagina. *Slightly*. His dick. Not *inside* her. Just on the tip of her clitoris. Surely that couldn't do any arm? Could it? Surely not... *'Dear God, let it be safe'*, she despaired. But seconds later, she wondered what did it matter? For although she didn't want to, she felt she was going to die anyway. And what would he do with her body? He said he would make sure *no one found her*. Had he been watching too much TV? Was he really that angry? Nico didn't seem the *physical* murderer type. Deliberately infecting women by having sex with them is one thing, but would he really kill her brutally there like that...? *Desperation.* It's a funny thing. And when ones pride is gone, and there's nothing left to live for and nothing left to care about... and when the source of his or her misery is there for the *taking-out*, there ain't no telling what one might do.

"Ok," he told her. "Get ready... here it comes... *mmmm.*" He hummed like a pervert.

Menna saw her life flashed in font of her eyes.

Morbid thoughts.

HIV.

Then death.

Then the motion of her breathless body being dragged to some dark lonely place. Left. Not found for years. Forever, even. It sent shivers down her spine.

Nico paused. Why was he pausing? Was he teasing? Or was he just prolonging the torture?

She glanced up to her bed. Maybe if he could just lay her there after she was dead. She loved her bed. *Comfort.* Not in some dark, desolate *not-to-be-discovered* place. *No*…. And it was then that she saw it… A single red rose.

"The rose… Nico… the rose… you brought… a rose?"

"It's not real." He licked her nipples. "It's a paper rose… you see… *the real ones die. Paper ones live forever.*"

She freaked. *'You have flipped. Totally,'* she thought, lying there beneath him, forgetting that she herself had done a few crazy things in the *not-so-far* past. To her though, it was *justice.*

Fear now, it seemed, had overpowered her *courage.* She wondered if anyone would hear her scream.

It was coming. Surely now… Hi dick.

No more stalling.

Getting closer… closer…

Towards her frightened vagina.

'Noooo! No, Nico, no! You bastard! Noooo!'… *Ugh!*"

Had she forgotten what he had said?… or was she just displaying *courage* over *fear*? … *'If you scream again… I'll kill you,'* he had said.

Whap! A blow to someone's head.

"Oh shit!"

Whap! Then another.

"Oh!"

Blood is dripping from a wrist.

"Oh…"

A body lay helpless… Not dead. Just helpless. Seemingly dying.

"Oh…"

What will the outcome be?

The most difficult part of attaining perfection, is finding something to do for an encore… And tomorrow? It would be another day. Yes. *Tomorrow would surely be another day.*

* * *

It was the dead of the night and Lawrence found himself raiding his fridge for a long cool drink. He couldn't sleep. The dream he had was pretty dramatic, and as he quenched his thirst, his mother's voice from his recent dream, and the real one from way back when in Antigua, drummed hi his ears. Her quoting of the scripture was like a personal damnation… *'If a man lieth with mankind, as he lieth with a woman, both of them have committed an abomination… 'If a man lieth with*

381

mankind, as he lieth with a woman, both of them have committed an
abomination!... 'If a man lieth with mankind, as he lieth with a
woman, both of them have committed an abomination!... abomination!
Abomination!...

His was the second time he dreamt about his mother's words since
the image of Lance and Clive's passionate session entered his head.

Chapter 21

℘ynthia pushed her key through her lock as she listened to the sound
of the Black Cab driving away. She lifted her suitcase above the
threshold then wheeled it into the corner of the porch. There were no
great need or urgency to unpack, so there it would stay until tomorrow.

Cynthia loved being home after any break away. She loved her
little house. After Menna had told her that she was coming back from
Jamaica, and after her tenant had found herself a place to go, she got a
decorating friend in to give it the facelift it needed for her re-
cohabitation. It was homely. *Hers*. And although Tricia tried this time
to persuade to give Canada a try, she didn't feel there was no place else
for her. Unless of course there was a gorgeous hunk waiting for her.
But there wasn't. So for her, her humble, cosy little house was the
epitome of *'Home Sweet Home'*.

Ten minutes later as she stirred a spoonful of sugar into her tea, her
answerphone blurted out messages. The first one was from Jeannette. It
would have been nice if the message had started 'Hope you had a nice
time in Canada,' but instead it rattled on about wanting her to
accompany her to a Singles night.

Cynthia took a sip of her tea and was about to sit out the rest of her
messages, when she was nearly choked on the warm liquid. The voice
of terror that emitted from her answerphone made her think twice
about sitting down. Her sister's terror-filled voice was hitting hard
against her ears: *'Jesus, Nico! Are you crazy?!'*...

"*Nico?*" Cynthia spoke to herself. "*Nico?*... Not *the* Nico? Surely
not."

'Maybe I am. Maybe you and your crew were a little crazy a few
weeks ago when you strung me up?'...

Cynthia discarded her tea and got closer to the machine.

'Nico... please don't... you're HIV positive. Please don't enter
me.'

"Oh, Jesus!" Cynthia panicked, remembering the date announced by the automated voice: she realised that it was the very day she flew to America.

'Like I said... what's the worry? You're gonna die anyway, so what's a little HIV between old lovers?... And try that sudden shit again, and I'll kill you quicker than I intended to.'

"Shit!" Cynthia dug into her bag in search of her mobile. Nervously, she dialled her sister's house phone but the answerphone kicked in. She clicked off and tried her mobile. *'It is impossible to connect your call. Please try again later,'* was what she got. "Shit!" She rewind the tape to where it had got to before she tried calling, and heard, *'Nico.'.... 'Noticed I 'low yuh wid di gun. I won't even restrain your wrists or anything.'* ... *Why? Is it not loaded?'... 'Find out for yourself. It's in your hand. Shoot me.'... 'Nico, you're hurting me.'... 'Really? You hurt me not so long ago. Have you forgotten? I thought you were so tough, nothing could ever hurt you.'* ... *'My wrist... it's bleeding. I'm losing blood.'*

"Oh my God!" Cynthia said, covering her mouth. "What shit have you got yourself into again, girl?" She contemplated. What should she do? Where was Menna then? Was she ok? Cynthia listened on... *'You're not listening. I said you're gonna die. Loosing a little blood is the least of it.'... 'You've really fucked me up, Menna.'... 'Aw!'... 'I can never face the public again. Not after that stringing up thing. Country Bwoy laughed at me! Faada Jarvis! Missa Chat Bout! Levi Clashington! Lady Mutiny and Sandra Irie! Every raas claat body who knows me!'... 'Yes, Nico but you...' ... 'Blow!'*

"Oh no!... Jesus! This man was giving my sister a battering." She dialled Menna's house phone again. This time she left a message. "Menz?! Menz, pick up, please! Where are you?! What was happening a week ago?! This message on my answerphone?... Menz, call me, please!...* Let me know if you're safe... *Please!*" Cynthia clicked off. Disillusioned and flattened from not hearing her sister's voice personally, she resumed listening to the gruesome tape. *'You get off on this shit don't you?' ... 'Maybe... I'm gonna make sure that no one find you when I'm done with you.'... 'What d'you mean?... Nico? What d'you...?' ... 'Nico... what d'you mean you're gonna make sure no one find you when you're done with me? ... 'What a way to go. This is fucking nice. Sweet. Mmmm... You are fucking sweet. Mmmm... Mmmm... Mmmm... Why do we have to die? Ohhhh...Whether you like it or not, I'm gonna enter you now...'... 'Nico, no! If you do, I swear*

I'll shoot you!' … 'Like I said… go ahead. I'm not restraining you. But make sure when you pull that trigger, I'm well and truly dead… and let me tell you this… if you scream again… I'll fucking kill you.'… Ok, get ready… here it comes… mmmm.'… … The rose… Nico… the rose… you brought a rose?'

Cynthia was baffled now. She listened on. *'It's not real. It's a paper rose… you see… the real ones die. Paper ones live forever.'*

"What the hell…?" Cynthia held her head. She paced around her living-room. And then the pivotal last cry from her sister ripped through her very soul… *'Noooo! No, Nico, no! You bastard! Noooo!'… Ugh!'*

"Jesus, Menna! No! No, Menna, no!… I hope that bastard hasn't hurt you! *No…. no… no…*" Not knowing what the hell she was doing, she dragged on her coat, grabbed her car keys and headed for the door.

"Start, you bastard, start!" She spoke to her car, which often mess about after being left for any length of time. Bingo. It started the third time. And if there was ever a good reason for breaking the speed limit, this one was it.

It was now 11:30pm. As Cynthia approached her sister's flat, she wished the neighbour that was so full of information could come now. If she had to, she would knock everybody up. This was her one and only sister.

When she got to the door, she stood for a few seconds. A chilling feeling told her *something* was *terribly* wrong. How could it not be? The terror on her answerphone was too gruesome for it to be ok. She pushed the key she had kept since living there. She could hear her own breathing. The flat was in darkness but still she called, "Menz?… Sis'?"… She felt for the switch and flicked the light on. "Menna!" She stopped when she got to the living-room. Droplets of blood on the wooden floor made her heart beat faster. "No… no…. No!" She felt the fear but did it anyway: walked to the bedroom. Her heart was beating like a drum. "Menz…" She didn't expect her to answer. "Oh, Lord! Ohhh Lord! Menna!" Menna wasn't there. She looked around the empty morbid room. A pool of dried blood in one corner: the end of a mobile phone charger set in it. A ruffled bed upon which a single red paper rose lay. "Oh my God," Cynthia whispered now. "He's killed her. Nico has killed my sister… but where is she? Where is her body?" She followed the droplets of blood and found that it trailed to the bathroom and to the living-room.

But it was when she ended the call to West Midland Police that Cynthia really sat down and cried.

* * *

Cynthia had to be slightly sedated when the investigating team of officers arrived. Giving credit where credit was due, they reached in less than ten minutes.

"Ms Jarrett," a police officer that had more gadgets bulging from his person than he could possibly need in any one day, said, "the tape on your answerphone?"

"Yes?"

"You haven't deleted it have you?"

"Of course not. Do I look stupid?"

He understood her temperament.

"He's killed my sister. I know it. But what the fuck has he done with her?"

"That's exactly what we're going to try and find out, Miss Jarrett. But first we have to listen to the tape. The forensic team is gathering information from all over the flat: DNA samples and what have you."

Cynthia watched as men in white attire trundled around her sister's flat, dusting up and dusting down, taking samples, fingerprints: anything they needed to solve the mystery of what really happened in her sister's flat that terrible night.

"Two of my officers will accompany you to your flat. They'll retrieve and take the tape away for scrutiny."

"Ok…" Cynthia burst into tears again. What am I going to do without her? It's not as if she's just away in Jamaica. The bastard has killed her… Jesus."

"Do you know where this *Nico* lives?" the officer asked.

"You guys should know?"

"Should we?"

"Yes. Years ago when my sister went away, I was staying at her flat. Nico kept pestering me. He wouldn't believe me when I told him she wasn't in the country. In the end it got so much, I had to call you, so unless he's moved, you should have a record of his address somewhere."

"What was his surname?"

"Nico Kaur. He's a Jamaican Indian… and anyway, you guys should know, Nico is a serial killer."

"He is… *what*?"

385

"A serial killer." There was a pause as the officers looked puzzled at each other, wondering if Cynthia was all there.

"… How d'you know that?"

"Nico is HIV positive. He knows it, but he goes around deliberately infecting women. Ok, it might not be killing with a knife a gun or bashing someone over the head in a dark alley, but it's still *killing*. Nico will have killed more people than any serial killer you guys have ever read about. Trust me." She wiped her eyes.

The officer looked again at his colleague, a butch-looking female with more bulges about her person then he himself. Lines of perplexity gathered on their foreheads. He jotted something down in his book.

"All done," a member of the forensic team said, "We should have all we want to start this investigation.".

"Ok, let's wrap it up," the strapping officer said.

"Miss Jarrett, are you ok to go with my officers now to your flat for the tape?"

"Yes."

"Shouldn't take a minute… and do you have anyone to stay with? You are clearly distressed."

Cynthia thought of Jeannette for a second, then she said, "No. I'll be fine. I just want to be alone… aren't you gonna ask the neighbours anything?"

"Yes. A few of my officers are doing that as we speak."

Minutes later, as Cynthia climbed into the back seat of the police car, she felt like a criminal. But that was the least of her problems. The main one goes without saying. Until they found Nico and put him behind bars where he belonged, she wouldn't be satisfied. But before that, they must find the body of her dear sister.

* * *

Nico sat in a small square room facing two Police Officers. He looked a little worse for wear. More than a little scraggly 'round the edges, you might say. He was losing that look he sported since he emerged from his mother's womb some years ago in Jamaica. A few good nights of sleep could have helped, but it wasn't happening. A shave too, but since West Midlands police picked him up at the crack of dawn, he had no time to remove the unruly mass of stubble that invaded his pretty-bwoy face.

After the usual preliminaries, the female officer took control:

"Do you know a Menna Jarrett, Mr Kaur?"

"Yes."

"And what is the relationship between you, Sir?"

Silence.

"For the benefit of the tape, Mr Kaur has evaded the last question."

"I'll ask you again, Mr Kaur, what *is* or *was* the relationship between you and Ms Menna Jarrett?"

"We were lovers."

"And when did this relationship end, Sir?"

"Five years ago. She left the country."

"And did it end on good terms, Sir?"

"No."

"Would you like to elaborate?"

"No."

"When was the last time you saw Ms Jarrett, Sir?"

Silence. He turned his face away.

"For the benefit of the tape Mr Kaur has evaded the last question."

"Three weeks ago," was his delayed response.

"You saw Ms Jarrett three weeks ago?"

"Yes."

"Where was that, Sir?"

"At her flat. She invited me round."

"She wanted to reconcile, did she?"

"No."

"Then what was the nature of the invitation?"

"I don't exactly want to talk about it."

"I see."

"And you're sure that three weeks ago was the last time you saw Ms Menna Jarrett?"

Pause. "Yes. Why?"

"Menna Jarrett has disappeared. We believe she might have been killed…"

"*Killed?*"

"Yes. And we also have reasons to believe you know something about it."

Nico sat back on his chair. He lifted his brows. "What reason have you got to believe I know anything about this?"

"Because you're lying, Mr Kaur. Three weeks ago wasn't the last time you saw Ms Menna Jarrett."

Nico was sweating. He ran his hands over his face and looked questioningly at the two officers. "I didn't kill anyone. You can't pin anything on me."

"So are you gonna tell us when you saw Ms Jarrett last?"

"I told you. Three weeks ago."

"Mr Kaur, my colleague is going to play you a tape. If at any time you want us to stop, please let us know. I think you should know that this tape was recorded only last Thursday. One week ago."

Nico looked puzzled. Confused. Irritated. *'What tape could this be?'* He wondered. But when the horror of that night was played out to him in broad daylight, he wondered no more... *'Jesus, Nico! Are you crazy?!'*... *'Maybe I am. Maybe you and your crew were a little crazy a few weeks ago when you strung me up?'*...

Nico held his head. He stood up... *'Nico... please don't... you're HIV positive. Please don't enter me.'*

He looked at the officers... *'Like I said... what's the worry? You're gonna die anyway, so what's a little HIV between old lovers?... And try that sudden shit again and I'll kill you quicker than I intended to.'*

"Stop it! Turn it off! Turn it off! Turn it of..." He fell to his knees, held his belly. Hung his head down and sobbed uncontrollably.

The male officer got up and went over to him. "Mr Kaur?"

"I didn't kill her." He looked up at the officer with pleading eyes. "I didn't kill her. You have to believe me."

"Could you sit back down on the chair, Mr Kaur?" He helped him up.

"You can't accuse me of killing someone until you find a body."

"And you've made sure of that haven't you, Sir?" the female officer resumed. "We have it all on tape. You said, *'I'm gonna make sure that no one find you when I'm done with you.'* So you will probably have a hard time proving that you didn't kill Ms Jarrett and disposed of her body."

"I didn't kill her! Are you deaf?!"

"Perhaps you can tell that to the judge, Mr Kaur." She stood up.

The male officer walked again towards Nico. "Nico Kaur, I'm arresting you for the suspected murder of Menna Jarrett. You do not have to say anything, but anything you say..."

"... No!!! You can't arrest me! You've got no body! I didn't kill her!"

The officer ignored Nico although his voice drummed his desperation into their heads.

The interview was wrapped up.

And like a prisoner of war, he was marched to a lonesome cell.

Once again, Nico felt like the day the doctor gave him the verdict of his HIV test.

His cell wasn't as warm as he would have liked it to be, but he was no stranger to a little cold.

"I didn't kill her," he said again when the officer turned the long key in the heavy cell door. "I didn't kill her."

* * *

Nico breathed a sigh of relief. He had to be released for the lack of sufficient evidence. With no body yet, and with the *coming-to-light* of another tiny bit of *something*, he could no longer be detained, but he knew full well he wasn't fully off the hook. That tape was too gruesome for everything to be suddenly ok. Until Menna's body is found, the Boys In Blue would be watching him. *Keenly.*

He couldn't take it. Not anymore. It seemed he had come to the end of the road. In the clear light of day, his deeds were upon him. As he sat in the living-room of his bachelor's pad, a drink in his hand and still smelling of the cell, he cast his mind back over the hundreds of women around Birmingham that he had deliberately dosed with the HIV virus...

The hundreds of others that they would have infected.

He thought of Pam: *God rest her soul. Beautiful, fun-loving, happy-go-lucky* Pam. She infected him.

Morag, the wife of a confused, money-driven bisexual black captain... Morag, to whom he had already given his real name, way back when at a jewellery party at his bredrin, Conteh's house.

Evadney. To whom he was *Sanchez.*

Bernadette. Another one who had his real name.

Sheree. To whom he was *Tom.*

Mitzi. To whom he was *Gregory.*

Lucy. To whom he was *Neville.*

Angie. To whom he was *Ricardo.*

And an added mountain of women whose names he couldn't remember. The knock-on effects would go on like a never-ending family tree. With *HIV* the new *DNA*: soon, a vast majority of the population of Birmingham will be *related. Trust.*

Nico sipped his drink.

He thought of his idrin, Conteh. Back in the days, it used to be *fun.*

389

Sex was *sex*, until the day they both took a sip from the same cup.

And *making love* was *making love*, until they both lost the love of their lives.

And when one day bitterness and the quest for revenge on the female population of Birmingham got hold of Nico, the course of history took a gruesome turn. Suddenly, it was changed... *forever*.

He thought of her now. *Menna*. The only woman he had ever *really* loved.

Menna...

Menna....

Menna...

He *hated* her strength, yet he *loved* it.

He couldn't reach her mind, but he tried.

Wanted to hold her forever.

Taste her...

Taste her...

Taste her until the life that was seeping away from him was replaced by the potent nectar of her *strength*. And in a perverse kind of way, he had tried to *own her*. And in his plan to take her life, he had believed he would do just that... *Own her*... *forever*.

Nico was at the end of his rope.

He was hot, yet a chill wind blew its blood-curdling gust around him.

It could have been *all so* different.

Chapter 22

"*H*eads are gonna roll, you know that don't you!" The shouting that echoed and bounced off every wall in the mental hospital made everyone sit up or even stood still and listen. "How the hell did you manage to lose her?! I can't see her taking her medication on the streets, can you?!" The Doctor in charge shouted.

Staff dashed everywhere looking in every hiding place, but Marcia had suddenly become the Scarlet Pimpernel. *Nowhere to be found*. No sir...

And heads were sure to roll...

On the inside...

And if they weren't careful, on the outside too...

390

For the lady was sick. And with no medication, there were no telling what she might do.

* * *

It had been two weeks now since her sister had gone missing, and Cynthia could count the hours of sleep she had had. And hearing that the main suspect was on the loose gave her no comfort at all. She had no family left but her brother Errol in Jamaica. Trying to call him to tell him what had happened had proved negative. Errol had proven somewhat un-contactable, so Cynthia gave up. She was drained. Work had understood and had given her as much time as she wanted to grieve, but grieving a death with no body must be the worst grieving ever. There would be no closure until Menna is found. She picked up again, for the tenth time, the picture of her only sister and hugged it. She wished she had half the *get-up-and-go* Menna had. She was strong. Vibrant. Ruthless at times, but she shone like the brightest star.

It was 8pm. Jeannette was on her way round but if the truth be told, Cynthia would rather be alone. She turned the radio on and found Father Jarvis there. He must have been covering for someone, for rightfully, that wasn't his slot. He helped. Warmed the edges of her heart a little. His cheerful voice told her that life goes on. But still, she had a long way to go. In fact, she hadn't even started. How could she? The limbo was killing.

The knock on the door prompted Cynthia to think that selfish, self-centred Jeannette must have managed to pull herself away from somebody else's man to come round to render a comforting word. Company. She walked to the door with her sister's photo still clutched close to her chest.

"Hey, girl! I hope you got that kettle on! An' some food! Mi hungry yuh si!"

Cynthia dropped the photo on the ground and the glass shattered all over the tiles in her porch. She lounged forward and grabbed the woman on her doorstep and landed a bitch punch in her face.

"Cynthia! What yuh doin'?!... Yuh mad?!" Menna said from the ground. She had fallen backwards over her suitcase and landed on her neck and shoulders in Cynthia's shrubbery.

Cynthia stood there covering her mouth. She couldn't understand why she reacted like that. "Menna! Are you alright?!"

"Am I alright?! I'm wondering about *you*, Sis'. What was that for?"

"Do you know what you put me though?… unless you're a ghost or something."

"What are you on about?"

"Jus' come inna di dyam house!"

Menna picked herself up.

"Where di fuck were you?" Cynthia asked, still perplexed.

Menna brushed herself off, heaved a full suitcase indoors for the second time in as two weeks. "What is it, Sis'? Yuh nearly kill mi? Have you been drinking?"

"Menna, where were you?" They were now in the living-room.

"I was in Canada with Clayton."

"Again?!"

"Yes."

"Menna that is a fucking selfish thing to do. And what was all that shit you left on my answerphone?"

"Cynth', let me sit down, cos I don't know *what* yuh talkin' 'bout."

"Menz, I walked in from America to find a message… You and Nico…"

She looked curiously at Cynthia.

"It's like he was killing you… Raping you… My machine picked up everything."

"Menna was baffled. "I didn't phone you then… I phoned you *after*. The next day when I decided to fly back to Canada, but your answerphone came on. I didn't leave a message. I planned to call you again from the airport but my damn mobile packed up completely. Then when I got to Canada and was about to call, I remembered that you would be in North Carolina for a week. Sorry, Cynth', but after that, things just got a bit busy."

"Things just got a bit busy? You are in Canada… another country… I don't know… and things just got a bit *busy*?"

"C'mon, Sis'. Lighten up. I'm here now."

"Jesus, Menna, you haven't got a clue what really went down, have you? And what the hell you mean you didn't phone me that day. It came from your phone. You and Nico's voices…"

Menna was still baffled. She paused. Looked down to the floor. She was thinking. Now she remembered. It was the only explanation she could give. When she had fallen, she hit her head on her mobile that was sat charging on her bedroom floor. That must have been it. It must have hit Cynthia's number by accident. "Oh, God. I think I know how that happened," she said, then went into the everlasting spiel of her ordeal with Nico.

Cynthia's mouth was wide open. "So… at the end of the tape? What was all that?"

"What?"

"Well I was just shitting myself when I heard you say *'Noooo! No, Nico, no! You bastard! Noooo!'*… Then there was a kind of *Ugh!*" Shit, I though that was it… I thought you were dead."

"I can't remember. That must have been when I found the strength to hit him. When I knew he was going to enter me. I had Nico's gun in my hand. It had no bullets. Not that I would have used it. I just whacked him hard over his head with it."

"Shit. What happened then?"

He was moaning and groaning. I wasn't gonna take no chances so he could overpower me again, so I bashed him hard again… he passed out. I thought he was dead."

"Jesus, Menna. Yuh t'ink yuh live inna some movie land or sop'n? This is Birmingham, girl… so what happened after that?"

"Ten minutes later the bastard came round. This time I held a gun to his head and promised him that this time I'd shoot. He could see it wasn't the one he came with and wasn't sure if it had bullets… I told him that I wouldn't shoot to kill. Just both his legs. I told him the police were on their way, and it was up to him if he wanted to escape. And that was when he dragged himself up and went."

"Oh my God… And what did the police say when they came?"

"What police? I didn't call them. I lied. I knew Nico wouldn't want to face the cops."

"Menna, it doesn't end there… Nico was arrested for your murder."

"What?"

"As far as the police are concerned, you're meant to be dead. I went to your flat. There was blood everywhere. After listening to the tape and seeing that, what was I supposed to think? I freaked, Menna. I had to call the police. Plus with no phone call from you… well…"

"Jesus. So I've wasted a whole lot of police time, then?"

"Yuh dyam right. We'll have to go down. You'll just have to tell them what you told me. The tape clearly showed that Nico was attacking you. If you want to, you can even press charges."

"Cynth', pressing charges against Nico is the least of my worries. I have better things to."

"But he tried to kill you, Menna."

"I suppose I tried to kill him too. It was my idea to string him up in the freezing cold outside Banana Baits…"

"What?!" Cynthia stared wide-eyed at her sister. Is that what he meant by *'I can never face the public again. Not after that stringing up thing'*?"

"Yeap."

"Is there a bottom to your depth, girl?"

"D'know."

"How did you manage that?"

"What? A bottomless depth? Or the stringing up of Nico?" she joked.

"The stringing up, silly."

"Me and a few others… I'll give you the run-down later."

"Gee, Menna…" Cynthia felt fits of laughter coming on. She couldn't control it

It was contagious and Menna caught it… "So you see," she said when the giggles had subsided, "he could have caught pneumonia."

"And you would be sorry for him?" Cynthia asked, wiping tears-of laughter from her eyes and spending the residue of laughter.

"No. I wouldn't be sorry for him. I would just have saved a lot more women from HIV and AIDS." She got up and walked to her sister's kitchen. "If you won't put the kettle on, *I* will."

Cynthia followed her. "So… apart from stringing up naked men, becoming a hero by triumphing against villains like Nico, then jumping on flights to Canada as if it was the number 47 bus, what else have you been doing, Sis'?"

"I'll tell you another day, Sis'… but you know I'll have to shoot you after, don't you?" she joked.

Cynthia started to giggle again. She couldn't stop.

"What is it now?" Menna asked, smiling again from the contagiousness of her sister's belly laugh.

"You! Ha! Ha!"

"What about me?"

"You! Ha! When I t'umped you down! Heh! Heh! Heh! Heh! Heyee!"

Menna left her tea-making alone. Hands akimbo, she said, "And you find that funny, do you?"

"Sorry, Sis', but I didn't realise I could punch so hard… Ha! Ha! Ha!"

"In the space of two weeks, I get a busted forehead, a slashed wrist then a bitch punch from my sister, and you think it's funny?" She smiled.

Cynthia was still chuckling.

Menna saw her sister now for much more than what she had ever seen her for. She was caring. Loving. She knew now that Cynthia loved her unconditionally. And she really wished she could buy her an everlasting dream to cling to. She kissed her teeth playfully as her sister emerged herself in amusement. "Yuh want a cuppa tea?"

"Yes, please, Menz." Cynthia dried her eyes.

The phone rang. It was Jeannette. *Would Cynthia mind if she didn't come. Melvin was coming over.*

"Who is Melvin?" Menna asked.

"A married guy she's seeing."

"Not that one where she stood next to his wife and bragged about her not knowing that she was in bed with her husband the night before."

"That's him."

But Cynthia didn't mind at all. Her sister was safe. That was all that mattered just then.

* * *

The police officer that found him was a Rookie... No *on-the-job* training could ever prepare him for this.

The ceiling was heaving under the pressure.

The rope was new and must have been bought for the sole, gruesome purpose.

He smelt of a prison cell.

The chair he kicked from beneath him must have hit the piled boxes of red paper roses, for they were scattered now, like a sea of peace offerings around his dangling feet.

Nico was a handsome man. Still a little scraggly from lack of sleep, but nonetheless, *handsome*. Not even death could take that away from him.

The last call was to his idrin, Conteh. *'Tell dem, Bredrin. Tell dem where to fin' mi. di door will be open. Mi love yuh, Bredrin... Mi love yuh.'*

As it was in the *metaphoric* sense, so it was in the *physical*: Nico had come to the end of his rope...

He tied a knot...

And hung himself.

And there they were… *A host of paper roses*. Still *living,* whilst Nico was *dead*. *'Paper roses…they never die… they live forever.'*

* * *

Sista Viola Prince kept her faith… Glad to be alive she prayed constantly.

Surviving such an attack from her own daughter was something, but now, the new worry of her escape played heavy on her mind. If she was safe, why didn't she come home? When she had visited her flat last, she could have sworn that Marcia had been there. Or else *who* would have sprayed an abundance of a man's fragrance? Jean-Paul Gaultier had lingered in every corner of her apartment.

* * *

"Hello! Hello!" Simone turned to find the attractive woman grinning at her. Grinning. Grinning. Grinning.

"Hello." Simone was in a bent position putting her shopping into the boot of her car in the car park above the market at the time. "Do I know you?"

"Hi," the lady said. *Grinning… Grinning… Grinning….*

Simone stood up straight.

She looked closely at the woman's face.

A creepy familiarity hit her. "Is something wrong?"

"Hi." *Grinning… Grinning… Grinning…*

Simone closed the boot of her car and walked briskly to the driving side. It was clear that there was something not quite right with the attractive lady.

"Hi." The lady drew nearer.

Simone climbed in and closed the door. She panicked now as she looked at her through the closed window.

'Is that really *her*?' Simone asked herself. 'Yes… it is… it *is* her… oh my God.'

"Hi." The lady waved at her through the glass. She looked harmless. Just spaced out.

And now Simone recalled the day she had watched the beautiful lady as she had stepped from a BMW Z3 Sport and walked confidently up her drive. *'Hi,'* the lady had said. *'You are beautiful.'* *'Who are you?* Simone had said. *'Where is he?'* was her reply. *'Where's who?'…* *'Conteh,'* she had said. *'Dear old Lover Boy, Conteh.'…*

'Excuse me?' Simone had perplexed. *'You mean he didn't tell you about me? My name is Marcia. You're Simone. I know.'*

Simone started her engine and put her car into reverse. She watched Marcia standing there and her heart went out to her. Slowly she released her clutch and gently pressed her accelerator pedal. Then she stopped. Pressed the bottom and wind her window down. "Are you ok, Marcia?"

"Yes. Yes. I'm fine," she said sharply.

"Ok," Simone said. She knew she wasn't, but what could she do?

She picked up her ticket and drove slowly towards the exit, and as she drove, she recalled again, the day Marcia came. *'Drink?'*... *'Brandy. Straight. Thank you.'*... *'Sit down, Marcia'*... *'No thank you. I'm not stopping... I fell in love you know. I didn't mean to, but I did. I've got everything. All I needed was someone to give me orgasms. All I needed. Just for him to make me come. Honest... But tell him I still want my fucking five grand back!'* And Marcia had switched again from a docile child to a she-devil, possessed with bitterness and hate. *'Your... five... grand?'* Simone had asked. *'I can see why he wouldn't leave you... No wonder. You're fucking beautiful.'* And Simone had never been so petrified in all her life. But her fear had heightened even more, when Marcia came towards her, slowly. She had stroked her face. *'He wouldn't leave you for me. You didn't know that did you? Said he loved you. Said he would never leave you. You bitch!'* Simone then found herself against the wall, her head hard against a ticking cuckoo clock. Strangely, Marcia's hands had propelled her breasts, gripping them so tight, she could hardly scream, her warm breath too close for comfort to her face. *'Liked these did he?'* Marcia had said in a deranged voice. *'Screwed him good did you? And I bet you have red silk sheets too, smelling of his after-shave.'* But the worst was when Marcia grabbed her private. A surge of bile had filled Simone's trembling mouth. *'What are you doing?'* Simone had shouted. *'Get off me!'* But within seconds, Marcia had switched again. *Docile.* She released her and said softly, *'I have to go, Simone. I have to go now.'*

Simone was jolted back to the here-and-now by the tooting of horns. In her deep thinking about Marcia, she had stopped her car at the car park's exit, not realising that a queue had built up behind her.

* * *

It was way past midnight… Sinister *visitors* were lurking in the dark, and the thought alone would send shivers up the spine of the *visited one,* for these visitors were lurking with grave intent.

Beneath an Autumn-bled tree and behind a fir tree outside Conteh's house, *one of them* crouched as if waiting for the victim of her planned ambush to appear. She didn't move much. Her plan was to knock, but the courage left ages ago.

And from behind the wheel of a car that she shouldn't really be driving, *the other* stared.

From different viewpoints, the women looked, not realising each other's presence.

One of them saw a father to her, and a father to her son: a man she had mistakenly slept with not knowing it was her own father. *Cerise.* In a few days time, a BA jet would be taking her, her son and her mother away from it all… But the memory?… It would stay. It could not be cut away. For the child would be a constant reminder.

And *Marcia*…

Dear old Marcia…

She was still possessed by his spell…

That *love-turned-to-hate* spell. She wanted him. No… not in the passionate sense. Not alive. *Dead… Dead… Dead.*

And as Conteh moved innocently across his mother's bedroom, his shadow silhouetting on her still proud nets, he would have shuddered at the thought of being *watched… Stalked… Wanted* for the crime of *'Acute devastation of the heart'.*

From behind the fir tree, Cerise held a knife in her hand.

Marcia held nothing…. You see, her weapon lay beneath her bed in her well-kept flat in Solihull. A bed behind which she had lain. *Still. Motionless*: as cops came looking for her, and went, unsuccessfully without her.

And so they sat there still outside his house. Both of them *looking… Looking… Waiting…* Even after he had drawn the curtains and turned the lights out…. Patiently… Patiently… they waited… waited… waited.

One sought the courage to knock…

The other relished the reality of stalking…

And tick… followed tock… followed tick… followed tock.

Then, Cerise climbed into her little car.

Her emergence from behind the bush alerted Marcia.

Cerise was going home. She pulled away... *Crying... Crying... Crying.*

But Marcia?... she stayed...

Looking at the darkened window as if she could see him. Once upon a time she was falling in love. Now...? She was simply falling apart. She laid her head against her headrest and drifted away from the there-and-then. Sleep took her. She entered into dream's darkness. *Insecurity.* Fading into time's dateless, timeless cuddles. *'Marcia!!! No!!! No!!'* The voice of her mother. Sista Viola Prince... And then... 'Marcia, No!'... And then...

Bring back, bring back,
Oh bring back my Bonnie to me, to me.
Bring back, bring back,
Oh bring back my Bonnie to me...

Chapter 23

"Thanks for agreeing to sell the house, Sis'." Conteh addressed both Sandra and Janet. He was sitting in the corner of Janet's settee an hour after picking at the Sunday dinner she had cooked for them all.

"No need to thank us, Conteh, that's what we planned to do as soon as you were ready," Janet told him. "It just feels so strange... the house we all grew up in, *gone.*"

"Well, you know what they say," Sandra added, "All good things must come to an end."

"I know," Conteh said, "I know... there's just one good thing I wish hadn't come to an end."

"What's that, Conteh?" Janet asked curiously.

"Nothing, Sis'. It's just me being selfish. Thinking about myself."

There was a cutting pause as the two sisters looked puzzling at each other.

"So where are you planning on going, Conteh?" Sandra asked.

"D'know, Sis'. Anywhere away from Birmingham. It's not the same without her."

"Oh God," Sandra said cynically, "Are you ever gonna get over Simone?"

"*No,*" he said assertively. "*Never.*"

"You've lost her, Bro'. Get over it," Janet said, though in a comforting voice. "Stop torturing yourself. Besides, even if there *was* a chance, Bro', you're HIV positive, she wouldn't…"

"Yes, but I haven't got *AIDS*. You know how it is… I might not even develop the thing."

"Bro, I don't know what yuh tellin' mi dat for. I'm not Simone."

"I think you're living in cuckoo land," Sandra threw in her opinion in her usual *straight-to-the-point* intense fashion. "I think you've been watching too much East Enders. Who d'you think you are, Mark Fowler?"

"Three nights running I dreamt of her, Sis'… we got back together… it felt so real… until I woke up."

"Damn right, *'until you woke up'*, Sandra replied. "We can all dream, Bro'. Simone is happily married to a gorgeous man… she loves him… you are HIV positive… the rest is history."

Janet gave her sister that usual *shut-the-fuck-up* look.

"*Well*," Sandra said, "he should have treated her better in the first place… stayed faithful. Then he wouldn't have lost her… nor would he have contracted the HIV virus."

Conteh got up and left the room. He loved his sister, but at times he wondered if her sense of compassion had crawled under a stone and died.

"D'you know, Sand'," Janet told Sandra, "your insensitivity is getting worse by the day."

"I don't think I'm insensitive. I just tell it like it is. You're just a permanent *Fairy Godmother* who cushions every Goddamn blow. Not that it is remotely possible, but how could he even *think* he could get her back?"

Janet kissed her teeth. "I don't know where you get it from, but I'm sure it ain't Mum."

"Has he told you what that last episode was about?" Sandra chose to ignore Janet's last comment.

"Him being tied up and left for days, you mean?"

"Ha! Ha! Ha!" Sandra couldn't help it even though it wasn't funny. The image of the dramatic night appeared again in her head.

"Shhhh!" Janet urged. She got up and walked to the door. Discreetly she peered out into the passage to make sure Conteh wasn't near, then she gently pushed the door shut. "He's not gonna say, but I think some score or the other was being settled. Some woman or women were being bitches. *She* or *they* tortured Conteh. It was no sex game."

"Ha! Ha! How d'you know that?"

"Did I say I *know* anything? I said I *think*."

"How's your back anyway," Sandra asked, remembering how her sister fell down the stairs after rushing to bring their brother a towel to cover his shame.

"It's ok now. I just hope I never have a fall like that again. *Jesus*."

"Our brother never ceases to bring drama into our lives, does he?" Sandra asked hypothetically with a cynical smile on her face.

"They were meant to be," Janet said out of the blue.

"Who?"

"Conteh and Simone... However their worlds might end up, those two were meant to be."

"Isn't that a little contradictory to what you said earlier?"

"No. I'm not back-tracking, I'm just saying they were meant to be. It doesn't mean that every couple that are *meant to be* together *are*, or *will be* together."

"And anyway," Sandra surmised, "even if Simone wasn't living the *happy-ever-after* with Lawrence, and she *did* decide to look at Conteh again, it wouldn't be fair. She could never really make love to him without a condom."

"True."

"And then there's the chance of him falling ill. Who would want to take that on?"

"Mmm," Janet said.

"And even if she decides to forget sex, it wouldn't be fair... how will she know how long he'll live?"

"How does anyone of us know how long we or anyone around us will live?" Janet asked. "How do we know if any of us will be eventually diagnosed with any life threatening illness?"

"God, you're morbid today aren't you?"

"No, it's true... I could walk across the road tomorrow and get knocked down by a double-decker bus, leaving all HIV positive people alive and kicking for years."

"You would love them to get back, wouldn't you, Sis'?" Sandra said. "That's why you're talking like that."

"You know, Sand'," Janet said, looking her sister in the eyes, "It's a hundred times better to live a few years with someone you truly love, than to live a lot of years with someone you don't."

"I hear what you saying, but isn't it a shame?... she *loves* Lawrence to the bones."

"I know. That's just it. And I can't see them ever being apart. He's sound."

"He *seems* sound, Janet. We can only judge people by the way we see them behave. Let's hope he's as *sound* as he *seems*, but sound or not, Conteh don't stand a hope in hell's chance..."

Suddenly, Conteh pushed the door and re-entered the room.

Thinking he had retreated to the spare room into which Janet had agreed for him to stay until he decided where he would go next, the girls were a little surprised to see him back.

"You haven't been listening to our conversation have you, Bro'?" Janet asked jokingly.

"Why? What have you been saying?" he asked, sitting in the corner of the settee from which he earlier withdrew. He stared deep and judgingly at his sisters.

Janet looked at Sandra. They both smiled.

"... It's true," Conteh said matter-of-factly.

"*What's* true?" they asked in unison.

"That it's a hundred times better to live a few years with someone you truly love, than to live a lot of years with someone you don't."

"You *have* been listening!" Sandra exalted.

"What else did you hear, Bro'?" Janet asked.

"He ignored her and said, "But she don't love me any more. And I know I don't have a hope in hell's chance, Sandra, but there's no harm in wishing."

"Cheer up, Bro'? Life's too short," Janet coaxed.

"Tell me about it," he replied, knowing his sister could not have realised her *no-pun-intended* remark.

"Most of the time my dreams come true. Good or bad, they come true. But I know this time it's just mocking me. I just know that if she was single, and I was the last man on earth, she still wouldn't consider it."

"Have you got any ice-cream, Sis'?" Sandra said, trying to change the subject.

"Yes. In the freezer... Are you gonna come to the Black and White Affair dance, Conteh?" Janet asked. "You said you would. You didn't come to the Red Affair. Father Jarvis is right, you need to get out more."

"Why not? I think I will."

"And pigs might fly," Sandra said, her head still inside her sister's freezer.

* * *

'I loved you in a way that I have never loved anyone before...' Marcia spoke at the crumpled mass of red silk she held like a comfort blanket in her hand. She spoke at it as if were Conteh. *'As intensely as I loved you, so you hurt me.'*

She sobbed. Christ, it had been years. You would have thought that the pain would have subsided just a little. And the red silk sheets; you would have thought she would have disposed of it.

'When we first met, I cried tears of joy... I was so happy... but you changed all that... you made me cry from hurt... anger.' She cuddled the sheet now as if it were him.

'You said you wanted me... yet you made me feel worthless...' She stretched out on her bedroom floor then scrunched her nude body up into a ball, wrapping, tying and tangling the memory-filled sheet around it.

'Said you loved me... but you couldn't leave her... first I loved you... then I hated you... love you! Hate you! Love you! Hate!...'

In her mind she saw her face. *Simone's face.* She wanted to *be* her. To become, just for a moment, maybe, what she was. Capture just a speck of her magic. In her mind, her own beauty was of no worth. No value. *'First you made me feel like I was in heaven... then... then... then you made me feel like a common whore!...* She raged... Then calmed... Then raged again. Then, as if it was her last ever words, she said in a vengeful whisper, ripping away at the already tattered red silk, *'Well, Sucker... though you have little power left... though you have just a morsel... I'm about to strip you of the little that makes you breathe.... Love... hate... bitter... sweet.'* She whimpered... Whined... Then, like an actress on a big stage, she rolled slowly onto her back, caressing her breasts with the *Jean-Paul-Gaultier-scented* silk. Finally, she tucked it gently between the meeting of her thighs. And *there*, she imagined him. *There*, she felt him. *There*, she wanted him... Conteh... Conteh... Conteh...

The brain...

The brain...

Oh the complex brain... How deadly the outcome when its rationale becomes totally unbalanced? *How deadly?... How devastatingly deadly?*

* * *

Scorcha yawned, stretched and eased listlessly into the *rhythm* of the night... The *rhythm* of *'rest'* that is.

The Dancehall Queen's body was seriously tired, and tonight, Black & White Affair or not, she was going *nowhere*. Dragging herself into her *'pit'* (as she called it) was a must, or she would crumple under the strain of *acute exhaustion*.

Every now and then it wouldn't be Scorcha who would tell herself that she was *mortal* as opposed to *iron*, but it would be her body that would spell it out loud and clear. And tonight it was shouting, *'Get your ass into bed, Darling, lest I crumble!'*

As she drifted into that well-needed slumber, she couldn't help thinking she would be missing a damn good night. Father Jarvis was playing. *Say no more.*

When there wasn't a sound-clash t'ing going on, like a faithful disciple, the lady would follow Father Jarvis to wherever his music would take him. And that was nuff places, since lately, it was difficult to imagine this DJ *sleeping*. Music had to be his food. *Seriously*. So there was no question that tomorrow, when ravers tell Scorcha how *'wicked'* the dance was, she would be gutted. But as it went, *gutted* was better than the thought of being picked up off the dance floor after flaking out from sheer exhaustion.

And now, as she drifted off, reaching that place just between the conscious and the semi-conscious: that place where *vivid imagination* lives, *family* was on her mind...

Her cousin Ikesha...

Gloria...

Kamilah...

And *Kunta... Kunta...* dear old *Kunta...*

And she had hoped there were some sweet sounds coming down... *wherever he was*. Her dream was about Kunta that night.

* * *

So as Scorcha snored, Father Jarvis was on the ball. No sleep for him tonight.

Winter had not yet set in, but it promised to be a cold one.

Warmth was needed in more ways than one, and everyone figured this was the place to be. They knew that Father Jarvis was the only DJ that could give a dance that would make the troubled ones forget their blues, and the Black & White Affair dance he had organised in the name of Love, Peace, Happiness and Prosperity promised to be the epitome of just that: *'Love, Peace, Happiness and Prosperity.'* Nothing more, nothing less.

Tickets were completely sold out, yet there would surely be people who would turn up wanting to pay on the door. Lots had gone on in the black community so far: *good, bad and indifferent things.* Yes, it had been an eventful year so far. Some would argue though, that a bigger dollop of *'Harmony'* wouldn't go amiss. So the *pulling-together* of faithful ravers under one roof would surely spread more love, laying a foundation for a new start, and this fun-loving DJ had it going on. *Chat bout.*

Anyone who was *anyone* was there, or was sure to pass through the doors of Banana Baits that Saturday night. Not much else was going on around Birmingham anyway. It was as if every DJ who was worth the mention had given up their own *planning* to support this event. They and their partners had already taken their places in comfortable corners of the club.

Most of the people who came to the Red Affair not so long ago were there. They recalled the amusing, yet devastating episode of *'the stringing-up of Nico'*, knowing full well that it would be a long time (if ever again) before such a block-buster event (or anything near) would present itself to them again.

Management hoped to be pleased with the takings on the bar.

Bongo Dee was security on the door. Remembering their last encounter, he nodded to Festus as he entered with Kizzy, Lijah and Gloria. Lucky for them all, Ikesha was staying with their children.

Reds, Faye and Roy followed them in. This was not a dance to be missed and not even the most *stiff-bodied* could resist.

Father Jarvis' voice, marinated with the sound of heavy baseline, pumped its way towards them as they climbed the stairs to the action-filled room.

Janet and Sandra followed a large group of *'Father-Jarvis-followers'* towards the entrance.

Even Sheree and Morag found their way to the exciting event. *Oh yes.* They needed something with a little more bounce and essence than the Belfry. Surely they would get it. Sheree was a little stiff, but Father Hovis would soon oil her bones with his musical lubricant. Morag couldn't move too well to the reggae beat. You see, the music would be *long gone*, and she would be *just coming*. And there were times too, when she would be gone, an' di music jus' ah come. Ah nuh not'n. Just as long as she found another Nico. It wouldn't be reggae music that she would be dancing to between the sheets, would it?

Time hadn't completely healed, or had even begun to wash away the memories of a ruined *matrimony*, but Yvonne had persuaded her friend Evadney to come out.

Poor Garnet had no choice. Tonight, he danced with criminals in a prison somewhere.

Lucy, dressed like Madonna, braised her way towards Bongo Dee. They weren't on speaking terms. Some *red rose* business. Nevertheless, the memory of his dick throbbed with the vividness of reality inside her. They spoke with their eyes as she eased into the club.

Heidi couldn't make it. A babysitter was to no avail.

Angie entered with a friend and searching eyes. She searched the dim room for Menna who had told her she *might* be there. But a last minute phone call would have confirmed that her *'might'* had turned into a definite *'chilling-out-at-home'* decision. Cynthia was doing the same.

Joya, Carmen and Colette, swung low like sweet chariots.

Lijah, finding himself a cosy corner for him and his queen, got more than a little flustered. You see, as he spread his arms around Gloria, he found that the two people that took up fixed positions either side of him were his worst nightmares. *Lucy* was to his left and *Bernadette* to his right. It wasn't intentional. Pure coincidental. They had not recognised him until minutes later of course. They soon moved away. Gloria was around, and there was a time and a place for everything.

Mitzi came too. Couldn't resist the hype. She had hoped Roy would take her, but he wasn't up to her *'leaning'*, so he chose to come with his family.

And there she was… *Jeannette*. All her baby fathers were at home or some place else with their women: later in the week, one or two might visit her for a bit of her usual *'give-away'*. And Cynthia wasn't her chauffer tonight; Jeannette had found a new friend to lean on. *Temporary*, but he would do. Hair done up to the nines, yet nothing in her brain beneath it, she walked through pretending she wasn't with her *temporary* friend. You see, the lights on the door were bright. The corner they would choose later would be much darker. They could never be sure *who* was looking.

And now… to seal the attendance list…the contrasting one…

The lady that spelt *trouble* better than *trouble* spelt itself…

It was a *Black & White* Affair, but this mysterious lady wore Red. *Red. Oh la la.*

She did not climb the few stairs that led to the dance floor. Instead, she stood in a corner below, where a sparing ray of light refused to shine.

It was 1am. Along with whatever else she held, she held her secluded corner. *Tight*…

… Now, from her corner, she watched him enter.

She knew he would come. *How* wasn't the issue… she just *knew* he would.

Conteh. He had come because that was to be his last rave-out in Birmingham for a very long time. He was moving out of the second city. *Feh real.* But for a man that was so *big on crowds*, suddenly, this crowd was *too damn big for him*. Still, he braved it. Dennis Brown licked out at him. *Music.* It was his first love. But it wouldn't be his last. *Simone. 'Where is she now?'* he wondered.

Father Jarvis spotted him. "Much love, Egyptian! Good to see you out, Bredrin! Nice! Nice!"

Janet and Sandra smiled from their corners. Good to see their brother emerged from the house at last.

Carmen, Colette and Joya's attention swayed towards the moving figure of their ex-lover as he made his way towards the small cosy area between the deck and the bar. If they hadn't known of his entry before, they knew then.

Conteh touched fist with Father Jarvis, then a few other DJs that stood around, then he eased himself into the corner by the bar. It held him. Kinda like a *'hiding-place'*, only it wasn't, for from her corner, the *mysterious lady in red* kept her eyes on him.

1:15am. *Lock down.* Lovers-rock sent every couple into a *'hol'-yuh-baby-tight'* position. Some serious foreplays were going down. *Dry sex. Groin-to-groin* an' t'ing.

"All who nuh 'ave a girl, fin' one!" Father Jarvis commanded. "Dis music too nice to waste, people! Yuh know w'at ah mean? Yeeees! Nice! Jus' grab a girl!"

Who could, *did.* Who couldn't, *moved alone.*

Conteh moved to the compelling beat. Attracting attention to himself wasn't in the game. His body was in Banana Baits, but his mind was on the other side of town. *Simone.* Why did he love her so much?

But as Conteh's mind set firmly on Simone, the *lady in red* set her feet firmly on the dance floor. Not to dance, however, but to tread its distance to where her prey stood. *Oh Lord.*

Sexy, yet deadly. She held a long object in her right hand. It looked like some kind of accessory. *'Couldn't you find a lady's umbrella?'* Bongo Dee had bantered earlier on the door. *'I like all things manly,'* she had said, winking at him. He liked that and eased her through with a smile. *Dyam flirt.*

A man eased sideways to make way for the lady's easy access to Conteh, not knowing her lethal intention.

Shit! Conteh clocked her! Saw her when she was practically upon him! Whoa!!

"D'you wanna dance?" she asked, holding him around his waist after leaning the long object into the corner. Before that, however, she had reached for something in the bag that hung around her shoulder.

"No... no... I's a'right. I'm not dancing." He was shaking like a leaf. He tried to ease her hand away from him, but her groin was now against his, and he had no room to move.

Father Jarvis glanced sideways and had convinced himself that Conteh was about to *rock-away*. How wrong. *How terribly wrong.*

"Why not?" she asked, still holding steadfast to him. "Are you refusing me?" He was wearing Jean-Paul Gaultier. *Shit.* He didn't know it but it turned her on.

Conteh tried again to ease her away from him, but when he felt the force of a protruding piece of metal in his right side, he danced. The corner he chose was seriously secluded. He had chosen it for his own *cradle*, but now it threatened to be his *grave.* Heaven help him.

"What are you doing?" he asked when he felt her right hand groping his balls from his left where no one had a chance of seeing. "Are you *crazy*?" He eased back, only to find the mouth of the small gun sticking in his back.

"We are all crazy, Conteh. This is a crazy fucking world."

"Ease off, Marcia." He grabbed her right arm and tried to stop her unzipping his trousers. *Jesus.*

"Release my fucking arm!" she commanded in his right ear.
He did.

"Now hold me... Look normal... We're dancing."
He did.

408

"Move and I'll *fucking* kill you," she whispered now into his ears.

"You can't do this?" he said when Marcia rolled his dick out of his trousers and started some serious manipulation shit. That was *not* normal. *No way.* But then the lady wasn't well. In more ways than one, Conteh's back was against the wall. He couldn't help it. It was natural. He began to rise. His knees became weak. Whoa!

Meanwhile, on the other side of the room, Carmen thought she could see Conteh having fun. *Dancing. Rubbing.* How dare he? Discretely, she moved across the room towards the cornered couple. She stood by them purposefully and ordered a drink. Conteh looked into her eyes. He was sweating. *Scared shit.* Carmen looked into his eyes. Then she leaned towards his right ears and said, "I see you're having fun."

Conteh said nothing. With his dick in Marcia's hand, and a pistol pushing hard against his back, he hoped Carmen wouldn't be in any long t'ing. He hoped she would just get her drink and go.

But Marcia did. *Said something*, that is. "What's your problem?" she asked Carmen.

"What?" Carmen asked, turning 'round and looking into her eyes, not knowing that the lady was not level-minded.

"He fucked you too, didn't he?" Marcia asked, still groping Conteh with her right hand and forcing her pistol with her left.

"Fuck you, bitch!" Carmen replied.

Marcia released Conteh. She stepped away slightly, leaving him shamefully vulnerable. He turned quickly into the corner, tucked himself in and zipped himself up, still not comprehending what was happening to him.

"*Bitch?!*" Marcia asked Carmen. "You're calling me a *Bitch?!*"

"And what are you gonna do about it, *Bitch?!*" Carmen asked, putting her drink down and turning to face Marcia.

These weren't children. They were two grown women.

Father Jarvis and all the surrounding DJs caught the gist of what was about to go down.

"Heye!!" Father Jarvis shouted. "Wha's di matta wid you?!... Dis dance is in the name of Peace, Love, Happiness ad Prosperity! Not in the name of war! No! No! Stop di fussin' an' fightin'!" But he had no clue that the rationality of this fussing was only one-sided.

After zipping himself up, Conteh had taken the opportunity to ease more towards the deck and away from the edge of the bar. The music went on and so did the two ladies. Marcia planted her gun-filled fist across Carmen's head. Caught unawares and on her sensitive temple, Carmen stumbled to the floor.

Father Jarvis stopped the music. The lights came on.

Now, Marcia held the small pistol towards whoever dared to challenge her.

"Shantamatilda!… Heaven help us!… What di…?" Father Jarvis was shocked.

"Bastards!!" Marcia shouted, reaching now for the so-called *umbrella*. Ripping the sophisticated red casing away from it, she revealed a deadly piece of metal.

"What the f…!" Conteh said under his breath. "Oh fuck!"

"Bastards!!!" Marcia shouted as if she was at war with everyone.

It was the dangling round of ammunition that hung like the milk-filled titties of a cow that made the whole club realise how much danger they were in. It was certainly no umbrella at all. No sir.

"Security!!!" somebody shouted.

But where was he? *Bongo Dee*. Someone else was temporarily holding the fort. Big and bold maybe, but at that present moment, he was *working*. Working his ass off. Under the stairs and in the dark. An old flame had sparked his fancy. An old flame who had no idea that *Nico* had *touched* someone that Bongo was *touching*. And before you know it, this old flame would *touch* someone else. And the rest would be history… So there you have it… a*nother one had bitten the HIV dust.*

Rat-a-tat-a-tat-a-tat-a-tat-a-tat-a-tat!!!!!

Now, it was the spending of ammunition that reached Bongo's ears just as he himself was *shooting* that alerted him. He pulled his dick out and his trousers up real fast and scampered towards the danger, leaving his conquest to emerge from their tryst with caution.

"Get down!" someone shouted. "Down! Down! Down!"

Rat-a-tat-a-tat-a-tat-a-tat-a-tat-a-tat!!!!!

"Nooooo! Help! Nooooo!"

Rat-a-tat-a-tat-a-tat-a-tat-a-tat-a-tat!!!!!

Where the hell did she get that deadly weapon? A pistol was bad enough, but it was obviously not enough.

"Conteh!!! I've got you now, Conteh!" the deranged lady shouted.

But she hadn't… Not touched him… not even the slightest graze… Saved by the deck, one could say. Like a rock-of-ages, it provided an ideal hiding-place for him and umpteen others who had buried themselves behind it.

Conteh was the chosen one, yet many had fallen in his place.

"G?!" Lijah called out when the confused gun-slinging female had walked fearlessly out of the room. "Yuh a'right?!"

"Yes... yes, I'm fine." Gloria replied.

Panic spread itself over the whole place.

"Festus?!" Lijah shouted again like a faithful shepherd, rounding up his sheep.

"Cool, man... Mi an' Kizzy cool."

"Reds?! Weh yuh deh?!" he shouted over the blanket of panic.

"Yeah, man. Mi deh yah!"

"Weh' Roy an' Faye deh?!"

"We're over here, Lijah. We're ok!" Roy shouted. And later he would be pleased to know that Mitzi had survived too. He didn't *want her*. But neither did her *want her dead*. Besides, Shari could not cope with another drama in her life.

Colette and Joya were *no more*. Like a pledge, they lay across each other. There was a time when they couldn't live together in peace, now, they were *dying together in someone else's war.*

Lucy lay upon the chest of a dread. She was dancing with him before the sting of the deadly bullets reached both. Now, blonde hair spread like a sheet over him, covering his face and his locks. They breathed *no more.*

Evadney and Yvonne had taken their last breaths together.

Funny, they were made from the same block, though they knew nothing of each other: Sheree lay uncannily upon Bernadette chest, simply because they stood next to each other in a dance. Morag lay to their left. They were all *no more.*

Janet and Sandra held onto their brother. Conteh stared into space. They were, all three, alive, but not kicking. Shock had gripped them all.

Angie was lucky. She had left only five minutes before the pandemonium.

"Oi!" Bongo Dee emitted a too-late call to Marcia as she strode towards the entrance, recognising the sounds of sirens. She turned towards him, made eye contact, then Rat-a-tat-a-tat-a-tat-a-tat-a-tat-a-tat!!!!! Now Bongo Dee was *no more.*

And moments later, well before the press had come like vultures, and before a myriad of boys-in-blue had arrived: when reality hit, the screams were enough to rip the heart away from the hardest of chests.

Ravers held onto bleeding limbs.

411

Unhurt comforted the *hurt*.

Blood flowed like rivers in a dream, its iron-fresh stench as high as it could ever be.

There were weeping.

Mourning.

Gnashing of teeth.

Knees had no time to bow.

Tongues, no time to confess.

Earlier they had laughed. Danced. Sipped various liquors from their glasses.

But then she came. *Marcia.*

And when she held the gun in her hand... the crowd laughed no more.

Something told her she had no choice.

Earlier the force of four policemen was no match for her, since she had gained strength ten-fold. She had got clean away and stayed away from their clutches long enough to create havoc like that.

Now, Marcia drifted away in the arms of a heavy dose of sedative... her sexy red number had lost it's appeal.

But like a message, *they* emerged, unscathed...

The chosen ones... The DJs... The well-needed entertainers.

What would we all do without them?

They emerged untouched...

Protected by a guiding angel...

Guided by the shield of Jah...

Father Jarvis...

Country Bwoy...

Mr Chat Bout...

Mr Sweetness...

DJ Clashington...

Lady Mutiny...

Sandra Irie...

. Federal G...

Rin-Tin-Tin...

Rankin' Trustus...

Skankie...

And the one, *Cyclone Quality.*

And there were more. The list was endless, but they all emerged from the unexpected carnage.

The message it seemed, was loud and clear... *'Go tell it on the mountains... over the hills and down below... shout it out to all those who are trying to shake it down... go tell them all... protect our DJs...* *'FOR REGGAE MUSIC MUST GO ON.'*

* * *

It was a whole month after the disaster at Banana Baits... There was a calm, yet the atmosphere could be sliced like a dense duccunnuh pudding.

Marcia was branded a *'threat to society'*. For a while, her freedom would be wishful thinking.

The press had had their field day.

Tongues had wagged.

Hearts were shattered, including that of Sista Viola Prince. After all, Marcia is still her daughter.

Lance had grieved, even though he had stopped loving Morag. No one deserved to go that way.

Bernadette and Lucy were bitches. And Lijah had wished them gone. But not like that. *No way.*

Lawrence was shocked and saddened about Sheree. A pest she was, but nonetheless, his ex. *'Don't worry,'* she had said on their last encounter, *'it's the last you'll see of me.'* And he had wondered if she had premonition of her own death. And he had felt awful too, for he had told himself that if he never saw her again, it would be his dream come true. Now, that dream was nothing but a terrible nightmare.

He felt for Lance too. Although love didn't live in their house, Morag was gone... forever.

Conteh had no words...

They had tortured him to a point of no-dignity, yet the deaths of Carmen, Colette and Joya were felt to his heart and soul. And he had known that their grandparents would take care of the children they had left.

Heidi had lost Bongo Dee, the father of her son. She would grieve for a while yet.

And what of the friends and families of the nameless?

Seconds. That was all it took. *Seconds* to beckon a sea of tears.

Everybody hurt... sometime. But this was the worst for a very long time.

* * *

413

It was in the Ruskin Hall that they gathered.

It was a long time coming.

A sea of *young* people spread their welcomed presence throughout the hall, outnumbering that of the older heads. It needed to be so. *Period*. Young trees needed to be trained while their vines are bendable, for when they are older they might not be able to depart from life's negative blights.

Their meeting was planned well before the latest disaster. They would touch upon it and other topics, but dealing with issues surrounding the youths of Birmingham was their main duty.

Gloria, Lijah, Reds, Festus, Kizzy, Roy, Faye and Mitzi came to give their support.

Kunta's friends stood in bunches of solidarity.

Miss Kryptonite: a loud *voice of reason* and positive female rapper had agreed to be a special guest at the meeting. She made no bones about saying what she felt about drugs. Guns. The destruction of young black people. And yes... the dreaded *black-on-black* killings: since we really are blind to see that the ones we hurt are our own goddamn selves.

Andre Johnson, aka STAL (*ST*reet *A*nthem *L*yricist), a young positive rapper was there to show his support. Young, talented and *need-no-one-to-tell-him-he-was-black*, his eyes were filled with dreams. But he knew that there were no use of dreaming without the presence of his young black brothers and sisters around. His lyrics were message-filled, and if his words could reach just *one* of his fellow-youths, he would have helped.

Ikesha and Shari had long gone known what time it was, and although lots of time had passed and a great deal more happened since the killing of her brother Kunta, time had only just permitted this well-needed gathering. At last they found a platform for their ***Don't Be Influenced*** meeting. Pleased about the turnout, they looked at each other and smiled. "Oh... if only Kunta could be here," Shari said to Ikesha. "If only," she replied. "If only." But since he was the main reason for this meeting, the question was a tricky one. A fine brother to Ikesha. An irreplaceable man to Shari. A precious son to Gloria and Lijah. A young man who had stopped living well before he had even started.

Shari had grown up fast. No choice. The sudden *taking* of her man, Kunta had made it so. She had two boys to think about. Menilek and Kunta Junior needed a strong mother. No time for sorrow-diving. A fine positive young woman, her head adorned in a vogue-like fashion of her own styling: a rich, vibrant-red material placed gracefully over a rich black, draped regally-chic around her neck. *It was Kunta's favourite*. It was his tribute. And how she loved him so.

Ikesha was ready for action. Her face said it, and her eyes oozed a kind of *'statement'*. A statement that was probably too deep for the untrained eye, or for anyone for that matter, to *read*. It was *passionate*. But not in the *bed* sense. No sir. A kind of *ready-for-action*, statement. Ready to draw out that *Peace, Love, Happiness* and *Prosperity* she knew was possible.

STAL was dressed in black. His eyes spoke *'volumes'* and his body language stated *'nuff'*. As always, he was as easy as Sunday mornings. Today he had come to *'reinforce'* a message. A message of *'fix-up'*.

"Hello everyone!" Ikesha started , throwing her voice zestfully out to the crowd. "Thank you all for coming... I hope that at the end of this meeting, the course of history will change somewhat..." She paused and looked around the crowd.... "It's time for us to wake up!... Smell the coffee!... Shake off the old head of destroying ourselves and put on the new head of maturity! Sense!"

Gloria looked on, proud.

The crown cheered.

Something seemed to be reaching.

"Let's not make no one change history for us!" she continued. "Let's do it ourselves! Another mother needn't cry! Another sister! Another girlfriend! Another dad!... *Grandmothers*" she dropped her voice solemnly now. "Grandfather... No... they needn't cry no more..."

A lump appeared in Gloria's throat.

"... Life is precious," Ikesha continued, "yet we're paying two many visits to the graveyards! Too many tear have fallen in the black community! I've lost a dear brother..." It was a grave sombreness that held her now. "*My best-friend*. Since that, an awful lot more young black people have fallen..." She forced back the tears and said, "They should be here!... They should be dancing!... Laughing!... Living!... Instead, they are lying in graveyards!... No! No! It's not funny! No one's laughing!..." She calmed a little... "I'm sure a few of you will have stories of your own to tell... Your own sorrows that you're bearing... Let's make a stand... We have become permanent headline fodder, feeding the nation with the latest news... Mothers?" she asked earnestly, "Fathers?... *Talk* to your youths... Youths! *listen* to your elders... Pride cometh before a fall... It's *our* destiny! Only *us* can control it! Let it go!... Let it go!... Let it go!... ***Don't Be Influenced!"***

Ikesha came to realise that her words were reaching. Perhaps this was the refreshing change that was needed. Words coming from someone whose age was not far off their own. A myriad of sombre faces looked back at her. She could feel the solidarity.

"And ladies!" she relented. "This meeting is not just about gun crimes in our city!... It is about us taking care of ourselves!... Literally! Among others, there is a drug out there called GHB... it is a rape drug. You've probably heard about it, but feel it can't happen to you!... Maybe you feel that that sort of thing only happen to girls that frequent the Broad Street haunts!... *No... It isn't so.... just be careful..."* Her eyes filled up.

Lijah got a little nervous. He wondered how far Ikesha would go on this one.

".... Self-preservation can only come from the *'self!...*"

The crowd applauded.

"... Let me see the hands of those people who *love* themselves!" Ikesha requested with confidence, and there was hardly anyone left without a hand in the air.

"We need to show that BLACK PEOPLE *CAN!* Let us stop being *statistics* all the time and start being *realistic*! We *can* make that change! It is true... at times we are much too blind to see that the ones we hurt are *you* and *me*! We can weed out all that!... but first we have to know how to *love* ourselves!..."

Young people touched fists.

Wrapped palms.

Hugged.

It was almost as if *positive deals* were being *sealed*. A new *PLEDGE*.

Now, Shari held the mike in her hand. She held it for a while before she could speak. She was speechless. Blown away. She had no idea that Ikesha could breath such passion to a crowd. It was as if someone had taken over her body and voice, and gave her the power to command solidarity between a host of young free-spirited youths. The applaud she got was never-ending. It went on, and on and on. And all Shari kept thinking was, *'I hope the youths we need to reach are here...'*

"Hi, everyone," Shari said when the cheer had subsided. "My name is Shari," she said in a calm, yet poignant tone. "I just want to say, I have two little boys, Menilek and Kunta Junior. Kunta, their father…" she welled up, "isn't here… First, he was pulled away by a devilish white substance… From the very moment he tasted, his life was wasted." Ikesha comforted her. "Then… the gun," she sobbed. "The gun… the gun took him…"

Reds put his head down. His heart wrenched. He was taken back to his own son, Damian, and coupled with the memory of Kunta, it wasn't good. But that wasn't all: he was *looking at* and *listening to* his daughter, a concept he hadn't gotten used to as yet. But he was proud to know that it was *his* blood that ran within her veins.

Mitzi glanced at Reds. It was almost as if she was reading his thoughts. And apart from that, she was seeing her daughter in a different light. She felt a little guilty about the way she treated Shari, and although it was too late, the fact that she robbed Reds of his *right* and his *privilege* to be a dad to her.

"… Please," Shari continued, "let's all make a stand for our precious black lives. There is no glory in self-destruction." She wiped her tears and gathered her voice. "Like Ikesha said, we have to *know* how to *love* ourselves… Let it go… Let it go… *Don't Be Influenced.*"

Now, Miss Kryptonite took the mike. She was the special guest, but it was her decision to speak last. She looked around the room for a few seconds before she began… "I came here tonight with a whole lot of stuff to say, but I don't know if I want to say them now… D'you know why?!" she asked with a hypothetic passion. "Because you've just *acted like you know!*… I *know* you've woken up!… I *know* you love yourselves!… I *know* you're tired of being some damn statistics!… I *know* that you know you're *children of the universe*!… I *know* you've smelt the coffee, so walk the right road, Bloods! Walk the right road!… Let it go!… *Don't Be Influenced!… Peace.*" She handed the mike to STAL in amidst a shower of applause, and the lenses from a BBC camera zoomed in. they had come to get the story.

STAL took the mike. "*RESPECT!…*" he said… "That's the first word. *YOURSELF!*… That's the second… How's that for a start, Bloods…?"

They cheered in agreement.

"… If we don't respect ourselves, no one is gonna respect us… If we disrespect ourselves, how can we expect others not to disrespect us? From respect comes Love!… Peace!… Happiness!… Prosperity!.. And only when we respect ourselves can we love ourselves!… And if we love ourselves, we will find it in us to love our fellow-youths! And only when we do, can we find peace, happiness and prosperity!..."

The crowd roared again and STAL hoped his words, like the others', were *'sinking in'*.

"... I'm not here to preach... just stating the obvious... *Pride* and *Persistence* is what we all need. Take *Pride* in yourselves. *Persist* at only positive things. Don't forget... *Pride and Persistence pays off!* Fact: It's all down to us, Bloods. Nobody else. I know it can be hard at times, but keep those chins up... it'll all happen in good time... Let it go! *Don't Be Influenced...Peace.*"

So young and yet so positive. And now, the roaring cheers gave him the backdrop for the appropriate track, rounding off his refreshing speech. Someone kicked off his backing-track and Andre eased into the track specially written for the event...

> *Some are distressed to the extent*
> *tear drops fall from their eyes*
> *Cos' being broke is da cause for their crimes*
> *But I tell dem it will happen all in good time*
> *So keep your chin up playa*
> *Don't bother waste your life on bitterness*
> *Keep saying those prayers...*

As if they knew what he was talking about, they cheered a heartfelt cheer.

> *... Looking da cake*
> *With more than da white icing*
> *sitting upon it*
> *We face da fact that life's frightening*
> *but we overcome it*
> *Duck for cover when da black clouds are coming*
> *But it's not about these crimes dat we over-commit...*

STAL needed no telling how the crowd felt. He could see... hear... feel... They swayed, whistled, cheered and pointed upwards, showing how much they were *feeling it.* Even Lijah, Gloria, Reds and Mitzi, who were real old-scholars moved to the *positive* wrap.

Ikesha and Shari were ready to shine. Both as beautiful as a brand new day, they had formed a kind of *'trinity'* with the young STAL.

Two rays of sunshine.

One fresh shower of rain.

An impressionable *'trio'*. Hopefully, together they'll make a *rainbow of hope*. For never before had it been so *needed*.

* * *

"**W**hat is it, Lijah?" Gloria asked a few days after the *D*on't *B*e *I*nfluenced meeting. She had found him lying alone in the back room.

"Just thinking, Babes."

"I wondered where you were. Anything you wanna tell me?"

"Just Papa Dread."

"Ok."

"He was one of the most positive elders in Birmingham, G. I wish he was here right now. He kept things together. You could always reason with him with your troubles."

"You have troubles?"

"No... No... I was just saying."

"I know. Papa Dread was a rock. Everybody loved him. Then he had to go and die on us, hey?"

Without words, Lijah stretched his hand towards her. He needed comfort. Only, he couldn't tell her how much. If only he could wish Bernadette away. For something told him she would be back.

And now, as Gloria lay in his arms, he placed his eyes on the picture of Haile Selassie. The picture that Papa Dread left him. And now, he read... *'Behold, how good and how pleasant it is for brethren to dwell together in Inity... It is like the precious ointment upon the head, that ran down upon the beard, even Aaron's head: that went down to the skirts of his garments;... As the dew of Hermon, and as the dew that descended upon the mountains of Zion: for there Jah commanded the blessing, even life for Ivermore.'*

* * *

'What will life in the USA really be like?' Jacqueline asked herself as she boarded the British Airways jet with her daughter and grandson. Not that she hadn't wondered before, but although all along she had viewed the migration as a refreshing change they all needed, today the reality of it all hit her like a ton of bricks. *'What if it don't work out?'* She glanced back, only to see that the strange, distant look had not disappeared from Cerise's eyes. The look that had been there for days.

She told herself that whatever it was, time would slowly dissolve it. *Hopefully*.

Tomorrow was gonna be another day.

* * *

Mitzi needed company… Her London flat was extremely lonely.

She couldn't stay at Shari's forever, and the isolation she was feeling was mixed with acute anxiety. It was almost inevitable, as the event of getting caught up in a mad shoot-up wasn't exactly an ordinary every-day one. They all had a narrow escape.

After the event, she had met several times with Roy to discuss the whole thing. She wanted much more, but cuddles were all he had offered. She had even contemplated buttering up to Reds, but it was almost as if she knew that *'the stone that the builder had once refused'* would now choose not to do any *'propping-up'*. Reds had pride. Oh yes… *Pride.*

Mitzi will surely survive.

Chapter 24

Sista Viola Prince pushed the door of the secure mental hospital once more. She was led there by security. Her beloved daughter, Marcia would be pleased to see her.

Unconditional. That's the love of a mother… *unconditional.*

* * *

Angie stirred her tea in a trance-like motion. It had been six weeks, but it was still kinda strange. She still couldn't get her head around how close she had come to being in the centre of that notorious mayhem weeks ago at Banana Baits when Marcia had struck, but worst of all, she had come to realise that she had she had taken a sip from a deadly cup. *Nico.*

What was the girl to do? The bullet was hard, but she had no choice but to *bite it.*

* * *

Mama Maya and Aunt Patricia were pleased to see Kizzy and the gang back in Jamaica. More than likely, the *'selling up and settling in Jamaica'* would happen. Lijah and Festus were all for it. And with the menacing Baby Face Glen out of the picture, Gloria and Kizzy could breathe easy.

Although it wasn't a perfect life, they were looking forward.

Although Gloria and Kizzy knew and accepted the fact that they both tasted the same man – *Baby Face Glen*, Gloria and Festus had not even the faintest idea that Lijah tasted Kizzy. *But which couple really know everything about each other?*

And Festus was none the wiser that dear Fari wasn't his son.

And Lijah still had no idea that Kizzy was his half sister.

Maybe, one day, they'll come out in the open. And if they do, they'll deal with each issue the best they can. But for now, their world just keeps on turning.

Ikesha didn't fancy moving to Jamaica. Not yet anyway. And something told them all, she was gonna be just fine.

But amidst it all, another wonder had happened: Aunt Patricia was getting on in age. Her heart wasn't exactly ready for it, but she had no choice but to deal with it. Among the bunch was Fiona, the daughter she had given up. A daughter she had told in a letter, how she came to *be*. Fiona had decided to wash her hands of her mother after examining her life, but it's never too late for a shower of rain. In the thick of life, everyone seems to eventually find his or her *'supper time'*. Everyone knows just when to *'come home'*.

***

'So what about Lijah and Gloria?' I hear you ask. *'Didn't Lijah copulate with Bernadette, dipping his wick into the oil that Nico had already dipped his?'*

Well, you see, it's just *one of those things*. That's just it. Nothing more, nothing less. Similar questions may well be directed to all ye who have no intention of rendering themselves *celibate*, and do not own a crystal ball. For as long as our lives are built on trust and trust alone, none of us can *really* be sure *if* or *when* Mr HIV is going to knock upon our doors. Bird flu might take our minds away from its quiet relentless storm for a short moment, but for every breath we take, HIV will claim another victim. The percentage of unanimous infected people in Birmingham alone, has risen since the last time you breathed. *Fact.*

It's the world we live in. Like it or not, we must put that in our pipes and smoke it.

People are *weak* and the carnal flesh temptingly *sweet*.

And what we don't know won't hurt us. Not until the day it slaps us in the face like the blistering vengeance of hell.

As we speak, at least five people you know are having affairs. They're not using protection, but still, they go home to their partners' beds... So Lijah and Gloria?... they're not alone. No sir... *Not in the least*.

* * *

It was inevitable, but when Reds and Shari had first sat down to talk, it was sure awkward. They were both mature people, so they both knew that the Daddy/daughter relationship had somewhat missed the boat. A *kinship* was however possible. They had pledged to take one day at a time. They weren't completely strangers, but needed time to handle their new relationship. And Reds had thought, *'I haven't much, but at least what I have will go to my blood-daughter and my grand-children'*.

Chapter 25

𝒩obody but Menna needed a bigger brain to take in all the shit that had been going down over the past three months. And it was exactly that: three months to the day since the terrible shooting at Banana Baits. Her and Cynthia had talked repeatedly about it, and wondered what would have happened if they had decided to go that night. *'We just weren't meant to go,'* Cynthia had said. *'It just weren't our time.'*

Still, they were still trying to come to terms with it all, even though Cynthia's friend Jeannette was *nearly* one of the victims. Jeannette had missed it by the skin of her teeth, since her *'borrowed'* partner shielded her from a wild bullet. Her screams could be heard above everyone else's, as the brother lay helpless across her chest. Irrelevant after such a horrific event, but Jeanette was in the arms of somebody else's guy. And had that disaster not taken place, Jeannette would have taken him home and given him *starter, main course* and *dessert*. And when she had had enough of him, he would have dragged his tired ass home, showered and crawled into bed just before his woman had finished her nightshift at the hospital where she worked. So, that night when the distressed nurse was called to the morgue, the grieving lady had no idea her man was at Banana Baits in the first place, let alone know that his blood had flown like torrents of red wine over Jeannette,

422

as she became trapped beneath him. She didn't know that, so it wouldn't hurt her. Only the lifeless body of her man mattered now.

Today, Menna and Cynthia had found some time to banter. *'Life goes on, after all,'* Menna had said. *'Moping won't help nothing. All I know,'* she had added, *'Conteh surely has got nine lives.'*... *'I don't think so,'* Cynthia had replied. *'I just think the one he's got is protected by the Almighty. Maybe He is giving him a second chance, so he can realise his naughty ways... Maybe He wants him to realise how much he hurt Simone.'*... *'You're such a philosopher,'* Menna had said, as she lightened up enough to tell her sister what she needed to tell her for a very long time.

"Sit down, Cynth'," Menna said, passing a glass of sweet white wine to her sister.

"Sit down? Bloody hell, Sis', what is it? You don't usually tell me to *sit down*? Shit, Menna, you're not dying are you?"

Menna chuckled. "No, Sis'. Not yet anyway. Far from it. I don't know if I'm *going to die* any time soon, I might be destined to be knocked down by a bus or something, I don't know... but *dying*?... no. There has been too much morbidity and dying going on around us lately. In fact, this little chat is about *living*."

"Living? What di hell yuh talkin' 'bout, girl?"

Cynthia had never failed to make Menna laugh with her dry sense-of-humour.

"A new life, Cynth'... me and you," Menna told her.

"Wha'?"

"Away from Birmingham, Cynth'. It's a great city but we've outgrown it. We need new pastures..."

"Speak for yourself," Cynthia said defensively. "I've already told Tricia I wasn't coming to North Carolina."

"... For me," Menna continued. "There are too many memories. I thought I was ready to come back, but I was wrong."

"Sis', I'm *not* going to Jamaica if that's what you're thinking. No way. Di man dem too rude. The last time I went on holiday, I was walking on the beach, and this man said to me, *'Whaap'n, daughta? Yuh pum-pum fat eeh? Mi cyan get a fuck aaffa yuh'?* " Cynthia did the action, the tone of a man's voice, *everything*.

Menna nearly choked on laughter. She was about to be serious with her *new life* talk, but she had no choice but to hold her belly and give way to the sudden attack of hysteria.

"And what did you say to him, Sis'?" she said, wiping her eyes.

Arms akimbo, Cynthia said, "Mi seh, *'Yes... mi pup-pum fat... an' it aggo stay fat, b'cause yuh would neva get a fuck aaffa mi. Go look fi a donkey or some dyam hole inna some wall'*." She spoke like a real Jamaican.

"What?!" Menna said, mouth opened wide. "That was a bit facety for you, wasn't it, Sis'? What if this guy had got angry and attacked you or something?"

"I know. I just didn't think at the time. I should have known better not to be so cheeky. I've had my share of backlashes. Like the time I went to an open-air dance and this guy asked me for a dance. When I refused, he cussed me and said, *'So whaap'n, yuh nuh dance wid man? Yuh is a lesbian or sop'n?'* He was getting really angry. Luckily, Errol stepped in."

Menna was falling over. She vaguely remembered her sister telling her that story, but today it seemed like a fresh one. Besides, she never tires of her sister's comedy.

"Then there was the time," Cynthia continued, as if she wasn't anxious to hear Menna's 'new life' speech, "I went to Spanish Town. A street vendor was selling shoes. He got really excited when I tried on a pair. He was so nice to me when I was trying it on. I suppose he thought I was *definitely* going to buy it. When I took it off, he said, *'Yuh want it, Mam?'* I said, *'No thank you.'* He said, *'So is weh di blood claat yuh was'e mi time fah!'* I was shocked. So with my cheeky self, I said, *'In England I can walk into any shop, try on any amount of shoes, walk out again without being under any obligation to buy.'* When he looked at me, I wondered what the hell possessed me to say that. He said, *'Don' tell mi 'bout no bombo claat Englan'! Go back ah yuh pussy claat Englan'... yuh likkle w'ite 'oman yuh!'*"

Menna couldn't' catch her breath for laughing.

Cynthia was giggling too. She carried on. "... Then I said to the man, *'Calm down. It's not nice to talk to your potential customers like that.'* By this time, he's flinging out his right arm at me, saying, *'G'weh! Yuh w'ite 'oman yuh! G'weh! Gwaan back ah Englan'! G'weh!'* By this time, everyone was looking. Cousin Charmaine was telling me, *'Come aan y'ear, Cynthia. Ah so dem stay. Dem nuh like w'en yuh try an' don' buy.'* Well you know me, Menz. I had to have the last say, so while he was there kissing his teeth and still cussing, I said, *'You are very rude. If you had let me finish, you would have realised that I wanted to buy that pair'...* I was pointing randomly to some shoes now, *'That pair... that pair... that pair... and that pair. But because you were so rude when I told you I didn't want the first pair, you've lost the sale of five'*. Well, his face was a sight to see. And so I went further up where he could see me. I bought three pairs of shoes from another vendor. I turned to see him looking. He was pig-sick."

Menna was even more creased up now. And when she had gained her composure she said, "But you could live in Jamaica, Sis'. I forgot how funny those stories were. You could give as good as you'd be getting. You are a force to be reckoned with."

"Yes, but it would only be a matter of time before someone box me down."

"Anyway," Menna said, "I've been living in Jamaica for the past five years now. There are lots and lots of nice, respectable men out there. They are not all rough and ragga. Those few you met don't speak for the whole Island. You could meet people like that right here in England. And not all guys chat you up by first referring to the fatness of yuh *pum-pum*." Menna laughed. The word *pum-pum* always had that effect on her. *Punani* was the other one. She wondered who invented them.

"Mmmm," Cynthia said sceptically. "Is that why the only guy you fucked in five years turned out to be Canadian?" she joked.

Menna smiled. "We won't go into that, Sis'. You just make me laugh. You should join the Blue Mountain Theatre crew. I'm gonna have a word with Lavern Archer. Maybe she can put a word in for you," she joked.

"A'right," Cynthia said. "Tell mi 'bout dis *new life* idea."

"You don't have to come, but I'd love it if you did."

"Come where?"

"Canada?"

"*Canada*? Don't you need nuff papers and all dat? Like America? All that green card shit?"

"Would you come, Sis'?... That's the question."

"Leave Birmingham?... *Whoooo...*"

"What yuh *whooooing* about? What would you be missing in Birmingham?... tell me."

"My friends."

"How many friends?... One?... *Jeannette,* who drops her nickers to other people's men at the drop of a hat, cries on your shoulders every Christmas because the man she happens to be with at the time has to spend it with his family?... Jeannette who spends more time on her hair, clothes and jewellery than her kids and uses her mother's house as a dumping-ground just so she sees the inside of a club every goddamn Saturday night…?"

"Menna?! That's a little bitchy isn't it?"

"… Do you mean *Jeannette* who lives off her *figure* since she has no *brain*, drops you every time she finds a new man?… And these men she finds every second, drop her as soon as they find out that she is not all sweetness and light, but a no-brain bimbo who has only her looks to live off… *Miss-every-man's-bed-warmer* come *pretending-to-be-Miss-Shit-Don'-t-Stink…"*

"Whoa!" Cynthia was shocked.

There was no stopping her. "… *Jeannette,* who juggles baby-fathers in and out of her bed like fingers juggle the keys of a piano?… *Jeannette* who can hardly wait for the other side of the bed to cool from her last fix before the other warmer climbs in?"

"Whoa!… *really* bitchy."

"Don't you mean, *really telling the truth*, Sis'?… Because you haven't told me I'm lying."

"Well…" Cynthia said, thinking.

"Cynthia, it's true and you know it. This is not about me being bitchy. It's the plain fact. I've read that girl for years, and I know she hasn't changed while I've been away in Jamaica. I don't bitch, I state facts. Jeannette is too damn superficial, Cynth'. A *friend* should be a *friend*. Not a fucking fair-weather user who only calls you to go out when there's no one else."

"Well… it's true. You're right."

"And she only visits you when you drives your car to pick her up,"

"True again."

"And can you remember the time she met the last guy, what's his name… *Ronald.* She dropped you in a flash. And to add to it, when this Ronald was putting you down, talking about how he didn't like her going around with you because he thought *you* was a bad influence and shit like that, the bitch didn't even put him straight! She just let him keep right on thinking that *you* were the bad one. What if you had gone right up to him and said, *'No Ronald. I might dance with men, but that's it. Your Miss-Shit-Don't Stink take them home and fuck them'.* How would she feel about that?"

"Menna?" Cynthia's chin dropped. She had no idea her sister had read Jeannette so well.

"I just don't like injustice, girl. And you knew all along that your sister don't beat around no goddamn bush."

"You could say that again." Cynthia took a big gulp of her wine.

"So... as I was saying, Sis'," Menna closed, '*what friends?*"

"Yes, but... *Canada?* To immigrate like that, we need money. It's a big upheaval, Sis'."

"Is *money* your only qualm?"

"Well it's a *big* qualm, wouldn't you say?"

"Well... in that case, let me pour you another drink."

Cynthia looked puzzled at her sister.

"We needed to have this chat for a while, but lots had been going on," Menna continued. "Not just the shooting thing at Banana Baits but lots more. I've also been busy sorting a few things."

Cynthia heaved herself to the edge of the settee. She had come to realise that her sister meant business. "God, Sis', you're a dark horse, I know that much... Talk to me Sis'."

"Can you remember a guy I worked with years ago?... *Peter*. Peter Walker. White guy. Worked with me at Key Chip then at his company Men's Bodies then with me at Black Star?"...

"Yes. I do. Skinny white guy."

"Well, not that skinny when I saw him last. I met up with him in Jamaica just before I came back. He travelled there more often than we change our fucking nickers..."

"A tell yuh one t'ing, Sis'," Cynthia interrupted, "You love that *F* word don't you. You'll wear it out if you're not careful," she joked. "Until you met Conteh, the most profanity that came out of your mouth was *bloody*. I noticed that it was after he came to your house and told you, over the candle-lit dinner you cooked him, that he was seeing that white girl, remember?"

"The fucka. And in his fucking telling, he forgot to tell me he had a black wife..."

"... Ok, Sis', c'mon, c'mon, don't start on that now, I'll never stop you. Get to the point. *Peter Walker*."

"... Anyway, Peter had become a big-time trafficker." She sipped her wine. "Cocaine. Straight off the Columbia ship, into holding..."

Cynthia's brain was trying to get the gist before Menna got to the end. "Yes! C'mon!"

"... Anyway, to cut a long story short, Peter ran a proposition by me. He wanted me to be a part of one of his runs. A real big one. And our brother Errol too. A few crooked Jamaican cops were gonna be involved... even a few airline pilots, believe it or not..."

"Really?"

"It scared me, Cynth'. Errol was all game, though."

"He would be."

"The plan was that an aircraft would travel from Jamaica, the lining of it baggage container packed with over 100kilos of class A drug, the street value of £10million."

"What?! How the hell would that be possible? All them sniffer dogs at airports an' t'ing?"

"Peter lived on the edge, Cynth'. He was very confident it would work. I'm no saint, but that was big... Anyway, as it went, the operation succeeded."

"No way..." Cynthia said in a low voice.

"... Yeap. Got through to its destination in Britain."

"Bloody hell."

"The plan was that in just one lick, Peter would sell his ware to a couple of guys. Big-timers. They would distribute it at another level. After that, it was no longer Peter's business."

"Bloody hell."

"Peter had always wanted to screw me... well you know that was never gonna happen. I let him live in hope. Used myself as a bait to catch this *money-hungry* fish."

"How, Menz?"

"I had a plan," Menna said with confidence. "I wanted to stop Peter in his tracks. I thought of the victims, new and old. The kids whose lives would be affected by this unthinkable amount of cocaine that would be eventually mixed with all kind of shit before it was passed down to them."

"So you went to the police, right?"

"That was the original plan. But things changed. Not that I didn't care about the kids anymore, but something new came up... I had a letter from Sharon... you remember Sharon, don't you? That blonde..."

"Yes, I do."

"The letter followed a text she had sent earlier... she must have sent it just before she died..."

"What?... she *died*?"

"Sharon died, Cynth'... I'll talk about that later."

"*Died*?!"

"Later, Cynth'... As I was saying, the letter stated that the shit that went down at Key Chip was all Peter's doing. She found out, and Peter paid her to shut up. She needed the money at the time, so she took it and shut up. By now, after reading the letter, I wanted to drive straight down to London and take the bastard out, but I calmed myself... waited... I wanted to look Peter in the eyes when I asked him about this."

Cynthia was aghast. "So. What did you intend to do after that?"

"Shoot the fucka and take at least some of his cash."

"Menna, are you crazy? *Shoot* him? Are you a gangster or sop'n?"

"As it happened," Menna continued, "Peter had confided in me... I knew when this big deal was scheduled to be done. He said everything would be clockwork. *'6pm sharp,'* he said, and by 6:30 everything would be done and dusted. The thought of Peter sitting in his London apartment with £10million worth of raw cash scared me."

"Yuh damn right. It's scaring me just listening to you." Cynthia smoothed her palm over the goose pimples that surfaces like piranhas on her arms.

"Anyway, I was supposed to be at Peter's around 7pm. He said after the deal he'd be alone. When he wasn't doing business, he was a bit of a loner, I know. Said he couldn't wait to wrap his around my sexy black ass. Said he just loves the way black women's asses pout outwards. Something to hold onto."

Cynthia laughed as her sister's pun in the middle of a serious conversation pulled her slightly from the suspense of it all.

"I was early. When I pulled up outside his apartment building, there were no movements, but after about ten minutes, two dodgy-looking characters emerged from the building. They were communicating. Somehow, I just *knew* they were connected to the deal. One, (seemingly the Don), kept going backwards and forwards to the front door of Peters apartment block. He was being let in and out again, after pressing the buzzer. I assumed Peter was letting him in. I was glad my windows were tinted. They couldn't see me, so they didn't know I was watching them..."

Cynthia covered her mouth. The image of it all, and the way Menna conveyed it was like something she would expect to see on TV.

"... After a while, they left. When I felt it was ok, I exit my car, locked it, walked up to Peter's building and buzzed him. *'Who is it?'* he asked. *'Its me, Peter... Menna,'* I said. *'Menna?'* he said in this real sexy voice, *'come in.'* He buzzed me in. His flat was on the ground floor. Well, Cynth', I nearly died when I entered his lounge."

"What?"

"You would have thought he would have put it away or something... On this big boardroom-like table, sat a massive silver case... Massive case. Not a size I'd seen before. It was wide open... The fucking thing was brimming with brand new notes... All in fifty-pound notes from what I could see... *'Peter?'* I said. *'Shit', are these real notes?'* *'As real as the fact that you are here, Menna. Just did the deal. I'm rich. Fucking, stinking rich!...'*

"Oh my God," Cynthia gasped.

'... Fact is,' Peter carried on telling me, *'I really don't need to do another traffic. I'm made for life. And it would even be better, Menna,'* he said, *'if you would share my life. I've always had a soft spot for you... you know that. We could have a nice life together.'*

"Shit... And what did you say?"

"By this time the man was pawing me. His hands were mauling my shoulders. Squeezing them. Well. You know how choosy I am. I couldn't stand it. I can't pretend when it comes to t'ings like that. Besides, I was blown away by the sight of all that raw cash. Nuff money... just sitting there... I was even convinced this cash turned Peter on. God, he could have raped me. No one even knew I was there. I could see his bulge getting bigger and bigger."

"Oh no, Menz. That Conteh has driven you crazy. Yuh put yuhself in some crazy situation since he messed with you."

"Anyway, I settled down a bit. We had a drink. Talked. It was around ten minutes to eight now, and just as Peter said to me, *'are you hungry',* his buzzer went."

"Oh no!" Cynthia was consumed by suspense.

"... He walked up to the intercom and asked who it was. A guy answered and Peter asked him to hold on. Apparently he was meant to be one of the guys who were there earlier. Peter clicked the case shut and told me to follow him and the case into the bedroom. Considering I pulled off a fucking robbery at a jewellery shop, and considering I went there with the intention to vent my anger at Peter by shooting him, girl I was so nervous."

"Shit! So what happened next? C'mon!"

"Peter said he didn't like the fact that the guy came back. He walked over and started clawing at the wall in the bedroom."

"Hey?"

"He had a cupboard built into the wall. Looking straight on, you couldn't even see that there was one. How he did it, I don't know, but all the edges were so perfectly flushed, it was unbelievable."

430

"Bloody hell..."

"The doorbell went again. My heartbeats were now racing so fast I thought my chest was gonna burst. *'Relax'*, Peter said as he placed the case in this secret cupboard and shut it. *'Stay here,'* he said. *'You can't be too careful. I just did a big deal. You can't really trust anyone in this game. There are vipers out there.'* And I thought, *'Vipers like you, Peter.'* Then I watched him leave the bedroom."

"Oh... my... God, this really sounds like something you see on TV."

"Anyway, minutes later I heard shouting coming from his living-room. Peter was arguing with this guy. This guy kept shouting, *'Where's the fucking money! Show me, you bastard! If I don't get it you're dead meat!'*... *'I haven't got it here!'* Peter kept saying. *'I despatched it off the premises minutes after the deal went down! I can't keep that sort a cash around!'*... *'But we've only just left you!'* the man was shouting. *'Yes! I know!'* Peter said, *'but like I said, I got rid of it literally minutes after you left!'*

"Shit!" Cynthia whispered.

"Well by this time," Menna said, "I felt sure that whoever this guy was, he was gonna start ripping the place apart. I felt sure he wouldn't believe Peter. I was pissing myself."

"What did you do?" Cynthia asked, almost desperately.

"I hid... in the cupboard... with the case. Shit. He didn't physically lock it. I remembered what he did to open it. I climbed in and pulled it shut. I nearly died. It was dark. Claustrophobic. I thought I was gonna have a panic attack. Remember when we were little and you locked me in the cupboard under the stairs for fun? This was a hundred times worse..."

Cynthia laughed.

"... So then I heard, *'Ok! Then take me to it, you bastard! Take me to wherever you dispatched it to!'*... And then... that was when I heard it."...

"What, Menz?"

"A bang... Not a loud bang, but a bang anyway. Then another... then silence."

"Shit!"

"Sis'... the moments after that must have been the longest wait of my entire life. *Silence... Darkness... Silence... Darkness...* it was killing. I wanted to come out of the cupboard but I was so afraid. Then after a while, I dared. I pushed it open and ventured out. I looked at my watch. 8:10. I hadn't really been in the cupboard that long, but being in that darkness, and with all that shit that was going on, it felt like a year. Anyway, heart beating, I tiptoed to the living-room… when I got there, I nearly fainted…"

"What?!"

"Peter and this guy were lying on the floor, Cynth'. It was horrible. I recognised the guy. He was one of the guys I saw talking outside the apartment building earlier. Peter was slumped over him. It looked as if they both managed to plug each other."

"Jesus… so you went with the intention of killing Peter, and someone did it for you."

"Yes, but although I don't know if I could *really* kill anyone when it came down to it, I still feel robbed even now. I was robbed of seeing the look in Peter's eyes after I ask him about the Key Chip fraud. I wanted to hear what he had to say to my face."

"Menna, that's the least of anything now. Besides, he would only deny it anyway. Worse now that Sharon is dead and couldn't challenge him."

"But anyway, just then, as I looked at Peter's face, I remembered something he said to me before… he said, 'I *will* make a financial killing, Menna… by *hook* or by *crook*'. And I couldn't help thinking, 'what a corny twist. You really *did* make that *financial killing* after all, didn't you, Peter'?"

"Never mind that, Sis', what happened next? C'mon. Shit, this is scary but it's exciting."

"Well, I don't know why, but I expected to see people outside. Surrounding the flat or something. I thought they must have heard it all… the shouting, the shots, everything. I thought any minute now, there would be sirens. Police. I thought they would be swarming the place, but apparently, Peter had soundproofed his walls, you know?… like studio walls?"

"Yeah?"

"So as it went, I was the only ears and eyes to the disaster that lay in front of me. I had to get away before anyone saw me. I was frightened. I wondered about CCTV cameras and things, so I breathed deeply and gathered my thoughts on how to move. I went into Peter's bedroom and looked in his wardrobe. I found what looked like a parker coat and an old trilby-type hat. I looked pretty stupid, but I put them on for disguise. Girl, that was the fastest I ever drove away from a scene. And it was only when I was quite a distance away that I remembered that I didn't even pull Peter's flat door shut. Anyone could have walked in after that and helped themselves to the contents of his flat."

"So… you left the cash in the secret cupboard?"

"Cynthia, have I got stupid written over my forehead?"

"You took it?!"

"Yes. But I gave it to a tramp I saw sitting on a corner in Shepherd's Bush."

"What?!"

"Well I hate to see people suffer poverty-wise."

"Menna… you gave a tramp £10million pounds?"

"Yeap. Just pulled up, tossed him the unlocked case and drove right on home to Birmingham."

Cynthia looked seriously disappointed. "Ok, if you must play Robin Sista Fuckin' Hood… well." Her voice dropped.

"Cynthia… there are times when I wonder about you," Menna said, reaching for the wine bottle. "The money is safely tucked away in Canada. Every last fucking cent."

"What?! How did?! What?! When?!"

"Anyway," Menna said, "before I tell you *what, how* and *when*, let me finish… The next day, after leaving Peter's flat, the killings were on the news, you must have heard it. Surely you remember the news about two guys found dead…"

"Was that them?! The other guy was somebody *Blacker*… "

"Yes… but that's not all. They said the CCTV picked up a guy running away from the block. And apparently, the CCTV weren't working before that, so as it went, I wasn't actually picked up going to, or leaving Peter's flat. Shit. I was so pleased about that, considering I had no disguise when I went in. My car was parked there too, remember?"

"God, that was close, Menna."

"Very… And there's more," Menna added.

"What?"

"The Police believed that the guy seen running away was responsible for the killings. He was even featured on Crime Watch."

"Well you know I don't watch that programme. It scares me."

"… But their ETD was way a little out," Menna said.

"ETD?"

"Estimated Time of Death… That guy was seen running away around 9pm, but like I told you, the shots went off around 8pm."

"So that mean they are looking for the wrong guy?" Cynthia asked.

"Not anymore, they're not... He now sleeps with worms."

"What?"

"The guy they were looking for is dead, Cynth'. You really don't watch the news do you?"

Cynthia's face was a question mark. "What are you going on about, Menz?"

"Remember the wedding reception killing? Evadney's wedding?"

"No way... Not the guy Garnet killed?"

"Yeap. *Baby Face Glen*. He must have been due for his share of the spoils from Peter. He must have gone there to see him. He was obviously running away for a reason. I'm surmising, but I think he might have got into the building somehow, went into the flat; since I didn't pull the door shut, saw the bodies and legged it. That must be when the CCTV picked him up. Straight away, he was a suspect. So the police were looking for him, but all they got was a dead man in a wedding suit in Birmingham."

"Jesus. I really didn't realise it was him," Cynthia said.

"No. Neither did Evadney. Perhaps if she had watched Crime Watch she would have known."

Cynthia paused to think. "Anyway, tell me how you got this money to Canada."

"Well, I'm sure you've heard of money laundering."

"Yes, but..."

"Well, you know it's a process whereby dirty money is made to look *clean* or *legal,* for that matter, right?"

"Menna, you are talking like a big-time criminal. What are you, *Ms Al Capone* or something?"

"No. *Ms In Control* actually... anyway, as I was saying. This dirty money goes through processes: placement, layering and disintegration and stuff."

"Listen. Don't baffle me, Sis', you are the one with the University degree. Just talk to me in Jamaican, will ya?"

"Well, excuse me. The last time I looked at your birth certificate, you were British."

Cynthia laughed.

"Money laundering is called what it is, Cynth', because *illegal*, or *dirty,* money is put through a cycle of transactions, or *washed*... not *literally* though..."

"I'm not that stupid, Menna. I hardly think it is actually put into a washing machine... Jesus. Gimme some credit."

"… Technically washed, so that it comes out the other end as legal, or clean, money. In other words, the source of the illegally obtained funds is obscured through a succession of transfers and deals in order that those same funds can eventually be made to appear as legitimate income."

"So… are you telling me you have £10million in a Canadian bank account waiting for you?"

"Waiting for *us*, Cynth'… waiting for *us*."

"But, How are you gonna explain to anyone how you came by so much dosh?… especially Clayton." Now Cynthia became the *voice of reason*.

"Cynth', she stretched the bottle of wine towards her sister's glass to top it up, "I have just signed a contract with Hot Covers Publishing, one of the biggest publishing houses around…"

"Really!… Christ, Menz, you don't tell me hardly anything anymore. You are so secretive."

"No. I've just changed a little. I wait to see light at the end of my tunnels before I shout."

Cynthia was thinking…"Yeah… but no one is gonna believe that a novel would gonna generate so much money, will they?"

"Warner Brothers," Menna said matter-of-factly, "have just asked Hot Covers for the film rights. They want to make the movie."

"What?!" Cynthia held her head with her wine-free hand. "Menna, when did all this happen? How come you keep so much from me, Sis'? I don't know if I know you any more."

"I'm telling you now, aren't I?"

"I really don't understand you anymore, Menna."

"Did you understand me before, Sis'?"… Anyway, as I was saying, whatever else cover do I need as a perfect money-spinning disguise? As far as Clayton is concerned, I've entered Canada with some savings. The money from the book and the film will follow. I just won't start spending until credits are rolling," she said with a glint in her eyes. "And even then, I won't be spending foolishly."

"And you won't feel guilty?… like you're living a lie?"

Menna smiled.

"Menna," Ms Voice Of Reason said, "I can't work this one out: nobody hates deceits and lies more than you. That's the reason you put Conteh and Nico through the mincer. So isn't it a little *double-standardish* to start off with Clayton on a secretive footing?"

"Cynth', I'm not gonna fuck out on Clayton. I'm just not gonna reveal the contents of my bank balance... Do you really think that I am going to know every last detail about Clayton?... Remember what Mum used to say... *'If you have four pounds, tell your man you have two.'* She did the same with dad. Did it kill him?... And I'm sure Dad didn't tell Mum about every breath he took either." She got up and wheeled her ass over to the drinks globe. The bottle of wine was all gone. She was celebrating. She needed the hard stuff.

Cynthia slumped into her seat. And before Menna realised that her sister had fainted - passed clean out, her glass had already acquired another treble shot of brandy. *Straight.* And before that too, the words, *'Here's to you, Conteh! Egyptian! Mr Vibes fucking Injection! I loved you, yuh fucka!'* were washed down by gulps of the strong liqueur. Now, she looked round to find the edge of her sister's glass. A toast was in order although her glass was near empty. But she soon forgot that. "Cynthia?! Cynth?!" She plunked her glass on the nearest surface, and the *slap-shake-prod* of her cheeks soon brought Cynthia round. "What happened to you?! Jesus! Yuh frighten di life outa mi, girl," she said, scolding Cynthia.

"Am I dreaming, Menz?" Cynthia asked dreamy eyed.

"No, Sis', you're not."

"You really have £10million in safe-heaven in Canada?"

"Well, no... just under. I had to pay a guy for his help in getting it there."

"Christ, this gets more intriguing... But is there such thing as a perfect crime, Sis'?" Cynthia asked, her mind working overtime.

"*Crime*? What *crime*? I went to see Peter. Someone shot him while I was hiding in his secret closet. I picked up his cash and left.... What *crime* did I commit?"

"You *stole*."

"Stole cash from a corpse?... If I had gone to the police, they would have probably tried to tie me in on the killings, the dodgy money, everything. So... I took the money and run."

"*Jesus*." Cynthia was still trying to grasp it all.

"Girl, you worry too much," Menna told her. "You're like Mum when she was alive."

"*Mum.*" Cynthia reflected for a while. "Mum wouldn't have liked this."

"I know. But I probably wouldn't have been so ruthless if she was alive."

"So, Menz?"...

"What, Sis'?"

"This guy you paid to get the money to Canada... how did...?"

"Yes, well, for a fee, I deployed the help of a gorgeous Italian named Mario."

"Hey?"

"I had seen Mario in the office of Key Chip before. By chance, I bumped into him at Heathrow Airport the day I flew in. He was playing at being a waiter. When he brought mine and Karen's coffee over, I knew I had seen him before..."

Cynthia listened tentatively, all the time wondering if her sister had undergone some sort of mind-transplant or something. Her sister was an ordinary black woman. As ordinary as any black woman that floated in an out of high street shops in Birmingham, and there she was spieling *movie material* from her lips.

"... I wanted to talk to Mario about the whole Key Chip thing... Find out if he knew anything." She chuckled. "Angie and this guy we met at the time thought I was chatting Mario up. As it turned out, in a weird twist of fate, Mario is *Mr Money Launderer* himself. Fuck. No wonder he was hanging around Peter who had other ways of ripping Key Chip off than a few fake accounts on my Ledger. Anyway, in the end, Mario ended up helping me with something I didn't even know I was gonna need him for: *Getting Peter's cash into Canada.* Shit.*" Menna cackled like a triumphant witch.

"Gees, Menz," Cynthia marvelled, "If you weren't the sister who I used to roll into the wet patch after I wet the bed when we were small, I would have said you were a genius."

"Oh... no mater, you can still call me *genius.*"

Cynthia smiled and shook her head.

"So you see," Menna surmised, "we've both got mean streaks after all."

"Mean streaks with a cause," Cynthia added.

"With a *cause*, Sis'. With a *cause*." Menna smiled. "But your *cause* made mum beat my ass every morning. Mine made you stinking rich."

"I still can't believe it though, Menz. Will we really get away with this?"

"Like I said, you worry too much. I just wish I could find you a man to go along with this cash. You need some regular *Vitamin S.* Cobwebs can grow you know."

"Hah! Hah! Hah!" Cynthia was reminded why she loved her sister so. "Don't be silly, sex is not all I want a man for."

"I'm only joking, Sis'. You're my sister. I know you want more than that. Why do you think I've been so worried about you finding a good man? You need life-long loving… the works."

"Pour me some a dat whisky," Cynthia said.

"Heye… Easy…" Menna said.

* * *

Conteh had passed by to see her… *Glenda*… Of late, his conscience had surfaced and it was pricking. *Sharp*.

She was having a sober day, and for the first time in a very long time they talked. He asked her forgiveness. The way he treated her was appalling, but she was no better. She too had searched for *gold*, but found *rubble. Ah nuh not'n.*

Glenda talked of Peter's death and Conteh detected a trace of regret in her voice. Maybe she was thinking that if she had stayed with Peter, he wouldn't have come to such an end. *Too late*, however.

That was a few days ago…

But now, as Conteh sat in his car outside Janet's place reflecting and thanking God he was breathing, the reckoning of events in his life so far was so surreal, it could be likened to a blockbuster movie. Yet, of all the happenings, he didn't know why he was transported to one special day in his and Simone's life: one day on their honeymoon when he had playfully asked her, *'Would you really love me in sickness and in health?'* And she had replied a sincere *'yes'*… *'And what if I develop a terminally ill condition tomorrow?… would you still stay with me?'* And she had replied, *'Of course I would'*, *'And what if I couldn't make love to you?'* he had asked, smiling at the seemingly remoteness of its likeliness. *'Conteh,'* Simone had replied, *'sex isn't everything. I love it, but I can live without it… and so can you.'* And he had laughed, thinking how ridiculous the statement was.

And now, as he closed his eyes and saw her face, he knew that the only person that Simone would be loving *'in sickness and in health'*, would be her dear husband, Lawrence. Life's a bitch, but there was nothing he could do about it.

So Conteh turned his mind now to the night at Banana Baits. Like everyone else who had survived the disaster that night, he was still having problems grasping the fact that it really happened. But unlike the others, somehow, he was strangled by guilt. Strangled at the

438

thought that he was the main player in the *'hell that had broken loose'* that night. And in his reflecting, he had captured all the other surreal events that led up to that crucial night, packaged them in one, and attributed it to *one day*. For it felt like it. *One day*. Like a cluster of heavy, dark clouds, the whole thing gathered in his head. Now, it spun round and round, threatening to take what was left of his sanity. Years of actions, reactions and knock-on effects rolled around in his mind as just *one day... One awful day... One day of judgement... One day of hell...* And he had seen it as *'The Day Hell Broke Loose'*.

'Lives are precious', he thought to himself, yet in his recalling he had seen lives as small stones of icicles hailing from the sky, hitting the earth, then disintegrating into nothingness. *'Where are they now?'* he asked himself. *'Heaven? Or hell?'*

He closed his eyes and counted...

Pam, the beautiful lady from whom he had contracted the HIV virus. *Dead.*

Nico, his best friend: a serial HIV infector who had gotten to the end of his rope and taken his own life. *Dead.*

Beverley, another victim of AIDS: a woman whom he had taken back to his wife's house while she was on a flight. *Dead.*

Carmen, Colette, Joya: his three baby-mothers who had died from bitterness long before the bullets from Marcia's gun, and well before the HIV virus had any time to develop into AIDS. *Dead.*

Sharon and *Melissa*: another two of his conquests: a blonde and a brunette who had decided to *'bow out gracefully'* in the name of *suicide*. If *gracefully* had anything to do with it, that is. *Dead.*

Evadney: who, herself, took a bullet caused by a rage he had triggered: a woman who once lived next door to him. A woman he couldn't resist satisfying, even though his wife Simone was next door. *Dead.*

Yvonne: Evadney's friend who died too on that same terrible night. *Dead.*

And what of the other he had known only via the grapevine? Not to look at, but by rumours: *Sheree*, some woman he had heard was after Simone's spotless husband. *Dead.*

Morag, a blonde who was married to a black captain. *Dead.*

Bernadette and *Lucy*, two women who had the same reason for menacing Lijah... *revenge*. Bernadette was *black*, Lucy *white*. But *menacing* has no colour. *Dead.*

Tracey, a blonde who had tasted Garnet, then decided that Bongo Dee's juice was sweeter. *'The blacker the berry, the sweeter the juice.'* *Dead.*

And what of *Bongo Dee*? *Dead.*

'Is this all real?' Conteh asked himself. *'Are these people really gone?'*

Then he remembered what his mother Gladys used to say... *'In the midst of life we are in death'...*

'But none of them had time to repent,' he told himself. *'And if it is so, that if your sin is as small as mustard seed, you still have no chance of entering the Kingdom of heaven, then... so be it.'*

Conteh stretched his legs, rubbed his eyes and tried to pull himself together. But when the r*eality* of where he had just been, finally sunk in, his heart pained. He wanted to shout, but it seemed the same thing that had taken his tears, had taken his voice. Now, a strange, yet comforting odour surrounded his aura. An odour only he could describe. A comforting one. One that took him back as far as he could remember. To when he was a small baby and his mother used to rock him close to her breast and sing, *'Hush Mama baby.'* Conteh was convinced that Gladys, along with The Almighty, were watching over him.

But without fail, as always, *she* was his final thought. *Simone.* Whatever else *had* or *would* happen in his life, he would always be lonely without her. In her hands, Simone held one half of his very being. Now, he sent his mind again to the night he had pulled up outside her house. He didn't know why. Just that he was driven to do it. And he had watched her dance with her husband, their silohetted harmony against the window mocking him into a tearful frenzy, Luther Vandross helping them to stir salt into his still gaping wound. And to top it all, Lawrence's gallant statue made him wish that he was lucky. *Why did he go*? It did nothing but brought back a whole lot of memories. Memories of the good times they had. It woke his pain. The moment reminded him of his loss. *'She should be in my arms,'* he had said. And when he had wondered what the hell he was doing there like a goddamn stalker, he pulled himself together and drove away.

* * *

There was a weird kind of silence in Lance's kitchen... From his lounge and through the silence, he could hear the clinking of a whisky bottle against a glass. It wasn't Morag. She was gone. Never to return.

Dead... Shot. He still could not comprehend, since he had no idea that the club she died in was even her scene. Obviously, she was in search of someone. Another black man. And where better to look than a club filled with them?

"Are you ok?" Clive asked, walking in with his glass of whisky.

"Yes…. Fine." Lance's voice could hardly be heard.

"Thought anymore about us moving in together?" Clive asked.

Lance looked at him. "It's a little early."

"Is it?"

"Yes. I need time."

"Time to get over Morag?"

"Yes."

"Ok…"

"Clive...?" Lance asked, gathering his thoughts. "Have you really considered what the world and his wife will have to say about us moving in together?"

"No, but you obviously have."

"Lots have happened, Clive." He sipped his whisky. "Let's take it slow."

Clive's face dropped. "I'm not rushing you. Take your time," he said.

"Sure," Lance said, stretching a hand towards Clive. "Sure."

Clive's mobile rang. "Listen, I have to meet someone. I'll be back later."

"Someone?"

"Yes. It's ok. Nothing to worry about. He's straight. Said he wants to talk to me about something."

"Right. What time will you be back?"

"Don't know." He kissed Lance's forehead. "Don't wait up though. After that I'm gonna pass by my house. Check on a few things."

"Ok. See you later." Lance got up. "I'm gonna take a shower."

* * *

The prison guard that found him wasn't at all surprised… The source of the knife that lodged itself with comfort in gut of the slumped corpse was no relevance just then. As far as the guard was concerned, it was a *payback* waiting to happen.

Conrad was found with his prison trousers down… And like a sorry uncooked sausage, his discarded dick lay pathetically by his side. It

441

was the ghastly thing that made the guard covered his eyes. Not a pretty sight.

For the last time, Conrad had tried his sodomite shit, only it was on the *wrong* man.

This man was much older than Lijah's youthful age way back when... much bigger than Festus' small frame... much more defiant to his ass being invaded. This man would rather to *kill* than to allow what was left of his spirit to be *killed*... Garnet... He had no regrets. An inmate had helped him to prepare... Briefed him on the character of the inmate he was about to share a cell with... supplied him with the avenging knife... And when Conrad had dared to hold him up against the wall, he had found strength ten-fold. Conrad had met his match. Oh yes. *'Every day yuh carry bucket to the well, one day the bottom will drop out'.*

'I'll take whatever punishment I must take,' Garnet had said after explaining his pending ordeal, *'but no man will ever violate me like that... no man. My ass was made for shitting.'*

Prisons... no beds of roses. None of Jah's children should pass through their doors.

Chapter 26

"*I*'m so pleased you have decided to leave Birmingham and come to live in Canada, Cynth'," Menna told her way into the long flight. "New place, fresh start and money in our pockets. Hopefully, you will find yourself a Canadian brother. In fact, who knows, you might just hit it off with Clayton's brother. He is meant to be flying in from Jamaica. *'A family reunion'*, Clayton said. Clayton's father will be there too... Wouldn't it be funny though?"

"What?" Cynthia asked. She was a little tired from the long flight.

"Me and you marrying the sons of a preacher-man."

Cynthia smiled. "I doubt it, Menz. I think my decision to marry someone so easy would be like pulling a dagger from a stone.... There was only one guy I ever felt that I would have ever considered marrying. I didn't even get to know him. I don't even think I told you about him. Met him at a dance years ago in Birmingham. I don't know, but I just felt he was the one."

"How come you've never told me about this guy then?" Menna asked curiously.

"I d'know. It was a long time ago. You were at Key Chip. It was about the time when you were having that trouble with that fraud thing... I didn't wanna bother you with some guy I had met, and anyway it was over in a flash, so..."

"Yes, but even after all that shit had blown over... we talked about other men... you could have mentioned it."

"Well, men come, and men go, Sis'."

"Yeah, but you said this guy felt *special*. I'd expect you to talk about someone you thought felt special."

"Yes. He felt special, but that's that. He's in the past. Spilt milk and all that...."

"So what happened, Cynth'?"

"He stayed at my flat after we got home from the dance. No nookies though. No way. You know I have never been quick at that. Then after he went back to London, BT cut my phone off. On top of that, I lost my diary with his number. I switched from BT after that, so that is how we lost contact. I don't even know if he had tried to call or nothing."

"Christ, Cynth, that's really weird."

"What?"

"Your story. It just sounds so familiar."

"Familiar to what?"

"You know when I came back?... when Angie came to pick me up from the airport?"

"Yes?"

"We got talking to a guy who told me a story just like that. He met some girl, blah, blah, blah... just like you told it."

"Yes, but there must be lots of stories like that, Menz. I doubt if that guy would be my Vincent."

"Vincent!"

"What!"

"That was his name... Vincent! Don't tell me that's a coincidence."

"Nuff Blackman name Vincent... Describe him."

"Tall. Muscular. Talks a lot. Quite good-looking. Couldn't place his accent though, and I didn't ask, I wanted to go. And I was afraid if I asked, Ang' and I would get the low-down on it all. He could really chat."

"Well, the only accent my Vincent had when I met him was a London accent."

"Yes, but he mentioned leaving England, so he travelled. But the accent wasn't of a particular dialect. It was like a mixture of quite a few."

"And he wasn't muscular. Fact is he was a bit gangly. But I liked him."

"No, this guy was *really* muscular. Looked as if he spent a lot of time in the gym."

"Well, I doubt it. In fact I can't imagine him with muscles."

"Cynthia, I couldn't imagine Peter Walker with muscles, but he developed them in abundance."

"Well…" Cynthia said, "We'll never know if weedy Vincent developed muscles, a mixture of accents and chats to strangers in airport lounges, will we?… I just hope things will be fine for us, Menz… in Canada."

"Don't tell me you're having second thoughts?"

"No, Sis'. I just hope this isn't a dream and that one day we're gonna have a sudden rude awakening."

"It's real, Cynth'. It isn't a dream. Besides, if you wanna pretend you're dreaming, why not? Dreams are nearly always better than reality anyway… unless of course they are nightmares."

"You know what?" Cynthia asked.

"What?"

"You always call me mother-hen, but right now I think you've taken over."

"And guess what?" Menna asked, as if she had come to the ultimate decision.

"What?"

"I've decided… I'm gonna tell Clayton the truth, the whole truth and nothing but."

"Yeah, right. And pigs are gonna start flying."

"I will. But I can guarantee he won't believe a word of it. He'll think I'm plotting another novel… Sis', I lay in bed last night running everything that happened in Birmingham since I reached back from Jamaica, to this present moment. It has all been so surreal, it would be hard for anyone who hadn't experienced it to believe it."

"Damn right," Cynthia said. "I'm sitting on this plane now, but I'm still waiting for someone to touch me and say, *'wake up'*."

Just then, the voice of the Captain alerted the ladies. The landing of the BA jet that had taken them from the drama-packed Birmingham to Canada would be in minutes. As if they had rehearsed it, the sisters reached for each other's hand and squeezed tight. "We're gonna be fine," Menna said. "We're gonna be fine."

"Yes," Cynthia second. "I reckon… We're gonna be fine,"

In the airport lounge Menna could see a curious head above all the other curious heads. She recognised Clayton straight away. His neck couldn't be stretched any further. Menna waved frantically at him until he saw her.

"Is that Clayton?" Cynthia asked.

"No, its Denzel Washington."

"Right. Well in that case, the guy standing next to him must be Wesley *fucking* Snipes?" Cynthia said through clenched teeth as if she thought the guy could hear her from such distance. "He's gorgeous, that's all I know."

"I don't know who he is," Menna said. "Clayton's brother, maybe? I told you he was due to fly in from Jamaica a few days ago."

Clayton walked towards Menna and her sister. The handsome stranger stood back, arms folded across his chest, giving off the sweetest, gentlest aura you could ever imagine.

Clayton held Menna and kissed her as if he had never kissed her before. "I missed you so much," he told her.

"Ditto," she bantered.

"Cynthia," he said, releasing Menna and kissing Cynthia's cheek, "welcome to Canada."

"Thanks. I hope I'll be happy here. It's a big change from Birmingham."

"I know, but I'm sure you'll like it. C'mon. My brother is waiting."

The trio walked towards the waiting hunk.

"Menna… Cynthia…" Clayton said, "this is my brother."

"Hi," Menna said stretching her hands towards the man's welcoming palm. She looked at him. He looked at her. "Haven't we… met?" Menna perplexed.

"I… think… we have. London. Heathrow Airport. In that little Patisserie…" the handsome man said.

Menna turned frantically to look at her sister, only to find her wide-eyed and chin-dropped. Cynthia was trembling nervously.

"Vincent!" Menna shouted, looking back at Vincent.

"Vincent?!" Cynthia said in a kind of whisper.

Vincent looked at Cynthia. *"Cyn…thia?!… Jesus!"*

"Vincent…" Cynthia was in a trance.

Clayton got a look in. "You guys know each other?"

"Cynthia...?" Vincent said again, ignoring his brother's question. "Will someone pinch me? Shit.... Shit... Holy shit."

"Right... er... right..." Menna was speechless...

"May I?" Vincent asked Cynthia.

"May you... *what?"*

But he replied only with the physical answer to his request. He picked her up, her chest squeezed tightly against his. He spun her round. And round. And round. She laughed. And laughed. And laughed. And when he placed her feet back on the ground, and when the airport lounge had stopped spinning, he said, "This is our second chance. It really is, Cynthia... this is our second chance. Do you realise that?"

"Yes. It's got to be."

"Let's make it the best of it," he said.

"And the last," she said. "The best and the last."

"Hey!" Menna bantered, looking at Clayton, "Get the feeling our limelight has been taken?"

"I do believe it has. But the world's is a big stage, Babes. There's room on it for us all. C'mon. Let's go. Vincent cook some real Jamaican food yuh si. Some yam, banana, dumplin, ackee, salt fish... you name it."

"You *cook?"* Cynthia asked Vincent with interest.

"What?" His sense of humour showed, "Is God a Black man?"

The roar of laughter took them all the way to Clayton's SUV. And all the way home, and thereafter, there were more laughter. And more. And more.

It felt like a dream...

A glorious dream...

But it wasn't. And even if it was, may they *never* wake up. There aren't many happy endings in this world these days, but this one is surely a whopper. So let the good times roll.

* * *

"Vincent and I shared different mothers," Clayton began in the telling of his brother's story. It was late. They were lying in bed together. "When I was two years old, my father went on an Evangelistic trip to England. He met a sista in the church. Well, I'm sure you know what I'm gonna say."

"I don't want to guess," Menna said.

446

"They had an affair and Vincent was conceived. I was ten years old before my mother got to hear about it. She found a letter from Vincent's mother. It caused a lot of problems between them, but they managed to keep it under cover."

"Oh dear," Menna said.

"Anyway," Clayton continued, "when I was 28, I went to visit my parents one Sunday for dinner. They told me that Vincent, then 26 years old, had contacted Dad. Rightly, he wanted to meet his father. There were no babies in the game now. We were all adults. Mum had no problem with it. When Vincent came, we got on great. Strange at first, but ok in the end. Vincent liked Canada. Said there wasn't much going on for him in England, and anyway, his mum had died very young."

"His mum died?"

"Yes. Sadly… Dad helped him to come over two years later. He couldn't really get settled with a girl. Every time he broke up with one, he kept talking about what might have happened if he had not lost contact with this *Cynthia* back in England. He felt sure she was the girl for him. Anyway, when one too many black women did him wrong, he decided to give a white girl a try. He met Michelle. They hit it off and got married when he was 33. But I still think he carried a torch for Cynthia all through his marriage. I don't know why the hell he didn't just go and try to look for her."

"I still can't believe they met up again. It's really weird," Menna said.

"I know. Fate, I suppose…. Anyway, at the time he was married to Michelle, I was married to Rose. Rose was beautiful. Clever. Worked for a top Accountancy firm in the City. Rose kept spending weekends away. Business trips. When it's not some office bonding shit, it was something else. You name it, it was happening. But I trusted her. I never suspected her of having an affair or anything like that, until one Friday evening. Not long after Rose had left for another office-bonding thing, an electrician mate of mine, Busta called me to say he saw Rose checking into a hotel with a white guy."

"Oh dear."

"It's funny, really. Busta was called out to the hotel to fix a problem with their electrics. He was standing on this ladder with his head up in the dark ceiling, when he saw this black woman checking in with a white man. As he looked closer, he saw it was my wife. He could see her as he looked down, but she could only see from his waist down, so she didn't know it was him."

"This is getting funny."

"When he called me and told me... well, first I laughed. Of course it *couldn't* be my wife, she was away on some bonding thing with her work... Anyway, he managed to convince me. I drove over to the hotel. I remember shaking like a leaf. My heart was racing. Busta met me at the entrance. "Are you sure?" I asked him. "How long have I known your wife?" he asked me. "I suppose I was hoping it was a mistake or something. Anyway, he could see I was about to burst, so he calmed me down. Asked me if I really wanted to see her in action. I was in two minds. My heart rate dropped after a drink from the hotel bar. And this is what I decided to do... I knew where her boss lived. David. Rich area. I have taken my wife there several times before when she   had to take him some paperwork or whatnot."

"You went there?"

"Yes. Anyway, when I got there, his wife opened the door. She knew Rose and me very well. Christmas parties, work dos etc. I asked if John was there. She said he was away on a business trip, in Vancouver, won't be back until late Sunday night. She asked me what it was. I asked her if I could come in. She was a bit apprehensive. Black man and that. When I first told her about her husband being in a sleazy hotel room with my wife she said, *'David?... My David?'* I said, *'Yes, your David.'* *'There must be some mistake,'* she said. After searching her mind, I expect she believed. I persuaded her to come and see for herself."

"And she came?"

"Yes.... When we got there, she asked the receptionist what room David O'reilly was in, and if he was there at that moment. We had already planned exactly what we'd do. We said we have some important paperwork for him. *'Yes, he is there, Mam, he just ordered room service,'* the receptionist said. *'Room 20,'* she said, *'the lift is to your right.'*

"Oh no. What a shock he's in for?" Menna said.

After three knocks, John shouted, *'Who is it?'* I changed my voice a little, just in case my wife recognised it. I said, *'Room service, Sir'.'*

When John opened the door in his dressing gown, his wife's face was picture. I just walked straight past him. His wife walked past him too. She followed me in. Maybe she wanted to physically *see* Rose... I found my wife in bed... lying there... Just lying there..."

"And what did you do?"

"Well, I must admit I could have killed her. I totally understood that minute, how someone could easily commit a crime of passion. Rose was so shocked, she couldn't move. She just held the sheets up to her neck, stared at me and trembled uncontrollably. I just stood there. Looking at her. Looking... Looking... Not saying a word. I suppose that frightened her more than if I spoke. Thoughts of murder were swimming in my head. But I made myself think consciously... All this time, David's wife was laying into him. Screaming... screaming. Slapping him... Then I couldn't help it. I don't know why I did it. I suppose I thought if I saw her nude, it would confirm it more. So I just yanked the sheets off her in one quick pull..."

"What?"

"Yeap... And there she was. Lying there in open shame. Nude. David had obviously just climbed out to get the door... He was about to fuck my wife. After that, it wasn't my wife I saw. It was a... *thing*. I don't know... I can't explain it. It was a weird feeling. I just kept thinking, *'how many times has this man fucked my wife?... Did she cover up?'*... All sorts."

"Deceit isn't good, is it?"

"No, Menna. Not good at all... It can twist anyone's brain up. Make you do things you never imagine you'd ever do..."

Menna felt her soul was on show just for a second.

"... I left the hotel that night and headed straight to Vincent's house. When I got there, he wasn't home. His wife Michelle was. I was so frustrated when she told me he wasn't there, I started to cry: something I hadn't done since I was ten years old. She told me to come in. Offered me a drink to calm me down. I told her what had happened. I suppose it was just the first person I saw... she started comforting me. Hugging me. At first it was just that. *Comfort.* But then she was coming on a bit stronger. I paused. I remember thinking, *'this isn't right.'* She was my brother's wife. I eased back, but she made a stronger advance. Started to touch me passionately. Kissing me... Yes, I knew I should have been stronger, but I was hurting. I was vulnerable. She was rubbing the inside of my thighs. I was confused. I started to rise. I wanted it then. It was just the moment. It could have been anyone with a comforting touch, I suppose. I became weak. Putty in her hands... She unzipped me... knelt down..."

"Lord, Lord," Menna emitted. "Don't tell me she..."

"… Before I knew it, my dick was in my brother's wife's mouth. And before I knew it, I was hammering her. From behind. Up against the worktop in the kitchen. She was making so much noise, none of us heard the keys turning in the door… My brother was home."

"He actually *caught you at it*?!"

"Right in the middle. Moving my ass… Michelle was actually coming. I thought I was a goner."

"Shit, Clayton, what happened?"

"He nearly killed me, Menna. My brother gave me the hiding of my life. How I escaped with my life, I don't know, but I did."

"Jesus… And what about Michelle, did he…?"

"He never touched her. Vincent wouldn't hit a woman, Menna. No way. That day proved it. I thought he was going to kill her after I left, but he never touched her. He told me, and Michelle confirmed it when I bumped into her a few weeks later. All he said to her was, *'Pack your things and leave'*. And that was it… They split, and Vincent went back to England. The truth is, I hoped he would have found the Cynthia he had talked so much about."

"Wow… *some story*."

"So, Menna, in the space of an hour and a half, three marriages got wrecked: mine, John's and my brother's. My mother was very angry with me for a while. Told me I was like my father. But I know I wasn't. I was just a broken man who the first female I started to tell my devastating news to, made sexual advances towards me. Started to show me sexual attention."

"So what made you and Vincent make up?"

"It was my father. You know I told you he was diagnosed with cancer?"

"Yeah?"

"Well he said it was his wish that me and Vincent should make piece before he goes. He said, *'Son, women come ten-to-the dozen, but you have one brother'*."

"I told him I would have no problem making peace with Vincent, but I couldn't be sure if Vincent would feel the same."

"And here you both are," Menna said.

"Yes… here we both are. I'm pleased. The family reunion is in a week's time at my parent's. But something else came out of it too."

"What's that?"

"We found out that Vincent shouldn't have married Michelle in the first place."

"Why?"

"Michelle was a prostitute. He had no idea. We found that out a year after the break-up. I hear she's now crippled with arthritis, and she's only thirty-eight. I suppose it's all those long, cold nights standing on the streets practically half-naked. It was bound to get her. Once the cold settle in your bones, well…"

"So where's Michelle now?"

"D'know. And I don't suppose Vincent wanna know either. It took him ages to get over the fact that the woman he had made his lawful wedded wife had slept with countless men for money. Which man could ever feel good about that? And which woman could ever feel good knowing she was once a prostitute? And the children. Fancy knowing that people know that your mother was a prostitute?"

"Clayton. I actually know a few women in Birmingham in their late fifties. Married with grown-up children. Of course they don't know that I know, but that was their lives. The oldest trick in the book, they call it. A few ended up marrying their pimps too. A few of them even tried their best to act as if they are the cream. I suppose as far as they're concerned, they are."

"Each to their own, I suppose," Clayton said.

"So all's well that ends well hey?" Menna surmised.

"I suppose so. Vincent got Cynthia, and I've got you…"

"And have you gotten over Rose?"

"Yes. Definitely… most definitely."

* * *

Meanwhile, in the dead of the night, and in a room two doors away, Vincent and Cynthia talked… and talked… and talked. And it looked as if the dawn would break and they would still be talking. They say, if two people are meant to be, time will surely bring them together. Even if it's in another life. But there they were… in this life… *together again*.

* * *

"So what about *you*, Menna? Anyone lingering in your head?" Clayton had asked after they resumed to the bedroom after they had taken a rest from talking to raid the kitchen for food. Like Cynthia and Vincent, it looked as if they would be talking all night.

Menna hesitated. Tried to remember if there ever was a time when she saw the world through *tinted-pretty-coloured* glasses. She couldn't.

Not even when she put her mind back to what she could remember as a child. *'The name of the game is survival'*, she told herself.

"No. No one lingering in your head."

"Anything exciting happened in your life worth telling then? Lately or in the past?"

"Me? Nah. Nothing."

"I don't believe that a woman with a boring life could write such an exciting book as *'Don't F**k With Me.'* There must be loads to tell."

"Well," Menna readied herself, "the honest truth is, there are loads to tell."

"You see, I knew it."

"But if I told you," she assured him, "you wouldn't believe none of it."

"Try me." He kissed her lips.

"Ok. Are you ready for this?"

"Shoot."

"Well… there was a man that I fell deeply in love with. For now, we'll call him *number 1*. He was married and have more women than he could ever manage…black and white… the lot."

"Ok…"

"He lied to me… told me he was single, so when I found out, I played him and his best mate, who we'll call *number 2*."

"How?"

"They were both my lovers. To *number 1*, I was *Menna*. To *number 2*, I was *Jade*."

"You are so funny." Clayton saw only the beauty of the lady and heard the clever way she was about to spin what he thought was a *playful yarn*. She was a writer. She wrote the most intriguing stories, so he knew she would narrate this story well.

"Anyway," she continued, "*number 1* riled me so bad, and I got real angry."

"Whoa!"

"I planned my strategy… I robbed the jewellers in front of his shop, disguised myself like a fucking mannequin, and walked into his shop… the bastard didn't even recognise me… I planted the evidence: loot and gun and all on him."

"Getting good, getting good," Clayton said, cuddling up to her.

"Then I tipped off the police… they checked him out. Found all the evidence in his safe… He got sent down."

"Remind me not to fuck with you then," Clayton joked, still believing she was spinning a yarn.

"Anyway, before that, these two guys both contracted the HIV virus from the best mate of the wife of *number 1*. I didn't get it, because I never slept with them unprotected."

"Go on," Clayton said, "you're doing good."

"Anyway, to cut a long story short, since I left Jamaica I had the urge to kick their asses some more: I gathered up a few other women who *number 1* had fucked with. We paid him a visit. Tortured him sexually... left him tied to his patio door for three days. *Nude*."

"Oh! Kinky!"

"I then lured *number 2* (who had become a serial HIV infector) going 'round giving different names to different women and infecting them deliberately) to my house. With the help of three of the same ladies, knocked him out, drove him to a popular nightspot and strung him up on a lamppost, nude, for all and sundry to see."

"Whoa!"

"I then went to London to see a white man who had pissed me off in the past... Way before I ever set eyes on number 1 and Number 2. While I was there, he got shot while I was hiding in his secret cupboard."

"Come on... you have to do better than that."

"So... I stole his Millions and left."

"Hah! Hah!... nice one, Menna."

"Later, the guy who we strung up nude on the lamppost tried to kill me in my flat... I got the better of him. I then came to see you here in Canada. Remember that cut on my wrist?"

"So, you didn't accidentally jab yourself on a knife that was sticking up, then?"

"No."

"Anyway, number 2 was arrested for my murder, as Cynthia thought I was dead. Later, he topped himself as he couldn't live with the shame, and the world was a safer place. And!... I got to keep the millions I stole from the dead white guy and..."

"...And now you're here with me."

"Yes... and now I'm here with you, my novel is hitting shelves all over the world, Warner Brothers has the film rights and so on and so forth..."

Clayton laughed. "So... in a nutshell, you used sledge-hammers to crack small nuts, right?"

"Damn right."

"Yeah right. Your spiel is a good way to steer anyone away from the truth, Menna. Weave them a yarn of plotted text. Well, you are a *writer*. What do I expect?"

"It's true, Clayton... never let it be said that I didn't tell you." She smiled at him. In a way, she felt a sense of relief. It felt as if she had done the right thing. Told it like it was, although she knew he would never believe her. But she was covered. If it ever came out, which she doubted, like she said, he could never say she didn't tell him.

"And you look so beautiful when you lie too." He kissed her.

"You see... I told you you wouldn't believe me."

"No, I don't believe you... but I tell you what?"

"What?"

"You need to write that shit. *Seriously*. As you were telling me all that, I saw it happening. Very dramatic. Write it Menna. *Seriously*. It'll knock 'Don't F**k With Me' off it's pedestal. The plot is brilliant. Warner Brothers would definitely want that one."

Menna could almost feel the glint that spurred into her eyes. "I might, Clayton," she stared into the distance and nodded her head approvingly. "I might just do that. I might... I might. One day when I'm old and grey. Then when I'm about to pop my clogs, I'd have it published. My grandchildren would benefit from the royalties."

"Why when you're old and grey? I'm serious, Menna. It's a great plot, you need to write it."

"Thank you," she whispered, climbing onto him.

Clayton smiled, dimmed the lights and peeled the sexy baby-doll from her body. And they both went to heaven... *again*.

* * *

A persistent pastor stretched out his hands to his congregation in a small Pentecostal church in Ealing, London. "Won't you come?" he beckoned. "The Lord is waiting to welcome you to His fold. Let not your heart be hardened. He will forgive all your sins. Just open your hearts and let Him in."

People walked in droves to the altar like humble lambs.

"God is real. Can't you feel Him *moving* in your souls?"

He focused now, on a man with sad eyes that had wandered in from the cold and had taken an empty seat in the back row. The man averted his eyes from the pastor's, his sins, he felt, too harsh to be bared.

"Won't you come," the pastor relented.

Why didn't he just go? The beckoning was clawing away at his heart. Besides, that was the reason he came.

"Open your hearts and let Him in..."

The pastor turned away now for a moment, but he could not have realised the joy in his eyes, when the lost man walked to the altar and knelt among the others.

"I will pray for you, brother," the pastor whispered, laying his palm across the man's forehead. "What is your name?" he asked, as if God wanted to know.

"Conteh," the man replied. "Conteh Gonzalez." The answer came with falling tears. "I was lost, but now I'm found. Blind, but now I see. But I know the Lord will forgive me."

"Aaaamen!" The pastor echoed his agreement and danced a circular dance. He settled into a whispered *'Hallelujah'*, then he continued, *'Dear Lord, I come before Thee again, with another Lamb that has finally found his way...'* He had found a *24carat-gold-sinner*, and was bringing him home, to glory.

Conteh felt special – almost as if his knees were the only ones on the sacred carpet. He looked around at the remaining bunch of kneelers, and wondered if they too, felt like the prodigal son. He looked down again. A tear fell onto his knuckles, beckoning two words: *'Jesus wept'*. It took him back with a vengeance, to when he was a mere ten years old. When he used to sing. And pray. And play the piano, bringing smiles to faces of approving brethren and sistren. His mind wandered around a little Pentecostal church, on the corner of Baxter Street, in Birmingham. The memories, disorientated, seeped from the crevices of his mind, like hot larva.

Conteh held a bible in his hand. Tight. He remembered one fresh track. A heart-wrenching track from Morgan Heritage: One that had never failed to touch him. And beneath the backdrop of the congregation's chatter, he could almost hear it:

'I'll be down by the river,
Waiting for the Good Lord to pass my way... Oh yeah...'

* * *

It was midnight. Two hours since Janet had climbed into bed.

Earlier she had chatted to her sister Sandra for the hundredth time about the shooting incident, thanking their lucky stars that they had survived it.

Her mind was alert.

Getting to sleep seemed like a distant wish.

You see, her mind was filled.

Actively it buzzed with a thought that had clung to her mind like a residing leech.

Not her brother's decision to move away from Birmingham...

Not the fact that Simone had spoken to her about her concern about the cramps in Lawrence's legs, which the doctor had told him was a circulation problem.

Not the shooting, nor its after effect: a cloud of sorrow that was clearing away much too slowly - like a heavy blanket of fog...

No...

The question that filled Janet's mind was...

'HOW MANY NICOS ARE THERE ROAMING
AROUND OUT THERE... FREELY... IN BIRMINGHAM?...
HOW MANY?'

The question blew her away to the land of uncertainty.

You see, Nico was most certainly *not alone*. No sir. And his invisible banner of the *'kiss of death'* will go on. It will be carried by many... for a very long time.

Heaven help us all.

Chapter 27

"Are you ok?" Simone asked Lawrence as they relaxed once again after dinner.

"Yes, Darling... fine."

"If I know the man I married, I don't think you are. I know a lot has happened lately.... That shooting thing at that club... what with Sheree and Morag getting killed, but you have been in that same vague, distant state ever since that night you went over to see Lance."

"Have I?"

"You know you have... you're not still dwelling on that drug-trafficking thing that Lance did are you?"

"No. I'm fine, Simone. Honestly."

"Or maybe you're worried about the cramps getting worse. If you're worried, Darling, I should go back to the doctors."

"Simone, I'm fine," he snapped. "… Sorry. I didn't' t mean to snap."

"When you're ready to tell me what's bothering you, I'll be ready to listen. I know you're troubled, but I can only ask."

Lawrence reached for her. She went towards him. They hugged. And like a force, she felt it. Something was *definitely* troubling him. Something, it seemed he wanted to, but couldn't tell her.

* * *

"What's yuh plans for the day?" Clive asked Lance as he emerged from the shower, drying his crutch.

"Nothing. Just relaxing. I thought you were doing the same."

"I was, but something came up," Clive said. "Business."

"Business?" Lance asked.

"Uh huh."

Lance looked at him. "You know, Clive, before we were so tight, you weren't so secretive. You used to tell me everything. Your business moves, everything. Now all I get is a two word reply."

"What's this?" Clive asked, his nude, toned body tantalising Lance. "Do I detect a bit of jealousy going on?"

"No… no… but I'm hoping that if there was ever anyone else, you'd tell me."

Clive pulled on his Calvin Klein underwear after creaming his body in some sexy, musky scented lotion. "I think you're getting paranoid, Lance." He splashed Jean-Paul Gaultier all over his body, and Lance couldn't help feeling a little insecure.

Lance didn't reply to Clive's last comment about him being paranoid. Instead he poured himself a drink, sat down and consulted the remote control.

"I'll see you later," Clive said ten minutes later.

And now, as Lance watched his Mercedes SLR pull off his drive, his heart sunk. He knew that a *pretty bwoy of a white First Officer* had recently been coming on to Clive. He had been watching things. He couldn't be too sure, but he felt his intuitions were right.

* * *

As far as Lawrence was concerned, early that morning, Simone had left for the long planned day out with an old friend, and she wouldn't be back until very late evening. But in fact, she was on her way to the airport to pick her mother up.

Considering he was so excited, Amari had done pretty well in keeping the *secret* of the *secret coming* of his grandma. It was meant to be the nicest surprise in a long while for Lawrence. This mother/son-in-law relationship must have been the best ever, since the whole world seemed to spend the longest time spinning off negative mother-in-law jokes. Lawrence loved Blanche and Blanche loved him. And Simone loved the way they hugged and exclaimed in loud exaltation and jump and waltz and acted like two grown kids when they see each other. *'In every real man,'* Blanche had said, *'there is a child inside wanting to play. Some will let that child out from time to time, but some will always play at being macho.'* The last surprise went well, and she knew that this one was well overdue. Besides, she figured Blanche might be just what he needed to heel his distant-mindedness.

It was late afternoon. Simone pulled up a little way from the house so the sound of her engine didn't announce her arrival. "We'll leave the luggage in the car for now," she told her mum and Amari. "We'll just go give Daddy his big surprise first."

Amari placed his finger over his lips as if it helped him to keep quiet. "C'mon grandma... tiptoe... don't let the keys rattle, Mum," he said.

"Ok, son," Simone whispered.

Blanche held her grandson's hand as she grinned a bright sunshine smile."

"You two stay outside, "Simone whispered, "I will go and tell him I've come back early because my friend wasn't well, but that I've also got something I want him to come and help me with. When he comes out, you can both shout, 'Surprise!"

"Ok, Mum," Amari whispered.

Blanche nodded and watched her daughter close the front door behind her, leaving them both on the doorstep. The excitement was unbearable. She couldn't wait to see her son-in-law, the sweet man who had brought happiness into her daughter's life.

Amari fidgeted with excitement as he gripped his grandma's hand.

"Darling?!" Simone shouted as she ran upstairs, already established her husband wasn't downstairs.

"Darling?!!" Lawrence's panicky voice shouted back. "How come you're back early?!" his panic-stricken voice said, and seconds later Simone realised why. Lawrence had not heard the door, and the seconds she took to reach their bedroom was much *too-little-too-late* for him to get his *ass* in shape. *Literally.*

"*Dar... ling?*" Simone gasped for breath.

"Darling?" Lawrence said. "I... I... thought..."

"What... what are you... *doing?*" Her eyes were as wide as saucers now.

"Darling... I... I can explain." But cramp held him. He could speak but he couldn't move.

"Who are *you...?*" Now, her forehead was riddled with countless lines of perplexity as she looked now at the person she could seriously kill there and then. The person who had wasted no time in springing from his *groin-to-ass* position when she had entered the room earlier.

"Oh, shit!" Lawrence, face-down upon their marital bed aggressed at the sudden, fierce cramps in both his legs that surrendered him immobile. "What a time for fucking cramps..." he mumbled as he averted his eyes from his wife's. What could he do? Apart from turning the clock back?... *nothing*.

"Simone covered her mouth as she watched him go... the third party, that is.

Earlier she had watched his back as he pulled on his clothes.

As his hard-on died.

As shame weighed heavily like sin on and around his shoulders.

As the thought of facing her and looking into her eyes would be the hardest thing he could ever do.

And as he trembled and shook, Clive was sure he could hear Simone's heart beating.

Now they were alone. Simone and her husband.

"Who is that man?"

Lawrence didn't answer.

Time was passing.

As her mother and son stood waiting patiently on the doorstep, wondering what was taking so long, Simone stared questioningly: not at her husband, but at her marital bed. Questions filled her head. '*Is this the first time?*' she wondered.

The cramp must have been excruciating.

It wouldn't subside.

Lawrence felt that his soul could be seen from his bare ass.

If only he could move.

Simone was still staring at her bed...

And there it was...

Her marital bedroom... alive with the gruesome sound of a piercing silence... *her bed... her bed... her bed...* far from cosy now, with the warmth of a body-heat that wasn't hers.

"Who is that, Grandma?" Amari asked, as Clive hurried out. He was surprised to see them standing there. His eyes met with Blanche's and along with the fragrance of Jean-Paul Gaultier, the breeze of his passing left her a readable message.

Now, Simone stared at a face she had loved.

A face that was now pleading with the weight of guilt.

"*Lawrence?*" she whispered low, failing to grasp her latest discovery.

"Oh, Baby." His eyes pleaded for forgiveness. "Baby... baby... baby... I have no words to explain."

She covered her mouth...

Mind confused...

It stretched back to the day they met...

'*How long*'... '*How long?*'... '*How long had it been going on?*'

'*How long had he been sleeping with men...?*'

The wondering wouldn't cease. It rang like an *out-of-control* alarm in her head.

Lawrence rubbed his legs. Rub. Rub. Rub. Severe cramp was now the master of his control.

"*Hoooooo!*" Simone screamed, though in a deep, dull hum.

"*Hoooooo!*" She held her belly for comfort as she fell now to her knees.

"*Hoooooo!*" Her heart was ripping away from its cavity.

She could feel it...

Surely it was bleeding?...

Surely it had broken up into a thousand pieces, never to be mended again...

"*Why?*" the sweet soul agonised. "*Why?*... What have I ever done so bad?"

Lawrence's eyes filled up. He wanted to wish it away. Her pain, that is. Turn the clock back. Wished he hadn't succumbed.

How could he convince her that it was the very first time?

How?

For it was... *the very first time.*

He loved her...

Truly...

Dearly...

He really did. It shouldn't have happened at all, but it did.

And he had not planned it to be in her bed. But explanations could stay. He was caught. *Simple*. In her bed. *Explanation*?... She wouldn't be listening.

"Mummy?!" the impatient voice of a sweet five-year-old rode the stairs.

Lawrence stood up. His feet were still not durable, but he was jolted by the voice of his son. He tried to stand. Shook his feet. Anything. He had to get dressed.

"Mummy, can we come now?! Where is Daddy?!"

"*We?*" Lawrence asked his wife.

Simone rose from her knees. She tried to find strength.

Lawrence reached for her.

"Don't touch me!" she said sternly, but still low, staring into his very soul. Hating his very existence. Asking questions. Stretching her mind way back, the same question came again like the plague... '*How long?*'... '*How long?*'... '*How long has this been going on?*'... Her heart pounded with anguish...

She walked out of the bedroom leaving the man she had adored fighting hard against his cramp as he pulled on his trousers.

Simone ascended the stairs in a daze. At the bottom, she saw her mother and son.

"Simone?" her mother asked. She had an old head. No use trying to fool Blanche.

"He's... he's... Lawrence is... *not well*, Mum."

Blanche turned her head upstairs.

"Daddy? What's wrong with Daddy?" Amari darted up the stairs, but Simone held him back. "Let Daddy rest, son. Let Daddy rest. You can see him later. If you let him rest, he'll be better soon."

"But why can't I...?"

"Shhhhh," Simone hugged him tight. "You'll see Daddy in a bit, son." She forced to maintain a level tone, and as she hugged the adorable child, bubbles of tears fell upon his unsuspecting back. She looked up now and spoke to her mother through a silent gaze.

"Oh, Dear, Lord," Blanche whispered. Left hand akimbo, right palm over her mouth, she wandered through to the living-room. She needed no spoken words: she had seen them right there in her daughter's eyes. Her intuitions were right. She had known by the look in the stranger's eyes as he walked past them earlier.

461

Simone and her mother were talking now. Only, one sat crying silently halfway up the stairs, while the other paced the distance of the living-room. Telepathically they spoke… *'Love him, but keep a little back for surprises. Your father has never failed to surprise me. I guess I surprised him at times too. No one is perfect. And no two days are the same. Today you can have sunshine, tomorrow a ruthless hurricane. The relics of some storms can be salvaged, while some, you'll just have to start right over again.'*

Simone took a deep breath. "C'mon, son," let's go make Gandma a nice cup of tea."

"Is Daddy sleeping?"

"Yes… Daddy is sleeping."

Simone wasn't as brave as she wished she was that day, but a verse from her favourite poem helped her by:

> *And whatever your labours and aspirations,*
> *in the noisy confusion of life,*
> *keep peace in your soul.*
> *With all its sham, drudgery, and broken dreams,*
> *it is still a beautiful world.*
> *Be cheerful. Strive to be happy.*

Once there lived a man who tried to live for society…He tried to fight against his inner *'self'*…

Tried to fight the emergence of his true sexuality…

And in his fighting, he had convinced himself that only a woman that was *perfect* in his eyes, could help him to overcome.

And he had wished that he could find that woman.

And then one day, he did… found her when he was least looking.

And he had known that heaven must have been missing an angel.

All others he had forsaken, and clung only to her.

They produced a beautiful son.

And in this man, this woman had found what she thought was a *perfect love.*

He was what she needed to obliterate the memories of a love that was deep, yet hurt too much to hold on to.

And when the *happily-ever-after* seemed more real than real could ever be, they rescued themselves in each other's warm and tender love.

But then, one day. One unsuspecting day, *it* came knocking. His *inner-self*, that is.

462

It came with a vengeance, triggered by the entangled images of his co-pilot, captured by the lenses of a camera pointed by an obsessed woman: a woman who wanted him to be the man she thought *she* knew.

And at these images he had looked... stared...

Imagined...

Wanted...

Lusted...

And yearned for an experience that pulled at his desires like a compulsive *'must'*.

And try as he may, he could never escape from himself.

Lawrence is what he is...

What he was...

And will always be...

Today...

Yesterday...

Always and forever... *Bisexual.*

* * *

Father Jarvis pulled his red Mercs into the seemingly waiting spot. He was pleased to see the queue that stretched for what seemed like miles outside the new Solid Lounge. When he had decided to kick out the blues with his *'Bring Back The Love'* dance, he knew it couldn't fail. Countless blessings were showering down from above. He could feel it. He had always felt that music was one of the main ingredients in life. And he knew too, that it must go on. *Seriously.*

The *'stand-in-until-we-arrive'* DJs were doing their things, but soon Father Jarvis and Country Bwoy would dominate the show.

"This feels good," Father Jarvis said as he walked through the door. He could almost feel the positive vibes. They hugged him like people would. "This feels real good," he mumbled again to himself. And deep within, he had known that the night was a tribute to all those who had passed on.

'Reggae bring back love
To the heart of the people
Reggae bring back sweet sweet love...
Seh reggae bring back love
To the heart of the people
Reggae bring back sweet sweet love...

* * *

Lawrence sat with his head in his hands and his ass in nothing but a pair of Calvin Klein's.

He had only just taken a shower and covered himself in the sensual fragrance of Amani Code. Simone loved it and had bought it for his last birthday.

The house was empty without his family. It was three days since he was caught *red-assed* with First Officer Clive Saunders upon his wife's bed.

'*Where were they?*' he wondered. He knew Blanche knew the whole story and would never stay under the same roof with him. '*What have I done?*' he asked himself for the hundredth time. '*Simone,*' he tormented. '*Where are you?… Where are you?*'

She wasn't taking his calls. She was obviously staying somewhere temporarily with his son and her mother. If only he could turn the clock back. Since she'd been gone, he was like a fish out of water, so when the doorbell rang, he thought any company would do, but the last person he expected to see was Lance.

"Lance, Hi…"

"Sorry to about turning up so unexpectedly, man."

"No worries," Lawrence said, feeling a little apprehensive. He didn't know why Lance was there. *Did he know? Did Clive tell him? Did he come to grovel about his stance never to be on the same flight with him again? Or did he need to talk some more about the untimely death of Morag? What?* "What brought you here?"

"Everything."

"*Everything?*"

"Look," Lance said, showing his need to come in, "Is Simone here? Can I…?"

"No. Simone's left me."

Lance stood still for a while. He was shocked. That was most unexpected. "… What did you say?"

"You heard me right, Lance… She's left me."

"Simone *left* you?"

"Yeap."

"What happened? You had a perfect…"

"Come in, Lance. You might as well."

Lance's face was riddled with questions. "What happened?" he asked again as he walked in. "Cos if you two were having problems you kept that real quiet."

"No... we weren't."

"So... what...?"

"Long story..."

"Right..." Though he was somewhat shocked and wanted to hear more, Lance couldn't help staring at Lawrence's body. And adorned in only a pair of boxers, there weren't much left to his imagination.

"Let me get some clothes on," Lawrence told him in a solemn voice. "Pour yuhself a drink."

"No need," Lance told him.

"*No need?*"

"No need to get dressed... you're... in your own house. Relax... Don't mind me."

Lawrence looked at him. "I know, but I will."

Lance clenched his fists. It was the first time he had ever seen Lawrence in just his boxers. "What happened to you and Simone? I know it can't be another woman. You're too damn loyal."

"No... no... I'll... go get dressed. Two minutes."

Lance was fighting with his desires. He got up. "That drink. Can I?"

"Yeah. Help yuhself man, I said."

He had to go past Lawrence to reach the drinks globe. "What yuh got?" He was clearly delaying him.

Lawrence walked towards the globe to look himself. He bent down to inspect its content, whilst Lance feasted his eyes on his strong, muscular back.

"Everything, by the looks of it," Lawrence said. "*Simone...* she topped up." Just uttering her name beckoned a devastating heartache.

"Are you ok, man?" Lance asked.

But somehow Lawrence couldn't answer. Grief buckled in his throat.

"Lawrence?" Lance bent down towards him.

"I've lost her, man... I can't believe I've lost her."

"What did you do, man? You two never argue. Whatever you did must have been pretty bad... that is assuming it was *your* fault."

Lawrence's tears came in abundance now.

"It's ok, man... It's ok... I don't know why she left, and you obviously don't want to say, but maybe she'll come back to you."

"I don't think so, Lance… I don't think she'll come back to me."
Tears were flowing down his chin.

"*Hey*… Lawrence," Lance coxed. "I've never seen you like this."
Now, falling to his knees, Lance cuddled his back. "*Hey*." As
Lawrence sobbed, he smoothed his right palm over his head, back and
shoulders. "*Hey*," he whispered. "She might come back." Now, he
brought Lawrence's head to his chest. "It's ok, Bro'… It's ok…"

Lawrence's sobs heightened…

Lance cuddled him tighter… tighter…

Kissed the side of his face… *Oh how he had wanted him so.*

Cupped his face in the palms of his hands…

Taboo…

Guided his lips to his…

Taboo…

Now, two masculine mouths *desiring*… *fumbling*… *finding*…
tasting… *devouring*…

Then, a pause…

A piercing look into each other's eyes…

Heat spread over their very existence…

Into each other's eyes they stared… *silently*… *silently*… No words
passing…

He wanted Lawrence… he had never dreamed he *ever could* or
ever would.

Lawrence needed his touch…. And it was much… much… much
too much to resist.

The bitterest taboo…

Then, like a synchronised force, their lips met with a ravenous
wanting.

Boxers, gone…

Lance's clothes discarded…

Firm touches…

Taboo!…

Strong embraces…

Taboo!…

Passionate kisses…

Entry… entry… entry…

The bitterest taboo!…

Why was Lawrence hearing his mother's voice?… *'If a man lieth
with mankind, as he lieth with a woman, both of them have committed
an abomination.'* And why was he forcing himself to shut it out?

"Ohhhh…" A muffled sound as the cushion he bit into took the full octave of his *pleasure-pain* sighs. "Ohhh…" As he felt, but refused to look now at the man that had wanted his very soul, now *digging deep* for his dignity. "Ohhh…" As he remembered where and when it started, and wondered where it would take him. "Ohhh…" *'If a man lieth with mankind, as he lieth with a woman…'* " Ohhh…" *'… both of them have committed an abomination'* Ohhh…" *Abomination!… Abomination!… Abomination!…*

Louder and louder, the voice of his *scripture-quoting* mother drummed in his head, as he sought rescue in the clutches of the swaddling cushion.

For Lance, a new moment had dawned. For he had always wanted to touch the man he had always viewed as Strong… Uprightness… Perfection.

He had always wanted to *touch* him… *taste* him… *hear* him hum in ecstasy… *see* his pleasure-filled face… hold him… hold him… *smell* his manly perspiration. Oh how he wanted him…wanted him…

Taboo… Taboo… The bitterest taboo…

* * *

"I called you," Clive said when Lance walked in that night after his encounter with Lawrence.

"Did you?"

"Yes. Didn't you check your mobile?"

"No. Not yet."

"Where did you go?"

"Quiet drink."

"Right…"

Lance was heading upstairs.

"Everything ok?" Clive asked.

"Yeah, fine. I just need a shower."

"I didn't know you had that fragrance?!" Clive shouted now to reach Lance who was now in the bathroom.

"What fragrance?!"

"The one you're wearing of course! Amani Code! The one Lawrence wears!"

"Oh… Right. I sprayed a few samples in Rackhams today! Don't know which one you're detecting!"

"Right! There's Chinese in the oven after your shower!"

"Nice. Thanks."

♣ ♣ Chapter 28 ♣ ♣

𝔗t was REM that pulled Conteh's heart apart as he lay on his settee, deep in thoughts. Perhaps he should have turned the radio off. Love songs can sometimes hurt you more than the hurt itself...

> *When the day is long and the night, the night is yours alone,*
> *When you're sure you've had enough of this life, well hang on.*
> *Don't let yourself go, everybody cries and everybody hurts*
> *sometimes...*

Apart from Janet and Sandra, the odd cousin or two, a few members of the Vibes Injection Crew who would take a spin down the motorway, or a neighbour two houses down, not many people visited Conteh. Not yet anyway. Give it time. Soon, Brother *This* and Sister *That* from the Ealing church would come in droves to make sure he wasn't lonely.

> *Sometimes everything is wrong. Now it's time to sing along.*
> *When your day is night alone, hold on, hold on*
> *If you feel like letting go, hold on*
> *When you think you've had too much of this life, well hang on...*

Moving to London was his choice. He needed a clean break from Birmingham: too many bad memories, though they were ones he had brought on himself. And although he could have found God anywhere, he found Him in London.

> *Everybody hurts. Take comfort in your friends.*
> *Everybody hurts. Don't throw your hand. Oh, no. Don't throw your*
> *hand.*
> *If you feel like you're alone, no, no, no, you are not alone...*

There were Brixton, Shepherds Bush and all the notorious black-populated areas, but Conteh chose Ealing. House prices were hard to mention, but lucky for him, the money from his share of the house he shared with Simone, plus that from the split share of his mother's house, made it possible to acquire an abode way above the size of a broom cupboard. First it felt lonely – it can't be easy for a notorious soundman to leave his roots and flee to another place, but peace was what he craved. And sometimes even to *live* is an act of courage.

If you're on your own in this life, the days and nights are long,
When you think you've had too much of this life to hang on...

Well, everybody hurts sometimes,
Everybody cries. And everybody hurts sometimes.
And everybody hurts sometimes. So, hold on, hold on.
Hold on, hold on. Hold on, hold on. Hold on, hold on.
Everybody hurts. You are not alone...

Everybody needs a bosom for a pillow, but apart from the Almighty's, only *one* bosom would do for him. She wasn't there, so he had lay with his thoughts across his soft leather settee, when they took him into a slumber.

Now, he rose reluctantly and rubbed the sleep from his eyes.

The knock at his door was ominous.

He wasn't expecting anyone.

There, through the transparency of a thick glass door, he saw them.

Two figures.

Who were they?

Slowly, he turned the key and opened the door.

Check... Surely not?

"Hi," the lady said.

"Hi... what?... what are you...?"

"Are you with someone?"

"No... no I'm not."

"Can we come in? It would be a shame to have travelled all this way..."

"Oh, sorry, of course you can. Come in, Babes. I'm ... I'm just a little shocked... come in... is everything ok?" He guided them into his living-room.

"No. Everything *isn't* ok," she told him.

But something tells him this was his day. She had come to him in times of trouble.

"Sit down... would you like a drink?"

"No thanks. I'm fine."

"What about you, Little Man?"

"No thank you. I'm fine."

"Would you just sit there and watch TV for a second while your mother and I have a little talk in the kitchen?"

"Ok."

Now, Conteh drifted on a dream towards the kitchen, an angel in tow. And when he got there he asked, "Can I... hold you?"

"Please do," she said, as if all other words were lost.

As if that was all she came for.

As if it would erase the memories of her latest findings.

Conteh put his arms around her and felt a tremor of relief.

And the track that emitted through the radio waves was uncannily appropriate, though it pulled at both their heartstrings.

When you're weary, feeling small...

He couldn't stop himself shaking.

His prayers were answered.

Once upon a time his hope was simply faith holding out its hand in the dark.

Once upon a time, behind the walls of his prison cell, he tried to cherish the dreams he had of her, knowing full well that was all it could ever be. *Dreams.*

Once upon a time he had *analysed* and *realised* the consequences of taking his prized possession for granted.

Once upon a time... once upon a time...

Simone laid her head upon his shoulder and let her tears fall freely down his back.

When tears are in your eyes...

"Him hurt yuh?" Conteh whispered.

Silence.

"He *has,* hasn't he?"

Silence.

Taking her silence for a yes, he reflected on how a few years ago, his *misfortune* was another man's fortune. Today, the table had turned. And there he was... wide awake... in a dream.

Gently, he eased her away from him almost in slow motion, then, he lifted her chin and kissed her falling tears.

I will dry them all, all...

'Dear God, show me how to make this right,' was his thought. "What did he do to you?" he asked in a low, calm voice, hoping that whatever it was, it would make his misdemeanour the tiniest blot on infidelity's landscape.

But she kept her eyes to the ground as uncontrollable sobs erupted from deep within her, pushing their way back into the living-room where her son sat.

"Mum?!... Don't cry, Mum!... Don't cry no more! Grandma said everything's gonna be ok!"

"I'm coming son. I'm coming."

Conteh looked at the beautiful woman that was crying in his arms. His heart melted, and his own problems flew away.

I'm on your side...

He pulled a tissue from a nearby box, and as he dried her eyes, so he kissed her. "Your mum's right... It's gonna be ok," he whispered. "I promise you... it's gonna be ok... did you know that destiny is our history pre-made?... even when we think it is us that control it?"

Oh, when times get rough
And friends just can't be found...

Now, he placed his lips upon hers and kissed her again. Passionately. Gone are the days when the saliva of an HIV infected person was cause for concern.

God had given him a second chance.

Simone had second it.

"I want to be there for you."

Like a bridge over troubled water,
I will lay me down...

This time she knew it was the real thing. For whether she wanted to admit it or not, they were meant to be. Nobody else could make her feel they way he did.

471

Like a bridge over troubled water,
I will lay me down...

And *this time* he knew that forgiveness was the strangest thing... the hardest gift for anyone to part with, yet the best gift of all. *Forgiveness*. It is unique... It has its limits. It's *'giving'* is of a *'personal'* choice. What one person will forgive, the other won't... But at that moment, Conteh realised that the forgiveness he was receiving was *blessed*. Sent from above. Lawrence's poison was now his meat. The table had turned... However he had stumbled upon it, (or *it* upon *him)*, this *'forgiveness'* had *'warmed his heart and cooled his sting'*... *This time... This time... This time...*

♣ END ♣

WRITERS' & ARTISTS' PROFILES...

'When you're born with the gift of creativity, nothing can stop the inspirational flow...'
WATCH THIS SPACE!!!

ANDRE JOHNSON is a *'Rapper with a cause'*. He is nineteen years old and was born in Birmingham, West Midlands. He is a Music & Media student at Gloucester College.

With a father that sings and a mother that writes, Andre's intense *dedication to*, and *passion for* music and lyric writing is somewhat inevitable: from a very early age when his piers pursued the everyday events that were second nature to youths of his age, Andre was never far from the confines of his bedroom, surrounded by mounds of paper, his pen, his mixing/sampling computer and his God-given inspiration. Today, his outstanding lyric writing and track sampling have emphasised a unique musical prowess that is proving to be at second to none.

Andre's quietly-confident nature, coupled with his raw talent are attributes that, if nurtured, could mark a significant place on the musical map. He has performed his work at numerous venues including Brighton, Bristol, Cheltenham and Gloucester, and his tracks have been played on 1-Xtra.

His album, featuring unique sample mixes from outstanding artists like Ann and Sonia, his Debut Album *'Pride And Persistence'* (featured in this novel) will be available from July, 2006 - Price £6.99.

Andre's mission is to use **Positive lyrics** to communicate with youths near and far. Two of his mottos are: *'Pride And Persistence Pay Off'*, and *'Put nothing into your body today, that it will detrimentally crave tomorrow'*.

To obtain a signed copy of Andre's (aka STAL) album, *'Pride And Persistence'*, please make your cheque or postal for £7.74 (£6.99 plus .75p P&P) and post to: **Xaymaca Books, PO Box 10886, Birmingham, West Midlands**.

SUE BROWN was born in Birmingham England of Jamaican parentage. She is the mother of three children and has been writing for over ten years.

In the late seventies and eighties, Sue was inspired by the works of prestigious Jamaican Dub poets the likes of Linton Kwesi Johnson, Prince Far-I and Michael Smith. However, it was not until 1994 that she wrote her first poem.

Discovering her newly found gift for poetry, Sue shared her talent with a friend: Poet and Writer Martin Glynn. Shortly after that Sue was taking part in her first live performance. Within months, she was performing in various events in and around the city, as well as nationally and internationally, appearing with the likes of the renowned Jean Binta Breeze, Moqapi Selassie, Kwame Dawes and Levi Tafari.

Her first poems where published in an anthology entitled *'Burning Words Flaming Images'*. Today, her work can be found in anthologies such as *'Hurricanes of Love'*, *'Griot'* and *'Saving The Seeds'*.

For the past five years Sue has been an active member of a Birmingham writers group: 'Writers Without Boarders'. In their latest publication, *'Saving The Seeds'* (produced by Cathy Perry - another of Birmingham's finest writers), just two of Sue's precious and moving poems *'Whose Identity'*, and *'Identity'* can be found.
From the stage, Sue oozes a Calm yet Powerful, Humble yet Majestic air, as her magnetic aura calls you, without effort, to *'listen'*.

Via Creative writing workshops, Sue uses poetry to explore ideas of self-expression, cultural identity and social behaviour, with aims to motivate, inspire, teach and educate. She has also successfully conducted various workshops in schools and community groups: independently as well as in conjunction with other artists, using various art forms.

Maintaining a long-standing collaboration with Birmingham based Book Communications, she contributes to the provision of services to the reading industry in primary and secondary schools, for children between the ages of five and seventeen-years-old.

From 1996 Sue has been an active Freelance workshop facilitator.
Below are just a few of her Commissions/performances:
- Black History Month, Youth and Book festivals, International women's festival, (cultural as well as social events).

- The Memorial Gates Project: writing material for schools nationally, focussing on the contributions of African, Asian and Caribbean war veterans in the 21st century conflicts.

- Birmingham's children's care homes: producing an anthology of poems.

- Adult Black Mental Health in Sandwell: producing an anthology of poems as well as visual art forms for an exhibition.

- Working with Birmingham's poet laureate, Julie Boden: to write and perform poetry inspired by The Opera of Bela Bartok Duke Bluebeard's Castle.

- 'Moving Here' project: Herbert Art Gallery and Museum, Coventry.

- Mothers of Creation, In Celebration of my Sisters and Birmingham's Annual Art Festival.

- Currently working with an African inspired rhythm band.

* * *

AVA MING has had several short stories anthologised and she was a commissioned writer for Stories on Stage at the Midlands Arts Centre in Birmingham.

As a broadcaster, Ava does voice-overs for adverts, trains new presenters and broadcasts a Sunday evening programme which showcases the best in Black Literature.

Ava's stage play *'A Caribbean Calypso Christmas'* was performed in 2004. She writes regularly for the BBC radio soap, 'Silver Street' and also writes plays for BBC Radio 4 and BBC 7.
Her first novel, **'Once Upon a Lie'** (which can be found in all good bookshops) was published by X Press Books in March 2005. Ava is currently working on her second book.

NORMAN SAMUDA-SMITH was born in Birmingham. The first black British born novelist to be published in contemporary UK in 1982, his novel *Bad Friday* was short listed for the Young Observer Fiction Prize that year. During the 1980's he acted with and was regularly commissioned to write plays for Ebony Arts Theatre Group, of which he was a founder member. His short story *Rasta Love* is one of seventeen featured in the award-winning anthology *Whispers in the Walls* published by Tindal Street Press in 2001.

His latest works *St Ann* and *I'm Beggin' You* will be found in the forthcoming collection, *The Heart of our Community*, published by: http://www.blackexpression2005.com/Anthology.html, an African/American publisher and information website.

St Ann was originally scribbled into a notebook in 1987 and dedicated to his Mother who lost her fight against cancer. It was written to fill his void when words of comfort failed.

I'm Beggin' You is a lament via someone who is homeless and trying to explain how he got in a mess; inspired by just buying the Big Issue from a dread in the city centre occasionally.

* * *

When **TREVOR THOMAS** answered his home phone in the early morning of August 2000, the last thing he expected to hear was that his new girlfriend had been arrested for money laundering. After all, she worked where he banked. Certain of her innocence, Trevor stood bail in the sum of £50,000. Considering his connection with the alleged money launderer, and being a Tax Consultant with a PhD in offshore tax planning, Trevor became a subject of interest to the police. They were particularly interested in the fact he knew how to *'hide money'*. Before long, he too was arrested for alleged *'money laundering'* crime. In the ensuing investigation, he lost his practice and his clients. However, Trevor managed to hold on to his sanity by writing the *'sensational'* and *'must read'* novel, *'The Laundryman'*...

'In the heart of city there is a man who processes the cash of the principal cocaine dealers in London. He launders their money. He turns dirty money into clean money and transfers it to anywhere in the world. One man. The police know of him because they have successfully infiltrated a number of the large drug cartels. That is, they know of his existence but they don't know 'who' he is or 'how' he operates. They have dubbed him 'The Laundryman.'

Dr Andrew Stuart is a highly respected international tax consultant, who yearns for the love of the beautiful, black and seemingly unattainable Tania Berkeley, the younger sister of his best friend BB. When Tania is arrested for money laundering, Stuart stands her bail, unaware of the fact that his 'act of chivalry' would set in motion a chain of events that would lead to his own arrest. Being an expert in offshore finance, a creator of offshore companies and trusts, the police want to believe they have 'caught their man'. However, one officer, DC Clarke, believes otherwise. The Laundryman, he argues, is cold, methodical, precise and unemotional. He would 'never' have stood bail for Tania Berkeley.

Enlisting the help of his fiercely loyal PA Anita Hume, his best friend BB, Tania's alcoholic lawyer Billy Carver and off-duty officer, DC Clarke, Dr Stuart attempts to clear his name. He must do what the police (with their huge resources and expertise) have been unable to do. He must identify and catch the Laundryman.

Without this novel, your bookshelf would be missing a 'masterpiece'. And when you have turned the last page, you will ask yourself, 'Is this just a brilliant work of fiction, or the most daring confession in the history of financial crime?'

To obtain a copy of this brilliant novel, visit www.Amazon.co.uk.
The Laundryman was published by Summara Books.

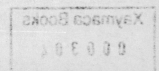
Xaymaca Books

000304

<u>**GRAND PRIZE DRAW!!!**</u>

Xaymaca Books is giving readers the chance to win £375.00 for all copies of 'THE DAY HELL BROKE LOOSE' bought between the 1st July, 2006 – 31st December, 2006.
1st prize of £200.00
2nd prize of £100.00
3rd prize of £50.00
4th prize of £25.00
Each novel sold between those dates will be number stamped. Purchasers are advised to keep their novels safe until the scheduled time of the draw.

<u>**LOGGING YOUR BOOK NUMBER AND DATE OF PURCHASE**</u>
To log the number stamped in your novel, and the date you purchased it, please email <u>xaymaca@book1.freeserve.co.uk</u> stating:
Your name, the number stamped in your book and where/when purchased.
Your information will be logged and you will be notified of when/where the draw will take place.
<u>**PERSONALISING YOUR NOVEL**</u>
When you purchase your novel, please endorse it by writing, 'This novel belongs to….. (your name)
<u>**TO CLAIM YOUR PRIZE**</u>
To claim your prize, you will need to show your novel. The info you emailed to Xaymaca Books will be matched to the novel you show, enabling you to claim your prize!
It is therefore advisable that you keep your novel safe, since it *'must'* be shown at the draw.
Lent books are often passed from hand to hand and are often not returned!
'SO DO NOT *LEND*, LET YOUR FRIENDS *SPEND!*'
Simply saying, '*My number was…*' won't be enough.
Ask your friends to obtain their own copies. This will give them the same chance as you to win a cash prize.
PS. If you cannot make the draw and your number is drawn, you will be notified via email or telephone, with a request to send your novel for proof.

Xaymaca Books

000304
'GOOD LUCK!'